THE NORSE SAGAS

PART 2

BY ANONYMOUS

The Laxdæla Saga
The Story of Burnt Njal
The Story of Gisli the Outlaw
The Saga of the Ere-Dwellers
The Saga of the Heath Slayings

NORSE LITERATURE SERIES
VOLUME 5

HENDERSON PUBLISHING

Norse Classics

The goal of this series is to provide an easy introduction to Norse literature for the novice. This series starts with the *Poetic and Prose Eddas*, which outline Norse mythology. It is followed by the *Heimskringla* is a semi-mythological historical account of the early medieval Norse kings. One important story in Norse and Germanic literature is the story of the Volsungs, which one will find elements of in the *Eddas*, volume four of this series in the *Saga of the Volsungs*, and of course, the *Nibelungenlied*. The *Nibelungenlied* in some sense is the Homeric epic of the Germans. In volumes 4, 5, and 6, one will find over 20 sagas compiled together here. These include stories of the first bishops of Iceland, Burnt Njal, Eirik the Red's journeys to North America, the Volsungs, Egil, and many more.

Here's an outline of the contents of this series:

Table of Contents

THE LAXDÆLA SAGA

Chapter 1
Of Ketill Flatnose and his Descendants, 9th Century A.D.

KETILL FLATNOSE was the name of a man. He was the son of Bjorn the Ungartered. Ketill was a mighty and high-born chieftain (hersir) in Norway. He abode in Raumsdale, within the folkland of the Raumsdale people, which lies between Southmere and Northmere. Ketill Flatnose had for wife Yngvild, daughter of Ketill Wether, who was a man of exceeding great worth. They had five children; one was named Bjorn the East-man, and another Helgi Bjolan. Thorunn the Horned was the name of one of Ketill's daughters, who was the wife of Helgi the Lean, son of Eyvind Eastman, and Rafarta, daughter of Kjarval, the Irish king. Unn "the Deep-minded" was another of Ketill's daughters, and was the wife of Olaf the White, son of Ingjald, who was son of Frodi the Valiant, who was slain by the Svertlings. Jorunn, "Men's Wit-breaker," was the name of yet another of Ketill's daughters. She was the mother of Ketill the Finn, who settled on land at Kirkby. His son was Asbjorn, father of Thorstein, father of Surt, the father of Sighat the Speaker-at-Law.

Chapter 2
Ketill and his Sons prepare to leave Norway

In the latter days of Ketill arose the power of King Harald the Fairhaired, in such a way that no folkland king or other great men could thrive in the land unless he alone ruled what title should be theirs. When Ketill heard that King Harald was minded to put to him the same choice as to other men of might–namely, not only to put up with his kinsmen being left unatoned, but to be made himself a hireling to boot–he calls together a meeting of his kinsmen, and began his speech in this wise: "You all know what dealings there have been between me and King Harald, the which there is no need of setting forth; for a greater need besets us, to wit, to take counsel as to the troubles that now are in store for us. I have true news of King Harald's enmity towards us, and to me it seems that we may abide no trust from that quarter. It seems to me that there are two choices left us, either to fly the land or to be slaughtered each in his own seat. Now, as for me, my will is rather to abide the same death that my kinsmen suffer, but I would not lead you by my wilfulness into so great a trouble, for I know the temper of my kinsmen and friends, that ye would not desert me, even though it would be some trial of manhood to follow me." Bjorn, the son of Ketill, answered: "I will make known my wishes at once. I will follow the example of noble men, and fly this land. For I deem myself no greater a man by abiding at home the thralls of King Harald, that they may chase me away from my own possessions, or that else I may have to come by utter death at their hands." At this there was made a good cheer, and they all thought it was spoken bravely. This counsel then was settled, that they should leave the country, for the sons of Ketill urged it much, and no one spoke against it. Bjorn and Helgi wished to go to Iceland, for they said they had heard many pleasing news thereof. They had been told that there was good land to be had there, and no need to pay money for it; they said there was plenty of whale and salmon and other fishing all the year round there. But Ketill said, "Into that fishing place I shall never come in my old age." So Ketill then told his mind, saying his desire was rather to go west over the sea, for there was a chance of getting a good livelihood. He knew lands there wide about, for there he had harried far and wide.

Chapter 3
Ketill's Sons go to Iceland

After that Ketill made a great feast, and at it he married his daughter Thorunn the Horned to Helgi the Lean, as has been said before. After that Ketill arrayed his journey west over the sea. Unn, his daughter, and many others of his relations went with him. That same summer Ketill's sons went to Iceland with Helgi, their brother-in-law. Bjorn, Ketill's son, brought his ship to the west coast of Iceland, to Broadfirth, and sailed up the firth along the southern shore, till he came to where a bay cuts into the land, and a high mountain stood on the ness on the inner side of the bay, but an island lay a little way off the land. Bjorn said that they should stay there for a while. Bjorn then went on land with a few men, and wandered along the coast, and but a narrow strip of land was there between fell and foreshore. This spot he thought suitable for habitation. Bjorn found the pillars of his temple washed up in a certain creek, and he thought that showed where he ought to build his house. Afterwards Bjorn took for himself all the land between Staff-river and Lavafirth, and abode in the place that ever after was called Bjornhaven. He was called Bjorn the Eastman. His wife, Gjaflaug, was the daughter of Kjallak the Old. Their sons were Ottar and Kjallak, whose son was Thorgrim, the father of Fight-Styr and Vemund, but the daughter of Kjallak was named Helga, who was the wife of Vestar of Eyr, son of Thorolf "Bladder-skull," who settled Eyr. Their son was Thorlak, father of Steinthor of Eyr. Helgi Bjolan brought his ship to the south of the land, and took all Keelness, between Kollafirth and Whalefirth, and lived at Esjuberg to old age. Helgi the Lean brought his ship to the north of the land, and took Islefirth, all along between Mastness and Rowanness, and lived at Kristness. From Helgi and Thornunn all the Islefirthers are sprung.

Chapter 4
Ketill goes to Scotland, A.D. 890

Ketill Flatnose brought his ship to Scotland, and was well received by the great men there; for he was a renowned man, and of high birth. They offered him there such station as he would like to take, and Ketill and his company of kinsfolk settled down there–all except Thorstein, his daughter's son, who forthwith betook himself to warring, and harried Scotland far and wide, and was always victorious. Later on he made peace with the Scotch, and got for his own one-half of Scotland. He had for wife Thurid, daughter of Eyvind, and sister of Helgi the Lean. The Scotch did not keep the peace long, but treacherously murdered him. Ari, Thorgil's son, the Wise, writing of his death, says that he fell in Caithness. Unn the Deep-minded was in Caithness when her son Thorstein fell. When she heard that Thorstein was dead, and her father had breathed his last, she deemed she would have no prospering in store there. So she had a ship built secretly in a wood, and when it was ready built she arrayed it, and had great wealth withal; and she took with her all her kinsfolk who were left alive; and men deem that scarce may an example be found that any one, a woman only, has ever got out of such a state of war with so much wealth and so great a following. From this it may be seen how peerless among women she was. Unn had with her many men of great worth and high birth. A man named Koll was one of the worthiest amongst her followers, chiefly owing to his descent, he being by title a "Hersir." There was also in the journey with Unn a man named Hord, and he too was also a man of high birth and of great worth. When she was ready, Unn took her ship to the Orkneys; there she stayed a little while, and there she married off Gro, the daughter of Thorstein the Red. She was the mother of Greilad, who married Earl Thorfinn, the son of Earl Turf-Einar, son of Rognvald Mere-Earl. Their son was Hlodvir, the father of Earl Sigurd, the father of Earl Thorfinn, and from them come all the kin of the Orkney Earls. After that Unn steered her ship to the Faroe Isles, and stayed there for some time. There she married off another daughter of Thorstein, named Olof, and from her sprung the noblest race of that land, who are called the Gate-Beards.

Chapter 5
Unn goes to Iceland, A.D. 895

Unn now got ready to go away from the Faroe Isles, and made it known to her shipmates that she was going to Iceland. She had with her Olaf "Feilan," the son of Thorstein, and those of his sisters who were unmarried. After that she put to sea, and, the weather being favourable, she came with her ship to the south of Iceland to Pumice-Course (Vikrarskeid). There they had their ship broken into splinters, but all the men and goods were saved. After that she went to find Helgi, her brother, followed by twenty men; and when she came there he went out to meet her, and bade her come stay with him with ten of her folk. She answered in anger, and said she had not known that he was such a churl; and she went away, being minded to find Bjorn, her brother in Broadfirth, and when he heard she was coming, he went to meet her with many followers, and greeted her warmly, and invited her and all her followers to stay with him, for he knew his sister's high-mindedness. She liked that right well, and thanked him for his lordly behaviour. She stayed there all the winter, and was entertained in the grandest manner, for there was no lack of means, and money was not spared. In the spring she went across Broadfirth, and came to a certain ness, where they ate their mid-day meal, and since that it has been called Daymealness, from whence Middlefell-strand stretches (eastward). Then she steered her ship up Hvammsfirth and came to a certain ness, and stayed there a little while. There Unn lost her comb, so it was afterwards called Combness. Then she went about all the Broadfirth-Dales, and took to her lands as wide as she wanted. After that Unn steered her ship to the head of the bay, and there her high-seat pillars were washed ashore, and then she deemed it was easy to know where she was to take up her abode. She had a house built there: it was afterwards called Hvamm, and she lived there. The same spring as Unn set up household at Hvamm, Koll married Thorgerd, daughter of Thorstein the Red. Unn gave, at her own cost, the bridal-feast, and let Thorgerd have for her dowry all Salmonriver-Dale; and Koll set up a household there on the south side of the Salmon-river. Koll was a man of the greatest mettle: their son was named Hoskuld.

Chapter 6

Unn Divides her Land

After that Unn gave to more men parts of her land-take. To Hord she gave all Hord-Dale as far as Skramuhlaups River. He lived at Hordabolstad (Hord-Lair-Stead), and was a man of the greatest mark, and blessed with noble offspring. His son was Asbjorn the Wealthy, who lived in Ornolfsdale, at Asbjornstead, and had to wife Thorbjorg, daughter of Midfirth-Skeggi. Their daughter was Ingibjorg, who married Illugi the Black, and their sons were Hermund and Gunnlaug Worm-tongue. They are called the Gilsbecking-race. Unn spoke to her men and said: "Now you shall be rewarded for all your work, for now I do not lack means with which to pay each one of you for your toil and good-will. You all know that I have given the man named Erp, son of Earl Meldun, his freedom, for far away was it from my wish that so high-born a man should bear the name of thrall." Afterwards Unn gave him the lands of Sheepfell, between Tongue River and Mid River. His children were Orm and Asgeir, Gunbjorn, and Halldis, whom Alf o' Dales had for wife. To Sokkolf Unn gave Sokkolfsdale, where he abode to old age. Hundi was the name of one of her freedmen. He was of Scottish kin. To him she gave Hundidale. Osk was the name of the fourth daughter of Thorstein the Red. She was the mother of Thorstein Swart, the Wise, who found the "Summer eeke." Thorhild was the name of a fifth daughter of Thorstein. She was the mother of Alf o' Dales, and many great men trace back their line of descent to him. His daughter was Thorgerd, wife of Ari Marson of Reekness, the son of Atli, the son of Ulf the Squinter and Bjorg, Eyvond's daughter, the sister of Helgi the Lean. From them come all the Reeknessings. Vigdis was the name of the sixth daughter of Thorstein the

Red. From her come the men of Headland of Islefirth.

Chapter 7
Of the Wedding of Olaf "Feilan," A.D. 920

Olaf "Feilan" was the youngest of Thorstein's children. He was a tall man and strong, goodly to look at, and a man of the greatest mettle. Unn loved him above all men, and made it known to people that she was minded to settle on Olaf all her belongings at Hvamm after her day. Unn now became very weary with old age, and she called Olaf "Feilan" to her and said: "It is on my mind, kinsman, that you should settle down and marry." Olaf took this well, and said he would lean on her foresight in that matter. Unn said: "It is chiefly in my mind that your wedding-feast should be held at the end of the summer, for that is the easiest time to get in all the means needed, for to me it seems a near guess that our friends will come hither in great numbers, and I have made up my mind that this shall be the last bridal feast arrayed by me." Olaf answered: "That is well spoken; but such a woman alone I mean to take to wife who shall rob thee neither of wealth nor rule (over thine own)." That same summer Olaf "Feilan" married Alfdis. Their wedding was at Hvamm. Unn spent much money on this feast, for she let be bidden thereto men of high degree wide about from other parts. She invited Bjorn and Helgi "Bjolan," her brothers, and they came with many followers. There came Koll o' Dales, her kinsman-in-law, and Hord of Hord-Dale, and many other great men. The wedding feast was very crowded; yet there did not come nearly so many as Unn had asked, because the Islefirth people had such a long way to come. Old age fell now fast upon Unn, so that she did not get up till mid-day, and went early to bed. No one did she allow to come to her for advice between the time she went to sleep at night and the time she was aroused, and she was very angry if any one asked how it fared with her strength. On this day Unn slept somewhat late; yet she was on foot when the guests came, and went to meet them and greeted her kinsfolk and friends with great courtesy, and said they had shown their affection to her in "coming hither from so far, and I specially name for this Bjorn and Helgi, but I wish to thank you all who are here assembled." After that Unn went into the hall and a great company with her, and when all seats were taken in the hall, every one was much struck by the lordliness of the feast. Then Unn said: "Bjorn and Helgi, my brothers, and all my other kindred and friends, I call witnesses to this, that this dwelling with all its belongings that you now see before you, I give into the hands of my kinsman, Olaf, to own and to manage." After that Unn stood up and said she would go to the bower where she was wont to sleep, but bade every one have for pastime whatever was most to his mind, and that ale should be the cheer of the common folk. So the tale goes, that Unn was a woman both tall and portly. She walked at a quick step out along the hall, and people could not help saying to each other how stately the lady was yet. They feasted that evening till they thought it time to go to bed. But the day after Olaf went to the sleeping bower of Unn, his grandmother, and when he came into the chamber there was Unn sitting up against her pillow, and she was dead. Olaf went into the hall after that and told these tidings. Every one thought it a wonderful thing, how Unn had upheld her dignity to the day of her death. So they now drank together Olaf's wedding and Unn's funeral honours, and the last day of the feast Unn was carried to the howe (burial mound) that was made for her. She was laid in a ship in the cairn, and much treasure with her, and after that the cairn was closed up. Then Olaf "Feilan" took over the household of Hvamm and all charge of the wealth there, by the advice of his kinsmen who were there. When the feast came to an end Olaf gave lordly gifts to the men most held in honour before they went away. Olaf became a mighty man and a great chieftain. He lived at Hvamm to old age.The children of Olaf and Alfdis were Thord Yeller, who married Hrodny, daughter of Midfirth Skeggi; and their sons were, Eyjolf the Grey, Thorarin Fylsenni, and Thorkell Kuggi. One daughter of Olaf Feilan was Thora, whom Thorstein Cod-biter, son of Thorolf Most-Beard, had for wife; their sons were Bork the Stout, and Thorgrim, father of Snori the Priest. Helga was another daughter of Olaf; she was the wife of Gunnar Hlifarson; their daughter was Jofrid, whom Thorodd, son of Tongue-Odd, had for wife, and afterwards Thorstein, Egil's son. Thorunn was the name of yet one of his daughters. She was the wife of Herstein, son of Thorkell Blund-Ketill's son. Thordis was the name of a third daughter of Olaf: she was the wife of Thorarin, the Speaker-at-Law, brother of Ragi. At that time, when Olaf was living at Hvamm, Koll o' Dales, his brother-in-law, fell ill and died. Hoskuld, the son of Koll, was young at the time of his father's death: he was fulfilled of wits before the tale of his years. Hoskuld was a hopeful man, and well made of body. He took over his father's goods and household. The homestead where Koll lived was named after him, being afterwards called Hoskuldstead. Hoskuld was soon in his householding blessed with friends, for that many supports stood thereunder, both kinsmen and friends whom Koll had gathered round him. Thorgerd, Thorstein's daughter, the mother of Hoskuld, was still a young woman and most goodly; she did not care for Iceland after the death of Koll. She told Hoskuld her son that she wished to go abroad, and take with her that share of goods which fell to her lot. Hoskuld said he took it much to heart that they should part, but he would not go against her in this any more than in anything else. After that Hoskuld bought the half-part in a ship that was standing beached off Daymealness, on behalf of his mother. Thorgerd betook herself on board there, taking with her a great deal of goods. After that Thorgerd put to sea and had a very good voyage, and arrived in Norway. Thorgerd had much kindred and many noble kinsmen there. They greeted her warmly, and gave her the choice of whatever she liked to take at their hands. Thorgerd was pleased at this, and said it was her wish to settle down in that land. She had not been a widow long before a man came forward to woo her. His name was Herjolf; he was a "landed man" as to title, rich, and of much account. Herjolf was a tall and strong man, but he was not fair of feature; yet the most high-mettled of men, and was of all men the best skilled at arms. Now as they sat taking counsel on this matter, it was Thorgerd's place to reply to it herself, as she was a widow; and, with the advice of her relations, she said she would not refuse the offer. So Thorgerd married Herjolf, and went with him to his home, and they loved each other dearly. Thorgerd soon showed by her ways that she was a woman of the greatest mettle, and Herjolf's manner of life was deemed much better and more highly to be honoured now that he had got such an one as she was for his wife.

Chapter 8
The Birth of Hrut and Thorgerd's Second Widowhood, A.D. 923

Herjolf and Thorgerd had not long been together before they had a son. The boy was sprinkled with water, and was given the name of Hrut. He was at an early age both big and strong as he grew up; and as to growth of body, he was goodlier than any man, tall and broad-shouldered, slender of waist, with fine limbs and well-made hands and feet. Hrut was of all men the fairest of feature, and like what Thorstein, his mother's father, had been, or like Ketill Flatnose. And all things taken together, he was a man of the greatest mettle. Herjolf now fell ill and died, and men deemed that a great loss. After that Thorgerd wished to go to Iceland to visit Hoskuld her son, for she still loved him best of all men, and Hrut was left behind well placed with his relations. Thorgerd arrayed her journey to Iceland, and went to find Hoskuld in his home in Salmonriver-Dale. He received his mother with honour. She was possessed of great wealth, and remained with Hoskuld to the day of her death. A few winters after Thorgerd came to Iceland she fell sick and died. Hoskuld took to himself all her money, but Hrut his brother owned one-half thereof.

Chapter 9
Hoskuld's Marriage, A.D. 935

At this time Norway was ruled by Hakon, Athelstan's fosterling. Hoskuld was one of his bodyguard, and stayed each year, turn and turn about, at Hakon's court, or at his own home, and was a very renowned man both in Norway and in Iceland. Bjorn was the name of a man who lived at Bjornfirth, where he had taken land, the firth being named after him. This firth cuts into the land north from Steingrim's firth, and a neck of land runs out between them. Bjorn was a man of high birth, with a great deal of money: Ljufa was the name of his wife. Their daughter was Jorunn: she was a most beautiful woman, and very proud and extremely clever, and so was thought the best match in all the firths of the West. Of this woman Hoskuld had heard, and he had heard besides that Bjorn was the wealthiest yeoman throughout all the Strands. Hoskuld rode from home with ten men, and went to Bjorn's house at Bjornfirth. He was well received, for to Bjorn his ways were well known. Then Hoskuld made his proposal, and Bjorn said he was pleased, for his daughter could not be better married, yet turned the matter over to her decision. And when the proposal was set before Jorunn, she answered in this way: "From all the reports I have heard of you, Hoskuld, I cannot but answer your proposal well, for I think that the woman would be well cared for who should marry you; yet my father must have most to say in this matter, and I will agree in this with his wishes." And the long and short of it was, that Jorunn was promised to Hoskuld with much money, and the wedding was to be at Hoskuldstead. Hoskuld now went away with matters thus settled, and home to his abode, and stays now at home until this wedding feast was to be held. Bjorn came from the north for the wedding with a brave company of followers. Hoskuld had also asked many guests, both friends and relations, and the feast was of the grandest. Now, when the feast was over each one returned to his home in good friendship and with seemly gifts. Jorunn Bjorn's daughter sits behind at Hoskuldstead, and takes over the care of the household with Hoskuld. It was very soon seen that she was wise and well up in things, and of manifold knowledge, though rather high-tempered at most times. Hoskuld and she loved each other well, though in their daily ways they made no show thereof. Hoskuld became a great chieftain; he was mighty and pushing, and had no lack of money, and was thought to be nowise less of his ways than his father, Koll. Hoskuld and Jorunn had not been married long before they came to have children. A son of theirs was named Thorliek. He was the eldest of their children. Bard was another son of theirs. One of their daughters was called Hallgerd, afterwards surnamed "Long-Breeks." Another daughter was called Thurid. All their children were most hopeful. Thorliek was a very tall man, strong and handsome, though silent and rough; and men thought that such was the turn of his temper, as that he would be no man of fair dealings, and Hoskuld often would say, that he would take very much after the race of the men of the Strands. Bard, Hoskuld's son, was most manly to look at, and of goodly strength, and from his appearance it was easy to see that he would take more after his father's people. Bard was of quiet ways while he was growing up, and a man lucky in friends, and Hoskuld loved him best of all his children. The house of Hoskuld now stood in great honour and renown. About this time Hoskuld gave his sister Groa in marriage to Velief the Old, and their son was "Holmgang"-Bersi.

Chapter 10
Of Viga Hrapp

Hrapp was the name of a man who lived in Salmon-river-Dale, on the north bank of the river on the opposite side to Hoskuldstead, at the place that was called later on Hrappstead, where there is now waste land. Hrapp was the son of Sumarlid, and was called Fight-Hrapp. He was Scotch on his father's side, and his mother's kin came from Sodor, where he was brought up. He was a very big, strong man, and one not willing to give in even in face of some odds; and for the reason that was most overbearing, and would never make good what he had misdone, he had had to fly from West-over-the-sea, and had bought the land on which he afterwards lived. His wife was named Vigdis, and was Hallstein's daughter; and their son was named Sumarlid. Her brother was named Thorstein Surt; he lived at Thorsness, as has been written before. Sumarlid was brought up there, and was a most promising young man. Thorstein had been married, but by this time his wife was dead. He had two daughters, one named Gudrid, and the other Osk. Thorkell trefill married Gudrid, and they lived in Svignaskard. He was a great chieftain, and a sage of wits; he was the son of Raudabjorn. Osk, Thorstein's daughter, was given in marriage to a man of Broadfirth named Thorarin. He was a valiant man, and very popular, and lived with Thorstein, his father-in-law, who was sunk in age and much in need of their care. Hrapp was disliked by most people, being overbearing to his neighbours; and at times he would hint to them that theirs would be a heavy lot as neighbours, if they held any other man for better than himself. All the goodmen took one counsel, and went to Hoskuld and told him their trouble. Hoskuld bade them tell him if Hrapp did any one any harm, "For he shall not plunder me of men or money."

Chapter 11
About Thord Goddi and Thorbjorn Skrjup

Thord Goddi was the name of a man who lived in Salmon-river-Dale on the northern side of the river, and his house was Vigdis called Goddistead. He was a very wealthy man; he had no children, and had bought the land he lived on. He was a neighbour of Hrapp's, and was very often badly treated by him. Hoskuld looked after him, so that he kept his dwelling in peace. Vigdis was the name of his wife. She was daughter of Ingjald, son of Olaf Feilan, and brother's daughter of Thord Yeller, and sister's daughter of Thorolf Rednose of Sheepfell. This Thorolf was a great hero, and in a very good position, and his kinsmen often went to him for protection. Vigdis had married more for money than high station. Thord had a thrall who had come to Iceland with him, named Asgaut. He was a big man, and shapely of body; and though he was called a thrall, yet few could be found his equal amongst those called freemen, and he knew well how to serve his master. Thord had many other thralls, though this one is the only one mentioned here. Thorbjorn was the name of a man. He lived in Salmon-river-Dale, next to Thord, up valley away from his homestead, and was called Skrjup. He was very rich in chattels, mostly in gold and silver. He was an huge man and of great strength. No squanderer of money on common folk was he. Hoskuld, Dalakoll's son, deemed it a drawback to his state that his house was worse built than he wished it should be; so he bought a ship from a Shetland man. The ship lay up in the mouth of the river Blanda. That ship he gets ready, and makes it known that he is going abroad, leaving Jorunn to take care of house and children. They now put out to sea, and all went well with them; and they hove somewhat southwardly into Norway, making Hordaland, where the market-town called Biorgvin was afterwards built. Hoskuld put up his ship, and had there great strength of kinsmen, though here they be not named. Hakon, the king, had then his seat in the Wick. Hoskuld did not go to the king, as his kinsfolk welcomed him with open arms. That winter all was quiet (in Norway).

Chapter 12
Hoskuld Buys a Slave Woman

There were tidings at the beginning of the summer that the king went with his fleet eastward to a tryst in Brenn-isles, to settle peace for his land, even as the law laid down should be done every third summer. This meeting was held between rulers with a view to settling such matters as kings had to adjudge–matters of international policy between Norway, Sweden, and Denmark. It was deemed a pleasure trip to go to this meeting, for thither came men from well-nigh all such lands as we know of. Hoskuld ran out his ship, being desirous also to go to the meeting; moreover, he had not been to see the king all the winter through. There was also a fair to be made for. At the meeting there were great crowds of people, and much amusement to be got–drinking, and games, and all sorts of entertainment. Nought, however, of great interest happened there. Hoskuld met many of his kinsfolk there who were come from Denmark. Now, one day as Hoskuld went out to disport himself with some other men, he saw a stately tent far away from the other booths. Hoskuld went thither, and into the tent, and there sat a man before him in costly raiment, and a Russian hat on his head. Hoskuld asked him his name. He said he was called Gilli: "But many call to mind the man if they hear my nickname–I am called Gilli the Russian." Hoskuld said he had often heard talk of him, and that he held him to be the richest of men that had ever belonged to the guild of merchants. Still Hoskuld spoke: "You must have things to sell such as we should wish to buy." Gilli asked what he and his companions wished to buy. Hoskuld said he should like to buy some bonds-woman, "if you have one to sell." Gilli answers: "There, you mean to give me trouble by this, in asking for things you don't expect me to have in stock; but it is not sure that follows." Hoskuld then saw that right across the booth there was drawn a curtain; and Gilli then lifted the curtain, and Hoskuld saw that there were twelve women seated behind the curtain. So Gilli said that Hoskuld should come on and have a look, if he would care to buy any of these women. Hoskuld did so. They sat all together across the booth. Hoskuld looks carefully at these women. He saw a woman sitting out by the skirt of the tent, and she was very ill-clad. Hoskuld thought, as far as he could see, this woman was fair to look upon. Then said Hoskuld, "What is the price of that woman if I should wish to buy her?" Gilli replied, "Three silver pieces is what you must weigh me out for her." "It seems to me," said Hoskuld, "that you charge very highly for this bonds-woman, for that is the price of three (such)." Then Gilli said, "You speak truly, that I value her worth more than the others. Choose any of the other eleven, and pay one mark of silver for her, this one being left in my possession." Hoskuld said, "I must first see how much silver there is in the purse I have on my belt," and he asked Gilli to take the scales while he searched the purse. Gilli then said, "On my side there shall be no guile in this matter; for, as to the ways of this woman, there is a great drawback which I wish, Hoskuld, that you know before we strike this bargain." Hoskuld asked what it was. Gilli replied, "The woman is dumb. I have tried in many ways to get her to talk, but have never got a word out of her, and I feel quite sure that this woman knows not how to speak." Then, said Hoskuld, "Bring out the scales, and let us see how much the purse I have got here may weigh." Gilli did so, and now they weigh the silver, and there were just three marks weighed. Then said Hoskuld, "Now the matter stands so that we can close our bargain. You take the money for yourself, and I will take the woman. I take it that you have behaved honestly in this affair, for, to be sure, you had no mind to deceive me herein." Hoskuld then went home to his booth. That same night Hoskuld went into bed with her. The next morning when men got dressed, spake Hoskuld, "The clothes Gilli the Rich gave you do not appear to be very grand, though it is true that to him it is more of a task to dress twelve women than it is to me to dress only one." After that Hoskuld opened a chest, and took out some fine women's clothes and gave them to her; and it was the saying of every one that she looked very well when she was dressed. But when the rulers had there talked matters over according as the law provided, this meeting was broken up. Then Hoskuld went to see King Hakon, and greeted him worthily, according to custom. The king cast a side glance at him, and said, "We should have taken well your greeting, Hoskuld, even if you had saluted us sooner; but so shall it be even now."

<h1 style="text-align:center">Chapter 13</h1>
<h2 style="text-align:center">Hoskuld Returns to Iceland, A.D. 948</h2>

After that the king received Hoskuld most graciously, and bade him come on board his own ship, and "be with us so long as you care to remain in Norway." Hoskuld answered: "Thank you for your offer; but now, this summer, I have much to be busy about, and that is mostly the reason I was so long before I came to see you, for I wanted to get for myself house-timber." The king bade him bring his ship in to the Wick, and Hoskuld tarried with the king for a while. The king got house-timber for him, and had his ship laden for him. Then the king said to Hoskuld, "You shall not be delayed here longer than you like, though we shall find it difficult to find a man to take your place." After that the king saw Hoskuld off to his ship, and said: "I have found you an honourable man, and now my mind misgives me that you are sailing for the last time from Norway, whilst I am lord over that land." The king drew a gold ring off his arm that weighed a mark, and gave it to Hoskuld; and he gave him for another gift a sword on which there was half a mark of gold. Hoskuld thanked the king for his gifts, and for all the honour he had done him. After that Hoskuld went on board his ship, and put to sea. They had a fair wind, and hove in to the south of Iceland; and after that sailed west by Reekness, and so by Snowfellness in to Broadfirth. Hoskuld landed at Salmon-river-Mouth. He had the cargo taken out of his ship, which he took into the river and beached, having a shed built for it. A ruin is to be seen now where he built the shed. There he set up his booths, and that place is called Booths'-Dale. After that Hoskuld had the timber taken home, which was very easy, as it was not far off. Hoskuld rode home after that with a few men, and was warmly greeted, as was to be looked for. He found that all his belongings had been kept well since he left. Jorunn asked, "What woman that was who journeyed with him?" Hoskuld answered, "You will think I am giving you a mocking answer when I tell you that I do not know her name." Jorunn said, "One of two things there must be: either the talk is a lie that has come to my ears, or you must have spoken to her so much as to have asked her her name." Hoskuld said he could not gainsay that, and so told her the truth, and bade that the woman should be kindly treated, and said it was his wish she should stay in service with them. Jorunn said, "I am not going to wrangle with the mistress you have brought out of Norway, should she find living near me no pleasure; least of all should I think of it if she is both deaf and dumb." Hoskuld slept with his wife every night after he came home, and had very little to say to the mistress. Every one clearly saw that there was something betokening high birth in the way she bore herself, and that she was no fool. Towards the end of the winter Hoskuld's mistress gave birth to a male child. Hoskuld was called, and was shown the child, and he thought, as others did, that he had never seen a goodlier or a more noble-looking child. Hoskuld was asked what the boy should be called. He said it should be named Olaf, for Olaf Feilan had died a little time before, who was his mother's brother. Olaf was far before other children, and Hoskuld bestowed great love on the boy. The next summer Jorunn said, "That the woman must do some work or other, or else go away." Hoskuld said she should wait on him and his wife, and take care of her boy besides. When the boy was two years old he had got full speech, and ran about like children of four years old. Early one morning, as Hoskuld had gone out to look about his manor, the weather being fine, and the sun, as yet little risen in the sky, shining brightly, it happened that he heard some voices of people talking; so he went down to where a little brook ran past the home-field slope, and he saw two people there whom he recognised as his son Olaf and his mother, and he discovered she was not speechless, for she was talking a great deal to the boy. Then Hoskuld went to her and asked her her name, and said it was useless for her to hide it any longer. She said so it should be, and they sat down on the brink of the field. Then she said, "If you want to know my name, I am called Melkorka." Hoskuld bade her tell him more of her kindred. She answered, "Myr Kjartan is the name of my father, and he is a king in Ireland; and I was taken a prisoner of war from there when I was fifteen winters old." Hoskuld said she had kept silence far too long about so noble a descent. After that Hoskuld went on, and told Jorunn what he had just found out during his walk. Jorunn said that she "could not tell if this were true," and said she had no fondness for any manner of wizards; and so the matter dropped. Jorunn was no kinder to her than before, but Hoskuld had somewhat more to say to her. A little while after this, when Jorunn was going to bed, Melkorka was undressing her, and put her shoes on the floor, when Jorunn took the stockings and smote her with them about the head. Melkorka got angry, and struck Jorunn on the nose with her fist, so that the blood flowed. Hoskuld came in and parted them. After that he let Melkorka go away, and got a dwelling ready for her up in Salmon-river-Dale, at the place that was afterwards called Melkorkastad, which is now waste land on the south of the Salmon river. Melkorka now set up household there, and Hoskuld had everything brought there that she needed; and Olaf, their son, went with her. It was soon seen that Olaf, as he grew up, was far superior to other men, both on account of his beauty and courtesy.

Chapter 14
The Murder of Hall, Ingjald's Brother

Ingjald was the name of a man. He lived in Sheepisles, that lie out in Broadfirth. He was called Sheepisles' Priest. He was rich, and a mighty man of his hand. Hall was the name of his brother. He was big, and had the makings of a man in him; he was, however, a man of small means, and looked upon by most people as an unprofitable sort of man. The brothers did not usually agree very well together. Ingjald thought Hall did not shape himself after the fashion of doughty men, and Hall thought Ingjald was but little minded to lend furtherance to his affairs. There is a fishing place in Broadfirth called Bjorn isles. These islands lie many together, and were profitable in many ways. At that time men went there a great deal for the fishing, and at all seasons there were a great many men there. Wise men set great store by people in outlying fishing-stations living peacefully together, and said that it would be unlucky for the fishing if there was any quarrelling; and most men gave good heed to this. It is told how one summer Hall, the brother of Ingjald, the Sheepisles' Priest, came to Bjorn isles for fishing. He took ship as one of the crew with a man called Thorolf. He was a Broadfirth man, and was well-nigh a penniless vagrant, and yet a brisk sort of a man. Hall was there for some time, and palmed himself off as being much above other men. It happened one evening when they were come to land, Hall and Thorolf, and began to divide the catch, that Hall wished both to choose and to divide, for he thought himself the greater man of the two. Thorolf would not give in, and there were some high words, and sharp things were said on both sides, as each stuck to his own way of thinking. So Hall seized up a chopper that lay by him, and was about to heave it at Thorolf's head, but men leapt between them and stopped Hall; but he was of the maddest, and yet unable to have his way as at this time. The catch of fish remained undivided. Thorolf betook himself away that evening, and Hall took possession of the catch that belonged to them both, for then the odds of might carried the day. Hall now got another man in Thorolf's place in the boat, and went on fishing as before. Thorolf was ill-contented with his lot, for he felt he had come to shame in their dealings together; yet he remained in the islands with the determination to set straight the humble plight to which he had been made to bow against his will. Hall, in the meantime, did not fear any danger, and thought that no one would dare to try to get even with him in his own country. So one fair-weather day it happened that Hall rowed out, and there were three of them together in the boat. The fish bit well through the day, and as they rowed home in the evening they were very merry. Thorolf kept spying about Hall's doings during the day, and is standing in the landing-place when Hall came to land. Hall rowed in the forehold of the boat, and leapt overboard, intending to steady the boat; and as he jumped to land Thorolf happens to be standing near, and forthwith hews at him, and the blow caught him on his neck against the shoulder, and off flew his head. Thorolf fled away after that, and Hall's followers were all in a flurried bustle about him. The story of Hall's murder was told all over the islands, and every one thought it was indeed great news; for the man was of high birth, although he had had little good luck. Thorolf now fled from the islands, for he knew no man there who would shelter him after such a deed, and he had no kinsmen he could expect help from; while in the neighbourhood were men from whom it might be surely looked for that they would beset his life, being moreover men of much power, such as was Ingjald, the Sheepisles' Priest, the brother of Hall. Thorolf got himself ferried across to the mainland. He went with great secrecy. Nothing is told of his journey, until one evening he came to Goddistead. Vigdis, the wife of Thord Goddi, was some sort of relation to Thorolf, and on that account he turned towards that house. Thorolf had also heard before how matters stood there, and how Vigdis was endowed with a good deal more courage than Thord, her husband. And forthwith the same evening that Thorolf came to Goddistead he went to Vigdis to tell her his trouble, and to beg her help. Vigdis answered his pleading in this way: "I do not deny our relationship, and in this way alone I can look upon the deed you have done, that I deem you in no way the worser man for it. Yet this I see, that those who shelter you will thereby have at stake their lives and means, seeing what great men they are who will be taking up the blood-suit. And Thord," she said, "my husband, is not much of a warrior; but the counsels of us women are mostly guided by little foresight if anything is wanted. Yet I am loath to keep aloof from you altogether, seeing that, though I am but a woman, you have set your heart on finding some shelter here." After that Vigdis led him to an outhouse, and told him to wait for her there, and put a lock on the door. Then she went to Thord, and said, "A man has come here as a guest, named Thorolf. He is some sort of relation of mine, and I think he will need to dwell here some long time if you will allow it." Thord said he could not away with men coming to put up at his house, but bade him rest there over the next day if he had no trouble on hand, but otherwise he should be off at his swiftest. Vigdis answered, "I have offered him already to stay on, and I cannot take back my word, though he be not in even friendship with all men." After that she told Thord of the slaying of Hall, and that Thorolf who was come there was the man who had killed him. Thord was very cross-grained at this, and said he well knew how that Ingjald would take a great deal of money from him for the sheltering that had been given him already, seeing that doors here have been locked after this man. Vigdis answered, "Ingjald shall take none of your money for giving one night's shelter to Thorolf, and he shall remain here all this winter through." Thord said, "In this manner you can checkmate me most thoroughly, but it is against my wish that a man of such evil luck should stay here." Still Thorolf stayed there all the winter. Ingjald, who had to take up the blood-suit for his brother, heard this, and so arrayed him for a journey into the Dales at the end of the winter, and ran out a ferry of his whereon they went twelve together. They sailed from the west with a sharp north-west wind, and landed in Salmon-river-Mouth in the evening. They put up their ferry-boat, and came to Goddistead in the evening, arriving there not unawares, and were cheerfully welcomed. Ingjald took Thord aside for a talk with him, and told him his errand, and said he had heard of Thorolf, the slayer of his brother, being there. Thord said there was no truth in that. Ingjald bade him not to deny it. "Let us rather come to a bargain together: you give up the man, and put me to no toil in the matter of getting at him. I have three marks of silver that you shall have, and I will overlook the offences you have brought on your hands for the shelter given to Thorolf." Thord thought the money fair, and had now a promise of acquittal of the offences for which he had hitherto most dreaded and for which he would have to abide sore loss of money. So he said, "I shall no doubt hear people speak ill of me for this, none the less this will have to be our bargain." They slept until it wore towards the latter end of the night, when it lacked an hour of day.

Chapter 15
Thorolf's Escape with Asgaut the Thrall

Ingjald and his men got up and dressed. Vigdis asked Thord what his talk with Ingjald had been about the evening before. Thord said they had talked about many things, amongst others how the place was to be ransacked, and how they should be clear of the case if Thorolf was not found there. "So I let Asgaut, my thrall, take the man away." Vigdis said she had no fondness for lies, and said she should be very loath to have Ingjald sniffing about her house, but bade him, however, do as he liked. After that Ingjald ransacked the place, and did not hit upon the man there. At that moment Asgaut came back, and Vigdis asked him where he had parted with Thorolf. Asgaut replied, "I took him to our sheephouses as Thord told me to." Vigdis replied, "Can anything be more exactly in Ingjald's way as he returns to his ship? nor shall any risk be run, lest they should have made this plan up between them last night. I wish you to go at once, and take him away as soon as possible. You shall take him to Sheepfell to Thorolf; and if you do as I tell you, you shall get something for it. I will give you your freedom and money, that you may go where you will." Asgaut agreed to this, and went to the sheephouse to find Thorolf, and bade him get ready to go at once. At this time Ingjald rode out of Goddistead, for he was now anxious to get his money's worth. As he was come down from the farmstead (into the plain) he saw two men coming to meet him; they were Thorolf and Asgaut. This was early in the morning, and there was yet but little daylight. Asgaut and Thorolf now found themselves in a hole, for Ingjald was on one side of them and the Salmon River on the other. The river was terribly swollen, and there were great masses of ice on either bank, while in the middle it had burst open, and it was an ill-looking river to try to ford. Thorolf said to Asgaut, "It seems to me we have two choices before us. One is to remain here and fight as well as valour and manhood will serve us, and yet the thing most likely is that Ingjald and his men will take our lives without delay; and the other is to tackle the river, and yet that, I think, is still a somewhat dangerous one." Asgaut said that Thorolf should have his way, and he would not desert him, "whatever plan you are minded to follow in this matter." Thorolf said, "We will make for the river, then," and so they did, and arrayed themselves as light as possible. After this they got over the main ice, and plunged into the water. And because the men were brave, and Fate had ordained them longer lives, they got across the river and upon the ice on the other side. Directly after they had got across, Ingjald with his followers came to the spot opposite to them on the other side of the river. Ingjald spoke out, and said to his companions, "What plan shall we follow now? Shall we tackle the river or not?" They said he should choose, and they would rely on his foresight, though they thought the river looked impassable. Ingjald said that so it was, and "we will turn away from the river;" and when Thorolf and Asgaut saw that Ingjald had made up his mind not to cross the river, they first wring their clothes and then make ready to go on. They went on all that day, and came in the evening to Sheepfell. They were well received there, for it was an open house for all guests; and forthwith that same evening Asgaut went to see Thorolf Rednose, and told him all the matters concerning their errand, "how Vigdis, his kinswoman, had sent him this man to keep in safety." Asgaut also told him all that had happened between Ingjald and Thord Goddi; therewithal he took forth the tokens Vigdis had sent. Thorolf replied thus, "I cannot doubt these tokens. I shall indeed take this man in at her request. I think, too, that Vigdis has dealt most bravely with this matter and it is a great pity that such a woman should have so feeble a husband. And you, Asgaut, shall dwell here as long as you like." Asgaut said he would tarry there for no length of time. Thorolf now takes unto him his namesake, and made him one of his followers; and Asgaut and they parted good friends, and he went on his homeward journey. And now to tell of Ingjald. He turned back to Goddistead when he and Thorolf parted. By that time men had come there from the nearest farmsteads at the summons of Vigdis, and no fewer than twenty men had gathered there already. But when Ingjald and his men came to the place, he called Thord to him, "You have dealt in a most cowardly way with me, Thord," says he, "for I take it to be the truth that you have got the man off." Thord said this had not happened with his knowledge; and now all the plotting that had been between Ingjald and Thord came out. Ingjald now claimed to have back his money that he had given to Thord. Vigdis was standing near during this talk, and said it had fared with them as was meet, and prayed Thord by no means to hold back this money, "For you, Thord," she said, "have got this money in a most cowardly way." Thord said she must needs have her will herein. After that Vigdis went inside, and to a chest that belonged to Thord, and found at the bottom a large purse. She took out the purse, and went outside with it up to where Ingjald was, and bade him take the money. Ingjald's brow cleared at that, and he stretched out his hand to take the purse. Vigdis raised the purse, and struck him on the nose with it, so that forthwith blood fell on the earth. Therewith she overwhelmed him with mocking words, ending by telling him that henceforth he should never have the money, and bidding him go his way. Ingjald saw that his best choice was to be off, and the sooner the better, which indeed he did, nor stopped in his journey until he got home, and was mightily ill at ease over his travel.

Chapter 16
Thord becomes Olaf's Foster Father, A.D. 950

About this time Asgaut came home. Vigdis greeted him, and asked him what sort of reception they had had at Sheepfell. He gave a good account of it, and told her the words wherewith Thorolf had spoken out his mind. She was very pleased at that. "And you, Asgaut," she said, "have done your part well and faithfully, and you shall now know speedily what wages you have worked for. I give you your freedom, so that from this day forth you shall bear the title of a freeman. Therewith you shall take the money that Thord took as the price for the head of Thorolf, my kinsman, and now that money will be better bestowed." Asgaut thanked her for her gift with fair words. The next summer Asgaut took a berth in Day-Meal-Ness, and the ship put to sea, and they came in for heavy gales, but not a long sea-voyage, and made Norway. After that Asgaut went to Denmark and settled there, and was thought a valiant and true man. And herewith comes to an end the tale of him. But after the plot Thord Goddi had made up with Ingjald, the Sheepisles priest, when they made up their minds to compass the death of Thorolf, Vigdis' kinsman, she returned that deed with hatred, and divorced herself from Thord Goddi, and went to her kinsfolk and told them the tale. Thord Yeller was not pleased at this; yet matters went off quietly. Vigdis did not take away with her from Goddistead any more goods than her own heirlooms. The men of Hvamm let it out that they meant to have for themselves one-half of the wealth that Thord was possessed of. And on hearing this he becomes exceeding faint-hearted, and rides forthwith to see Hoskuld to tell him of his troubles. Hoskuld said, "Times have been that you have been terror-struck, through not having with such overwhelming odds to deal." Then Thord offered Hoskuld money for his help, and said he would not look at the matter with a niggard's eye. Hoskuld said, "This is clear, that you will not by peaceful consent allow any man to have the enjoyment of your wealth." Answers Thord, "No, not quite that though; for I fain would that you should take over all my goods. That being settled, I will ask to foster your son Olaf, and leave him all my wealth after my days are done; for I have no heir here in this land, and I think my means would be better bestowed then, than that the kinsmen of Vigdis should grab it." To this Hoskuld agreed, and had it bound by witnesses. This Melkorka took heavily, deeming the fostering too low. Hoskuld said she ought not to think that, "for Thord is an old man, and childless, and I wish Olaf to have all his money after his day, but you can always go to see him at any time you like." Thereupon Thord took Olaf to him, seven years old, and loved him very dearly. Hearing this, the men who had on hand the case against Thord Goddi thought that now it would be even more difficult than before to lay claim to the money. Hoskuld sent some handsome presents to Thord Yeller, and bade him not be angry over this, seeing that in law they had no claim on Thord's money, inasmuch as Vigdis had brought no true charges against Thord, or any such as justified desertion by her. "Moreover, Thord was no worse a man for casting about for counsel to rid himself of a man that had been thrust upon his means, and was as beset with guilt as a juniper bush is with prickles." But when these words came to Thord from Hoskuld, and with them large gifts of money, then Thord allowed himself to be pacified, and said he thought the money was well placed that Hoskuld looked after, and took the gifts; and all was quiet after that, but their friendship was rather less warm than formerly. Olaf grew up with Thord, and became a great man and strong. He was so handsome that his equal was not to be found, and when he was twelve years old he rode to the Thing meeting, and men in other countrysides looked upon it as a great errand to go, and to wonder at the splendid way he was made. In keeping herewith was the manner of Olaf's war-gear and raiment, and therefore he was easily distinguished from all other men. Thord got on much better after Olaf came to live with him. Hoskuld gave Olaf a nickname, and called him Peacock, and the name stuck to him.

Chapter 17
About Viga Hrapp's Ghost, A.D. 950

The tale is told of Hrapp that he became most violent in his behaviour, and did his neighbours such harm that they could hardly hold their own against him. But from the time that Olaf grew up Hrapp got no hold of Thord. Hrapp had the same temper, but his powers waned, in that old age was fast coming upon him, so that he had to lie in bed. Hrapp called Vigdis, his wife, to him, and said, "I have never been of ailing health in life," said he, "and it is therefore most likely that this illness will put an end to our life together. Now, when I am dead, I wish my grave to be dug in the doorway of my fire hall, and that I be put: thereinto, standing there in the doorway; then I shall be able to keep a more searching eye on my dwelling." After that Hrapp died, and all was done as he said, for Vigdis did not dare do otherwise. And as evil as he had been to deal with in his life, just so he was by a great deal more when he was dead, for he walked again a great deal after he was dead. People said that he killed most of his servants in his ghostly appearances. He caused a great deal of trouble to those who lived near, and the house of Hrappstead became deserted. Vigdis, Hrapp's wife, betook herself west to Thorstein Swart, her brother. He took her and her goods in. And now things went as before, in that men went to find Hoskuld, and told him all the troubles that Hrapp was doing to them, and asked him to do something to put an end to this. Hoskuld said this should be done, and he went with some men to Hrappstead, and has Hrapp dug up, and taken away to a place near to which cattle were least likely to roam or men to go about. After that Hrapp's walkings-again abated somewhat. Sumarlid, Hrapp's son, inherited all Hrapp's wealth, which was both great and goodly. Sumarlid set up household at Hrappstead the next spring; but after he had kept house there for a little time he was seized of frenzy, and died shortly afterwards. Now it was the turn of his mother, Vigdis, to take there alone all this wealth; but as she would not go to the estate of Hrappstead, Thorstein Swart took all the wealth to himself to take care of. Thorstein was by then rather old, though still one of the most healthy and hearty of men.

Chapter 18
Of the Drowning of Thorstein Swart

At that time there rose to honour among men in Thorness, the kinsmen of Thorstein, named Bork the Stout and his brother, Thorgrim. It was soon found out how these brothers would fain be the greatest men there, and were most highly accounted of. And when Thorstein found that out, he would not elbow them aside, and so made it known to people that he wished to change his abode, and take his household to Hrappstead, in Salmon-river-Dale. Thorstein Swart got ready to start after the spring Thing, but his cattle were driven round along the shore. Thorstein got on board a ferry-boat, and took twelve men with him; and Thorarin, his brother-in-law, and Osk, Thorstein's daughter, and Hild, her daughter, who was three years old, went with them too. Thorstein fell in with a high south-westerly gale, and they sailed up towards the roosts, and into that roost which is called Coal-chest-Roost, which is the biggest of the currents in Broadfirth. They made little way sailing, chiefly because the tide was ebbing, and the wind was not favourable, the weather being squally, with high wind when the squalls broke over, but with little wind between whiles. Thorstein steered, and had the braces of the sail round his shoulders, because the boat was blocked up with goods, chiefly piled-up chests, and the cargo was heaped up very high; but land was near about, while on the boat there was but little way, because of the raging current against them. Then they sailed on to a hidden rock, but were not wrecked. Thorstein bade them let down the sail as quickly as possible, and take punt poles to push off the ship. This shift was tried to no avail, because on either board the sea was so deep that the poles struck no bottom; so they were obliged to wait for the incoming tide, and now the water ebbs away under the ship. Throughout the day they saw a seal in the current larger by much than any others, and through the day it would be swimming round about the ship, with flappers none of the shortest, and to all of them it seemed that in him there were human eyes. Thorstein bade them shoot the seal, and they tried, but it came to nought. Now the tide rose; and just as the ship was getting afloat there broke upon them a violent squall, and the boat heeled over, and every one on board the boat was drowned, save one man, named Gudmund, who drifted ashore with some timber. The place where he was washed up was afterwards called Gudmund's Isles. Gudrid, whom Thorkell Trefill had for wife, was entitled to the inheritance left by Thorstein, her father. These tidings spread far and near of the drowning of Thorstein Swart, and the men who were lost there. Thorkell sent straightway for the man Gudmund, who had been washed ashore, and when he came and met Thorkell, he (Thorkell) struck a bargain with him, to the end that he should tell the story of the loss of lives even as he (Thorkell) was going to dictate it to him. Gudmund agreed. Thorkell now asked him to tell the story of this mishap in the hearing of a good many people. Then Gudmund spake on this wise: "Thorstein was drowned first, and then his son-in-law, Thorarin"–so that then it was the turn of Hild to come in for the money, as she was the daughter of Thorarin. Then he said the maiden was drowned, because the next in inheritance to her was Osk, her mother, and she lost her life the last of them, so that all the money thus came to Thorkell Trefill, in that his wife Gudrid must take inheritance after her sister. Now this tale is spread abroad by Thorkell and his men; but Gudmund ere this had told the tale in somewhat another way. Now the kinsmen of Thorarin misdoubted this tale somewhat, and said they would not believe it unproved, and claimed one-half of the heritage against Thorkell; but Thorkell maintained it belonged to him alone, and bade that ordeal should be taken on the matter, according to their custom. This was the ordeal at that time, that men had had to pass under "earth-chain," which was a slip of sward cut loose from the soil, but both ends thereof were left adhering to the earth, and the man who should go through with the ordeal should walk thereunder. Thorkell Trefill now had some misgivings himself as to whether the deaths of the people had indeed taken place as he and Gudmund had said the second time. Heathen men deemed that on them rested no less responsibility when ceremonies of this kind had to be gone through than Christian men do when ordeals are decreed. He who passed under "earth-chain" cleared himself if the sward-slip did not fall down upon him. Thorkell made an arrangement with two men that they should feign quarrelling over something or another, and be close to the spot when the ordeal was being gone through with, and touch the sward-slip so unmistakably that all men might see that it was they who knocked it down. After this comes forward he who was to go through with the ordeal, and at the nick of time when he had got under the "earth-chain," these men who had been put up to it fall on each other with weapons, meeting close to the arch of the sward-slip, and lie there fallen, and down tumbles the "earth-chain", as was likely enough. Then men rush up between them and part them, which was easy enough, for they fought with no mind to do any harm. Thorkell Trefill then asked people as to what they thought about the ordeal, and all his men now said that it would have turned out all right if no one had spoilt it. Then Thorkell took all the chattels to himself, but the land at Hrapstead was left to lie fallow.

Chapter 19
Hrut Comes to Iceland

Now of Hoskuld it is to be told that his state is one of great honour, and that he is a great chieftain. He had in his keep a great deal of money that belonged to his (half) brother, Hrut, Herjolf's son. Many men would have it that Hoskuld's means would be heavily cut into if he should be made to pay to the full the heritage of his (Hrut's) mother. Hrut was of the bodyguard of King Harald, Gunnhild's son, and was much honoured by him, chiefly for the reason that he approved himself the best man in all deeds of manly trials, while, on the other hand, Gunnhild, the Queen, loved him so much that she held there was not his equal within the guard, either in talking or in anything else. Even when men were compared, and noblemen therein were pointed to, all men easily saw that Gunnhild thought that at the bottom there must be sheer thoughtlessness, or else envy, if any man was said to be Hrut's equal. Now, inasmuch as Hrut had in Iceland much money to look after, and many noble kinsfolk to go and see, he desired to go there, and now arrays his journey for Iceland. The king gave him a ship at parting, and said he had proved a brave man and true. Gunnhild saw Hrut off to his ship, and said, "Not in a hushed voice shall this be spoken, that I have proved you to be a most noble man, in that you have prowess equal to the best man here in this land, but are in wits a long way before them". Then she gave him a gold ring and bade him farewell. Whereupon she drew her mantle over her head and went swiftly home. Hrut went on board his ship, and put to sea. He had a good breeze, and came to Broadfirth. He sailed up the bay, up to the island, and, steering in through Broadsound, he landed at Combness, where he put his gangways to land. The news of the coming of this ship spread about, as also that Hrut, Herjolf's son, was the captain. Hoskuld gave no good cheer to these tidings, and did not go to meet Hrut. Hrut put up his ship, and made her snug. He built himself a dwelling, which since has been called Combness. Then he rode to see Hoskuld, to get his share of his mother's inheritance. Hoskuld said he had no money to pay him, and said his mother had not gone without means out of Iceland when she met with Herjolf. Hrut liked this very ill, but rode away, and there the matter rested. All Hrut's kinsfolk, excepting Hoskuld, did honour to Hrut. Hrut now lived three winters at Combness, and was always demanding the money from Hoskuld at the Thing meetings and other law gatherings, and he spoke well on the matter. And most men held that Hrut had right on his side. Hoskuld said that Thorgerd had not married Herjolf by his counsel, and that he was her lawful guardian, and there the matter dropped. That same autumn Hoskuld went to a feast at Thord Goddi's, and hearing that, Hrut rode with twelve men to Hoskuldstead and took away twenty oxen, leaving as many behind. Then he sent some men to Hoskuld, telling them where he might search for the cattle. Hoskuld's house-carles sprang forthwith up, and seized their weapons, and words were sent to the nearest neighbours for help, so that they were a party of fifteen together, and they rode each one as fast as they possibly could. Hrut and his followers did not see the pursuit till they were a little way from the enclosure at Combness. And forthwith he and his men jumped off their horses, and tied them up, and went forward unto a certain sandhill. Hrut said that there they would make a stand, and added that though the money claim against Hoskuld sped slowly, never should that be said that he had run away before his thralls. Hrut's followers said that they had odds to deal with. Hrut said he would never heed that; said they should fare all the worse the more they were in number. The men of Salmon-river-Dale now jumped off their horses, and got ready to fight. Hrut bade his men not trouble themselves about the odds, and goes for them at a rush. Hrut had a helmet on his head, a drawn sword in one hand and a shield in the other. He was of all men the most skilled at arms. Hrut was then so wild that few could keep up with him. Both sides fought briskly for a while; but the men of Salmon-river-Dale very soon found that in Hrut they had to deal with one for whom they were no match, for now he slew two men at every onslaught. After that the men of Salmon-river-Dale begged for peace. Hrut replied that they should surely have peace. All the house-carles of Hoskuld who were yet alive were wounded, and four were killed. Hrut then went home, being somewhat wounded himself; but his followers only slightly or not at all, for he had been the foremost in the fight. The place has since been called Fight-Dale where they fought. After that Hrut had the cattle killed. Now it must be told how Hoskuld got men together in a hurry when he heard of the robbery and rode home. Much at the same time as he arrived his house-carles came home too, and told how their journey had gone anything but smoothly. Hoskuld was wild with wrath at this, and said he meant to take at Hrut's hand no robbery or loss of lives again, and gathered to him men all that day. Then Jorunn, his wife, went and talked to him, and asked him what he had made his mind up to. He said, "It is but little I have made up my mind to, but I fain would that men should oftener talk of something else than the slaying of my house-carles". Jorunn answered, "You are after a fearful deed if you mean to kill such a man as your brother, seeing that some men will have it that it would not have been without cause if Hrut had seized these goods even before this; and now he has shown that, taking after the race he comes from, he means no longer to be an outcast, kept from what is his own. Now, surely he cannot have made up his mind to try his strength with you till he knew that he might hope for some backing-up from the more powerful among men; for, indeed, I am told that messages have been passing in quiet between Hrut and Thord Yeller. And to me, at least, such matters seem worthy of heed being paid to them. No doubt Thord will be glad to back up matters of this kind, seeing how clear are the bearings of the case. Moreover you know, Hoskuld, that since the quarrel between Thord Goddi and Vigdis, there has not been the same fond friendship between you and Thord Yeller as before, although by means of gifts you staved off the enmity of him and his kinsmen in the beginning. I also think, Hoskuld," she said, "that in that matter, much to the trial of their temper, they feel they have come off worst at the hands of yourself and your son, Olaf. Now this seems to me the wiser counsel: to make your brother an honourable offer, for there a hard grip from greedy wolf may be looked for. I am sure that Hrut will take that matter in good part, for I am told he is a wise man, and he will see that that would be an honour to both of you." Hoskuld quieted down greatly at Jorunn's speech, and thought this was likely to be true. Then men went between them who were friends of both sides, bearing words of peace from Hoskuld to Hrut. Hrut received them well, and said he would indeed make friends with Hoskuld, and added that he had long been ready for their coming to terms as behoved kinsmen, if but Hoskuld had been willing to grant him his right. Hrut also said he was ready to do honour to Hoskuld for what he on his side had misdone. So now these matters were shaped and settled between the brothers, who now take to living together in good brotherhood from this time forth. Hrut now looks after his homestead, and became mighty man of his ways. He did not mix himself up in general things, but in whatever matter he took a part he would have his own way. Hrut now moved his dwelling, and abode to old age at a place which now is called Hrutstead. He made a temple in his home-field, of which the remains are still to be seen. It is called Trolls' walk now, and there is the high road. Hrut married a woman named Unn, daughter of Mord Fiddle. Unn left him, and thence sprang the quarrels between the men of Salmon-river-Dale and the men of Fleetlithe. Hrut's second wife was named Thorbjorg. She was Armod's daughter. Hrut married a third wife, but her we do not name. Hrut had sixteen sons and ten daughters by these two wives. And men say that one summer Hrut rode to the Thing meeting, and fourteen of his sons were with him. Of this mention is made, because it was thought a sign of greatness and might. All his sons were right goodly men.

Chapter 20

Melkorka's Marriage and Olaf the Peacock's Journey, A.D. 955

Hoskuld now remained quietly at home, and began now to sink into old age, and his sons were now all grown up. Thorliek sets up household of his own at a place called Combness, and Hoskuld handed over to him his portion. After that he married a woman named Gjaflaug, daughter of Arnbjorn, son of Sleitu Bjorn, and Thordaug, the daughter of Thord of Headland. It was a noble match, Gjaflaug being a very beautiful and high-minded woman. Thorliek was not an easy man to get on with, but was most warlike. There was not much friendship between the kinsmen Hrut and Thorliek. Bard Hoskuld's son stayed at home with his father, looked after the household affairs no less than Hoskuld himself. The daughters of Hoskuld do not have much to do with this story, yet men are known who are descended from them. Olaf, Hoskuld's son, was now grown up, and was the handsomest of all men that people ever set eyes on. He arrayed himself always well, both as to clothes and weapons. Melkorka, Olaf's mother, lived at Melkorkastead, as has been told before. Hoskuld looked less after Melkorka's household ways than he used to do, saying that that matter concerned Olaf, her son. Olaf said he would give her such help as he had to offer her. Melkorka thought Hoskuld had done shamefully by her, and makes up her mind to do something to him at which he should not be over pleased. Thorbjorn Skrjup had chiefly had on hand the care of Melkorka's household affairs. He had made her an offer of marriage, after she had been an householder for but a little while, but Melkorka refused him flatly. There was a ship up by Board-Ere in Ramfirth, and Orn was the name of the captain. He was one of the bodyguard of King Harald, Gunnhild's son. Melkorka spoke to Olaf, her son, and said that she wished he should journey abroad to find his noble relations, "For I have told the truth that Myrkjartan is really my father, and he is king of the Irish and it would be easy for you betake you on board the ship that is now at Board-Ere." Olaf said, "I have spoken about it to my father, but he seemed to want to have but little to do with it; and as to the manner of my foster-father's money affairs, it so happens that his wealth is more in land or cattle than in stores of islandic market goods." Melkorka said, "I cannot bear your being called the son of a slave-woman any longer; and if it stands in the way of the journey, that you think you have not enough money, then I would rather go to the length even of marrying Thorbjorn, if then you should be more willing than before to betake yourself to the journey. For I think he will be willing to hand out to you as much wares as you think you may need, if I give my consent to his marrying me. Above all I look to this, that then Hoskuld will like two things mightily ill when he comes to hear of them, namely, that you have gone out of the land, and that I am married." Olaf bade his mother follow her own counsel. After that Olaf talked to Thorbjorn as to how he wished to borrow wares of him, and a great deal thereof. Thorbjorn answered, "I will do it on one condition, and that is that I shall marry Melkorka for them; it seems to me, you will be as welcome to my money as to that which you have in your keep." Olaf said that this should then be settled; whereupon they talked between them of such matters as seemed needful, but all these things they agreed should be kept quiet. Hoskuld wished Olaf to ride with him to the Thing. Olaf said he could not do that on account of household affairs, as he also wanted to fence off a grazing paddock for lambs by Salmon River. Hoskuld was very pleased that he should busy himself with the homestead. Then Hoskuld rode to the Thing; but at Lambstead a wedding feast was arrayed, and Olaf settled the agreement alone. Olaf took out of the undivided estate thirty hundred ells' worth of wares, and should pay no money for them. Bard,

Hoskuld's son, was at the wedding, and was a party with them to all these doings. When the feast was ended Olaf rode off to the ship, and found Orn the captain, and took berth with him. Before Olaf and Melkorka parted she gave him a great gold finger-ring, and said, "This gift my father gave me for a teething gift, and I know he will recognise it when he sees it." She also put into his hands a knife and a belt, and bade him give them to her nurse: "I am sure she will not doubt these tokens." And still further Melkorka spake, "I have fitted you out from home as best I know how, and taught you to speak Irish, so that it will make no difference to you where you are brought to shore in Ireland." After that they parted. There arose forthwith a fair wind, when Olaf got on board, and they sailed straightway out to sea.

Chapter 21
Olaf the Peacock goes to Ireland, A.D. 955

Now Hoskuld came back from the Thing and heard these tidings, and was very much displeased. But seeing that his near akin were concerned in the matter, he quieted down and let things alone. Olaf and his companions had a good voyage, and came to Norway. Orn urges Olaf to go to the court of King Harald, who, he said, bestowed goodly honour on men of no better breeding than Olaf was. Olaf said he thought he would take that counsel. Olaf and Orn now went to the court, and were well received. The king at once recognised Olaf for the sake of his kindred, and forthwith bade him stay with him. Gunnhild paid great heed to Olaf when she knew he was Hrut's brother's son; but some men would have it, that she took pleasure in talking to Olaf without his needing other people's aid to introduce him. As the winter wore on, Olaf grew sadder of mood. Orn asked him what was the matter of his sorrow? Olaf answered, "I have on hand a journey to go west over the sea; and I set much store by it and that you should lend me your help, so that it may be undertaken in the course of next summer." Orn bade Olaf not set his heart on going, and said he did not know of any ships going west over the sea. Gunnhild joined in their talk, and said, "Now I hear you talk together in a manner that has not happened before, in that each of you wants to have his own way!" Olaf greeted Gunnhild well, without letting drop their talk. After that Orn went away, but Gunnhild and Olaf kept conversing together. Olaf told her of his wish, and how much store he set by carrying it out, saying he knew for certain that Myrkjartan, the king, was his mother's father. Then Gunnhild said, "I will lend you help for this voyage, so that you may go on it as richly furnished as you please." Olaf thanked her for her promise. Then Gunnhild had a ship prepared and a crew got together, and bade Olaf say how many men he would have to go west over the sea with him. Olaf fixed the number at sixty; but said that it was a matter of much concern to him, that such a company should be more like warriors than merchants. She said that so it should be; and Orn is the only man mentioned by name in company with Olaf on this journey. The company were well fitted out. King Harald and Gunnhild led Olaf to his ship, and they said they wished to bestow on him their good-luck over and above other friendship they had bestowed on him already. King Harald said that was an easy matter; for they must say that no goodlier a man had in their days come out of Iceland. Then Harald the king asked how old a man he was. Olaf answered, "I am now eighteen winters." The king replied, "Of exceeding worth, indeed, are such men as you are, for as yet you have left the age of child but a short way behind; and be sure to come and see us when you come back again." Then the king and Gunnhild bade Olaf farewell. Then Olaf and his men got on board, and sailed out to sea. They came in for unfavourable weather through the summer, had fogs plentiful, and little wind, and what there was was unfavourable; and wide about the main they drifted, and on most on board fell "sea-bewilderment." But at last the fog lifted over-head; and the wind rose, and they put up sail. Then they began to discuss in which direction Ireland was to be sought; and they did not agree on that. Orn said one thing, and most of the men went against him, and said that Orn was all bewildered: they should rule who were the greater in number. Then Olaf was asked to decide. He said, "I think we should follow the counsel of the wisest; for the counsels of foolish men I think will be of all the worse service for us in the greater number they gather together." And now they deemed the matter settled, since Olaf spake in this manner; and Orn took the steering from that time. They sailed for days and nights, but always with very little wind. One night the watchmen leapt up, and bade every one wake at once, and said they saw land so near that they had almost struck on it. The sail was up, but there was but little wind. Every one got up, and Orn bade them clear away from the land, if they could. Olaf said, "That is not the way out of our plight, for I see reefs all about astern; so let down the sail at once, and we will take our counsel when there is daylight, and we know what land this is." Then they cast anchors, and they caught bottom at once. There was much talk during the night as to where they could be come to; and when daylight was up they recognised that it was Ireland. Orn said, "I don't think we have come to a good place, for this is far away from the harbours or market-towns, whose strangers enjoy peace; and we are now left high and dry, like sticklebacks, and near enough, I think, I come to the laws of the Irish in saying that they will lay claim to the goods we have on board as their lawful prize, for as flotsam they put down ships even when sea has ebbed out shorter from the stern (than here)." Olaf said no harm would happen, "But I have seen that to-day there is a gathering of men up inland; so the Irish think, no doubt, the arrival of this ship a great thing. During the ebb-tide to-day I noticed that there was a dip, and that out of the dip the sea fell without emptying it out; and if our ship has not been damaged, we can put out our boat and tow the ship into it." There was a bottom of loam where they had been riding at anchor, so that not a plank of the ship was damaged. So Olaf and his men tow their boat to the dip, cast anchor there. Now, as day drew on, crowds drifted down to the shore. At last two men rowed a boat out to the ship. They asked what men they were who had charge of that ship, and Olaf answered, speaking in Irish, to their inquiries.

When the Irish knew they were Norwegians they pleaded their law, and bade them give up their goods; and if they did so, they would do them no harm till the king had sat in judgment on their case. Olaf said the law only held good when merchants had no interpreter with them. "But I can say with truth these are peaceful men, and we will not give ourselves up untried." The Irish then raised a great war-cry, and waded out into the sea, and wished to drag the ship, with them on board, to the shore, the water being no deeper than reaching up to their armpits, or to the belts of the tallest. But the pool was so deep where the ship was floating that they could not touch the bottom. Olaf bade the crew fetch out their weapons, and range in line of battle from stem to stern on the ship; and so thick they stood, that shield overlapped shield all round the ship, and a spear-point stood out at the lower end of every shield. Olaf walked fore to the prow, and was thus arrayed: he had a coat of mail, and a gold-reddened helmet on his head; girt with a sword with gold-inlaid hilt, and in his hand a barbed spear chased and well engraved. A red shield he had before him, on which was drawn a lion in gold. When the Irish saw this array fear shot through their hearts, and they thought it would not be so easy a matter as they had thought to master the booty. So now the Irish break their journey, and run all together to a village near. Then there arose great murmur in the crowd, as they deemed that, sure enough, this must be a warship, and that they must expect many others; so they sent speedily word to the king, which was easy, as he was at that time a short way off, feasting. Straightway he rides with a company of men to where the ship was. Between the land and the place where the ship lay afloat the space was no greater than that one might well hear men talking together. Now Olaf stood forth in the same arrayal whereof is written before, and men marvelled much how noble was the appearance of the man who was the captain of the ship. But when the shipmates of Olaf see how a large company of knights rides towards them, looking a company of the bravest, they grow hushed, for they deemed here were great odds to deal with. But when Olaf heard the murmur which went round among his followers, he bade them take heart, "For now our affairs are in a fair way; the Irish are now greeting Myrkjartan, their king." Then they rode so near to the ship, that each could hear what the other said. The king asked who was the master of the ship. Olaf told his name, and asked who was the valiant-looking knight with whom he then was talking. He answered, "I am called Myrkjartan." Olaf asked, "Are you then a king of the Irish?" He said he was. Then the king asked Olaf for news commonly talked of, and Olaf gave good answers as to all news he was asked about. Then the king asked whence they had put to sea, and whose men they were. And still the king asked, more searchingly than before, about Olaf's kindred, for the king found that this man was of haughty bearing, and would not answer any further than the king asked. Olaf said, "Let it be known to you that we ran our ship afloat from the coast of Norway, and these are of the bodyguard of King Harald, the son of Gunnhild, who are here on board. And as for my race, I have, sire, to tell you this, that my father lives in Iceland, and is named Hoskuld, a man of high birth; but of my mother's kindred, I think you must have seen many more than I have. For my mother is called Melkorka, and it has been told me as a truth that she is your daughter, king. Now, this has driven me upon this long journey, and to me it is a matter most weighty what answer you give in my case." The king then grew silent, and had a converse with his men. The wise men asked the king what might be the real truth of the story that this man was telling. The king answered, "This is clearly seen in this Olaf, that he is high-born man, whether he be a kinsman of mine or not, as well as this, that of all men he speaks the best of Irish." After that the king stood up, and said, "Now I will give answer to your speech, in so far as we grant to you and all your shipmates peace; but on the kinship you claim with us, we must talk more before I give answer to that." After that they put out their gangways to the shore, and Olaf and his followers went on land from the ship; and the Irish now marvel much how warrior-like these men are. Olaf greeted the king well, taking off his helmet and bowing to the king, who welcomes Olaf with all fondness. Thereupon they fall to talking together, Olaf pleading his case again in a speech long and frank; and at the end of his speech he said he had a ring on his hand that Melkorka had given him at parting in Iceland, saying "that you, king, gave it her as a tooth gift." The king took and looked at the ring, and his face grew wondrous red to look at; and then the king said, "True enough are the tokens, and become by no means less notable thereby that you have so many of your mother's family features, and that even by them you might be easily recognised; and because of these things I will in sooth acknowledge your kinship, Olaf, by the witnessing of these men that here are near and hear my speech. And this shall also follow that I will ask you to my court, with all your suite, but the honour of you all will depend thereon of what worth as a man I find you to be when I try you more." After that the king orders riding-horses to be given to them, and appoints men to look after their ship, and to guard the goods belonging to them. The King now rode to Dublin, and men thought this great tidings, that with the king should be journeying the son of his daughter, who had been carried off in war long ago when she was only fifteen winters old. But most startled of all at these tidings was the foster-mother of Melkorka, who was then bed-ridden, both from heavy sickness and old age; yet she walked with no staff even to support her, to meet Olaf. The king said to Olaf, "Here is come Melkorka's foster-mother, and she will wish to hear all the tidings you can tell about Melkorka's life." Olaf took her with open arms, and set the old woman on his knee, and said her foster-daughter was well settled and in a good position in Iceland. Then Olaf put in her hands the knife and the belt, and the old woman recognised the gifts, and wept for joy, and said it was easy to see that Melkorka's son was one of high mettle, and no wonder, seeing what stock he comes of. The old woman was strong and well, and in good spirits all that winter. The king was seldom at rest, for at that time the lands in the west were at all times raided by war-bands. The king drove from his land that winter both Vikings and raiders. Olaf was with his suite in the king's ship, and those who came against them thought his was indeed a grim company to deal with. The king talked over with Olaf and his followers all matters needing counsel, for Olaf proved himself to the king both wise and eager-minded in all deeds of prowess. But towards the latter end of the winter the king summoned a Thing, and great numbers came. The king stood up and spoke. He began his speech thus: "You all know that last autumn there came hither a man who is the son of my daughter, and high-born also on his father's side; and it seems to me that Olaf is a man of such prowess and courage that here such men are not to be found. Now I offer him my kingdom after my day is done, for Olaf is much more suitable for a ruler than my own sons." Olaf thanked him for this offer with many graceful and fair words, and said he would not run the risk as to how his sons might behave when Myrkjartan was no more; said it was better to gain swift honour than lasting shame; and added that he wished to go to Norway when ships could safely journey from land to land, and that his mother would have little delight in life if he did not return to her. The king bade Olaf do as he thought best. Then the Thing was broken up. When Olaf's ship was ready, the king saw him off on board; and gave him a spear chased with gold, and a gold-bedecked sword, and much money besides. Olaf begged that he might take Melkorka's foster-mother with him; but the king said there was no necessity for that, so she did not go. Then Olaf got on board his ship, and he and the king parted with the greatest friendship. Then Olaf sailed out to sea. They had a good voyage, and made land in Norway; and Olaf's journey became very famous. They set up their ship; and Olaf got horses for himself, and went, together with his followers, to find King Harald.

Chapter 22
Olaf the Peacock comes Home to Iceland, A.D. 957

Olaf Hoskuldson then went to the court of King Harald. The king gave him a good welcome, but Gunnhild a much better. With many fair words they begged him to stay with them, and Olaf agreed to it, and both he and Orn entered the king's court. King Harald and Gunnhild set so great a store by Olaf that no foreigner had ever been held in such honour by them. Olaf gave to the king and Gunnhild many rare gifts, which he had got west in Ireland. King Harald gave Olaf at Yule a set of clothes made out of scarlet stuff. So now Olaf stayed there quietly all the winter. In the spring, as it was wearing on, Olaf and the king had a conversation together, and Olaf begged the king's leave to go to Iceland in the summer, "For I have noble kinsfolk there I want to go and see." The king answered, "It would be more to my mind that you should settle down with us, and take whatever position in our service you like best yourself." Olaf thanked the king for all the honour he was offering him, but said he wished very much to go to Iceland, if that was not against the king's will. The king answered, "Nothing shall be done in this in an unfriendly manner to you, Olaf. You shall go out to Iceland in the summer, for I see you have set your heart on it; but neither trouble nor toil shall you have over your preparations, for

I will see after all that," and thereupon they part talking. King Harald had a ship launched in the spring; it was a merchant ship, both great and good. This ship the king ordered to be laden with wood, and fitted out with full rigging. When the ship was ready the king had Olaf called to him, and said, "This ship shall be your own, Olaf, for I should not like you to start from Norway this summer as a passenger in any one else's ship." Olaf thanked the king in fair words for his generosity. After that Olaf got ready for his journey; and when he was ready and a fair wind arose, Olaf sailed out to sea, and King Harald and he parted with the greatest affection. That summer Olaf had a good voyage. He brought his ship into Ramfirth, to Board-Ere. The arrival of the ship was soon heard of, and also who the captain was. Hoskuld heard of the arrival of Olaf, his son, and was very much pleased, and rode forthwith north to Hrutafjord with some men, and there was a joyful meeting between the father and son. Hoskuld invited Olaf to come to him, and Olaf said he would agree to that; so he set up his ship, but his goods were brought (on horseback) from the north. And when this business was over Olaf himself rode with twelve men home to Hoskuldstead, and Hoskuld greeted his son joyfully, and his brothers also received him fondly, as well as all his kinsfolk; but between Olaf and Bard was love the fondest. Olaf became very renowned for this journey; and now was proclaimed the descent of Olaf, that he was the daughter's son of Myrkjartan, king of Ireland. The news of this spread over the land, as well as of the honour that mighty men, whom he had gone to see, had bestowed on him. Melkorka came soon to see Olaf, her son, and Olaf greeted her with great joy. She asked about many things in Ireland, first of her father and then of her other relations. Olaf replied to everything she asked. Then she asked if her foster-mother still lived. Olaf said she was still alive. Melkorka asked why he had not tried to give her the pleasure of bringing her over to Iceland. Olaf replied, "They would not allow me to bring your foster-mother out of Ireland, mother." "That may be so," she replied, and it could be seen that this she took much to heart. Melkorka and Thorbjorn had one son, who was named Lambi. He was a tall man and strong, like his father in looks as well as in temper. When Olaf had been in Iceland a month, and spring came on, father and son took counsel together. "I will, Olaf," said Hoskuld, "that a match should be sought for you, and that then you should take over the house of your foster-father at Goddistead, where still there are great means stored up, and that then you should look after the affairs of that household under my guidance." Olaf answered, "Little have I set my mind on that sort of thing hitherto; besides, I do not know where that woman lives whom to marry would mean any great good luck to me. You must know I shall look high for a wife. But I see clearly that you would not have broached this matter till you had made up your mind as to where it was to end." Hoskuld said, "You guess that right. There is a man named Egil. He is Skallagrim's son. He lives at Borg, in Borgarfjord. This Egil has a daughter who is called Thorgerd, and she is the woman I have made up my mind to woo on your behalf, for she is the very best match in all Borgarfjord, and even if one went further afield. Moreover, it is to be looked for, that an alliance with the Mere-men would mean more power to you." Olaf answered, "Herein I shall trust to your foresight, for if this match were to come off it would be altogether to my liking. But this you must bear in mind, father, that should this matter be set forth, and not come off, I should take it very ill." Hoskuld answered, "I think I shall venture to bring the matter about." Olaf bade him do as he liked. Now time wears on towards the Thing. Hoskuld prepares his journey from home with a crowded company, and Olaf, his son, also accompanies him on the journey. They set up their booth. A great many people were there. Egil Skallagrim's son was at the Thing. Every one who saw Olaf remarked what a handsome man he was, and how noble his bearing, well arrayed as he was as to weapons and clothes.

Chapter 23
The Marriage of Olaf Peacock and Thorgerd, the Daughter of Egil, A.D. 959

It is told how one day the father and son, Hoskuld and Olaf, went forth from their booth to find Egil. Egil greeted them well, for he and Hoskuld knew each other very well by word of mouth. Hoskuld now broaches the wooing on behalf of Olaf, and asks for the hand of Thorgerd. She was also at the Thing. Egil took the matter well, and said he had always heard both father and son well spoken of, "and I also know, Hoskuld," said Egil, "that you are a high-born man and of great worth, and Olaf is much renowned on account of his journey, and it is no wonder that such men should look high for a match, for he lacks neither family nor good looks; but yet this must be talked over with Thorgerd, for it is no man's task to get Thorgerd for wife against her will." Hoskuld said, "I wish, Egil, that you would talk this over with your daughter." Egil said that that should be done. Egil now went away to find his daughter, and they talked together. Egil said, "There is here a man named Olaf, who is Hoskuld's son, and he is now one of the most renowned of men. Hoskuld, his father, has broached a wooing on behalf of Olaf, and has sued for your hand; and I have left that matter mostly for you to deal with. Now I want to know your answer. But it seems to me that it behoves you to give a good answer to such a matter, for this match is a noble one." Thorgerd answered, "I have often heard you say that you love me best of all your children, but now it seems to me you make that a falsehood if you wish me to marry the son of a bonds-woman, however goodly and great a dandy he may be." Egil said, "In this matter you are not so well up, as in others. Have you not heard that he is the son of the daughter of Myrkjartan, king of Ireland? so that he is much higher born on his mother's side than on his father's, which, however, would be quite good enough for us." Thorgerd would not see this; and so they dropped the talk, each being somewhat of a different mind. The next day Egil went to Hoskuld's booth. Hoskuld gave him a good welcome, and so they fell a-talking together.

Hoskuld asked how this wooing matter had sped. Egil held out but little hope, and told him all that had come to pass. Hoskuld said it looked like a closed matter, "Yet I think you have behaved well." Olaf did not hear this talk of theirs. After that Egil went away. Olaf now asks, "How speeds the wooing?" Hoskuld said, "It pointed to slow speed on her side." Olaf said, "It is now as I told you, father, that I should take it very ill if in answer (to the wooing) I should have to take shaming words, seeing that the broaching of the wooing gives undue right to the wooed. And now I shall have my way so far, that this shall not drop here. For true is the saw, that 'others' errands eat the wolves'; and now I shall go straightway to Egil's booth." Hoskuld bade him have his own way. Olaf now dressed himself in this way, that he had on the scarlet clothes King Harald had given him, and a golden helmet on his head, and the gold-adorned sword in his hand that King Myrkjartan had given him. Then Hoskuld and Olaf went to Egil's booth. Hoskuld went first, and Olaf followed close on his heels. Egil greeted him well, and Hoskuld sat down by him, but Olaf stood up and looked about him. He saw a woman sitting on the dais in the booth, she was goodly and had the looks of one of high degree, and very well dressed. He thought to himself this must be Thorgerd, Egil's daughter. Olaf went up to the dais and sat down by her. Thorgerd greeted the man, and asked who he was. Olaf told his own and his father's name, and "You must think it very bold that the son of a slave should dare to sit down by you and presume to talk to you!" She said, "You cannot but mean that you must be thinking you have done deeds of greater daring than that of talking to women." Then they began to talk together, and they talked all day. But nobody heard their conversation. And before they parted Egil and Hoskuld were called to them; and the matter of Olaf's wooing was now talked over again, and Thorgerd came round to her father's wish. Now the affair was all easily settled and the betrothal took place. The honour was conceded to the Salmon-river-Dale men that the bride should be brought home to them, for by law the bride-groom should have gone to the bride's home to be married. The wedding was to take place at Hoskuldstead when seven weeks summer had passed. After that Egil and Hoskuld separated. The father and son rode home to Hoskuldstead, and all was quiet the rest of the summer. After that things were got ready for the wedding at Hoskuldstead, and nothing was spared, for means were plentiful. The guests came at the time settled, and the Burgfirthmen mustered in a great company. Egil was there, and Thorstein, his son. The bride was in the journey too, and with her a chosen company out of all the countryside. Hoskuld had also a great company awaiting them. The feast was a brave one, and the guests were seen off with good gifts on leaving. Olaf gave to Egil the sword, Myrkjartan's gift, and Egil's brow brightened greatly at the gift. Nothing in the way of tidings befell, and every one went home.

Chapter 24
The Building of Herdholt, A. D. 960

Olaf and Thorgerd lived at Hoskuldstead and loved each other very dearly; it was easily seen by every one that she was a woman of very high mettle, though she meddled little with every-day things, but whatever Thorgerd put her hand to must be carried through as she wished. Olaf and Thorgerd spent that winter turn and turn about at Hoskuldstead, or with Olaf's foster-father. In the spring Olaf took over the household business at Goddistead. The following summer Thord fell ill, and the illness ended in his death. Olaf had a cairn raised over him on the ness that runs out into the Salmon-river and is called Drafn-ness, with a wall round which is called Howes-garth. After that liegemen crowded to Olaf and he became a great chieftain. Hoskuld was not envious of this, for he always wished that Olaf should be consulted in all great matters. The place Olaf owned was the stateliest in Salmon-river-Dale. There were two brothers with Olaf, both named An. One was called An the White and the other An the Black. They had a third brother who was named Beiner the Strong. These were Olaf's smiths, and very valiant men. Thorgerd and Olaf had a daughter who was named Thurid. The land that Hrapp had owned all lay waste, as has been told before. Olaf thought that it lay well and set before his father his wishes on the matter; how they should send down to Trefill with this errand, that Olaf wished to buy the land and other things thereto belonging at Hrappstead. It was soon arranged and the bargain settled, for Trefill saw that better was one crow in the hand than two in the wood. The bargain arranged was that Olaf should give three marks of silver for the land; yet that was not fair price, for the lands were wide and fair and very rich in useful produce, such as good salmon fishing and seal catching. There were wide woods too, a little further up than Hoskuldstead, north of the Salmon-river, in which was a space cleared, and it was well-nigh a matter of certainty that the flocks of Olaf would gather together there whether the weather was hard or mild. One autumn it befell that on that same hill Olaf had built a dwelling of the timber that was cut out of the forest, though some he got together from drift-wood strands. This was a very lofty dwelling. The buildings stood empty through the winter. The next spring Olaf went thither and first gathered together all his flocks which had grown to be a great multitude; for, indeed, no man was richer in live stock in all Broadfirth. Olaf now sent word to his father that he should be standing out of doors and have a look at his train as he was moving to his new home, and should give him his good wishes. Hoskuld said so it should be. Olaf now arranged how it should be done. He ordered that all the shiest of his cattle should be driven first and then the milking live stock, then came the dry cattle, and the pack horses came in the last place; and men were ranged with the animals to keep them from straying out of straight line. When the van of the train had got to the new homestead, Olaf was just riding out of Goddistead and there was nowhere a gap breaking the line. Hoskuld stood outside his door together with those of his household. Then Hoskuld spake, bidding Olaf his son welcome and abide all honour to this new dwelling of his, "And somehow my mind forebodes me that this will follow, that for a long time his name will be remembered." Jorunn his wife said, "Wealth enough the slave's son has got for his name to be long remembered." At the moment that the house-carles had unloaded the pack horses Olaf rode into the place. Then he said, "Now you shall have your curiosity satisfied with regard to what you have been talking about all the winter, as to what this place shall be called; it shall be called Herdholt." Every one thought this a very happy name, in view of what used to happen there. Olaf now sets up his household at Herdholt, and a stately one it soon became, and nothing was lacking there. And now the honour of Olaf greatly increased, there being many causes to bring it about: Olaf was the most beloved of men, for whatever he had to do with affairs of men, he did so that all were well contented with their lot. His father backed him up very much towards being a widely honoured man, and Olaf gained much in power from his alliance with the Mere-men. Olaf was considered the noblest of all Hoskuld's sons. The first winter that Olaf kept house at Herdholt, he had many servants and workmen, and work was divided amongst the house-carles; one looked after the dry cattle and another after the cows. The fold was out in the wood, some way from the homestead. One evening the man who looked after the dry cattle came to Olaf and asked him to make some other man look after the neat and "set apart for me some other work." Olaf answered, "I wish you to go on with this same work of yours." The man said he would sooner go away. "Then you think there is something wrong," said Olaf. "I will go this evening with you when you do up the cattle, and if I think there is any excuse for you in this I will say nothing about it, but otherwise you will find that your lot will take some turn for the worse." Olaf took his gold-set spear, the king's gift, in his hand, and left home, and with him the house-carle. There was some snow on the ground. They came to the fold, which was open, and Olaf bade the house-carle go in. "I will drive up the cattle and you tie them up as they come in." The house-carle went to the fold-door. And all unawares Olaf finds him leaping into his open arms. Olaf asked why he went on so terrified? He replied, "Hrapp stands in the doorway of the fold, and felt after me, but I have had my fill of wrestling with him." Olaf went to the fold door and struck at him with his spear. Hrapp took the socket of the spear in both hands and wrenched it aside, so that forthwith the spear shaft broke. Olaf was about to run at Hrapp but he disappeared there where he stood, and there they parted, Olaf having the shaft and Hrapp the spear-head. After that Olaf and the house-carle tied up the cattle and went home. Olaf saw the house-carle was not to blame for his grumbling. The next morning Olaf went to where Hrapp was buried and had him dug up. Hrapp was found undecayed, and there Olaf also found his spear-head. After that he had a pyre made and had Hrapp burnt on it, and his ashes were flung out to sea. After that no one had any more trouble with

Hrapp's ghost.

Chapter 25

About Hoskuld's Sons

Now Hoskuld's sons shall be told about. Thorliek, Hoskuld's son, had been a great seafarer, and taken service with men in lordly station when he was on his merchant voyages before he settled down as a householder, and a man of mark he was thought to be. He had also been on Viking raids, and given good account of himself by reason of his courage. Bard, Hoskuld's son, had also been a seafarer, and was well accounted of wherever he went, for he was the best of brave men and true, and a man of moderation in all things. Bard married a Broadfirth woman, named Astrid, who came of a good stock. Bard's son was named Thorarin, and his daughter Gudney, who married Hall, the son of Fight Styr, and from them are descended many great families. Hrut, Herjolf's son, gave a thrall of his, named Hrolf, his freedom, and with it a certain amount of money, and a dwelling-place where his land joined with Hoskuld's. And it lay so near the landmark that Hrut's people had made a mistake in the matter, and settled the freedman down on the land belonging to Hoskuld. He soon gained there much wealth. Hoskuld took it very much to heart that Hrut should have placed his freedman right up against his ear, and bade the freedman pay him money for the lands he lived on "for it is mine own." The freedman went to Hrut and told him all they had spoken together. Hrut bade him give no heed, and pay no money to Hoskuld. "For I do not know," he said, "to which of us the land belonged." So the freedman went home, and goes on with his household just as before. A little later, Thorliek, Hoskuld's son, went at the advice of his father to the dwelling of the freedman and took him and killed him, and Thorliek claimed as his and his father's own all the money the freedman had made. Hrut heard this, and he and his sons liked it very ill. They were most of them grown up, and the band of kinsmen was deemed a most forbidding one to grapple with. Hrut fell back on the law as to how this ought to turn out, and when the matter was searched into by lawyers, Hrut and his son stood at but little advantage, for it was held a matter of great weight that Hrut had set the freedman down without leave on Hoskuld's land, where he had made money, Thorliek having slain the man within his and his father's own lands. Hrut took his lot very much to heart; but things remained quiet. After that Thorliek had a homestead built on the boundary of Hrut and Hoskuld's lands, and it was called Combness. There Thorliek lived for a while, as has been told before. Thorliek begat a son of his wife. The boy was sprinkled with water and called Bolli. He was at an early age a very promising man.

Chapter 26
The Death of Hoskuld, A.D. 985

Hoskuld, Koll o' Dales' son, fell ill in his old age, and he sent for his sons and other kinsfolk, and when they were come Hoskuld spoke to the brothers Bard and Thorliek, and said, "I have taken some sickness, and as I have not been much in the way of falling ill before, I think this may bring me to death; and now, as you know, you are both begotten in wedlock, and are entitled to all inheritance left by me. But there is a third son of mine, one who is not born in wedlock, and I will ask you brothers to allow him, Olaf to wit, to be adopted, so that he take of my means one-third with you." Bard answered first, and said that he would do as his father wished, "for I look for honour from Olaf in every way, the more so the wealthier he becomes." Then Thorliek said, "It is far from my wish that Olaf be adopted; he has plenty of money already; and you, father, have for a long time given him a great deal, and for a very long time dealt unevenly with us. I will not freely give up the honour to which I am born." Hoskuld said, "Surely you will not rob me of the law that allows me to give twelve ounces to my son, seeing how high-born Olaf is on his mother's side." To this Thorliek now agreed. Then Hoskuld took the gold ring, Hakon's gift, that weighed a mark, and the sword, King's gift whereon was half a mark of gold, and gave them to Olaf, his son, and therewith his good luck and that of the family, saying he did not speak in this way because he did not know well enough that the luck had already come to him. Olaf took his gifts, and said he would risk how Thorliek would like it. Thorliek liked it very ill, and thought that Hoskuld had behaved in a very underhand way to him. Olaf said, "I shall not give up the gifts, Thorliek, for you agreed to the gift in the face of witnesses; and I shall run the risk to keep it." Bard said he would obey his father's wishes. After that Hoskuld died, and his death was very much grieved for, in the first place by his sons, and next by all his relations and friends. His sons had a worthy cairn made for him; but little money was put into it with him. And when this was over, the brothers began to talk over the matter of preparing an "arvale" (burial feast) after their father, for at that time such was the custom. Olaf said, "It seems to me that we should not be in a hurry about preparing this feast, if it is to be as noble as we should think right; now the autumn is very far worn, and the ingathering of means for it is no longer easy; most people who have to come a long way would find that a hard matter in the autumn days; so that it is certain that many would not come of the men we most should like to see. So I will now make the offer, next summer at the Thing, to bid men to the feast, and I will bear one-third of the cost of the wassail." The brothers agreed to that, and Olaf now went home. Thorliek and Bard now share the goods between them. Bard had the estate and lands, which was what most men held to, as he was the most popular; but Thorliek got for his share more of the chattels. Olaf and Bard got on well together, but Olaf and Thorliek rather snappishly. Now the next winter passed, and summer comes, and time wears on towards the Thing. The sons of Hoskuld got ready to go to the Thing. It was soon seen clearly enough how Olaf took the lead of the brothers. When they got to the Thing they set up three booths, and make themselves comfortable in a handsome manner.

Chapter 27

The Funeral Feast for Hoskuld

It is told how one day when people went to the law rock Olaf stood up and asked for a hearing, and told them first of the death of his father, "and there are now here many men, kinsmen and friends of his. It is the will of my brothers that I ask you to a funeral feast in memory of Hoskuld our father. All you chieftains, for most of the mightier men are such, as were bound by alliances to him, I let it be known that no one of the greater men shall go away giftless. And herewith I bid all the farmers and any who will accept–rich or poor–to a half month's feast at Hoskuldstead ten weeks before the winter." And when Olaf finished his speech good cheer was made thereto, and his bidding was looked upon as a right lordly one. And when Olaf came home to the booth he told his brothers what he had settled to do. The brothers were not much pleased, and thought that this was going in for far too much state. After the Thing the brothers rode home and the summer now wears on. Then the brothers got ready for the feast, and Olaf put forward unstintedly his third part, and the feast was furnished with the best of provisions. Great stores were laid in for this feast, for it was expected many folk would come. And when the time came it is said that most of the chief men came that were asked. There were so many that most men say that there could not be far short of nine hundred (1080). This is the most crowded burial feast that has been in Iceland, second to that which the sons of Hialti gave at the funeral of their father, at which time there were 1440 guests. But this feast was of the bravest in every way, and the brothers got great honour therefrom, Olaf being at the head of the affair throughout. Olaf took even share with his brothers in the gifts; and gifts were bestowed on all the chiefs. When most of the men had gone away Olaf went to have a talk with Thorliek his brother, and said, "So it is, kinsman, as you know, that no love has been lost between us; now I would beg for a better understanding in our brotherhood. I know you did not like when I took the heirlooms my father gave me on his dying day. Now if you think yourself wronged in this, I will do as much for gaining back your whole good-will as to give fostering to your son. For it is said that ever he is the lesser man who fosters another's child." Thorliek took this in good part, and said, as was true, that this was honourably offered. And now Olaf took home Bolli, the son of Thorliek, who at this time was three winters old. They parted now with the utmost affection, and Bolli went home to Herdholt with Olaf. Thorgerd received him well, and Bolli grew up there and was loved no less than their own children.

Chapter 28
The Birth of Kjartan, Olaf's Son, A.D. 978

Olaf and Thorgerd had a son, and the boy was sprinkled with water and a name was given him, Olaf letting him be called Kjartan after Myrkjartan his mother's father. Bolli and Kjartan were much of an age. Olaf and Thorgerd had still more children; three sons were called Steinthor and Halldor and Helgi, and Hoskuld was the name of the youngest of Olaf's sons. The daughters of Olaf and his wife were named Bergthora, Thorgerd, and Thorbjorg. All their children were of goodly promise as they grew up. At that time Holmgang Bersi lived in Saurby at an abode called Tongue. He comes to see Olaf and asked for Halldor his son to foster. Olaf agreed to this and Halldor went home with him, being then one winter old. That summer Bersi fell ill, and lay in bed for a great part of the summer. It is told how one day, when all the men were out haymaking at Tongue and only they two, Bersi and Halldor, were left in the house, Halldor lay in his cradle and the cradle fell over under the boy and he fell out of it on to the floor, and Bersi could not get to him. Then Bersi said this ditty:

> Here we both lie
> In helpless plight,
> Halldor and I,
> Have no power left us;
> Old age afflicts me,
> Youth afflicts you,
> You will get better
> But I shall get worse.

Later on people came in and picked Halldor up off the floor, and Bersi got better. Halldor was brought up there, and was a tall man and doughty looking. Kjartan, Olaf's son, grew up at home at Herdholt. He was of all men the goodliest of those who have been born in Iceland. He was striking of countenance and fair of feature, he had the finest eyes of any man, and was light of hue. He had a great deal of hair as fair as silk, falling in curls; he was a big man, and strong, taking after his mother's father Egil, or his uncle Thorolf. Kjartan was better proportioned than any man, so that all wondered who saw him. He was better skilled at arms than most men; he was a deft craftsman, and the best swimmer of all men. In all deeds of strength he was far before others, more gentle than any other man, and so engaging that every child loved him; he was light of heart, and free with his money. Olaf loved Kjartan best of all his children. Bolli, his foster-brother, was a great man, he came next to Kjartan in all deeds of strength and prowess; he was strong, and fair of face and courteous, and most warrior-like, and a great dandy. The foster-brothers were very fond of each other. Olaf now remained quietly in his home, and for a good many years.

Chapter 29
Olaf's Second Journey to Norway, A.D. 975

It is told how one spring Olaf broke the news to Thorgerd that he wished to go out voyaging–"And I wish you to look after our household and children." Thorgerd said she did not much care about doing that; but Olaf said he would have his way. He bought a ship that stood up in the West, at Vadill. Olaf started during the summer, and brought his ship to Hordaland. There, a short way inland, lived a man whose name was Giermund Roar, a mighty man and wealthy, and a great Viking; he was an evil man to deal with, but had now settled down in quiet at home, and was of the bodyguard of Earl Hakon. The mighty Giermund went down to his ship and soon recognised Olaf, for he had heard him spoken of before. Giermund bade Olaf come and stay with him, with as many of his men as he liked to bring. Olaf accepted his invitation, and went there with seven men. The crew of Olaf went into lodgings about Hordaland. Giermund entertained Olaf well. His house was a lofty one, and there were many men there, and plenty of amusement all the winter. And towards the end of the winter Olaf told Giermund the reason of his voyage, which was that he wished to get for himself some house-timber, and said he set great store by obtaining timber of a choice kind. Giermund said, "Earl Hakon has the best of woods, and I know quite well if you went to see him you would be made welcome to them, for the Earl receives well, men who are not half so well-bred as you, Olaf, when they go to see him." In the spring Olaf got ready to go and find Hakon Earl; and the Earl gave him exceeding good welcome, and bade Olaf stay with him as long as he liked. Olaf told the Earl the reason of his journey, "And I beg this of you, sir, that you give us permission to cut wood for house-building from your forests." The Earl answered, "You are welcome to load your ship with timber, and I will give it you. For I think it no every-day occurrence when such men as you come from Iceland to visit me." At parting the Earl gave him a gold-inlaid axe, and the best of keepsakes it was; and therewith they parted in the greatest friendship. Giermund in the meantime set stewards over his estates secretly, and made up his mind to go to Iceland in the summer in Olaf's ship. He kept this secret from every one. Olaf knew nothing about it till Giermund brought his money to Olaf's ship, and very great wealth it was. Olaf said, "You should not have gone in my ship if I had known of this before-hand, for I think there are those in Iceland for whom it would be better never to have seen you. But since you have come with so much goods, I cannot drive you out like a straying cur." Giermund said, "I shall not return for all your high words, for I mean to be your passenger." Olaf and his got on board, and put out to sea. They had a good voyage and made Broadfirth, and they put out their gangways and landed at Salmon-river-Mouth. Olaf had the wood taken out of his ship, and the ship put up in the shed his father had made. Olaf then asked Giermund to come and stay with him. That summer Olaf had a fire-hall built at Herdholt, a greater and better than had ever been seen before. Noble legends were painted on its wainscoting and in the roof, and this was so well done that the hall was thought even more beautiful when the hangings were not up. Giermund did not meddle with every-day matters, but was uncouth to most people. He was usually dressed in this way–he wore a scarlet kirtle below and a grey cloak outside, and a bearskin cap on his head, and a sword in his hand. This was a great weapon and good, with a hilt of walrus tooth, with no silver on it; the brand was sharp, and no rust would stay thereon. This sword he called Footbiter, and he never let it out of his hands. Giermund had not been there long before he fell in love with Thured, Olaf's daughter, and proposed to Olaf for her hand; but he gave him a straight refusal. Then Giermund gave some money to Thorgerd with a view to gaining the match. She took the money, for it was offered unstintedly. Then Thorgerd broached the matter to Olaf, and said she thought their daughter could not be better married, "for he is a very brave man, wealthy and high-mettled." Then Olaf answered, "I will not go against you in this any more than in other things, though I would sooner marry Thured to some one else." Thorgerd went away and thought her business had sped well, and now told Giermund the upshot of it. He thanked her for her help and her determination, and Giermund broached the wooing a second time to Olaf, and now won the day easily. After that Giermund and Thured were betrothed, and the wedding was to be held at the end of the winter at Herdholt. The wedding feast was a very crowded one, for the new hall was finished. Ulf Uggason was of the bidden guests, and he had made a poem on Olaf Hoskuldson and of the legends that were painted round the hall, and he gave it forth at the feast. This poem is called the "House Song," and is well made. Olaf rewarded him well for the poem. Olaf gave great gifts to all the chief men who came. Olaf was considered to have gained in renown by this feast.

Chapter 30
About Giermund and Thured, A.D. 978

Giermund and Thured did not get on very well together, and little love was lost between them on either side. When Giermund had stayed with Olaf three winters he wished to go away, and gave out that Thured and his daughter Groa should remain behind. This little maid was by then a year old, and Giermund would not leave behind any money for them. This the mother and daughter liked very ill, and told Olaf so. Olaf said, "What is the matter now, Thorgerd? is the Eastman now not so bounteous as he was that autumn when he asked for the alliance?" They could get Olaf to do nothing, for he was an easygoing man, and said the girl should remain until she wished to go, or knew how in some way to shift for herself. At parting Olaf gave Giermund the merchant ship all fitted out. Giermund thanked him well therefor, and said it was a noble gift. Then he got on board his ship, and sailed out of the Salmon-river-Mouth by a north-east breeze, which dropped as they came out to the islands. He now lies by Oxe-isle half a month without a fair wind rising for a start. At that time Olaf had to leave home to look after his foreshore drifts. Then Thured, his daughter, called to his house-carles, and bade them come with her. She had the maid Groa with her, and they were a party of ten together. She lets run out into the water a ferry-boat that belonged to Olaf, and Thured bade them sail and row down along Hvamfirth, and when they came out to the islands she bade them put out the cock-boat that was in the ferry. Thured got into the boat with two men, and bade the others take care of the ship she left behind until she returned. She took the little maid in her arms, and bade the men row across the current until they should reach the ship (of Giermund). She took a gimlet out of the boat's locker, and gave it to one of her companions, and bade him go to the cockle-boat belonging to the merchant ship and bore a hole in it so as to disable it if they needed it in a hurry. Then she had herself put ashore with the little maid still in her arms. This was at the hour of sunrise. She went across the gangway into the ship, where all men were asleep. She went to the hammock where Giermund slept. His sword Footbiter hung on a peg pole. Thured now sets the little maid in the hammock, and snatched off Footbiter and took it with her. Then she left the ship and rejoined her companions. Now the little maid began to cry, and with that Giermund woke up and recognised the child, and thought he knew who must be at the bottom of this. He springs up wanting to seize his sword, and misses it, as was to be expected, and then went to the gunwale, and saw that they were rowing away from the ship. Giermund called to his men, and bade them leap into the cockle-boat and row after them. They did so, but when they got a little way they found how the coal-blue sea poured into them, so they went back to the ship. Then Giermund called Thured and bade her come back and give him his sword Footbiter, "and take your little maid, and with her as much money as you like." Thured answered, "Would you rather than not have the sword back?" Giermund answered, "I would give a great deal of money before I should care to let my sword go." Thured answered, "Then you shall never have it again, for you have in many ways behaved cowardly towards me, and here we shall part for good." Then Giermund said, "Little luck will you get with the sword." Thured said she would take the risk of that. "Then I lay thereon this spell," said Giermund, "That this sword shall do to death the man in your family in who would be the greatest loss, and in a manner most ill-fated." After that Thured went home to Herdholt. Olaf had then come home, and showed his displeasure at her deed, yet all was quiet. Thured gave Bolli, her cousin, the sword Footbiter, for she loved him in no way less than her brothers. Bolli bore that sword for a long time after. After this Giermund got a favourable wind, and sailed out to sea, and came to Norway in the autumn. They sailed one night on to some hidden rocks before Stade, and then Giermund and all his crew perished. And that is the end of all there is to tell about Giermund.

Chapter 31
Thured's Second Marriage, A.D. 980

Olaf Hoskuldson now stayed at home in much honour, as has been told before. There was a man named Gudmund, who was the son of Solmund, and lived at Asbjornness north in Willowdale. He wooed Thured, and got her and a great deal of wealth with her. Thured was a wise woman, high-tempered and most stirring. Their sons were called Hall and Bard and Stein and Steingrim. Gudrun and Olof were their daughters. Thorbjorg, Olaf's daughter, was of women the most beautiful and stout of build. She was called Thorbjorg the Stout, and was married west in Waterfirth to Asgier, the son of Knott. He was a noble man. Their son was Kjartan, father of Thorvald, the father of Thord, the father of Snorri, the father of Thorvald, from whom is sprung the Waterfirth race. Afterwards, Vermund, the son of Thorgrim, had Thorbjorg for wife. Their daughter was Thorfinna, whom Thorstein Kuggason had for wife. Bergthora, Olaf's daughter, was married west in Deepfirth to Thorhall the Priest. Their son was Kjartan, father of Smith-Sturla, the foster son of Thord Gilson. Olaf Peacock had many costly cattle. He had one very good ox named Harri; it was dapple-grey of coat, and bigger than any other of his cattle. It had four horns, two great and fair ones, the third stood straight up, and a fourth stood out of its forehead, stretching down below its eyes. It was with this that he opened the ice in winter to get water. He scraped snow away to get at pasture like a horse. One very hard winter he went from Herdholt into the Broadfirth-Dales to a place that is now called Harristead. There he roamed through the winter with sixteen other cattle, and got grazing for them all. In the spring he returned to the home pastures, to the place now called Harris'-Lair in Herdholt land. When Harri was eighteen winters old his ice-breaking horn fell off, and that same autumn Olaf had him killed. The next night Olaf dreamed that a woman came to him, and she was great and wrathful to look at. She spoke and said, "Are you asleep?" He said he was awake. The woman said, "You are asleep, though it comes to the same thing as if you were awake. You have had my son slain, and let him come to my hand in a shapeless plight, and for this deed you shall see your son, blood-stained all over through my doing, and him I shall choose thereto whom I know you would like to lose least of all." After that she disappeared, and Olaf woke up and still thought he saw the features of the woman. Olaf took the dream very much to heart, and told it to his friends, but no one could read it to his liking. He thought those spoke best about this matter who said that what had appeared to him was only a dream or fancy.

Chapter 32
Of Osvif Helgeson

Osvif was the name of a man. He was the son of Helgi, who was the son of

Ottar, the son of Bjorn the Eastman, who was the son of Ketill Flatnose, the son of Bjorn Buna. The mother of Osvif was named Nidbiorg. Her mother was Kadlin, the daughter of Ganging-Hrolf, the son of Ox-Thorir, who was a most renowned "Hersir" (war-lord) east in Wick. Why he was so called, was that he owned three islands with eighty oxen on each. He gave one island and its oxen to Hakon the King, and his gift was much talked about. Osvif was a great sage. He lived at Laugar in Salingsdale. The homestead of Laugar stands on the northern side of Salingsdale-river, over against Tongue. The name of his wife was Thordis, daughter of Thjodolf the Low. Ospak was the name of one of their sons. Another was named Helgi, and a third Vandrad, and a fourth Jorrad, and a fifth Thorolf. They were all doughty men for fighting. Gudrun was the name of their daughter. She was the goodliest of women who grew up in Iceland, both as to looks and wits. Gudrun was such a woman of state that at that time whatever other women wore in the way of finery of dress was looked upon as children's gewgaws beside hers. She was the most cunning and the fairest spoken of all women, and an open-handed woman withal. There was a woman living with Osvif who was named Thorhalla, and was called the Chatterer. She was some sort of relation to Osvif. She had two sons, one named Odd and the other Stein. They were muscular men, and in a great measure the hardest toilers for Osvif's household. They were talkative like their mother, but ill liked by people; yet were upheld greatly by the sons of Osvif. At Tongue there lived a man named Thorarin, son of Thorir Sæling (the Voluptuous). He was a well-off yeoman, a big man and strong. He had very good land, but less of live stock. Osvif wished to buy some of his land from him, for he had lack of land but a multitude of live stock. So this then came about that Osvif bought of the land of Thorarin all the tract from Gnupaskard along both sides of the valley to Stack-gill, and very good and fattening land it was. He had on it an out-dairy. Osvif had at all times a great many servants, and his way of living was most noble. West in Saurby is a place called Hol, there lived three kinsmen-in-law–Thorkell the Whelp and Knut, who were brothers, they were very well-born men, and their brother-in-law, who shared their household with them, who was named Thord. He was, after his mother, called Ingun's-son. The father of Thord was Glum Gierison. Thord was a handsome and valiant man, well knit, and a great man of law-suits. Thord had for wife the sister of Thorkell and Knut, who was called Aud, neither a goodly nor a bucksome woman. Thord loved her little, as he had chiefly married her for her money, for there a great wealth was stored together, and the household flourished from the time that Thord came to have hand in it with them.

Chapter 33
Of Gest Oddleifson and Gudrun's Dreams

Gest Oddleifson lived west at Bardastrand, at Hagi. He was a great chieftain and a sage; was fore-seeing in many things and in good friendship with all the great men, and many came to him for counsel. He rode every summer to the Thing, and always would put up at Hol. One time it so happened once more that Gest rode to the Thing and was a guest at Hol. He got ready to leave early in the morning, for the journey was a long one and he meant to get to Thickshaw in the evening to Armod, his brother-in-law's, who had for wife Thorunn, a sister of Gest's. Their sons were Ornolf and Haldor. Gest rode all that day from Saurby and came to the Sælingsdale spring, and tarried there for a while. Gudrun came to the spring and greeted her relative, Gest, warmly. Gest gave her a good welcome, and they began to talk together, both being wise and of ready speech. And as the day was wearing on, Gudrun said, "I wish, cousin, you would ride home with us with all your followers, for it is the wish of my father, though he gave me the honour of bearing the message, and told me to say that he would wish you to come and stay with us every time you rode to or from the west." Gest received the message well, and thought it a very manly offer, but said he must ride on now as he had purposed. Gudrun said, "I have dreamt many dreams this winter; but four of the dreams do trouble my mind much, and no man has been able to explain them as I like, and yet I ask not for any favourable interpretation of them." Gest said, "Tell me your dreams, it may be that I can make something of them." Gudrun said, "I thought I stood out of doors by a certain brook, and I had a crooked coif on my head, and I thought it misfitted me, and I wished to alter the coif, and many people told me I should not do so, but I did not listen to them, and I tore the hood from my head, and cast it into the brook, and that was the end of that dream." Then Gudrun said again, "This is the next dream. I thought I stood near some water, and I thought there was a silver ring on my arm. I thought it was my own, and that it fitted me exceeding well. I thought it was a most precious thing, and long I wished to keep it. But when I was least aware of it, the ring slipped off my arm and into the water, and nothing more did I see of it afterwards. I felt this loss much more than it was likely I should ever feel the loss of a mere keepsake. Then I awoke." Gest answered this alone: "No lesser a dream is that one." Gudrun still spoke: "This is the third dream, I thought I had a gold ring on my hand, which I thought belonged to me, and I thought my loss was now made good again. And the thought entered my mind that I would keep this ring longer than the first; but it did not seem to me that this keepsake suited me better than the former at anything like the rate that gold is more precious than silver. Then I thought I fell, and tried to steady myself with my hand, but then the gold ring struck on a certain stone and broke in two, and the two pieces bled. What I had to bear after this felt more like grief than regret for a loss. And it struck me now that there must have been some flaw in the ring, and when I looked at the pieces I thought I saw sundry more flaws in them; yet I had a feeling that if I had taken better care of it, it might still have been whole; and this dream was no longer." Gest said, "The dreams are not waning." Then said Gudrun, "This is my fourth dream. I thought I had a helm of gold upon my head, set with many precious stones. And I thought this precious thing belonged to me, but what I chiefly found fault with was that it was rather too heavy, and I could scarcely bear it, so that I carried my head on one side; yet I did not blame the helm for this, nor had I any mind to part with it. Yet the helm tumbled from my head out into Hvammfirth, and after that I awoke. Now I have told you all my dreams." Gest answered, "I clearly see what these dreams betoken; but you will find my unravelling savouring much of sameness, for I must read them all nearly in the same way. You will have four husbands, and it misdoubts me when you are married to the first it will be no love match. Inasmuch as you thought you had a great coif on your head and thought it ill-fitting, that shows you will love him but little. And whereas you took it off your head and cast it into the water, that shows that you will leave him. For that, men say, is 'cast on to the sea,' when a man loses what is his own, and gets nothing in return for it." And still Gest spake: "Your second dream was that you thought you had a silver ring on your arm, and that shows you will marry a nobleman whom you will love much, but enjoy him for but a short time, and I should not wonder if you lose him by drowning. That is all I have to tell of that dream. And in the third dream you thought you had a gold ring on your hand; that shows you will have a third husband; he will not excel the former at the rate that you deemed this metal more rare and precious than silver; but my mind forebodes me that by that time a change of faith will have come about, and your husband will have taken the faith which we are minded to think is the more exalted. And whereas you thought the ring broke in two through some misheed of yours, and blood came from the two pieces, that shows that this husband of yours will be slain, and then you will think you see for the first time clearly all the flaws of that match." Still Gest went on to say: "This is your fourth dream, that you thought you had a helm on your head, of gold set with precious stones, and that it was a heavy one for you to bear. This shows you will have a fourth husband who will be the greatest nobleman (of the four), and will bear somewhat a helm of awe over you. And whereas you thought it tumbled out into Hvammfirth, it shows that that same firth will be in his way on the last day of his life. And now I go no further with this dream." Gudrun sat with her cheeks blood red whilst the dreams were unravelled, but said not a word till Gest came to the end of his speech. Then said Gudrun, "You would have fairer prophecies in this matter if my delivery of it into your hands had warranted; have my thanks all the same for unravelling the dreams. But it is a fearful thing to think of, if all this is to come to pass as you say." Gudrun then begged Gest would stay there the day out, and said that he and Osvif would have many wise things to say between them. He answered, "I must ride on now as I have made up my mind. But bring your father my greeting and tell him also these my words, that the day will come when there will be a shorter distance between Osvif's and my dwellings, and then we may talk at ease, if then we are allowed to converse together." Then Gudrun went home and Gest rode away. Gest met a servant of Olaf's by the home-field fence, who invited Gest to Herdholt, at the bidding of Olaf. Gest said he would go and see Olaf during the day, but would stay (the night) at Thickshaw. The servant returned home and told Olaf so. Olaf had his horse brought and rode with several men out to meet Gest. He and Gest met up at Lea-river. Olaf greeted him well and asked him in with all his followers. Gest thanked him for the invitation, and said he would ride up to the homestead and have a look and see how he was housed, but he must stay with Armod. Gest tarried but a little while, yet he saw over the homestead and admired it and said, "No money has been spared for this place." Olaf rode away with Gest to the Salmon-river. The foster-brothers had been swimming there during the day, and at this sport the sons of Olaf mostly took the lead. There were many other young men from the other houses swimming too. Kjartan and Bolli leapt out of the water as the company rode down and were nearly dressed when Olaf and Gest came up to them. Gest looked at these young men for a while, and told Olaf where Kjartan was sitting as well as Bolli, and then Gest pointed his spear shaft to each one of Olaf's sons and named by name all of them that were there. But there were many other handsome young men there who had just left off swimming and sat on the river-bank with Kjartan and Bolli. Gest said he did not discover the family features of Olaf in any of these young men. Then said Olaf: "Never is there too much said about your wits, Gest, knowing, as you do, men you have never seen before. Now I wish you to tell me which of those young men will be the mightiest man." Gest replied, "That will fall out much in keeping with your own love, for Kjartan will be the most highly accounted of so long as he lives." Then Gest smote his horse and rode away. A little while after Thord the Low rode up to his side, and said, "What has now come to pass, father, that you are shedding tears?" Gest answered, "It is needless to tell it, yet I am loath to keep silence on matters that will happen in your own days. To me it will not come unawares if Bolli one day should have at his feet the head of Kjartan slain, and should by the deed bring about his own death, and this is an ill thing to know of such sterling men." Then they rode on to the Thing, and it was an uneventful meeting.

Chapter 34
Gudrun's First Marriage, A.D. 989

Thorvald was the name of a man, son of Haldor Garpdale's Priest. He lived at Garpsdale in Gilsfirth, a wealthy man, but not much of a hero. At the Thing he wooed Gudrun, Osvif's daughter, when she was fifteen years old. The matter was not taken up in a very adverse manner, yet Osvif said that against the match it would tell, that he and Gudrun were not of equal standing. Thorvald spoke gently, and said he was wooing a wife, not money. After that Gudrun was betrothed to Thorvald, and Osvif settled alone the marriage contract, whereby it was provided that Gudrun should alone manage their money affairs straightway when they came into one bed, and be entitled to one-half thereof as her own, whether their married life were long or short. He should also buy her jewels, so that no woman of equal wealth should have better to show. Yet he should retain his farm-stock unimpaired by such purchases. And now men ride home from the Thing. Gudrun was not asked about it, and took it much to heart; yet things went on quietly. The wedding was at Garpsdale, in Twinmonth (latter part of August to the latter part of September). Gudrun loved Thorvald but little, and was extravagant in buying finery. There was no jewel so costly in all the West-firths that Gudrun did not deem it fitting that it should be hers, and rewarded Thorvald with anger if he did not buy it for her, however dear it might be. Thord, Ingun's son, made himself very friendly with Thorvald and Gudrun, and stayed with them for long times together, and there was much talk of the love of Thord and Gudrun for each other. Once upon a time Gudrun bade Thorvald buy a gift for her, and Thorvald said she showed no moderation in her demands, and gave her a box on the ear. Then said Gudrun, "Now you have given me that which we women set great store by having to perfection—a fine colour in the cheeks—and thereby have also taught me how to leave off importuning you." That same evening Thord came there. Gudrun told him about the shameful mishandling, and asked him how she should repay it. Thord smiled, and said: "I know a very good counsel for this: make him a shirt with such a large neck-hole that you may have a good excuse for separating from him, because he has a low neck like a woman." Gudrun said nothing against this, and they dropped their talk. That same spring Gudrun separated herself from Thorvald, and she went home to Laugar. After that the money was divided between Gudrun and Thorvald, and she had half of all the wealth, which now was even greater than before (her marriage). They had lived two winters together. That same spring Ingun sold her land in Crookfirth, the estate which was afterwards called Ingunstead, and went west to Skalmness. Glum Gierison had formerly had her for wife, as has been before written. At that time Hallstein the Priest lived at Hallsteinness, on the west side of Codfirth. He was a mighty man, but middling well off as regards friends.

Chapter 35
Gudrun's Second Marriage, A.D. 991

Kotkell was the name of a man who had only come to Iceland a short time before, Grima was the name of his wife. Their sons were Hallbjorn Whetstone-eye, and Stigandi. These people were natives of Sodor. They were all wizards and the greatest of enchanters. Hallstein Godi took them in and settled them down at Urdir in Skalm-firth, and their dwelling there was none of the best liked. That summer Gest went to the Thing and went in a ship to Saurby as he was wont. He stayed as guest at Hol in Saurby. The brothers-in-law found him in horses as was their former wont. Thord Ingunson was amongst the followers of Gest on this journey and came to Laugar in Salingsdale. Gudrun Osvif's daughter rode to the Thing, and Thord Ingunson rode with her. It happened one day as they were riding over Blueshaw-heath, the weather being fine, that Gudrun said, "Is it true, Thord, that your wife Aud always goes about in breeches with gores in the seat, winding swathings round her legs almost to her feet?" Thord said, "He had not noticed that." "Well, then, there must be but little in the tale," said Gudrun, "if you have not found it out, but for what then is she called Breeches Aud?" Thord said, "I think she has been called so for but a short time." Gudrun answered, "What is of more moment to her is that she bear the name for a long time hereafter." After that people arrived at the Thing and no tidings befell there. Thord spent much time in Gest's booth and always talked to Gudrun. One day Thord Ingunson asked Gudrun what the penalty was for a woman who went about always in breeches like men. Gudrun replied, "She deserves the same penalty as a man who is dressed in a shirt with so low a neck that his naked breast be seen–separation in either case." Then Thord said, "Would you advise me to proclaim my separation from Aud here at the Thing or in the country by the counsel of many men? For I have to deal with high-tempered men who will count themselves as ill-treated in this affair." Gudrun answered after a while, "For evening waits the idler's suit." Then Thord sprang up and went to the law rock and named to him witnesses, declared his separation from Aud, and gave as his reason that she made for herself gored breeches like a man. Aud's brothers disliked this very much, but things kept quiet. Then Thord rode away from the Thing with the sons of Osvif. When Aud heard these tidings, she said, "Good! Well, that I know that I am left thus single." Then Thord rode, to divide the money, west into Saurby and twelve men with him, and it all went off easily, for Thord made no difficulties as to how the money was divided. Thord drove from the west unto Laugar a great deal of live stock. After that he wooed Gudrun and that matter was easily settled; Osvif and Gudrun said nothing against it. The wedding was to take place in the tenth week of the summer, and that was a right noble feast. Thord and Gudrun lived happily together. What alone withheld Thorkell Whelp and Knut from setting afoot a lawsuit against Thord Ingunson was, that they got no backing up to that end. The next summer the men of Hol had an out-dairy business in Hvammdale, and Aud stayed at the dairy. The men of Laugar had their out-dairy in Lambdale, which cuts westward into the mountains off Salingsdale. Aud asked the man who looked after the sheep how often he met the shepherd from Laugar. He said nearly always as was likely since there was only a neck of land between the two dairies. Then said Aud, "You shall meet the shepherd from Laugar to-day, and you can tell me who there are staying at the winter-dwelling or who at the dairy, and speak in a friendly way of Thord as it behoves you to do." The boy promised to do as she told him. And in the evening when the shepherd came home Aud asked what tidings he brought. The shepherd answered, "I have heard tidings which you will think good, that now there is a broad bedroom-floor between the beds of Thord and Gudrun, for she is at the dairy and he is swinging at the rear of the hall, he and Osvif being two together alone at the winter-dwelling." "You have espied well," said she, "and see to have saddled two horses at the time when people are going to bed." The shepherd did as she bade him. A little before sunset Aud mounted, and was now indeed in breeches. The shepherd rode the other horse and could hardly keep up with her, so hard did she push on riding. She rode south over Salingsdale-heath and never stopped before she got to the home-field fence at Laugar. Then she dismounted, and bade the shepherd look after the horses whilst she went to the house. Aud went to the door and found it open, and she went into the fire-hall to the locked-bed in the wall. Thord lay asleep, the door had fallen to, but the bolt was not on, so she walked into the bedroom. Thord lay asleep on his back. Then Aud woke Thord, and he turned on his side when he saw a man had come in. Then she drew a sword and thrust it at Thord and gave him great wounds, the sword striking his right arm and wounding him on both nipples. So hard did she follow up the stroke that the sword stuck in the bolster. Then Aud went away and to her horse and leapt on to its back, and thereupon rode home. Thord tried to spring up when he got the blow, but could not, because of his loss of blood. Then Osvif awoke and asked what had happened, and Thord told that he had been wounded somewhat. Osvif asked if he knew who had done the deed on him, and got up and bound up his wounds. Thord said he was minded to think that Aud had done it. Osvif offered to ride after her, and said she must have gone on this errand with few men, and her penalty was ready-made for her. Thord said that should not be done at all, for she had only done what she ought to have done. Aud got home at sunrise, and her brothers asked her where she had been to. Aud said she had been to Laugar, and told them what tidings had befallen in her journey. They were pleased at this, and said that too little was likely to have been done by her. Thord lay wounded a long time. His chest wound healed well, but his arm grew no better for work than before (i.e. when it first was wounded). All was now quiet that winter. But in the following spring Ingun, Thord's mother, came west from Skalmness. Thord greeted her warmly: she said she wished to place herself under his protection, and said that Kotkell and his wife and sons were giving her much trouble by stealing her goods, and through witchcraft, but had a strong support in Hallstein the Priest. Thord took this matter up swiftly, and said he should have the right of these thieves no matter how it might displease Hallstein. He got speedily ready for the journey with ten men, and Ingun went west with him. He got a ferry-boat out of Tjaldness. Then they went to Skalmness. Thord had put on board ship all the chattels his mother owned there, and the cattle were to be driven round the heads of the firths. There were twelve of them altogether in the boat, with Ingun and another woman. Thord and ten men went to Kotkell's place. The sons of Kotkell were not at home. He then summoned Kotkell and Grima and their sons for theft and witchcraft, and claimed outlawry as award. He laid the case to the Althing, and then returned to his ship. Hallbjorn and Stigandi came home when Thord had got out but a little way from land, and Kotkell told his sons what had happened there. The brothers were furious at that, and said that hitherto people had taken care not to show them in so barefaced a manner such open enmity. Then Kotkell had a great spell-working scaffold made, and they all went up on to it, and they sang hard twisted songs that were enchantments. And presently a great tempest arose. Thord, Ingun's son, and his companions, continued out at sea as he was, soon knew that the storm was raised against him. Now the ship is driven west beyond Skalmness, and Thord showed great courage with seamanship. The men who were on land saw how he threw overboard all that made up the boat's lading, saving the men; and the people who were on land expected Thord would come to shore, for they had passed the place that was the rockiest; but next there arose a breaker on a rock a little way from the shore that no man had ever known to break sea before, and smote the ship so that forthwith up turned keel uppermost. There Thord and all his followers were drowned, and the ship was broken to pieces, and the keel was washed up at a place now called Keelisle. Thord's shield was washed up on an island that has since been called Shieldisle. Thord's body and the bodies of his followers were all washed ashore, and a great howe was raised over their corpses at the place now called Howesness.

Chapter 36
About Kotkell and Grima

These tidings spread far and wide, and were very ill-spoken of; they were accounted of as men of doomed lives, who wrought such witchcraft as that which Kotkell and his had now shown. Gudrun took the death of Thord sorely to heart, for she was now a woman not hale, and coming close to her time. After that Gudrun gave birth to a boy, who was sprinkled with water and called Thord. At that time Snorri the Priest lived at Holyfell; he was a kinsman and a friend of Osvif's, and Gudrun and her people trusted him very much. Snorri went thither (to Laugar), being asked to a feast there. Then Gudrun told her trouble to Snorri, and he said he would back up their case when it seemed good to him, but offered to Gudrun to foster her child to comfort her. This Gudrun agreed to, and said she would rely on his foresight. This Thord was surnamed the Cat, and was father of the poet Stúf. After that Gest Oddleifson went to see Hallstein, and gave him choice of two things, either that he should send away these wizards or he said that he would kill them, "and yet it comes too late." Hallstein made his choice at once, and bade them rather be off, and put up nowhere west of Daleheath, adding that it was more justly they ought to be slain. After that Kotkell and his went away with no other goods than four stud-horses. The stallion was black; he was both great and fair and very strong, and tried in horse-fighting. Nothing is told of their journey till they came to Combeness, to Thorliek, Hoskuld's son. He asked to buy the horses from them, for he said that they were exceeding fine beasts. Kotkell replied, "I'll give you the choice. Take you the horses and give me some place to dwell in here in your neighbourhood." Thorliek said, "Will the horses not be rather dear, then, for I have heard tell you are thought rather guilty in this countryside?" Kotkell answers, "In this you are hinting at the men of Laugar." Thorliek said that was true. Then Kotkell said, "Matters point quite another way, as concerning our guilt towards Gudrun and her brothers, than you have been told; people have overwhelmed us with slander for no cause at all. Take the horses, nor let these matters stand in the way. Such tales alone are told of you, moreover, as would show that we shall not be easily tripped up by the folk of this countryside, if we have your help to fall back upon." Thorliek now changed his mind in this matter, for the horses seemed fair to him, and Kotkell pleaded his case cunningly; so Thorliek took the horses, and gave them a dwelling at Ludolfstead in Salmon-river-Dale, and stocked them with farming beasts. This the men of Laugar heard, and the sons of Osvif wished to fall forthwith on Kotkell and his sons; but Osvif said, "Let us take now the counsel of Priest Snorri, and leave this business to others, for short time will pass before the neighbours of Kotkell will have brand new cases against him and his, and Thorliek, as is most fitting, will abide the greatest hurt from them. In a short while many will become his enemies from whom heretofore he has only had good will. But I shall not stop you from doing whatever hurt you please to Kotkell and his, if other men do not come forward to drive them out of the countryside or to take their lives, by the time that three winters have worn away." Gudrun and her brothers said it should be as he said. Kotkell and his did not do much in working for their livelihood, but that winter they were in no need to buy hay or food; but an unbefriended neighbourhood was theirs, though men did not see their way to disturbing their dwelling because of Thorliek.

Chapter 37
About Hrut and Eldgrim, A.D. 995

One summer at the Thing, as Thorliek was sitting in his booth, a very big man walked into the booth. He greeted Thorliek, who took well the greeting of this man and asked his name and whence he was. He said he was called Eldgrim, and lived in Burgfirth at a place called Eldgrimstead—but that abode lies in the valley which cuts westward into the mountains between Mull and Pigtongue, and is now called Grimsdale. Thorliek said, "I have heard you spoken of as being no small man." Eldgrim said, "My errand here is that I want to buy from you the stud-horses, those valuable ones that Kotkell gave you last summer." Thorliek answered, "The horses are not for sale." Eldgrim said, "I will offer you equally many stud-horses for them and some other things thrown in, and many would say that I offer you twice as much as the horses are worth." Thorliek said, "I am no haggler, but these horses you will never have, not even though you offer three times their worth." Eldgrim said, "I take it to be no lie that you are proud and self-willed, and I should, indeed, like to see you getting a somewhat less handsome price for them than I have now offered you, and that you should have to let the horses go none the less." Thorliek got angered at these words, and said, "You need, Eldgrim, to come to closer quarters if you mean to frighten out me the horses." Eldgrim said, "You think it unlikely that you will be beaten by me, but this summer I shall go and see the horses, and we will see which of us will own them after that." Thorliek said, "Do as you like, but bring up no odds against me." Then they dropped their talk. The man who heard this said that for this sort of dealing together here were two just fitting matches for each other. After that people went home from the Thing, and nothing happened to tell tidings of. It happened one morning early that a man looked out at Hrutstead at goodman Hrut's, Herjolf's son's, and when he came in Hrut asked what news he brought. He said he had no other tidings to tell save that he saw a man riding from beyond Vadlar towards where Thorliek's horses were, and that the man got off his horse and took the horses. Hrut asked where the horses were then, and the house-carle replied, "Oh, they have stuck well to their pasture, for they stood as usual in your meadows down below the fence-wall." Hrut replied, "Verily, Thorliek, my kinsman, is not particular as to where he grazes his beasts; and I still think it more likely that it is not by his order that the horses are driven away." Then Hrut sprang up in his shirt and linen breeches, and cast over him a grey cloak and took in his hand his gold inlaid halberd that King Harald had given him. He went out quickly and saw where a man was riding after horses down below the wall. Hrut went to meet him, and saw that it was Eldgrim driving the horses. Hrut greeted him, and Eldgrim returned his greeting, but rather slowly. Hrut asked him why he was driving the horses. Eldgrim replied, "I will not hide it from you, though I know what kinship there is between you and Thorliek; but I tell you I have come after these horses, meaning that he shall never have them again. I have also kept what I promised him at the Thing, that I have not gone after the horses with any great company." Hrut said, "That is no deed of fame to you to take away the horses while Thorliek lies in his bed and sleeps; you would keep best what you agreed upon if you go and meet himself before you drive the horses out of the countryside." Eldgrim said, "Go and warn Thorliek if you wish, for you may see I have prepared myself in such a manner as that I should like it well if we were to meet together, I and Thorliek," and therewith he brandished the barbed spear he had in his hand. He had also a helmet on his head, and a sword girded on his side, and a shield on his flank, and had on a chain coat. Hrut said, "I think I must seek for something else than to go to Combeness for I am heavy of foot; but I mean not to allow Thorliek to be robbed if I have means thereto, no matter how little love there may go with our kinship." Eldgrim said, "And do you mean to take the horses away from me?" Hrut said, "I will give you other stud-horses if you will let these alone, though they may not be quite so good as these are." Eldgrim said, "You speak most kindly, Hrut, but since I have got hold of Thorliek's horses you will not pluck them out of my hands either by bribes or threats." Hrut replied, "Then I think you are making for both of us the choice that answers the worst." Eldgrim now wanted to part, and gave the whip to his horse, and when Hrut saw that, he raised up his halberd and struck Eldgrim through the back between the shoulders so that the coat of mail was torn open and the halberd flew out through the chest, and Eldgrim fell dead off his horse, as was only natural. After that Hrut covered up his body at the place called Eldgrim's-holt south of Combeness. Then Hrut rode over to Combeness and told Thorliek the tidings. Thorliek burst into a rage, and thought a great shame had been done him by this deed, while Hrut thought he had shown him great friendship thereby. Thorliek said that not only had he done this for an evil purpose, but that, moreover, no good would come in return for it. Hrut said that Thorliek must do what pleased him, and so they parted in no loving kindness. Hrut was eighty years old when he killed Eldgrim, and he was considered by that deed to have added much to his fame. Thorliek thought that Hrut was none the worthier of any good from him for being more renowned for this deed, for he held it was perfectly clear he would have himself have got the better of Eldgrim if they had had a trial of arms between them, seeing how little was needed to trip Eldgrim up. Thorliek now went to see his tenants Kotkell and Grima, and bade them do something to the shame of Hrut. They took this up gladly, and said they were quite ready to do so. Thorliek now went home. A little later they, Kotkell and Grima and their sons, started on a journey from home, and that was by night. They went to Hrut's dwelling, and made great incantations there, and when the spell-working began, those within were at a loss to make out what could be the reason of it; but sweet indeed was that singing they heard. Hrut alone knew what these goings-on meant, and bade no man look out that night, "and let every one who may keep awake, and no harm will come to us if that counsel is followed." But all the people fell asleep. Hrut watched longest, and at last he too slept. Kari was the name of a son of Hrut, and he was then twelve winters old. He was the most promising of all Hrut's sons, and Hrut loved him much. Kari hardly slept at all, for to him the play was made; he did not sleep very soundly, and at last he got up and looked out, and walked in the direction of the enchantment, and fell down dead at once. Hrut awoke in the morning, as also did his household, and missed his son, who was found dead a short way from the door. This Hrut felt as the greatest bereavement, and had a cairn raised over Kari. Then he rode to Olaf Hoskuldson and told him the tidings of what had happened there. Olaf was madly wroth at this, and said it showed great lack of forethought that they had allowed such scoundrels as Kotkell and his family to live so near to him, and said that Thorliek had shaped for himself an evil lot by dealing as he had done with Hrut, but added that more must have been done than Thorliek had ever could have wished. Olaf said too that forthwith Kotkell and his wife and sons must be slain, "late though it is now." Olaf and Hrut set out with fifteen men. But when Kotkell and his family saw the company of men riding up to their dwelling, they took to their heels up to the mountain. There Hallbjorn Whetstone-eye was caught and a bag was drawn over his head, and while some men were left to guard him others went in pursuit of Kotkell, Grima, and Stigandi up on the mountain. Kotkell and Grima were laid hands on on the neck of land between Hawkdale and Salmon-river-Dale, and were stoned to death and a heap of stones thrown up over them, and the remains are still to be seen, being called Scratch-beacon. Stigandi took to his heels south over the neck towards Hawkdale, and there got out of their sight. Hrut and his sons went down to the sea with Hallbjorn, and put out a boat and rowed out from land with him, and they took the bag off his head and tied a stone round his neck. Hallbjorn set gloating glances on the land, and the manner of his look was nowise of the goodliest. Then Hallbjorn said, "It was no day of bliss when we, kinsfolk, came to this Combeness and met with Thorliek. And this spell I utter," says he, "that Thorliek shall from henceforth have but few happy days, and that all who fill his place have a troublous life there." And this spell, men deem, has taken great effect. After that they drowned him, and rowed back to land.

A little while afterwards Hrut went to find Olaf his kinsman, and told him that he would not leave matters with Thorliek as they stood, and bade him furnish him with men to go and make a house-raid on Thorliek. Olaf replied, "It is not right that you two kinsmen should be laying hands on each other; on Thorliek's behalf this has turned out a matter of most evil luck. I would sooner try and bring about peace between you, and you have often waited well and long for your good turn." Hrut said, "It is no good casting about for this; the sores between us two will never heal up; and I should like that from henceforth we should not both live in Salmon-river-Dale." Olaf replied, "It will not be easy for you to go further against Thorliek than I am willing to allow; but if you do it, it is not unlikely that dale and hill will meet." Hrut thought he now saw things stuck hard and fast before him; so he went home mightily ill pleased; but all was quiet or was called so. And for that year men kept quiet at home.

Chapter 38
The Death of Stigandi. Thorliek leaves Iceland

Now, to tell of Stigandi, he became an outlaw and an evil to deal with. Thord was the name of a man who lived at Hundidale; he was a rich man, but had no manly greatness. A startling thing happened that summer in Hundidale, in that the milking stock did not yield much milk, but a woman looked after the beast there. At last people found out that she grew wealthy in precious things, and that she would disappear long and often, and no one knew where she was. Thord brought pressure to bear on her for confession, and when she got frightened she said a man was wont to come and meet her, "a big one," she said, "and in my eyes very handsome." Thord then asked how soon the man would come again to meet her, and she said she thought it would be soon. After that Thord went to see Olaf, and told him that Stigandi must be about, not far away from there, and bade him bestir himself with his men and catch him. Olaf got ready at once and came to Hundidale, and the bonds-woman was fetched for Olaf to have talk of her. Olaf asked her where the lair of Stigandi was. She said she did not know. Olaf offered to pay her money if she would bring Stigandi within reach of him and his men; and on this they came to a bargain together. The next day she went out to herd her cattle, and Stigandi comes that day to meet her. She greeted him well, and offers to look through (the hair of) his head. He laid his head down on her knee, and soon went to sleep. Then she slunk away from under his head, and went to meet Olaf and his men, and told them what had happened. Then they went towards Stigandi, and took counsel between them as to how it should not fare with him as his brother, that he should cast his glance on many things from which evil would befall them. They take now a bag, and draw it over his head. Stigandi woke at that, and made no struggle, for now there were many men to one. The sack had a slit in it, and Stigandi could see out through it the slope on the other side; there the lay of the land was fair, and it was covered with thick grass. But suddenly something like a whirlwind came on, and turned the sward topsy-turvy, so that the grass never grew there again. It is now called Brenna. Then they stoned Stigandi to death, and there he was buried under a heap of stones. Olaf kept his word to the bonds-woman, and gave her her freedom, and she went home to Herdholt. Hallbjorn Whetstone-eye was washed up by the surf a short time after he was drowned. It was called Knorstone where he was put in the earth, and his ghost walked about there a great deal. There was a man named Thorkell Skull who lived at Thickshaw on his father's inheritance. He was a man of very dauntless heart and mighty of muscle. One evening a cow was missing at Thickshaw, and Thorkell and his house-carle went to look for it. It was after sunset, but was bright moonlight. Thorkell said they must separate in their search, and when Thorkell was alone he thought he saw the cow on a hill-rise in front of him, but when he came up to it he saw it was Whetstone-eye and no cow. They fell upon each in mighty strength. Hallbjorn kept on the defensive, and when Thorkell least expected it he crept down into the earth out of his hands. After that Thorkell went home. The house-carle had come home already, and had found the cow. No more harm befell ever again from Hallbjorn.

Thorbjorn Skrjup was dead by then, and so was Melkorka, and they both lie in a cairn in Salmon-river-Dale. Lambi, their son, kept house there after them. He was very warrior-like, and had a great deal of money. Lambi was more thought of by people than his father had been, chiefly because of his mother's relations; and between him and Olaf there was fond brotherhood. Now the winter next after the killing of Kotkell passed away. In the spring the brothers Olaf and Thorliek met, and Olaf asked if Thorliek was minded to keep on his house. Thorliek said he was. Olaf said, "Yet I would beg you, kinsman, to change your way of life, and go abroad; you will be thought an honourable man whereever you come; but as to Hrut, our kinsman, I know he feels how your dealings with him come home to him. And it is little to my mind that the risk of your sitting so near to each other should be run any longer. For Hrut has a strong run of luck to fall back upon, and his sons are but reckless bravos. On account of my kinship I feel I should be placed in a difficulty if you, my kinsman, should come to quarrel in full enmity." Thorliek replied, "I am not afraid of not being able to hold myself straight in the face of Hrut and his sons, and that is no reason why I should depart the country. But if you, brother, set much store by it, and feel yourself in a difficult position in this matter, then, for your words I will do this; for then I was best contented with my lot in life when I lived abroad. And I know you will not treat my son Bolli any the worse for my being nowhere near; for of all men I love him the best." Olaf said, "You have, indeed, taken an honourable course in this matter, if you do after my prayer; but as touching Bolli, I am minded to do to him henceforth as I have done hitherto, and to be to him and hold him no worse than my own sons." After that the brothers parted in great affection. Thorliek now sold his land, and spent his money on his journey abroad. He bought a ship that stood up in Daymealness; and when he was full ready he stepped on board ship with his wife and household. That ship made a good voyage, and they made Norway in the autumn. Thence he went south to Denmark, as he did not feel at home in Norway, his kinsmen and friends there being either dead or driven out of the land. After that Thorliek went to Gautland. It is said by most men that Thorliek had little to do with old age; yet he was held a man of great worth throughout life. And there we close the story of Thorliek.

Chapter 39
Of Kjartan's Friendship for Bolli

At that time, as concerning the strife between Hrut and Thorliek, it was ever the greatest gossip throughout the Broadfirth-Dales how that Hrut had had to abide a heavy lot at the hands of Kotkell and his sons. Then Osvif spoke to Gudrun and her brothers, and bade them call to mind whether they thought now it would have been the best counsel aforetime then and there to have plunged into the danger of dealing with such "hell-men" (terrible people) as Kotkell and his were. Then said Gudrun, "He is not counsel-bereft, father, who has the help of thy counsel." Olaf now abode at his manor in much honour, and all his sons are at home there, as was Bolli, their kinsman and foster-brother. Kjartan was foremost of all the sons of Olaf. Kjartan and Bolli loved each other the most, and Kjartan went nowhere that Bolli did not follow. Often Kjartan would go to the Sælingdale-spring, and mostly it happened that Gudrun was at the spring too. Kjartan liked talking to Gudrun, for she was both a woman of wits and clever of speech. It was the talk of all folk that of all men who were growing up at the time Kjartan was the most even match for Gudrun. Between Olaf and Osvif there was also great friendship, and often they would invite one another, and not the less frequently so when fondness was growing up between the young folk. One day when Olaf was talking to Kjartan, he said: "I do not know why it is that I always take it to heart when you go to Laugar and talk to Gudrun. It is not because I do not consider Gudrun the foremost of all other women, for she is the one among womenkind whom I look upon as a thoroughly suitable match for you. But it is my foreboding, though I will not prophesy it, that we, my kinsmen and I, and the men of Laugar will not bring altogether good luck to bear on our dealings together." Kjartan said he would do nothing against his father's will where he could help himself, but he hoped things would turn out better than he made a guess to. Kjartan holds to his usual ways as to his visits (to Laugar), and Bolli always went with him, and so the next seasons passed.

Chapter 40
Kjartan and Bolli Voyage to Norway, A.D. 996

Asgeir was the name of a man, he was called Eider-drake. He lived at Asgeir's-river, in Willowdale; he was the son of Audun Skokul; he was the first of his kinsmen who came to Iceland; he took to himself Willowdale. Another son of Audun was named Thorgrim Hoaryhead; he was the father of Asmund, the father of Gretter. Asgeir Eider-drake had five children; one of his sons was called Audun, father of Asgeir, father of Audun, father of Egil, who had for wife Ulfeid, the daughter of Eyjolf the Lame; their son was Eyjolf, who was slain at the All Thing. Another of Asgeir's sons was named Thorvald; his daughter was Wala, whom Bishop Isleef had for wife; their son was Gizor, the bishop. A third son of Asgeir was named Kalf. All Asgeir's sons were hopeful men. Kalf Asgeirson was at that time out travelling, and was accounted of as the worthiest of men. One of Asgeir's daughters was named Thured; she married Thorkell Kuggi, the son of Thord Yeller; their son was Thorstein. Another of Asgeir's daughters was named Hrefna; she was the fairest woman in those northern countrysides and very winsome. Asgeir was a very mighty man. It is told how one time Kjartan Olafson went on a journey south to Burgfirth. Nothing is told of his journey before he got to Burg. There at that time lived Thorstein, Egil's son, his mother's brother. Bolli was with him, for the foster-brothers loved each other so dearly that neither thought he could enjoy himself if they were not together. Thorstein received Kjartan with loving kindness, and said he should be glad for his staying there a long rather than a short time. So Kjartan stayed awhile at Burg. That summer there was a ship standing up in Steam-river-Mouth, and this ship belonged to Kalf Asgeirson, who had been staying through the winter with Thorstein, Egil's son. Kjartan told Thorstein in secret that his chief errand to the south then was, that he wished to buy the half of Kalf's ship, "for I have set my mind on going abroad," and he asked Thorstein what sort of a man he thought Kalf was. Thorstein said he thought he was a good man and true. "I can easily understand," said Thorstein, "that you wish to see other men's ways of life, and your journey will be remarkable in one way or another, and your kinsfolk will be very anxious as to how the journey may speed for you." Kjartan said it would speed well enough. After that Kjartan bought a half share in Kalf's ship, and they made up half-shares partnership between them; Kjartan was to come on board when ten weeks of summer had passed. Kjartan was seen off with gifts on leaving Burg, and he and Bolli then rode home. When Olaf heard of this arrangement he said he thought Kjartan had made up his mind rather suddenly, but added that he would not foreclose the matter. A little later Kjartan rode to Laugar to tell Gudrun of his proposed journey abroad. Gudrun said, "You have decided this very suddenly, Kjartan," and she let fall sundry words about this, from which Kjartan got to understand that Gudrun was displeased with it. Kjartan said, "Do not let this displease you.

I will do something else that shall please you." Gudrun said, "Be then a man of your word, for I shall speedily let you know what I want." Kjartan bade her do so. Gudrun said, "Then, I wish to go out with you this summer; if that comes off, you would have made amends to me for this hasty resolve, for I do not care for Iceland." Kjartan said, "That cannot be, your brothers are unsettled yet, and your father is old, and they would be bereft of all care if you went out of the land; so you wait for me three winters." Gudrun said she would promise nothing as to that matter, and each was at variance with the other, and therewith they parted. Kjartan rode home. Olaf rode to the Thing that summer, and Kjartan rode with his father from the west out of Herdholt, and they parted at North-river-Dale. From thence Kjartan rode to his ship, and his kinsman Bolli went along with him. There were ten Icelanders altogether who went with Kjartan on this journey, and none would part with him for the sake of the love they bore him. So with this following Kjartan went to the ship, and Kalf Asgeirson greeted them warmly. Kjartan and Bolli took a great many goods with them abroad. They now got ready to start, and when the wind blew they sailed out along Burgfirth with a light and good breeze, and then out to sea. They had a good journey, and got to Norway to the northwards and came into Thrandhome, and fell in with men there and asked for tidings. They were told that change of lords over the land had befallen, in that Earl Hakon had fallen and King Olaf Tryggvason had come in, and all Norway had fallen under his power. King Olaf was ordering a change of faith in Norway, and the people took to it most unequally. Kjartan and his companions took their craft up to Nidaross. At that time many Icelanders had come to Norway who were men of high degree. There lay beside the landing-stage three ships, all owned by Icelanders. One of the ships belonged to Brand the Bounteous, son of Vermund Thorgrimson. And another ship belonged to Hallfred the Trouble-Bard. The third ship belonged to two brothers, one named Bjarni, and the other Thorhall; they were sons of Broad-river-Skeggi, out of Fleetlithe in the east. All these men had wanted to go west to Iceland that summer, but the king had forbidden all these ships to sail because the Icelanders would not take the new faith that he was preaching. All the Icelanders greeted Kjartan warmly, but especially Brand, as they had known each other already before. The Icelanders now took counsel together and came to an agreement among themselves that they would refuse this faith that the king preached, and all the men previously named bound themselves together to do this. Kjartan and his companions brought their ship up to the landing-stage and unloaded it and disposed of their goods. King Olaf was then in the town. He heard of the coming of the ship and that men of great account were on board. It happened one fair-weather day in the autumn that the men went out of the town to swim in the river Nid. Kjartan and his friends saw this. Then Kjartan said to his companions that they should also go and disport themselves that day. They did so. There was one man who was by much the best at this sport. Kjartan asked Bolli if he felt willing to try swimming against the townsman. Bolli answered,

"I don't think I am a match for him." "I cannot think where your courage can now have got to," said Kjartan, "so I shall go and try." Bolli replied, "That you may do if you like." Kjartan then plunges into the river and up to this man who was the best swimmer and drags him forthwith under and keeps him down for awhile, and then lets him go up again. And when they had been up for a long while, this man suddenly clutches Kjartan and drags him under; and they keep down for such a time as Kjartan thought quite long enough, when up they come a second time. Not a word had either to say to the other. The third time they went down together, and now they keep under for much the longest time, and Kjartan now misdoubted him how this play would end, and thought he had never before found himself in such a tight place; but at last they come up and strike out for the bank. Then said the townsman, "Who is this man?" Kjartan told him his name. The townsman said, "You are very deft at swimming. Are you as good at other deeds of prowess as at this?" Kjartan answered rather coldly, "It was said when I was in Iceland that the others kept pace with this one. But now this one is not worth much." The townsman replied, "It makes some odds with whom you have had to do. But why do you not ask me anything?" Kjartan replied, "I do not want to know your name." The townsman answered, "You are not only a stalwart man, but you bear yourself very proudly as well, but none the less you shall know my name, and with whom you have been having a swimming match. Here is Olaf the king, the son of Tryggvi." Kjartan answered nothing, but turned away forthwith without his cloak. He had on a kirtle of red scarlet. The king was then well-nigh dressed; he called to Kjartan and bade him not go away so soon. Kjartan turned back, but rather slowly. The king then took a very good cloak off his shoulders and gave it to Kjartan, saying he should not go back cloakless to his companions. Kjartan thanked the king for the gift, and went to his own men and showed them the cloak. His men were nowise pleased as this, for they thought Kjartan had got too much into the king's power; but matters went on quietly. The weather set in very hard that autumn, and there was a great deal of frost, the season being cold. The heathen men said it was not to be wondered at that the weather should be so bad; "it is all because of the newfangled ways of the king and this new faith that the gods are angry." The Icelanders kept all together in the town during the winter, and Kjartan took mostly the lead among them. On the weather taking a turn for the better, many people came to the town at the summons of King Olaf. Many people had become Christians in Thrandhome, yet there were a great many more who withstood the king. One day the king had a meeting out at Eyrar, and preached the new faith to men–a long harangue and telling. The people of Thrandhome had a whole host of men, and in turn offered battle to the king. The king said they must know that he had had greater things to cope with than fighting there with churls out of Thrandhome. Then the good men lost heart and gave the whole case into the king's power, and many people were baptized then and there. After that, the meeting came to an end. That same evening the king sent men to the lodgings of the Icelanders, and bade them get sure knowledge of what they were saying. They did so. They heard much noise within. Then Kjartan began to speak, and said to Bolli, "How far are you willing, kinsman, to take this new faith the king preaches?" "I certainly am not willing thereto," said Bolli, "for their faith seems to me to be most feeble." Kjartan said, "Did ye not think the king was holding out threats against those who should be unwilling to submit to his will?" Bolli answered, "It certainly seemed to me that he spoke out very clearly that they would have to take exceeding hard treatment at his hands." "I will be forced under no one's thumb," said Kjartan, "while I have power to stand up and wield my weapons. I think it most unmanly, too, to be taken like a lamb in a fold or a fox in a trap. I think that is a better thing to choose, if a man must die in any case, to do first some such deed as shall be held aloft for a long time afterwards." Bolli said, "What will you do?" "I will not hide it from you," Kjartan replied; "I will burn the king in his hall." "There is nothing cowardly in that," said Bolli; "but this is not likely to come to pass, as far as I can see. The king, I take it, is one of great good luck and his guardian spirit mighty, and, besides, he has a faithful guard watching both day and night." Kjartan said that what most men failed in was daring, however valiant they might otherwise be. Bolli said it was not so certain who would have to be taunted for want of courage in the end. But here many men joined in, saying this was but an idle talk. Now when the king's spies had overheard this, they went away and told the king all that had been said. The next morning the king wished to hold a meeting, and summoned all the Icelanders to it; and when the meeting was opened the king stood up and thanked men for coming, all those who were his friends and had taken the new faith. Then he called to him for a parley the Icelanders. The king asked them if they would be baptized, but they gave little reply to that. The king said they were making for themselves the choice that would answer the worst. "But, by the way, who of you thought it the best thing to do to burn me in my hall?" Then Kjartan answered, "You no doubt think that he who did say it would not have the pluck to confess it; but here you can see him." "I can indeed see you," said the king, "man of no small counsels, but it is not fated for you to stand over my head, done to death by you; and you have done quite enough that you should be prevented making a vow to burn more kings in their houses yet, for the reason of being taught better things than you know and because I do not know whether your heart was in your speech, and that you have bravely acknowledged it, I will not take your life. It may also be that you follow the faith the better the more outspoken you are against it; and I can also see this, that on the day you let yourself be baptized of your own free will, several ships' crews will on that day also take the faith. And I think it likely to happen that your relations and friends will give much heed to what you speak to them when you return to Iceland. And it is in my mind that you, Kjartan, will have a better faith when you return from Norway than you had when you came hither. Go now in peace and safety wheresoever you like from the meeting. For the time being you shall not be tormented into Christianity, for God says that He wills that no one shall come to Him unwillingly." Good cheer was made at the king's speech, though mostly from the Christian men; but the heathen left it to Kjartan to answer as he liked. Kjartan said, "We thank you, king, that you grant safe peace unto us, and the way whereby you may most surely draw us to take the faith is, on the one hand, to forgive us great offences, and on the other to speak in this kindly manner on all matters, in spite of your this day having us and all our concerns in your power even as it pleases you. Now, as for myself, I shall receive the faith in Norway on that understanding alone that I shall give some little worship to Thor the next winter when I get back to Iceland." Then the king said and smiled, "It may be seen from the mien of Kjartan that he puts more trust in his own weapons and strength than in Thor and Odin." Then the meeting was broken up. After a while many men egged the king on to force Kjartan and his followers to receive the faith, and thought it unwise to have so many heathen men near about him. The king answered wrathfully, and said he thought there were many Christians who were not nearly so well-behaved as was Kjartan or his company either, "and for such one would have long to wait." The king caused many profitable things to be done that winter; he had a church built and the market-town greatly enlarged. This church was finished at Christmas. Then Kjartan said they should go so near the church that they might see the ceremonies of this faith the Christians followed; and many fell in, saying that would be right good pastime. Kjartan with his following and Bolli went to the church; in that train was also Hallfred and many other Icelanders. The king preached the faith before the people, and spoke both long and tellingly, and the Christians made good cheer at his speech. And when Kjartan and his company went back to their chambers, a great deal of talk arose as to how they had liked the looks of the king at this time, which Christians accounted of as the next greatest festival. "For the king said, so that we might hear, that this night was born the Lord, in whom we are now to believe, if we do as the king bids us." Kjartan says: "So greatly was I taken with the looks of the king when I saw him for the first time, that I knew at once that he was a man of the highest excellence, and that feeling has kept steadfast ever since, when I have seen him at folk-meetings, and that but by much the best, however, I liked the looks of him to-day; and I cannot help thinking that the turn of our concerns hangs altogether on our believing Him to be the true God in whom the king bids us to believe, and the king cannot by any means be more eager in wishing that I take this faith than I am to let myself be baptized. The only thing that puts off my going straightway to see the king now is that the day is far spent, and the king, I take it, is now at table; but that day will be delayed, on which we, companions, will let ourselves all be baptized." Bolli took to this kindly, and bade Kjartan alone look to their affairs. The king had heard of the talk between Kjartan and his people before the tables were cleared away, for he had his spies in every chamber of the heathens. The king was very glad at this, and said, "In Kjartan has come true the saw: 'High tides best for happy signs.'" And the first thing the next morning early, when the king went to church, Kjartan met him in the street with a great company of men. Kjartan greeted the king with great cheerfulness, and said he had a pressing errand with him. The king took his greeting well, and said he had had a thoroughly clear news as to what his errand must be, "and that matter will be easily settled by you." Kjartan begged they should not delay fetching the water, and said that a great deal would be needed. The king answered and smiled. "Yes, Kjartan," says he, "on this matter I do not think your eager-mindedness would part us, not even if you put the price higher still." After that Kjartan and Bolli were baptized and all their crew, and a multitude of other men as well. This was on the second day of Yule before Holy Service. After that the king invited Kjartan to his Yule feast with Bolli his kinsman. It is the tale of most men that Kjartan on the day he laid aside his white baptismal-robes became a liegeman of the king's, he and Bolli both. Hallfred was not baptized that day, for he made it a point that the king himself should be his godfather, so the king put it off till the next day. Kjartan and Bolli stayed with Olaf the king the rest of the winter. The king held Kjartan before all other men for the sake of his race and manly prowess, and it is by all people said that Kjartan was so winsome that he had not a single enemy within the court. Every one said that there had never before come from Iceland such a man as Kjartan. Bolli was also one of the most stalwart of men, and was held in high esteem by all good men. The winter now passes away, and, as spring came on, men got ready for their journeys, each as he had a mind to.

Chapter 41
Bolli returns to Iceland, A.D. 999

Kalf Asgeirson went to see Kjartan and asks what he was minded to do that summer. Kjartan said, "I have been thinking chiefly that we had better take our ship to England, where there is a good market for Christian men. But first I will go and see the king before I settle this, for he did not seem pleased at my going on this journey when we talked about it in the spring." Then Kalf went away and Kjartan went to speak to the king, greeting him courteously. The king received him most kindly, and asked what he and his companion (Kalf) had been talking about. Kjartan told what they had mostly in mind to do, but said that his errand to the king was to beg leave to go on this journey. "As to that matter, I will give you your choice, Kjartan. Either you will go to Iceland this summer, and bring men to Christianity by force or by expedients; but if you think this too difficult a journey, I will not let you go away on any account, for you are much better suited to serve noble men than to turn here into a chapman." Kjartan chose rather to stay with the king than to go to Iceland and preach the faith to them there, and said he could not be contending by force against his own kindred. "Moreover, it would be more likely that my father and other chiefs, who are near kinsmen of mine, would go against thy will with all the less stubbornness the better beholden I am under your power." The king said, "This is chosen both wisely and as beseems a great man." The king gave Kjartan a whole set of new clothes, all cut out of scarlet cloth, and they suited him well; for people said that King Olaf and Kjartan were of an even height when they went under measure. King Olaf sent the court priest, named Thangbrand, to Iceland. He brought his ship to Swanfirth, and stayed with Side-Hall all the winter at Wash-river, and set forth the faith to people both with fair words and harsh punishments. Thangbrand slew two men who went most against him. Hall received the faith in the spring, and was baptized on the Saturday before Easter, with all his household; then Gizor the White let himself be baptized, so did Hjalti Skeggjason and many other chiefs, though there were many more who spoke against it; and then dealings between heathen men and Christians became scarcely free of danger. Sundry chiefs even took counsel together to slay Thangbrand, as well as such men who should stand up for him. Because of this turmoil Thangbrand ran away to Norway, and came to meet King Olaf, and told him the tidings of what had befallen in his journey, and said he thought Christianity would never thrive in Iceland. The king was very wroth at this, and said that many Icelanders would rue the day unless they came round to him. That summer Hjalti Skeggjason was made an outlaw at the Thing for blaspheming the gods. Runolf Ulfson, who lived in Dale, under Isles'-fells, the greatest of chieftains, upheld the lawsuit against him. That summer Gizor left Iceland and Hjalti with him, and they came to Norway, and went forthwith to find King Olaf. The king gave them a good welcome, and said they had taken a wise counsel; he bade them stay with him, and that offer they took with thanks. Sverling, son of Runolf of Dale, had been in Norway that winter, and was bound for Iceland in the summer. His ship was floating beside the landing stage all ready, only waiting for a wind. The king forbade him to go away, and said that no ships should go to Iceland that summer. Sverling went to the king and pleaded his case, and begged leave to go, and said it mattered a great deal to him, that they should not have to unship their cargo again. The king spake, and then he was wroth: "It is well for the son of a sacrificer to be where he likes it worst." So Sverling went no whither. That winter nothing to tell of befell. The next summer the king sent Gizor and Hjalti Skeggjason to Iceland to preach the faith anew, and kept four men back as hostages Kjartan Olafson, Halldor, the son of Gudmund the Mighty, Kolbein, son of Thord the priest of Frey, and Sverling, son of Runolf of Dale. Bolli made up his mind to journey with Gizor and Hjalti, and went to Kjartan, his kinsman, and said, "I am now ready to depart; I should wait for you through the next winter, if next summer you were more free to go away than you are now. But I cannot help thinking that the king will on no account let you go free. I also take it to be the truth that you yourself call to mind but few of the things that afford pastime in Iceland when you sit talking to Ingibjorg, the king's sister." She was at the court of King Olaf, and the most beautiful of all the women who were at that time in the land. Kjartan said, "Do not say such things, but bear my greeting to both my kinsfolk and friends."

Chapter 42
Bolli makes love to Gudrun, A.D. 1000

After that Kjartan and Bolli parted, and Gizor and Hjalti sailed from Norway and had a good journey, and came to the Westmen's Isles at the time the Althing was sitting, and went from thence to the mainland, and had there meetings and parleys with their kinsmen. Thereupon they went to the Althing and preached the faith to the people in an harangue both long and telling, and then all men in Iceland received the faith. Bolli rode from the Thing to Herdholt in fellowship with his uncle Olaf, who received him with much loving-kindness. Bolli rode to Laugar to disport himself after he had been at home for a short time, and a good welcome he had there. Gudrun asked very carefully about his journey and then about Kjartan. Bolli answered right readily all Gudrun asked, and said there were no tidings to tell of his journey. "But as to what concerns Kjartan there are, in truth, the most excellent news to be told of his ways of life, for he is in the king's bodyguard, and is there taken before every other man; but I should not wonder if he did not care to have much to do with this country for the next few winters to come." Gudrun then asked if there was any other reason for it than the friendship between Kjartan and the king. Bolli then tells what sort of way people were talking about the friendship of Kjartan with Ingibjorg the king's sister, and said he could not help thinking the king would sooner marry Ingibjorg to Kjartan than let him go away if the choice lay between the two things. Gudrun said these were good tidings, "but Kjartan would be fairly matched only if he got a good wife." Then she let the talk drop all of a sudden and went away and was very red in the face; but other people doubted if she really thought these tidings as good as she gave out she thought they were. Bolli remained at home in Herdholt all that summer, and had gained much honour from his journey; all his kinsfolk and acquaintances set great store by his valiant bearing; he had, moreover, brought home with him a great deal of wealth. He would often go over to Laugar and while away time talking to Gudrun. One day Bolli asked Gudrun what she would answer if he were to ask her in marriage. Gudrun replied at once, "No need for you to bespeak such a thing, Bolli, for I cannot marry any man whilst I know Kjartan to be still alive." Bolli answered, "I think then you will have to abide husbandless for sundry winters if you are to wait for Kjartan; he might have chosen to give me some message concerning the matter if he set his heart at all greatly on it." Sundry words they gave and took, each at variance with the other. Then Bolli rode home.

Chapter 43
Kjartan comes back to Iceland, A.D. 1001

A little after this Bolli talked to his uncle Olaf, and said, "It has come to this, uncle, that I have it in mind to settle down and marry, for I am now grown up to man's estate. In this matter I should like to have the assistance of your words and your backing-up, for most of the men hereabouts are such as will set much store by your words." Olaf replied, "Such is the case with most women, I am minded to think, that they would be fully well matched in you for a husband. And I take it you have not broached this matter without first having made up your mind as to where you mean to come down." Bolli said, "I shall not go beyond this countryside to woo myself a wife whilst there is such an goodly match so near at hand. My will is to woo Gudrun, Osvif's daughter, for she is now the most renowned of women." Olaf answered, "Ah, that is just a matter with which I will have nothing to do. To you it is in no way less well known, Bolli, than to me, what talk there was of the love between Kjartan and Gudrun; but if you have set your heart very much on this, I will put no hindrance in the way if you and Osvif settle the matter between you. But have you said anything to Gudrun about it?" Bolli said that he had once hinted at it, but that she had not given much heed to it, "but I think, however, that Osvif will have most to say in the matter." Olaf said Bolli could go about the business as it pleased himself. Not very long after Bolli rode from home with Olaf's sons, Halldor and Steinthor; there were twelve of them together. They rode to Laugar, and Osvif and his sons gave them a good welcome. Bolli said he wished to speak to Osvif, and he set forth his wooing, and asked for the hand of Gudrun, his daughter. Osvif answered in this wise, "As you know, Bolli, Gudrun is a widow, and has herself to answer for her, but, as for myself, I shall urge this on." Osvif now went to see Gudrun, and told her that Bolli Thorliekson had come there, "and has asked you in marriage; it is for you now to give the answer to this matter. And herein I may speedily make known my own will, which is, that Bolli will not be turned away if my counsel shall avail." Gudrun answered, "You make a swift work of looking into this matter; Bolli himself once bespoke it before me, and I rather warded it off, and the same is still uppermost in my mind." Osvif said, "Many a man will tell you that this is spoken more in overweening pride than in wise forethought if you refuse such a man as is Bolli. But as long as I am alive, I shall look out for you, my children, in all affairs which I know better how to see through things than you do." And as Osvif took such a strong view of the matter, Gudrun, as far as she was concerned, would not give an utter refusal, yet was most unwilling on all points. The sons of Osvif's urged the matter on eagerly, seeing what great avail an alliance with Bolli would be to them; so the long and short of the matter was that the betrothal took place then and there, and the wedding was to be held at the time of the winter nights. Thereupon Bolli rode home and told this settlement to Olaf, who did not hide his displeasure thereat. Bolli stayed on at home till he was to go to the wedding. He asked his uncle to it, but Olaf accepted it nowise quickly, though, at last, he yielded to the prayers of Bolli. It was a noble feast this at Laugar. Bolli stayed there the winter after. There was not much love between Gudrun and Bolli so far as she was concerned. When the summer came, and ships began to go and come between Iceland and Norway, the tidings spread to Norway that Iceland was all Christian. King Olaf was very glad at that, and gave leave to go to Iceland unto all those men whom he had kept as hostages, and to fare whenever they liked. Kjartan answered, for he took the lead of all those who had been hostages, "Have great thanks, Lord King, and this will be the choice we take, to go and see Iceland this summer." Then King Olaf said, "I must not take back my word, Kjartan, yet my order pointed rather to other men than to yourself, for in my view you, Kjartan, have been more of a friend than a hostage through your stay here. My wish would be, that you should not set your heart on going to Iceland though you have noble relations there; for, I take it, you could choose for yourself such a station in life in Norway, the like of which would not be found in Iceland." Then Kjartan answered, "May our Lord reward you, sire, for all the honours you have bestowed on me since I came into your power, but I am still in hopes that you will give leave to me, no less than to the others you have kept back for a while." The king said so it should be, but avowed that it would be hard for him to get in his place any untitled man such as Kjartan was. That winter Kalf Asgeirson had been in Norway and had brought, the autumn before, west-away from England, the ship and merchandise he and Kjartan had owned. And when Kjartan had got leave for his journey to Iceland Kalf and he set themselves to get the ship ready. And when the ship was all ready Kjartan went to see Ingibjorg, the king's sister. She gave him a cheery welcome, and made room for him to sit beside her, and they fell a-talking together, and Kjartan tells Ingibjorg that he has arranged his journey to Iceland. Then Ingibjorg said, "I am minded to think, Kjartan, that you have done this of your own wilfulness rather than because you have been urged by men to go away from Norway and to Iceland." But thenceforth words between them were drowned in silence. Amidst this Ingibjorg turns to a "mead-cask" that stood near her, and takes out of it a white coif inwoven with gold and gives it to Kjartan, saying, that it was far too good for Gudrun Osvif's daughter to fold it round her head, yet "you will give her the coif as a bridal gift, for I wish the wives of the Icelanders to see as much as that she with whom you have had your talks in Norway comes of no thrall's blood." It was in a pocket of costly stuff, and was altogether a most precious thing. "Now I shall not go to see you off," said Ingibjorg. "Fare you well, and hail!" After that Kjartan stood up and embraced Ingibjorg, and people told it as a true story that they took it sorely to heart being parted. And now Kjartan went away and unto the king, and told the king he now was ready for his journey. Then the king led Kjartan to his ship and many men with him, and when they came to where the ship was floating with one of its gangways to land, the king said, "Here is a sword, Kjartan, that you shall take from me at our parting; let this weapon be always with you, for my mind tells me you will never be a 'weapon-bitten' man if you bear this sword." It was a most noble keepsake, and much ornamented. Kjartan thanked the king with fair words for all the honour and advancement he had bestowed on him while he had been in Norway. Then the king spoke,

"This I will bid you, Kjartan, that you keep your faith well." After that they parted, the king and Kjartan in dear friendship, and Kjartan stepped on board his ship. The king looked after him and said, "Great is the worth of Kjartan and his kindred, but to cope with their fate is not an easy matter."

Chapter 44
Kjartan comes home, A.D. 1001

Now Kjartan and Kalf set sail for the main. They had a good wind, and were only a short time out at sea. They hove into White-river, in Burgfirth. The tidings spread far and wide of the coming of Kjartan. When Olaf, his father, and his other kinsfolk heard of it they were greatly rejoiced. Olaf rode at once from the west out of the Dales and south to Burgfirth, and there was a very joyful meeting between father and son. Olaf asked Kjartan to go and stay with him, with as many of his men as he liked to bring. Kjartan took that well, and said that there only of all places in Iceland he meant to abide. Olaf now rides home to Herdholt, and Kjartan remained with his ship during the summer. He now heard of the marriage of Gudrun, but did not trouble himself at all over it; but that had heretofore been a matter of anxiety to many. Gudmund, Solmund's son, Kjartan's brother-in-law, and Thurid, his sister, came to his ship, and Kjartan gave them a cheery welcome. Asgeir Eider-drake came to the ship too to meet his son Kalf, and journeying with him was Hrefna his daughter, the fairest of women. Kjartan bade his sister Thurid have such of his wares as she liked, and the same Kalf said to Hrefna. Kalf now unlocked a great chest and bade them go and have a look at it. That day a gale sprang up, and Kjartan and Kalf had to go out to moor their ship, and when that was done they went home to the booths. Kalf was the first to enter the booth, where Thurid and Hrefna had turned out most of the things in the chest. Just then Hrefna snatched up the coif and unfolded it, and they had much to say as to how precious a thing it was. Then Hrefna said she would coif herself with it, and Thurid said she had better, and Hrefna did so. When Kalf saw that he gave her to understand that she had done amiss, and bade her take it off at her swiftest. "For that is the one thing that we, Kjartan and I, do not own in common." And as he said this Kjartan came into the booth. He had heard their talk, and fell in at once and told them there was nothing amiss. So Hrefna sat still with the head-dress on. Kjartan looked at her heedfully and said, "I think the coif becomes you very well, Hrefna," says he, "and I think it fits the best that both together, coif and maiden, be mine." Then Hrefna answered, "Most people take it that you are in no hurry to marry, and also that the woman you woo, you will be sure to get for wife." Kjartan said it would not matter much whom he married, but he would not stand being kept long a waiting wooer by any woman. "Now I see that this gear suits you well, and it suits well that you become my wife." Hrefna now took off the head-dress and gave it to Kjartan, who put it away in a safe place. Gudmund and Thurid asked Kjartan to come north to them for a friendly stay some time that winter, and Kjartan promised the journey. Kalf Asgeirson betook himself north with his father. Kjartan and he now divided their partnership, and that went off altogether in good-nature and friendship. Kjartan also rode from his ship westward to the Dales, and they were twelve of them together. Kjartan now came home to Herdholt, and was joyfully received by everybody. Kjartan had his goods taken to the west from the ship during the autumn. The twelve men who rode with Kjartan stayed at Herdholt all the winter. Olaf and Osvif kept to the same wont of asking each other to their house, which was that each should go to the other every other autumn. That autumn the wassail was to be at Laugar, and Olaf and all the Herdholtings were to go thither. Gudrun now spoke to Bolli, and said she did not think he had told her the truth in all things about the coming back of Kjartan. Bolli said he had told the truth about it as best he knew it. Gudrun spoke little on this matter, but it could be easily seen that she was very displeased, and most people would have it that she still was pining for Kjartan, although she tried to hide it. Now time glides on till the autumn feast was to be held at Laugar. Olaf got ready and bade Kjartan come with him. Kjartan said he would stay at home and look after the household. Olaf bade him not to show that he was angry with his kinsmen. "Call this to mind, Kjartan, that you have loved no man so much as your foster-brother Bolli, and it is my wish that you should come, for things will soon settle themselves between you, kinsmen, if you meet each other." Kjartan did as his father bade him. He took the scarlet clothes that King Olaf had given him at parting, and dressed himself gaily; he girded his sword, the king's gift, on; and he had a gilt helm on his head, and on his side a red shield with the Holy Cross painted on it in gold; he had in his hand a spear, with the socket inlaid with gold. All his men were gaily dressed. There were in all between twenty and thirty men of them. They now rode out of Herdholt and went on till they came to Laugar. There were a great many men gathered together already.

Chapter 45
Kjartan marries Hrefna, A.D. 1002

Bolli, together with the sons of Osvif, went out to meet Olaf and his company, and gave them a cheery welcome. Bolli went to Kjartan and kissed him, and Kjartan took his greeting. After that they were seen into the house, Bolli was of the merriest towards them, and Olaf responded to that most heartily, but Kjartan was rather silent. The feast went off well. Now Bolli had some stud-horses which were looked upon as the best of their kind. The stallion was great and goodly, and had never failed at fight; it was light of coat, with red ears and forelock. Three mares went with it, of the same hue as the stallion. These horses Bolli wished to give to Kjartan, but Kjartan said he was not a horsey man, and could not take the gift. Olaf bade him take the horses, "for these are most noble gifts." Kjartan gave a flat refusal. They parted after this nowise blithely, and the Herdholtings went home, and all was quiet. Kjartan was rather gloomy all the winter, and people could have but little talk of him. Olaf thought this a great misfortune. That winter after Yule Kjartan got ready to leave home, and there were twelve of them together, bound for the countrysides of the north. They now rode on their way till they came to Asbjornness, north in Willowdale, and there Kjartan was greeted with the greatest blitheness and cheerfulness. The housing there was of the noblest. Hall, the son of Gudmund, was about twenty winters old, and took much after the kindred of the men of Salmon-river-Dale; and it is all men's say, there was no more valiant-looking a man in all the north land. Hall greeted Kjartan, his uncle, with the greatest blitheness. Sports are now at once started at Asbjornness, and men were gathered together from far and near throughout the countrysides, and people came from the west from Midfirth and from Waterness and Waterdale all the way and from out of Longdale, and there was a great gathering together. It was the talk of all folk how strikingly Kjartan showed above other men. Now the sports were set going, and Hall took the lead. He asked Kjartan to join in the play, "and I wish, kinsman, you would show your courtesy in this." Kjartan said, "I have been training for sports but little of late, for there were other things to do with King Olaf, but I will not refuse you this for once." So Kjartan now got ready to play, and the strongest men there were chosen out to go against him. The game went on all day long, but no man had either strength or litheness of limb to cope with Kjartan. And in the evening when the games were ended, Hall stood up and said, "It is the wish and offer of my father concerning those men who have come from the farthest hither, that they all stay here over night and take up the pastime again to-morrow." At this message there was made a good cheer, and the offer deemed worthy of a great man. Kalf Asgeirson was there, and he and Kjartan were dearly fond of each other. His sister Hrefna was there also, and was dressed most showily. There were over a hundred (i.e. over 120) men in the house that night. And the next day sides were divided for the games again. Kjartan sat by and looked on at the sports. Thurid, his sister, went to talk to him, and said, "It is told me, brother, that you have been rather silent all the winter, and men say it must be because you are pining after Gudrun, and set forth as a proof thereof that no fondness now is shown between you and Bolli, such as through all time there had been between you. Do now the good and befitting thing, and don't allow yourself to take this to heart, and grudge not your kinsman a good wife. To me it seems your best counsel to marry, as you bespoke it last summer, although the match be not altogether even for you, where Hrefna is, for such a match you cannot find within this land. Asgeir, her father, is a noble and a high-born man, and he does not lack wealth wherewith to make this match fairer still; moreover, another daughter of his is married to a mighty man. You have also told me yourself that Kalf Asgeirson is the doughtiest of men, and their way of life is of the stateliest. It is my wish that you go and talk to Hrefna, and I ween you will find that there great wits and goodliness go together." Kjartan took this matter up well, and said she had ably pleaded the case. After this Kjartan and Hrefna are brought together that they may have their talk by themselves, and they talked together all day. In the evening Thurid asked Kjartan how he liked the manner in which Hrefna turned her speech. He was well pleased about it, and said he thought the woman was in all ways one of the noblest as far as he could see. The next morning men were sent to Asgeir to ask him to Asbjornness. And now they had a parley between them on this affair, and Kjartan wooed Hrefna, Asgeir's daughter. Asgeir took up the matter with a good will, for he was a wise man, and saw what an honourable offer was made to them. Kalf, too, urged the matter on very much, saying, "I will not let anything be spared (towards the dowry)." Hrefna, in her turn, did not make unwilling answers, but bade her father follow his own counsel. So now the match was covenanted and settled before witnesses. Kjartan would hear of nothing but that the wedding should be held at Herdholt, and Asgeir and Kalf had nothing to say against it. The wedding was then settled to take place at Herdholt when five weeks of summer had passed. After that Kjartan rode home with great gifts. Olaf was delighted at these tidings, for Kjartan was much merrier than before he left home. Kjartan kept fast through Lent, following therein the example of no man in this land; and it is said he was the first man who ever kept fast in this land. Men thought it so wonderful a thing that Kjartan could live so long without meat, that people came over long ways to see him. In a like manner Kjartan's other ways went beyond those of other men. Now Easter passed, and after that Kjartan and Olaf made ready a great feast. At the appointed time Asgeir and Kalf came from the north as well as Gudmund and Hall, and altogether there were sixty men. Olaf and Kjartan had already many men gathered together there. It was a most brave feast, and for a whole week the feasting went on. Kjartan made Hrefna a bridal gift of the rich head-dress, and a most famous gift was that; for no one was there so knowing or so rich as ever to have seen or possessed such a treasure, for it is the saying of thoughtful men that eight ounces of gold were woven into the coif. Kjartan was so merry at the feast that he entertained every one with his talk, telling of his journey. Men did marvel much how great were the matters that entered into that tale; for he had served the noblest of lords–King Olaf Tryggvason. And when the feast was ended Kjartan gave Gudmund and Hall good gifts, as he did to all the other great men. The father and son gained great renown from this feast. Kjartan and Hrefna loved each other very dearly.

Chapter 46
Feast at Herdholt and the Loss of Kjartan's Sword, A.D. 1002

Olaf and Osvif were still friends, though there was some deal of ill-will between the younger people. That summer Olaf had his feast half a month before winter. And Osvif was also making ready a feast, to be held at "Winter-nights," and they each asked the other to their homes, with as many men as each deemed most honourable to himself. It was Osvif's turn to go first to the feast at Olaf's, and he came to Herdholt at the time appointed. In his company were Bolli and Gudrun and the sons of Osvif. In the morning one of the women on going down the hall was talking how the ladies would be shown to their seats. And just as Gudrun had come right against the bedroom wherein Kjartan was wont to rest, and where even then he was dressing and slipping on a red kirtle of scarlet, he called out to the woman who had been speaking about the seating of the women, for no one else was quicker in giving the answer, "Hrefna shall sit in the high seat and be most honoured in all things so long as I am alive." But before this Gudrun had always had the high seat at Herdholt and everywhere else. Gudrun heard this, and looked at Kjartan and flushed up, but said nothing. The next day Gudrun was talking to Hrefna, and said she ought to coif herself with the head-dress, and show people the most costly treasure that had ever come to Iceland. Kjartan was near, but not quite close, and heard what Gudrun said, and he was quicker to answer than Hrefna. "She shall not coif herself with the headgear at this feast, for I set more store by Hrefna owning the greatest of treasures than by the guests having it to feast thereon their eyes at this time." The feast at Olaf's was to last a week. The next day Gudrun spoke on the sly to Hrefna, and asked her to show her the head-dress, and Hrefna said she would. The next day they went to the out-bower where the precious things were kept, and Hrefna opened a chest and took out the pocket of costly stuff, and took from thence the coif and showed it to Gudrun. She unfolded the coif and looked at it a while, but said no word of praise or blame. After that Hrefna put it back, and they went to their places, and after that all was joy and amusement. And the day the guests should ride away Kjartan busied himself much about matters in hand, getting change of horses for those who had come from afar, and speeding each one on his journey as he needed. Kjartan had not his sword "King's-gift" with him while he was taken up with these matters, yet was he seldom wont to let it go out of his hand. After this he went to his room where the sword had been, and found it now gone. He then went and told his father of the loss. Olaf said, "We must go about this most gently. I will get men to spy into each batch of them as they ride away," and he did so. An the White had to ride with Osvif's company, and to keep an eye upon men turning aside, or baiting. They rode up past Lea-shaws, and past the homesteads which are called Shaws, and stopped at one of the homesteads at Shaws, and got off their horses. Thorolf, son of Osvif, went out from the homestead with a few other men. They went out of sight amongst the brushwood, whilst the others tarried at the Shaws' homestead. An followed him all the way unto Salmon-river, where it flows out of Sælingsdale, and said he would turn back there. Thorolf said it would have done no harm though he had gone nowhere at all. The night before a little snow had fallen so that footprints could be traced. An rode back to the brushwood, and followed the footprints of Thorolf to a certain ditch or bog. He groped down with his hand, and grasped the hilt of a sword. An wished to have witnesses with him to this, and rode for Thorarin in Sælingsdale Tongue, and he went with An to take up the sword. After that An brought the sword back to Kjartan. Kjartan wrapt it in a cloth, and laid it in a chest. The place was afterwards called Sword-ditch, where An and Thorarin had found the "King's-gift." This was all kept quiet. The scabbard was never found again. Kjartan always treasured the sword less hereafter than heretofore. This affair Kjartan took much to heart, and would not let the matter rest there. Olaf said, "Do not let it pain you; true, they have done a nowise pretty trick, but you have got no harm from it. We shall not let people have this to laugh at, that we make a quarrel about such a thing, these being but friends and kinsmen on the other side." And through these reasonings of Olaf, Kjartan let matters rest in quiet. After that Olaf got ready to go to the feast at Laugar at "winter nights," and told Kjartan he must go too. Kjartan was very unwilling thereto, but promised to go at the bidding of his father. Hrefna was also to go, but she wished to leave her coif behind. "Goodwife," Thorgerd said, "whenever will you take out such a peerless keepsake if it is to lie down in chests when you go to feasts?" Hrefna said, "Many folk say that it is not unlikely that I may come to places where I have fewer people to envy me than at Laugar." Thorgerd said, "I have no great belief in people who let such things fly here from house to house." And because Thorgerd urged it eagerly Hrefna took the coif, and Kjartan did not forbid it when he saw how the will of his mother went. After that they betake themselves to the journey and came to Laugar in the evening, and had a goodly welcome there. Thorgerd and Hrefna handed out their clothes to be taken care of. But in the morning when the women should dress themselves Hrefna looked for the coif and it was gone from where she had put it away. It was looked for far and near, and could not be found. Gudrun said it was most likely the coif had been left behind at home, or that she had packed it so carelessly that it had fallen out on the way. Hrefna now told Kjartan that the coif was lost. He answered and said it was no easy matter to try to make them take care of things, and bade her now leave matters quiet; and told his father what game was up. Olaf said, "My will is still as before, that you leave alone and let pass by this trouble and I will probe this matter to the bottom in quiet; for I would do anything that you and Bolli should not fall out. Best to bind up a whole flesh, kinsman," says he. Kjartan said, "I know well, father, that you wish the best for everybody in this affair; yet I know not whether I can put up with being thus overborne by these folk of Laugar." The day that men were to ride away from the feast Kjartan raised his voice and said, "I call on you, Cousin Bolli, to show yourself more willing henceforth than hitherto to do to us as behoves a good man and true. I shall not set this matter forth in a whisper, for within the knowledge of many people it is that a loss has befallen here of a thing which we think has slipped into your own keep. This harvest, when we gave a feast at Herdholt, my sword was taken; it came back to me, but not the scabbard. Now again there has been lost here a keepsake which men will esteem a thing of price. Come what may, I will have them both back." Bolli answered, "What you put down to me, Kjartan, is not my fault, and I should have looked for anything else from you sooner than that you would charge me with theft." Kjartan says, "I must think that the people who have been putting their heads together in this affair are so near to you that it ought to be in your power to make things good if you but would. You affront us far beyond necessity, and long we have kept peaceful in face on your enmity. But now it must be made known that matters will not rest as they are now." Then Gudrun answered his speech and said, "Now you rake up a fire which it would be better should not smoke. Now, let it be granted, as you say, that there be some people here who have put their heads together with a view to the coif disappearing. I can only think that they have gone and taken what was their own. Think what you like of what has become of the head-dress, but I cannot say I dislike it though it should be bestowed in such a way as that Hrefna should have little chance to improve her apparel with it henceforth." After that they parted heavy of heart, and the Herdholtings rode home. That was the end of the feasts, yet everything was to all appearances quiet. Nothing was ever heard of the head-dress. But many people held the truth to be that Thorolf had burnt it in fire by the order of Gudrun, his sister. Early that winter Asgeir Eider-drake died. His sons inherited his estate and chattels.

Chapter 47
Kjartan goes to Laugar

After Yule that winter Kjartan got men together, and they mustered sixty men altogether. Kjartan did not tell his father the reason of his journey, and Olaf asked but little about it. Kjartan took with him tents and stores, and rode on his way until he came to Laugar. He bade his men get off their horses, and said that some should look after the horses and some put up the tents. At that time it was the custom that outhouses were outside, and not so very far away from the dwelling-house, and so it was at Laugar. Kjartan had all the doors of the house taken, and forbade all the inmates to go outside, and for three nights he made them do their errands within the house. After that Kjartan rode home to Herdholt, and each of his followers rode to his own home. Olaf was very ill-pleased with this raid, but Thorgerd said there was no reason for blame, for the men of Laugar had deserved this, yea, and a still greater shame. Then Hrefna said, "Did you have any talk with any one at Laugar, Kjartan?" He answered, "There was but little chance of that," and said he and Bolli had exchanged only a few words. Then Hrefna smiled and said, "It was told me as truth that you and Gudrun had some talk together, and I have likewise heard how she was arrayed, that she had coifed herself with the head-dress, and it suited her exceeding well." Kjartan answered, and coloured up, and it was easy to see he was angry with her for making a mockery of this. "Nothing of what you say, Hrefna, passed before my eyes, and there was no need for Gudrun to coif herself with the head-dress to look statelier than all other women." Thereat Hrefna dropped the talk. The men of Laugar bore this exceedingly ill, and thought it by much a greater and worse disgrace than if Kjartan had even killed a man or two of them. The sons of Osvif were the wildest over this matter, but Bolli quieted them rather. Gudrun was the fewest-spoken on the matter, yet men gathered from her words that it was uncertain whether any one took it as sorely to heart as she did. Full enmity now grows up between the men of Laugar and the Herdholtings. As the winter wore on Hrefna gave birth to a child, a boy, and he was named Asgier. Thorarin, the goodman of Tongue, let it be known that he wished to sell the land of Tongue. The reason was that he was drained of money, and that he thought ill-will was swelling too much between the people of the countryside, he himself being a friend of either side. Bolli thought he would like to buy the land and settle down on it, for the men of Laugar had little land and much cattle. Bolli and Gudrun rode to Tongue at the advice of Osvif; they thought it a very handy chance to be able to secure this land so near to themselves, and Osvif bade them not to let a small matter stand in the way of a covenant. Then they (Bolli and Gudrun) bespoke the purchase with Thorarin, and came to terms as to what the price should be, and also as to the kind wherein it should be paid, and the bargain was settled with Thorarin. But the buying was not done in the presence of witnesses, for there were not so many men there at the time as were lawfully necessary. Bolli and Gudrun rode home after that. But when Kjartan Olafson hears of these tidings he rides off with twelve men, and came to Tongue early one day. Thorarin greeted him well, and asked him to stay there. Kjartan said he must ride back again in the morning, but would tarry there for some time. Thorarin asked his errand, and Kjartan said, "My errand here is to speak about a certain sale of land that you and Bolli have agreed upon, for it is very much against my wishes if you sell this land to Bolli and Gudrun." Thorarin said that to do otherwise would be unbecoming to him, "For the price that Bolli has offered for the land is liberal, and is to be paid up speedily." Kjartan said, "You shall come in for no loss even if Bolli does not buy your land; for I will buy it at the same price, and it will not be of much avail to you to speak against what I have made up my mind to have done. Indeed it will soon be found out that I shall want to have the most to say within this countryside, being more ready, however, to do the will of others than that of the men of Laugar." Thorarin answered, "Mighty to me will be the master's word in this matter, but it would be most to my mind that this bargain should be left alone as I and Bolli have settled it." Kjartan said, "I do not call that a sale of land which is not bound by witnesses. Now you do one of two things, either sell me the lands on the same terms as you agreed upon with the others, or live on your land yourself." Thorarin chooses to sell him the land, and witnesses were forthwith taken to the sale, and after the purchase Kjartan rode home. That same evening this was told at Laugar. Then Gudrun said, "It seems to me, Bolli, that Kjartan has given you two choices somewhat harder than those he gave Thorarin–that you must either leave the countryside with little honour, or show yourself at some meeting with him a good deal less slow than you have been heretofore." Bolli did not answer, but went forthwith away from this talk. All was quiet now throughout what was left of Lent. The third day after Easter Kjartan rode from home with one other man, on the beach, for a follower. They came to Tongue in the day. Kjartan wished Thorarin to ride with them to Saurby to gather in debts due to him, for Kjartan had much money-at-call in these parts. But Thorarin had ridden to another place. Kjartan stopped there awhile, and waited for him. That same day Thorhalla the Chatterbox was come there. She asked Kjartan where he was minded to go. He said he was going west to Saurby. She asked, "Which road will you take?" Kjartan replied, "I am going by Sælingsdale to the west, and by Swinedale from the west." She asked how long he would be. Kjartan answered, "Most likely I shall be riding from the west next Thursday (the fifth day of the week)." "Would you do an errand for me?" said Thorhalla. "I have a kinsman west at Whitedale and Saurby; he has promised me half a mark's worth of homespun, and I would like you to claim it for me, and bring it with you from the west." Kjartan promised to do this. After this Thorarin came home, and betook himself to the journey with them. They rode westward over Sælingsdale heath, and came to Hol in the evening to the brothers and sister there. There Kjartan got the best of welcomes, for between him and them there was the greatest friendship. Thorhalla the Chatterbox came home to Laugar that evening. The sons of Osvif asked her who she had met during the day. She said she had met Kjartan Olafson. They asked where he was going. She answered, telling them all she knew about it, "And never has he looked braver than now, and it is not wonderful at all that such men should look upon everything as low beside themselves;" and Thorhalla still went on, "and it was clear to me that Kjartan liked to talk of nothing so well as of his land bargain with Thorarin." Gudrun spoke, "Kjartan may well do things as boldly as it pleases him, for it is proven that for whatever insult he may pay others, there is none who dares even to shoot a shaft at him." Present at this talk of Gudrun and Thorhalla were both Bolli and the sons of Osvif. Ospak and his brothers said but little, but what there was, rather stinging for Kjartan, as was always their way. Bolli behaved as if he did not hear, as he always did when Kjartan was spoken ill of, for his wont was either to hold his peace, or to gainsay them.

Chapter 48
The Men of Laugar and Gudrun plan an Ambush for Kjartan, A.D. 1003

Kjartan spent the fourth day after Easter at Hol, and there was the greatest merriment and gaiety. The night after An was very ill at ease in his sleep, so they waked him. They asked him what he had dreamt. He answered, "A woman came to me most evil-looking and pulled me forth unto the bedside. She had in one hand a short sword, and in the other a trough; she drove the sword into my breast and cut open all the belly, and took out all my inwards and put brushwood in their place. After that she went outside." Kjartan and the others laughed very much at this dream, and said he should be called An "brushwood belly," and they caught hold of him and said they wished to feel if he had the brushwood in his stomach. Then Aud said, "There is no need to mock so much at this; and my counsel is that Kjartan do one of two things: either tarry here longer, or, if he will ride away, then let him ride with more followers hence than hither he did." Kjartan said, "You may hold An 'brushwood belly' a man very sage as he sits and talks to you all day, since you think that whatever he dreams must be a very vision, but go I must, as I have already made up my mind to, in spite of this dream." Kjartan got ready to go on the fifth day in Easter week; and at the advice of Aud, so did Thorkell Whelp and Knut his brother. They rode on the way with Kjartan a band of twelve together. Kjartan came to Whitedale and fetched the homespun for Thorhalla Chatterbox as he had said he would. After that he rode south through Swinedale. It is told how at Laugar in Sælingsdale Gudrun was early afoot directly after sunrise. She went to where her brothers were sleeping. She roused Ospak and he woke up at once, and then too the other brothers. And when Ospak saw that there was his sister, he asked her what she wanted that she was up so early. Gudrun said she wanted to know what they would be doing that day. Ospak said he would keep at rest, "for there is little work to do." Gudrun said, "You would have the right sort of temper if you were the daughters of some peasant, letting neither good nor bad be done by you. Why, after all the disgrace and shame that Kjartan has done to you, you none the less lie quietly sleeping, though he rides past this place with but one other man. Such men indeed are richly endowed with the memory of swine. I think it is past hoping that you will ever have courage enough to go and seek out Kjartan in his home, if you dare not meet him now that he rides with but one other man or two; but here you sit at home and bear yourselves as if you were hopeful men; yea, in sooth there are too many of you." Ospak said she did not mince matters and it was hard to gainsay her, and he sprang up forthwith and dressed, as did also each of the brothers one after the other. Then they got ready to lay an ambush for Kjartan. Then Gudrun called on Bolli to bestir him with them. Bolli said it behoved him not for the sake of his kinship with Kjartan, set forth how lovingly Olaf had brought him up. Gudrun answered, "Therein you speak the truth, but you will not have the good luck always to do what pleases all men, and if you cut yourself out of this journey, our married life must be at an end." And through Gudrun's harping on the matter Bolli's mind swelled at all the enmity and guilts that lay at the door of Kjartan, and speedily he donned his weapons, and they grew a band of nine together. There were the five sons of Osvif—Ospak, Helgi, Vandrad, Torrad, and Thorolf. Bolli was the sixth and Gudlaug, the son of Osvif's sister, the hopefullest of men, the seventh. There were also Odd and Stein, sons of Thorhalla Chatterbox. They rode to Swinedale and took up their stand beside the gill which is called Goat-gill. They bound up their horses and sat down. Bolli was silent all day, and lay up on the top of the gill bank. Now when Kjartan and his followers were come south past Narrowsound, where the dale begins to widen out, Kjartan said that Thorkell and the others had better turn back. Thorkell said they would ride to the end of the dale. Then when they came south past the out-dairies called Northdairies Kjartan spake to the brothers and bade them not to ride any farther. "Thorolf the thief," he said, "shall not have that matter to laugh at that I dare not ride on my way with few men." Thorkell Whelp said, "We will yield to you in not following you any farther; but we should rue it indeed not to be near if you should stand in need of men to-day." Then Kjartan said, "Never will Bolli, my kinsman, join hands with plotters against my life. But if the sons of Osvif lie in wait for me, there is no knowing which side will live to tell the tale, even though I may have some odds to deal with." Thereupon the brothers rode back to the west.

Chapter 49
The Death of Kjartan

Now Kjartan rode south through the dale, he and they three together, himself, An the Black, and Thorarin. Thorkell was the name of a man who lived at Goat-peaks in Swinedale, where now there is waste land. He had been seeing after his horses that day, and a shepherd of his with him. They saw the two parties, the men of Laugar in ambush and Kjartan and his where they were riding down the dale three together. Then the shepherd said they had better turn to meet Kjartan and his; it would be, quoth he, a great good hap to them if they could stave off so great a trouble as now both sides were steering into. Thorkell said, "Hold your tongue at once. Do you think, fool as you are, you will ever give life to a man to whom fate has ordained death? And, truth to tell, I would spare neither of them from having now as evil dealings together as they like. It seems to me a better plan for us to get to a place where we stand in danger of nothing, and from where we can have a good look at their meeting, so as to have some fun over their play. For all men make a marvel thereof, how Kjartan is of all men the best skilled at arms. I think he will want it now, for we two know how overwhelming the odds are." And so it had to be as Thorkell wished. Kjartan and his followers now rode on to Goat-gill. On the other hand the sons of Osvif misdoubt them why Bolli should have sought out a place for himself from where he might well be seen by men riding from the west. So they now put their heads together, and, being of one mind that Bolli was playing them false, they go for him up unto the brink and took to wrestling and horse-playing with him, and took him by the feet and dragged him down over the brink. But Kjartan and his followers came up apace as they were riding fast, and when they came to the south side of the gill they saw the ambush and knew the men. Kjartan at once sprung off his horse and turned upon the sons of Osvif. There stood near by a great stone, against which Kjartan ordered they should wait the onset (he and his). Before they met Kjartan flung his spear, and it struck through Thorolf's shield above the handle, so that therewith the shield was pressed against him, the spear piercing the shield and the arm above the elbow, where it sundered the main muscle, Thorolf dropping the shield, and his arm being of no avail to him through the day. Thereupon Kjartan drew his sword, but he held not the "King's-gift." The sons of Thorhalla went

at Thorarin, for that was the task allotted to them. That outset was a hard one,
for Thorarin was mightily strong, and it was hard to tell which would outlast
the other. Osvif's sons and Gudlaug set on Kjartan, they being five together,
and Kjartan and An but two. An warded himself valiantly, and would ever
be going in front of Kjartan. Bolli stood aloof with Footbiter. Kjartan smote
hard, but his sword was of little avail (and bent so), he often had to straighten
it under his foot. In this attack both the sons of Osvif and An were wounded,
but Kjartan had no wound as yet. Kjartan fought so swiftly and dauntlessly
that Osvif's sons recoiled and turned to where An was. At that moment An
fell, having fought for some time, with his inwards coming out. In this attack
Kjartan cut off one leg of Gudlaug above the knee, and that hurt was enough
to cause death. Then the four sons of Osvif made an onset on Kjartan, but he
warded himself so bravely that in no way did he give them the chance of any
advantage. Then spake Kjartan, "Kinsman Bolli, why did you leave home if
you meant quietly to stand by? Now the choice lies before you, to help one
side or the other, and try now how Footbiter will do." Bolli made as if he did
not hear. And when Ospak saw that they would no how bear Kjartan over, he
egged on Bolli in every way, and said he surely would not wish that shame to
follow after him, to have promised them his aid in this fight and not to grant it
now. "Why, heavy enough in dealings with us was Kjartan then, when by none
so big a deed as this we had offended him; but if Kjartan is now to get away
from us, then for you, Bolli, as even for us, the way to exceeding hardships will
be equally short." Then Bolli drew Footbiter, and now turned upon Kjartan.
Then Kjartan said to Bolli, "Surely thou art minded now, my kinsman, to do a
dastard's deed; but oh, my kinsman, I am much more fain to take my death
from you than to cause the same to you myself." Then Kjartan flung away his
weapons and would defend himself no longer; yet he was but slightly wounded,
though very tired with fighting. Bolli gave no answer to Kjartan's words, but all
the same he dealt him his death-wound. And straightway Bolli sat down under
the shoulders of him, and Kjartan breathed his last in the lap of Bolli. Bolli
rued at once his deed, and declared the manslaughter due to his hand. Bolli
sent the sons of Osvif into the countryside, but he stayed behind together with
Thorarin by the dead bodies. And when the sons of Osvif came to Laugar they
told the tidings. Gudrun gave out her pleasure thereat, and then the arm of
Thorolf was bound up; it healed slowly, and was never after any use to him.
The body of Kjartan was brought home to Tongue, but Bolli rode home to
Laugar. Gudrun went to meet him, and asked what time of day it was. Bolli
said it was near noontide. Then spake Gudrun, "Harm spurs on to hard deeds
(work); I have spun yarn for twelve ells of homespun, and you have killed
Kjartan." Bolli replied, "That unhappy deed might well go late from my mind
even if you did not remind me of it." Gudrun said "Such things I do not count
among mishaps. It seemed to me you stood in higher station during the year
Kjartan was in Norway than now, when he trod you under foot when he came
back to Iceland. But I count that last which to me is dearest, that Hrefna will

not go laughing to her bed to-night." Then Bolli said and right wroth he was, "I think it is quite uncertain that she will turn paler at these tidings than you do; and I have my doubts as to whether you would not have been less startled if I had been lying behind on the field of battle, and Kjartan had told the tidings." Gudrun saw that Bolli was wroth, and spake, "Do not upbraid me with such things, for I am very grateful to you for your deed; for now I think I know that you will not do anything against my mind." After that Osvif's sons went and hid in an underground chamber, which had been made for them in secret, but Thorhalla's sons were sent west to Holy-Fell to tell Snorri Godi the Priest these tidings, and therewith the message that they bade him send them speedily all availing strength against Olaf and those men to whom it came to follow up the blood-suit after Kjartan. At Sælingsdale Tongue it happened, the night after the day on which the fight befell, that An sat up, he who they had all thought was dead. Those who waked the bodies were very much afraid, and thought this a wondrous marvel. Then An spake to them, "I beg you, in God's name, not to be afraid of me, for I have had both my life and my wits all unto the hour when on me fell the heaviness of a swoon. Then I dreamed of the same woman as before, and methought she now took the brushwood out of my belly and put my own inwards in instead, and the change seemed good to me." Then the wounds that An had were bound up and he became a hale man, and was ever afterwards called An Brushwood-belly. But now when Olaf Hoskuld's son heard these tidings he took the slaying of Kjartan most sorely to heart, though he bore it like a brave man. His sons wanted to set on Bolli forthwith and kill him. Olaf said, "Far be it from me, for my son is none the more atoned to me though Bolli be slain; moreover, I loved Kjartan before all men, but as to Bolli, I could not bear any harm befalling him. But I see a more befitting business for you to do. Go ye and meet the sons of Thorhalla, who are now sent to Holy-Fell with the errand of summoning up a band against us. I shall be well pleased for you to put them to any penalty you like." Then Olaf's sons swiftly turn to journeying, and went on board a ferry-boat that Olaf owned, being seven of them together, and rowed out down Hvamsfirth, pushing on their journey at their lustiest. They had but little wind, but fair what there was, and they rowed with the sail until they came under Scoreisle, where they tarried for some while and asked about the journeyings of men thereabouts. A little while after they saw a ship coming from the west across the firth, and soon they saw who the men were, for there were the sons of Thorhalla, and Halldor and his followers boarded them straightway. They met with no resistance, for the sons of Olaf leapt forthwith on board their ships and set upon them. Stein and his brother were laid hands on and beheaded overboard. The sons of Olaf now turn back, and their journey was deemed to have sped most briskly.

Chapter 50
The End of Hrefna. The Peace Settled, A.D. 1003

Olaf went to meet Kjartan's body. He sent men south to Burg to tell Thorstein

Egilson these tidings, and also that he would have his help for the blood-suit; and if any great men should band themselves together against him with the sons of Osvif, he said he wanted to have the whole matter in his own hands. The same message he sent north to Willowdale, to Gudmund, his son-in-law, and to the sons of Asgeir; with the further information that he had charged as guilty of the slaying of Kjartan all the men who had taken part in the ambush, except Ospak, son of Osvif, for he was already under outlawry because of a woman who was called Aldis, the daughter of Holmganga-Ljot of Ingjaldsand. Their son was Ulf, who later became a marshal to King Harold Sigurdsson, and had for wife Jorunn, the daughter of Thorberg. Their son was Jon, father of Erlend the Laggard, the father of Archbishop Egstein. Olaf had proclaimed that the blood-suit should be taken into court at Thorness Thing. He had Kjartan's body brought home, and a tent was rigged over it, for there was as yet no church built in the Dales. But when Olaf heard that Thorstein had bestirred him swiftly and raised up a band of great many men, and that the Willowdale men had done likewise, he had men gathered together throughout all the Dales, and a great multitude they were. The whole of this band Olaf sent to Laugar, with this order: "It is my will that you guard Bolli if he stand in need thereof, and do it no less faithfully than if you were following me; for my mind misgives me that the men from beyond this countryside, whom, coming soon, we shall be having on our hands, will deem that they have somewhat of a loss to make up with Bolli." And when he had put the matter in order in this manner, Thorstein, with his following, and also the Willowdale men, came on, all wild with rage. Hall Gudmund's son and Kalf Asgeirson egged them on most to go and force Bolli to let search be made for the sons of Osvif till they should be found, for they could be gone nowhere out of the countryside. But because Olaf set himself so much against their making a raid on Laugar, messages of peace were borne between the two parties, and Bolli was most willing, and bade Olaf settle all terms on his behalf, and Osvif said it was not in his power to speak against this, for no help had come to him from Snorri the Priest. A peace meeting, therefore, took place at Lea-Shaws, and the whole case was laid freely in Olaf's hand. For the slaughter of Kjartan there were to come such fines and penalties as Olaf liked. Then the peace meeting came to an end. Bolli, by the counsel of Olaf, did not go to this meeting. The award should be made known at Thorness Thing. Now the Mere-men and Willowdale men rode to Herdholt. Thorstein Kuggison begged for Asgeir, son of Kjartan, to foster, as a comfort to Hrefna. Hrefna went north with her brothers, and was much weighed down with grief, nevertheless she bore her sorrow with dignity, and was easy of speech with every man. Hrefna took no other husband after Kjartan. She lived but a little while after coming to the north; and the tale goes that she died of a broken heart.

Chapter 51
Osvif's Sons are Banished

Kjartan's body lay in state for a week in Herdholt. Thorstein Egilson had had a church built at Burg. He took the body of Kjartan home with him, and Kjartan was buried at Burg. The church was newly consecrated, and as yet hung in white. Now time wore on towards the Thorness Thing, and the award was given against Osvif's sons, who were all banished the country. Money was given to pay the cost of their going into exile, but they were forbidden to come back to Iceland so long as any of Olaf's sons, or Asgeir, Kjartan's son, should be alive. For Gudlaug, the son of Osvif's sister, no weregild (atonement) should be paid, because of his having set out against, and laid ambush for, Kjartan, neither should Thorolf have any compensation for the wounds he had got. Olaf would not let Bolli be prosecuted, and bade him ransom himself with a money fine. This Halldor and Stein, and all the sons of Olaf, liked mightily ill, and said it would go hard with Bolli if he was allowed to stay in the same countryside as themselves. Olaf saw that would work well enough as long as he was on his legs. There was a ship in Bjornhaven which belonged to Audun Cable-hound. He was at the Thing, and said, "As matters stand, the guilt of these men will be no less in Norway, so long as any of Kjartan's friends are alive." Then Osvif said, "You, Cable-hound, will be no soothsayer in this matter, for my sons will be highly accounted of among men of high degree, whilst you, Cable-hound, will pass, this summer, into the power of trolls." Audun Cable-hound went out a voyage that summer and the ship was wrecked amongst the Faroe Isles and every man's child on board perished, and Osvif's prophecy was thought to have come thoroughly home. The sons of Osvif went abroad that summer, and none ever came back again. In such a manner the blood-suit came to an end that Olaf was held to have shown himself all the greater a man, because where it was due, in the case of the sons of Osvif, to wit, he drove matters home to the very bone, but spared Bolli for the sake of their kinship. Olaf thanked men well for the help they had afforded him. By Olaf's counsel Bolli bought the land at Tongue. It is told that Olaf lived three winters after Kjartan was slain. After he was dead his sons shared the inheritance he left behind. Halldor took over the manor of Herdholt. Thorgerd, their mother, lived with Halldor; she was most hatefully-minded towards Bolli, and thought the reward he paid for his fostering a bitter one.

Chapter 52
The Killing of Thorkell of Goat's Peak

In the spring Bolli and Gudrun set up householding at Sælingsdale-Tongue, and it soon became a stately one. Bolli and Gudrun begat a son. To that boy a name was given, and he was called Thorleik; he was early a very fine lad, and a right nimble one. Halldor Olafson lived at Herdholt, as has before been written, and he was in most matters at the head of his brothers. The spring that Kjartan was slain Thorgerd Egil's daughter placed a lad, as kin to her, with Thorkell of Goat-Peaks, and the lad herded sheep there through the summer. Like other people he was much grieved over Kjartan's death. He could never speak of Kjartan if Thorkell was near, for he always spoke ill of him, and said he had been a "white" man and of no heart; he often mimicked how Kjartan had taken his death-wound. The lad took this very ill, and went to Herdholt and told Halldor and Thorgerd and begged them to take him in. Thorgerd bade him remain in his service till the winter. The lad said he had no strength to bear being there any longer. "And you would not ask this of me if you knew what heart-burn I suffer from all this." Then Thorgerd's heart turned at the tale of his grief, and she said that as far as she was concerned, she would make a place for him there. Halldor said, "Give no heed to this lad, he is not worth taking in earnest." Then Thorgerd answered, "The lad is of little account," says she, "but Thorkell has behaved evilly in every way in this matter, for he knew of the ambush the men of Laugar laid for Kjartan, and would not warn him, but made fun and sport of their dealings together, and has since said many unfriendly things about the matter; but it seems a matter far beyond you brothers ever to seek revenge where odds are against you, now that you cannot pay out for their doings such scoundrels as Thorkell is." Halldor answered little to that, but bade Thorgerd do what she liked about the lad's service. A few days after Halldor rode from home, he and sundry other men together. He went to Goat-Peaks, and surrounded Thorkell's house. Thorkell was led out and slain, and he met his death with the utmost cowardice. Halldor allowed no plunder, and they went home when this was done. Thorgerd was well pleased over this deed, and thought this reminder better than none. That summer all was quiet, so to speak, and yet there was the greatest ill-will between the sons of Olaf and Bolli. The brothers bore themselves in the most unyielding manner towards Bolli, while he gave in to his kinsmen in all matters as long as he did not lower himself in any way by so doing, for he was a very proud man. Bolli had many followers and lived richly, for there was no lack of money. Steinthor, Olaf's son, lived in Danastead in Salmon-river-Dale. He had for wife Thurid, Asgeir's daughter, who had before been married to Thorkell Kuggi. Their son was Steinthor, who was called "Stone-grig."

Chapter 53
Thorgerd's Egging, A.D. 1007

The next winter after the death of Olaf Hoskuldson, Thorgerd, Egil's daughter, sent word to her son Steinthor that he should come and meet her. When the mother and son met she told him she wished to go up west to Saurby, and see her friend Aud. She told Halldor to come too. They were five together, and Halldor followed his mother. They went on till they came to a place in front of the homestead of Sælingsdale Tongue. Then Thorgerd turned her horse towards the house and asked, "What is this place called?" Halldor answered, "You ask this, mother, not because you don't know it. This place is called Tongue." "Who lives here?" said she. He answered, "You know that, mother." Thorgerd said and snorted, "I know that well enough," she said. "Here lives Bolli, the slayer of your brother, and marvellously unlike your noble kindred you turn out in that you will not avenge such a brother as Kjartan was; never would Egil, your mother's father, have behaved in such a manner; and a piteous thing it is to have dolts for sons; indeed, I think it would have suited you better if you had been your father's daughter and had married. For here, Halldor, it comes to the old saw: 'No stock without a duffer,' and this is the ill-luck of Olaf I see most clearly, how he blundered in begetting his sons. This I would bring home to you, Halldor," says she, "because you look upon yourself as being the foremost among your brothers. Now we will turn back again, for all my errand here was to put you in mind of this, lest you should have forgotten it already." Then Halldor answered, "We shall not put it down as your fault, mother, if this should slip out of our minds." By way of answer Halldor had few words to say about this, but his heart swelled with wrath towards Bolli. The winter now passed and summer came, and time glided on towards the Thing. Halldor and his brothers made it known that they will ride to the Thing. They rode with a great company, and set up the booth Olaf had owned. The Thing was quiet, and no tidings to tell of it. There were at the Thing from the north the Willowdale men, the sons of Gudmund Solmundson. Bardi Gudmundson was then eighteen winters old; he was a great and strong man. The sons of Olaf asked Bardi, their nephew, to go home with them, and added many pressing words to the invitation. Hall, the son of Gudmund, was not in Iceland then. Bardi took up their bidding gladly, for there was much love between those kinsmen. Bardi rode west from the Thing with the sons of Olaf. They came home to Herdholt, and Bardi tarried the rest of the summer time.

Chapter 54
Halldor prepares to avenge Kjartan

Now Halldor told Bardi in secret that the brothers had made up their minds to set on Bolli, for they could no longer withstand the taunts of their mother. "And we will not conceal from you, kinsman Bardi, that what mostly lay behind the invitation to you was this, that we wished to have your help and fellowship." Then Bardi answered, "That will be a matter ill spoken of, to break the peace on one's own kinsmen, and on the other hand it seems to me nowise an easy thing to set on Bolli. He has many men about him and is himself the best of fighters, and is not at a loss for wise counsel with Gudrun and Osvif at his side. Taking all these matters together they seem to me nowise easy to overcome." Halldor said, "There are things we stand more in need of than to make the most of the difficulties of this affair. Nor have I broached it till I knew that it must come to pass, that we make earnest of wreaking revenge on Bolli. And I hope, kinsman, you will not withdraw from doing this journey with us." Bardi answered, "I know you do not think it likely that I will draw back, neither do I desire to do so if I see that I cannot get you to give it up yourselves." "There you do your share in the matter honourably," said Halldor, "as was to be looked for from you." Bardi said they must set about it with care. Halldor said he had heard that Bolli had sent his house-carles from home, some north to Ramfirth to meet a ship and some out to Middlefell strand. "It is also told me that Bolli is staying at the out-dairy in Sælingsdale with no more than the house-carles who are doing the haymaking. And it seems to me we shall never have a better chance of seeking a meeting with Bolli than now." So this then Halldor and Bardi settled between them. There was a man named Thorstein the Black, a wise man and wealthy; he lived at Hundidale in the Broadfirth-Dales; he had long been a friend of Olaf Peacock's. A sister of Thorstein was called Solveig; she was married to a man who was named Helgi, who was son of Hardbein. Helgi was a very tall and strong man, and a great sailor; he had lately come to Iceland, and was staying with his brother-in-law Thorstein. Halldor sent word to Thorstein the Black and Helgi his brother-in-law, and when they were come to Herdholt Halldor told them what he was about, and how he meant to carry it out, and asked them to join in the journey with him. Thorstein showed an utter dislike of this undertaking, saying, "It is the most heinous thing that you kinsmen should go on killing each other off like that; and now there are but few men left in your family equal to Bolli." But though Thorstein spoke in this wise it went for nought. Halldor sent word to Lambi, his father's brother, and when he came and met Halldor he told him what he was about, and Lambi urged hard that this should be carried out. Goodwife Thorgerd also egged them on eagerly to make an earnest of their journey, and said she should never look upon Kjartan as avenged until Bolli paid for him with his life. After this they got ready for the journey. In this raid there were the four sons of Olaf and the fifth was Bardi. There were the sons of Olaf, Halldor, Steinthor, Helgi, and Hoskuld, but Bardi was Gudmund's son. Lambi was the sixth, the seventh was Thorstein, and the eighth Helgi, his brother-in-law, the ninth An Brushwood-belly. Thorgerd betook herself also to the raid with them; but they set themselves against it, and said that such were no journeys for women. She said she would go indeed, "For so much I know of you, my sons, that whetting is what you want." They said she must have her own way.

Chapter 55
The Death of Bolli

After that they rode away from home out of Herdholt, the nine of them together, Thorgerd making the tenth. They rode up along the foreshore and so to Lea-shaws during the early part of the night. They did not stop before they got to Sælingsdale in the early morning tide. There was a thick wood in the valley at that time. Bolli was there in the out-dairy, as Halldor had heard. The dairy stood near the river at the place now called Bolli's-tofts. Above the dairy there is a large hill-rise stretching all the way down to Stack-gill. Between the mountain slope above and the hill-rise there is a wide meadow called Barni; it was there Bolli's house-carles were working. Halldor and his companions rode across Ran-meads unto Oxgrove, and thence above Hammer-Meadow, which was right against the dairy. They knew there were many men at the dairy, so they got off their horses with a view to biding the time when the men should leave the dairy for their work. Bolli's shepherd went early that morning after the flocks up into the mountain side, and from there he saw the men in the wood as well as the horses tied up, and misdoubted that those who went on the sly in this manner would be no men of peace. So forthwith he makes for the dairy by the straightest cut in order to tell Bolli that men were come there. Halldor was a man of keen sight. He saw how that a man was running down the mountain side and making for the dairy. He said to his companions that "That must surely be Bolli's shepherd, and he must have seen our coming; so we must go and meet him, and let him take no news to the dairy." They did as he bade them. An Brushwood-belly went the fastest of them and overtook the man, picked him up, and flung him down. Such was that fall that the lad's back-bone was broken. After that they rode to the dairy. Now the dairy was divided into two parts, the sleeping-room and the byre. Bolli had been early afoot in the morning ordering the men to their work, and had lain down again to sleep when the house-carles went away. In the dairy therefore there were left the two, Gudrun and Bolli. They awoke with the din when they got off their horses, and they also heard them talking as to who should first go on to the dairy to set on Bolli. Bolli knew the voice of Halldor, as well as that of sundry more of his followers. Bolli spoke to Gudrun, and bade her leave the dairy and go away, and said that their meeting would not be such as would afford her much pastime. Gudrun said she thought such things alone would befall there worthy of tidings as she might be allowed to look upon, and held that she would be of no hurt to Bolli by taking her stand near to him. Bolli said that in this matter he would have his way, and so it was that Gudrun went out of the dairy; she went down over the brink to a brook that ran there, and began to wash some linen. Bolli was now alone in the dairy; he took his weapon, set his helm on his head, held a shield before him, and had his sword, Footbiter, in his hand: he had no mail coat. Halldor and his followers were talking to each other outside as to how they should set to work, for no one was very eager to go into the dairy. Then said An Brushwood-belly, "There are men here in this train nearer in kinship to Kjartan than I am, but not one there will be in whose mind abides more steadfastly than in mine the event when Kjartan lost his life. When I was being brought more dead than alive home to Tongue, and Kjartan lay slain, my one thought was that I would gladly do Bolli some harm whenever I should get the chance.So I shall be the first to go into the dairy." Then Thorstein the Black answered, "Most valiantly is that spoken; but it would be wiser not to plunge headlong beyond heed, so let us go warily now, for Bolli will not be standing quiet when he is beset; and however underhanded he may be where he is, you may make up your mind for a brisk defence on his part, strong and skilled at arms as he is. He also has a sword that for a weapon is a trusty one." Then An went into the dairy hard and swift, and held his shield over his head, turning forward the narrower part of it. Bolli dealt him a blow with Footbiter, and cut off the tail-end of the shield, and clove An through the head down to the shoulder, and forthwith he gat his death. Then Lambi went in; he held his shield before him, and a drawn sword in his hand. In the nick of time Bolli pulled Footbiter out of the wound, whereat his shield veered aside so as to lay him open to attack. So Lambi made a thrust at him in the thigh, and a great wound that was. Bolli hewed in return, and struck Lambi's shoulder, and the sword flew down along the side of him, and he was rendered forthwith unfit to fight, and never after that time for the rest of his life was his arm any more use to him. At this brunt Helgi, the son of Hardbien, rushed in with a spear, the head of which was an ell long, and the shaft bound with iron. When Bolli saw that he cast away his sword, and took his shield in both hands, and went towards the dairy door to meet Helgi. Helgi thrust at Bolli with the spear right through the shield and through him. Now Bolli leaned up against the dairy wall, and the men rushed into the dairy, Halldor and his brothers, to wit, and Thorgerd went into the dairy as well. Then spoke Bolli, "Now it is safe, brothers, to come nearer than hitherto you have done," and said he weened that defence now would be but short. Thorgerd answered his speech, and said there was no need to shrink from dealing unflinchingly with Bolli, and bade them "walk between head and trunk." Bolli stood still against the dairy wall, and held tight to him his kirtle lest his inside should come out. Then Steinthor Olafson leapt at Bolli, and hewed at his neck with a large axe just above his shoulders, and forthwith his head flew off. Thorgerd bade him "hale enjoy hands," and said that Gudrun would have now a while a red hair to trim for Bolli. After that they went out of the dairy. Gudrun now came up from the brook, and spoke to Halldor, and asked for tidings of what had befallen in their dealings with Bolli. They told her all that had happened. Gudrun was dressed in a kirtle of "rám"-stuff, and a tight-fitting woven bodice, a high bent coif on her head, and she had tied a scarf round her with dark-blue stripes, and fringed at the ends. Helgi Hardbienson went up to Gudrun, and caught hold of the scarf end, and wiped the blood off the spear with it, the same spear with which he had thrust Bolli through. Gudrun glanced at him and smiled slightly. Then Halldor said, "That was blackguardly and gruesomely done." Helgi bade him not be angry about it, "For I am minded to think that under this scarf end abides undoer of my life." Then they took their horses and rode away. Gudrun went along with them talking with them for a while, and then she turned back.

Chapter 56
Bolli Bollison is born, A.D. 1008

The followers of Halldor now fell a-talking how that Gudrun must think but little of the slaying of Bolli, since she had seen them off chatting and talked to them altogether as if they had done nothing that she might take to heart.

Then Halldor answered, "That is not my feeling, that Gudrun thinks little of Bolli's death; I think the reason of her seeing us off with a chat was far rather, that she wanted to gain a thorough knowledge as to who the men were who had partaken in this journey. Nor is it too much said of Gudrun that in all mettle of mind and heart she is far above other women. Indeed, it is only what might be looked for that Gudrun should take sorely to heart the death of Bolli, for, truth to tell, in such men as was Bolli there is the greatest loss, though we kinsmen, bore not about the good luck to live in peace together." After that they rode home to Herdholt. These tidings spread quickly far and wide and were thought startling, and at Bolli's death there was the greatest grief. Gudrun sent straightway men to Snorri the Priest, for Osvif and she thought that all their trust was where Snorri was. Snorri started quickly at the bidding of Gudrun and came to Tongue with sixty men, and a great ease to Gudrun's heart his coming was. He offered her to try to bring about a peaceful settlement, but Gudrun was but little minded on behalf of Thorleik to agree to taking money for the slaughter of Bolli. "It seems to me, Snorri, that the best help you can afford me," she said, "is to exchange dwellings with me, so that I be not next-door neighbour to the Herdholtings." At that time Snorri had great quarrels with the dwellers at Eyr, but said he would do this for the sake of his friendship with Gudrun. "Yet, Gudrun, you will have to stay on this year at Tongue." Snorri then made ready to go away, and Gudrun gave him honourable gifts. And now Snorri rides away, and things went pretty quietly on that year. The next winter after the killing of Bolli Gudrun gave birth to a child; it was a male, and he was named Bolli. He was at an early age both big and goodly, and Gudrun loved him very much. Now as the winter passed by and the spring came the bargain took place which had been bespoken in that Snorri and Gudrun changed lands. Snorri went to Tongue and lived there for the rest of his life, and Gudrun went to Holyfell, she and Osvif, and there they set up a stately house. There Thorleik and Bolli, the sons of Gudrun, grew up. Thorleik was four years old at the time when Bolli his father was slain.

Chapter 57
About Thorgils Hallason, A.D. 1018

There was a man named Thorgils Hallason; he was known by his mother's name, as she lived longer than his father, whose name was Snorri, son of Alf o' Dales. Halla, Thorgil's mother, was daughter of Gest Oddliefson. Thorgils lived in Horddale at a place called Tongue. Thorgils was a man great and goodly of body, the greatest swaggerer, and was spoken of as one of no fairness in dealings with men. Between him and Snorri the Priest there was often little love lost, for Snorri found Thorgils both meddlesome and flaunting of demeanour. Thorgils would get up many errands on which to go west into the countryside, and always came to Holyfell offering Gudrun to look after her affairs, but she only took the matter quietly and made but little of it all. Thorgils asked for her son Thorleik to go home with him, and he stayed for the most part at Tongue and learnt law from Thorgils, for he was a man most skilled in law-craft. At that time Thorkell Eyjolfson was busy in trading journeys; he was a most renowned man, and of high birth, and withal a great friend of Snorri the Priest. He would always be staying with Thorstein Kuggison, his kinsman, when he was out here (in Iceland). Now, one time when Thorkell had a ship standing up in Vadil, on Bardistrand, it befell, in Burgfirth, that the son of Eid of Ridge was killed by the sons of Helga from Kropp. Grim was the name of the man who had done the manslaughter, and that of his brother was Nial, who was drowned in White-river; a little later on Grim was outlawed to the woods because of the manslaughter, and he lay out in the mountains whilst he was under the award of outlawry. He was a great man and strong. Eid was then very old when this happened, so the case was not followed up. People blamed Thorkell very much that he did not see matters righted. The next spring when Thorkell had got his ship ready he went south across Broadfirth-country, and got a horse there and rode alone, not stopping in his journey till he got as far as Ridge, to Eid, his kinsman. Eid took him in joyfully. Thorkell told him his errand, how that he would go and find Grim his outlaw, and asked Eid if he knew at all where his lair was. Eid answered, "I am nowise eager for this; it seems to me you have much to risk as to how the journey may speed, seeing that you will have to deal with a man of Hel's strength, such as Grim. But if you will go, then start with many men, so that you may have it all your own way." "That to me is no prowess," said Thorkell, "to draw together a great company against one man. But what I wish is, that you would lend me the sword Skofnung, for then I ween I shall be able to overcome a mere runagate, be he never so mighty a man of his hands." "You must have your way in this," said Eid, "but it will not come to me unawares, if, some day, you should come to rue this wilfulness. But inasmuch as you will have it that you are doing this for my sake, what you ask for shall not be withheld, for I think Skofnung well bestowed if you bear it. But the nature of the sword is such that the sun must not shine upon its hilt, nor must it be drawn if a woman should be near. If a man be wounded by the sword the hurt may not be healed, unless the healing-stone that goes with the sword be rubbed thereon." Thorkell said he would pay careful heed to this, and takes over the sword, asking Eid to point out to him the way to where Grim might have his lair. Eid said he was most minded to think that Grim had his lair north on Twodays-Heath by the Fishwaters. Then Thorkell rode northward upon the heath the way which Eid did point out to him, and when he had got a long way onward over the heath he saw near some great water a hut, and makes his way for it.

Chapter 58
Thorkell and Grim, and their Voyage Abroad

Thorkell now comes to the hut, he sees where a man is sitting by the water at the mouth of a brook, where he was line-fishing, and had a cloak over his head. Thorkell leapt off his horse and tied it up under the wall of the hut. Then he walks down to the water to where the man was sitting. Grim saw the shadow of a man cast on the water, and springs up at once. By then Thorkell had got very nearly close up to him, and strikes at him. The blow caught him on his arm just above the wolf-joint (the wrist), but that was not a great wound. Grim sprang forthwith upon Thorkell, and they seized each other wrestling-wise, and speedily the odds of strength told, and Thorkell fell and Grim on the top of him. Then Grim asked who this man might be. Thorkell said that did not at all matter to him. Grim said, "Now things have befallen otherwise than you must have thought they would, for now your life will be in my power." Thorkell said he would not pray for peace for himself, "for lucklessly I have taken this in hand." Grim said he had had enough mishaps for him to give this one the slip, "for to you some other fate is ordained than that of dying at this our meeting, and I shall give you your life, while you repay me in whatever kind you please." Now they both stand up and walk home to the hut. Thorkell sees that Grim was growing faint from loss of blood, so he took Skofnung's-stone and rubbed it on, and ties it to the arm of Grim, and it took forthwith all smarting pain and swelling out of the wound. They stayed there that night. In the morning Thorkell got ready to go away, and asked if Grim would go with him. He said that sure enough that was his will. Thorkell turns straightway westward without going to meet Eid, nor halted he till he came to Sælingsdale Tongue. Snorri the Priest welcomes him with great blitheness. Thorkell told him that his journey had sped lucklessly. Snorri said it had turned out well, "for Grim looks to me a man endowed with good luck, and my will is that you make matters up with him handsomely. But now, my friend, I would like to counsel you to leave off trade-journeyings, and to settle down and marry, and become a chief as befits your high birth." Thorkell answered, "Often your counsels have stood me in good stead," and he asked if Snorri had bethought him of the woman he should woo. Snorri answers, "You must woo the woman who is the best match for you, and that woman is Gudrun, Osvif's daughter." Thorkell said it was true that a marriage with her would be an honourable one. "But," says he, "I think her fierce heart and reckless-mindedness weigh heavily, for she will want to have her husband, Bolli, avenged. Besides, it is said that on this matter there is some understanding between her and Thorgils Hallason, and it may be that this will not be altogether to his liking. Otherwise, Gudrun pleases me well." Snorri said, "I will undertake to see that no harm shall come to you from Thorgils; but as to the revenge for Bolli, I am rather in hopes that concerning that matter some change will have befallen before these seasons (this year) are out." Thorkell answered, "It may be that these be no empty words you are speaking now. But as to the revenge of Bolli, that does not seem to me more likely to happen now than it did a while ago, unless into that strife some of the greater men may be drawn." Snorri said, "I should be well pleased to see you go abroad once more this summer, to let us see then what happens." Thorkell said so it should be, and they parted, leaving matters where they now stood. Thorkell went west over Broadfirth-country to his ship. He took Grim with him abroad. They had a good summer-voyage, and came to the south of Norway. Then Thorkell said to Grim, "You know how the case stands, and what things happened to bring about our acquaintance, so I need say nothing about that matter; but I would fain that it should turn out better than at one time it seemed likely it would. I have found you a valiant man, and for that reason I will so part from you, as if I had never borne you any grudge. I will give you as much merchandise as you need in order to be able to join the guild of good merchants. But do not settle down here in the north of this land, for many of Eid's kinsmen are about on trading journeys who bear you heavy ill-will." Grim thanked him for these words, and said he could never have thought of asking for as much as he offered. At parting Thorkell gave to Grim a goodly deal of merchandise, and many men said that this deed bore the stamp of a great man. After that Grim went east in the Wick, settled there, and was looked upon as a mighty man of his ways; and therewith comes to an end what there is to be told about Grim. Thorkell was in Norway through the winter, and was thought a man of much account; he was exceeding wealthy in chattels. Now this matter must be left for a while, and the story must be taken up out in Iceland, so let us hear what matters befell there for tidings to be told of whilst Thorkell was abroad.

Chapter 59
Gudrun demands Revenge for Bolli, A.D. 1019

In "Twinmonth" that summer Gudrun, Osvif's daughter, went from home up into the Dales. She rode to Thickshaw; and at this time Thorleik was sometimes at Thickshaw with the sons of Armod Halldor and Ornolf, and sometimes Tongue with Thorgils. The same night Gudrun sent a man to Snorri Godi saying that she wished to meet him without fail the next day. Snorri got ready at once and rode with one other man until he came to Hawkdale-river; on the northern side of that river stands a crag by the river called Head, within the land of Lea-Shaw. At this spot Gudrun had bespoken that she and Snorri should meet. They both came there at one and the same time. With Gudrun there was only one man, and he was Bolli, son of Bolli; he was now twelve years old, but fulfilled of strength and wits was he, so much so, that many were they who were no whit more powerful at the time of ripe manhood; and now he carried Footbiter. Snorri and Gudrun now fell to talking together; but Bolli and Snorri's follower sat on the crag and watched people travelling up and down the countryside. When Snorri and Gudrun had asked each other for news, Snorri inquired on what errand he was called, and what had come to pass lately that she sent him word so hurriedly. Gudrun said, "Truth to tell, to me is ever fresh the event which I am about to bring up, and yet it befell twelve years ago; for it is about the revenge of Bolli I wish to speak, and it ought not to take you unawares. I have called it to your mind from time to time. I must also bring this home to you that to this end you have promised me some help if I but waited patiently, but now I think it past hope that you will give any heed to our case. I have now waited as long as my temper would hold out, and I must have whole-hearted counsel from you as to where this revenge is to be brought home." Snorri asked what she chiefly had in her mind's eye. Gudrun said, "It is my wish that all Olaf's sons should not go scatheless." Snorri said he must forbid any onset on the men who were not only of the greatest account in the countryside, but also closely akin to those who stand nearest to back up the revenge; and it is high time already that these family feuds come to an end. Gudrun said, "Then Lambi shall be set upon and slain; for then he, who is the most eager of them for evil, would be put out of the way." Snorri said, "Lambi is guilty enough that he should be slain; but I do not think Bolli any the more revenged for that; for when at length peace should come to be settled, no such disparity between them would be acknowledged as ought to be due to Bolli when the manslaughters of both should come up for award." Gudrun spoke, "It may be that we shall not get our right out of the men of Salmon-river-Dale, but some one shall pay dear for it, whatever dale he may dwell in. So we shall turn upon Thorstein the Black, for no one has taken a worse share in these matters than he." Snorri spake, "Thorstein's guilt against you is the same as that of the other men who joined in the raid against Bolli, but did not wound him. But you leave such men to sit by in quiet on whom it seems to me revenge wrought would be revenge indeed, and who, moreover, did take the life of Bolli, such as was Helgi Hardbienson." Gudrun said, "That is true, but I cannot be sure that, in that case, all these men against whom I have been stirring up enmity will sit quietly by doing nothing." Snorri said, "I see a good way to hinder that. Lambi and Thorstein shall join the train of your sons, and that is a fitting ransom for those fellows, Lambi and Thorstein; but if they will not do this, then I shall not plead for them to be let off, whatever penalty you may be pleased to put upon them." Gudrun spake: "How shall we set about getting these men that you have named to go on this journey?" Snorri spake: "That is the business of them who are to be at the head of the journey." Gudrun spake: "In this we must have your foresight as to who shall rule the journey and be the leader." Then Snorri smiled and said, "You have chosen your own men for it." Gudrun replied, "You are speaking of Thorgils." Snorri said so it was. Gudrun spake: I have talked the matter over already with Thorgils, but now it is as good as all over, for he gave me the one choice, which I would not even look at. He did not back out of undertaking to avenge Bolli, if he could have me in marriage in return; but that is past all hope, so I cannot ask him to go this journey." Snorri spoke: "On this I will give you a counsel, for I do not begrudge Thorgils this journey. You shall promise marriage to him, yet you shall do it in language of this double meaning, that of men in this land you will marry none other but Thorgils, and that shall be holden to, for Thorkell Eyjolfson is not, for the time being, in this land, but it is he whom I have in my mind's eye for this marriage." Gudrun spake: "He will see through this trick." Snorri answered, "Indeed he will not see through it, for Thorgils is better known for foolhardiness than wits. Make the covenant with but few men for witnesses, and let Halldor, his foster-brother, be there, but not Ornolf, for he has more wits, and lay the blame on me if this will not work out." After that they parted their talk and each bade the other farewell, Snorri riding home, and Gudrun unto Thickshaw. The next morning Gudrun rode from Thickshaw and her sons with her, and when they ride west along Shawstrand they see that men are riding after them. They ride on quickly and catch them up swiftly, and lo, there was Thorgils Hallason. They greeted each other well, and now ride on in the day all together, out to Holyfell.

Chapter 60
The Egging of Gudrun

A few nights after Gudrun had come home she called her sons to her to have a talk with them in her orchard; and when they were come there they saw how there were lying out some linen clothes, a shirt and linen breeches, and they were much stained with blood. Then spake Gudrun: "These same clothes you see here cry to you for your father's revenge. I will not say many words on this matter, for it is past hope that you will heed an egging-on by words alone if you bring not home to your minds such hints and reminders as these." The brothers were much startled as this, and at what Gudrun had to say; but yet this way they made answer that they had been too young to seek for revenge without a leader; they knew not, they felt, how to frame a counsel for themselves or others either. "But we might well bear in mind what we have lost." Gudrun said, "They would be likely to give more thought to horse-fights or sports." After that they went away. The next night the brothers could not sleep. Thorgils got aware of this, and asked them what was the matter. They told him all the talk they had had with their mother, and this withal that they could no longer bear their grief or their mother's taunts. "We will seek revenge," said Bolli, "now that we brothers have come to so ripe an age that men will be much after us if we do not take the matter in hand." The next day Gudrun and Thorgils had a talk together, and Gudrun started speaking in this wise: "I am given to think, Thorgils, that my sons brook it ill to sit thus quietly on any longer without seeking revenge for their father's death. But what mostly has delayed the matter hitherto is that up to now I deemed Thorleik and Bolli too young to be busy in taking men's lives. But need enough there has been to call this to mind a good long time before this." Thorgils answered, "There is no use in your talking this matter over with me, because you have given a flat denial to 'walking with me' (marrying me). But I am in just the same frame of mind as I have been before, when we have had talks about this matter. If I can marry you, I shall not think twice about killing either or both of the two who had most to do with the murder of Bolli." Gudrun spoke: "I am given to think that to Thorleik no man seems as well fitted as you to be the leader if anything is to be done in the way of deeds of hardihood. Nor is it a matter to be hidden from you that the lads are minded to go for Helgi Hardbienson the 'Bareserk,' who sits at home in his house in Skorridale misdoubting himself of nothing."

Thorgils spake: "I never care whether he is called Helgi or by any other name, for neither in Helgi nor in any one else do I deem I have an over-match in strength to deal with. As far as I am concerned, the last word on this matter is now spoken if you promise before witnesses to marry me when, together with your sons, I have wreaked the revenge." Gudrun said she would fulfil all she should agree to, even though such agreement were come to before few men to witness it. "And," said she, "this then we shall settle to have done." Gudrun bade be called thither Halldor, Thorgils' foster-brother, and her own sons. Thorgils bade that Ornolf should also be with them. Gudrun said there was no need of that, "For I am more doubtful of Ornolf's faithfulness to you than I think you are yourself." Thorgils told her to do as she liked. Now the brothers come and meet Gudrun and Thorgils, Halldor being also at the parley with them. Gudrun now sets forth to them that "Thorgils has said he will be the leader in this raid against Helgi Hardbienson, together with my sons, for revenge of Bolli, and Thorgils has bargained in return for this undertaking to get me for wife. Now I avow, with you to witness, that I promise this to Thorgils, that of men in this land I shall marry none but him, and I do not purpose to go and marry in any other land." Thorgils thought that this was binding enough, and did not see through it. And now they broke up their talk. This counsel is now fully settled that Thorgils must betake himself to this journey. He gets ready to leave Holyfell, and with him the sons of Gudrun, and they rode up into the Dales and first to the homestead at Tongue.

Chapter 61
Of Thorstein the Black and Lambi

The next Lord's day a leet was held, and Thorgils rode thither with his company, Snorri Godi was not at the leet, but there was a great many people together. During the day Thorgils fetched up Thorstein the Black for a talk with him, and said, "As you know, you were one in the onset by the sons of Olaf when Bolli was slain, and you have made no atonement for your guilt to his sons. Now although a long time is gone since those things befell, I think their mind has not given the slip to the men who were in that raid. Now, these brothers look in this light upon the matter, that it beseem them least, by reason of kinship, to seek revenge on the sons of Olaf; and so the brothers purpose to turn for revenge upon Helgi Hardbienson, for he gave Bolli his death-wound. So we ask this of you, Thorstein, that you join in this journey with the brothers, and thus purchase for yourself peace and good-will." Thorstein replied, "It beseems me not at all to deal in treason with Helgi, my brother-in-law, and I would far rather purchase my peace with as much money as it would be to their honour to take." Thorgils said, "I think it is but little to the mind of the brothers to do aught herein for their own gain; so you need not hide it away from yourself, Thorstein, that at your hands there lie two choices: either to betake yourself to this journey, or to undergo the harshest of treatments from them as soon as they may bring it about; and my will is, that you take this choice in spite of the ties that bind you to Helgi; for when men find themselves in such straits, each must look after himself." Thorstein spake: "Will the same choice be given to more of the men who are charged with guilt by the sons of Bolli?" Thorgils answered, "The same choice will be put to Lambi." Thorstein said he would think better of it if he was not left the only one in this plight. After that Thorgils called Lambi to come and meet him, and bade Thorstein listen to their talk. He said, "I wish to talk over with you, Lambi, the same matter that I have set forth to Thorstein; to wit, what amends you are willing to make to the sons of Bolli for the charges of guilt which they have against you? For it has been told me as true that you wrought wounds on Bolli; but besides that, you are heavily guilt-beset, in that you urged it hard that Bolli should be slain; yet, next to the sons of Olaf, you were entitled to some excuse in the matter." Then Lambi asked what he would be asked to do. Thorgils said the same choice would be put to him as to Thorstein, "to join with the brothers in this journey." Lambi said, "This I think an evil price of peace and a dastardly one, and I have no mind for this journey." Then said Thorstein, "It is not the only thing open to view, Lambi, to cut so quickly away from this journey; for in this matter great men are concerned, men of much worth, moreover, who deem that they have long had to put up with an unfair lot in life. It is also told me of Bolli's sons that they are likely to grow into men of high mettle, and that they are exceeding masterful; but the wrong they have to wreak is great. We cannot think of escaping from making some amends after such awful deeds. I shall be the most open to people's reproaches for this by reason of my alliance with Helgi. But I think most people are given to 'setting all aside for life,' and the trouble on hand that presses hardest must first be thrust out of the way." Lambi said, "It is easy to see what you urge to be done, Thorstein; and I think it well befitting that you have your own way in this matter, if you think that is the only way you see open, for ours has been a long partnership in great troubles. But I will have this understood if I do go into this business, that my kinsmen, the sons of Olaf, shall be left in peace if the revenge on Helgi shall be carried out." Thorgils agreed to this on behalf of the brothers. So now it was settled that Lambi and Thorstein should betake themselves to the journey with Thorgils; and they bespoke it between them that they should come early on the third day (Tuesday) to Tongue, in Hord-Dale. After that they parted. Thorgils rode home that evening to Tongue. Now passes on the time within which it was bespoken they should come to Tongue. In the morning of the third day (Tuesday), before sunrise, Thorstein and Lambi came to Tongue, and Thorgils gave them a cheerful welcome.

Chapter 62
Thorgils and his Followers leave Home

Thorgils got himself ready to leave home, and they all rode up along Hord-Dale, ten of them together. There Thorgils Hallason was the leader of the band. In that train the sons of Bolli, Thorleik and Bolli, and Thord the Cat, their brother, was the fourth, the fifth was Thorstein the Black, the sixth Lambi, the seventh and eighth Haldor and Ornolf, the ninth Svein, and the tenth Hunbogi. Those last were the sons of Alf o' Dales. They rode on their way up to Sweeping-Pass, and across Long-waterdale, and then right across Burgfirth. They rode across North-river at Isleford, but across White-river at Bankford, a short way down from the homestead of By. Then they rode over Reekdale, and over the neck of land to Skorradale, and so up through the wood in the neighbourhood of the farmstead of Water-Nook, where they got off their horses, as it was very late in the evening. The homestead of Water-Nook stands a short way from the lake on the south side of the river. Thorgils said to his followers that they must tarry there over night, "and I will go to the house and spy and see if Helgi be at home. I am told Helgi has at most times very few men with him, but that he is of all men the wariest of himself, and sleeps on a strongly made lock-bed." Thorgils' followers bade him follow his own foresight. Thorgils now changed his clothes, and took off his blue cloak, and slipped on a grey foul-weather overall. He went home to the house. When he was come near to the home-field fence he saw a man coming to meet him, and when they met Thorgils said, "You will think my questions strange, comrade, but whose am I come to in this countryside, and what is the name of this dwelling, and who lives here?" The man answered, "You must be indeed a wondrous fool and wit-bereft if you have not heard Helgi Hardbienson spoken of, the bravest of warriors, and a great man withal." Thorgils next asked how far Helgi took kindly to unknown people coming to see him, such as were in great need of help. He replied, "In that matter, if truth is told, only good can be said of Helgi, for he is the most large-hearted of men, not only in giving harbour to comers, but also in all his high conduct otherwise." "Is Helgi at home now?" asked Thorgils; "I should like to ask him to take me in." The other then asks what matters he had on his hands. Thorgils answered, "I was outlawed this summer at the Thing, and I want to seek for myself the help of some such man as is a mighty one of his hands and ways, and I will in return offer my fellowship and service. So now you take me home to the house to see Helgi." "I can do that very well, to show you home," he said, "for you will be welcome to quarters for the night, but you will not see Helgi, for he is not at home." Then Thorgils asked where he was. The man answered, "He is at his out-dairy called Sarp." Thorgils asked where that was, and what men were with him. He said his son Hardbien was there, and two other men, both outlaws, whom he had taken in to shelter. Thorgils bade him show the nearest way to the dairy, "for I want to meet Helgi at once, when I can get to him and plead my errand to him." The house-carle did so and showed him the way, and after that they parted. Thorgils returned to the wood to his companions, and told them what he had found out about Helgi. "We must tarry here through the night, and not go to the dairy till to-morrow morning." They did as he ordained, and in the morning Thorgils and his band rode up through the wood till they were within a short way from the dairy. Then Thorgils bade them get off their horses and eat their morning meal, and so they did, and kept them for a while.

Chapter 63
The Description of his Enemies brought to Helgi

Now we must tell what happened at the dairy where Helgi was, and with him the men that were named before. In the morning Helgi told his shepherd to go through the woods in the neighbourhood of the dairy and look out for people passing, and take heed of whatever else he saw, to tell news of, "for my dreams have gone heavily to-night." The lad went even as Helgi told him. He was away awhile, and when he came back Helgi asked what he had seen to tell tidings of. He answered, "I have seen what I think is stuff for tidings." Helgi asked what that was. He said he had seen men, "and none so few either, and I think they must have come from beyond this countryside." Helgi spoke: "Where were they when you saw them, and what were they doing, or did you take heed of the manner of raiment, or their looks?" He answered, "I was not so much taken aback at the sight as not to mind those matters, for I knew you would ask about them." He also said they were but short away from the dairy, and were eating their morning meal. Helgi asked if they sat in a ring or side by side in a line. He said they sat in a ring, on their saddles. Helgi said, "Tell me now of their looks, and I will see if I can guess from what they looked like who the men may be." The lad said, "There sat a man in a stained saddle, in a blue cloak. He was great of growth, and valiant-looking; he was bald in front and somewhat 'tooth-bare.'" Helgi said, "I know that man clearly from your tale. There you have seen Thorgils Hallason, from west out of Hord-Dale. I wonder what he wants with us, the hero." The lad spoke: "Next to him sat a man in a gilded saddle; he had on a scarlet kirtle, and a gold ring on his arm, and a gold-embroidered fillet was tied round his head. This man had yellow hair, waving down over his shoulders; he was fair of hue, with a knot on his nose, which was somewhat turned up at the tip, with very fine eyes–blue-eyed and swift-eyed, and with a glance somewhat restless, broad-browed and full-cheeked; he had his hair cut across his forehead. He was well grown as to breadth of shoulders and depth of chest. He had very beautiful hands, and strong-looking arms. All his bearing was courteous, and, in a word, I have never seen a man so altogether doughty-looking. He was a young-looking man too, for his lips had grown no beard, but it seemed to me he was aged by grief." Then Helgi answers: "You have paid a careful heed, indeed, to this man, and of much account he must needs be; yet this man, I think, I have never seen, so I must make a guess at it who he is. There, I think, must have been Bolli Bollison, for I am told he has in him the makings of a man." Then the lad went on: "Next there sat a man on an enamelled saddle in a yellow green kirtle; he had a great finger ring on his hand. This man was most goodly to behold, and must still be young of age; his hair was auburn and most comely, and in every way he was most courtly." Helgi answers, "I think I know who this man is, of whom you have now been telling. He must be Thorleik Bollison, and a sharp and mindful man you are."

The lad said again, "Next sat a young man; he was in a blue kirtle and black breeches, and his tunic tucked into them. This man was straight-faced, light of hair, with a goodly-featured face, slender and graceful." Helgi answered, "I know that man, for I must have seen him, though at a time when he was quite young; for it must be Thord Thordson, fosterling of Snorri the Priest. And a very courtly band they have, the Westfirthers. What is there yet to tell?" Then the lad said, "There sat a man on a Scotch saddle, hoary of beard and very sallow of hue, with black curly hair, somewhat unsightly and yet warrior like; he had on a grey pleated cape." Helgi said, "I clearly see who that man is; there is Lambi, the son of Thorbjorn, from Salmon-river-Dale; but I cannot think why he should be in the train of these brothers." The lad spake: "There sat a man on a pommelled saddle, and had on a blue cloak for an overall, with a silver ring on his arm; he was a farmer-looking sort of man and past the prime of life, with dark auburn long curly hair, and scars about his face." "Now the tale grows worse by much," said Helgi, "for there you must have seen Thorstein the Black, my brother-in-law; and a wondrous thing indeed I deem it, that he should be in this journey, nor would I ever offer him such a home-raid. But what more is there still to tell?" He answered, "Next there sat two men like each other to look upon, and might have been of middle age; most brisk they looked, red of hair, freckled of face, yet goodly to behold." Helgi said, "I can clearly understand who those men are. There are the sons of Armod, foster-brothers of Thorgils, Halldor and Ornolf. And a very trustworthy fellow you are. But have you now told the tale of all the men you saw?" He answered, "I have but little to add now. Next there sat a man and looked out of the circle; he was in a plate-corselet and had a steel cap on his head, with a brim a hand's breadth wide; he bore a shining axe on his shoulder, the edge of which must have measured an ell in length. This man was dark of hue, black-eyed, and most viking like." Helgi answered, "I clearly know this man from your tale. There has been Hunbogi the Strong, son of Alf o' Dales. But what I find so hard to make out is, what they want journeying with such a very picked company." The lad spoke again: "And still there sat a man next to this strong-looking one, dark auburn of hair, thick-faced and red-faced, heavy of brow, of a tall middle size." Helgi said, "You need not tell the tale further, there must have been Svein, son of Alf o' Dales, brother of Hunbogi. Now it would be as well not to stand shiftless in the face of these men; for near to my mind's foreboding it is, that they are minded to have a meeting with me or ever they leave this countryside; moreover, in this train there are men who would hold that it would have been but due and meet, though this our meeting should have taken a good long time before this. Now all the women who are in the dairy slip on quickly men's dress and take the horses that are about the dairy and ride as quickly as possible to the winter dwelling; it may be that those who are besetting us about will not know whether men or women be riding there; they need give us only a short respite till we bring men together here, and then it is not so certain on which side the outlook will be most hopeful." The women now rode off, four together. Thorgils misdoubts him lest news of their coming may have reached Helgi, and so bade the others take their horses and ride after them at their swiftest, and so they did, but before they mounted a man came riding up to them openly in all men's sight. He was small of growth and all on the alert, wondrously swift of glance and had a lively horse. This man greeted Thorgils in a familiar manner, and Thorgils asked him his name and family and also whence he had come. He said his name was Hrapp, and he was from Broadfirth on his mother's side. "And then I grew up, and I bear the name of Fight-Hrapp, with the name follows that I am nowise an easy one to deal with, albeit I am small of growth; but I am a southlander on my father's side, and have tarried in the south for some winters. Now this is a lucky chance, Thorgils, I have happened of you here, for I was minded to come and see you anyhow, even though I should find it a business somewhat hard to follow up. I have a trouble on hand; I have fallen out with my master, and have had from him a treatment none of the best; but it goes with the name, that I will stand no man such shameful mishandling, so I made an outset at him, but I guess I wounded him little or not at all, for I did not wait long enough to see for myself, but thought myself safe when I got on to the back of this nag, which I took from the goodman." Hrapp says much, but asks for few things; yet soon he got to know that they were minded to set on Helgi, and that pleased him very much, and he said they would not have to look for him behind.

Chapter 64
The Death of Helgi, A.D. 1019

Thorgils and his followers, as soon as they were on horseback, set off at a hard ride, and rode now out of the wood. They saw four men riding away from the dairy, and they rode very fast too. Seeing this, some of Thorgils' companions said they had better ride after them at their swiftest. Then said Thorleik Bollison, "We will just go to the dairy and see what men are there, for I think it less likely that these be Helgi and his followers. It seems to me that those are only women." A good many of them gainsaid this. Thorgils said that Thorleik should rule in the matter, for he knew that he was a very far-sighted man. They now turned to the dairy. Hrapp rode first, shaking the spear-stick he carried in his hand, and thrusting it forward in front of himself, and saying now was high time to try one's self. Helgi and his followers were not aware of anything till Thorgils and his company had surrounded the dairy. Helgi and his men shut the door, and seized their weapons. Hrapp leapt forthwith upon the roof of the dairy, and asked if old Reynard was in. Helgi answered, "You will come to take for granted that he who is here within is somewhat hurtful, and will know how to bite near the warren." And forthwith Helgi thrust his spear out through the window and through Hrapp, so that he fell dead to earth from the spear. Thorgils bade the others go heedfully and beware of mishaps, "for we have plenty of means wherewith to get the dairy into our power, and to overcome Helgi, placed as he is now, for I am given to think that here but few men are gathered together." The dairy was rigged over one roof-beam, resting on two gables so that the ends of the beam stuck out beyond each gable; there was a single turf thatch on the house, which had not yet grown together. Then Thorgils told some of his men to go to the beam ends, and pull them so hard that either the beam should break or else the rafters should slip in off it, but others were to guard the door lest those within should try and get out. Five they were, Helgi and his within the dairy–Hardbien, his son, to wit, he was twelve years old–his shepherd and two other men, who had come to him that summer, being outlaws–one called Thorgils, and the other Eyolf. Thorstein the Black and Svein, son of Alf o' Dales, stood before the door. The rest of the company were tearing the roof off the dairy. Hunbogi the Strong and the sons of Armod took one end of the beam, Thorgils, Lambi, and Gudrun's sons the other end. They now pull hard at the beam till it broke asunder in the middle; just at this Hardbien thrust a halberd out through where the door was broken, and the thrust struck the steel cap of Thorstein the Black and stuck in his forehead, and that was a very great wound. Then Thorstein said, as was true, that there were men before them. Next Helgi leapt so boldly out of the door so that those nearest shrunk aback. Thorgils was standing near, and struck after him with a sword, and caught him on the shoulder and made a great wound. Helgi turned to meet him, and had a wood-axe in his hand, and said, "Still the old one will dare to look at and face weapons," and therewith he flung the axe at Thorgils, and the axe struck his foot, and a great wound that was. And when Bolli saw this he leapt forward at Helgi with Footbiter in his hand, and thrust Helgi through with it, and that was his death-blow. Helgi's followers leapt out of the dairy forthwith, and Hardbien with them. Thorleik Bollison turned against Eyolf, who was a strong man. Thorleik struck him with his sword, and it caught him on the leg above the knee and cut off his leg, and he fell to earth dead. Hunbogi the Strong went to meet Thorgils, and dealt a blow at him with an axe, and it struck the back of him, and cut him asunder in the middle. Thord Cat was standing near where Hardbien leapt out, and was going to set upon him straightway, but Bolli rushed forward when he saw it, and bade no harm be done to Hardbien. "No man shall do a dastard's work here, and Hardbien shall have life and limbs spared." Helgi had another son named Skorri. He was brought up at Gugland in Reekdale the southernmost.

Chapter 65
Of Gudrun's Deceit

After these deeds Thorgils and his band rode away over the neck to Reekdale, where they declared these manslaughters on their hands. Then they rode the same way eastward as they had ridden from the west, and did not stop their journey till they came to Hord-Dale. They now told the tidings of what had happened in their journey, which became most famous, for it was thought a great deed to have felled such a hero as was Helgi. Thorgils thanked his men well for the journey, and the sons of Bolli did the same. And now the men part who had been in Thorgils' train; Lambi rode west to Salmon-river-Dale, and came first to Herdholt and told his kinsmen most carefully the tidings of what had happened in Skorradale. They were very ill-pleased with his journey and laid heavy reproaches upon him, saying he had shown himself much more of the stock of Thorbjorn "Skrjup" than of that of Myrkjartan, the Irish king. Lambi was very angry at their talk, and said they knew but little of good manners in overwhelming him with reproaches, "for I have dragged you out of death," says he. After that they exchanged but few words, for both sides were yet more fulfilled of ill-will than before. Lambi now rode home to his manor. Thorgils Hallason rode out to Holyfell, and with him the sons of Gudrun and his foster-brothers Halldor and Ornolf. They came late in the evening to Holyfell, when all men were in bed. Gudrun rose up and bade the household get up and wait upon them. She went into the guest-chamber and greeted Thorgils and all the others, and asked for tidings. Thorgils returned Gudrun's greeting; he had laid aside his cloak and his weapons as well, and sat then up against the pillars. Thorgils had on a red-brown kirtle, and had round his waist a broad silver belt. Gudrun sat down on the bench by him. Then Thorgils said this stave–

> "To Helgi's home a raid we led,
> Gave ravens corpse-repast to swallow,
> We dyed shield-wands with blood all red,
> As Thorleik's lead our band did follow.
> And at our hands there perished three
> Keen helmet-stems, accounted truly
> As worthies of the folk–and we
> Claim Bolli now's avenged full duly."

Gudrun asked them most carefully for the tidings of what had happened on their journey. Thorgils told her all she wished. Gudrun said the journey had been most stirringly carried out, and bade them have her thanks for it. After that food was set before them, and after they had eaten they were shown to bed, and slept the rest of the night. The next day Thorgils went to talk to Gudrun, and said, "Now the matter stands thus, as you know, Gudrun, that I have brought to an end the journey you bade me undertake, and I must claim that, in a full manly wise, that matter has been turned out of hand; you will also call to mind what you promised me in return, and I think I am now entitled to that prize." Then Gudrun said, "It is not such a long time since we last talked together that I should have forgotten what we said, and my only aim is to hold to all I agreed to as concerning you. Or what does your mind tell you as to how matters were bespoken between us?" Thorgils said she must remember that, and Gudrun answered, "I think I said that of men within this land I would marry none but you; or have you aught to say against that?" Thorgils said she was right. "That is well then," said Gudrun, "that our memory should be one and the same on this matter. And I will not put it off from you any longer, that

I am minded to think that it is not fated to me to be your wife. Yet I deem that I fulfil to you all uttered words, though I marry Thorkell Eyjolfson, who at present is not in this land." Then Thorgils said, and flushed up very much, "Clearly I do see from whence that chill wave comes running, and from thence cold counsels have always come to me. I know that this is the counsel of Snorri the Priest." Thorgils sprang up from this talk and was very angry, and went to his followers and said he would ride away. Thorleik disliked very much that things should have taken such a turn as to go against Thorgils' will; but Bolli was at one with his mother's will herein. Gudrun said she would give Thorgils some good gifts and soften him by that means, but Thorleik said that would be of no use, "for Thorgils is far too high-mettled a man to stoop to trifles in a matter of this sort." Gudrun said in that case he must console himself as best he could at home. After this Thorgils rode from Holyfell with his foster-brothers. He got home to Tongue to his manor mightily ill at ease over his lot.

Chapter 66

Osvif and Gest die

That winter Osvif fell ill and died, and a great loss that was deemed, for he had been the greatest of sages. Osvif was buried at Holyfell, for Gudrun had had a church built there. That same winter Gest Oddliefson fell ill, and as the sickness grew heavy on him, he called to him Thord the Low, his son, and said, "My mind forebodes me that this sickness will put an end to our living together. I wish my body to be carried to Holyfell, for that will be the greatest place about these countrysides, for I have often seen a light burning there." Thereupon Gest died. The winter had been very cold, and there was much ice about, and Broadfirth was laid under ice so far out that no ship could get over it from Bardistrand. Gest's body lay in state two nights at Hegi, and that very night there sprang up such a gale that all the ice was drawn away from the land, and the next day the weather was fair and still. Then Thord took a ship and put Gest's body on board, and went south across Broadfirth that day, and came in the evening to Holyfell. Thord had a good welcome there, and stayed there through the night. In the morning Gest's body was buried, and he and Osvif rested in one grave. So Gest's soothsaying was fulfilled, in that now it was shorter between them than at the time when one dwelt at Bardistrand and the other in Sælingsdale. Thord the Low then went home as soon as he was ready. That next night a wild storm arose, and drove the ice on to the land again, where it held on long through the winter, so that there was no going about in boats. Men thought this most marvellous, that the weather had allowed Gest's body to be taken across when there was no crossing before nor afterwards during the winter.

Chapter 67
The Death of Thorgils Hallason, A.D. 1020

Thorarin was the name of a man who lived at Longdale: he was a chieftain, but not a mighty one. His son was named Audgisl, and was a nimble sort of a man. Thorgils Hallason took the chieftainship from them both, father and son. Audgisl went to see Snorri Godi, and told him of this unfairness, and asked him to help. Snorri answered only by fair words, and belittled the whole affair; but answered, "Now that Halla's-grig is getting too forward and swaggering. Will Thorgils then happen on no man that will not give in to him in everything? No doubt he is a big man and doughty, but men as good as he is have also been sent to Hel." And when Audgisl went away Snorri gave him an inlaid axe. The next spring Thorgils Hallason and Thorstein the Black went south to Burgfirth, and offered atonement to the sons of Helgi and his other kinsmen, and they came to terms of peace on the matter, and fair honour was done (to Helgi's side). Thorstein paid two parts of the atonement for the manslaughter, and the third part Thorgils was to pay, payment being due at the Thing. In the summer Thorgils rode to the Thing, but when he and his men came to the lava field by Thingvellir, they saw a woman coming to meet them, and a mighty big one she was. Thorgils rode up to her, but she turned aside, and said this—

> "Take care
> If you go forward,
> And be wary
> Of Snorri's wiles,
> No one can escape,
> For so wise is Snorri."

And after that she went her way. Then Thorgils said, "It has seldom happened so before, when luck was with me, that you were leaving the Thing when I was riding to it." He now rode to the Thing and to his own booth. And through the early part the Thing was quiet. It happened one day during the Thing that folk's clothes were hung out to dry. Thorgils had a blue hooded cloak, which was spread out on the booth wall, and men heard the cloak say thus—

> "Hanging wet on the wall,
> A hooded cloak knows a braid (trick);
> I do not say he does not know two,
> He has been lately washed."

This was thought a most marvellous thing. The next day Thorgils went west over the river to pay the money to the sons of Helgi. He sat down on the lava above the booths, and with him was his foster-brother Halldor and sundry more of them were there together. The sons of Helgi came to the meeting.

Thorgils now began to count out the money. Audgisl Thorarinson came near, and when Thorgils had counted ten Audgisl struck at him, and all thought they heard the head say eleven as it flew off the neck. Audgisl ran to the booth of the Waterfirthers and Halldor rushed after him and struck him his death-blow in the door of the booth. These tidings came to the booth of Snorri Godi how Thorgils was slain. Snorri said, "You must be mistaken; it must be that Thorgils Hallason has slain some one." The man replied, "Why, the head flew off his trunk." "Then perhaps it is time," said Snorri. This manslaughter was peacefully atoned, as is told in the Saga of Thorgils Hallason.

Chapter 68
Gudrun's Marriage with Thorkell Eyjolfson

The same summer that Thorgils Hallason was killed a ship came to Bjorn's-haven. It belonged to Thorkell Eyjolfson. He was by then such a rich man that he had two merchant ships on voyages. The other ship came to Ramfirth to Board-Eyr; they were both laden with timber. When Snorri heard of the coming of Thorkell he rode at once to where the ship was. Thorkell gave him a most blithe welcome; he had a great deal of drink with him in his ship, and right unstintedly it was served, and many things they found to talk about. Snorri asked tidings of Norway, and Thorkell told him everything well and truthfully. Snorri told in return the tidings of all that had happened here while Thorkell had been away. "Now it seems to me," said Snorri, "you had better follow the counsel I set forth to you before you went abroad, and should give up voyaging about and settle down in quiet, and get for yourself the same woman to wife of whom we spoke then." Thorkell replied, "I understand what you are driving at; everything we bespoke then is still uppermost in my mind, for indeed I begrudge me not the noblest of matches could it but be brought about." Snorri spake, "I am most willing and ready to back that matter up on your behalf, seeing that now we are rid of both the things that seemed to you the most troublesome to overcome, if you were to get Gudrun for wife at all, in that Bolli is revenged and Thorgils is out of the way." Thorkell said, "Your counsels go very deep, Snorri, and into this affair I go heart and soul." Snorri stayed in the ship several nights, and then they took a ten-oared boat that floated alongside of the merchant ship and got ready with five-and-twenty men, and went to Holyfell. Gudrun gave an exceeding affectionate welcome to Snorri, and a most goodly cheer they had; and when they had been there one night Snorri called Gudrun to talk to him, and spake, "Matters have come to this, that I have undertaken this journey for my friend Thorkell, Eyjolf's son, and he has now come here, as you see, and his errand hither is to set forth the wooing of you. Thorkell is a man of noble degree. You know yourself all about his race and doings in life, nor is he short of wealth either. To my mind, he is now the one man west about here who is most likely to become a chieftain, if to that end he will put himself forward. Thorkell is held in great esteem when he is out there, but by much is he more honoured when he is in Norway in the train of titled men." Then answers Gudrun: "My sons Thorleik and Bolli must have most to say in this matter; but you, Snorri, are the third man on whom I shall most rely for counsels in matters by which I set a great store, for you have long been a wholesome guide to me." Snorri said he deemed it a clear case that Thorkell must not be turned off. Thereupon Snorri had the sons of Gudrun called in, and sets forth the matter to them, laying down how great an help Thorkell might afford them by reason of his wealth and wise foresight; and smoothly he framed his speech on this matter. Then Bolli answered: "My mother will know how most clearly to see through this matter, and herein I shall be of one mind with her own will. But, to be sure, we shall deem it wise to set much store by your pleading this matter, Snorri, for you have done to us mightily well in many things." Then Gudrun spake: "In this matter we will lean most on Snorri's foresight, for to us your counsels have been wholesome." Snorri urged the matter on by every word he spoke, and the counsel taken was, that Gudrun and Thorkell should be joined in marriage. Snorri offered to have the wedding at his house; and Thorkell, liking that well, said: "I am not short of means, and I am ready to furnish them in whatever measure you please." Then Gudrun spake: "It is my wish that the feast be held here at Holyfell. I do not blench at standing the cost of it, nor shall I call upon Thorkell or any one else to trouble themselves about this matter." "Often, indeed, you show, Gudrun," said Snorri, "that you are the most high-mettled of women." So this was now settled that the wedding should take place when it lacked six weeks of summer. At matters thus settled Snorri and Thorkell went away, Snorri going home and Thorkell to his ship, and he spent the summer, turn and turn about, at Tongue or at his ship. Time now wore on towards the wedding feast. Gudrun made great preparation with much ingatherings. Snorri came to the feast together with Thorkell, and they brought with them well-nigh sixty men, and a very picked company that was, for most of the men were in dyed raiments. Gudrun had well-nigh a hundred and twenty first-bidden guests. The brothers Bolli and Thorleik, with the first-bidden guests, went to meet Snorri and his train; and to him and his fellowship was given a right cheery welcome, and their horses are taken in hand, as well as their clothes. They were shown into the guest-chamber, and Thorkell and Snorri and their followers took seats on the bench that was the upper one, and Gudrun's guests sat on the lower.

Chapter 69
The Quarrel about Gunnar at the Feast

That autumn Gunnar, the slayer of Thridrandi, had been sent to Gudrun for "trust and keep," and she had taken him in, his name being kept secret. Gunnar was outlawed because of the slaying of Thridrandi, Geitir's son, as is told in the Niard-wickers' Saga. He went about much "with a hidden head," for that many great men had their eyes upon him. The first evening of the feast, when men went to wash, a big man was standing by the water; he was broad of shoulder and wide of chest, and this man had a hat on his head. Thorkell asked who he was. He named himself as it seemed best to him. Thorkell says: "I think you are not speaking the truth; going by what the tale tells you would seem more like to Gunnar, the slayer of Thridrandi. And if you are so great a hero as other men say, you will not keep hidden your name." Then said Gunnar: "You speak most eagerly on this matter; and, truth to tell, I think I have no need to hide myself from you. You have rightly named your man; but then, what have you chiefly bethought yourself of having done to me?" Thorkell said he would like that he should soon know it, and spake to his men, ordering them to lay hands on him. Gudrun sat on the dais at the upper end of the hall, together with other women all becoifed with white linen, and when she got aware of this she rises up from the bridal bench and calls on her men to lend Gunnar help, and told them to give quarter to no man who should show any doubtful behaviour. Gudrun had the greatest number of followers, and what never was meant to happen seemed like to befall. Snorri Godi went between both sides and bade them allay this storm. "The one thing clearly to be done by you, Thorkell, is not to push things on so hotly; and now you can see what a stirring woman Gudrun is, as she overrules both of us together." Thorkell said he had promised his namesake, Thorleik Geitir's son, that he would kill Gunnar if he came into the countrysides of the west. "And he is my greatest friend," Snorri spake. "You are much more in duty bound to act as we wish; and for yourself, it is a matter of the greatest importance, for you will never find such another woman as Gudrun, however far you may seek." And because of Snorri's reasoning, and seeing that he spoke the truth, Thorkell quieted down, and Gunnar was sent away that evening. The feast now went forward well and bravely, and when it was over the guests got ready to go away. Thorkell gave to Snorri very rich gifts, and the same to all the chief men. Snorri asked Bolli Bollison to go home with him, and to live with him as long as he liked. Bolli accepted this with thanks, and rides home to Tongue. Thorkell now settled down at Holyfell, and took in hand the affairs of the household, and it was soon seen that he was no worse a hand at that than at trade-voyaging. He had the hall pulled down in the autumn and a new one built, which was finished when the winter set in, and was both large and lofty. Between Gudrun and Thorkell dear love now grew up, and so the winter passed on. In the spring Gudrun asked how Thorkell was minded to look out for Gunnar the slayer of Thridrandi. He said that Gudrun had better take the management of that matter, "for you have taken it so hard in hand, that you will put up with nothing but that he be sent away with honour." Gudrun said he guessed aright: "I wish you to give him a ship, and therewithal such things as he cannot do without." Thorkell said and smiled, "You think nothing small on most matters, Gudrun, and would be ill served if you had a mean-minded man for a husband; nor has that ever been your heart's aim. Well, this shall be done after your own will"–and carried out it was. Gunnar took the gifts most gratefully. "I shall never be so 'long-armed' as to be able to repay all this great honour you are doing to me," he said. Gunnar now went abroad and came to Norway, and then went to his own estates. Gunnar was exceeding wealthy, most great-hearted, and a good and true man withal.

Chapter 70
Thorleik goes to Norway

Thorkell Eyjolfson became a great chieftain; he laid himself out much for friendships and honours. He was a masterful man within his own countryside, and busied himself much about law-suits; yet of his pleadings at court there is no tale to tell here. Thorkell was the richest man in Broadfirth during his lifetime next after Snorri. Thorkell kept his house in good order. He had all the houses at Holyfell rebuilt large and strong. He also had the ground of a church marked out, and gave it out that he had made up his mind to go abroad and fetch timber for the building of his church. Thorkell and Gudrun had a son who was called Gellir; he looked early most likely to turn out well. Bolli Bollison spent his time turn and turn about at Tongue or Holyfell, and Snorri was very fond of him. Thorleik his brother lived at Holyfell. These brothers were both tall and most doughty looking, Bolli being the foremost in all things. Thorkell was kind to his stepsons, and Gudrun loved Bolli most of all her children. He was now sixteen, and Thorleik twenty years old. So, once on a time, Thorleik came to talk to his stepfather and his mother, and said he wished to go abroad. "I am quite tired of sitting at home like a woman, and I wish that means to travel should be furnished to me." Thorkell said, "I do not think I have done against you two brothers in anything since our alliance began. Now, I think it is the most natural thing that you should yearn to get to know the customs of other men, for I know you will be counted a brisk man wheresoever you may come among doughty men." Thorleik said he did not want much money, "for it is uncertain how I may look after matters, being young and in many ways of an unsettled mind." Thorkell bade him have as much as he wanted. After that Thorkell bought for Thorleik a share in a ship that stood up in Daymeal-Ness, and saw him off to his ship, and fitted him well out with all things from home. Thorleik journeyed abroad that summer. The ship arrived in Norway. The lord over the land then was King Olaf the Holy. Thorleik went forthwith to see King Olaf, who gave him a good welcome; he knew Thorleik from his kindred, and so asked him to stay with him. Thorleik accepted with thanks, and stayed with the king that winter and became one of his guard, and the king held him in honour. Thorleik was thought the briskest of men, and he stayed on with King Olaf for several months. Now we must tell of Bolli Bollison. The spring when he was eighteen years old he spoke to his stepfather and his mother, and said that he wished they would hand him out his father's portion. Gudrun asked him what he had set his mind on doing, since he asked them to give him this money. Bolli answered, "It is my wish that a woman be wooed on my behalf, and I wish," said Bolli, "that you, Thorkell, be my spokesman and carry this through." Thorkell asked what woman it was Bolli wished to woo. Bolli answered, "The woman's name is Thordis, and she is the daughter of Snorri the Priest; she is the woman I have most at heart to marry; I shall be in no hurry to marry if I do not get this one for wife. And I set a very great store by this matter being carried out." Thorkell answered, "My help is quite welcome to you, my son, if you think that if I follow up this matter much weight lies thereon. I think the matter will be easily got over with Snorri, for he will know well enough how to see that a fair offer is made him by such as you." Gudrun said, "I will say at once, Thorkell, that I will let spare nothing so that Bolli may but have the match that pleases him, and that for two reasons, first, that I love him most, and then he has been the most whole-hearted of my children in doing my will." Thorkell gave it out that he was minded to furnish Bolli off handsomely. "It is what for many reasons is due to him, and I know, withal, that in Bolli a good husband will be purchased." A little while after Thorkell and Bolli went with a good many followers to Tongue. Snorri gave to them a kind and blithe welcome, and they were treated to the very best of cheers at Snorri's hands. Thordis, the daughter of Snorri, was at home with her father; she was a woman both goodly and of great parts. When they had been a few nights at Tongue Thorkell broached the wooing, bespeaking on behalf of Bolli an alliance with Snorri by marriage with Thordis, his daughter. Snorri answers, "It is well you come here on this errand; it is what I might have looked for from you. I will answer the matter well, for I think Bolli one of the most hopeful of men, and that woman I deem well given in marriage who is given in marriage to him. It will, however, tell most in this matter, how far this is to Thordis' own mind; for she shall marry such a man only on whom she sets her heart." This matter coming before Thordis she answered suchwise as that therein she would lean on the foresight of her father, saying she would sooner marry Bolli, a man from within her own countryside, than a stranger from farther away. And when Snorri found that it was not against her wish to go with Bolli, the affair was settled and the betrothal took place. Snorri was to have the feast at his house about the middle of summer. With that Thorkell and Bolli rode home to Holyfell, and Bolli now stayed at home till the time of the wedding-feast. Then Thorkell and Bolli array themselves to leave home, and with them all the men who were set apart therefor, and a crowded company and the bravest band that was. They then rode on their way and came to Tongue, and had a right hearty welcome there. There were great numbers there, and the feast was of the noblest, and when the feast comes to an end the guests get ready to depart. Snorri gave honourable gifts to Thorkell, yea and to both of them, him and Gudrun, and the same to his other friends and relations. And now each one of those who had gone to the feast rode to his own home. Bolli abode at Tongue, and between him and Thordis dear love sprang speedily up. Snorri did all he could to entertain Bolli well, and to him he was even kinder than to his own children. Bolli received all this gratefully, and remained at Tongue that year in great favour. The next summer a ship came to White-river. One-half of the ship belonged to Thorleik Bollison and the other half of it belonged to some Norwegian man. When Bolli heard of the coming of his brother he rode south to Burgfirth and to the ship. The brothers greeted each other joyfully. Bolli stayed there for several nights, and then both brothers ride together west to Holyfell; Thorkell takes them in with the greatest blitheness, as did also Gudrun, and they invited Thorleik to stay with them for the winter, and that he took with thanks. Thorleik tarried at Holyfell awhile, and then he rode to White-river and lets his ship be beached and his goods be brought to the West. Thorleik had had good luck with him both as to wealth and honours, for that he had become the henchman of that noblest of lords, King Olaf. He now stayed at Holyfell through the winter, while Bolli tarried at Tongue.

Chapter 71
The Peace between the Sons of Bolli and the Sons of Olaf, A.D. 1026

That winter the brothers would always be meeting, having talks together, and took no pleasure in games or any other pastime; and one time, when Thorleik was at Tongue, the brothers talked day and night together. Snorri then thought he knew that they must be taking counsel together on some very great matter, so he went and joined the talk of the brothers. They greeted him well, but dropped their talk forthwith. He took their greeting well; and presently Snorri spoke: "What are you taking counsels about so that ye heed neither sleep nor meat?" Bolli answers: "This is no framing of counsels, for that talk is one of but little mark which we talk together." Now Snorri found that they wanted to hide from him all that was in their minds, yet misdoubted him, that they must be talking chiefly of things from which great troubles might arise, in case they should be carried out. He (Snorri) spoke to them: "This I misdoubt me now, that it be neither a vain thing nor a matter of jest you are talking about for such long hours together, and I hold you quite excused, even if such should be the case. Now, be so good as to tell it me and not to hide it away from me. We shall not, when gathered all together, be worse able to take counsel in this matter, for that I shall nowhere stand in the way of anything going forward whereby your honour grows the greater." Thorleik thought Snorri had taken up their case in a kindly manner, and told him in a few words their wishes, and how they had made up their minds to set on the sons of Olaf, and to put them to sore penalties; they said that now they lacked of nothing to bring the sons of Olaf to terms of equality, since Thorleik was a liegeman of King Olaf, and Bolli was the son-in-law of such a chief as Snorri was. Snorri answered in this way: "For the slaying of Bolli enough has come in return, in that the life of Helgi Hardbeinson was paid therefor; the troubles of men have been far too great already, and it is high time that now at last they be put a stop to." Bolli said, "What now, Snorri? are you less keen now to stand by us than you gave out but a little while ago? Thorleik would not have told you our mind as yet if he had first taken counsel with me thereon. And when you claim that

Helgi's life has come in revenge for Bolli, it is a matter well known to men that a money fine was paid for the slaying of Helgi, while my father is still unatoned for." When Snorri saw he could not reason them into a change of mind, he offered them to try to bring about a peaceful atonement between them and the sons of Olaf, rather than that any more manslaughters should befall; and the brothers agreed to this. Then Snorri rode with some men to Herdholt. Halldor gave him a good welcome, and asked him to stay there, but Snorri said he must ride back that night. "But I have an urgent errand with you." So they fell to talking together, and Snorri made known his errand, saying it had come to his knowledge that Thorleik and Bolli would put up with it no longer that their father should be unatoned at the hands of the sons of Olaf. "And now I would endeavour to bring about peace, and see if an end cannot be put to the evil luck that besets you kinsmen." Halldor did not flatly refuse to deal further with the case. "I know only too well that Thorgils Hallason and Bolli's sons were minded to fall on me and my brothers, until you turned elsewhere their vengeance, so that thence-forward it seemed to them best to slay Helgi Hardbeinson. In these matters you have taken a good part, whatever your counsels may have been like in regard to earlier dealings between us kinsmen." Snorri said, "I set a great store by my errand turning out well and that it might be brought about which I have most at heart, that a sound peace should be settled between you kinsmen; for I know the minds of the men who have to deal with you in this case so well, that they will keep faithfully to whatever terms of peace they agree to." Halldor said, "I will undertake this, if it be the wish of my brothers, to pay money for the slaying of Bolli, such as shall be awarded by the umpires chosen, but I bargain that there be no outlawing of anybody concerned, nor forfeiture of my chieftainship or estate; the same claim I make in respect of the estates my brothers are possessed of, and I make a point of their being left free owners thereof whatever be the close of this case, each side to choose their own umpire." Snorri answered, "This is offered well and frankly, and the brothers will take this choice if they are willing to set any store by my counsel." Thereupon Snorri rode home and told the brothers the outcome of his errand, and that he would keep altogether aloof from their case if they would not agree to this. Bolli bade him have his own way, "And I wish that you, Snorri, be umpire on our behalf." Then Snorri sent to Halldor to say that peaceful settlement was agreed to, and he bade them choose an umpire against himself. Halldor chose on his behalf Steinthor Thorlakson of Eyr. The peace meeting should be at Drangar on Shawstrand, when four weeks of summer were passed. Thorleik Bollison rode to Holyfell, and nothing to tell tidings of befell that winter, and when time wore unto the hour bespoken for the meeting, Snorri the Priest came there with the sons of Bolli, fifteen together in all; Steinthor and his came with the same number of men to the meeting. Snorri and Steinthor talked together and came to an agreement about these matters. After that they gave out the award, but it is not told how much money they awarded; this, however, is told, that the money was readily paid and the peace well holden to. At the Thorness Thing the fines were paid out; Halldor gave Bolli a good sword, and Steinthor Olafson gave Thorleik a shield, which was also a good gift. Then the Thing was broken up, and both sides were thought to have gained in esteem from these affairs.

Chapter 72
Bolli and Thorleik go abroad, A. D. 1029

After the peace between Bolli and Thorleik and the sons of Olaf had been settled and Thorleik had been one winter in Iceland, Bolli made it known that he was minded to go abroad. Snorri, dissuading him, said, "To us it seems there is a great risk to be run as to how you may speed; but if you wish to have in hand more than you have now, I will get you a manor and stock it for you; therewithal I shall hand over to you chieftainship over men and uphold you for honours in all things; and that, I know, will be easy, seeing that most men bear you good-will." Bolli said, "I have long had it in my mind to go for once into southern lands; for a man is deemed to grow benighted if he learns to know nothing farther afield than what is to be seen here in Iceland." And when Snorri saw that Bolli had set his mind on this, and that it would come to nought to try to stop him, he bade him take as much money as he liked for his journey. Bolli was all for having plenty of money, "for I will not," he said, "be beholden to any man either here or in any foreign land." Then Bolli rode south to Burgfirth to White-river and bought half of a ship from the owners, so that he and his brother became joint owners of the same ship. Bolli then rides west again to his home. He and Thordis had one daughter whose name was Herdis, and that maiden Gudrun asked to bring up. She was one year old when she went to Holyfell. Thordis also spent a great deal of her time there, for Gudrun was very fond of her.

Chapter 73
Bolli's Voyage

Now the brothers went both to their ship. Bolli took a great deal of money abroad with him. They now arrayed the ship, and when everything was ready they put out to sea. The winds did not speed them fast, and they were a long time out at sea, but got to Norway in the autumn, and made Thrandheim in the north. Olaf, the king, was in the east part of the land, in the Wick, where he had made ingatherings for a stay through the winter. And when the brothers heard that the king would not come north to Thrandheim that autumn, Thorleik said he would go east along the land to meet King Olaf. Bolli said, "I have little wish to drift about between market towns in autumn days; to me that is too much of worry and restraint. I will rather stay for the winter in this town. I am told the king will come north in the spring, and if he does not then I shall not set my face against our going to meet him." Bolli has his way in the matter, and they put up their ship and got their winter quarters. It was soon seen that

Bolli was a very pushing man, and would be the first among other men; and in that he had his way, for a bounteous man was he, and so got speedily to be highly thought of in Norway. Bolli kept a suite about him during the winter at Thrandheim, and it was easily seen, when he went to the guild meeting-places, that his men were both better arrayed as to raiment and weapons than other townspeople. He alone also paid for all his suite when they sat drinking in guild halls, and on a par with this were his openhandedness and lordly ways in other matters. Now the brothers stay in the town through the winter. That winter the king sat east in Sarpsborg, and news spread from the east that the king was not likely to come north. Early in the spring the brothers got their ship ready and went east along the land. The journey sped well for them, and they got east to Sarpsborg, and went forthwith to meet King Olaf. The king gave a good welcome to Thorleik, his henchman, and his followers. Then the king asked who was that man of stately gait in the train of Thorleik; and Thorleik answered, "He is my brother, and is named Bolli." "He looks, indeed, a man of high mettle," said the king. Thereupon the king asks the brothers to come and stay with him, and that offer they took with thanks, and spend the spring with the king. The king was as kind to Thorleik as he had been before, yet he held Bolli by much in greater esteem, for he deemed him even peerless among men. And as the spring went on, the brothers took counsel together about their journeys. And Thorleik asked Bolli if he was minded to go back to Iceland during the summer, "or will you stay on longer here in Norway?" Bolli answered, "I do not mean to do either. And sooth to say, when I left Iceland, my thought was settled on this, that people should not be asking for news of me from the house next door; and now I wish, brother, that you take over our ship." Thorleik took it much to heart that they should have to part. "But you, Bolli, will have your way in this as in other things." Their matter thus bespoken they laid before the king, and he answered thus: "Will you not tarry with us any longer, Bolli?" said the king. "I should have liked it best for you to stay with me for a while, for I shall grant you the same title that I granted to Thorleik, your brother." Then Bolli answered: "I should be only too glad to bind myself to be your henchman, but I must go first whither I am already bent, and have long been eager to go, but this choice I will gladly take if it be fated to me to come back." "You will have your way as to your journeyings, Bolli," says the king, "for you Icelanders are self-willed in most matters. But with this word I must close, that I think you, Bolli, the man of greatest mark that has ever come from Iceland in my days." And when Bolli had got the king's leave he made ready for his journey, and went on board a round ship that was bound south for Denmark. He also took a great deal of money with him, and sundry of his followers bore him company. He and King Olaf parted in great friendship, and the king gave Bolli some handsome gifts at parting. Thorleik remained behind with King Olaf, but Bolli went on his way till he came south to Denmark. That winter he tarried in Denmark, and had great honour there of mighty men; nor did he bear himself there in any way less lordly than while he was in Norway. When Bolli had been a winter in Denmark he started on his journey out into foreign countries, and did not halt in his journey till he came to Micklegarth (Constantinople). He was there only a short time before he got himself into the Varangian Guard, and, from what we have heard, no Northman had ever gone to take war-pay from the Garth king before Bolli, Bolli's son. He tarried in Micklegarth very many winters, and was thought to be the most valiant in all deeds that try a man, and always went next to those in the forefront. The Varangians accounted Bolli most highly of whilst he was with them in Micklegarth.

Chapter 74
Thorkell Eyjolfson goes to Norway

Now the tale is to be taken up again where Thorkell Eyjolfson sits at home in lordly way. His and Gudrun's son, Gellir, grew up there at home, and was early both a manly fellow and winning. It is said how once upon a time Thorkell told Gudrun a dream he had had. "I dreamed," he said, "that I had so great a beard that it spread out over the whole of Broadfirth." Thorkell bade her read his dream. Gudrun said, "What do you think this dream betokens?" He said, "To me it seems clear that in it is hinted that my power will stand wide about the whole of Broadfirth." Gudrun said, "Maybe that such is the meaning of it, but I rather should think that thereby is betokened that you will dip your beard down into Broadfirth." That same summer Thorkell runs out his ship and gets it ready for Norway. His son, Gellir, was then twelve winters old, and he went abroad with his father. Thorkell makes it known that he means to fetch timber to build his church with, and sails forthwith into the main sea when he was ready. He had an easy voyage of it, but not a very short one, and they hove into Norway northwardly. King Olaf then had his seat in Thrandheim, and Thorkell sought forthwith a meeting with King Olaf, and his son Gellir with him. They had there a good welcome. So highly was Thorkell accounted of that winter by the king, that all folk tell that the king gave him not less than one hundred marks of refined silver. The king gave to Gellir at Yule a cloak, the most precious and excellent of gifts. That winter King Olaf had a church built in the town of timber, and it was a very great minster, all materials thereto being chosen of the best. In the spring the timber which the king gave to Thorkell was brought on board ship, and large was that timber and good in kind, for Thorkell looked closely after it. Now it happened one morning early that the king went out with but few men, and saw a man up on the church which then was being built in the town. He wondered much at this, for it was a good deal earlier than the smiths were wont to be up. Then the king recognised the man, and, lo! there was Thorkell Eyjolfson taking the measure of all the largest timber, crossbeams, sills, and pillars. The king turned at once thither, and said: "What now, Thorkell, do you mean after these measurements to shape the church timber which you are taking to Iceland?" "Yes, in truth, sire," said Thorkell. Then said King Olaf, "Cut two ells off every main beam, and that church will yet be the largest built in Iceland." Thorkell answered, "Keep your timber yourself if you think you have given me too much, or your hand itches to take it back, but not an ell's length shall I cut off it. I shall both know how to go about and how to carry out getting other timber for me." Then says the king most calmly, "So it is, Thorkell, that you are not only a man of much account, but you are also now making yourself too big, for, to be sure, it is too overweening for the son of a mere peasant to try to vie with us. But it is not true that I begrudge you the timber, if only it be fated to you to build a church therewith; for it will never be large enough for all your pride to find room to lie inside it. But near it comes to the foreboding of my mind, that the timber will be of little use to men, and that it will be far from you ever to get any work by man done with this timber." After that they ceased talking, and the king turned away, and it was marked by people that it misliked him how Thorkell accounted as of nought what he said. Yet the king himself did not let people get the wind of it, and he and Thorkell parted in great good-will. Thorkell got on board his ship and put to sea. They had a good wind, and were not long out about the main. Thorkell brought his ship to Ramfirth, and rode soon from his ship home to Holyfell, where all folk were glad to see him. In this journey Thorkell had gained much honour. He had his ship hauled ashore and made snug, and the timber for the church he gave to a caretaker, where it was safely bestowed, for it could not be brought from the north this autumn, as he was at all time full of business. Thorkell now sits at home at his manor throughout the winter. He had Yule-drinking at Holyfell, and to it there came a crowd of people; and altogether he kept up a great state that winter. Nor did Gudrun stop him therein; for she said the use of money was that people should increase their state therewith; moreover, whatever Gudrun must needs be supplied with for all purposes of high-minded display, that (she said) would be readily forthcoming (from her husband). Thorkell shared that winter amongst his friends many precious things he had brought with him out to Iceland.

Chapter 75
Thorkell and Thorstein and Halldor Olafson, A.D. 1026

That winter after Yule Thorkell got ready to go from home north to Ramfirth to bring his timber from the north. He rode first up into the Dales and then to Lea-shaws to Thorstein, his kinsman, where he gathered together men and horses. He afterwards went north to Ramfirth and stayed there awhile, taken up with the business of his journey, and gathered to him horses from about the firth, for he did not want to make more than one journey of it, if that could be managed. But this did not speed swiftly, and Thorkell was busy at this work even into Lent. At last he got under way with the work, and had the wood dragged from the north by more than twenty horses, and had the timber stacked on Lea-Eyr, meaning later on to bring it in a boat out to Holyfell. Thorstein owned a large ferry-boat, and this boat Thorkell was minded to use for his homeward voyage. Thorkell stayed at Lea-shaws through Lent, for there was dear friendship between these kinsmen. Thorstein said one day to Thorkell, they had better go to Herdholt, "for I want to make a bid for some land from Halldor, he having but little money since he paid the brothers the weregild for their father, and the land being just what I want most." Thorkell bade him do as he liked; so they left home a party of twenty men together. They come to Herdholt, and Halldor gave them good welcome, and was most free of talk with them. There were few men at home, for Halldor had sent his men north to Steingrims-firth, as a whale had come ashore there in which he owned a share. Beiner the Strong was at home, the only man now left alive of those who had been there with Olaf, the father of Halldor. Halldor had said to Beiner at once when he saw Thorstein and Thorkell riding up, "I can easily see what the errand of these kinsmen is—they are going to make me a bid for my land, and if that is the case they will call me aside for a talk; I guess they will seat themselves each on either side of me; so, then, if they should give me any trouble you must not be slower to set on Thorstein than I on Thorkell. You have long been true to us kinsfolk. I have also sent to the nearest homesteads for men, and at just the same moment I should like these two things to happen: the coming in of the men summoned, and the breaking up of our talk." Now as the day wore on, Thorstein hinted to Halldor that they should all go aside and have some talk together, "for we have an errand with you." Halldor said it suited him well. Thorstein told his followers they need not come with them, but Beiner went with them none the less, for he thought things came to pass very much after what Halldor had guessed they would. They went very far out into the field. Halldor had on a pinned-up cloak with a long pin brooch, as was the fashion then. Halldor sat down on the field, but on either side of him each of these kinsmen, so near that they sat well-nigh on his cloak; but Beiner stood over them with a big axe in his hand. Then said Thorstein, "My errand here is that I wish to buy land from you, and I bring it before you now because my kinsman Thorkell is with me; I should think that this would suit us both well, for I hear that you are short of money, while your land is costly to husband. I will give you in return an estate that will beseem you, and into the bargain as much as we shall agree upon." In the beginning Halldor took the matter as if it were not so very far from his mind, and they exchanged words concerning the terms of the purchase; and when they felt that he was not so far from coming to terms, Thorkell joined eagerly in the talk, and tried to bring the bargain to a point. Then Halldor began to draw back rather, but they pressed him all the more; yet at last it came to this, that he was the further from the bargain the closer they pressed him. Then said Thorkell, "Do you not see, kinsman Thorstein, how this is going? Halldor has delayed the matter for us all day long, and we have sat here listening to his fooling and wiles. Now if you want to buy the land we must come to closer quarters." Thorstein then said he must know what he had to look forward to, and bade Halldor now come out of the shadow as to whether he was willing to come to the bargain. Halldor answered, "I do not think I need keep you in the dark as to this point, that you will have to go home to-night without any bargain struck." Then said Thorstein, "Nor do I think it needful to delay making known to you what we have in our mind to do; for we, deeming that we shall get the better of you by reason of the odds on our side, have bethought us of two choices for you: one choice is, that you do this matter willingly and take in return our friendship; but the other, clearly a worse one, is, that you now stretch out your hand against your own will and sell me the land of Herdholt." But when Thorstein spoke in this outrageous manner, Halldor leapt up so suddenly that the brooch was torn from his cloak, and said, "Something else will happen before I utter that which is not my will." "What is that?" said Thorstein. "A pole-axe will stand on your head from one of the worst of men, and thus cast down your insolence and unfairness." Thorkell answered, "That is an evil prophecy, and I hope it will not be fulfilled; and now I think there is ample cause why you, Halldor, should give up your land and have nothing for it." Then Halldor answered, "Sooner you will be embracing the sea-tangle in Broadfirth than I sell my land against my own will." Halldor went home after that, and the men he had sent for came crowding up to the place. Thorstein was of the wrothest, and wanted forthwith to make an onset on Halldor. Thorkell bade him not to do so, "for that is the greatest enormity at such a season as this; but when this season wears off, I shall not stand in the way of his and ours clashing together." Halldor said he was given to think he would not fail in being ready for them. After that they rode away and talked much together of this their journey; and Thorstein, speaking thereof, said that, truth to tell, their journey was most wretched. "But why, kinsman Thorkell, were you so afraid of falling on Halldor and putting him to some shame?" Thorkell answered, "Did you not see Beiner, who stood over you with the axe reared aloft? Why, it was an utter folly, for forthwith on seeing me likely to do anything, he would have driven that axe into your head." They rode now home to Lea-shaws; and Lent wears and Passion Week sets in.

Chapter 76
The Drowning of Thorkell, A.D. 1026

On Maundy Thursday, early in the morning, Thorkell got ready for his journey. Thorstein set himself much against it: "For the weather looks to me uncertain," said he. Thorkell said the weather would do all right. "And you must not hinder me now, kinsman, for I wish to be home before Easter." So now Thorkell ran out the ferry-boat, and loaded it. But Thorstein carried the lading ashore from out the boat as fast as Thorkell and his followers put it on board. Then Thorkell said, "Give over now, kinsman, and do not hinder our journey this time; you must not have your own way in this." Thorstein said, "He of us two will now follow the counsel that will answer the worst, for this journey will cause the happening of great matters." Thorkell now bade them farewell till their next meeting, and Thorstein went home, and was exceedingly downcast. He went to the guest-house, and bade them lay a pillow under his head, the which was done. The servant-maid saw how the tears ran down upon the pillow from his eyes. And shortly afterwards a roaring blast struck the house, and Thorstein said, "There, we now can hear roaring the slayer of kinsman Thorkell." Now to tell of the journey of Thorkell and his company: they sail this day out, down Broadfirth, and were ten on board. The wind began to blow very high, and rose to full gale before it blew over. They pushed on their way briskly, for the men were most plucky. Thorkell had with him the sword Skofnung, which was laid in the locker. Thorkell and his party sailed till they came to Bjorn's isle, and people could watch them journey from both shores. But when they had come thus far, suddenly a squall caught the sail and overwhelmed the boat. There Thorkell was drowned and all the men who were with him. The timber drifted ashore wide about the islands, the corner-staves (pillars) drove ashore in the island called Staff-isle. Skofnung stuck fast to the timbers of the boat, and was found in Skofnungs-isle. That same evening that Thorkell and his followers were drowned, it happened at Holyfell that Gudrun went to the church, when other people had gone to bed, and when she stepped into the lich-gate she saw a ghost standing before her. He bowed over her and said, "Great tidings, Gudrun." She said, "Hold then your peace about them, wretch." Gudrun went on to the church, as she had meant to do, and when she got up to the church she thought she saw that Thorkell and his companions were come home and stood before the door of the church, and she saw that water was running off their clothes. Gudrun did not speak to them, but went into the church, and stayed there as long as it seemed good to her. After that she went to the guest-room, for she thought Thorkell and his followers must have gone there; but when she came into the chamber, there was no one there. Then Gudrun was struck with wonder at the whole affair. On Good Friday Gudrun sent her men to find out matters concerning the journeying of Thorkell and his company, some up to Shawstrand and some out to the islands. By then the flotsam had already come to land wide about the islands and on both shores of the firth. The Saturday before Easter the tidings got known and great news they were thought to be, for Thorkell had been a great chieftain. Thorkell was eight-and-forty years old when he was drowned, and that was four winters before Olaf the Holy fell. Gudrun took much to heart the death of Thorkell, yet bore her bereavement bravely. Only very little of the church timber could ever be gathered in. Gellir was now fourteen years old, and with his mother he took over the business of the household and the chieftainship. It was soon seen that he was made to be a leader of men. Gudrun now became a very religious woman. She was the first woman in Iceland who knew the Psalter by heart. She would spend long time in the church at nights saying her prayers, and Herdis, Bolli's daughter, always went with her at night. Gudrun loved Herdis very much. It is told that one night the maiden Herdis dreamed that a woman came to her who was dressed in a woven cloak, and coifed in a head cloth, but she did not think the woman winning to look at. She spoke, "Tell your grandmother that I am displeased with her, for she creeps about over me every night, and lets fall down upon me drops so hot that I am burning all over from them. My reason for letting you know this is, that I like you somewhat better, though there is something uncanny hovering about you too. However, I could get on with you if I did not feel there was so much more amiss with Gudrun." Then Herdis awoke and told Gudrun her dream. Gudrun thought the apparition was of good omen. Next morning Gudrun had planks taken up from the church floor where she was wont to kneel on the hassock, and she had the earth dug up, and they found blue and evil-looking bones, a round brooch, and a wizard's wand, and men thought they knew then that a tomb of some sorceress must have been there; so the bones were taken to a place far away where people were least likely to be passing.

Chapter 77

The Return of Bolli, A.D. 1030

When four winters were passed from the drowning of Thorkell Eyjolfson a ship came into Islefirth belonging to Bolli Bollison, most of the crew of which were Norwegians. Bolli brought out with him much wealth, and many precious things that lords abroad had given him. Bolli was so great a man for show when he came back from this journey that he would wear no clothes but of scarlet and fur, and all his weapons were bedight with gold: he was called Bolli the Grand. He made it known to his shipmasters that he was going west to his own countrysides, and he left his ship and goods in the hands of his crew. Bolli rode from the ship with twelve men, and all his followers were dressed in scarlet, and rode on gilt saddles, and all were they a trusty band, though Bolli was peerless among them. He had on the clothes of fur which the Garth-king had given him, he had over all a scarlet cape; and he had Footbiter girt on him, the hilt of which was dight with gold, and the grip woven with gold; he had a gilded helmet on his head, and a red shield on his flank, with a knight painted on it in gold. He had a dagger in his hand, as is the custom in foreign lands; and whenever they took quarters the women paid heed to nothing but gazing at Bolli and his grandeur, and that of his followers. In this state Bolli rode into the western parts all the way till he came to Holyfell with his following. Gudrun was very glad to see her son. Bolli did not stay there long till he rode up to Sælingsdale Tongue to see Snorri, his father-in-law, and his wife Thordis, and their meeting was exceeding joyful. Snorri asked Bolli to stay with him with as many of his men as he liked. Bolli accepted the invitation gratefully, and was with Snorri all the winter, with the men who had ridden from the north with him. Bolli got great renown from this journey. Snorri made it no less his business now to treat Bolli with every kindness than death when he was with him before.

Chapter 78
The Death of Snorri, and the End, A.D. 1031

When Bolli had been one winter in Iceland Snorri the Priest fell ill. That illness did not gain quickly on him, and Snorri lay very long abed. But when the illness gained on him, he called to himself all his kinsfolk and affinity, and said to Bolli, "It is my wish that you shall take over the manor here and the chieftainship after my day, for I grudge honours to you no more than to my own sons, nor is there within this land now the one of my sons who I think will be the greatest man among them, Halldor to wit." Thereupon Snorri breathed his last, being seventy-seven years old. That was one winter after the fall of St. Olaf, so said Ari the Priest "Deep-in-lore." Snorri was buried at Tongue. Bolli and Thordis took over the manor of Tongue as Snorri had willed it, and Snorri's sons put up with it with a good will. Bolli grew a man of great account, and was much beloved. Herdis, Bolli's daughter, grew up at Holyfell, and was the goodliest of all women. Orm, the son of Hermund, the son of Illugi, asked her in marriage, and she was given in wedlock to him; their son was Kodran, who had for wife Gudrun, the daughter of Sigmund. The son of Kodran was Hermund, who had for wife Ulfeid, the daughter of Runolf, who was the son of Bishop Kelill; their sons were Kelill, who was Abbot of Holyfell, and Reinn and Kodran and Styrmir; their daughter was Thorvor, whom Skeggi, Bard's son, had for wife, and from whom is come the stock of the Shaw-men. Ospak was the name of the son of Bolli and Thordis. The daughter of Ospak was Gudrun, whom Thorarin, Brand's son, had to wife. Their son was Brand, who founded the benefice of Housefell. Gellir, Thorleik's son, took to him a wife, and married Valgerd, daughter of Thorgils Arison of Reekness. Gellir went abroad, and took service with King Magnus the Good, and had given him by the king twelve ounces of gold and many goods besides. The sons of Gellir were Thorkell and Thorgils, and a son of Thorgils was Ari the "Deep-in-lore." The son of Ari was named Thorgils, and his son was Ari the Strong. Now Gudrun began to grow very old, and lived in such sorrow and grief as has lately been told. She was the first nun and recluse in Iceland, and by all folk it is said that Gudrun was the noblest of women of equal birth with her in this land. It is told how once upon a time Bolli came to Holyfell, for Gudrun was always very pleased when he came to see her, and how he sat by his mother for a long time, and they talked of many things. Then Bolli said, "Will you tell me, mother, what I want very much to know? Who is the man you have loved the most?" Gudrun answered, "Thorkell was the mightiest man and the greatest chief, but no man was more shapely or better endowed all round than Bolli. Thord, son of Ingun, was the wisest of them all, and the greatest lawyer; Thorvald I take no account of." Then said Bolli, "I clearly understand that what you tell me shows how each of your husbands was endowed, but you have not told me yet whom you loved the best. Now there is no need for you to keep that hidden any longer." Gudrun answered, "You press me hard, my son, for this, but if I must needs tell it to any one, you are the one I should first choose thereto." Bolli bade her do so. Then Gudrun said, "To him I was worst whom I loved best." "Now," answered Bolli, "I think the whole truth is told," and said she had done well to tell him what he so much had yearned to know. Gudrun grew to be a very old woman, and some say she lost her sight. Gudrun died at Holyfell, and there she rests. Gellir, Thorkell's son, lived at Holyfell to old age, and many things of much account are told of him; he also comes into many Sagas, though but little be told of him here. He built a church at Holyfell, a very stately one, as Arnor, the Earls' poet, says in the funeral song which he wrote about Gellir, wherein he uses clear words about that matter. When Gellir was somewhat sunk into his latter age, he prepared himself for a journey away from Iceland. He went to Norway, but did not stay there long, and then left straightway that land and "walked" south to Rome to "see the holy apostle Peter." He was very long over this journey; and then journeying from the south he came into Denmark, and there he fell ill and lay in bed a very long time, and received all the last rites of the church, whereupon he died, and he rests at Roskild. Gellir had taken Skofnung with him, the sword that had been taken out of the barrow of Holy Kraki, and never after could it be got back. When the death of Gellir was known in Iceland, Thorkell, his son, took over his father's inheritance at Holyfell. Thorgils, another of Gellir's sons, was drowned in Broadfirth at an early age, with all hands on board. Thorkell Gellirson was a most learned man, and was said to be of all men the best stocked of lore. Here is the end of the Saga of the men of Salmon-river-Dale.

THE STORY OF BURNT NJAL

Chapter 1
Of Fiddle Mord

There was a man named Mord whose surname was Fiddle; he was the son of Sigvat the Red, and he dwelt at the "Vale" in the Rangrivervales. He was a mighty chief, and a great taker up of suits, and so great a lawyer that no judgments were thought lawful unless he had a hand in them. He had an only daughter, named Unna. She was a fair, courteous and gifted woman, and that was thought the best match in all the Rangrivervales.

Now the story turns westward to the Broadfirth dales, where, at Hauskuldstede, in Laxriverdale, dwelt a man named Hauskuld, who was Dalakoll's son, and his mother's name was Thorgerda. He had a brother named Hrut, who dwelt at Hrutstede; he was of the same mother as Hauskuld, but his father's name was Heriolf. Hrut was handsome, tall and strong, well skilled in arms, and mild of temper; he was one of the wisest of men — stern towards his foes, but a good counsellor on great matters. It happened once that Hauskuld bade his friends to a feast, and his brother Hrut was there, and sat next him. Hauskuld had a daughter named Hallgerda, who was playing on the floor with some other girls. She was fair of face and tall of growth, and her hair was as soft as silk; it was so long, too, that it came down to her waist. Hauskuld called out to her, "Come hither to me, daughter". So she went up to him, and he took her by the chin, and kissed her; and after that she went away.

Then Hauskuld said to Hrut, "What dost thou think of this maiden? Is she not fair?" Hrut held his peace. Hauskuld said the same thing to him a second time, and then Hrut answered, "Fair enough is this maid, and many will smart for it, but this I know not, whence thief's eyes have come into our race". Then Hauskuld was wroth, and for a time the brothers saw little of each other.

Chapter 2
Hrut Woos Unna

It happened once that those brothers, Hauskuld and Hrut, rode to the Althing, and there was much people at it. Then Hauskuld said to Hrut, "One thing I wish, brother, and that is, that thou wouldst better thy lot and woo thyself a wife."

Hrut answered, "That has been long on my mind, though there always seemed to be two sides to the matter; but now I will do as thou wishest; whither shall we turn our eyes?"

Hauskuld answered, "Here now are many chiefs at the Thing, and there is plenty of choice, but I have already set my eyes on a spot where a match lies made to thy hand. The woman's name is Unna, and she is a daughter of Fiddle Mord one of the wisest of men. He is here at the Thing, and his daughter too, and thou mayest see her if it pleases thee."

Now the next day, when men were going to the High Court, they saw some well-dressed women standing outside the booths of the men from the Rangrivervales, Then Hauskuld said to Hrut —

"Yonder now is Unna, of whom I spoke; what thinkest thou of her?"

"Well," answered Hrut; "but yet I do not know whether we should get on well together."

After that they went to the High Court, where Fiddle Mord was laying down the law as was his wont, and alter he had done he went home to his booth.

Then Hauskuld and Hrut rose, and went to Mord's booth. They went in and found Mord sitting in the innermost part of the booth, and they bade him "good day". He rose to meet them, and took Hauskuld by the hand and made him sit down by his side, and Hrut sat next to Hauskuld, So after they had talked much of this and that, at last Hauskuld said, "I have a bargain to speak to thee about; Hrut wishes to become thy son-in-law, and buy thy daughter, and I, for my part, will not be sparing in the matter".

Mord answered, "I know that thou art a great chief, but thy brother is unknown to me".

"He is a better man than I," answered Hauskuld.

"Thou wilt need to lay down a large sum with him, for she is heir to all I leave behind me," said Mord.

"There is no need," said Hauskuld, "to wait long before thou hearest what I give my word he shall have. He shall have Kamness and Hrutstede, up as far as Thrandargil, and a trading-ship beside, now on her voyage."

Then said Hrut to Mord, "Bear in mind, now, husband, that my brother has praised me much more than I deserve for love's sake; but if after what thou hast heard, thou wilt make the match, I am willing to let thee lay down the terms thyself".

Mord answered, "I have thought over the terms; she shall have sixty hundreds down, and this sum shall be increased by a third more in thine house, but if ye two have heirs, ye shall go halves in the goods".

Then said Hrut, "I agree to these terms, and now let us take witness". After that they stood up and shook hands, and Mord betrothed his daughter Unna to Hrut, and the bridal feast was to be at Mord's house, half a month after Midsummer.

Now both sides ride home from the Thing, and Hauskuld and Hrut ride westward by Hallbjorn's beacon. Then Thiostolf, the son of Biorn Gullbera of Reykiardale, rode to meet them, and told them how a ship had come out from Norway to the White River, and how aboard of her was Auzur, Hrut's father's brother, and he wished Hrut to come to him as soon as ever he could. When Hrut heard this, he asked Hauskuld to go with him to the ship, so Hauskuld went with his brother, and when they reached the ship, Hrut gave his kinsman Auzur a kind and hearty welcome. Auzur asked them into his booth to drink, so their horses were unsaddled, and they went in and drank, and while they were drinking, Hrut said to Auzur, "Now, kinsman, thou must ride west with me, and stay with me this winter."

"That cannot be, kinsman, for I have to tell thee the death of thy brother Eyvind, and he has left thee his heir at the Gula Thing, and now thy foes will seize thy heritage, unless thou comest to claim it."

"What's to be done now, brother?" said Hrut to Hauskuld, "for this seems a hard matter, coming just as I have fixed my bridal day."

"Thou must ride south," said Hauskuld, "and see Mord, and ask him to change the bargain which ye two have made, and to let his daughter sit for thee three winters as thy betrothed, but I will ride home and bring down thy wares to the ship."

Then said Hrut, "My wish is that thou shouldest take meal and timber, and whatever else thou needest out of the lading". So Hrut had his horses brought out, and he rode south, while Hauskuld rode home west. Hrut came east to the Rangrivervales to Mord, and had a good welcome, and he told Mord all his business, and asked his advice what he should do.

"How much money is this heritage?" asked Mord, and Hrut said it would come to a hundred marks, if he got it all.

"Well," said Mord, "that is much when set against what I shall leave behind me, and thou shalt go for it, if thou wilt."

After that they broke their bargain, and Unna was to sit waiting for Hrut three years as his betrothed. Now Hrut rides back to the ship, and stays by her during the summer, till she was ready to sail, and Hauskuld brought down all Hrut's wares and money to the ship, and Hrut placed all his other property in Hauskuld's hands to keep for him while he was away. Then Hauskuld rode home to his house, and a little while after they got a fair wind and sail away to sea. They were out three weeks, and the first land they made was Hern, near Bergen, and so sail eastward to the Bay.

Chapter 3
Hrut and Gunnhillda, King's Mother

At that time Harold Grayfell reigned in Norway; he was the son of Eric Blood-axe, who was the son of Harold Fairhair; his mother's name was Gunnhillda, a daughter of Auzur Toti, and they had their abode east, at the King's Crag. Now the news was spread, how a ship had come thither east into the Bay, and as soon as Gunnhillda heard of it, she asked what men from Iceland were aboard, and they told her Hrut was the man's name, Auzur's brother's son. Then Gunnhillda said, "I see plainly that he means to claim his heritage, but there is a man named Soti, who has laid his hands on it".

After that she called her waiting-man, whose name was Augmund, and said—

"I am going to send thee to the Bay to find out Auzur and Hint, and tell them that I ask them both to spend this winter with me. Say, too, that I will be their friend, and if Hrut will carry out my counsel, I will see after his suit, and anything else he takes in hand, and I will speak a good word, too, for him to the king."

After that he set off and found them; and as soon as they knew that he was Gunnhillda's servant, they gave him good welcome. He took them aside and told them his errand, and after that they talked over their plans by themselves. Then Auzur said to Hrut —

"Methinks, kinsman, here is little need for long talk, our plans are ready made for us; for I know Gunnhillda's temper; as soon as ever we say we will not go to her she will drive us out of the land, and take all our goods by force; but if we go to her, then she will do us such honour as she has promised."

Augmund went home, and when he saw Gunnhillda, he told her how his errand had ended, and that they would come, and Gunnhillda said —

"It is only what was to be looked for; for Hrut is said to be a wise and well-bred man; and now do thou keep a sharp look out, and tell me as soon as ever they come to the town."

Hrut and Auzur went east to the King's Crag, and when they reached the town, their kinsmen and friends went out to meet and welcome them. They asked, whether the king were in the town, and they told them he was. After that they met Augmund, and he brought them a greeting from Gunnhillda, saying, that she could not ask them to her house before they had seen the king, lest men should say, "I make too much of them". Still she would do all she could for them, and she went on, "tell Hrut to be outspoken before the king, and to ask to be made one of his body-guard"; "and here," said Augmund, "is a dress of honour which she sends to thee, Hrut, and in it thou must go in before the king". After that he went away.

The next day Hrut said —

"Let us go before the king."

"That may well be," answered Auzur.

So they went, twelve of them together, and all of them friends or kinsmen, and came into the hall where the king sat over his drink. Hrut went first and bade the king "good day," and the king, looking steadfastly at the man who was well-dressed, asked him his name. So he told his name.

"Art thou an Icelander?" said the king.

He answered, "Yes".

"What drove thee hither to seek us?"

Then Hrut answered —

"To see your state, lord; and, besides, because I have a great matter of inheritance here in the land, and I shall have need of your help, if I am to get my rights."

The king said —

"I have given my word that every man shall have lawful justice here in Norway; but hast thou any other errand in seeking me?"

"Lord!" said Hrut, "I wish you to let me live in your court, and become one of your men."

At this the king holds his peace, but Gunnhillda said —

"It seems to me as if this man offered you the greatest honour, for me thinks if there were many such men in the body-guard, it would be well filled."

"Is he a wise man?" asked the king.

"He is both wise and willing," said she.

"Well," said the king, "methinks my mother wishes that thou shouldst have the rank for which thou askest, but for the sake of our honour and the custom of the land, come to me in half a month's time, and then thou shalt be made one of my body-guard. Meantime, my mother will take care of thee, but then come to me."

Then Gunnhillda said to Augmund —

"Follow them to my house, and treat them well."

So Augmund went out, and they went with him, and he brought them to a hall built of stone, which was hung with the most beautiful tapestry, and there too was Gunnhillda's high-seat.

Then Augmund said to Hrut —

"Now will be proved the truth of all that I said to thee from Gunnhillda. Here is her high-seat, and in it thou shalt sit, and this seat thou shalt hold, though she comes herself into the hall."

After that he made them good cheer, and they had sat down but a little while when Gunnhillda came in. Hrut wished to jump up and greet her.

"Keep thy seat!" she says, "and keep it too all the time thou art my guest."

Then she sat herself down by Hrut, and they fell to drink, and at even she said —

"Thou shalt be in the upper chamber with me to-night, and we two together."

"You shall have your way," he answers.

After that they went to sleep, and she locked the door inside. So they slept that night, and in the morning fell to drinking again. Thus they spent their life all that half-month, and Gunnhillda said to the men who were there —

"Ye shall lose nothing except your lives if you say to any one a word of how Hrut and I are going on."

[When the half-month was over] Hrut gave her a hundred ells of household woollen and twelve rough cloaks, and Gunnhillda thanked him for his gifts. Then Hrut thanked her and gave her a kiss and went away. She bade him "farewell". And next day he went before the king with thirty men after him and bade the king "good-day". The king said —

"Now, Hrut, thou wilt wish me to carry out towards thee what I promised."

So Hrut was made one of the king's body-guard, and he asked, "Where shall I sit?"

"My mother shall settle that," said the king.

Then she got him a seat in the highest room, and he spent the winter with the king in much honour.

Chapter 4
Of Hrut's Cruise

When the spring came he asked about Soti, and found out he had gone south to Denmark with the inheritance. Then Hrut went to Gunnhillda and tells her what Soti had been about. Gunnhillda said —

"I will give thee two long-ships, full manned, and along with them the bravest men. Wolf the Unwashed, our overseer of guests; but still go and see the king before thou settest off."

Hrut did so; and when he came before the king, then he told the king of Soti's doings, and how he had a mind to hold on after him.

The king said, "What strength has my mother handed over to thee?"

"Two long-ships and Wolf the Unwashed to lead the men," says Hrut.

"Well given," says the king. "Now I will give thee other two ships, and even then thou'lt need all the strength thou'st got."

After that he went down with Hrut to the ship, and said "fare thee well". Then Hrut sailed away south with his crews.

Chapter 5
Atli Arnvid Son's Slaying

There was a man named Atli, son of Arnvid, Earl of East Gothland. He had kept back the taxes from Hacon Athelstane's foster child, and both father and son had fled away from Jemtland to Gothland. After that, Atli held on with his followers out of the Mælar by Stock Sound, and so on towards Denmark, and now he lies out in resound. He is an outlaw both of the Dane-King and of the Swede-King. Hrut held on south to the Sound, and when he came into it he saw many ships in the Sound. Then Wolf said —

"What's best to be done now, Icelander?"

"Hold on our course," says Hrut, " 'for nothing venture, nothing have'. My ship and Auzur's shall go first, but thou shalt lay thy ship where thou likest."

"Seldom have I had others as a shield before me," says Wolf, and lays his galley side by side with Hrut's ship; and so they hold on through the Sound. Now those who are in the Sound see that ships are coming up to them, and they tell Atli.

He answered, "Then maybe there'll be gain to be got".

After that men took their stand on board each ship; "but my ship," says Atli, "shall be in the midst of the fleet".

Meantime Hrut's ships ran on, and as soon as either side could hear the other's hail, Atli stood up and said —

"Ye fare unwarily. Saw ye not that war-ships were in the Sound? But what's the name of your chief?"

Hrut tells his name.

"Whose man art thou?" says Atli.

"One of king Harold Grayfell's body-guard."

Atli said, "'Tis long since any love was lost between us, father and son, and your Norway kings".

"Worse luck for thee," says Hrut.

"Well," says Atli, "the upshot of our meeting will be, that thou shalt not be left alive to tell the tale;" and with that he caught up a spear and hurled it at Hrut's ship, and the man who stood before it got his death. After that the battle began, and they were slow in boarding Hrut's ship. Wolf, he went well forward, and with him it was now cut, now thrust. Atli's bowman's name was Asolf; he sprung up on Hrut's ship, and was four men's death before Hrut was ware of him; then he turned against him, and when they met, Asolf thrust at and through Hrut's shield, but Hrut cut once at Asolf, and that was his death-blow. Wolf the Unwashed saw that stroke, and called out —

"Truth to say, Hrut, thou dealest big blows, but thou'st much to thank Gunnhillda for."

"Something tells me," says Hrut, "that thou speakest with a 'fey' mouth."

Now Atli sees a bare place for a weapon on Wolf, and shot a spear through him, and now the battle grows hot: Atli leaps up on Hrut's ship, and clears it fast round about, and now Auzur turns to meet him, and thrust at him, but fell down full length on his back, for another man thrust at him. Now Hrut turns to meet Atli: he cut at once at Hrut's shield, and clove it all in two, from top to point; just then Atli got a blow on his hand from a stone, and down fell his sword. Hrut caught up the sword, and cut his foot from under him. After that he dealt him his death-blow. There they took much goods, and brought away with them two ships which were best, and stayed there only a little while. But meantime Soti and his crew had sailed past them, and he held on his course back to Norway, and made the land at Limgard's side. There Soti went on shore, and there he met Augmund, Gunnhillda's page; he knew him at once, and asks —

"How long meanest thou to be here?"

"Three nights," says Soti.

"Whither away, then?" says Augmund.

"West, to England," says Soti, "and never to come back again to Norway while Gunnhillda's rule is in Norway."

Augmund went away, and goes and finds Gunnhillda, for she was a little way off at a feast, and Gudred, her son, with her. Augmund told Gunnhillda what Soti meant to do, and she begged Gudred to take his life. So Gudred set off at once, and came unawares on Soti, and made them lead up the country, and hang him there. But the goods he took, and brought them to his mother, and she got men to carry them all down to the King's Crag, and after that she went thither herself.

Hrut came back towards autumn, and had gotten great store of goods. He went at once to the king, and had a hearty welcome. He begged them to take whatever they pleased of his goods, and the king took a third. Gunnhillda told Hrut how she had got hold of the inheritance, and had Soti slain. He thanked her, and gave her half of all he had.

Chapter 6
Hrut Sails out to Iceland

Hrut stayed with the king that winter in good cheer, but when spring came he grew very silent. Gunnhillda finds that out, and said to him when they two were alone together —

"Art thou sick at heart?"

"So it is," said Hrut, "as the saying runs — 'Ill goes it with those who are born on a barren land.'"

"Wilt thou to Iceland?" she asks.

"Yes," he answered.

"Hast thou a wife out there?" she asked; and he answers, "No".

"But I am sure that is true," she says; and so they ceased talking about the matter.

[Shortly after] Hrut went before the king and bade him "good day"; and the king said, "What dost thou want now, Hrut?"

"I am come to ask, lord, that you give me leave to go to Iceland."

"Will thine honour be greater there than here?" asks the king.

"No, it will not," said Hrut; "but every one must win the work that is set before him."

"It is pulling a rope against a strong man," said Gunnhillda, "so give him leave to go as best suits him."

There was a bad harvest that year in the land, yet Gunnhillda gave Hrut as much meal as he chose to have; and now he busks him to sail out to Iceland, and Auzur with him; and when they were all-boun, Hrut went to find the king and Gunnhillda. She led him aside to talk alone, and said to him —

"Here is a gold ring which I will give thee;" and with that she clasped it round his wrist.

"Many good gifts have I had from thee," said Hrut.

Then she put her hands round his neck and kissed him, and said —

"If I have as much power over thee as I think, I lay this spell on thee that thou mayest never have any pleasure in living with that woman on whom thy heart is set in Iceland, but with other women thou mayest get on well enough, and now it is like to go well with neither of us; — but thou hast not believed what I have been saying."

Hrut laughed when he heard that, and went away; after that he came before the king and thanked him; and the king spoke kindly to him, and bade him "farewell". Hrut went straight to his ship, and they had a fair wind all the way until they ran into Borgarfirth.

As soon as the ship was made fest to the land, Hrut rode west home, but Auzur stayed by the ship to unload her, and lay her up. Hrut rode straight to Hauskuldstede, and Hauskuld gave him a hearty welcome, and Hrut told him all about his travels. After that they sent men east across the rivers to tell Fiddle Mord to make ready for the bridal feast; but the two brothers rode to the ship, and on the way Hauskuld told Hrut how his money matters stood, and his goods had gained much since he was away. Then Hrut said —

"The reward is less worth than it ought to be, but I will give thee as much meal as thou needst for thy household next winter."

Then they drew the ship on land on rollers, and made her snug in her shed, but all the wares on board her they carried away into the Dales westward. Hrut stayed at home at Hrutstede till winter was six weeks off, and then the brothers made ready, and Auzur with them, to ride to Hrut's wedding. Sixty men ride with them, and they rode east till they came to Rangriver plains. There they found a crowd of guests, and the men took their seats on benches down the length of the hall, but the women were seated on the cross benches on the dais, and the bride was rather downcast. So they drank out the feast and it went off well. Mord pays down his daughter's portion, and she rides west with her husband and his train. So they ride till they reach home. Hrut gave over everything into her hands inside the house, and all were pleased at that; but for all that she and Hrut did not pull well together as man and wife, and so things went on till spring, and when spring came Hrut had a journey to make to the Westfirths, to get in the money for which he had sold his wares; but before he set off his wife says to him—

"Dost thou mean to be back before men ride to the Thing?"

"Why dost thou ask?" said Hrut.

"I will ride to the Thing," she said, "to meet my father."

"So it shall be," said he, "and I will ride to the Thing along with thee."

"Well and good," she says.

After that Hrut rode from home west to the Firths, got in all his money, and laid it out anew, and rode home again. When he came home he busked him to ride to the Thing, and made all his neighbours ride with him. His brother Hauskuld rode among the rest. Then Hrut said to his wife —

"If thou hast as much mind now to go to the Thing as thou saidst a while ago, busk thyself and ride along with me."

She was not slow in getting herself ready, and then they all rode to the Thing. Unna went to her father's booth, and he gave her a hearty welcome, but she seemed somewhat heavy-hearted, and when he saw that he said to her —

"I have seen thee with a merrier face. Hast thou anything on thy mind?"

She began to weep, and answered nothing. Then he said to her again, "Why dost thou ride to the Thing, if thou wilt not tell me thy secret? Dost thou dislike living away there in the west?"

Then she answered him —

"I would give all I own in the world that I had never gone thither."

"Well!" said Mord, "I'll soon get to the bottom of this." Then he sends men to fetch Hauskuld and Hrut, and they came straightway; and when they came in to see Mord, he rose up to meet them and gave them a hearty welcome, and asked them to sit down. Then they talked a long time in a friendly way, and at last Mord said to Hauskuld —

"Why does my daughter think so ill of life in the west yonder?"

"Let her speak out," said Hrut, "if she has anything to lay to my charge."

But she brought no charge against him. Then Hrut made them ask his neighbours and household how he treated her, and all bore him good witness, saying that she did just as she pleased in the house.

Then Mord said, "Home thou shalt go, and be content with thy lot; for all the witness goes better for him than for thee".

After that Hrut rode home from the Thing, and his wife with him, and all went smoothly between them that summer; but when spring came it was the old story over again, and things grew worse and worse as the spring went on. Hrut had again a journey to make west to the Firths, and gave out that he would not ride to the Althing, but Unna his wife said little about it. So Hrut went away west to the Firths.

Chapter 7
Unna separates from Hrut

Now the time for the Thing was coming on, Unna spoke to Sigmund Auzur's son, and asked if he would ride to the Thing with her; he said he could not ride if his kinsman Hrut set his face against it.

"Well!" says she, "I spoke to thee because I have better right to ask this from thee than from any one else."

He answered, "I will make a bargain with thee: thou must promise to ride back west with me, and to have no underhand dealings against Hrut or myself".

So she promised that, and then they rode to the Thing. Her father Mord was at the Thing, and was very glad to see her, and asked her to stay in his booth while the Thing lasted, and she did so.

"Now," said Mord, "what hast thou to tell me of thy mate, Hrut?"

Then she sung him a song, in which she praised Hrut's liberality, but said he was not master of himself. She herself was ashamed to speak out.

Mord was silent a short time, and then said —

"Thou hast now that on thy mind I see, daughter, which thou dost not wish that any one should know save myself, and thou wilt trust to me rather than any one else to help thee out of thy trouble."

Then they went aside to talk, to a place where none could overhear what they said; and then Mord said to his daughter —

"Now tell me all that is between you two, and don't make more of the matter than it is worth."

"So it shall be," she answered, and sang two songs, in which she revealed the cause of their misunderstanding; and when Mord pressed her to speak out, she told him how she and Hrut could not live together, because he was spell-bound, and that she wished to leave him.

"Thou didst right to tell me all this," said Mord, "and now I will give thee a piece of advice, which will stand thee in good stead, if thou canst carry it out to the letter. First of all, thou must ride home from the Thing, and by that time thy husband will have come back, and will be glad to see thee; thou must he blithe and buxom to him, and he will think a good change has come over thee, and thou must show no signs of coldness or ill-temper, but when spring comes thou must sham sickness, and take to thy bed. Hrut will not lose time in guessing what thy sickness can be, nor will he scold thee at all, but he will rather beg every one to take all the care they can of thee. After that he will set off west to the Firths, and Sigmund with him, for he will have to flit all his goods home from the Firths west, and he will be away till the summer is far spent. But when men ride to the Thing, and after all have ridden from the Dales that mean to ride thither, then thou must rise from thy bed and summon men to go along with thee to the Thing; and when thou art all-boun, then shalt thou go to thy bed, and the men with thee who are to bear thee company, and thou shalt take witness before thy husband's bed, and declare thyself separated from him by such a lawful separation as may hold good according to the judgment of the Great Thing, and the laws of the land; and at the man's door [the main door of the house] thou shalt take the same witness. After that ride away, and ride over Laxriverdale Heath, and so on over Holtbeacon Heath; for they will look for thee by way of Hrutfirth. And so ride on till thou comest to me; then I will see after the matter. But into his hands thou shalt never come more."

Now she rides home from the Thing, and Hrut had come back before her, and made her hearty welcome. She answered him kindly, and was blithe and forbearing towards him. So they lived happily together that half-year; but when spring came she fell sick, and kept her bed. Hrut set off west to the Firths, and bade them tend her well before he went. Now, when the time for the Thing comes, she busked herself to ride away, and did in every way as had been laid down for her; and then she rides away to the Thing. The country folk looked for her, but could not find her. Mord made his daughter welcome, and asked her if she had followed his advice; and she says, "I have not broken one tittle of it".

Then she went to the Hill of Laws, and declared herself separated from Hrut; and men thought this strange news. Unna went home with her father, and never went west from that day forward.

Chapter 8
Mord Claims his Goods from Hrut

Hrut came home, and knit his brows when he heard his wife was gone, but yet kept his feelings well in hand, and stayed at home all that half-year, and spoke to no one on the matter. Next summer he rode to the Thing, with his brother Hauskuld, and they had a great following. But when he came to the Thing, he asked whether Fiddle Mord were at the Thing, and they told him he was; and all thought they would come to words at once about their matter, but it was not so. At last, one day when the brothers and others who were at the Thing went to the Hill of Laws, Mord took witness and declared that he had a money-suit against Hrut for his daughter's dower, and reckoned the amount at ninety hundreds in goods, calling on Hrut at the same time to pay and hand it over to him, and asking for a fine of three marks. He laid the suit in the Quarter Court, into which it would come by law, and gave lawful notice, so that all who stood on the Hill of Laws might hear.

But when he had thus spoken, Hrut said —

"Thou hast undertaken this suit, which belongs to thy daughter, rather for the greed of gain and love of strife than in kindliness and manliness. But I shall have something to say against it; for the goods which belong to me are not yet in thy hands. Now, what I have to say is this, and I say it out, so that all who hear me on this hill may bear witness: I challenge thee to fight on the island; there on one side shall be laid all thy daughter's dower, and on the other I will lay down goods worth as much, and whoever wins the day shall have both dower and goods; but if thou wilt not fight with me, then thou shalt give up all claim to these goods."

Then Mord held his peace, and took counsel with his friends about going to fight on the island, and Jorund the priest gave him an answer.

"There is no need for thee to come to ask us for counsel in this matter, for thou knowest if thou fightest with Hrut thou wilt lose both life and goods. He has a good cause, and is besides mighty in himself and one of the boldest of men."

Then Mord spoke out, that he would not fight with Hrut, and there arose a great shout and hooting on the hill, and Mord got the greatest shame by his suit.

After that men ride home from the Thing, and those brothers Hauskuld and Hrut ride west to Reykiardale, and turned in as guests at Lund, where Thiostolf, Biorn Gullbera's son, then dwelt. There had been much rain that day, and men got wet, so long-fires were made down the length of the hall. Thiostolf, the master of the house, sat between Hauskuld and Hrut, and two boys, of whom Thiostolf had the rearing, were playing on the floor, and a girl was playing with them. They were great chatterboxes, for they were too young to know better. So one of them said —

"Now, I will be Mord, and summon thee to lose thy wife because thou hast not been a good husband to her."

Then the other answered —

"I will be Hrut, and I call on thee to give up all claim to thy goods, if thou darest not to fight with me."

This they said several times, and all the household burst out laughing. Then Hauskuld got wroth, and struck the boy who called himself Mord with a switch, and the blow fell on his face, and graced the skin.

"Get out with thee," said Hauskuld to the boy, "and make no game of us;" but Hrut said, "Come hither to me," and the boy did so. Then Hrut drew a ring from his finger and gave it to him, and said —

"Go away, and try no man's temper henceforth."

Then the boy went away saying —

"Thy manliness I will bear in mind all my life."

From this matter Hrut got great praise, and after that they went home; and that was the end of Mord's and Hrut's quarrel.

Chapter 9
Thorwald gets Hallgerda to Wife

Now, it must be told how Hallgerda, Hauskuld's daughter, grows up, and is the fairest of women to look on; she was tall of stature, too, and therefore she was called "Longcoat". She was fair-haired, and had so much of it that she could hide herself in it; but she was lavish and hard-hearted. Her foster-father's name was Thiostolf; he was a South islander by stock; he was a strong man, well skilled in arms, and had slain many men, and made no atonement in money for one of them. It was said, too, that his rearing had not bettered Hallgerda's temper.

There was a man named Thorwald; he was Oswif's son, and dwelt out on Middlefells strand, under the Fell. He was rich and well to do, and owned the islands called Bear-isles, which lie out in Broadfirth, whence he got meal and stock fish. This Thorwald was a strong and courteous man, though somewhat hasty in temper. Now, it fell out one day that Thorwald and his father were talking together of Thorwald's marrying, and where he had best look for a wife, and it soon came out that he thought there wasn't a match fit for him far or near.

"Well," said Oswif, "wilt thou ask for Hallgerda Longcoat, Hauskuld's daughter?"

"Yes! I will ask for her," said Thorwald.

"But that is not a match that will suit either of you," Oswif went on to say, "for she has a will of her own, and thou art stern-tempered and unyielding."

"For all that I will try my luck there," said Thorwald, "so it's no good trying to hinder me."

"Ay!" said Oswif, "and the risk is all thine own."

After that they set off on a wooing journey to Hauskuldstede, and had a hearty welcome. They were not long in telling Hauskuld their business, and began to woo; then Hauskuld answered —

"As for you, I know how you both stand in the world, but for my own part I will use no guile towards you. My daughter has a hard temper, but as to her looks and breeding you can both see for yourselves."

"Lay down the terms of the match," answered Thorwald, "for I will not let her temper stand in the way of our bargain."

Then they talked over the terms of the bargain, and Hauskuld never asked his daughter what she thought of it, for his heart was set on giving her away, and so they came to an understanding as to the terms of the match. After that Thorwald betrothed himself to Hallgerda, and rode away home when the matter was settled.

Chapter 10
Hallgerda's Wedding

Hauskuld told Hallgerda of the bargain he had made, and she said —

"Now that has been put to the proof which I have all along been afraid of, that thou lovest me not so much as thou art always saying, when thou hast not thought it worth while to tell me a word of all this matter. Besides, I do not think the match as good a one as thou hast always promised me."

So she went on, and let them know in every way that she thought she was thrown away.

Then Hauskuld said —

"I do not set so much store by thy pride as to let it stand in the way of my bargains; and my will, not thine, shall carry the day if we fell out on any point."

"The pride of all you kinsfolk is great," she said, "and so it is not wonderful if I have some of it."

With that she went away, and found her foster-father Thiostolf, and told him what was in store for her, and was very heavy-hearted. Then Thiostolf said —

"Be of good cheer, for thou wilt be married a second time, and then they will ask thee what thou thinkest of the match; for I will do in all things as thou wishest, except in what touches thy father or Hrut."

After that they spoke no more of the matter, and Hauskuld made ready the bridal feast, and rode off to ask men to it. So he came to Hrutstede and called Hrut out to speak with him. Hrut went out, and they began to talk, and Hauskuld told him the whole story of the bargain, and bade him to the feast, saying —

"I should be glad to know that thou dost not feel hurt though I did not tell thee when the bargain was being made."

"I should be better pleased," said Hrut, "to have nothing at all to do with it; for this match will bring luck neither to him nor to her; but still I will come to the feast if thou thinkest it will add any honour to thee."

"Of course I think so," said Hauskuld, and rode off home.

Oswif and Thorwald also asked men to come, so that no fewer than one hundred guests were asked.

There was a man named Swan, who dwelt in Bearfirth, which lies north from Steingrimsfirth. This Swan was a great wizard, and he was Hallgerda's mother's brother. He was quarrelsome, and hard to deal with, but Hallgerda asked him to the feast, and sends Thiostolf to him; so he went, and it soon got to friendship between him and Swan.

Now men come to the feast, and Hallgerda sat upon the cross-bench, and she was a very merry bride. Thiostolf was always talking to her, though he sometimes found time to speak to Swan, and men thought their talking strange.

The feast went off well, and Hauskuld paid down Hallgerda's portion with the greatest readiness. After he had done that, he said to Hrut —

"Shall I bring out any gifts beside?"

"The day will come," answered Hrut, "when thou wilt have to waste thy goods for Hallgerda's sake, so hold thy hand now."

Chapter 11
Thorwald's Slaying

Thorwald rode home from the bridal feast, and his wife with him, and Thiostolf, who rode by her horse's side, and still talked to her in a low voice. Oswif turned to his son and said —

"Art thou pleased with thy match? and how went it when ye talked together?"

"Well," said he, "she showed all kindness to me. Thou mightst see that by the way she laughs at every word I say."

"I don't think her laughter so hearty as thou dost," answered Oswif, "but this will be put to the proof by and by."

So they ride on till they come home, and at night she took her seat by her husband's side, and made room for Thiostolf next herself on the inside. Thiostolf and Thorwald had little to do with each other, and few words were thrown away between them that winter, and so time went on. Hallgerda was prodigal and grasping, and there was nothing that any of their neighbours had that she must not have too, and all that she had, no matter whether it were her own or belonged to others, she waited. But when the spring came there was a scarcity in the house, both of meal and stock fish, so Hallgerda went up to Thorwald and said —

"Thou must not be sitting indoors any longer, for we want for the house both meal and fish."

"Well," said Thorwald, "I did not lay in less for the house this year than I laid in before, and then it used to last till summer."

"What care I," said Hallgerda, "if thou and thy father have made your money by starving yourselves."

Then Thorwald got angry and gave her a blow on the face and drew blood, and went away and called his men and ran the skiff down to the shore. Then six of them jumped into her and rowed out to the Bear-isles, and began to load her with meal and fish.

Meantime it is said that Hallgerda sat out of doors heavy at heart. Thiostolf went up to her and saw the wound on her face, and said —

"Who has been playing thee this sorry trick?"

"My husband Thorwald," she said, "and thou stoodst aloof, though thou wouldst not if thou hadst cared at all for me."

"Because I knew nothing about it," said Thiostolf, "but I will avenge it."

Then he went away down to the shore and ran out a six-oared boat, and held in his hand a great axe that he had with a haft overlaid with iron. He steps into the boat and rows out to the Bear-isles, and when he got there all the men had rowed away but Thorwald and his followers, and he stayed by the skiff to load her, while they brought the goods down to him. So Thiostolf came up just then and jumped into the skiff and began to load with him, and after a while he said—

"Thou canst do but little at this work, and that little thou dost badly."

"Thinkest thou thou canst do it better?" said Thorwald.

"There's one thing to be done which I can do better than thou," said Thiostolf, and then he went on —

"The woman who is thy wife has made a bad match, and you shall not live much longer together."

Then Thorwald snatched up a fishing-knife that lay by him, and made a stab at Thiostolf; he had lifted his axe to his shoulder and dashed it down. It came on Thorwald's arm and crushed the wrist, but down fell the knife. Then Thiostolf lifted up his axe a second time and gave Thorwald a blow on the head, and he fell dead on the spot.

Chapter 12
Thiostolf's Flight

While this was going on, Thorwald's men came down with their load, but Thiostolf was not slow in his plans. He hewed with both hands at the gunwale of the skiff and cut it down about two planks; then he leapt into his boat, but the dark blue sea poured into the skiff, and down she went with all her freight. Down too sank Thorwald's body, so that his men could not see what had been done to him, but they knew well enough that he was dead, Thiostolf rowed away up the firth, but they shouted after him wishing him ill luck. He made them no answer, but rowed on till he got home, and ran the boat up on the beach, and went up to the house with his axe, all bloody as it was, on his shoulder. Hallgerda stood out of doors, and said —

"Thine axe is bloody; what hast thou done?"

"I have done now what will cause thee to be wedded a second time."

"Thou tellest me then that Thorwald is dead?" she said.

"So it is," said he, "and now look out for my safety."

"So I will," she said; "I will send thee north to Bearfirth, to Swanshol, and Swan, my kinsman, will receive thee with open arms. He is so mighty a man that no one will seek thee thither."

So he saddled a horse that she had, and jumped on his back, and rode off north to Bearfirth, to Swanshol, and Swan received him with open arms, and said —

"That's what I call a man who does not stick at trifles! And now I promise thee if they seek thee here, they shall get nothing but the greatest shame."

Now, the story goes back to Hallgerda, and how she behaved. She called on Liot the black, her kinsman, to go with her, and bade him saddle their horses, for she said — "I will ride home to my father".

While he made ready for their journey, she went to her chests and unlocked them, and called all the men of her house about her, and gave each of them some gift; but they all grieved at her going. Now she rides home to her father; and he received her well, for as yet he had not heard the news. But Hrut said to Hallgerda —

"Why did not Thorwald come with thee?" and she answered —

"He is dead."

Then Said Hauskuld —

"That was Thiostolf's doing?"

"It was," she said.

"Ah!" said Hauskuld, "Hrut was not for wrong when he told me that this bargain would draw mickle misfortune after it. But there's no good in troubling one's self about a thing that's done and gone."

Now the story must go back to Thorwald's mates, how there they ate, and how they begged the loan of a boat to get to the mainland. So a boat was lent them at once, and they rowed up the firth to Reykianess, and found Oswif, and told him these tidings.

He said, "Ill luck is the end of ill redes, and now I see how it has all gone. Hallgerda must have sent Thiostolf to Bearfirth, but she herself must have ridden home to her father. Let us now gather folk and follow him up thither north." So they did that, and went about asking for help, and got together many men. And then they all rode off to Steingrims river, and so on to Liotriverdale and Selriverdale, till they came to Bearfirth.

Now Swan began to speak, and gasped much. "Now Oswif's fetches are seeking us out." Then up sprung Thiostolf, but Swan said, "Go thou out with me, there won't be need of much". So they went out both of them, and Swan took a goatskin and wrapped it about his own head, and said, "Become mist and fog, become fright and wonder mickle to all those who seek thee".

Now, it must be told how Oswif, his friends, and his men are riding along the ridge; then came a great mist against them, and Oswif said, "This is Swan's doing; 'twere well if nothing worse followed". A little after a mighty darkness came before their eyes, so that they could see nothing, and then they fell off their horses' backs, and lost their horses, and dropped their weapons, and went over head and ears into bogs, and some went astray into the wood, till they were on the brink of bodily harm. Then Oswif said, "If I could only find my horse and weapons, then I'd turn back"; and he had scarce spoken these words than they saw somewhat, and found their horses and weapons. Then many still egged the others on to look after the chase once more; and so they did, and at once the same wonders befell them, and so they fared thrice. Then Oswif said, "Though the course be not good, let us still turn back. Now, we will take counsel a second time, and what now pleases my mind best, is to go and find Hauskuld, and ask atonement for my son; for there's hope of honour where there's good store of it."

So they rode thence to the Broadfirth dales, and there is nothing to be told about them till they come to Hauskuldstede, and Hrut was there before them. Oswif called out Hauskuld and Hrut, and they both went out and bade him good-day. After that they began to talk. Hauskuld asked Oswif whence he came. He said he had set out to search for Thiostolf, but couldn't find him. Hauskuld said he must have gone north to Swanshol, "and thither it is not every man's lot to go to find him".

"Well," says Oswif, "I am come hither for this, to ask atonement for my son from thee."

Hauskuld answered — "I did not slay thy son, nor did I plot his death; still it may be forgiven thee to look for atonement somewhere".

"Nose is next of kin, brother, to eyes," said Hrut, "and it is needful to stop all evil tongues, and to make him atonement for his son, and so mend thy daughter's state, for that will only be the case when this suit is dropped, and the less that is said about it the better it will be."

Hauskuld said — "Wilt thou undertake the award?"

"That I will," says Hrut, "nor will I shield thee at all in my award; for if the truth must be told thy daughter planned his death."

Then Hrut held his peace some little while, and afterwards he stood up, and said to Oswif — "Take now my hand in handsel as a token that thou lettest the suit drop".

So Oswif stood up and said — "This is not an atonement on equal terms when thy brother utters the award, but still thou (speaking to Hrut) hast behaved so well about it that I trust thee thoroughly to make it" Then he stood up and took Hauskuld's hand, and came to an atonement in the matter, on the understanding that Hrut was to make up his mind and utter the award before Oswif went away. After that, Hrut made his award, and said — "For the slaying of Thorwald I award two hundred in silver" — that was then thought a good price for a man — "and thou shalt pay it down at once, brother, and pay it too with an open hand".

Hauskuld did so, and then Hrut said to Oswif — "I will give thee a good cloak which I brought with me from foreign lands".

He thanked him for his gift, and went home well pleased at the way in which things had gone.

After that Hauskuld and Hrut came to Oswif to share the goods, and they and Oswif came to a good agreement about that too, and they went home with their share of the goods, and Oswif is now out of our story. Hallgerda begged Hauskuld to let her come back home to him, and he gave her leave, and for a long time there was much talk about Thorwald's slaying. As for Hallgerda'a goods they went on growing till they were worth a great sum.

Chapter 13
Glum's Wooing

Now three brothers are named in the story. One was called Thorarin, the second Ragi, and the third Glum. They were the sons of Olof the Halt, and were men of much worth and of great wealth in goods. Thorarin's surname was Ragi's brother; he had the Speakership of the Law after Rafn Heing's son. He was a very wise man, and lived at Varmalek, and he and Glum kept house together. Glum had been long abroad; he was a tall, strong, handsome man. Ragi their brother was a great man-slayer. Those brothers owned in the south Engey and Laugarness. One day the brothers Thorarin and Glum were talking together, and Thorarin asked Glum whether he meant to go abroad, as was his wont.

He answered — "I was rather thinking now of leaving off trading voyages".

"What hast thou then in thy mind? Wilt thou woo thee a wife?"

"That I will," says he, "if I could only get myself well matched."

Then Thorarin told off all the women who were unwedded in Borgarfirth, and asked him if he would have any of these — "Say the word, and I will ride with thee!"

But Glum answered — "I will have none of these".

"Say then the name of her thou wishest to have," says Thorarin.

Glum answered — "If thou must know, her name is Hallgerda, and she is Hauskuld's daughter away west in the dales".

"Well," says Thorarin, "'tis not with thee as the saw says, 'be warned by another's woe'; for she was wedded to a man, and she plotted his death."

Glum said — "May be such ill-luck will not befall her a second time, and sure I am she will not plot my death. But now, if thou wilt show me any honour, ride along with me to woo her."

Thorarin said — "There's no good striving against it, for what must be is sure to happen". Glum often talked the matter over with Thorarin, but he put it off a long time. At last it came about that they gathered men together and rode off ten in company, west to the dales, and came to Hauskuldstede. Hauskuld gave them a hearty welcome, and they stayed there that night. But early next morning, Hauskuld sends Hrut, and he came thither at once; and Hauskuld was out of doors when he rode into the "town". Then Hauskuld told Hrut what men had come thither.

"What may it be they want?" asked Hrut

"As yet," says Hauskuld, "they have not let out to me that they have any business."

"Still," says Hrut, "their business must be with thee. They will ask the hand of thy daughter, Hallgerda. If they do, what answer wilt thou make?"

"What dost thou advise me to say?" says Hauskuld.

"Thou shalt answer well," says Hrut; "but still make a clean breast of all the good and all the ill thou knowest of the woman."

But while the brothers were talking thus, out came the guests. Hauskuld greeted them well, and Hrut bade both Thorarin and his brothers good morning. After that they all began to talk, and Thorarin said —

"I am come hither, Hauskuld, with my brother Glum on this errand, to ask for Hallgerda thy daughter, at the hand of my brother Glum. Thou must know that he is a man of worth."

"I know well," says Hauskuld, "that ye are both of you powerful and worthy men; but I must tell you right out, that I chose a husband for her before, and that turned out most unluckily for us."

Thorarin answered — "We will not let that stand in the way of the bargain; for one oath shall not become all oaths, and this may prove to be a good match, though that turned out ill; besides Thiostolf had most hand in spoiling it".

Then Hrut spoke: "Now I will give you a bit of advice — this: if ye will not let all this that has already happened to Hallgerda stand in the way of the match, mind you do not let Thiostolf go south with her if the match comes off, and that he is never there longer than three nights at a time, unless Glum gives him leave, but fall an outlaw by Glum's hand without atonement if he stay there longer. Of course, it shall be in Glum's power to give him leave; but he will not if he takes my advice. And now this match, shall not be fulfilled, as the other was, without Hallgerda's knowledge. She shall now know the whole course of this bargain, and see Glum, and herself settle whether she will have him or not; and then she will not be able to lay the blame on others if it does not turn out well. And all this shall be without craft or guile."

Then Thorarin said — "Now, as always, it will prove best if thy advice be taken".

Then they sent for Hallgerda, and she came thither, and two women with her. She had on a cloak of rich blue wool, and under it a scarlet kirtle, and a silver girdle round her waist, but her hair came down on both sides of her bosom, and she had turned the locks up under her girdle. She sat down between Hrut and her father, and she greeted them all with kind words, and spoke well and boldly, and asked what was the news. After that she ceased speaking.

Then Glum said — "There has been some talk between thy father and my brother Thorarin and myself about a bargain. It was that I might get thee, Hallgerda, if it be thy will, as it is theirs; and now, if thou art a brave woman, thou wilt say right out whether the match is at all to thy mind; but if thou hast anything in thy heart against this bargain with us, then we will not say anything more about it."

Hallgerda said — "I know well that you are men of worth and might, ye brothers. I know too that now I shall be much better wedded than I was before; but what I want to know is, what you have said already about the match, and how far you have given your words in the matter. But so far as I now see of thee, I think I might love thee well if we can but hit it off as to temper."

So Glum himself told her all about the bargain, and left nothing out, and then he asked Hauskuld and Hrut whether he had repeated it right. Hauskuld said he had; and then Hallgerda said — "Ye have dealt so well with me in this matter, my father and Hrut, that I will do what ye advise, and this bargain shall be struck as ye have settled it".

Then Hrut said — "Methinks it were best that Hauskuld and I should name witnesses, and that Hallgerda should betroth herself, if the Lawman thinks that right and lawful".

"Right and lawful it is," says Thorarin.

After that Hallgerda's goods were valued, and Glum was to lay down as much against them, and they were to go shares, half and half, in the whole. Then Glum bound himself to Hallgerda as his betrothed, and they rode away home south; but Hauskuld was to keep the wedding-feast at his house. And now all is quiet till men ride to the wedding.

Chapter 14
Glum's Wedding

Those brothers gathered together a great company, and they were all picked men. They rode west to the dales and came to Hauskuldstede, and there they found a great gathering to meet them. Hauskuld and Hrut, and their friends, filled one bench, and the bridegroom the other. Hallgerda sat upon the cross-bench on the dais, and behaved well. Thiostolf went about with his axe raised in air, and no one seemed to know that he was there, and so the wedding went off well. But when the feast was over, Hallgerda went away south with Glum and his brothers. So when they came south to Varmalek, Thorarin asked Hallgerda if she would undertake the housekeeping, "No, I will not," she said. Hallgerda kept her temper down that winter, and they liked her well enough. But when the spring came, the brothers talked about their property, and Thorarin said — "I will give up to you the house at Varmalek, for that is readiest to your hand, and I will go down south to Laugarness and live there, but Engey we will have both of us in common".

Glum was willing enough to do that. So Thorarin went down to the south of that district, and Glum and his wife stayed behind there, and lived in the house at Varmalek.

Now Hallgerda got a household about her; she was prodigal in giving, and grasping in getting. In the summer she gave birth to a girl. Glum asked her what name it was to have.

"She shall be called after my father's mother, and her name shall be Thorgerda," for she came down from Sigurd Fafnir's-bane on the father's side, according to the family pedigree.

So the maiden was sprinkled with water, and had this name given her, and there she grew up, and got like her mother in looks and feature. Glum and Hallgerda agreed well together, and so it went on for a while. About that time these tidings were heard from the north and Bearfirth, how Swan had rowed out to fish in the spring, and a great storm came down on him from the east, and how he was driven ashore at Fishless, and he and his men were there lost. But the fishermen who were at Kalback thought they saw Swan go into the fell at Kalbackshorn, and that he was greeted well; but some spoke against that story, and said there was nothing in it. But this all knew that he was never seen again either alive or dead. So when Hallgerda heard that, she thought she had a great loss in her mother's brother. Glum begged Thorarin to change lands with him, but he said he would not; "but," said he, "if I outlive you, I mean to have Varmalek to myself". When Glum told this to Hallgerda, she said, "Thorarin has indeed a right to expect this from us".

Chapter 15
Thiostolf goes to Glum's House

Thiostolf had beaten one of Hauskuld's house-carles, so he drove him away. He took his horse and weapons, and said to Hauskuld —

"Now, I will go away and never come back."

"All will be glad at that," says Hauskuld.

Thiostolf rode till he came to Varmalek, and there he got a hearty welcome from Hallgerda, and not a bad one from Glum. He told Hallgerda how her father had driven him away, and begged her to give him her help and countenance. She answered him by telling him she could say nothing about his staying there before she had seen Glum about it.

"Does it go well between you?" he says.

"Yes," she says, "our love runs smooth enough."

After that she went to speak to Glum, and threw her arms round his neck and said —

"Wilt thou grant me a boon which I wish to ask of thee?"

"Grant it I will," he says, "if it be right and seemly; but what is it thou wishest to ask?"

"Well," she said, "Thiostolf has been driven away from the west, and what I want thee to do is to let him stay here; but I will not take it crossly if it is not to thy mind."

Glum said — "Now that thou behavest so well, I will grant thee thy boon; but I tell thee, if he takes to any ill he shall be sent off at once".

She goes then to Thiostolf and tells him, and he answered —

"Now, thou art still good, as I had hoped."

After that he was there, and kept himself down a little white, but then it was the old story, he seemed to spoil all the good he found; for he gave way to no one save to Hallgerda alone, but she never took his side in his brawls with others. Thorarin, Glum's brother, blamed him for letting him be there, and said ill luck would come of it, and all would happen as had happened before if he were there. Glum answered him well and kindly, but still kept on in his own way.

Chapter 16
Glum's Sheep Hunt

Now once on a time when autumn came, it happened that men had hard work to get their flocks home, and many of Glum's wethers were missing. Then Glum said to Thiostolf —

"Go thou up on the fell with my house-carles and see if ye cannot find out anything about the sheep."

"'Tis no business of mine," says Thiostolf, "to hunt up sheep, and this one thing is quite enough to hinder it. I won't walk in thy thralls' footsteps. But go thyself, and then I'll go with thee."

About this they had many words. The weather was good, and Hallgerda was sitting out of doors. Glum went up to her and said —

"Now Thiostolf and I have had a quarrel, and we shall not live much longer together." And so he told her all that they had been talking about.

Then Hallgerda spoke up for Thiostolf, and they had many words about him. At last Glum gave her a blow with his hand, and said —

"I will strive no longer with thee," and with that he went away.

Now she loved him much, and could not calm herself, but wept out loud. Thiostolf went up to her and said —

"This is sorry sport for thee, and so it must not be often again."

"Nay," she said, "but thou shalt not avenge this, nor meddle at all whatever passes between Glum and me."

He went off with a spiteful grin.

Chapter 17
Glum's Slaying

Now Glum called men to follow him, and Thiostolf got ready and went with them. So they went up South Reykiardale and then up along by Baugagil and so south to Crossfell. But some of his band he sent to the Sulafells, and they all found very many sheep. Some of them, too, went by way of Scoradale, and it came about at last that those twain, Glum and Thiostolf, were left alone together. They went south from Crossfell and found there a flock of wild sheep, and they went from the south towards the fell, and tried to drive them down; but still the sheep got away from them up on the fell. Then each began to scold the other, and Thiostolf said at last that Glum had no strength save to tumble about in Hallgerda's arms.

Then Glum said —

"'A man's foes are those of his own house.' Shall I take upbraiding from thee, runaway thrall as thou art?"

Thiostolf said —

"Thou shalt soon have to own that I am no thrall, for I will not yield an inch to thee."

Then Glum got angry, and cut at him with his hand-axe, but he threw his axe in the way, and the blow fell on the haft with a downward stroke and bit into it about the breadth of two fingers. Thiostolf cut at him at once with his axe, and smote him on the shoulder, and the stroke hewed asunder the shoulderbone and collarbone, and the wound bled inwards. Glum grasped at Thiostolf with his left hand so fast that he fell; but Glum could not hold him, for death came over him. Then Thiostolf covered his body with stones, and took off his gold ring. Then he went straight to Varmalek. Hallgerda was sitting out of doors, and saw that his axe was bloody. He said —

"I know not what thou wilt think of it, but I tell thee Glum is slain."

"That must be thy deed?" she says.

"So it is," he says.

She laughed and said —

"Thou dost not stand for nothing in this sport."

"What thinkest thou is best to be done now?" he asked.

"Go to Hrut, my father's brother," she said, "and let him see about thee."

"I do not know," says Thiostolf, "whether this is good advice; but still I will take thy counsel in this matter."

So he took his horse, and rode west to Hrutstede that night. He binds his horse at the back of the house, and then goes round to the door, and gives a great knock. After that he walks round the house, north about. It happened that Hrut was awake. He sprang up at once, and put on his jerkin and pulled on his shoes. Then he took up his sword, and wrapped a cloak about his left arm, up as far as the elbow. Men woke up just as he went out; there he saw a tall stout man at the back of the house, and knew it was Thiostolf. Hrut asked him what news.

"I tell thee Glum is slain," says Thiostolf.

"Who did the deed?" says Hrut.

"I slew him," says Thiostolf.

"Why rodest thou hither?" says Hrut.

"Hallgerda sent me to thee," says Thiostolf.

"Then she has no hand in this deed," says Hrut, and drew his sword. Thiostolf saw that, and would not be behind hand, so he cuts at Hrut at once. Hrut got out of the way of the stroke by a quick turn, and at the same time struck the back of the axe so smartly with a side-long blow of his left hand, that it flew out of Thiostolf's grasp. Then Hrut made a blow with the sword in his right hand at Thiostolf's leg, just above the knee, and cut it almost off so that it hung by a little piece, and sprang in upon him at the same time, and thrust him hard back. After that he smote him on the head, and dealt him his death-blow. Thiostolf fell down on his back at full length, and then out came Hrut's men, and saw the tokens of the deed. Hrut made them take Thiostolf away, and throw stones over his body, and then he went to find Hauskuld, and told him of Glum's slaying, and also of Thiostolf's. He thought it harm that Glum was dead and gone, but thanked him for killing Thiostolf. A little while after, Thorarin Ragi's brother hears of his brother Glum's death, then he rides with eleven men behind him west to Hauskuldstede, and Hauskuld welcomed him with both hands, and he is there the night. Hauskuld sent at once for Hrut to come to him, and he went at once, and next day they spoke much of the slaying of Glum, and Thorarin said — "Wilt thou make me any atonement for my brother, for I have had a great loss?"

Hauskuld answered — "I did not slay thy brother, nor did my daughter plot his death; but as soon as ever Hrut knew it he slew Thiostolf".

Then Thorarin held his peace, and thought the matter had taken a bad turn. But Hrut said — "Let us make his journey good; he has indeed had a heavy loss, and if we do that we shall be well spoken of. So let us give him gifts, and then he will be our friend ever afterwards."

So the end of it was that those brothers gave him gifts, and he rode back south. He and Hallgerda changed homesteads in the spring, and she went south to Laugarness and he to Varmalek. And now Thorarin is out of the story.

Chapter 18
Fiddle Mord's Death

Now it must be told how Fiddle Mord took a sickness and breathed his last; and that was thought great scathe. His daughter Unna took all the goods he left behind him. She was then still unmarried the second time. She was very lavish, and unthrifty of her property; so that her goods and ready money wasted away, and at last she had scarce anything left but land and stock.

Chapter 19
Gunnar comes into the Story

There was a man whose name was Gunnar. He was one of Unna's kinsmen, and his mother's name was Rannveig. Gunnar's father was named Hamond. Gunnar Hamond's son dwelt at Lithend, in the Fleetlithe. He was a tall man in growth, and a strong man — best skilled in arms of all men. He could cut or thrust or shoot if he chose as well with his left as with his right hand, and he smote so swiftly with his sword, that three seemed to flash through the air at once. He was the best shot with the bow of all men, and never missed his mark. He could leap more than his own height, with all his war-gear, and as far backwards as forwards. He could swim like a seal, and there was no game in which it was any good for anyone to strive with him; and so it has been said that no man was his match. He was handsome of feature, and fair skinned. His nose was straight, and a little turned up at the end. He was blue-eyed and bright-eyed, and ruddy-cheeked. His hair thick, and of good hue, and hanging down in comely curls. The most courteous of men was he, of sturdy frame and strong will, bountiful and gentle, a fast friend, but hard to please when making them. He was wealthy in goods. His brother's name was Kolskegg; he was a tall strong man, a noble fellow, and undaunted in everything. Another brother's name was Hjort; he was then in his childhood. Orm Skogarnef was a base-born brother of Gunnar's; he does not come into this story. Arnguda was the name of Gunnar's sister. Hroar, the priest at Tongue, had her to wife.

Chapter 20
Of Njal and his Children

There was a man whose name was Njal. He was the son of Thorgeir Gelling, the son of Thorolf. Njal's mother's name was Asgerda. Njal dwelt at Bergthorsknoll in the land-isles; he had another homestead on Thorolfsfell. Njal was wealthy in goods, and handsome of face; no beard grew on his chin. He was so great a lawyer, that his match was not to be found. Wise too he was, and foreknowing and foresighted. Of good counsel, and ready to give it, and all that he advised men was sure to be the best for them to do. Gentle and generous, he unravelled every man's knotty points who came to see him about them. Bergthora was his wife's name; she was Skarphedinn's daughter, a very high-spirited, brave-hearted woman, but somewhat hard-tempered. They had six children, three daughters and three sons, and they all come afterwards into this story.

Chapter 21
Unna goes to see Gunnar

Now it must be told how Unna had lost all her ready money. She made her way to Lithend, and Gunnar greeted his kinswoman well. She stayed there that night, and the next morning they sat out of doors and talked. The end of their talk was that she told him how heavily she was pressed for money.

"This is a bad business," he said.

"What help wilt thou give me out of my distress?" she asked.

He answered — "Take as much money as thou needest from what I have out at interest".

"Nay," she said, "I will not waste thy goods."

"What then dost thou wish?"

"I wish thee to get back my goods out of Hrut's hands," she answered.

"That, methinks, is not likely," said he, "when thy father could not get them back, and yet he was a great lawyer, but I know little about law."

She answered — "Hrut pushed that matter through rather by boldness than by law; besides, my father was old, and that was why men thought it better not to drive things to the uttermost. And now there is none of my kinsmen to take this suit up if thou hast not daring enough."

"I have courage enough," he replied, "to get these goods back; but I do not know how to take the suit up."

"Well!" she answered, "go and see Njal of Bergthorsknoll, he will know how to give thee advice. Besides, he is a great friend of thine."

"'Tis like enough he will give me good advice, as he gives it to every one else," says Gunnar.

So the end of their talk was, that Gunnar undertook her cause, and gave her the money she needed for her housekeeping, and after that she went home.

Now Gunnar rides to see Njal, and he made him welcome, and they began to talk at once.

Then Gunnar said — "I am come to seek a bit of good advice from thee".

Njal replied — "Many of my friends are worthy of this, but still I think I would take more pains for none than for thee".

Gunnar said — "I wish to let thee know that I have undertaken to get Unna's goods back from Hrut".

"A very hard suit to undertake," said Njal, "and one very hazardous how it will go; but still I will get it up for thee in the way I think likeliest to succeed, and the end will be good if thou breakest none of the rules I lay down; if thou dost, thy life is in danger."

"Never fear; I will break none of them," said Gunnar.

Then Njal held his peace for a little while, and after that he spoke as follows:—

Chapter 22
Njal's Advice

"I have thought over the suit, and it will do so. Thou shalt ride from home with two men at thy back. Over all thou shalt have a great rough cloak, and under that, a russet kirtle of cheap stuff, and under all, thy good clothes. Thou must take a small axe in thy hand, and each of you must have two horses, one fat, the other lean. Thou shalt carry hardware and smith's work with thee hence, and ye must ride off early to-morrow morning, and when ye are come across Whitewater westwards, mind and slouch thy hat well over thy brows. Then men will ask who is this tall man, and thy mates shall say — 'Here is Huckster Hedinn the Big, a man from Eyjafirth, who is going about with smith's work for sale'. This Hedinn is ill-tempered and a chatterer — a fellow who thinks he alone knows everything. Very often he snatches back his wares, and flies at men if everything is not done as he wishes. So thou shalt ride west to Borgarfirth offering all sorts of wares for sale, and be sure often to cry off thy bargains, so that it will be noised abroad that Huckster Hedinn is the worst of men to deal with, and that no lies have been told of his bad behaviour. So thou shalt ride to Northwaterdale, and to Hrutfirth, and Laxriverdale, till thou comest to Hauskuldstede. There thou must stay a night, and sit in the lowest place, and hang thy head down. Hauskuld will tell them all not to meddle nor make with Huckster Hedinn, saying he is a rude unfriendly fellow. Next morning thou must be off early and go to the farm nearest Hrutstede. There thou must offer thy goods for sale, praising up all that is worst, and tinkering up the faults. The master of the house will pry about and find out the faults. Thou must snatch the wares away from him, and speak ill to him. He will say — 'Twas not to be hoped that thou wouldst behave well to him, when thou behavest ill to every one else. Then thou shalt fly at him, though it is not thy wont, but mind and spare thy strength, that thou mayest not be found out. Then a man will be sent to Hrutstede to tell Hrut he had best come and part you. He will come at once and ask thee to his house, and thou must accept his offer. Thou shalt greet Hrut, and he will answer well. A place will be given thee on the lower bench over against Hrut's high-seat. He will ask if thou art from the North, and thou shalt answer that thou art a man of Eyjafirth. He will go on to ask if there are very many famous men there. 'Shabby fellows enough and to spare,' thou must answer. 'Dost thou know Reykiardale and the parts about?' he will ask. To which thou must answer — 'I know all Iceland by heart.'"

" 'Are there any stout champions left in Reykiardale?' he will ask. 'Thieves and scoundrels,' thou shalt answer. Then Hrut will smile and think it sport to listen. You two will go on to talk of the men in the Eastfirth Quarter, and thou must always find something to say against them. At last your talk will come to Rangrivervale, and then thou must say, there is small choice of men left in those parts since Fiddle Mord died. At the same time sing some stave to please Hrut, for I know thou art a skald. Hrut will ask what makes thee say there is never a man to come in Mord's place; and then thou must answer, that he was so wise a man and so good a taker up of suits, that he never made a false step in upholding his leadership. He will ask — 'Dost thou know how matters fared between me and him?'

" 'I know all about it,' thou must reply, 'he took thy wife from thee, and thou hadst not a word to say.'

"Then Hrut will ask — 'Dost thou not think it was some disgrace to him when he could not get back his goods, though he set the suit on foot?'

" 'I can answer thee that well enough,' thou must say, 'Thou challengedst him to single combat; but he was old, and so his friends advised him not to fight with thee, and then they let the suit fall to the ground.'

" 'True enough,' Hrut will say. 'I said so, and that passed for law among foolish men; but the suit might have been taken up again at another Thing if he had the heart.'

" 'I know all that,' thou must say.

"Then he will ask — 'Dost thou know anything about law?'

" 'Up in the North I am thought to know something about it,' thou shalt say. 'But still I should like thee to tell me how this suit should be taken up.'

" 'What suit dost thou mean?' he will ask.

" 'A suit,' thou must answer, 'which does not concern me. I want to know how a man must set to work who wishes to get back Unna's dower.'

"Then Hrut will say — 'In this suit I must be summoned so that I can hear the summons, or I must be summoned here in my lawful house'.

" 'Recite the summons, then,' thou must say, and I will say it after thee.'

"Then Hrut will summon himself; and mind and pay great heed to every word he says. After that Hrut will bid thee repeat the summons, and thou must do so, and say it all wrong, so that no more than every other word is right.

"Then Hrut will smile and not mistrust thee, but say that scarce a word is right. Thou must throw the blame on thy companions, and say they put thee out, and then thou must ask him to say the words first, word by word, and to let thee say the words after him. He will give thee leave, and summon himself in the suit, and thou shalt summon after him there and then, and this time say every word right. When it is done, ask Hrut if that were rightly summoned, and he will answer 'there is no flaw to be found in it'. Then thou shalt say in a loud voice, so that thy companions may hear —

" 'I summon thee in the suit which Unna Mord's daughter has made over to me with her plighted hand.'

"But when men are sound asleep, you shall rise and take your bridles and saddles, and tread softly, and go out of the house, and put your saddles on your fat horses in the fields, and so ride off on them, but leave the others behind you. You must ride up into the hills away from the home pastures and stay there three nights, for about so long will they seek you. After that ride home south, riding always by night and resting by day. As for us we will then ride this summer to the Thing, and help thee in thy suit." So Gunnar thanked Njal, and first of all rode home.

Chapter 23
Huckster Hedinn

Gunnar rode from home two nights afterwards, and two men with him; they rode along until they got on Bluewoodheath, and then men on horseback met them and asked who that tall man might be of whom so little was seen. But his companions said it was Huckster Hedinn. Then the others said a worse was not to be looked for behind, when such a man as he went before. Hedinn at once made as though he would have set upon them, but yet each went their way. So Gunnar went on doing everything as Njal had laid it down for him, and when he came to Hauskuldstede he stayed there the night, and thence he went down the dale till he came to the next farm to Hrutstede. There he offered his wares for sale, and Hedinn fell at once upon the farmer. This was told to Hrut, and he sent for Hedinn, and Hedinn went at once to see Hrut, and had a good welcome. Hrut seated him over against himself, and their talk went pretty much as Njal had guessed; but when they came to talk of Rangrivervale, and Hrut asked about the men there, Gunnar sung this stave —

> Men in sooth are slow to find, —
> So the people speak by stealth,
> Often this hath reached my ears, -
> All through Rangar's rolling vales.
> Still I trow that Fiddle Mord,
> Tried his hand in fight of yore;
> Sure was never gold-bestower,
> Such a man for might and wit.

Then Hrut said, "Thou art a skald, Hedinn. But hast thou never heard how things went between me and Mord?" Then Hedinn sung another stave —

> Once I ween I heard the rumour,
> How the Lord of rings bereft thee;
> From thine arms earth's offspring tearing,
> Trickful he and trustful thou.
> Then the men, the buckler-bearers,
> Begged the mighty gold-begetter,
> Sharp sword oft of old he reddened,
> Not to stand in strife with thee.

So they went on, till Hrut, in answer told him how the suit must be taken up, and recited the summons. Hedinn repeated it all wrong, and Hrut burst out laughing, and had no mistrust. Then he said, Hrut must summon once more, and Hrut did so. Then Hedinn repeated the summons a second time, and this time right, and called his companions to witness how he summoned Hrut in a suit which Unna Mord's daughter had made over to him with her plighted hand. At night he went to sleep like other men, but as soon as ever Hrut was sound asleep, they took their clothes and arms, and went out and came to their horses, and rode off across the river, and so up along the bank by Hiardarholt till the dale broke off among the hills, and so there they are upon the fells between Laxriverdale and Hawkdale, having got to a spot where no one could find them unless he had fallen on them by chance.

Hauskuld wakes up that night at Hauskuldstede, and roused all his household, "I will tell you my dream," he said. "I thought I saw a great bear go out of this house, and I knew at once this beast's match was not to be found; two cubs followed him, wishing well to the bear, and they all made for Hrutstede, and went into the house there. After that I woke. Now I wish to ask if any of you saw aught about yon tall man."

Then one man answered him — "I saw how a golden fringe and a bit of scarlet cloth peeped out at his arm, and on his right arm he had a ring of gold".

Hauskuld said — "This beast is no man's fetch, but Gunnar's of Lithend, and now methinks I see all about it. Up! let us ride to Hrutstede." And they did so. Hrut lay in his locked bed, and asks who have come there? Hauskuld tells who he is, and asked what guests might be there in the house.

"Only Huckster Hedinn is here," says Hrut.

"A broader man across the back, it will be, I fear," says Hauskuld, "I guess here must have been Gunnar of Lithend."

"Then there has been a pretty trial of cunning," says Hrut.

"What has happened?" says Hauskuld.

"I told him how to take up Unna's suit, and I summoned myself and he summoned after, and now he can use this first step in the suit, and it is right in law."

"There has, indeed, been a great falling off of wit on one side," said Hauskuld, "and Gunnar cannot have planned it all by himself; Njal must be at the bottom of this plot, for there is not his match for wit in all the land."

Now they look for Hedinn, but he is already off and away; after that they gathered folk, and looked for them three days, but could not find them. Gunnar rode south from the fell to Hawkdale and so east of Skard, and north to Holtbeaconheath, and so on until he got home.

Chapter 24
Gunnar and Hrut Strive at the Thing

Gunnar rode to the Althing, and Hrut and Hauskuld rode thither too with a very great company. Gunnar pursues his suit, and began by calling on his neighbours to bear witness, but Hrut and his brother had it in their minds to make an onslaught on him, but they mistrusted their strength.

Gunnar next went to the court of the men of Broadfirth, and bade Hrut listen to his oath and declaration of the cause of the suit, and to all the proofs which he was about to bring forward. After that he took his oath, and declared his case. After that he brought forward his witnesses of the summons, along with his witnesses that the suit had been handed over to him. All this time Njal was not at the court. Now Gunnar pursued his suit till he called on the defendant to reply. Then Hrut took witness, and said the suit was naught, and that there was a flaw in the pleading; he declared that it had broken down because Gunnar had failed to call those three witnesses which ought to have been brought before the court. The first, that which was taken before the marriage-bed, the second, before the man's door, the third, at the Hill of Laws. By this time Njal was come to the court and said the suit and pleading might still he kept alive if they chose to strive in that way.

"No," says Gunnar, "I will not have that; I will do the same to Hrut as he did to Mord my kinsman; — or, are those brothers Hrut and Hauskuld so near that they may hear my voice?"

"Hear it we can," says Hrut. "What dost thou wish?"

Gunnar said — "Now all men here present be ear-witnesses, that I challenge thee Hrut to single combat, and we shall fight to-day on the holm, which is here in Axewater. But if thou wilt not fight with me, then pay up all the money this very day."

After that Gunnar sung a stave —

> Yes, so must it be, this morning —
> Now my mind is full of fire —
> Hrut with me on yonder island
> Raises roar of helm and shield.
> All that hear my words bear witness,
> Warriors grasping Woden's guard,
> Unless the wealthy wight down payeth
> Dower of wife with flowing veil.

After that Gunnar went away from the court with all his followers. Hrut and Hauskuld went home too, and the suit was never pursued nor defended from that day forth. Hrut said, as soon as he got inside the booth, "This has never happened to me before, that any man has offered me combat and I have shunned it".

"Then thou must mean to fight," says Hauskuld, "but that shall not be if I have my way; for thou comest no nearer to Gunnar than Mord would have come to thee, and we had better both of us pay up the money to Gunnar."

After that the brothers asked the householders of their own country what they would lay down, and they one and all said they would lay down as much as Hrut wished.

"Let us go then," says Hauskuld, "to Gunner's booth, and pay down the money out of hand." That was told to Gunnar, and he went out into the doorway of the booth, and Hauskuld said —

"Now it is thine to take the money."

Gunnar said —

"Pay it down, then, for I am ready to take it."

So they paid down the money truly out of hand, and then Hauskuld said — "Enjoy it now, as thou hast gotten it". Then Gunnar sang another stave —

> Men who wield the blade of battle
> Hoarded wealth may well enjoy,
> Guileless gotten this at least,
> Golden meed I fearless take;
> But if we for woman's quarrel,
> Warriors born to brandish sword,
> Glut the wolf with manly gore,
> Worse the lot of both would be.

Hrut answered — "Ill will be thy meed for this".

"Be that as it may," says Gunnar.

Then Hauskuld and his brother went home to their booth, and he had much upon his mind, and said to Hrut —

"Will this unfairness of Gunnar's never be avenged?"

"Not so," says Hrut; "'twill be avenged on him sure enough, but we shall have no share nor profit in that vengeance. And after all it is most likely that he will turn to our stock to seek for friends."

After that they left off speaking of the matter. Gunnar showed Njal the money, and he said — "The suit has gone off well".

"Ay," says Gunnar, "but it was all thy doing."

Now men rode home from the Thing, and Gunnar got very great honour from the suit. Gunnar handed over all the money to Unna, and would have none of it, but said he thought he ought to look for more help from her and her kin hereafter than from other men. She said, so it should be.

Chapter 25
Unna's Second Wedding

There was a man named Valgard, he kept house at Hof by Rangriver, he was the son of Jorund the Priest, and his brother was Wolf Aurpriest. Those brothers. Wolf Aurpriest, and Valgard the guileful, set off to woo Unna, and she gave herself away to Valgard without the advice of any of her kinsfolk. But Gunnar and Njal, and many others thought ill of that, for he was a cross-grained man and had few friends. They begot between them a son, whose name was Mord, and he is long in this story. When he was grown to man's estate, he worked ill to his kinsfolk, but worst of all to Gunnar. He was a crafty man in his temper, but spiteful in his counsels.

Now we will name Njal's sons. Skarphedinn was the eldest of them. He was a tall man in growth and strong withal; a good swordsman; he could swim like a seal, the swiftest-footed of men, and bold and dauntless; he had a great flow of words and quick utterance; a good skald too; but still for the most part he kept himself well in hand; his hair was dark brown, with crisp curly locks; he had good eyes; his features were sharp, and his face ashen pale, his nose turned up and his front teeth stuck out, and his mouth was very ugly. Still he was the most soldier-like of men.

Grim was the name of Njal's second son. He was fair of face and wore his hair long. His hair was dark, and he was comelier to look on than Skarphedinn. A tall strong man.

Helgi was the name of Njal's third son. He too was fair of face and had fine hair. He was a strong man and well-skilled in arms. He was a man of sense and knew well how to behave. They were all unwedded at that time, Njal's sons.

Hauskuld was the fourth of Njal's sons. He was base-born. His mother was Rodny, and she was Hauskuld's daughter, the sister of Ingialld of the Springs.

Njal asked Skarphedinn one day if he would take to himself a wife. He bade his father settle the matter. Then Njal asked for his hand Thorhilda, the daughter of Ranvir of Thorolfsfell, and that was why they had another homestead there after that. Skarphedinn got Thorhilda, but he stayed still with his father to the end. Grim wooed Astrid of Deepback; she was a widow and very wealthy. Grim got her to wife, and yet lived on with Njal.

Chapter 26
Of Asgrim and his Children

There was a man named Asgrim. He was Ellidagrim's son. The brother of Asgrim Ellidagrim's son was Sigfus.

Asgrim had two sons, and both of them were named Thorhall. They were both hopeful men. Grim was the name of another of Asgrim's sons, and Thorhalla was his daughter's name. She was the fairest of women, and well behaved.

Njal came to talk with his son Helgi, and said, "I have thought of a match for thee, if thou wilt follow my advice".

"That I will surely," says he, "for I know that thou both meanest me well, and canst do well for me; but whither hast thou turned thine eyes?"

"We will go and woo Asgrim Ellidagrim's son's daughter, for that is the best choice we can make."

Chapter 27
Helgi Njal's Son's Wooing

A little after they rode out across Thurso water, and fared till they came into Tongue. Asgrim was at home, and gave them a hearty welcome; and they were there that night. Next morning they began to talk, and then Njal raised the question of the wooing, and asked for Thorhalla for his son Helgi's hand. Asgrim answered that well, and said there were no men with whom he would be more willing to make this bargain than with them. They fell a-talking then about terms, and the end of it was that Asgrim betrothed his daughter to Helgi, and the bridal day was named. Gunnar was at that feast, and many other of the best men. After the feast Njal offered to foster in his house Thorhall, Asgrim's son, and he was with Njal long after. He loved Njal more than his own father. Njal taught him law, so that he became the greatest lawyer in Iceland in those days.

Chapter 28
Hallvard comes out to Iceland

There came a ship out from Norway, and ran into Arnbæl's Oyce, and the master of the ship was Hallvard, the white, a man from the Bay. He went to stay at Lithend, and was with Gunnar that winter, and was always asking him to fare abroad with him. Gunnar spoke little about it, but yet said more unlikely things might happen; and about spring he went over to Bergthorsknoll to find out from Njal whether he thought it a wise step in him to go abroad.

"I think it is wise," says Njal; "they will think thee there an honourable man, as thou art."

"Wilt thou perhaps take my goods into thy keeping while I am away, for I wish my brother Kolskegg to fare with me; but I would that thou shouldst see after my household along with my mother."

"I will not throw anything in the way of that," says Njal; "lean on me in this thing as much as thou likest."

"Good go with thee for thy words," says Gunnar, and he rides then home.

The Easterling [the Norseman Hallvard] fell again to talk with Gunnar that he should fare abroad. Gunnar asked if he had ever sailed to other lands? He said he had sailed to every one of them that lay between Norway and Russia, and so, too, I have sailed to Biarmaland.

"Wilt thou sail with me eastward ho?" says Gunnar.

"That I will of a surety," says he.

Then Gunnar made up his mind to sail abroad with him. Njal took all Gunnar's goods into his keeping.

Chapter 29
Gunnar goes Abroad

So Gunnar fared abroad, and Kolskegg with him. They sailed first to Tnsberg, and were there that winter. There had then been a shift of rulers in Norway, Harold Grayfell was then dead, and so was Gunnhillda. Earl Hacon the Bad, Sigurd's son, Hacon's son, Gritgarth's son, then ruled the realm. The mother of Hacon was Bergliot, the daughter of Earl Thorir. Her mother was Olof harvest-heal. She was Harold Fair-hair's daughter.

Hallvard asks Gunnar if he would make up his mind to go to Earl Hacon?

"No; I will not do that," says Gunnar. "Hast thou ever a long-ship?"

"I have two," he says.

"Then I would that we two went on warfare; and let us get men to go with us."

"I will do that," says Hallvard.

After that they went to the Bay, and took with them two ships, and fitted them out thence. They had good choice of men, for much praise was said of Gunnar.

"Whither wilt thou first fare?" says Gunnar.

"I wish to go south-east to Hisingen, to see my kinsman Oliver," says Hallvard.

"What dost thou want of him?" says Gunnar.

He answered — "He is a fine brave fellow, and he will be sure to get us some more strength for our voyage".

"Then let us go thither," says Gunnar.

So, as soon as they were "boun," they held on east to Hisingen, and had there a hearty welcome. Gunnar had only been there a short time ere Oliver made much of him. Oliver asks about his voyage, and Hallvard says that Gunnar wishes to go a-warfaring to gather goods for himself.

"There's no use thinking of that," says Oliver, "when ye have no force."

"Well," says Hallvard, "then you may add to it."

"So I do mean to strengthen Gunnar somewhat," says Oliver; "and though thou reckonest thyself my kith and kin, I think there is more good in him."

"What force, now, wilt thou add to ours?" he asks.

"Two long-ships, one with twenty, and the other with thirty seats for rowers."

"Who shall man them?" asks Hallvard.

"I will man one of them with my own house-carles, and the freemen around shall man the other. But still I have found out that strife has come into the river, and I know not whether ye two will be able to get away; for they are in the river."

"Who?" says Hallvard.

"Brothers twain," says Oliver; "one's name is Vandil and the other's Karli, sons of Sjolf the Old, east away out of Gothland."

Hallvard told Gunnar that Oliver had added some ships to theirs, and Gunnar was glad at that. They busked them for their voyage thence, till they were "all-boun". Then Gunnar and Hallvard went before Oliver, and thanked him; he bade them fare warily for the sake of those brothers.

Chapter 30
Gunnar goes A-sea-roving

So Gunnar held on out of the river, and he and Kolskegg were both on board one ship. But Hallvard was on board another. Now, they see the ships before them, and then Gunnar spoke, and said —

"Let us be ready for anything if they turn towards us! but else let us have nothing to do with them."

So they did that, and made all ready on board their ships. The others patted their ships asunder, and made a fareway between the ships. Gunnar fared straight on between the ships, but Vandil caught up a grappling-iron, and cast it between their ships and Gunnar's ship, and began at once to drag it towards him.

Oliver had given Gunnar a good sword; Gunnar now drew it, and had not yet put on his helm. He leapt at once on the forecastle of Vandil's ship, and gave one man his death-blow. Karli ran his ship alongside the other side of Gunnar's ship, and hurled a spear athwart the deck, and aimed at him about the waist. Gunnar sees this, and turned him about so quickly, that no eye could follow him, and caught the spear with his left hand, and hurled it back at Karli's ship, and that man got his death who stood before it. Kolskegg snatched up a grapnel and casts it at Karli's ship, and the fluke fell inside the hold, and went out through one of the planks, and in rushed the coal-blue sea, and all the men sprang on board other ships.

Now Gunnar leapt back to his own ship, and then Hallvard came up, and now a great battle arose. They saw now that their leader was unflinching, and every man did as well as he could. Sometimes Gunnar smote with the sword, and sometimes he hurled the spear, and many a man had his bane at his hand. Kolskegg backed him well. As for Karli, he hastened in a ship to his brother Vandil, and thence they fought that day. During the day Kolskegg took a rest on Gunnar's ship, and Gunnar sees that. Then he sung a song —

> For the eagle ravine-eager,
> Raven of my race, to-day
> Better surely hast thou catered,
> Lord of gold, than for thyself;
> Here the morn come greedy ravens,
> Many a rill of wolf to sup,

> But thee burning thirst down-beareth,
> Prince of battle's Parliament!

After that Kolskegg took a beaker full of mead, and drank it off and went on fighting afterwards; and so it came about that those brothers sprang up on the ship of Vandil and his brother, and Kolskegg went on one side, and Gunnar on the other. Against Gunnar came Vandil, and smote at once at him with his sword, and the blow fell on his shield. Gunnar gave the shield a twist as the sword pierced it, and broke it short off at the hilt. Then Gunnar smote back at Vandil, and three swords seemed to be aloft, and Vandil could not see how to shun the blow. Then Gunnar cut both his legs from under him, and at the same time Kolskegg ran Karli through with a spear. After that they took great war spoil.

Thence they held on south to Denmark, and thence east to Smoland, and had victory wherever they went. They did not come back in autumn. The next summer they held on to Reval, and fell in there with sea-rovers, and fought at once, and won the fight. After that they steered east to Osel, and lay there somewhile under a ness. There they saw a man coming down from the ness above them; Gunnar went on shore to meet the man, and they had a talk. Gunnar asked him his name, and he said it was Tofi. Gunnar asked again what he wanted.

"Thee I want to see," says the man. "Two warships lie on the other side under the ness, and I will tell thee who command them: two brothers are the captains — one's name is Hallgrim, and the other's Kolskegg. I know them to be mighty men of war; and I know too that they have such good weapons that the like are not to be had. Hallgrim has a bill which he had made by seething-spells; and this is what the spells say, that no weapon shall give him his death-blow save that bill. That thing follows it too that it is known at once when a man is to be slain with that bill, for something sings in it so loudly that it may be heard a long way off — such a strong nature has that bill in it."

Then Gunnar sang a song —

> Soon shall I that spearhead seize,
> And the bold sea-rover slay,
> Him whose blows on headpiece ring,
> Heaper up of piles of dead.
> Then on Endil's courser bounding,
> O'er the sea-depths I will ride,
> While the wretch who spells abuseth,
> Life shall lose in Sigar's storm.

"Kolskegg has a short sword; that is also the best of weapons. Force, too, they have — a third more than ye. They have also much goods, and have stowed them away on land, and I know clearly where they are. But they have sent a spy-ship off the ness, and they know all about you. Now they are getting themselves ready as fast as they can; and as soon as they are 'boun,' they mean to run out against you. Now you have either to row away at once, or to busk yourselves as quickly as ye can; but if ye win the day, then I will lead you to all their store of goods."

Gunnar gave him a golden finger-ring, and went afterwards to his men and told them that war-ships lay on the other side of the ness, "and they know all about us; so let us take to our arms, and busk us well, for now there is gain to be got".

Then they busked them; and just when they were boun they see ships coming up to them. And now a fight sprung up between them, and they fought long, and many men fell. Gunnar slew many a man. Hallgrim and his men leapt on board Gunnar's ship, Gunnar turns to meet him, and Hallgrim thrust at him with his bill. There was a boom athwart the ship, and Gunnar leapt nimbly back over it, Gunnar's shield was just before the boom, and Hallgrim thrust his bill into it, and through it, and so on into the boom. Gunnar cut at Hallgrim's arm hard, and lamed the forearm, but the sword would not bite. Then down fell the bill, and Gunnar seized the bill, and thrust Hallgrim through, and then sang a song —

> Slain is he who spoiled the people,
> Lashing them with flashing steel:
> Heard have I how Hallgrim's magic
> Helm-rod forged in foreign land;
> All men know, of heart-strings doughty,
> How this bill hath come to me,
> Deft in fight, the wolf's dear feeder.
> Death alone us two shall part.

And that vow Gunnar kept, in that he bore the bill while he lived. Those namesakes [the two Kolskeggs] fought together, and it was a near thing which would get the better of it. Then Gunnar came up, and gave the other Kolskegg his death-blow. After that the sea-rovers begged for mercy. Gunnar let them have that choice, and he let them also count the slain, and take the goods which the dead men owned, but he gave the others whom he spared their arms and their clothing, and bade them be off to the lands that fostered them. So they went off and Gunnar took all the goods that were left behind.

Tofi came to Gunnar after the battle, and offered to lead him to that store of goods which the sea-rovers had stowed away, and said that it was both better and larger than that which they had already got.

Gunnar said he was willing to go, and so he went ashore, and Tofi before him, to a wood, and Gunnar behind him. They came to a place where a great heap of wood was piled together. Tofi says the goods were under there, then they tossed off the wood, and found under it both gold and silver, clothes and good weapons. They bore those goods to the ships, and Gunnar asks Tofi in what way he wished him to repay him.

Tofi answered, "I am a Dansk man by race, and I wish thou wouldst bring me to my kinsfolk".

Gunnar asks why he was there away east?

"I was taken by sea-rovers," says Tofi, "and they put me on land here in Osel, and here I have been ever since."

Chapter 31

Gunnar goes to King Harold Gorm's Son and Earl Hacon

Gunnar took Tofi on board, and said to Kolskegg and Hallvard, "Now we will hold our course for the north lands".

They were well pleased at that, and bade him have his way. So Gunnar sailed from the east with much goods. He had ten ships, and ran in with them to Heidarby in Denmark. King Harold Gorm's son was there up the country, and he was told about Gunnar, and how too that there was no man his match in all Iceland. He sent men to him to ask him to come to him, and Gunnar went at once to see the king, and the king made him a hearty welcome, and sat him down next to himself. Gunnar was there half a month. The king made himself sport by letting Gunnar prove himself in divers feats of strength against his men, and there were none that were his match even in one feat.

Then the king said to Gunnar, "It seems to me as though thy peer is not to be found far or near," and the king offered to get Gunnar a wife, and to raise him to great power if he would settle down there.

Gunnar thanked the king for his offer and said — "I will first of all sail back to Iceland to see my friends and kinsfolk".

"Then thou wilt never come back to us," says the king.

"Fate will settle that, lord," says Gunnar.

Gunnar gave the king a good long-ship, and much goods besides, and the king gave him a robe of honour, and golden-seamed gloves, and a fillet with a knot of gold on it, and a Russian hat.

Then Gunnar fared north to Hisingen. Oliver welcomed him with both hands, and he gave back to Oliver his ships, with their lading, and said that was his share of the spoil. Oliver took the goods, and said Gunnar was a good man and true, and bade him stay with him some while. Hallvard asked Gunnar if he had a mind to go to see Earl Hacon. Gunnar said that was near his heart, "for now I am somewhat proved, but then I was not tried at all when thou badest me do this before".

After that they fared north to Drontheim to see Earl Hacon, and he gave Gunnar a hearty welcome, and bade him stay with him that winter, and Gunnar took that offer, and every man thought him a man of great worth. At Yule the Earl gave him a gold ring.

Gunnar set his heart on Bergliota, the Earl's kinswoman, and it was often to be seen from the Earl's way, that he would have given her to him to wife if

Gunnar had said anything about that.

Chapter 32
Gunnar comes out to Iceland

When the spring came, the Earl asks Gunnar what course he meant to take. He said he would go to Iceland. The Earl said that had been a bad year for grain, "and there will be little sailing out to Iceland, but still thou shalt have meal and timber both in thy ship".

Gunnar fitted out his ship as early as he could, and Hallvard fared out with him and Kolskegg. They came out early in the summer, and made Arnbæl's Oyce before the Thing met.

Gunnar rode home from the ship, but got men to strip her and lay her up. But when they came home all men were glad to see them. They were blithe and merry to their household, nor had their haughtiness grown while they were away.

Gunnar asks if Njal were at home; and he was told that he was at home; then he let them saddle his horse, and those brothers rode over to Bergthorsknoll.

Njal was glad at their coming, and begged them to stay there that night, and Gunnar told him of his voyages.

Njal said he was a man of the greatest mark, "and thou hast been much proved; but still thou wilt be more tried hereafter; for many will envy thee".

"With all men I would wish to stand well," says Gunnar.

"Much bad will happen," says Njal, "and thou wilt always have some quarrel to ward off."

"So be it, then," says Gunnar, "so that I have a good ground on my side."

"So will it be too," says Njal, "if thou hast not to smart for others."

Njal asked Gunnar if he would ride to the Thing. Gunnar said he was going to ride thither, and asks Njal whether he were going to ride; but he said he would not ride thither, "and if I had my will thou wouldst do the like".

Gunnar rode home, and gave Njal good gifts, and thanked him for the care he had taken of his goods, Kolskegg urged him on much to ride to the Thing, saying, "There thy honour will grow, for many will flock to see thee there".

"That has been little to my mind," says Gunnar, "to make a show of myself; but I think it good and right to meet good and worthy men."

Hallvard by this time was also come thither, and offered to ride to the Thing with them.

Chapter 33
Gunnar's Wooing

So Gunnar rode, and they all rode. But when they came to the Thing they were so well arrayed that none could match them in bravery; and men came out of every booth to wonder at them. Gunnar rode to the booths of the men of Rangriver, and was there with his kinsmen. Many men came to see Gunnar, and ask tidings of him; and he was easy and merry to all men, and told them all they wished to hear.

It happened one day that Gunnar went away from the Hill of Laws, and passed by the booths of the men from Mossfell; then he saw a woman coming to meet him, and she was in goodly attire; but when they met she spoke to Gunnar at once. He took her greeting well, and asks what woman she might be. She told him her name was Hallgerda, and said she was Hauskuld's daughter, Dalakoll's son. She spoke up boldly to him, and bade him tell her of his voyages; but he said he would not gainsay her a talk. Then they sat them down and talked. She was so clad that she had on a red kirtle, and had thrown over her a scarlet cloak trimmed with needlework down to the waist. Her hair came down to her bosom, and was both fair and full. Gunnar was clad in the scarlet clothes which King Harold Gorm's son had given him; he had also the gold ring on his arm which Earl Hacon had given him.

So they talked long out loud, and at last it came about that he asked whether she were unmarried. She said, so it was, "and there are not many who would run the risk of that".

"Thinkest thou none good enough for thee?"

"Not that," she says, "but I am said to be hard to please in husbands."

"How wouldst thou answer were I to ask for thee?"

"That can not be in thy mind," she says.

"It is though," says he.

"If thou hast any mind that way, go and see my father."

After that they broke off their talk.

Gunnar went straightway to the Dalesmen's booths, and met a man outside the doorway, and asks whether Hauskuld were inside the booth?

The man says that he was. Then Gunnar went in, and Hauskuld and Hrut made him welcome. He sat down between them, and no one could find out from their talk that there had ever been any misunderstanding between them. At last Gunnar's speech turned thither; how these brothers would answer if he asked for Hallgerda?

"Well," says Hauskuld, "if that is indeed thy mind."

Gunnar says that he is in earnest, "but we so parted last time, that many would think it unlikely that we should ever be bound together".

"How thinkest thou, kinsman Hrut?" says Hauskuld.

Hrut answered, "Methinks this is no even match".

"How dost thou make that out?" says Gunnar.

Hrut spoke — "In this wise will I answer thee about this matter, as is the very truth. Thou art a brisk brave man, well to do, and unblemished; but she is much mixed up with ill report, and I will not cheat thee in anything."

"Good go with thee for thy words," says Gunnar, "but still I shall hold that for true, that the old feud weighs with ye, if ye will not let me make this match."

"Not so," says Hrut, "'tis more because I see that thou art unable to help thyself; but though we make no bargain, we would still be thy friends."

"I have talked to her about it," says Gunnar, "and it is not far from her mind."

Hrut says — "I know that you have both set your hearts on this match; and, besides, ye two are those who run the most risk as to how it turns out".

Hrut told Gunnar unasked all about Hallgerda's temper, and Gunnar at first thought that there was more than enough that was wanting; but at last it came about that they struck a bargain.

Then Hallgerda was sent for, and they talked over the business when she was by, and now, as before, they made her betroth herself. The bridal feast was to be at Lithend, and at first they were to set about it secretly; but the end after all was that every one knew of it.

Gunnar rode home from the Thing, and came to Bergthorsknoll, and told Njal of the bargain he had made. He took it heavily.

Gunnar asks Njal why he thought this so unwise?

"Because from her," says Njal, "will arise all kind of ill if she comes hither east."

"Never shall she spoil our friendship," says Gunnar.

"Ah! but yet that may come very near," says Njal; "and, besides, thou wilt have always to make atonement for her."

Gunnar asked Njal to the wedding, and all those as well whom he wished should be at it from Njal's house.

Njal promised to go; and after that Gunnar rode home, and then rode about the district to bid men to his wedding.

Chapter 34
Of Thrain Sigfus' Son

There was a man named Thrain, he was the son of Sigfus, the son of Sighvat the Red. He kept house at Gritwater on Fleetlithe. He was Gunnar's kinsman, and a man of great mark. He had to wife Thorhilda Skaldwife; she had a sharp tongue of her own, and was giving to jeering. Thrain loved her little. He and his wife were bidden to the wedding, and she and Bergthora, Skarphedinn's daughter, Njal's wife, waited on the guests with meat and drink.

Kettle was the name of the second son of Sigfus; he kept house in the Mark, east of Markfleet. He had to wife Thorgerda, Njal's daughter. Thorkell was the name of the third son of Sigfus; the fourth's name was Mord; the fifth's Lambi; the sixth's Sigmund; the seventh's Sigurd. These were all Gunnar's kinsmen, and great champions. Gunnar bade them all to the wedding.

Gunnar had also bidden Valgard the guileful, and Wolf Aurpriest, and their sons Runolf and Mord.

Hauskuld and Hrut came to the wedding with a very great company, and the sons of Hauskuld, Torleik, and Olof, were there; the bride, too, came along with them, and her daughter Thorgerda came also, and she was one of the fairest of women; she was then fourteen winters old. Many other women were with her, and besides there were Thorkatla Asgrim Ellidagrim's son's daughter, and Njal's two daughters, Thorgerda and Helga.

Gunnar had already many guests to meet them, and he thus arranged his men. He sat on the middle of the bench, and on the inside, away from him, Thrain Sigfus' son, then Wolf Aurpriest, then Valgard the guileful, then Mord and Runolf, then the other sons of Sigfus, Lambi sat outermost of them.

Next to Gunnar on the outside, away from him, sat Njal, then Skarphedinn, then Helgi, then Grim, then Hauskuld Njal's son, then Hafr the Wise, then Ingialld from the Springs, then the sons of Thorir from Holt away east. Thorir would sit outermost of the men of mark, for every one was pleased with the seat he got.

Hauskuld, the bride's father, sat on the middle of the bench over against Gunnar, but his sons sat on the inside away from him; Hrut sat on the outside away from Hauskuld, but it is not said how the others were placed. The bride sat in the middle of the cross-bench on the dais; but on one hand of her sat her daughter Thorgerda, and on the other Thorkatla Asgrim Ellidagrim's son's daughter.

Thorhillda went about waiting on the guests, and Bergthora bore the meat on the board.

Now Thrain Sigfus' son kept staring at Thorgerda Glum's daughter; his wife Thorhillda saw this, and she got wroth, and made a couplet upon him.

"Thrain," she says,

> "Gaping mouths are no wise good,
> Goggle eyne are in thy head,"

He rose at once up from the board, and said he would put Thorhillda away, "I will not bear her jibes and jeers any longer;" and he was so quarrelsome about this, that he would not be at the feast unless she were driven away. And so it was, that she went away; and now each man sat in his place, and they drank and were glad.

Then Thrain began to speak — "I will not whisper about that which is in my mind. This I will ask thee, Hauskuld Dalakoll's son, wilt thou give me to wife Thorgerda, thy kinswoman?"

"I do not know that," says Hauskuld; "methinks thou art ill parted from the one thou hadst before. But what kind of man is he, Gunnar?"

Gunnar answers — "I will not say aught about the man, because he is near of kin; but say thou about him, Njal," says Gunnar, "for all men will believe it".

Njal spoke, and said — "That is to be said of this man, that the man is well to do for wealth, and a proper man in all things. A man, too, of the greatest mark; so that ye may well make this match with him."

Then Hauskuld spoke — "What thinkest thou we ought to do, kinsman Hrut?"

"Thou mayst make the match, because it is an even one for her," says Hrut.

Then they talk about the terms of the bargain, and are soon of one mind on all points.

Then Gunnar stands up, and Thrain too, and they go to the cross-bench. Gunnar asked that mother and daughter whether they would say yes to this bargain. They said they would find no fault with it, and Hallgerda betrothed her daughter. Then the places of the women were shifted again, and now Thorhalla sate between the brides. And now the feast sped on well, and when it was over, Hauskuld and his company ride west, but the men of Rangriver rode to their own abode. Gunnar gave many men gifts, and that made him much liked.

Hallgerda took the housekeeping under her, and stood up for her rights in word and deed. Thorgerda took to housekeeping at Gritwater, and was a good housewife.

Chapter 35
The visit to Bergthorsknoll

Now it was the custom between Gunnar and Njal, that each made the other a feast, winter and winter about, for friendship's sake; and it was Gunnar's turn to go to feast at Njal's. So Gunnar and Hallgerda set off for Bergthorsknoll, and when they got there Helgi and his wife were not at home. Njal gave Gunnar and his wife a hearty welcome, and when they had been there a little while, Helgi came home with Thorhalla his wife. Then Bergthora went up to the cross-bench, and Thorhalla with her, and Bergthora said to Hallgerda —

"Thou shalt give place to this woman."

She answered — "To no one will I give place, for I will not be driven into the corner for any one".

"I shall rule here," said Bergthora, After that Thorhalla sat down, and Bergthora went round the table with water to wash the guests' hands. Then Hallgerda took hold of Bergthora's hand, and said —

"There's not much to choose, though, between you two. Thou hast hang-nails on every finger, and Njal is beardless."

"That's true," says Bergthora, "yet neither of us finds fault with the other for it; but Thorwald, thy husband, was not beardless, and yet thou plottedst his death."

Then Hallgerda said — "It stands me in little stead to have the bravest man in Iceland if thou dost not avenge this, Gunnar!"

He sprang up and strode across away from the board, and said — "Home I will go, and it were more seemly that thou shouldest wrangle with those of thine own household, and not under other men's roofs; but as for Njal, I am his debtor for much honour, and never will I be egged on by thee like a fool".

After that they set off home.

"Mind this, Bergthora," said Hallgerda, "that we shall meet again."

Bergthora said she should not be better off for that. Gunnar said nothing at all, but went home to Lithend, and was there at home all the winter. And now the summer was running on towards the Great Thing.

Chapter 36
Kol Slew Swart

Gunnar rode away to the Thing, but before he rode from home he said to Hallgerda — "Be good now while I am away, and show none of thine ill temper in anything with which my friends have to do".

"The trolls take thy friends," says Hallgerda.

So Gunnar rode to the Thing, and saw it was not good to come to words with her. Njal rode to the Thing too, and all his sons with him.

Now it must be told of what tidings happened at home. Njal and Gunnar owned a wood in common at Redslip; they had not shared the wood, but each was wont to hew in it as he needed, and neither said a word to the other about that. Hallgerda's grieve's name was Kol; he had been with her long, and was one of the worst of men. There was a man named Swart; he was Njal's and Bergthora's house-carle; they were very fond of him. Now Bergthora told him that he must go up into Redslip and hew wood; but she said — "I will get men to draw home the wood".

He said he would do the work she set him to win; and so he went up into Redslip, and was to be there a week.

Some gangrel men came to Lithend from the east across Markfleet, and said that Swart had been in Redslip, and hewn wood, and done a deal of work.

"So," says Hallgerda, "Bergthora must mean to rob me in many things, but I'll take care that he does not hew again."

Rannveig, Gunnar's mother, heard that, and said — "There have been good housewives before now, though they never set their hearts on manslaughter".

Now the night wore away, and early next morning Hallgerda came to speak to Kol, and said — "I have thought of some work for thee"; and with that she put weapons into his hands, and went on to say — "Fare thou to Redslip; there wilt thou find Swart".

"What shall I do to him?" he says.

"Askest thou that when thou art the worst of men?" she says. "Thou shalt kill him."

"I can get that done," he says, "but 'tis more likely that I shall lose my own life for it."

"Everything grows big in thy eyes," she says, "and thou behavest ill to say this after I have spoken up for thee in everything. I must get another man to do this if thou darest not."

He took the axe, and was very wroth, and takes a horse that Gunnar owned, and rides now till he comes east of Markfleet. There he got off and bided in the wood, till they had carried down the firewood, and Swart was left alone behind. Then Kol sprang on him, and said — "More folk can hew great strokes than thou alone"; and so he laid the axe on his head, and smote him his death-blow, and rides home afterwards, and tells Hallgerda of the slaying.

She said — "I shall take such good care of thee, that no harm shall come to thee".

"May be so," says he, "but I dreamt all the other way as I slept ere I did the deed."

Now they come up into the wood, and find Swart slain, and bear him home. Hallgerda sent a man to Gunnar at the Thing to tell him of the slaying. Gunnar said no hard words at first of Hallgerda to the messenger, and men knew not at first whether he thought well or ill of it. A little after he stood up, and bade his men go with him: they did so, and fared to Njal's booth. Gunnar sent a man to fetch Njal, and begged him to come out. Njal went out at once, and he and Gunnar fell a-talking, and Gunnar said —

"I have to tell thee of the slaying of a man, and my wife and my grieve Kol were those who did it; but Swart, thy house-carle, fell before them."

Njal held his peace while he told him the whole story. Then Njal spoke —

"Thou must take heed not to let her have her way in everything."

Gunnar said — "Thou thyself shall settle the terms".

Njal spoke again — "'Twill be hard work for thee to atone for all Hallgerda's mischief; and somewhere else there will be a broader trail to follow than this which we two now have a share in, and yet, even here there will be much awanting before all be well; and herein we shall need to bear in mind the friendly words that passed between us of old; and something tells me that thou wilt come well out of it, but still thou wilt be sore tried".

Then Njal took the award into his own hands from Gunnar, and said —

"I will not push this matter to the uttermost; thou shalt pay twelve ounces of silver; but I will add this to my award, that if anything happens from our homestead about which thou hast to utter an award, thou wilt not be less easy in thy terms".

Gunnar paid up the money out of hand, and rode home afterwards. Njal, too, came home from the Thing, and his sons. Bergthora saw the money, and said —

"This is very justly settled; but even as much money shall be paid for Kol as time goes on."

Gunnar came home from the Thing and blamed Hallgerda. She said, better men lay unatoned in many places, Gunnar said, she might have her way in beginning a quarrel, "but how the matter is to be settled rests with me".

Hallgerda was for ever chattering of Swart's slaying, but Bergthora liked that ill. Once Njal and her sons went up to Thorolfsfell to see about the housekeeping there, but that selfsame day this thing happened when Bergthora was out of doors: she sees a man ride up to the house on a black horse. She stayed there and did not go in, for she did not know the man. That man had a spear in his hand, and was girded with a short sword. She asked this man his name.

"Atli is my name," says he.

She asked whence he came.

"I am an Eastfirther," he says.

"Whither shalt thou go?" she says.

"I am a homeless man," says he, "and I thought to see Njal and Skarphedinn, and know if they would take me in."

"What work is handiest to thee?" says she.

"I am a man used to field-work," he says, "and many things else come very handy to me; but I will not hide from thee that I am a man of hard temper and it has been many a man's lot before now to bind up wounds at my hand."

"I do not blame thee," she says, "though thou art no milksop."

Atli said — "Hast thou any voice in things here?"

"I am Njal's wife," she says, "and I have as much to say to our housefolk as he."

"Wilt thou take me in then?" says he.

"I will give thee thy choice of that," says she. "If thou wilt do all the work that I set before thee, and that though I wish to send thee where a man's life is at stake."

"Thou must have so many men at thy beck," says he, "that thou wilt not need me for such work."

"That I will settle as I please," she says.

"We will strike a bargain on these terms," says he.

Then she took him into the household. Njal and his sons came home and asked Bergthora what man that might be?

"He is thy house-carle," she says, "and I took him in." Then she went on to say he was no sluggard at work.

"He will be a great worker enough, I daresay," says Njal, "but I do not know whether he will be such a good worker."

Skarphedinn was good to Atli.

Njal and his sons ride to the Thing in the course of the summer; Gunnar was also at the Thing.

Njal took out a purse of money.

"What money is that, father?"

"Here is the money that Gunnar paid me for our house-carle last summer."

"That will come to stand thee in some stead," says Skarphedinn, and smiled as he spoke.

Chapter 37
The Slaying of Kol, whom Atli Slew

Now we must take up the story, and say that Atli asked Bergthora what work he should do that day.

"I have thought of some work for thee," she says; "thou shall go and look for Kol until thou find him; for now shalt thou slay him this very day, if thou wilt do my will."

"This work is well fitted," says Atli, "for each of us two are bad fellows; but still I will so lay myself out for him that one or other of us shall die."

"Well mayest thou fare," she says, "and thou shalt not do this deed for nothing."

He took his weapons and his horse, and rode up to Fleetlithe, and there met men who were coming down from Lithend. They were at home east in the Mark. They asked Atli whither he meant to go? He said he was riding to look for an old jade. They said that was a small errand for such a workman, "but still 'twould be better to ask those who have been about last night".

"Who are they?" says he.

"Killing-Kol," say they, "Hallgerda's house-carle, fared from the fold just now, and has been awake all night."

"I do not know whether I dare to meet him," says Atli, "he is bad-tempered, and may be that I shall let another's wound be my warning."

"Thou bearest that look beneath the brows as though thou wert no coward," they said, and showed him where Kol was.

Then he spurred his horse and rides fast, and when he meets Kol, Atli said to him —

"Go the pack-saddle bands well?"

"That's no business of thine, worthless fellow, nor of any one else whence thou comest."

Atli said — "Thou hast something behind that is earnest work, but that is to die".

After that Atli thrust at him with his spear, and struck him about his middle. Kol swept at him with his axe, but missed him, and fell off his horse, and died at once.

Atli rode till he met some of Hallgerda's workmen, and said, "Go ye up to the horse yonder, and look to Kol, for he has fallen off, and is dead".

"Hast thou slain him?" say they.

"Well, 'twill seem to Hallgerda as though he has not fallen by his own hand."

After that Atli rode home and told Bergthora; she thanked him for this deed, and for the words which he had spoken about it.

"I do not know," says he, "what Njal will think of this."

"He will take it well upon his hands," she says, "and I will tell thee one thing as a token of it, that he has earned away with him to the Thing the price of that thrall which we took last spring, and that money will now serve for Kol; but though peace be made thou must still beware of thyself, for Hallgerda will keep no peace."

"Wilt thou send at all a man to Njal to tell him of the slaying?"

"I will not," she says, "I should like it better that Kol were unatoned."

Then they stopped talking about it.

Hallgerda was told of Kol's slaying, and of the words that Atli had said. She said Atli should be paid off for them. She sent a man to the Thing to tell Gunnar of Kol's slaying; he answered little or nothing, and sent a man to tell Njal. He too made no answer, but Skarphedinn said —

"Thralls are men of more mettle than of yore; they used to fly at each other and fight, and no one thought much harm of that; but now they will do naught but kill," and as he said this he smiled.

Njal pulled down the purse of money which hung up in the booth, and went out; his sons went with him to Gunnar's booth.

Skarphedinn said to a man who was in the doorway of the booth —

"Say thou to Gunnar that my father wants to see him."

He did so, and Gunnar went out at once and gave Njal a hearty welcome. After that they began to talk.

"'Tis ill done," says Njal, "that my housewife should have broken the peace, and let thy house-carle be slain."

"She shall not have blame for that," says Gunnar.

"Settle the award thyself," says Njal.

"So I will do," say Gunnar, "and I value those two men at an even price, Swart and Kol. Thou shalt pay me twelve ounces in silver."

Njal took the purse of money and handed it to Gunnar. Gunnar knew the money, and saw it was the same that he had paid Njal. Njal went away to his booth, and they were just as good friends as before. When Njal came home, he blamed Bergthora; but she said she would never give way to Hallgerda. Hallgerda was very cross with Gunnar, because he had made peace for Kol's slaying, Gunnar told her he would never break with Njal or his sons, and she flew into a great rage; but Gunnar took no heed of that, and so they sat for that year, and nothing noteworthy happened.

Chapter 38
The Killing of Atli the Thrall

Next spring Njal said to Atli — "I wish that thou wouldst change thy abode to the east firths, so that Hallgerda may not put an end to thy life".

"I am not afraid of that," says Atli, "and I will willingly stay at home if I have the choice."

"Still that is less wise," says Njal.

"I think it better to lose my life in thy house than to change my master; but this I will beg of thee, if I am slain, that a thrall's price shall not be paid for me."

"Thou shalt be atoned for as a free man; but perhaps Bergthora will make thee a promise which she will fulfil, that revenge, man for man, shall be taken for thee."

Then he made up his mind to be a hired servant there.

Now it must be told of Hallgerda that she sent a man west to Bearfirth, to fetch Brynjolf the Unruly, her kinsman. He was a base son of Swan, and he was one of the worst of men. Gunnar knew nothing about it. Hallgerda said he was well fitted to be a grieve. So Brynjolf came from the west, and Gunnar asked what he was to do there? He said he was going to stay there.

"Thou wilt not better our household," says Gunnar, "after what has been told me of thee, but I will not turn away any of Hallgerda's kinsmen, whom she wishes to be with her."

Gunnar said little, but was not unkind to him, and so things went on till the Thing. Gunnar rides to the Thing and Kolskegg rides too, and when they came to the Thing they and Njal met, for he and his sons were at the Thing, and all went well with Gunnar and them.

Bergthora said to Atli — "Go thou up into Thorolfsfell and work there a week".

So he went up thither, and was there on the sly, and burnt charcoal in the wood.

Hallgerda said to Brynjolf — "I have been told Atli is not at home, and he must be winning work on Thorolfsfell".

"What thinkest thou likeliest that he is working at?" says he.

"At something in the wood," she says.

"What shall I do to him?" he asks.

"Thou shalt kill him," says she.

He was rather slow in answering her, and Hallgerda said —

"'Twould grow less in Thiostolf's eyes to kill Atli if he were alive."

"Thou shalt have no need to goad me on much more," he says, and then he seized his weapons, and takes his horse and mounts, and rides to Thorolfsfell. There he saw a great reek of coal smoke east of the homestead, so he rides thither, and gets off his horse and ties him up, but he goes where the smoke was thickest. Then he sees where the charcoal pit is, and a man stands by it. He saw that he had thrust his spear in the ground by him. Brynjolf goes along with the smoke right up to him, but he was eager at his work, and saw him not. Brynjolf gave him a stroke on the head with his axe, and he turned so quick round that Brynjolf loosed his hold of the axe, and Atli grasped the spear, and hurled it after him. Then Brynjolf cast himself down on the ground, but the spear flew away over him.

"Lucky for thee that I was not ready for thee," says Atli, "but now Hallgerda will be well pleased, for thou wilt tell her of my death; but it is a comfort to know that thou wilt have the same fate soon; but come now, take thy axe which has been here."

He answered him never a word, nor did he take the axe before he was dead. Then he rode up to the house on Thorolfsfell, and told of the slaying, and after that rode home and told Hallgerda. She sent men to Bergthorsknoll, and let them tell Bergthora, that now Kol's slaying was paid for.

After that Hallgerda sent a man to the Thing to tell Gunnar of Atli's killing.

Gunnar stood up, and Kolskegg with him, and Kolskegg said —

"Unthrifty will Hallgerda's kinsmen be to thee."

Then they go to see Njal, and Gunnar said —

"I have to tell thee of Atli's killing." He told him also who slew him, and went on, "and now I will bid thee atonement for the deed, and thou shall make the award thyself".

Njal said — "We two have always meant never to come to strife about anything; but still I cannot make him out a thrall".

Gunnar said that was all right, and stretched out his hand.

Njal named his witnesses, and they made peace on those terms.

Skarphedinn said, "Hallgerda does not let our house-carles die of old age".

Gunnar said — "Thy mother will take care that blow goes for blow between the houses".

"Ay, ay," says Njal, "there will be enough of that work."

After that Njal fixed the price at a hundred in silver, but Gunnar paid it down at once. Many who stood by said that the award was high; Gunnar got wroth, and said that a full atonement was often paid for those who were no brisker men than Atli.

With that they rode home from the Thing.

Bergthora said to Njal when she saw the money — "Thou thinkest thou hast fulfilled thy promise, but now my promise is still behind".

"There is no need that thou shouldst fulfil it," says Njal.

"Nay," says she, "thou hast guessed it would be so; and so it shall be."

Hallgerda said to Gunnar —

"Hast thou paid a hundred in silver for Atli's slaying, and made him a free man?"

"He was free before," says Gunnar, "and besides, I will not make Njal's household outlaws who have forfeited their rights."

"There's not a pin to choose between you," she said, "for both of you are so blate."

"That's as things prove," says he.

Then Gunnar was for a long time very short with her, till she gave way to him; and now all was still for the rest of that year; in the spring Njal did not increase his household, and now men ride to the Thing about summer.

Chapter 39
The Slaying of Brynjolf the Unruly

There was a man named Thord, he was surnamed Freedmanson. Sigtrygg was his father's name, and he had been the freedman of Asgerd, and he was drowned in Markfleet. That was why Thord was with Njal afterwards. He was a tall man and a strong, and he had fostered all Njal's sons. He had set his heart on Gudfinna Thorolf's daughter, Njal's kinswoman; she was housekeeper at home there, and was then with child.

Now Bergthora came to talk with Thord Freedmanson; she said —

"Thou shalt go to kill Brynjolf, Hallgerda's kinsman."

"I am no man-slayer," he says, "but still I will do what ever thou wilt."

"This is my will," she says.

After that he went up to Lithend, and made them call Hallgerda out, and asked where Brynjolf might be.

"What's thy will with him?" she says.

"I want him to tell me where he has hidden Atli's body; I have heard say that he has buried it badly."

She pointed to him, and said he was down yonder in Acretongue.

"Take heed," says Thord, "that the same thing does not befall him as befell Atli."

"Thou art no man-slayer," she says, "and so nought will come of it even if ye two do meet."

"Never have I seen man's blood, nor do I know how I should feel if I did," he says, and gallops out of the "town" and down to Acretongue.

Rannveig, Gunnar's mother, had heard their talk.

"Thou goadest his mind much, Hallgerda," she says, "but I think him a dauntless man, and that thy kinsman will find."

They met on the beaten way, Thord and Brynjolf; and Thord said — "Guard thee, Brynjolf, for I will do no dastard's deed by thee".

Brynjolf rode at Thord, and smote at him with his axe. He smote at him at the same time with his axe, and hewed in sunder the haft just above Brynjolf s hands, and then hewed at him at once a second time, and struck him on the collarbone, and the blow went straight into his trunk. Then he fell from horseback, and was dead on the spot.

Thord met Hallgerda'a herdsman, and gave out the slaying as done by his hand, and said where he lay, and bade him tell Hallgerda of the slaying. After that he rode home to Bergthorsknoll, and told Bergthora of the slaying, and other people too.

"Good luck go with thy hands," she said.

The herdsman told Hallgerda of the slaying; she was snappish at it, and said much ill would come of it, if she might have her way.

Chapter 40
Gunnar and Njal make Peace about Brynjolf's Slaying

Now these tidings come to the Thing, and Njal made them tell him the tale thrice, and then he said —

"More men now become man-slayers than I weened."

Skarphedinn spoke — "That man, though, must have been twice fey," he says, "who lost his life by our foster-father's hand, who has never seen man's blood. And many would think that we brothers would sooner have done this deed with the turn of temper that we have."

"Scant apace wilt thou have," says Njal, "ere the like befalls thee; but need will drive thee to it."

Then they went to meet Gunnar, and told him of the slaying. Gunnar spoke and said that was little manscathe, "but yet he was a free man".

Njal offered to make peace at once, and Gunnar said yes, and he was to settle the terms himself. He made his award there and then, and laid it at one hundred in silver. Njal paid down the money on the spot, and they were at peace after that.

Chapter 41
Sigmund comes out to Iceland

There was a man whose name was Sigmund. He was the son of Lambi, the son of Sighvat the Red. He was a great voyager, and a comely and a courteous man; tall too, and strong. He was a man of proud spirit, and a good skald, and well trained in most feats of strength. He was noisy and boisterous, and given to jibes and mocking. He made the land east in Hornfirth. Skiolld was the name of his fellow-traveller; he was a Swedish man, and ill to do with. They took horse and rode from the east out of Hornfirth, and did not draw bridle before they came to Lithend, in the Fleetlithe. Gunnar gave them a hearty welcome, for the bonds of kinship were close between them. Gunnar begged Sigmund to stay there that winter, and Sigmund said he would take the offer if Skiolld his fellow might be there too.

"Well, I have been so told about him," said Gunnar, "that he is no better of thy temper; but as it is, thou rather needest to have it bettered. This, too, is a bad house to stay at, and I would just give both of you a bit of advice, my kinsmen, not to fire up at the egging on of my wife Hallgerda; for she takes much in hand that is far from my will."

"His hands are clean who warns another," says Sigmund.

"Then mind the advice given thee," says Gunnar, "for thou art sure to be sore tried; and go along always with me, and lean upon my counsel."

After that they were in Gunnar's company. Hallgerda was good to Sigmund; and it soon came about that things grew so warm that she loaded him with money, and tended him no worse than her own husband; and many talked about that, and did not know what lay under it.

One day Hallgerda said to Gunnar — "It is not good to be content with that hundred in silver which thou tookest for my kinsman Brynjolf. I shall avenge him if I may," she says.

Gunnar said he had no mind to bandy words with her, and went away. He met Kolskegg, and said to him, "Go and see Njal; and tell him that Thord must beware of himself though peace has been made, for, methinks, there is faithlessness somewhere".

He rode off and told Njal, but Njal told Thord, and Kolskegg rode home, and Njal thanked them for their faithfulness.

Once on a time they two were out in the "town," Njal and Thord; a he-goat was wont to go up and down in the "town," and no one was allowed to drive him away. Then Thord spoke and said —

"Well, this is a wondrous thing!"

"What is it that thou see'st that seems after a wondrous fashion?" says Njal.

"Methinks the goat lies here in the hollow, and he is all one gore of blood."

Njal said that there was no goat there, nor anything else.

"What is it then?" says Thord.

"Thou must be a 'fey' man," says Njal, "and thou must have seen the fetch that follows thee, and now be ware of thyself."

"That will stand me in no stead," says Thord, "if death is doomed for me."

Then Hallgerda came to talk with Thrain Sigfus' son, and said — "I would think thee my son-in-law indeed," she says, "if thou slayest Thord Freedman-son".

"I will not do that," he says, "for then I shall have the wrath of my kinsman Gunnar; and besides, great things hang on this deed, for this slaying would soon be avenged."

"Who will avenge it?" she asks; "is it the beardless carle?"

"Not so," says he; "his sons will avenge it."

After that they talked long and low, and no man knew what counsel they took together.

Once it happened that Gunnar was not at home, but those companions were. Thrain had come in from Gritwater, and then he and they and Hallgerda sat out of doors and talked. Then Hallgerda said —

"This have ye two brothers in arms, Sigmund and Skiolld, promised to slay Thord Freedmanson; but Thrain thou hast promised me that thou wouldst stand by them when they did the deed."

They all acknowledged that they had given her this promise.

"Now I will counsel you how to do it," she says: "Ye shall ride east into Hornfirth after your goods, and come home about the beginning of the Thing, but if ye are at home before it begins, Gunnar will wish that ye should ride to the Thing with him. Njal will be at the Thing and his sons and Gunnar, but then ye two shall slay Thord."

They all agreed that this plan should be carried out. After that they busked them east to the Firth, and Gunnar was not aware of what they were about, and Gunnar rode to the Thing. Njal sent Thord Freedmanson away east under Eyjafell, and bade him be away there one night. So he went east, but he could not get back from the east, for the Fleet had risen so high that it could not be crossed on horseback ever so far up. Njal waited for him one night, for he had meant him to have ridden with him; and Njal said to Bergthora, that she must send Thord to the Thing as soon as ever he came home. Two nights after, Thord came from the east, and Bergthora told him that he must ride to the Thing, "but first thou shalt ride up into Thorolfsfell and see about the farm there, and do not be there longer than one or two nights."

Chapter 42
The Slaying of Thord Freedsmanson

Then Sigmund came from the east and those companions. Hallgerda told them that Thord was at home, but that he was to ride straightway to the Thing after a few nights' space. "Now ye will have a fair chance at him," he says, "but if this goes off, ye will never get nigh him". Men came to Lithend from Thorolfsfell, and told Hallgerda that Thord was there. Hallgerda went to Thrain Sigfus' son, and his companions, and said to him, "Now is Thord on Thorolfsfell, and now your best plan is to fall on him and kill him as he goes home".

"That we will do," says Sigmund. So they went out, and took their weapons and horses and rode on the way to meet him. Sigmund said to Thrain, "Now thou shalt have nothing to do with it; for we shall not need all of us".

"Very well, so I will," says he.

Then Thord rode up to them a little while after, and Sigmund said to him —

"Give thyself up," he says, "for now shalt thou die."

"That shall not be," says Thord, "come thou to single combat with me."

"That shall not be either," says Sigmund, "we will make the most of our numbers; but it is not strange that Skarphedinn is strong, for it is said that a fourth of a foster-child's strength comes from the foster-father."

"Thou wilt feel the force of that," says Thord, "for Skarphedinn will avenge me."

After that they fall on him, and he breaks a spear of each of them, so well did he guard himself. Then Skiolld cut off his hand, and he still kept them off with his other hand for some time, till Sigmund thrust him through. Then he fell dead to earth. They threw over him turf and stones; and Thrain said — "We have won an ill work, and Njal's sons will take this slaying ill when they hear of it".

They ride home and tell Hallgerda. She was glad to hear of the slaying, but Rannveig, Gunnar's mother, said —

"It is said 'but a short while is hand fain of blow,' and so it will be here; but still Gunnar will set thee free from this matter. But if Hallgerda makes thee take another fly in thy mouth, then that will be thy bane."

Hallgerda sent a man to Bergthorsknoll, to tell the slaying, and another man to the Thing, to tell it to Gunnar. Bergthora said she would not fight against Hallgerda with ill worth about such a matter; "that," quoth she, "would be no revenge for so great a quarrel".

Chapter 43
Njal and Gunnar make Peace for the Slaying of Thord

But when the messenger came to the Thing to tell Gunnar of the slaying, then Gunnar said —

"This has happened ill, and no tidings could come to my ears which I should think worse; but yet we will now go at once and see Njal. I still hope he may take it well, though he be sorely tried."

So they went to see Njal, and called him to come out and talk to them. He went out at once to meet Gunnar, and they talked, nor were there any more men by at first than Kolskegg.

"Hard tidings have I to tell thee," says Gunnar; "the slaying of Thord Freedmanson, and I wish to offer thee self-doom for the slaying."

Njal held his peace some while, and then said —

"That is well offered, and I will take it; but yet it is to be looked for, that I shall have blame from my wife or from my sons for that, for it will mislike them much; but still I will run the risk, for I know that I have to deal with a good man and true; nor do I wish that any breach should arise in our friendship on my part."

"Wilt thou let thy sons be by, pray?" says Gunnar.

"I will not," says Njal, "for they will not break the peace which I make, but if they stand by while we make it, they will not pull well together with us."

"So it shall be," says Gunnar. "See thou to it alone."

Then they shook one another by the hand, and made peace well and quickly.

Then Njal said — "The award that I make is two hundred in silver, and that thou wilt think much".

"I do not think it too much," says Gunnar, and went home to his booth.

Njal's sons came home, and Skarphedinn asked whence that great sum of money came, which his father held in his hand.

Njal said — "I tell you of your foster-father's Thord's slaying, and we two, Gunnar and I, have now made peace in the matter, and he has paid an atonement for him as for two men".

"Who slew him?" says Skarphedinn.

"Sigmund and Skiolld, but Thrain was standing near too," says Njal.

"They thought they had need of much strength," says Skarphedinn, and sang a song —

> Bold in deeds of derring-do,
> Burdeners of ocean's steeds,
> Strength enough it seems they needed
> All to slay a single man;
> When shall we our hands uplift?
> We who brandish burnished steel -
> Famous men erst reddened weapons,
> When? if now we quiet sit?

"Yes! when shall the day come when we shall lift our hands?"

"That will not be long off," says Njal, "and then thou shalt not be baulked; but still, methinks, I set great store on your not breaking this peace that I have made."

"Then we will not break it," says Skarphedinn, "but if anything arises between us, then we will bear in mind the old feud."

"Then I will ask you to spare no one," says Njal.

Chapter 44
Sigmund Mocks Njal and his Sons

Now men ride home from the Thing; and when Gunnar came home, he said to Sigmund —

"Thou art a more unlucky man than I thought, and turnest thy good gifts to thine own ill. But still I have made peace for thee with Njal and his sons; and now, take care that thou dost not let another fly come into thy mouth. Thou art not at all after my mind, thou goest about with jibes and jeers, with scorn and mocking; but that is not my turn of mind. That is why thou gettest on so well with Hallgerda, because ye two have your minds more alike."

Gunnar scolded him a long time, and he answered him well, and said he would follow his counsel more for the time to come than he had followed it hitherto. Gunnar told him then they might get on together. Gunnar and Njal kept up their friendship though the rest of their people saw little of one another. It happened once that some gangrel women came to Lithend from Bergthorsknoll; they were great gossips and rather spiteful tongued. Hallgerda had a bower, and sate often in it, and there sate with her daughter Thorgerda, and there too were Thrain and Sigmund, and a crowd of women. Gunnar was not there nor Kolskegg. These gangrel women went into the bower, and Hallgerda greeted them, and made room for them; then she asked them for news, but they said they had none to tell. Hallgerda asked where they had been over night; they said at Bergthorsknoll.

"What was Njal doing?" she says.

"He was hard at work sitting still," they said.

"What were Njal's sons doing?" she says; "they think themselves men at any rate."

"Tall men they are in growth," they say, "but as yet they are all untried; Skarphedinn whetted an axe, Grim fitted a spearhead to the shaft, Helgi rivetted a hilt on a sword, Hauskuld strengthened the handle of a shield."

"They must be bent on some great deed," says Hallgerda.

"We do not know that," they say.

"What were Njal's house-carles doing?" she asks.

"We don't know what some of them were doing, but one was carting dung up the hill-side."

"What good was there in doing that?" she asks.

"He said it made the swathe better there than any where else," they reply. "Witless now is Njal," says Hallgerda, "though he knows how to give counsel on every thing."

"How so?" they ask.

"I will only bring forward what is true to prove it," says she; "why doesn't he make them cart dung over his beard that he may be like other men? Let us call him 'the beardless carle': but his sons we will call 'dung-beardlings'; and now do pray give some stave about them, Sigmund, and let us get some good by thy gift of song."

"I am quite ready to do that," says he, and sang these verses —

Lady proud with hawk in hand.
Prithee why should dungbeard boys,
Reft of reason, dare to hammer

Handle fast on battle shield?
For these lads of loathly feature -
Lady scattering swanbath's beams —
Shall not shun this ditty shameful
Which I shape upon them now.

He the beardless carle shall listen
While I lash him with abuse,
Loon at whom our stomachs sicken.
Soon shall hear these words of scorn;
Far too nice for such base fellows
Is the name my bounty gives,
E'n my muse her help refuses,
Making mirth of dungbeard boys.

Here I find a nickname fitting
For those noisome dungbeard boys -
Loath am I to break my bargain
Linked with such a noble man —
Knit we all our taunts together -
Known to me is mind of man —
Call we now with outburst common,
Him, that churl, the beardless carle.

"Thou art a jewel indeed," says Hallgerda; "how yielding thou art to what I ask!"

Just then Gunnar came in. He had been standing outside the door of the bower, and heard all the words that had passed. They were in a great fright when they saw him come in, and then all held their peace, but before there had been bursts of laughter.

Gunnar was very wroth, and said to Sigmund, "thou art a foolish man, and one that cannot keep to good advice, and thou revilest Njal's sons, and Njal himself who is most worth of all; and this thou doest in spite of what thou hast already done. Mind, this will be thy death. But if any man repeats these words that thou hast spoken, or these verses that thou hast made, that man shall be sent away at once, and have my wrath beside."

But they were all so sore afraid of him, that no one dared to repeat those words. After that he went away, but the gangrel women talked among themselves, and said that they would get a reward from Bergthora if they told her all this. They went then away afterwards down thither, and took Bergthora aside and told her the whole story of their own free will.

Bergthora spoke and said, when men sate down to the board, "Gifts have been given to all of you, father and sons, and ye will be no true men unless ye repay them somehow".

"What gifts are these?" asks Skarphedinn.

"You, my sons," says Bergthora, "have got one gift between you all. Ye are nick-named 'Dung-beardlings,' but my husband 'the beardless carle.'"

"Ours is no woman's nature," says Skarphedinn, "that we should fly into a rage at every little thing."

"And yet Gunnar was wroth for your sakes," says she, "and he is thought to be good-tempered. But if ye do not take vengeance for this wrong, ye will avenge no shame."

"The carline, our mother, thinks this fine sport," says Skarphedinn, and smiled scornfully as he spoke, but still the sweat burst out upon his brow, and red flecks came over his cheeks, but that was not his wont. Grim was silent and bit his lip. Helgi made no sign, and he said never a word. Hauskuld went off with Bergthora; she came into the room again, and fretted and foamed much.

Njal spoke and said, "'slow and sure,' says the proverb, mistress! and so it is with many things, though they try men's tempers, that there are always two sides to a story, even when vengeance is taken".

But at even when Njal was come into his bed, he heard that an axe came against the panel and rang loudly, but there was another shut bed, and there the shields were hung up, and he sees that they are away. He said, "who have taken down our shields?"

"Thy sons went out with them," says Bergthora.

Njal pulled his shoes on his feet, and went out at once, and round to the other side of the house, and sees that they were taking their course right up the slope; he said, "whither away, Skarphedinn?"

"To look after thy sheep," he answers.

"You would not then be armed," said Njal, "if you meant that, and your errand must be something else."

Then Skarphedinn sang a song —

> Squanderer of hoarded wealth,
> Some there are that own rich treasure,
> Ore of sea that clasps the earth,
> And yet care to count their sheep;
> Those who forge sharp songs of mocking,
> Death songs, scarcely can possess
> Sense of sheep that crop the grass;
> Such as these I seek in fight;

and said afterwards —

"We shall fish for salmon, father."

"'Twould be well then if it turned out so that the prey does not get away from you."

They went their way, but Njal went to his bed, and he said to Bergthora, "Thy sons were out of doors all of them, with arms, and now thou must have egged them on to something".

"I will give them my heartfelt thanks," said Bergthora, "if they tell me the slaying of Sigmund."

Chapter 45
The Slaying of Sigmund and Skiolld

Now they, Njal's sons, fare up to Fleetlithe, and were that night under the Lithe, and when the day began to break, they came near to Lithend. That same morning both Sigmund and Skiolld rose up and meant to go to the stud-horses; they had bits with them, and caught the horses that were in the "town" and rode away on them. They found the stud-horses between two brooks. Skarphedinn caught sight of them, for Sigmund was in bright clothing. Skarphedinn said, "See you now the red elf yonder, lads?" They looked that way, and said they saw him.

Skarphedinn spoke again: "Thou, Hauskuld, shalt have nothing to do with it, for thou wilt often be sent about alone without due heed; but I mean Sigmund for myself; methinks that is like a man; but Grim and Helgi, they shall try to slay Skiolld".

Hauskuld sat him down, but they went until they came up to them. Skarphedinn said to Sigmund —

"Take thy weapons and defend thyself; that is more needful now, than to make mocking songs on me and my brothers."

Sigmund took up his weapons, but Skarphedinn waited the while. Skiolld turned against Grim and Helgi, and they fell hotly to fight. Sigmund had a helm on his head, and a shield at his side, and was girt with a sword, his spear was in his hand; now he turns against Skarphedinn, and thrusts at once at him with his spear, and the thrust came on his shield. Skarphedinn dashes the spearhaft in two, and lifts up his axe and hews at Sigmund, and cleaves his shield down to below the handle. Sigmund drew his sword and cut at Skarphedinn, and the sword cuts into his shield, so that it stuck fast. Skarphedinn gave the shield such a quick twist, that Sigmund let go his sword. Then Skarphedinn hews at Sigmund with his axe, the "Ogress of war". Sigmund had on a corselet, the axe came on his shoulder. Skarphedinn cleft the shoulder-blade right through, and at the same time pulled the axe towards him, Sigmund fell down on both knees, but sprang up again at once.

"Thou hast lifted low to me already," says Skarphedinn, "but still thou shalt fall upon thy mother's bosom ere we two part."

"Ill is that then," says Sigmund.

Skarphedinn gave him a blow on his helm, and after that dealt Sigmund his death-blow.

Grim cut off Skiolld's foot at the ankle-joint, but Helgi thrust him through with his spear, and he got his death there and then.

Skarphedinn saw Hallgerda's shepherd, just as he had hewn off Sigmund's head; he handed the head to the shepherd, and bade him bear it to Hallgerda, and said she would know whether that head had made jeering songs about them, and with that he sang a song.

> Here! this head shall thou, that heapest
> Hoards from ocean-caverns won,
> Bear to Hallgerd with my greeting,
> Her that hurries men to fight;
> Sure am I, O firewood splitter!
> That yon spendthrift knows it well,
> And will answer if it ever
> Uttered mocking songs on us.

The shepherd casts the head down as soon as ever they parted, for he dared not do so while their eyes were on him. They fared along till they met some men down by Markfleet, and told them the tidings. Skarphedinn gave himself out as the slayer of Sigmund; and Grim and Helgi as the slayers of Skiolld; then they fared home and told Njal the tidings. He answers them —

"Good luck to your hands! Here no self-doom will come to pass as things stand."

Now we must take up the story, and say that the shepherd came home to Lithend. He told Hallgerda the tidings.

"Skarphedinn put Sigmund's head into my hands," he says, "and bade me bring it thee; but I dared not do it, for I knew not how thou wouldst like that."

"'Twas ill that thou didst not do that," she says; "I would have brought it to Gunnar, and then he would have avenged his kinsman, or have to bear every man's blame."

After that she went to Gunnar and said, "I tell thee of thy kinsman Sigmund's slaying: Skarphedinn slew him, and wanted them to bring me the head".

"Just what might be looked for to befall him," says Gunnar, "for ill redes bring ill luck, and both you and Skarphedinn have often done one another spiteful turns".

Then Gunnar went away; he let no steps be taken towards a suit for man-slaughter, and did nothing about it. Hallgerda often put him in mind of it, and kept saying that Sigmund had fallen unatoned. Gunnar gave no heed to that.

Now three Things passed away, at each of which men thought that he would follow up the suit: then a knotty point came on Gunnar's hands, which he knew not how to set about, and then he rode to find Njal. He gave Gunnar a hearty welcome. Gunnar said to Njal, "I am come to seek a bit of good counsel at thy hands about a knotty point".

"Thou art worthy of it," says Njal, and gave him counsel what to do. Then Gunnar stood up and thanked him. Njal then spoke and said, and took Gunnar by the hand, "Over long hath thy kinsman Sigmund been unatoned". "He has been long ago atoned," says Gunnar, "but still I will not fling back the honour offered me."

Gunnar had never spoken an ill word of Njal's sons. Njal would have nothing else than that Gunnar should make his own award in the matter. He awarded two hundred in silver, but let Skiolld fall without a price. They paid down all the money at once.

Gunnar declared this their atonement at the Thingskala Thing, when most men were at it, and laid great weight on the way in which they (Njal and his sons) had behaved; he told too those bad words which cost Sigmund his life, and no man was to repeat them or sing the verses, but if any sung them, the man who uttered them was to fall without atonement.

Both Gunnar and Njal gave each other their words that no such matters should ever happen that they would not settle among themselves; and this pledge was well kept ever after, and they were always friends.

Chapter 46
Of Gizur the White and Geir the Priest

There was a man named Gizur the White; he was Teit's son; Kettlebjorn the Old's son, of Mossfell. Gizur the White kept house at Mossfell, and was a great chief. That man is also named in this story, whose name was Geir the priest; his mother was Thorkatla, another daughter of Kettlebjorn the Old of Mossfell. Geir kept house at Lithe. He and Gizur backed one another in every matter. At that time Mord Valgard's son kept house at Hof on the Rangrivervales; he was crafty and spiteful. Valgard his father was then abroad, but his mother was dead. He was very envious of Gunnar of Lithend. He was wealthy, so far as goods went, but had not many friends.

Chapter 47
Of Otkell in Kirkby

There was a man named Otkell; he was the son of Skarf, the son of Hallkell, who fought with Gorm of Gormness, and felled him on the holm. This Hallkell and Kettlebjorn the Old were brothers.

Otkell kept house at Kirkby; his wife's name was Thorgerda; she was a daughter of Mar, the son of Runolf, the son of Naddad of the Faroe isles. Otkell was wealthy in goods. His son's name was Thorgeir; he was young in years, and a bold dashing man.

Skamkell was the name of another man; he kept house at another farm called Hof; he was well off for money, but he was a spiteful man and a liar; quarrelsome too, and ill to deal with. He was Otkell's friend. Hallkell was the name of Otkell's brother; he was a tall strong man, and lived there with Otkell; their brother's name was Hallbjorn the White; he brought out to Iceland a thrall, whose name was Malcolm; he was Irish and had not many friends.

Hallbjorn went to stay with Otkell, and so did his thrall Malcolm. The thrall was always saying that he should think himself happy if Otkell owned him. Otkell was kind to him, and gave him a knife and belt, and a full suit of clothes, but the thrall turned his hand to any work that Otkell wished.

Otkell wanted to make a bargain with his brother for the thrall; he said he would give him the thrall, but said too, that he was a worse treasure than he thought. And as soon as Otkell owned the thrall, then he did less and less work. Otkell often said outright to Hallbjorn, that he thought the thrall did little work; and he told Otkell that there was worse in him yet to come.

At that time came a great scarcity, so that men fell short both of meat and hay, and that spread over all parts of Iceland. Gunnar shared his hay and meat with many men; and all got them who came thither, so long as his stores lasted. At last it came about that Gunnar himself fell short both of hay and meat. Then Gunnar called on Kolskegg to go along with him; he called too on Thrain Sigfus' son, and Lambi Sigurd's son. They fared to Kirkby, and called Otkell out. He greeted them, and Gunnar said, "It so happens that I am come to deal with thee for hay and meat, if there be any left".

Otkell answers, "There is store of both, but I will sell thee neither".

"Wilt thou give me them then," says Gunnar, "and run the risk of my paying thee back somehow?"

"I will not do that either," says Otkell.

Skamkell all the while was giving him bad counsel.

Then Thrain Sigfus' son said, "It would serve him right if we take both hay and meat and lay down the worth of them instead".

Skamkell answered, "All the men of Mossfell must be dead and gone then, if ye, sons of Sigfus, are to come and rob them".

"I will have no hand in any robbery," says Gunnar.

"Wilt thou buy a thrall of me?" says Otkell.

"I'll not spare to do that," says Gunnar. After that Gunnar bought the thrall, and fared away as things stood.

Njal hears of this, and said, "Such things are ill done, to refuse to let Gunnar buy; and it is not a good outlook for others if such men as he cannot get what they want".

"What's the good of thy talking so much about such a little matter?" says Bergthora; "far more like a man would it be to let him have both meat and hay, when thou lackest neither of them."

"That is clear as day," says Njal, "and I will of a surety supply his need somewhat."

Then he fared up to Thorolfsfell, and his sons with him, and they bound hay on fifteen horses; but on five horses they had meat. Njal came to Lithend, and called Gunnar out. He greeted them kindly.

"Here is hay and meat," said Njal, "which I will give thee; and my wish is, that thou shouldst never look to any one else than to me if thou standest in need of any thing."

"Good are thy gifts," says Gunnar, "but methinks thy friendship is still more worth, and that of thy sons."

After that Njal fared home, and now the spring passes away.

Chapter 48
How Hallgerda makes Malcolm Steal from Kirkby

Now Gunnar is about to ride to the Thing, but a great crowd of men from the Side east turned in as guests at his house.

Gunnar bade them come and be his guests again, as they rode back from the Thing; and they said they would do so.

Now they ride to the Thing, and Njal and his sons were there. That Thing was still and quiet.

Now we must take up the story, and say that Hallgerda comes to talk with Malcolm the thrall.

"I have thought of an errand to send thee on," she says; "thou shalt go to Kirkby."

"And what shall I do there?" he says.

"Thou shalt steal from thence food enough to load two horses, and mind and have butter and cheese; but thou shalt lay fire in the storehouse, and all will think that it has arisen out of heedlessness, but no one will think that there has been theft."

"Bad have I been," said the thrall, "but never have I been a thief."

"Hear a wonder!" says Hallgerda, "thou makest thyself good, thou that hast been both thief and murderer; but thou shalt not dare to do aught else than go, else will I let thee be slain."

He thought he knew enough of her to be sure that she would so do if he went not; so he took at night two horses and laid pack-saddles on them, and went his way to Kirkby. The house-dog knew him and did not bark at him, and ran and fawned on him. After that he went to the storehouse and loaded the two horses with food out of it, but the storehouse he burnt, and the dog he slew.

He went up along by Rangriver, and his shoe-thong snapped; so he takes his knife and makes the shoe right, but he leaves the knife and belt lying there behind him.

He fares till he comes to Lithend; then he misses the knife, but dares not to go back.

Now he brings Hallgerda the food, and she showed herself well pleased at it.

Next morning when men came out of doors at Kirkby there they saw great scathe. Then a man was sent to the Thing to tell Otkell, he bore the loss well, and said it must have happened because the kitchen was next to the storehouse; and all thought that that was how it happened.

Now men ride home from the Thing, and many rode to Lithend. Hallgerda set food on the hoard, and in came cheese and butter. Gunnar knew that such food was not to be looked for in his house, and asked Hallgerda whence it came?

"Thence," she says, "whence thou mightest well eat of it; besides, it is no man's business to trouble himself with housekeeping."

Gunnar got wroth and said, "Ill indeed is it if I am a partaker with thieves"; and with that he gave her a slap on the cheek.

She said she would bear that slap in mind and repay it if she could.

So she went off and he went with her, and then all that was on the board was cleared away, but flesh-meat was brought in instead, and all thought that was because the flesh was thought to have been got in a better way.

Now the men who had been at the Thing fare away.

Chapter 49
Of Skamkell's Evil Counsel

Now we must tell of Skamkell. He rides after some sheep up along Rangriver, and he sees something shining in the path. He finds a knife and belt, and thinks he knows both of them. He fares with them to Kirkby; Otkell was out of doors when Skamkell came. He spoke to him and said —

"Knowest thou aught of these pretty things?"

"Of a surety," says Otkell, "I know them."

"Who owns them?" asks Skamkell.

"Malcolm the thrall," says Otkell.

"Then more shall see and know them than we two," says Skamkell, "for true will I be to thee in counsel."

They showed them to many men, and all knew them. Then Skamkell said —

"What counsel wilt thou now take?"

"We shall go and see Mord Valgard's son," answers Otkell, "and seek counsel of him."

So they went to Hof, and showed the pretty things to Mord, and asked him if he knew them?

He said he knew them well enough, but what was there in that? "Do you think you have a right to look for anything at Lithend?"

"We think it hard for us," says Skamkell, "to know what to do, when such mighty men have a hand in it."

"That is so, sure enough," says Mord, "but yet I will get to know those things out of Gunnar's household, which none of you will ever know."

"We would give thee money," they say, "if thou wouldst search out this thing."

"That money I shall buy full dear," answered Mord, "but still, perhaps, it may be that I will look at the matter."

They gave him three marks of silver for lending them his help.

Then he gave them this counsel, that women should go about from house to house with small wares, and give them to the housewives, and mark what was given them in return.

"For," he says, "'tis the turn of mind of all men first to give away what has been stolen, if they have it in their keeping, and so it will be here also, if this hath happened by the hand of man. Ye shall then come and show me what has been given to each in each house, and I shall then be free from further share in this matter, if the truth comes to light."

To this they agreed, and went home afterwards.

Mord sends women about the country, and they were away half a month. Then they came back, and had big bundles. Mord asked where they had most given them?

They said that at Lithend most was given them, and Hallgerda had been most bountiful to them.

He asked what was given them there?

"Cheese," say they.

He begged to see it, and they showed it to him, and it was in great slices. These he took and kept.

A little after, Mord fared to see Otkell, and bade that he would bring Thorgerda's cheese-mould; and when that was done, he laid the slices down in it, and lo! they fitted the mould in every way.

Then they saw, too, that a whole cheese had been given to them.

Then Mord said, "Now may ye see that Hallgerda must have stolen the cheese"; and they all passed the same judgment; and then Mord said, that now he thought he was free of this matter.

After that they parted.

Shortly after Kolskegg fell to talking with Gunnar, and said —

"Ill is it to tell, but the story is in every man's mouth, that Hallgerda must have stolen, and that she was at the bottom of all that great scathe that befell at Kirkby."

Gunnar said that he too thought that must be so. "But what is to be done now?"

Kolskegg answered, "That wilt think it thy most bounden duty to make atonement for thy wife's wrong, and methinks it were best that thou farest to see Otkell, and makest him a handsome offer."

"This is well spoken," says Gunnar, "and so it shall be."

A little after Gunnar sent after Thrain Sigfus' son, and Lambi Sigurd's son, and they came at once.

Gunnar told them whither he meant to go, and they were well pleased. Gunnar rode with eleven men to Kirkby, and called Otkell out. Skamkell was there too, and said, "I will go out with thee, and it will be best now to have the balance of wit on thy side. And I would wish to stand closest by thee when thou needest it most, and now this will be put to the proof. Methinks it were best that thou puttest on an air of great weight."

Then they, Otkell and Skamkell, and Hallkell and Hallbjorn, went out all of them.

They greeted Gunnar, and he took their greeting well. Otkell asks whither he meant to go?

"No farther than here," says Gunnar, "and my errand hither is to tell thee about that bad mishap — how it arose from the plotting of my wife and that thrall whom I bought from thee."

"'Tis only what was to be looked for," says Hallbjorn.

"Now I will make thee a good offer," says Gunnar, "and the offer is this, that the best men here in the country round settle the matter."

"This is a fair-sounding offer," said Skamkell, "but an unfair and uneven one. Thou art a man who has many friends among the householders, but Otkell has not many friends."

"Well," says Gunnar, "then I will offer thee that I shall make an award, and utter it here on this spot, and so we will settle the matter, and my good-will shall follow the settlement. But I will make thee an atonement by paying twice the worth of what was lost."

"This choice shalt thou not take," said Skamkell; "and it is unworthy to give up to him the right to make his own award, when thou oughtest to have kept it for thyself."

So Otkell said, "I will not give up to thee, Gunnar, the right to make thine own award."

"I see plainly," said Gunnar, "the help of men who will be paid off for it one day I daresay; but come now, utter an award for thyself."

Otkell leant toward Skamkell and said, "What shall I answer now?"

"This thou shalt call a good offer, but still put thy suit into the hands of Gizur the White, and Geir the priest, and then many will say this, that thou behavest like Hallkell, thy grandfather, who was the greatest of champions."

"Well offered is this, Gunnar," said Otkell, "but still my will is thou wouldst give me time to see Gizur the White."

"Do now whatever thou likest in the matter," said Gunnar; "but men will say this, that thou couldst not see thine own honour when thou wouldst have none of the choices I offer thee."

Then Gunnar rode home, and when he had gone away, Hallbjorn said, "Here I see how much man differs from man. Gunnar made thee good offers, but thou wouldst take none of them; or how dost thou think to strive with Gunnar in a quarrel, when no one is his match in fight. But now he is still so kind-hearted a man that it may be he will let these offers stand, though thou art only ready to take them afterwards. Methinks it were best that thou farest to see Gizur the White and Geir the priest now this very hour."

Otkell let them catch his horse, and made ready in every way. Otkell was not sharpsighted, and Skamkell walked on the way along with him, and said to Otkell—

"Methought it strange that thy brother would not take this toil from thee, and now I will make thee an offer to fare instead of thee, for I know that the journey is irksome to thee."

"I will take that offer," says Otkell, "but mind and be as truthful as ever thou canst."

"So it shall be," says Skamkell.

Then Skamkell took his horse and cloak, but Otkell walks home.

Hallbjorn was out of doors, and said to Otkell —

"Ill is it to have a thrall for one's bosom friend, and we shall rue this for ever that thou hast turned back, and it is an unwise step to send the greatest liar on an errand, of which one may so speak that men's lives hang on it."

"Thou wouldst be sore afraid," says Otkell, "if Gunnar had his bill aloft, when thou art so scared now."

"No one knows who will be most afraid then," said Hallbjorn; "but this thou wilt have to own, that Gunnar does not lose much time in brandishing his bill when he is wroth."

"Ah!" said Otkell, "ye are all of you for yielding but Skamkell."

And then they were both wroth.

Chapter 50
Of Skamkell's Lying

Skamkell came to Mossfell, and repeated all the offers to Gizur.

"It so seems to me," says Gizur, "as though these have been bravely offered; but why took he not these offers?"

"The chief cause was," answers Skamkell, "that all wished to show thee honour, and that was why he waited for thy utterance; besides, that is best for all."

So Skamkell stayed there the night over, but Gizur sent a man to fetch Geir the priest; and he came there early. Then Gizur told him the story and said —

"What course is to be taken now?"

"As thou no doubt hast already made up thy mind — to make the best of the business for both sides."

"Now we will let Skamkell tell his tale a second time, and see how he repeats it."

So they did that, and Gizur said —

"Thou must have told this story right; but still I have seen thee to be the wickedest of men, and there is no faith in faces if thou turnest out well."

Skamkell fared home, and rides first to Kirkby and calls Otkell out. He greets Skamkell well, and Skamkell brought him the greeting of Gizur and Geir.

"But about this matter of the suit," he says, "there is no need to speak softly, how that it is the will of both Gizur and Geir that this suit should not be settled in a friendly way. They gave that counsel that a summons should be set on foot, and that Gunnar should be summoned for having partaken of the goods, but Hallgerda for stealing them."

"It shall be done," said Otkell, "in everything as they have given counsel."

"They thought most of this," says Skamkell, "that thou hadst behaved so proudly; but as for me, I made as great a man of thee in everything as I could."

Now Otkell tells all this to his brothers, and Hallbjorn said —

"This must be the biggest lie."

Now the time goes on until the last of the summoning days before the Althing came.

Then Otkell called on his brothers and Skamkell to ride on the business of the summons to Lithend.

Hallbjorn said he would go, but said also that they would rue this summoning as time went on.

Now they rode twelve of them together to Lithend, but when they came into the "town," there was Gunnar out of doors, and knew naught of their coming till they had ridden right up to the house.

He did not go indoors then, and Otkell thundered out the summons there and then; but when they had made an end of the summoning Skamkell said —

"Is it all right, master?"

"Ye know that best," says Gunnar, "but I will put thee in mind of this journey one of these days, and of thy good help."

"That will not harm us," says Skamkell, "if thy bill be not aloft."

Gunnar was very wroth and went indoors, and told Kolskegg, and Kolskegg said —

"Ill was it that we were not out of doors; they should have come here on the most shameful journey, if we had been by."

"Everything bides its time," says Gunnar; "but this journey will not turn out to their honour."

A little after Gunnar went and told Njal.

"Let it not worry thee a jot," said Njal, "for this will be the greatest honour to thee, ere this Thing comes to an end. As for us, we will all back thee with counsel and force."

Gunnar thanked him and rode home.

Otkell rides to the Thing, and his brothers with him and Skamkell.

Chapter 51
Of Gunnar

Gunnar rode to the Thing and all the sons of Sigfus; Njal and his sons too, they all went with Gunnar; and it was said that no band was so well knit and hardy as theirs.

Gunnar went one day to the booth of the Dalemen; Hrut was by the booth and Hauskuld, and they greeted Gunnar well. Now Gunnar tells them the whole story of the suit up to that time.

"What counsel gives Njal?" asks Hrut.

"He bade me seek you brothers," says Gunnar, "and said he was sure that he and you would look at the matter in the same light."

"He wishes then," says Hrut, "that I should say what I think for kinship's sake; and so it shall be. Thou shalt challenge Gizur the White to combat on the island, if they do not leave the whole award to thee; but Kolskegg shall challenge Geir the Priest. As for Otkell and his crew, men must be got ready to fall on them; and now we have such great strength all of us together, that thou mayst carry out whatever thou wilt."

Gunnar went home to his booth and told Njal.

"Just what I looked for," said Njal.

Wolf Aurpriest got wind of this plan, and told Gizur, and Gizur said to Otkell—

"Who gave thee that counsel that thou shouldst summon Gunnar?"

"Skamkell told me that was the counsel of both Geir the priest and thyself."

"But where is that scoundrel," says Gizur, "who has thus lied?"

"He lies sick up at our booth," says Otkell.

"May he never rise from his bed," says Gizur, "Now we must all go to see Gunnar, and offer him the right to make his own award; but I know not whether he will take that now."

Many men spoke ill of Skamkell, and he lay sick all through the Thing.

Gizur and his friends went to Gunnar's booth; their coming was known, and Gunnar was told as he sat in his booth, and then they all went out and stood in array.

Gizur the White came first, and after a while he spoke and said —

"This is our offer — that thou, Gunnar, makest thine own award in this suit."

"Then," says Gunnar, "it was no doubt far from thy counsel that I was summoned."

"I gave no such counsel," says Gizur, "neither I nor Geir."

"Then thou must clear thyself of this charge by fitting proof."

"What proof dost thou ask?" says Gizur.

"That thou takest an oath," says Gunnar.

"That I will do," says Gizur, "if thou wilt take the award into thine own hands."

"That was the offer I made a while ago," says Gunnar; "but now, methinks, I have a greater matter to pass judgment on."

"It will not be right to refuse to make thine own award," said Njal; "for the greater the matter, the greater the honour in making it."

"Well," said Gunnar, "I will do this to please my friends, and utter my award; but I give Otkell this bit of advice, never to give me cause for quarrel hereafter."

Then Hrut and Hauskuld were sent for, and they came thither, and then Gizur the White and Geir the priest took their oaths; but Gunnar made his award, and spoke with no man about it, and afterwards he uttered it as follows: —

"This is my award," he says; "first, I lay it down that the storehouse must be paid for, and the food that was therein; but for the thrall, I will pay thee no fine, for that thou hiddest his faults; but I award him back to thee; for as the saying is, 'Birds of a feather flock most together'. Then, on the other hand, I see that thou hast summoned me in scorn and mockery, and for that I award to myself no less a sum than what the house that was burnt and the stores in it were worth; but if ye think it better that we be not set at one again, then I will let you have your choice of that, but if so I have already made up my mind what I shall do, and then I will fulfil my purpose."

"What we ask," said Gizur, "is that thou shouldst not be hard on Otkell, but we beg this of thee, on the other hand, that thou wouldst be his friend."

"That shall never be," said Gunnar, "so long as I live; but he shall have Skamkell's friendship; on that he has long leant."

"Well," answers Gizur, "we will close with thee in this matter, though thou alone layest down the terms."

Then all this atonement was made and hands were shaken on it, and Gunnar said to Otkell —

"It were wiser to go away to thy kinsfolk; but if thou wilt be here in this country, mind that thou givest me no cause of quarrel."

"That is wholesome counsel," said Gizur; "and so he shall do."

So Gunnar had the greatest honour from that suit, and afterwards men rode home from the Thing.

Now Gunnar sits in his house at home, and so things are quiet for a while.

Chapter 52
Of Runolf, the son of Wolf Aurpriest

There was a man named Runolf, the son of Wolf Aurpriest, he kept house at the Dale, east of Markfleet. He was Otkell's guest once when he rode from the Thing. Otkell gave him an ox, all black, without a spot of white, nine winters old. Runolf thanked him for the gift, and bade him come and see him at home whenever he chose to go; and this bidding stood over for some while, so that he had not paid the visit. Runolf often sent men to him and put him in mind that he ought to come; and he always said he would come, but never went.

Now Otkell had two horses, dun coloured, with a black stripe down the back; they were the best steeds to ride in all the country round, and so fond of each other, that whenever one went before, the other ran after him.

There was an Easterling staying with Otkell, whose name was Audulf; he had set his heart on Signy Otkell's daughter. Audulf was a tall man in growth, and strong.

Chapter 53
How Otkell rode over Gunnar

It happened next spring that Otkell said that they would ride east to the Dale, to pay Runolf a visit, and all showed themselves well pleased at that. Skamkell and his two brothers, and Audulf and three men more, went along with Otkell. Otkell rode one of the dun horses, but the other ran loose by his side. They shaped their course east towards Markfleet; and now Otkell gallops ahead, and now the horses race against each other, and they break away from the path up towards the Fleetlithe.

Now, Otkell goes faster than he wished, and it happened that Gunnar had gone away from home out of his house all alone; and he had a corn-sieve in one hand, but in the other a hand-axe. He goes down to his seed field and sows his corn there, and had laid his cloak of fine stuff and his axe down by his aide, and so he sows the corn a while.

Now, it must be told how Otkell rides faster than he would. He had spurs on his feet, and so he gallops down over the ploughed field, and neither of them sees the other; and just as Gunnar stands upright, Otkell rides down upon him, and drives one of the spurs into Gunnar's ear, and gives him a great gash, and it bleeds at once much.

Just then Otkell's companions rode up.

"Ye may see, all of you," says Gunnar, "that thou hast drawn my blood, and it is unworthy to go on so. First thou hast summoned me, but now thou treadest me under foot, and ridest over me."

Skamkell said, "Well it was no worse, master, but thou wast not one whit less wroth at the Thing, when thou tookest the self-doom and clutchedst thy bill."

Gunnar said, "When we two next meet thou shalt see the bill." After that they part thus, and Skamkell shouted out and said, "Ye ride hard, lads!"

Gunnar went home, and said never a word to any one about what had happened, and no one thought that this wound could have come by man's doing.

It happened, though, one day that he told it to his brother Kolskegg, and Kolskegg said —

"This thou shalt tell to more men, so that it may not be said that thou layest blame on dead men; for it will be gainsaid if witnesses do not know beforehand what has passed between you."

Then Gunnar told it to his neighbours, and there was little talk about it at first.

Otkell comes east to the Dale, and they get a hearty welcome there, and sit there a week.

Skamkell told Runolf all about their meeting with Gunnar, and how it had gone off; and one man had happened to ask how Gunnar behaved.

"Why," said Skamkell, "if it were a low-born man it would have been said that he had wept."

"Such things are ill spoken," says Runolf, "and when ye two next meet, thou wilt have to own that there is no voice of weeping in his frame of mind; and it will be well if better men have not to pay for thy spite. Now it seems to me best when ye wish to go home that I should go with you, for Gunnar will do me no harm."

"I will not have that," says Otkell; "but I will ride across the Fleet lower down."

Runolf gave Otkell good gifts, and said they should not see one another again.

Otkell bade him then to bear his sons in mind if things turned out so.

Chapter 54
The Fight at Rangriver

Now we must take up the story, and say that Gunnar was out of doors at Lithend, and sees his shepherd galloping up to the yard. The shepherd rode straight into the "town"; and Gunnar said, "Why ridest thou so hard?"

"I would be faithful to thee," said the man; "I saw men riding down along Markfleet, eight of them together, and four of them were in coloured clothes."

Gunnar said, "That must be Otkell".

The lad said, "I have often heard many temper-trying words of Skamkell's; for Skamkell spoke away there East at Dale, and said that thou sheddest tears when they rode over thee; but I tell it thee because I cannot bear to listen to such speeches of worthless men".

"We must not be word-sick," says Gunnar, "but from this day forth thou shalt do no other work than what thou choosest for thyself."

"Shall I say aught of this to Kolskegg thy brother?" asked the shepherd.

"Go thou and sleep," says Gunnar; "I will tell Kolskegg."

The lad laid him down and fell asleep at once, but Gunnar took the shepherd's horse and laid his saddle on him; he took his shield, and girded him with his sword, Oliver's gift; he sets his helm on his head; takes his bill, and something sung loud in it, and his mother, Rannveig, heard it. She went up to him and said, "Wrathful art thou now, my son, and never saw I thee thus before".

Gunnar goes out, and drives the butt of his spear into the earth, and throws himself into the saddle, and rides away.

His mother, Rannveig, went into the sitting-room, where there was a great noise of talking.

"Ye speak loud," she says, "but yet the bill gave a louder sound when Gunnar went out."

Kolskegg heard what she said, and spoke, "This betokens no small tidings".

"That is well," says Hallgerda, "now they will soon prove whether he goes away from them weeping."

Kolskegg takes his weapons and seeks him a horse, and rides after Gunnar as fast as he could.

Gunnar rides across Acretongue, and so to Geilastofna, and thence to Rangriver, and down the stream to the ford at Hof. There were some women at the milking-post there. Gunnar jumped off his horse and tied him up. By this time the others were riding up towards him; there were flat stones covered with mud in the path that led down to the ford.

Gunnar called out to them and said, "Now is the time to guard yourselves; here now is the bill, and here now ye will put it to the proof whether I shed one tear for all of you".

Then they all of them sprang off their horses' backs and made towards Gunnar. Hallbjorn was the foremost.

"Do not thou come on," says Gunnar; "thee last of all would I harm; but I will spare no one if I have to fight to my life."

"That I cannot do," says Hallbjorn; "thou wilt strive to kill my brother for all that, and it is a shame if I sit idly by." And as he said this he thrust at Gunnar with a great spear which he held in both hands.

Gunnar threw his shield before the blow, but Hallbjorn pierced the shield through. Gunnar thrust the shield down so hard that it stood fast in the earth, but he brandished his sword so quickly that no eye could follow it, and he made a blow with the sword, and it fell on Hallbjorn's arm above the wrist, so that it cut it off.

Skamkell ran behind Gunnar's back and makes a blow at him with a great axe. Gunnar turned short round upon him and parries the blow with the bill, and caught the axe under one of its horns with such a wrench that it flew out of Skamkell's hand away into the river.

Then Gunnar sang a song.

> Once thou askedst, foolish fellow,
> Of this man, this sea-horse racer,
> When as fast as feet could foot it
> Forth ye fled from farm of mine,
> Whether that were rightly summoned?
> Now with gore the spear we redden,
> Battle-eager and avenge us
> Thus on thee, vile source of strife.

Gunnar gives another thrust with his bill, and through Skamkell, and lifts him up and casts him down in the muddy path on his head.

Audulf the Easterling snatches up a spear and launches it at Gunnar. Gunnar caught the spear with his hand in the air, and hurled it back at once, and it flew through the shield and the Easterling too, and so down into the earth.

Otkell smites at Gunnar with his sword, and aims at his leg just below the knee, but Gunnar leapt up into the air and he misses him. Then Gunnar thrusts at him the bill, and the blow goes through him.

Then Kolskegg comes up, and rushes at once at Hallkell and dealt him his death-blow with his short sword. There and then they slay eight men.

A woman who saw all this, ran home and told Mord, and besought him to part them.

"They alone will be there," he says, "of whom I care not though they slay one another."

"Thou canst not mean to say that," she says, "for thy kinsman Gunnar, and thy friend Otkell will be there."

"Baggage that thou art," he says, "thou art always chattering," and so he lay still indoors while they fought.

Gunnar and Kolskegg rode home after this work, and they rode hard up along the river bank, and Gunnar slipped off his horse and came down on his feet.

Then Kolskegg said, "Hard now thou ridest, brother!"

"Ay," said Gunnar, "that was what Skamkell said when he uttered those very words when they rode over me."

"Well! thou hast avenged that now," says Kolskegg.

"I would like to know," says Gunnar, "whether I am by so much the less brisk and bold than other men, because I think more of killing men than they?"

Chapter 55
Njal's advice to Gunnar

Now those tidings are heard far and wide, and many say that they thought they had not happened before it was likely. Gunnar rode to Bergthorsknoll and told Njal of these deeds.

Njal said, "Thou hast done great things, but thou hast been sorely tried."

"How will it now go henceforth?" says Gunnar.

"Wilt thou that I tell thee what hath not yet come to pass?" asks Njal. "Thou wilt ride to the Thing, and thou wilt abide by my counsel and get the greatest honour from this matter. This will be the beginning of thy manslayings."

"But give me some cunning counsel," says Gunnar.

"I will do that," says Njal: "never slay more than one man in the same stock, and never break the peace which good men and true make between thee and others, and least of all in such a matter as this."

Gunnar said, "I should have thought there was more risk of that with others than with me."

"Like enough," says Njal, "but still thou shalt so think of thy quarrels that, if that should come to pass of which I have warned thee, then thou wilt have but a little while to live; but otherwise, thou wilt come to be an old man."

Gunnar said, "Dost thou know what will be thine own death?"

"I know it," says Njal.

"What?" asks Gunnar.

"That," says Njal, "which all would be the last to think."

After that Gunnar rode home.

A man was sent to Gizur the White and Geir the priest, for they had the blood-feud after Otkell. Then they had a meeting, and had a talk about what was to be done; and they were of one mind that the quarrel should be followed up at law. Then some one was sought who would take the suit up, but no one was ready to do that.

"It seems to me," says Gizur, "that now there are only two courses, that one of us two undertakes the suit, and then we shall have to draw lots who it shall be, or else the man will be unatoned. We may make up our minds, too, that this will be a heavy suit to touch; Gunnar has many kinsmen and is much beloved; but that one of us who does not draw the lot shall ride to the Thing and never leave it until the suit comes to an end."

After that they drew lots, and Geir the priest drew the lot to take up the suit.

A little after, they rode from the west over the river, and came to the spot where the meeting had been by Rangriver, and dug up the bodies, and took witness to the wounds. After that they gave lawful notice and summoned nine neighbours to bear witness in the suit.

They were told that Gunnar was at home with about thirty men; then Geir the priest asked whether Gizur would ride against him with one hundred men.

"I will not do that," says he, "though the balance of force is great on our side."

After that they rode back home. The news that the suit was set on foot was spread all over the country, and the saying ran that the Thing would be very noisy and stormy.

Chapter 56
Gunnar and Geir the Priest strive at the Thing

There was a man named Skapti. He was the son of Thorod. That father and son were great chiefs, and very well skilled in law. Thorod was thought to be rather crafty and guileful. They stood by Gizur the White in every quarrel.

As for the Lithemen and the dwellers by Rangriver, they came in a great body to the Thing. Gunnar was so beloved that all said with one voice that they would back him.

Now they all come to the Thing and fit up their booths. In company with Gizur the White were these chiefs: Skapti Thorod's son, Asgrim Ellidagrim's son, Oddi of Kidberg, and Halldor Ornolf's son.

Now one day men went to the Hill of Laws, and then Geir the priest stood up and gave notice that he had a suit of manslaughter against Gunnar for the slaying of Otkell. Another suit of manslaughter he brought against Gunnar for the slaying of Hallbjorn the white; then too he went on in the same way as to the slaying of Audulf, and so too as to the slaying of Skamkell. Then too he laid a suit of manslaughter against Kolskegg for the slaying of Hallkell.

And when he had given due notice of all his suits of manslaughter it was said that he spoke well. He asked, too, in what Quarter court the suits lay, and in what house in the district the defendants dwelt. After that men went away from the Hill of Laws, and so the Thing goes on till the day when the courts were to be set to try suits. Then either side gathered their men together in great strength.

Geir the priest and Gizur the White stood at the court of the men of Rangriver looking north, and Gunnar and Njal stood looking south towards the court.

Geir the priest bade Gunnar to listen to his oath, and then he took the oath, and afterwards declared his suit.

Then he let men bear witness of the notice given of the suit; then he called upon the neighbours who were to form the inquest to take their seats; then he called on Gunnar to challenge the inquest; and then he called on the inquest to utter their finding. Then the neighbours who were summoned on the inquest went to the court and took witness, and said that there was a bar to their finding in the suit as to Audulf's slaying, because the next of kin who ought to follow it up was in Norway, and so they had nothing to do with that suit.

After that they uttered their finding in the suit as to Otkell, and brought in Gunnar as truly guilty of killing him.

Then Geir the priest called on Gunnar for his defence, and took witness of all the steps in the suit which had been proved.

Then Gunnar, in his turn, called on Geir the priest to listen to his oath, and to the defence which he was about to bring forward in the suit. Then he took the oath and said —

"This defence I make to this suit, that I took witness and outlawed Otkell before my neighbours for that bloody wound which I got when Otkell gave me a hurt with his spur; but thee, Geir the priest, I forbid by a lawful protest made before a priest to pursue this suit, and so, too, I forbid the judges to hear it; and with this I make all the steps hitherto taken in this suit void and of none-effect. I forbid thee by a lawful protest, a full, fair, and binding protest, as I have a right to forbid thee by the common custom of the Thing and by the law of the land."

"Besides, I will tell thee something else which I mean to do," says Gunnar.

"What!" says Geir, "wilt thou challenge me to the island as thou art wont, and not bear the law?"

"Not that," says Gunnar; "I shall summon thee at the Hill of Laws for that thou calledst those men on the inquest who had no right to deal with Audulf's slaying, and I will declare thee for that guilty of outlawry."

Then Njal said, "Things must not take this turn, for the only end of it will be that this strife will be carried to the uttermost. Each of you, as it seems to me, has much on his side. There are some of these manslaughters, Gunnar, about which thou canst say nothing to hinder the court from finding thee guilty; but thou hast set on foot a suit against Geir, in which he, too, must be found guilty. Thou too, Geir the priest, shalt know that this suit of outlawry which hangs over thee shall not fall to the ground if thou wilt not listen to my words."

Thorod the priest said, "It seems to us as though the most peaceful way would be that a settlement and atonement were come to in the suit. But why sayest thou so little, Gizur the White?"

"It seems to me," says Gizur, "as though we shall need to have strong props for our suit; we may see, too, that Gunnar's friends stand near him, and so the best turn for us that things can take will be that good men and true should utter an award on the suit, if Gunnar so wills it."

"I have ever been willing to make matters up," says Gunnar; "and, besides, ye have much wrong to follow up, but still I think I was hard driven to do as I did."

And now the end of those suits was, by the counsel of the wisest men, that all the suits were put to arbitration; six men were to make this award, and it was uttered there and then at the Thing.

The award was that Skamkell should be unatoned. The blood money for Otkell's death was to be set off against the hurt Gunnar got from the spur; and as for the rest of the manslaughters, they were paid for after the worth of the men, and Gunnar's kinsmen gave money so that all the fines might be paid up at the Thing.

Then Geir the priest and Gizur the White went up and gave Gunnar pledges that they would keep the peace in good faith.

Gunnar rode home from the Thing, and thanked men for their help, and gave gifts to many, and got the greatest honour from the suit.

Now Gunnar sits at home in his honour.

Chapter 57
Of Starkad and his Sons

There was a man named Starkad; he was a son of Bork the waxy-toothed-blade, the son of Thorkell clubfoot, who took the land round about Threecorner as the first settler. His wife's name was Hallbera. The sons of Starkad and Hallbera were these: Thorgeir and Bork and Thorkell. Hildigunna the leech was their sister.

They were very proud men in temper, hard-hearted and unkind. They treated men wrongfully.

There was a man named Egil; he was a son of Kol, who took land as a settler between Storlek and Reydwater. The brother of Egil was Aunund of Witchwood, father of Hall the strong, who was at the slaying of Holt-Thorir with the sons of Kettle the smooth-tongued.

Egil kept house at Sandgil; his sons were these: Kol and Ottar and Hauk. Their mother's name was Steinvor; she was Starkad's sister.

Egil's sons were tall and strifeful; they were most unfair men. They were always on one side with Starkad's sons. Their sister was Gudruna nightsun, and she was the best-bred of women.

Egil had taken into his house two Easterlings; the one's name was Thorir and the other's Thorgrim. They were not long come out hither for the first time, and were wealthy and beloved by their friends; they were well skilled in arms, too, and dauntless in everything.

Starkad had a good horse of chesnut hue, and it was thought that no horse was his match in fight. Once it happened that these brothers from Sandgil were away under the Threecorner. They had much gossip about all the householders in the Fleetlithe, and they fell at last to asking whether there was any one that would fight a horse against them.

But there were some men there who spoke so as to flatter and honour them, that not only was there no one who would dare do that, but that there was no one that had such a horse.

Then Hildigunna answered, "I know that man who will dare to fight horses with you".

"Name him," they say.

"Gunnar has a brown horse," she says, "and he will dare to fight his horse against you, and against any one else."

"As for you women," they say, "you think no one can be Gunnar's match; but though Geir the priest or Gizur the White have come off with shame from before him, still it is not settled that we shall fare in the same way."

"Ye will fare much worse," she says; and so there arose out of this the greatest strife between them. Then Starkad said —

"My will is that ye try your hands on Gunnar last of all; for ye will find it hard work to go against his good luck."

"Thou wilt give us leave, though, to offer him a horse-fight?"

"I will give you leave, if ye play him no trick."

They said they would be sure to do what their father said.

Now they rode to Lithend; Gunnar was at home, and went out, and Kolskegg and Hjort went with him, and they gave them a hearty welcome, and asked whither they meant to go?

"No farther than hither," they say. "We are told that thou hast a good horse, and we wish to challenge thee to a horse-fight."

"Small stories can go about my horse," says Gunnar; "he is young and untried in every way."

"But still thou wilt be good enough to have the fight, for Hildigunna guessed that thou wouldst be easy in matching thy horse."

"How came ye to talk about that?" says Gunnar.

"There were some men," say they, "who were sure that no one would dare to fight his horse with ours."

"I would dare to fight him," says Gunnar; "but I think that was spitefully said."

"Shall we look upon the match as made, then?" they asked.

"Well, your journey will seem to you better if ye have your way in this; but still I will beg this of you, that we so fight our horses that we make sport for each other, but that no quarrel may arise from it, and that ye put no shame upon me; but if ye do to me as ye do to others, then there will be no help for it but that I shall give you such a buffet as it will seem hard to you to put up with. In a word, I shall do then just as ye do first."

Then they ride home. Starkad asked how their journey had gone off; they said that Gunnar had made their going good.

"He gave his word to fight his horse, and we settled when and where the horse-fight should be; but it was plain in everything that he thought he fell short of us, and he begged and prayed to get off."

"It will often be found," says Hildigunna, "that Gunnar is slow to be drawn into quarrels, but a hard hitter if he cannot avoid them."

Gunnar rode to see Njal, and told him of the horse-fight, and what words had passed between them, "But how dost thou think the horse-fight will turn out?"

"Thou wilt be uppermost," says Njal, "but yet many a man's bane will arise out of this fight."

"Will my bane perhaps come out of it?" asks Gunnar.

"Not out of this," says Njal; "but still they will bear in mind both the old and the new feud who fate against thee, and thou wilt have naught left, for it but to yield."

Then Gunnar rode home.

Chapter 58
How Gunnar's Horse Fought

Just then Gunnar heard of the death of his father-in-law Hauskuld; a few nights after, Thorgerda, Thrain's wife, was delivered at Gritwater, and gave birth to a boy child. Then she sent a man to her mother, and bade her choose whether it should be called Glum or Hauskuld. She bade call it Hauskuld. So that name was given to the boy.

Gunnar and Hallgerda had two sons, the one's name was Hogni and the other's Grani. Hogni was a brave man of few words, distrustful and slow to believe, but truthful.

Now men ride to the horse-fight, and a very great crowd is gathered together there. Gunnar was there and his brothers, and the sons of Sigfus. Njal and all his sons. There too was come Starkad and his sons, and Egil and his sons, and they said to Gunnar that now they would lead the horses together.

Gunner said, "That was well".

Skarphedinn said, "Wilt thou that I drive thy horse, kinsman Gunnar?"

"I will not have that," says Gunnar.

"It wouldn't be amiss though," says Skarphedinn; "we are hot-headed on both sides."

"Ye would say or do little," says Gunnar, "before a quarrel would spring up; but with me it will take longer, though it will be all the same in the end."

After that the horses were led together; Gunnar busked him to drive his horse, but Skarphedinn led him out. Gunnar was in a red kirtle, and had about his loins a broad belt, and a great riding-rod in his hand.

Then the horses run at one another, and bit each other long, so that there was no need for any one to touch them, and that was the greatest sport.

Then Thorgeir and Kol made up their minds that they would push their horse forward just as the horses rushed together, and see if Gunnar would fall before him.

Now the horses ran at one another again, and both Thorgeir and Kol ran alongside their horse's flank.

Gunnar pushes his horse against them, and what happened in a trice was this, that Thorgeir and his brother fall down flat on their backs, and their horse a-top of them.

Then they spring up and rush at Gunnar, Gunnar swings himself free and seizes Kol, casts him down on the field, so that he lies senseless, Thorgeir Starkad's son smote Gunnar's horse such a blow that one of his eyes started out. Gunnar smote Thorgeir with his riding-rod, and down falls Thorgeir senseless; but Gunnar goes to his horse, and said to Kolskegg, "Cut off the horse's head; he shall not live a maimed and blemished beast".

So Kolskegg cut the head off the horse.

Then Thorgeir got on his feet and took his weapons, and wanted to fly at Gunnar, but that was stopped, and there was a great throng and crush.

Skarphedinn said, "This crowd wearies me, and it is far more manly that men should fight it out with weapons"; and so he sang a song, —

> At the Thing there is a throng;
> Past all bounds the crowding comes;
> Hard 'twill be to patch up peace
> 'Twixt the men: this wearies me;
> Worthier is it far for men
> Weapons red with gore to stain;
> I for one would sooner tame
> Hunger huge of cub of wolf.

Gunnar was still, so that one man held him, and spoke no ill words.

Njal tried to bring about a settlement, or to get pledges of peace; but Thorgeir said he would neither give nor take peace; far rather, he said, would he see Gunnar dead for the blow.

Kolskegg said, "Gunnar has before now stood too fast than that he should have fallen for words alone, and so it will be again".

Now men ride away from the horse-field, every one to his home. They make no attack on Gunnar, and so that half-year passed away. At the Thing, the summer after, Gunnar met Olaf the peacock, his cousin, and he asked him to come and see him, but yet bade him beware of himself; "For," says he, "they will do us all the harm they can, and mind and fare always with many men at thy back".

He gave him much good counsel beside, and they agreed that there should be the greatest friendship between them.

Chapter 59
Of Asgrim and Wolf Uggis' son

Asgrim Ellidagrim's son had a suit to follow up at the Thing against Wolf Uggis' son. It was a matter of inheritance, Asgrim took it up in such a way as was seldom his wont; for there was a bar to his suit, and the bar was this, that he had summoned five neighbours to bear witness, when he ought to have summoned nine. And now they have this as their bar.

Then Gunnar spoke and said, "I will challenge thee to single combat on the island, Wolf Uggis' son, if men are not to get their rights by law; and Njal and my friend Helgi would like that I should take some share in defending thy cause, Asgrim, if they were not here themselves."

"But," says Wolf, "this quarrel is not one between thee and me."

"Still it shall be as good as though it were," says Gunnar.

And the end of the suit was, that Wolf had to pay down all the money.

Then Asgrim said to Gunnar, "I will ask thee to come and see me this summer, and I will ever be with thee in lawsuits, and never against thee".

Gunnar rides home from the Thing, and a little while after, he and Njal met, Njal besought Gunnar to be ware of himself, and said he had been told that those away under the Threecorner meant to fall on him, and bade him never go about with a small company, and always to have his weapons with him. Gunnar said so it should be, and told him that Asgrim had asked him to pay him a visit, "and I mean to go now this harvest."

"Let no men know before thou farest how long thou wilt be away," said Njal; "but, besides, I beg thee to let my sons ride with thee, and then no attack will be made on thee."

So they settled that among themselves.

"Now the summer wears away till it was eight weeks to winter," and then Gunnar says to Kolskegg, "Make thee ready to ride, for we shall ride to a feast at Tongue".

"Shall we say anything about it to Njal's sons?" said Kolskegg.

"No," says Gunnar; "they shall fall into no quarrels for me."

Chapter 60
An Attack against Gunnar Agreed on

They rode three together, Gunnar and his brothers. Gunnar had the bill and his sword, Oliver's gift; but Kolskegg had his short sword; Hjort, too, had proper weapons.

Now they rode to Tongue, and Asgrim gave them a hearty welcome, and they were there some while. At last they gave it out that they meant to go home there and then. Asgrim gave them good gifts, and offered to ride east with them, but Gunnar said there was no need of any such thing; and so he did not go.

Sigurd Swinehead was the name of a man who dwelt by Thurso water. He came to the farm under the Threecorner, for he had given his word to keep watch on Gunnar's doings, and so he went and told them of his journey home; "and," quoth he, "there could never be a finer chance than just now, when he has only two men with him".

"How many men shall we need to have to lie in wait for him?" says Starkad.

"Weak men shall be as nothing before him," he says; "and it is not safe to have fewer than thirty men."

"Where shall we lie in wait?"

"By Knafahills," he says; "there he will not see us before he comes on us."

"Go thou to Sandgil and tell Egil that fifteen of them must busk themselves thence, and now other fifteen will go hence to Knafahills."

Thorgeir said to Hildigunna, "This hand shall show thee Gunnar dead this very night".

"Nay, but I guess," says she, "that thou wilt hang thy head after ye two meet."

So those four, father and sons, fare away from the Threecorner, and eleven men besides, and they fared to Knafahills, and lay in wait there.

Sigurd Swinehead came to Sandgil and said, "Hither am I sent by Starkad and his sons to tell thee, Egil, that ye, father and sons, must fare to Knafahills to lie in wait for Gunnar".

"How many shall we fare in all?" says Egil.

"Fifteen, reckoning me," he says.

Kol said, "Now I mean to try my hand on Kolskegg".

"Then I think thou meanest to have a good deal on thy hands," says Sigurd.

Egil begged his Easterlings to fare with them. They said they had no quarrel with Gunnar; "and besides," says Thorir, "ye seem to need much help here, when a crowd of men shall go against three men".

Then Egil went away and was wroth.

Then the mistress of the house said to the Easterling: "In an evil hour hath my daughter Gudruna humbled herself, and broken the point of her maidenly pride, and lain by thy side as thy wife, when thou wilt not dare to follow thy father-in-law, and thou must be a coward," she says.

"I will go," he says, "with thy husband, and neither of us two shall come back."

After that he went to Thorgrim his messmate, and said, "Take thou now the keys of my chests; for I shall never unlock them again. I bid thee take for thine own whatever of our goods thou wilt; but sail away from Iceland, and do not think of revenge for me. But if thou dost not leave the land, it will be thy death."

So the Easterling joined himself to their band.

Chapter 61
Gunnar's Dream

Now we must go back and say that Gunnar rides east over Thurso water, but when he had gone a little way from the river he grew very drowsy, and bade them lie down and rest there.

They did so. He fell fast asleep, and struggled much as he slumbered.

Then Kolskegg said, "Gunnar dreams now". But Hjort said, "I would like to wake him".

"That shall not be," said Kolskegg, "but he shall dream his dream out".

Gunnar lay a very long while, and threw off his shield from him, and he grew very warm. Kolskegg said, "What hast thou dreamt, kinsman?"

"That have I dreamt," says Gunnar, "which if I had dreamt it there I would never have ridden with so few men from Tongue."

"Tell us thy dream," says Kolskegg.

Then Gunnar sang a song.

> Chief, that chargest foes in fight!
> Now I fear that I have ridden
> Short of men from Tongue, this harvest;
> Raven's fast I sure shall break.
> Lord, that scatters Ocean's fire!
> This at least, I long to say,
> Kite with wolf shall fight for marrow,
> Ill I dreamt with wandering thought.

"I dreamt, methought, that I was riding on by Knafahills, and there I thought I saw many wolves, and they all made at me; but I turned away from them straight towards Rangriver, and then methought they pressed hard on me on all sides, but I kept them at bay, and shot all those that were foremost, till they came so close to me that I could not use my bow against them. Then I took my sword, and I smote with it with one hand, but thrust at them with my bill with the other. Shield myself then I did not, and methought then I knew not what shielded me. Then I slew many wolves, and thou, too, Kolskegg; but Hjort methought they pulled down, and tore open his breast, and one methought had his heart in his maw; but I grew so wroth that I hewed that wolf asunder just below the brisket, and after that methought the wolves turned and fled. Now my counsel is, brother Hjort, that thou ridest back west to Tongue."

"I will not do that," says Hjort; "though I know my death is sure, I will stand by thee still."

Then they rode and came east by Knafahills, and Kolskegg said —

"Seest thou, kinsman! many spears stand up by the hills, and men with weapons."

"It does not take me unawares," says Gunnar, "that my dream comes true."

"What is best to be done now?" says Kolskegg; "I guess thou wilt not run away from them."

"They shall not have that to jeer about," says Gunnar, "but we will ride on down to the ness by Rangriver; there is some vantage ground there."

Now they rode on to the ness, and made them ready there, and as they rode on past them Kol called out and said —

"Whither art thou running to now, Gunnar?"

But Kolskegg said, "Say the same thing farther on when this day has come to an end".

Chapter 62
The Slaying of Hjort and Fourteen Men

After that Starkad egged on his men, and then they turn down upon them into the ness. Sigurd Swinehead came first and had a red targe, but in his other hand he held a cutlass. Gunnar sees him and shoots an arrow at him from his bow; he held the shield up aloft when he saw the arrow flying high, and the shaft passes through the shield and into his eye, and so came out at the nape of his neck, and that was the first man slain.

A second arrow Gunnar shot at Ulfhedinn, one of Starkad's men, and that struck him about the middle and he fell at the feet of a yeoman, and the yeoman over him. Kolskegg cast a stone and struck the yeoman on the head, and that was his death-blow.

Then Starkad said, "'Twill never answer our end that he should use his bow, but let us come on well and stoutly". Then each man egged on the other, and Gunnar guarded himself with his bow and arrows as long as he could; after that he throws them down, and then he takes his bill and sword and fights with both hands. There is long the hardest fight, but still Gunnar and Kolskegg slew man after man.

Then Thorgeir Starkad's son said, "I vowed to bring Hildigunna thy head, Gunnar."

Then Gunnar sang a song —

> Thou, that battle-sleet down bringeth,
> Scarce I trow thou speakest truth;
> She, the girl with golden armlets,
> Cannot care for such a gift;
> But, O serpent's hoard despoiler!
> If the maid must have my head —
> Maid whose wrist Rhine's fire wreatheth,
> Closer come to crash of spear.

"She will not think that so much worth having," says Gunnar; "but still to get it thou wilt have to come nearer!"

Thorgeir said to his brothers —

"Let us run all of us upon him at once; he has no shield and we shall have his life in our hands."

So Bork and Thorkel both ran forward and were quicker than Thorgeir. Bork made a blow at Gunnar, and Gunnar threw his bill so hard in the way that the sword flew out of Bork's hand; then he sees Thorkel standing on his other hand within stroke of sword. Gunnar was standing with his body swayed a little on one side, and he makes a sweep with his sword, and caught Thorkel on the neck, and off flew his head.

Kol Egil's son said, "Let me get at Kolskegg," and turning to Kolskegg he said, "This I have often said, that we two would be just about an even match in fight".

"That we can soon prove," says Kolskegg.

Kol thrust at him with his spear; Kolskegg had just slain a man and had his hands full, and so he could not throw his shield before the blow, and the thrust came upon his thigh, on the outside of the limb and went through it.

Kolskegg turned sharp round, and strode towards him, and smote him with his short sword on the thigh, and cut off his leg, and said, "Did it touch thee or not?"

"Now," says Kol, "I pay for being bare of my shield."

So he stood a while on his other leg and looked at the stump.

"Thou needest not to look at it," said Kolskegg; "'tis even as thou seest, the leg is off."

Then Kol fell down dead.

But when Egil sees this, he runs at Gunnar and makes a cut at him; Gunnar thrusts at him with the bill and struck him in the middle, and Gunnar hoists him up on the bill and hurls him out into Rangriver.

Then Starkad said, "Wretch that thou art indeed, Thorir Easterling, when thou sittest by; but thy host and father-in-law Egil is slain."

Then the Easterling sprung up and was very wroth. Hjort had been the death of two men, and the Easterling leapt on him and smote him full on the breast. Then Hjort fell down dead on the spot.

Gunnar sees this and was swift to smite at the Easterling, and cuts him asunder at the waist.

A little while after Gunnar hurls the bill at Bork, and struck him in the middle, and the bill went through him and stuck in the ground.

Then Kolskegg cut off Hauk Egil's son's head, and Gunnar smites off Otter's hand at the elbow-joint. Then Starkad said —

"Let us fly now. We have not to do with men!"

Gunnar said, "Ye two will think it a sad story if there is naught on you to show that ye have both been in the battle".

Then Gunnar ran after Starkad and Thorgeir, and gave them each a wound. After that they parted; and Gunnar and his brothers had then wounded many men who got away from the field, but fourteen lost their lives, and Hjort the fifteenth.

Gunnar brought Hjort home, laid out on his shield, and he was buried in a cairn there. Many men grieved for him, for he had many dear friends.

Starkad came home, too, and Hildigunna dressed his wounds and Thorgeir's, and said, "Ye would have given a great deal not to have fallen out with Gunnar".

"So we would," says Starkad.

Chapter 63
Njal's counsel to Gunnar

Steinvor, at Sandgil, besought Thorgrim the Easterling to take in hand the care of her goods, and not to sail away from Iceland, and so to keep in mind the death of his messmate and kinsman.

"My messmate Thorir," said he, "foretold that I should fall by Gunnar's hand if I stayed here in the land, and he must have foreseen that when he foreknew his own death."

"I will give thee," she says, "Gudruna my daughter to wife, and all my goods into the bargain."

"I knew not," he said, "that thou wouldest pay such a long price."

After that they struck the bargain that he shall have her, and the wedding feast was to be the next summer.

Now Gunnar rides to Bergthorsknoll, and Kolskegg with him. Njal was out of doors and his sons, and they went to meet Gunnar and gave them a hearty welcome. After that they fell a-talking, and Gunnar said —

"Hither am I come to seek good counsel and help at thy hand."

"That is thy due," said Njal.

"I have fallen into a great strait," says Gunnar, "and slain many men, and I wish to know what thou wilt make of the matter?"

"Many will say this," said Njal, "that thou hast been driven into it much against thy will; but now thou shalt give me time to take counsel with myself."

Then Njal went away all by himself, and thought over a plan, and came back and said —

"Now have I thought over the matter somewhat, and it seems to me as though this must be carried through — if it be carried through at all — with hardihood and daring. Thorgeir has got my kinswoman Thorfinna with child, and I will hand over to thee the suit for seduction. Another suit of outlawry against Starkad I hand over also to thee, for having hewn trees in my wood on the Threecorner ridge. Both these suits shalt thou take up. Thou shalt fare too to the spot where ye fought, and dig up the dead, and name witnesses to the wounds, and make all the dead outlaws, for that they came against thee with that mind to give thee and thy brothers wounds or swift death. But if this be tried at the Thing, and it be brought up against thee that thou first gave Thorgeir a blow, and so mayest neither plead thine own cause nor that of others, then I will answer in that matter, and say that I gave thee back thy rights at the Thingskala-Thing, so that thou shouldest be able to plead thine own suit as well as that of others, and then there will be an answer to that point. Thou shalt also go to see Tyrfing of Berianess, and he must hand over to thee a suit against Aunund of Witchwood, who has the blood feud after his brother Egil."

Then first of all Gunnar rode home; but a few nights after Njal's sons and Gunnar rode thither where the bodies were, and dug them up that were buried there. Then Gunnar summoned them all as outlaws for assault and treachery, and rode home after that.

Chapter 64
Of Valgard and Mord

That same harvest Valgard the guileful came out to Iceland, and fared home to Hof. Then Thorgeir went to see Valgard and Mord, and told them what a strait they were in if Gunnar were to be allowed to make all those men outlaws whom he had slain.

Valgard said that must be Njal's counsel, and yet every thing had not come out yet which he was likely to have taught him.

Then Thorgeir begged those kinsmen for help and backing, but they held out a long while, and at last asked for and got a large sum of money.

That, too, was part of their plan, that Mord should ask for Thorkatla, Gizur the White's daughter, and Thorgeir was to ride at once west across the river with Valgard and Mord.

So the day after they rode twelve of them together and came to Mossfell. There they were heartily welcomed, and they put the question to Gizur about the wooing, and the end of it was that the match should be made, and the wedding feast was to be in half a month's space at Mossfell.

They ride home, and after that they ride to the wedding, and there was a crowd of guests to meet them, and it went off well. Thorkatla went home with Mord and took the housekeeping in hand but Valgard went abroad again the next summer.

Now Mord eggs on Thorgeir to set his suit on foot against Gunnar, and Thorgeir went to find Aunund; he bids him now to begin a suit for manslaughter for his brother Egil and his sons; "but I will begin one for the manslaughter of my brothers, and for the wounds of myself and my father".

He said he was quite ready to do that, and then they set out, and give notice of the manslaughter, and summon nine neighbours who dwelt nearest to the spot where the deed was done. This beginning of the suit was heard of at Lithend; and then Gunnar rides to see Njal, and told him, and asked what he wished them to do next.

"Now," says Njal, "thou shalt summon those who dwell next to the spot, and thy neighbours; and call men to witness before the neighbours, and choose out Kol as the slayer in the manslaughter of Hjort thy brother: for that is lawful and right; then thou shalt give notice of the suit for manslaughter at Kol's hand, though he be dead. Then shall thou call men to witness, and summon the neighbours to ride to the Althing to bear witness of the fact, whether they, Kol and his companions, were on the spot, and in onslaught when Hjort was slain. Thou shalt also summon Thorgeir for the suit of seduction, and Aunund at the suit of Tyrfing."

Gunnar now did in everything as Njal gave him counsel. This men thought a strange beginning of suits, and now these matters come before the Thing.

Gunnar rides to the Thing, and Njal's sons and the sons of Sigfus. Gunnar had sent messengers to his cousins and kinsmen, that they should ride to the Thing, and come with as many men as they could, and told them that this matter would lead to much strife. So they gathered together in a great band from the west.

Mord rode to the Thing and Runolf of the Dale, and those under the Threecorner, and Aunund of Witchwood. But when they come to the Thing, they join them in one company with Gizur the White and Geir the priest.

Chapter 65
Of Fines and Atonements

Gunnar, and the sons of Sigfus, and Njal's sons, went altogether in one band, and they marched so swiftly and closely that men who came in their way had to take heed lest they should get a fall; and nothing was so often spoken about over the whole Thing as these great lawsuits.

Gunnar went to meet his cousins, and Olaf and his men greeted him well. They asked Gunnar about the fight, but he told them all about it, and was just in all he said; he told them, too, what steps he had taken since.

Then Olaf said, "'Tis worth much to see how close Njal stands by thee in all counsel".

Gunnar said he should never be able to repay that, but then he begged them for help; and they said that was his due.

Now the suits on both sides came before the court, and each pleads his cause.

Mord asked — "How it was that a man could have the right to set a suit on foot who, like Gunnar, had already made himself an outlaw by striking Thorgeir a blow?"

"Wast thou," answered Njal, "at Thingskala-Thing last autumn?"

"Surely I was," says Mord.

"Heardest thou," asks Njal, "how Gunnar offered him full atonement? Then I gave back Gunnar his right to do all lawful deeds."

"That is right and good law," says Mord, "but how does the matter stand if Gunnar has laid the slaying of Hjort at Kol's door, when it was the Easterling that slew him?"

"That was right and lawful," says Njal, "when he chose him as the slayer before witnesses."

"That was lawful and right, no doubt," says Mord; "but for what did Gunnar summon them all as outlaws?"

"Thou needest not to ask about that," says Njal, "when they went out to deal wounds and manslaughter."

"Yes," says Mord, "but neither befell Gunnar."

"Gunnar's brothers," said Njal, "Kolskegg and Hjort, were there, and one of them got his death and the other a flesh wound."

"Thou speakest nothing but what is law," says Mord, "though it is hard to abide by it."

Then Hjallti Skeggis son of Thursodale, stood forth and said —

"I have had no share in any of your lawsuits; but I wish to know whether thou wilt do something, Gunnar, for the sake of my words and friendship."

"What askest thou?" says Gunnar.

"This," he says, "that ye lay down the whole suit to the award and judgment of good men and true."

"If I do so," said Gunnar, "then thou shalt never be against me, whatever men I may have to deal with."

"I will give my word to that," says Hjallti.

After that he tried his best with Gunnar's adversaries, and brought it about that they were all set at one again. And after that each side gave the other pledges of peace; but for Thorgeir's wound came the suit for seduction, and for the hewing in the wood, Starkad's wound. Thorgeir's brothers were atoned for by half fines, but half fell away for the onslaught on Gunnar. Egil's staying and Tyrfing's lawsuit were set off against each other. For Hjort's slaying, the slaying of Kol and of the Easterling were to come, and as for all the rest, they were atoned for with half fines.

Njal was in this award, and Asgrim Ellidagrim's son, and Hjallti Skeggi's son.

Njal had much money out at interest with Starkad, and at Sandgil too, and he gave it all to Gunnar to make up these fines.

So many friends had Gunnar at the Thing, that he not only paid up there and then all the fines on the spot, but gave besides gifts to many chiefs who had lent him help; and he had the greatest honour from the suit; and all were agreed in this, that no man was his match in all the South Quarter.

So Gunnar rides home from the Thing and sits there in peace, but still his adversaries envied him much for his honour.

Chapter 66
Of Thorgeir Otkell's Son

Now we must tell of Thorgeir Otkell's son; he grew up to be a tall strong man, true-hearted and guileless, but rather too ready to listen to fair words. He had many friends among the best men, and was much beloved by his kinsmen.

Once on a time Thorgeir Starkad's son had been to see his kinsman Mord.

"I can ill brook," he says, "that settlement of matters which we and Gunnar had, but I have bought thy help so long as we two are above ground; I wish thou wouldest think out some plan and lay it deep; this is why I say it right out, because I know that thou art Gunnar's greatest foe, and he too thine. I will much increase thine honour if thou takest pains in this matter."

"It will always seem as though I were greedy of gain, but so it must be. Yet it will be hard to take care that thou mayest not seem to be a truce-breaker, or peace-breaker, and yet carry out thy point. But now I have been told that

Kolskegg means to try a suit, and regain a fourth part of Moeidsknoll, which was paid to thy father as an atonement for his son. He has taken up this suit for his mother, but this too is Gunnar's counsel, to pay in goods and not to let the land go. We must wait till this comes about, and then declare that he has broken the settlement made with you. He has also taken a cornfield from Thorgeir Otkell's son, and so broken the settlement with him too. Thou shalt go to see Thorgeir Otkell's son, and bring him into the matter with thee, and then fall on Gunnar; but if ye fail in aught of this, and cannot get him hunted down, still ye shall set on him over and over again, I must tell thee that Njal has 'spaed' his fortune, and foretold about his life, if he slays more than once in the same stock, that it would lead him to his death, if it so fell out that he broke the settlement made after the deed. Therefore shalt thou bring Thorgeir into the suit, because he has already slain his father; and now, if ye two are together in an affray, thou shalt shield thyself; but he will go boldly on, and then Gunnar will slay him. Then he has slain twice in the same stock, but thou shalt fly from the fight. And if this is to drag him to his death he will break the settlement afterwards, and so we may wait till then."

After that Thorgeir goes home and tells his father secretly. Then they agreed among themselves that they should work out this plot by stealth.

Chapter 67
Of Thorgeir Starkad's Son

Sometime after Thorgeir Starkad's son fared to Kirkby to see his namesake, and they went aside to speak, and talked secretly all day; but at the end Thorgeir Starkad's son, gave his namesake a spear inlaid with gold, and rode home afterwards; they made the greatest friendship the one with the other.

At the Thingskala-Thing in the autumn, Kolskegg laid claim to the land at Moeidsknoll, but Gunnar took witness, and offered ready money, or another piece of land at a lawful price to those under the Threecorner.

Thorgeir took witness also, that Gunnar was breaking the settlement made between them.

After that the Thing was broken up, and so the next year wore away.

Those namesakes were always meeting, and there was the greatest friendship between them. Kolskegg spoke to Gunnar and said —

"I am told that there is great friendship between those namesakes, and it is the talk of many men that they will prove untrue, and I would that thou wouldst be ware of thyself."

"Death will come to me when it will come," says Gunnar, "wherever I may be, if that is my fate."

Then they left off talking about it.

About autumn, Gunnar gave out that they would work one week there at home, and the next down in the isles, and so make an end of their haymaking. At the same time, he let it be known that every man would have to leave the house, save himself and the women.

Thorgeir under Threecorner goes to see his namesake, but as soon as they met they began to talk after their wont, and Thorgeir Starkad's son, said —

"I would that we could harden our hearts and fall on Gunnar."

"Well," says Thorgeir Otkell's son, "every struggle with Gunnar has had but one end, that few have gained the day; besides, methinks it sounds ill to be called a peace-breaker."

"They have broken the peace, not we," says Thorgeir Starkad's son. "Gunnar took away from thee thy cornfield; and he has taken Moeidsknoll from my father and me."

And so they settle it between them to fall on Gunnar; and then Thorgeir said that Gunnar would be all alone at home in a few nights' space, "and then thou shalt come to meet me with eleven men, but I will have as many".

After that Thorgeir rode home.

Chapter 68
Of Njal and those Namesakes

Now when Kolskegg and the house-carles had been three nights in the isles, Thorgeir Starkad's son had news of that, and sends word to his namesake that he should come to meet him on Threecorner ridge.

After that Thorgeir of the Threecorner busked him with eleven men; he rides up on the ridge and there waits for his namesake.

And now Gunnar is at home in his house, and those namesakes ride into a wood hard by. There such a drowsiness came over them that they could do naught else but sleep. So they hung their shields up in the boughs, and tethered their horses, and laid their weapons by their sides.

Njal was that night up in Thorolfsfell, and could not sleep at all, but went out and in by turns.

Thorhilda asked Njal why he could not sleep?

"Many things now flit before my eyes," said he; "I see many fetches of Gunnar's bitter foes, and what is very strange is this, they seem to be mad with rage, and yet they fare without plan or purpose."

A little after, a man rode up to the door and got off his horse's back and went in, and there was come the shepherd of Thorhilda and her husband.

"Didst thou find the sheep?" she asked.

"I found what might be more worth," said he.

"What was that?" asked Njal.

"I found twenty-four men up in the wood yonder; they had tethered their horses, but slept themselves. Their shields they had hung up in the boughs."

But so closely had he looked at them that he told of all their weapons and war-gear and clothes, and then Njal knew plainly who each of them must have been, and said to him —

"'Twere good hiring if there were many such shepherds; and this shall ever stand to thy good; but still I will send thee on an errand."

He said at once he would go.

"Thou shalt go," says Njal, "to Lithend and tell Gunnar that he must fare to Gritwater, and then send after men; but I will go to meet with those who are in the wood and scare them away. This thing hath well come to pass, so that they shall gain nothing by this journey, but lose much."

The shepherd set off and told Gunnar as plainly as he could the whole story. Then Gunnar rode to Gritwater and summoned men to him.

Now it is to be told of Njal how he rides to meet these namesakes.

"Unwarily ye lie here," he says, "or for what end shall this journey have been made? And Gunnar is not a man to be trifled with. But if the truth must be told then, this is the greatest treason. Ye shall also know this, that Gunnar is gathering force, and he will come here in the twinkling of an eye, and slay you all, unless ye ride away home."

They bestirred them at once, for they were in great fear, and took their weapons, and mounted their horses and galloped home under the Threecorner.

Njal fared to meet Gunnar and bade him not to break up his company.

"But I will go and seek for an atonement; now they will be finely frightened; but for this treason no less a sum shall be paid when one has to deal with all of them, than shall be paid for the slaying of one or other of those namesakes, though such a thing should come to pass. This money I will take into my keeping, and so lay it out that it may be ready to thy hand when thou hast need of it."

Chapter 69
Olaf the Peacock's Gifts to Gunnar

Gunnar thanked Njal for his aid, and Njal rode away under the Threecorner, and told those namesakes that Gunnar would not break up his band of men before he had fought it out with them.

They began to offer terms for themselves, and were full of dread, and bade Njal to come between them with an offer of atonement.

Njal said that could only be if there were no guile behind. Then they begged him to have a share in the award, and said they would hold to what he awarded.

Njal said he would make no award unless it were at the Thing, and unless the best men were by; and they agreed to that.

Then Njal came between them, so that they gave each other pledges of peace and atonement.

Njal was to utter the award, and to name as his fellows those whom he chose.

A little while after those namesakes met Mord Valgard's son, and Mord blamed them much for having laid the matter in Njal's hands, when he was Gunnar's great friend. He said that would turn out ill for them.

Now men ride to the Althing after their wont, and now both sides are at the Thing.

Njal begged for a hearing, and asked all the best men who were come thither, what right at law they thought Gunnar had against those namesakes for their treason. They said they thought such a man had great right on his side.

Njal went on to ask, whether he had a right of action against all of them, or whether the leaders had to answer for them all in the suit?

They say that most of the blame would fall on the leaders, but a great deal still on them all.

"Many will say this," said Mord, "that it was not without a cause when Gunnar broke the settlement made with those namesakes."

"That is no breach of settlement," says Njal, "that any man should take the law against another; for with law shall our land be built up and settled, and with lawlessness wasted and spoiled."

Then Njal tells them that Gunnar had offered land for Moeidsknoll, or other goods.

Then those namesakes thought they had been beguiled by Mord, and scolded him much, and said that this fine was all his doing.

Njal named twelve men as judges in the suit, and then every man paid a hundred in silver who had gone out, but each of those namesakes two hundred.

Njal took this money into his keeping, but either side gave the other pledges of peace, and Njal gave out the terms.

Then Gunnar rode from the Thing west to the Dales, till he came to Hjardarholt, and Olaf the peacock gave him a hearty welcome. There he sat half a month, and rode far and wide about the Dales, and all welcomed him with joyful hands. But at their parting Olaf said —

"I will give thee three things of price, a gold ring, and a cloak which Moorkjartan the Erse king owned, and a hound that was given me in Ireland; he is big, and no worse follower than a sturdy man. Besides, it is part of his nature that he has man's wit, and he will bay at every man whom he knows is thy foe, but never at thy friends; he can see, too, in any man's face, whether he means thee well or ill, and he will lay down his life to be true to thee. This hound's name is Sam."

After that he spoke to the hound, "Now shalt thou follow Gunnar, and do him all the service thou canst".

The hound went at once to Gunnar and laid himself down at his feet.

Olaf bade Gunnar to be ware of himself, and said he had many enviers, "For now thou art thought to be a famous man throughout all the land".

Gunnar thanked him for his gifts and good counsel, and rode home.

Now Gunnar sits at home for some time, and all is quiet.

Chapter 70
Mord's Counsel

A little after, those namesakes and Mord met, and they were not at all of one mind. They thought they had lost much goods for Mord's sake, but had got nothing in return; and they bade him set on foot some other plot which might do Gunnar harm.

Mord said so it should be. "But now this is my counsel, that thou, Thorgeir Otkell's son shouldest beguile Ormilda, Gunnar's kinswoman; but Gunnar will let his displeasure grow against thee at that, and then I will spread that story abroad that Gunnar will not suffer thee to do such things."

"Then ye two shall some time after make an attack on Gunnar, but still ye must not seek him at home, for there is no thinking of that while the hound is alive."

So they settled this plan among them that it should be brought about.

Thorgeir began to turn his steps towards Ormilda, and Gunnar thought that ill, and great dislike arose between them.

So the winter wore away. Now comes the summer, and their secret meetings went on oftener than before.

As for Thorgeir of the Threecorner and Mord, they were always meeting; and they plan an onslaught on Gunnar, when he rides down to the isles to see after the work done by his house-carles.

One day Mord was ware of it when Gunnar rode down to the isles, and sent a man off under the Threecorner to tell Thorgeir that then would be the likeliest time to try to fall on Gunnar.

They bestirred them at once, and fare thence twelve together, but when they came to Kirkby there they found thirteen men waiting for them.

Then they made up their minds to ride down to Rangriver and lie in wait there for Gunnar.

But when Gunnar rode up from the isles, Kolskegg rode with him. Gunnar had his bow and his arrows and his bill. Kolskegg had his short sword and weapons to match.

Chapter 71
The Slaying of Thorgeir Otkell's Son

That token happened as Gunnar and his brother rode up towards Rangriver, that much blood burst out on the bill.

Kolskegg asked what that might mean.

Gunnar says, "If such tokens took place in other lands, it was called 'wound-drops,' and Master Oliver told me also that this only happened before great fights".

So they rode on till they saw men sitting by the river on the other side, and they had tethered their horses.

Gunnar said, "Now we have an ambush".

Kolskegg answered, "Long have they been faithless; but what is best to be done now?"

"We will gallop up alongside them to the ford," says Gunnar, "and there make ready for them."

The others saw that and turned at once towards them.

Gunnar strings his bow, and takes his arrows and throws them on the ground before him, and shoots as soon as ever they come within shot; by that Gunnar wounded many men, but some he slew.

Then Thorgeir Otkell's son spoke and said, "This is no use; let us make for him as hard as we can".

They did so, and first went Aunund the fair, Thorgeir's kinsman. Gunnar hurled the bill at him, and it fell on his shield and clove it in twain, but the bill rushed through Aunund. Augmund Shockhead rushed at Gunnar behind his back. Kolskegg saw that and cut off at once both Augmund's legs from under him, and hurled him out into Rangriver, and he was drowned there and then.

Then a hard battle arose; Gunnar cut with one hand and thrust with the other. Kolskegg slew some men and wounded many.

Thorgeir's Starkad's son called out to his namesake, "It looks very little as though thou hadst a father to avenge".

"True it is," he answers, "that I do not make much way, but yet thou hast not followed in my footsteps; still I will not bear thy reproaches."

With that he rushes at Gunnar in great wrath, and thrust his spear through his shield, and so on through his arm.

Gunnar gave the shield such a sharp twist that the spearhead broke short off at the socket. Gunnar sees that another man was come within reach of his sword, and he smites at him and deals him his death-blow. After that, he clutches his bill with both hands; just then Thorgeir Otkell's son had come near him with a drawn sword, and Gunnar turns on him in great wrath, and drives the bill through him, and lifts him up aloft, and casts him out into Rangriver, and he drifts down towards the ford, and stuck fast there on a stone; and the name of that ford has since been Thorgeir's ford.

Then Thorgeir Starkad's son said, "Let us fly now; no victory will be fated to us this time".

So they all turned and fled from the field.

"Let us follow them up now," says Kolskegg, "and take thou thy bow and arrows, and thou wilt come within bow-shot of Thorgeir Starkad's son."

Then Gunnar sang a song.

> Reaver of rich river-treasure,
> Plundered will our purses be,
> Though to-day we wound no other
> Warriors wight in play of spears;
> Aye, if I for all these sailors
> Lowly lying, fines must pay —
> This is why I hold my hand,
> Hearken, brother dear, to me.

"Our purses will be emptied," says Gunnar, "by the time that these are atoned for who now lie here dead."

"Thou wilt never lack money," says Kolskegg; "but Thorgier will never leave off before he compasses thy death."

Gunnar sung another song.

Lord of water-skates that skim
Sea-king's fields, more good as he,
Shedding wounds' red stream, must stand
In my way ere I shall wince.
I, the golden armlets' warder,
Snakelike twined around my wrist,
Ne'er shall shun a foeman's faulchion
Flashing bright in din of fight.

"He, and a few more as good as he," says Gunnar, "must stand in my path ere I am afraid of them."

After that they ride home and tell the tidings.

Hallgerda was well pleased to hear them, and praised the deed much.

Rannveig said, "May be the deed is good; but somehow," she says, "I feel too downcast about it to think that good can come of it."

Chapter 72
Of the Suits for Manslaughter at the Thing

These tidings were spread far and wide, and Thorgeir's death was a great grief to many a man. Gizur the White and his men rode to the spot and gave notice of the manslaughter, and called the neighbours on the inquest to the Thing. Then they rode home west.

Njal and Gunnar met and talked about the battle. Then Njal said to Gunnar—

"Now be ware of thyself! Now hast thou slain twice in the same stock; and so now take heed to thy behaviour, and think that it is as much as thy life is worth, if thou dost not hold to the settlement that is made."

"Nor do I mean to break it in any way," says Gunnar, "but still I shall need thy help at the Thing."

"I will hold to my faithfulness to thee," said Njal, "till my death day."

Then Gunnar rides home. Now the Thing draws near; and each side gather a great company; and it is a matter of much talk at the Thing how these suits will end.

Those two, Gizur the White, and Geir the priest, talked with each other as to who should give notice of the suit of manslaughter after Thorgeir, and the end of it was that Gizur took the suit on his hand, and gave notice of it at the Hill of Laws, and spoke in these words: —

"I gave notice of a suit for assault laid down by law against Gunnar Hamond's son; for that he rushed with an onslaught laid down by law on Thorgeir Otkell's son, and wounded him with a body wound, which proved a death wound, so that Thorgeir got his death."

"I say on this charge he ought to become a convicted outlaw, not to be fed, not to be forwarded, not to be helped or harboured in any need."

"I say that his goods are forfeited, half to me and half to the men of the Quarter, whose right it is by law to seize the goods of outlaws."

"I give notice of this charge in the Quarter Court, into which this suit ought by law to come."

"I give this lawful notice in the hearing of all men at the Hill of Laws."

"I give notice now of this suit, and of full forfeiture and outlawry against Gunnar Hamond's son."

A second time Gizur took witness, and gave notice of a suit against Gunnar Hamond's son, for that he had wounded Thorgeir Otkell's son with a body wound which was a death wound, and from which Thorgeir got his death, on such and such a spot when Gunnar first sprang on Thorgeir with an onslaught, laid down by law.

After that he gave notice of this declaration as he had done of the first. Then he asked in what Quarter Court the suit lay, and in what house in the district the defendant dwelt.

When that was over men left the Hill of Laws, and all said that he spoke well.

Gunnar kept himself well in hand and said little or nothing.

Now the Thing wears away till the day when the courts were to be set.

Then Gunnar stood looking south by the court of the men of Rangriver, and his men with him.

Gizur stood looking north, and calls his witnesses, and bade Gunnar to listen to his oath, and to his declaration of the suit, and to all the steps and proofs which he meant to bring forward. After that he took his oath, and then he brought forward the suit in the same shape before the court, as he had given notice of it before. Then he made them bring forward witness of the notice, then he bade the neighbours on the inquest to take their seats, and called upon Gunnar to challenge the inquest.

Chapter 73
Of the Atonement

Then Njal spoke and said —

"Now I can no longer sit still and take no part. Let us go to where the neighbours sit on the inquest."

They went thither and challenged four neighbours out of the inquest, but they called on the five that were left to answer the following question in Gunnar's favour "whether those namesakes had gone out with that mind to the place of meeting to do Gunnar a mischief if they could?"

But all bore witness at once that so it was.

Then Njal called this a lawful defence to the suit, and said he would bring forward proof of it unless they gave over the suit to arbitration.

Then many chiefs joined in praying for an atonement, and so it was brought about that twelve men should utter an award in the matter.

Then either side went and handselled this settlement to the other. Afterwards the award was made, and the sum to be paid settled, and it was all to be paid down then and there at the Thing.

But besides, Gunnar was to go abroad and Kolskegg with him, and they were to be away three winters; but if Gunnar did not go abroad when he had a chance of a passage, then he was to be slain by the kinsmen of those whom he had killed.

Gunnar made no sign, as though he thought the terms of atonement were not good. He asked Njal for that money which he had handed over to him to keep. Njal had laid the money out at interest and paid it down all at once, and it just came to what Gunnar had to pay for himself.

Now they ride home. Gunnar and Njal rode both together from the Thing, and then Njal said to Gunnar —

"Take good care, messmate, that thou keepest to this atonement, and bear in mind what we have spoken about; for though thy former journey abroad brought thee to great honour, this will be a far greater honour to thee. Thou wilt come back with great glory, and live to be an old man, and no man here will then tread on thy heel; but if thou dost not fare away, and so breakest thy atonement, then thou wilt be slain here in the land, and that is ill knowing for those who are thy friends."

Gunnar said he had no mind to break the atonement, and he rides home and told them of the settlement.

Rannveig said it was well that he fared abroad, for then they must find some one else to quarrel.

Chapter 74
Kolskegg goes Abroad

Thrain Sigfus' son said to his wife that he meant to fare abroad that summer. She said that was well. So he took his passage with Hogni the white.

Gunnar took his passage with Arnfin of the Bay; and Kolskegg was to go with him.

Grim And Helgi, Njal's sons, asked their father's leave to go abroad too, and Njal said —

"This foreign voyage ye will find hard work, so hard that it will be doubtful whether ye keep your lives; but still ye two will get some honour and glory, but it is not unlikely that a quarrel will arise out of your journey when ye come back."

Still they kept on asking their father to let them go, and the end of it was that he bade them go if they chose.

Then they got them a passage with Bard the black, and Olaf Kettle's son of Elda; and it is the talk of the whole country that all the better men in that district were leaving it.

By this time Gunnar's sons, Hogni and Grani, were grown up; they were men of very different turn of mind. Grani had much of his mother's temper, but Hogni was kind and good.

Gunnar made men bear down the wares of his brother and himself to the ship, and when all Gunnar's baggage had come down, and the ship was all but "boun," then Gunnar rides to Bergthorsknoll, and to other homesteads to see men, and thanked them all for the help they had given him.

The day after he gets ready early for his journey to the ship, and told all his people that he would ride away for good and all, and men took that much to heart, but still they said that they looked to his coming back afterwards.

Gunnar threw his arms round each of the household when he was "boun," and every one of them went out of doors with him; he leans on the butt of his spear and leaps into the saddle, and he and Kolskegg ride away.

They ride down along Markfleet, and just then Gunnar's horse tripped and threw him off. He turned with his face up towards the Lithe and the homestead at Lithend, and said —

"Fair is the Lithe; so fair that it has never seemed to me so fair; the corn fields are white to harvest, and the home mead is mown; and now I will ride back home, and not fare abroad at all."

"Do not this joy to thy foes," says Kolskegg, "by breaking thy atonement, for no man could think thou wouldst do thus, and thou mayst be sure that all will happen as Njal has said."

"I will not go away any whither," says Gunnar, "and so I would thou shouldest do too."

"That shall not be," says Kolskegg; "I will never do a base thing in this, nor in anything else which is left to my good faith; and this is that one thing that could tear us asunder; but tell this to my kinsmen and to my mother, that I never mean to see Iceland again, for I shall soon learn that thou art dead, brother, and then there will be nothing left to bring me back."

So they parted there and then. Gunnar rides home to Lithend, but Kolskegg rides to the ship, and goes abroad.

Hallgerda was glad to see Gunnar when he came home, but his mother said little or nothing.

Now Gunnar sits at home that fall and winter, and had not many men with him.

Now the winter leaves the farmyard. Olaf the peacock asked Gunnar and Hallgerda to come and stay with him; but as for the farm, to put it into the hands of his mother and his son Hogni.

Gunnar thought that a good thing at first, and agreed to it, but when it came to the point he would not do it.

But at the Thing next summer, Gizur the White, and Geir the priest, gave notice of Gunnar's outlawry at the Hill of Laws; and before the Thing broke up Gizur summoned all Gunnar's foes to meet in the "Great Rift". He summoned Starkad under the Threecorner, and Thorgeir his son; Mord and Valgard the guileful; Geir the priest and Hjalti Skeggi's son; Thorbrand and Asbrand, Thorleik's sons; Eyjulf, and Aunund his son, Aunund of Witchwood and Thorgrim the Easterling of Sandgil.

Then Gizur spoke and said, "I will make you all this offer, that we go out against Gunnar this summer and slay him".

"I gave my word to Gunnar," said Hjalti, "here at the Thing, when he showed himself most willing to yield to my prayer, that I would never be in any attack upon him; and so it shall be."

Then Hjalti went away, but those who were left behind made up their minds to make an onslaught on Gunnar, and shook hands on the bargain, and laid a fine on any one that left the undertaking.

Mord was to keep watch and spy out when there was the best chance of falling on him, and they were forty men in this league, and they thought it would be a light thing for them to hunt down Gunnar, now that Kolskegg was away, and Thrain and many other of Gunnar's friends.

Men ride from the Thing, and Njal went to see Gunnar, and told him of his outlawry, and how an onslaught was planned against him.

"Me thinks thou art the best of friends," says Gunnar; "thou makest me aware of what is meant."

"Now," says Njal, "I would that Skarphedinn should come to thy house, and my son Hauskuld; they will lay down their lives for thy life."

"I will not," says Gunnar, "that thy sons should be slain for my sake, and thou hast a right to look for other things from me."

"All thy care will come to nothing," says Njal; "quarrels will turn thitherward where my sons are as soon as thou art dead and gone."

"That is not unlikely," says Gunnar, "but still it would mislike me that they fell into them for me; but this one thing I will ask of thee, that ye see after my son Hogni, but I say naught of Grani, for he does not behave himself much after my mind."

Njal rode home, and gave his word to do that.

It is said that Gunnar rode to all meetings of men, and to all lawful Things, and his foes never dared to fall on him.

And so some time went on that he went about as a free and guiltless man.

Chapter 75
The Riding to Lithend

Next autumn Mord Valgard's son, sent word that Gunnar would be all alone at home, but all his people would be down in the isles to make an end of their haymaking. Then Gizur the White and Geir the priest rode east over the rivers as soon as ever they heard that, and so east across the sands to Hof. Then they sent word to Starkad under the Threecorner, and there they all met who were to fall on Gunnar, and took counsel how they might best bring it about.

Mord said that they could not come on Gunnar unawares, unless they seized the farmer who dwelt at the next homestead, whose name was Thorkell, and made him go against his will with them to lay hands on the hound Sam, and unless he went before them to the homestead to do this.

Then they set out east for Lithend, but sent to fetch Thorkell. They seized him and bound him, and gave him two choices — one that they would slay him, or else he must lay hands on the hound; but he chooses rather to save his life, and went with them.

There was a beaten sunk road, between fences, above the farm yard at Lithend, and there they halted with their band. Master Thorkell went up to the homestead, and the tyke lay on the top of the house, and he entices the dog away with him into a deep hollow in the path. Just then the hound sees that there are men before them, and he leaps on Thorkell and tears his belly open.

Aunund of Witchwood smote the hound on the head with his axe, so that the blade sunk into the brain. The hound gave such a great howl that they thought it passing strange, and he fell down dead.

Chapter 76
Gunnar's slaying

Gunnar woke up in his hall and said —

"Thou hast been sorely treated, Sam, my fosterling, and this warning is so meant that our two deaths will not be far apart."

Gunnar's hall was made all of wood, and roofed with beams above, and there were window-slits under the beams that carried the roof, and they were fitted with shutters.

Gunnar slept in a loft above the hall, and so did Hallgerda and his mother.

Now when they were come near to the house they knew not whether Gunnar were at home, and bade that some one would go straight up to the house and see if he could find out. But the rest sat them down on the ground.

Thorgrim the Easterling went and began to climb up on the hall; Gunnar sees that a red kirtle passed before the windowslit, and thrusts out the bill, and smote him on the middle. Thorgrim's feet slipped from under him, and he dropped his shield, and down he toppled from the roof.

Then he goes to Gizur and his band as they sat on the ground.

Gizur looked at him and said —

"Well, is Gunnar at home?"

"Find that out for yourselves," said Thorgrim; "but this I am sure of, that his bill is at home," and with that he fell down dead.

Then they made for the buildings. Gunnar shot out arrows at them, and made a stout defence, and they could get nothing done. Then some of them got into the out-houses and tried to attack him thence, but Gunnar found them out with his arrows there also, and still they could get nothing done.

So it went on for while, then they took a rest, and made a second onslaught. Gunnar still shot out at them, and they could do nothing, and fell off the second time. Then Gizur the White said-

"Let us press on harder; nothing comes of our onslaught."

Then they made a third bout of it, and were long at it, and then they fell off again.

Gunnar said, "There lies on arrow outside on the wall, and it is one of their shafts; I will shoot at them with it, and it will be a shame to them if they get a hurt from their own weapons".

His mother said, "Do not so, my son; nor rouse them again when they have already fallen off from the attack".

But Gunnar caught up the arrow and shot it after them, and struck Eylif Aunund's son, and he got a great wound; he was standing all by himself, and they knew not that he was wounded.

"Out came an arm yonder," says Gizur, "and there was a gold ring on it, and took an arrow from the roof and they would not look outside for shafts if there were enough in doors; and now ye shall make a fresh onslaught."

"Let us burn him house and all," said Mord.

"That shall never be," says Gizur, "though I knew that my life lay on it; but it is easy for thee to find out some plan, such a cunning man as thou art said to be."

Some ropes lay there on the ground, and they were often used to strengthen the roof. Then Mord said — "Let us take the ropes and throw one end over the end of the carrying beams, but let us fasten the other end to these rocks and twist them tight with levers, and so pull the roof off the hall."

So they took the ropes and all lent a hand to carry this out, and before Gunnar was aware of it, they had pulled the whole roof off the hall.

Then Gunnar still shoots with his bow so that they could never come nigh him. Then Mord said again that they must burn the house over Gunnar's head. But Gizur said —

"I know not why thou wilt speak of that which no one else wishes, and that shall never be."

Just then Thorbrand Thorleik's son sprang up on the roof, and cuts asunder Gunnar's bowstring. Gunnar clutches the bill with both hands, and turns on him quickly and drives it through him, and hurls him down on the ground.

Then up sprung Asbrand his brother. Gunnar thrusts at him with the bill, and he threw his shield before the blow, but the bill passed clean through the shield and broke both his arms, and down he fell from the wall.

Gunnar had already wounded eight men and slain those twain. By that time Gunnar had got two wounds, and all men said that he never once winced either at wounds or death.

Then Gunnar said to Hallgerda, "Give me two locks of thy hair, and ye two, my mother and thou, twist them together into a bowstring for me."

"Does aught lie on it?" she says.

"My life lies on it," he said; "for they will never come to close quarters with me if I can keep them off with my bow."

"Well!" she says, "now I will call to thy mind that slap on the face which thou gavest me; and I care never a whit whether thou holdest out a long while or a short."

Then Gunnar sang a song —

> Each who hurls the gory javelin
> Hath some honour of his own,

> Now my helpmeet wimple-hooded
> Hurries all my fame to earth.
> No one owner of a war-ship
> Often asks for little things,
> Woman, fond of Frodi's flour,
> Wends her hand as she is wont.

"Every one has something to boast of," says Gunnar, "and I will ask thee no more for this."

"Thou behavest ill," said Rannveig, "and this shame shall long be had in mind."

Gunnar made a stout and bold defence, and now wounds other eight men with such sore wounds that many lay at death's door. Gunnar keeps them all off until he fell worn out with toil. Then they wounded him with many and great wounds, but still he got away out of their hands, and held his own against them a while longer, but at last it came about that they slew him.

Of this defence of his, Thorkell the Skald of Gta-Elf sang in the verses which follow —

> We have heard how south in Iceland
> Gunnar guarded well himself,
> Boldly battle's thunder wielding,
> Fiercest Iceman on the wave;
> Hero of the golden collar,
> Sixteen with the sword he wounded;
> In the shock that Odin loveth,
> Two before him lasted death.

But this is what Thormod Olaf's son sang —

> None that scattered sea's bright sunbeams,
> Won more glorious fame than Gunnar,
> So runs fame of old in Iceland,
> Fitting fame of heathen men;
> Lord of fight when helms were crashing,
> Lives of foeman twain he took,
> Wielding bitter steel he sorely
> Wounded twelve, and four besides.

Then Gizur spoke and said: "We have now laid low to earth a mighty chief, and hard work has it been, and the fame of this defence of his shall last as long as men live in this land".

After that he went to see Rannveig and said, "Wilt thou grant us earth here for two of our men who are dead, that they may lie in a cairn here?"

"All the more willingly for two," she says, "because I wish with all my heart I had to grant it to all of you."

"It must be forgiven thee," he says, "to speak thus, for thou hast had a great loss."

Then he gave orders that no man should spoil or rob anything there.

After that they went away.

Then Thorgeir Starkad's son said, "We may not be in our house at home for the sons of Sigfus, unless thou Gizur or thou Geir be here south some little while".

"This shall be so," says Gizur, and they cast lots, and the lot fell on Geir to stay behind.

After that he came to the Point, and set up his house there; he had a son whose name was Hroald; he was base born, and his mother's name was Biartey; he boasted that he had given Gunnar his death-blow. Hroald was at the Point with his father.

Thorgeir Starkad's son boasted of another wound which he had given to Gunnar.

Gizur sat at home at Mossfell. Gunnar's slaying was heard of, and ill spoken of throughout the whole country, and his death was a great grief to many a man.

Chapter 77
Gunnar Sings a Song Dead

Njal could ill brook Gunnar's death, nor could the sons of Sigfus brook it either.

They asked whether Njal thought they had any right to give notice of a suit of manslaughter for Gunnar, or to set the suit on foot.

He said that could not be done, as the man had been outlawed; but said it would be better worth trying to do something to wound their glory, by slaying some men in vengeance after him.

They cast a cairn over Gunnar, and made him sit upright in the cairn. Rannveig would not hear of his bill being buried in the cairn, but said he alone should have it as his own, who was ready to avenge Gunnar. So no one took the bill.

She was so hard on Hallgerda, that she was on the point of killing her; and she said that she had been the cause of her son's slaying.

Then Hallgerda fled away to Gritwater, and her son Grani with her, and they shared the goods between them; Hogni was to have the land at Lithend and the homestead on it, but Grani was to have the land let out on lease.

Now this token happened at Lithend, that the neat-herd and the serving-maid were driving cattle by Gunnar's cairn. They thought that he was merry, and that he was singing inside the cairn. They went home and told Rannveig, Gunnar's mother, of this token, but she bade them go and tell Njal.

Then they went over to Bergthorsknoll and told Njal, but he made them tell it three times over.

After that, he had a long talk all alone with Skarphedinn; and Skarphedinn took his weapons and goes with them to Lithend.

Rannveig and Hogni gave him a hearty welcome, and were very glad to see him. Rannveig asked him to stay there some time, and he said he would.

He and Hogni were always together, at home and abroad. Hogni was a brisk, brave man, well-bred and well-trained in mind and body, but distrustful and slow to believe what he was told, and that was why they dared not tell him of the token.

Now those two, Skarphedinn and Hogni, were out of doors one evening by Gunnar's cairn on the south side. The moon and stars were shining clear and bright, but every now and then the clouds drove over them. Then all at once they thought they saw the cairn standing open, and lo! Gunnar had turned himself in the cairn and looked at the moon. They thought they saw four lights burning in the cairn, and none of them threw a shadow. They saw that Gunnar was merry, and he wore a joyful face. He sang a song, and so loud, that it might have been heard though they had been farther off.

> He that lavished rings in largesse,
> When the fight's red rain-drops fell,
> Bright of face, with heart-strings hardy,
> Hogni's father met his fate;
> Then his brow with helmet shrouding,
> Bearing battle-shield, he spake,
> "I will die the prop of battle,
> Sooner die than yield an inch.
> Yes, sooner die than yield an inch".

After that the cairn was shut up again.

"Wouldst thou believe these tokens if Njal or I told them to thee?" says Skarphedinn.

"I would believe them," he says, "if Njal told them, for it is said he never lies."

"Such tokens as these mean much," says Skarphedinn, "when he shows himself to us, he who would sooner die than yield to his foes; and see how he has taught us what we ought to do."

"I shall be able to bring nothing to pass," says Hogni, "unless thou wilt stand by me."

"Now," says Skarphedinn, "will I bear in mind how Gunnar behaved after the slaying of your kinsman Sigmund; now I will yield you such help as I may. My father gave his word to Gunnar to do that whenever thou or thy mother had need of it."

After that they go home to Lithend.

Chapter 78
Gunnar of Lithend Avenged

Now we shall set off at once," says Skarphedinn, "this very night; for if they learn that I am here, they will be more wary of themselves."

"I will fulfil thy counsel," says Hogni.

After that they took their weapons when all men were in their beds. Hogni takes down the bill, and it gave a sharp ringing sound.

Rannveig sprang up in great wrath and said —

"Who touches the bill, when I forbade every one to lay hand on it?"

"I mean," says Hogni, "to bring it to my father, that he may bear it with him to Valhalla, and have it with him when the warriors meet."

"Rather shalt thou now bear it," she answered, "and avenge thy father; for the bill has spoken of one man's death or more."

Then Hogni went out, and told Skarphedinn all the words that his grandmother had spoken.

After that they fare to the Point, and two ravens flew along with them all the way. They came to the Point while it was still night. Then they drove the flock before them up to the house, and then Hroald and Tjorfi ran out and drove the flock up the hollow path, and had their weapons with them.

Skarphedinn sprang up and said, "Thou needest not to stand and think if it be really as it seems. Men are here."

Then Skarphedinn smites Tjorfi his death-blow. Hroald had a spear in his hand, and Hogni rushes at him; Hroald thrusts at him, but Hogni hewed asunder the spear-shaft with his bill, and drives the bill through him.

After that they left them there dead, and turn away thence under the Three-corner.

Skarphedinn jumps up on the house and plucks the grass, and those who were inside the house thought it was cattle that had come on the roof. Starkad and Thorgeir took their weapons and upper clothing, and went out and round about the fence of the yard. But when Starkad sees Skarphedinn he was afraid, and wanted to turn back.

Skarphedinn cut him down by the fence. Then Hogni comes against Thorgeir and slays him with the bill.

Thence they went to Hof, and Mord was outside in the field, and begged for mercy, and offered them full atonement.

Skarphedinn told Mord the slaying of those four men, and sang a song.

> Four who wielded warlike weapons
> We have slain, all men of worth,
> Them at once, gold-greedy fellow,
> Thou shalt follow on the spot;
> Let us press this pinch-purse so,
> Pouring fear into his heart;
> Wretch! reach out to Gunnar's son
> Right to settle all disputes.

"And the like journey," says Skarphedinn, "shalt thou also fare, or hand over to Hogni the right to make his own award, if he will take these terms."

Hogni said his mind had been made up not to come to any terms with the slayers of his father; but still at last he took the right to make his own award from Mord.

Chapter 79
Hogni takes an Atonement for Gunnar's Death

Njal took a share in bringing those who had the blood-feud after Starkad and Thorgeir to take an atonement, and a district meeting was called together, and men were chosen to make the award, and every matter was taken into account, even the attack on Gunnar, though he was an outlaw; but such a fine as was awarded, all that Mord paid; for they did not close their award against him before the other matter was already settled, and then they set off one award against the other.

Then they were all set at one again, but at the Thing there was great talk, and the end of it was, that Geir the priest and Hogni were set at one again, and that atonement they held to ever afterwards.

Geir the priest dwelt in the Lithe till his death-day, and he is out of the story.

Njal asked as a wife for Hogni Alfeida the daughter of Weatherlid the Skald, and she was given away to him. Their son was Ari, who sailed for Shetland, and took him a wife there; from him is come Einar the Shetlander, one of the briskest and boldest of men.

Hogni kept up his friendship with Njal, and he is now out of the story.

Chapter 80
Of Kolskegg: How He was Baptised

Now it is to be told of Kolskegg how he comes to Norway, and is in the Bay east that winter. But the summer after he fares east to Denmark, and bound himself to Sweyn Forkbeard the Dane-king, and there he had great honour.

One night he dreamt that a man came to him; he was bright and glistening, and he thought he woke him up. He spoke, and said to him —

"Stand up and come with me."

"What wilt thou with me?" he asks.

"I will get thee a bride, and thou shalt be my knight."

He thought he said yea to that, and after that he woke up.

Then he went to a wizard and told him the dream, but he read it so that he should fare to southern lands and become God's knight.

Kolskegg was baptised in Denmark, but still he could not rest there, but fared east to Russia, and was there one winter. Then he fared thence out to Micklegarth, and there took service with the Emperor. The last that was heard of him was, that he wedded a wife there, and was captain over the Varangians, and stayed there till his death-day; and he, too, is out of this story.

Chapter 81
Of Thrain: How He Slew Kol

Now we must take up the story, and say how Thrain Sigfus' son came to Norway. They made the land north in Helgeland, and held on south to Drontheim, and so to Hlada. But as soon as Earl Hacon heard of that, he sent men to them, and would know what men were in the ship. They came back and told him who the men were. Then the Earl sent for Thrain Sigfus' son, and he went to see him. The Earl asked of what stock he might be. He said that he was Gunnar of Lithend's near kinsman. The Earl said —

"That shall stand thee in good stead; for I have seen many men from Iceland, but none his match."

"Lord," said Thrain, "is it your will that I should be with you this winter?"

The Earl took to him, and Thrain was there that winter, and was thought much of.

There was a man named Kol, he was a great sea-rover. He was the son of Asmund Ashside, east out of Smoland. He lay east in the Gta-Elf, and had five ships, and much force.

Thence Kol steered his course out of the river to Norway, and landed at Fold, in the bight of the "Bay," and came on Hallvard Soti unawares, and found him in a loft. He kept them off bravely till they set fire to the house, then he gave himself up; but they slew him, and took there much goods, and sailed thence to Ldese.

Earl Hacon heard these tidings, and made them make Kol an outlaw over all his realm, and set a price upon his head.

Once on a time it so happened that the Earl began to speak thus —

"Too far off from us now is Gunnar of Lithend. He would slay my outlaw if he were here; but now the Icelanders will slay him, and it is ill that he hath not fared to us."

Then Thrain Sigfus' son answered —

"I am not Gunnar, but still I am near akin to him, and I will undertake this voyage."

The Earl said, "I should be glad of that, and thou shalt be very well fitted out for the journey".

After that his son Eric began to speak, and said —

"Your word, father, is good to many men, but fulfilling it is quite another thing. This is the hardest undertaking; for this sea-rover is tough and ill to deal with, wherefore thou wilt need to take great pains, both as to men and ships for this voyage."

Thrain said, "I will set out on this voyage, though it looks ugly".

After that the Earl gave him five ships, and all well trimmed and manned. Along with Thrain was Gunnar Lambi's son, and Lambi Sigurd's son. Gunnar was Thrain's brother's son, and had come to him young, and each loved the other much.

Eric, the Earl's son, went heartily along with them, and looked after strength for them, both in men and weapons, and made such changes in them as he thought were needful. After they were "boun," Eric got them a pilot. Then they sailed south along the land; but wherever they came to land, the Earl allowed them to deal with whatever they needed as their own.

So they held on east to Ldese, and then they heard that Kol was gone to Denmark. Then they shaped their course south thither; but when they came south to Helsingborg, they met men in a boat, who said that Kol was there just before them, and would be staying there for a while.

One day when the weather was good, Kol saw the ships as they sailed up towards him, and said he had dreamt of Earl Hacon the night before, and told his people he was sure these must be his men, and bade them all to take their weapons.

After that they busked them, and a fight arose; and they fought long, so that neither side had the mastery.

Then Kol sprang up on Thrain's ship, and cleared the gangways fast, and slays many men. He had a gilded helm.

Now Thrain sees that this is no good, and now he eggs on his men to go along with him, but he himself goes first and meets Kol.

Kol hews at him, and the blow fell on Thrain's shield, and cleft it down from top to bottom. Then Kol got a blow on the arm from a stone, and then down fell his sword.

Thrain hews at Kol, and the stroke came on his leg so that it cut it off. After that they slew Kol, and Thrain cut off his head, and they threw the trunk overboard, but kept his head.

There they took much spoil, and then they held on north to Drontheim, and go to see the Earl.

The Earl gave Thrain a hearty welcome, and he showed the Earl Kol's head, but the Earl thanked him for that deed.

Eric said it was worth more than words alone, and the Earl said so it was, and bade them come along with him.

They went thither, where the Earl had made them make a good ship that was not made like a common long-ship. It had a vulture's head, and was much carved and painted.

"Thou art a great man for show, Thrain," said the Earl, "and so have both of you, kinsmen, been, Gunnar and thou; and now I will give thee this ship, but it is called the 'Vulture'. Along with it shall go my friendship; and my will is that thou stayest with me as long as thou wilt."

He thanked him for his goodness, and said he had no longing to go to Iceland just yet.

The Earl had a journey to make to the marches of the land to meet the Swede-king. Thrain went with him that summer, and was a shipmaster and

steered the Vulture, and sailed so fast that few could keep up with him, and
he was much envied. But it always came out that the Earl laid great store on
Gunnar, for he set down sternly all who tried Thrain's temper.

So Thrain was all that winter with the Earl, but next spring the Earl asked
Thrain whether he would stay there or fare to Iceland; but Thrain said he had
not yet made up his mind, and said that he wished first to know tidings from
Iceland.

The Earl said that so it should be as he thought it suited him best; and
Thrain was with the Earl.

Then those tidings were heard from Iceland, which many thought great
news, the death of Gunnar of Lithend. Then the Earl would not that Thrain
should fare out to Iceland, and so there he stayed with him.

Chapter 82
Njal's Sons Sail Abroad

Now it must be told how Njal's sons, Grim and Helgi, left Iceland the same
summer that Thrain and his fellows went away; and in the ship with them were
Olaf Kettle's son of Elda, and Bard the black. They got so strong a wind from
the north that they were driven south into the main; and so thick a mist came
over them that they could not tell whither they were driving, and they were out
a long while. At last they came to where was a great ground sea, and thought
then they must be near land. So then Njal's sons asked Bard if he could tell at
all to what land they were likely to be nearest.

"Many lands there are," said he, "which we might hit with the weather we
have had — the Orkneys, or Scotland, or Ireland."

Two nights after, they saw land on both boards, and a great surf running
up in the firth. They cast anchor outside the breakers, and the wind began to
fall; and next morning it was calm. Then they see thirteen ships coming out to
them.

Then Bard spoke and said, "What counsel shall we take now, for these men
are going to make an onslaught on us?"

So they took counsel whether they should defend themselves or yield, but
before they could make up their minds, the Vikings were upon them. Then
each side asked the other their names, and what their leaders were called. So
the leaders of the chapmen told their names, and asked back who led that
host. One called himself Gritgard, and the other Snowcolf, sons of Moldan of
Duncansby in Scotland, kinsmen of Malcolm the Scot king.

"And now," says Gritgard, "we have laid down two choices, one that ye go
on shore, and we will take your goods; the other is, that we fall on you and slay
every man that we can catch."

"The will of the chapmen," answers Helgi, "is to defend themselves."

But the chapmen called out, "Wretch that thou art to speak thus! What
defence can we make? Lading is less than life."

But Grim, he fell upon a plan to shout out to the Vikings, and would not let them hear the bad choice of the chapmen.

Then Bard and Olaf said, "Think ye not that these Icelanders will make game of you sluggards; take rather your weapons and guard your goods".

So they all seized their weapons, and bound themselves, one with another, never to give up so long as they had strength to fight.

Chapter 83
Of Kari Solmund's Son

Then the Vikings shot at them and the fight began, and the chapmen guard themselves well. Snowcolf sprang aboard and at Olaf, and thrust his spear through his body, but Grim thrust at Snowcolf with his spear, and so stoutly, that he fell over-board. Then Helgi turned to meet Grim, and they too drove down all the Vikings as they tried to board, and Njal's sons were ever where there was most need. Then the Vikings called out to the chapmen and bade them give up, but they said they would never yield. Just then some one looked seaward, and there they see ships coming from the south round the Ness, and they were not fewer than ten, and they row hard and steer thitherwards. Along their sides were shield on shield, but on that ship that came first stood a man by the mast, who was clad in a silken kirtle, and had a gilded helm, and his hair was both fair and thick; that man had a spear inlaid with gold in his hand.

He asked, "Who have here such an uneven game?"

Helgi tells his name, and said that against them are Gritgard and Snowcolf.

"But who are your captains?" he asks.

Helgi answered, "Bard the black, who lives, but the other, who is dead and gone, was called Olaf".

"Are ye men from Iceland?" says he.

"Sure enough we are," Helgi answers.

He asked whose sons they were, and they told him, then he knew them and said —

"Well known names have ye all, father and sons both."

"Who art thou?" asks Helgi.

"My name is Kari, and I am Solmund's son."

"Whence comest thou?" says Helgi.

"From the Southern Isles."

"Then thou art welcome," says Helgi, "if thou wilt give us a little help."

"I'll give ye all the help ye need," says Kari; "but what do ye ask?"

"To fall on them," says Helgi.

Kari says that so it shall be. So they pulled up to them, and then the battle began the second time; but when they had fought a little while, Kari springs up on Snowcolf's ship; he turns to meet him and smites at him with his sword. Kari leaps nimbly backwards over a beam that lay athwart the ship, and Snowcolf smote the beam so that both edges of the sword were hidden. Then Kari smites at him, and the sword fell on his shoulder, and the stroke was so mighty that he cleft in twain shoulder, arm, and all, and Snowcolf got his death there and then. Gritgard hurled a spear at Kari, but Kari saw it and sprang up aloft, and the spear missed him. Just then Helgi and Grim came up both to meet Kari, and Helgi springs on Gritgard and thrusts his spear through him, and that was his death blow; after that they went round the whole ship on both boards, and then men begged for mercy. So they gave them all peace, but took all their goods. After that they ran all the ships out under the islands.

Chapter 84
Of Earl Sigurd

Sigurd was the name of an earl who ruled over the Orkneys; he was the son of Hlodver, the son of Thorfinn the scull-splitter, the son of Turf-Einar, the son of Rognvald, Earl of M[oe]ren, the son of Eystein the noisy. Kari was one of Earl Sigurd's body-guard, and had just been gathering scatts in the Southern Isles from Earl Gilli. Now Kari asks them to go to Hrossey, and said the Earl would take to them well. They agreed to that, and went with Kari and came to Hrossey. Kari led them to see the Earl, and said what men they were.

"How came they," says the Earl, "to fall upon thee?"

"I found them," says Kari, "in Scotland's Firths, and they were fighting with the sons of Earl Moldan, and held their own so well that they threw themselves about between the bulwarks, from side to side, and were always there where the trial was greatest, and now I ask you to give them quarters among your body-guard."

"It shall be as thou choosest," says the Earl, "thou hast already taken them so much by the hand."

Then they were there with the Earl that winter, and were worthily treated, but Helgi was silent as the winter wore on. The Earl could not tell what was at the bottom of that, and asked why he was so silent, and what was on his mind.

"Thinkest thou it not good to be here?"

"Good, methinks, it is here," he says.

"Then what art thou thinking about?" asks the Earl.

"Hast thou any realm to guard in Scotland?" asks Helgi.

"So we think," says the Earl, "but what makes thee think about that, or what is the matter with it?"

"The Scots," says Helgi, "must have taken your steward's life, and stopped all the messengers; that none should cross the Pentland Firth."

"Hast thou the second sight?" said the Earl.

"That has been little proved," answers Helgi.

"Well," says the Earl, "I will increase thy honour if this be so, otherwise thou shalt smart for it."

"Nay," says Kari, "Helgi is not that kind of man, and like enough his words are sooth, for his father has the second sight."

After that the Earl sent men south to Straumey to Arnljot, his steward there, and after that Arnljot sent them across the Pentland Firth, and they spied out and learnt that Earl Hundi and Earl Melsnati had taken the life of Havard in Thraswick, Earl Sigurd's brother-in-law. So Arnljot sent word to Earl Sigurd to come south with a great host and drive those earls out of his realm, and as soon as the Earl heard that, he gathered together a mighty host from all the isles.

Chapter 85

The Battle with the Earls

After that the Earl set out south with his host, and Kari went with him, and Njal's sons too. They came south to Caithness. The Earl had these realms in Scotland, Ross and Moray, Sutherland, and the Dales. There came to meet them men from those realms, and said that the Earls were a short way off with a great host. Then Earl Sigurd turns his host thither, and the name of that place is Duncansness, above which they met, and it came to a great battle between them. Now the Scots had let some of their host go free from the main battle, and these took the Earl's men in flank, and many men fell there till Njal's sons turned against the foe, and fought with them and put them to flight; but still it was a hard fight, and then Njal's sons turned back to the front by the Earl's standard, and fought well. Now Kari turns to meet Earl Melsnati, and Melsnati hurled a spear at him, but Kari caught the spear and threw it back and through the Earl. Then Earl Hundi fled, but they chased the fleers until they learnt that Malcolm was gathering a host at Duncansby. Then the Earl took counsel with his men, and it seemed to all the best plan to turn back, and not to fight with such a mighty land force; so they turned back. But when the Earl came to Straumey they shared the battle-spoil. After that he went north to Hrossey, and Njal's sons and Kari followed him. Then the Earl made a great feast, and at that feast he gave Kari a good sword, and a spear inlaid with gold; but he gave Helgi a gold ring and a mantle, and Grim a shield and sword. After that he took Helgi and Grim into his body-guard, and thanked them for their good help. They were with the Earl that winter and the summer after, till Kari went sea-roving; then they went with him, and harried far and wide that summer, and everywhere won the victory. They fought against Godred, King of Man, and conquered him; and after that they fared back, and had gotten much goods. Next winter they were still with the Earl, and when the spring came Njal's sons asked leave to go to Norway. The Earl said they should go or not as they pleased, and he gave them a good ship and smart men. As for Kari, he said he must come that summer to Norway with Earl Hacon's scatts, and then they would meet; and so it fell out that they gave each other their word to meet. After that Njal's sons put out to sea and sailed for Norway, and made the land north near Drontheim.

Chapter 86
Hrapp's Voyage from Iceland

There was a man named Kolbein, and his surname was Arnljot's son; he was a man from Drontheim; he sailed out to Iceland that same summer in which Kolskegg and Njal's sons went abroad. He was that winter east in Broaddale; but the spring after, he made his ship ready for sea in Gautawick; and when men were almost "boun," a man rowed up to them in a boat, and made the boat fast to the ship, and afterwards he went on board the ship to see Kolbein.

Kolbein asked that man for his name.

"My name is Hrapp," says he.

"What wilt thou with me?" says Kolbein.

"I wish to ask thee to put me across the Iceland main."

"Whose son art thou?" asks Kolbein.

"I am a son of Aurgunleid, the son of Geirolf the fighter."

"What need lies on thee," asked Kolbein, "to drive thee abroad?"

"I have slain a man," says Hrapp.

"What manslaughter was that," says Kolbein, "and what men have the blood-feud?"

"The men of Weaponfirth," says Hrapp, "but the man I slew was Aurlyg, the son of Aurlyg, the son of Roger the white."

"I guess this," says Kolbein, "that he will have the worst of it who bears thee abroad."

"I am the friend of my friend," said Hrapp, "but when ill is done to me I repay it. Nor am I short of money to lay down for my passage."

Then Kolbein took Hrapp on board, and a little while after a fair breeze sprung up, and they sailed away on the sea.

Hrapp ran short of food at sea, and then he sate him down at the mess of those who were nearest to him. They sprang up with ill words, and so it was that they came to blows, and Hrapp, in a trice, has two men under him.

Then Kolbein was told, and he bade Hrapp to come and share his mess, and he accepted that.

Now they come off the sea, and lie outside off Agdirness.

Then Kolbein asked where that money was which he had offered to pay for his fare?

"It is out in Iceland," answers Hrapp.

"Thou wilt beguile more men than me, I fear," says Kolbein; "but now I will forgive thee all the fare."

Hrapp bade him have thanks for that. "But what counsel dost thou give as to what I ought to do?"

"That first of all," he says, "that thou goest from the ship as soon as ever thou canst, for all Easterlings will bear thee bad witness; but there is yet another bit of good counsel which I will give thee, and that is, never to cheat thy master."

Then Hrapp went on shore with his weapons, and he had a great axe with an iron-bound haft in his hand.

He fares on and on till he comes to Gudbrand of the Dale. He was the greatest friend of Earl Hacon. They two had a shrine between them, and it was never opened but when the Earl came thither. That was the second greatest shrine in Norway, but the other was at Hlada.

Thrand was the name of Gudbrand's son, but his daughter's name was Gudruna.

Hrapp went in before Gudbrand, and hailed him well. He asked whence he came and what was his name. Hrapp told him about himself, and how he had sailed abroad from Iceland.

After that he asks Gudbrand to take him into his household as a guest.

"It does not seem," said Gudbrand, "to look on thee, as though thou wert a man to bring good luck."

"Methinks, then," says Hrapp, "that all I have heard about thee has been great lies; for it is said that thou takest every one into thy house that asks thee; and that no man is thy match for goodness and kindness, far or near; but now I shall have to speak against that saying, if thou dost not take me in."

"Well, thou shalt stay here," said Gudbrand.

"To what seat wilt thou show me?" says Hrapp.

"To one on the lower bench, over against my high seat."

Then Hrapp went and took his seat. He was able to tell of many things, and so it was at first that Gudbrand and many thought it sport to listen to him; but still it came about that most men thought him too much given to mocking, and the end of it was that he took to talking alone with Gudruna, so that many said that he meant to beguile her.

But when Gudbrand was aware of that, he scolded her much for daring to talk alone with him, and bade her beware of speaking aught to him if the whole household did not hear it. She gave her word to be good at first, but still it was soon the old story over again as to their talk. Then Gudbrand got Asvard, his overseer, to go about with her, out of doors and in, and to be with her wherever she went. One day it happened that she begged for leave to go into the nut-wood for a pastime, and Asvard went along with her. Hrapp goes to seek for them and found them, and took her by the hand, and led her away alone.

Then Asvard went to look for her, and found them both together stretched on the grass in a thicket.

He rushes at them, axe in air, and smote at Hrapp's leg, but Hrapp gave himself a second turn, and he missed him. Hrapp springs on his feet as quick as he can, and caught up his axe. Then Asvard wished to turn and get away, but Hrapp hewed asunder his backbone.

Then Gudruna said, "Now hast thou done that deed which will hinder thy stay any Longer with my father; but still there is something behind which he will like still less, for I go with child".

"He shall not learn this from others," says Hrapp, "but I will go home and tell him both these tidings."

"Then," she says, "thou will not come away with thy life."

"I will run the risk of that," he says.

After that he sees her back to the other women, but he went home. Gudbrand sat in his high seat, and there were few men in the hall.

Hrapp went in before him, and bore his axe high.

"Why is thine axe bloody?" asks Gudbrand.

"I made it so by doing a piece of work on thy overseer Asvard's back," says Hrapp.

"That can be no good work," says Gudbrand; "thou must have slain him."

"So it is, be sure," says Hrapp.

"What did ye fall out about?" asks Gudbrand.

"Oh!" says Hrapp, "what you would think small cause enough. He wanted to hew off my leg."

"What hast thou done first?" asked Gudbrand.

"What he had no right to meddle with," says Hrapp.

"Still thou wilt tell me what it was."

"Well!" said Hrapp, "if thou must know, I lay by thy daughter's side, and he thought that bad."

"Up men!" cried Gudbrand, "and take him. He shall be slain out of hand."

"Very little good wilt thou let me reap of my son-in-lawship," says Hrapp, "but thou hast not so many men at thy back as to do that speedily."

Up they rose, but he sprang out of doors. They run after him, but he got away to the wood, and they could not lay hold of him.

Then Gudbrand gathers people, and lets the wood be searched; but they find him not, for the wood was great and thick.

Hrapp fares through the wood till he came to a clearing; there he found a house, and saw a man outside cleaving wood.

He asked that man for his name, and he said his name was Tofi.

Tofi asked him for his name in turn, and Hrapp told him his true name.

Hrapp asked why the householder had set up his abode so far from other men?

"For that here," he says, "I think I am less likely to have brawls with other men."

"It is strange how we beat about the bush in out talk," says Hrapp, "but I will first tell thee who I am. I have been with Gudbrand of the Dale, but I ran away thence because I slew his overseer; but now I know that we are both of us bad men; for thou wouldst not have come hither away from other men unless thou wert some man's outlaw. And now I give thee two choices, either that I will tell where thou art, or that we two have between us, share and share alike, all that is here."

"This is even as thou sayest," said the householder; "I seized and carried off this woman who is here with me, and many men have sought for me."

Then he led Hrapp in with him; there was a small house there, but well built.

The master of the house told his mistress that he had taken Hrapp into his company.

"Most men will get ill luck from this man," she says; "but thou wilt have thy way."

So Hrapp was there after that. He was a great wanderer, and was never at home. He still brings about meetings with Gudruna; her father and brother, Thrand and Gudbrand, lay in wait for him, but they could never get nigh him, and so all that year passed away.

Gudbrand sent and told Earl Hacon what trouble he had had with Hrapp, and the Earl let him be made an outlaw, and laid a price upon his head. He said too, that he would go himself to look after him; but that passed off, and the Earl thought it easy enough for them to catch him when he went about so unwarily.

Chapter 87
Thrain took to Hrapp

That same summer Njal's sons fared to Norway from the Orkneys, as was before written, and they were there at the fair during the summer. Then Thrain Sigfus' son busked his ship for Iceland, and was all but "boun". At that time Earl Hacon went to a feast at Gudbrand's house. That night Killing-Hrapp came to the shrine of Earl Hacon and Gudbrand, and he went inside the house, and there he saw Thorgerda Shrinebride sitting, and she was as tall as a full-grown man. She had a great gold ring on her arm, and a wimple on her head; he strips her of her wimple, and takes the gold ring from off her. Then he sees Thor's car, and takes from him a second gold ring; a third he took from Irpa; and then dragged them all out, and spoiled them of all their gear.

After that he laid fire to the shrine, and burnt it down, and then he goes away just as it began to dawn. He walks across a ploughed field, and there six men sprung up with weapons, and fall upon him at once; but he made a stout defence, and the end of the business was that he slays three men, but wounds Thrand to the death, and drives two to the woods, so that they could bear no news to the Earl. He then went up to Thrand and said —

"It is now in my power to slay thee if I will, but I will not do that; and now I will set more store by the ties that are between us than ye have shown to me."

Now Hrapp means to turn back to the wood, but now he sees that men have come between him and the wood, so he dares not venture to turn thither, but lays him down in a thicket, and so lies there a while.

Earl Hacon and Gudbrand went that morning early to the shrine and found it burnt down; but the three gods were outside, stripped of all their bravery.

Then Gudbrand began to speak, and said —

"Much might is given to our gods, when here they have walked of themselves out of the fire!"

"The gods can have naught to do with it," says the Earl; "a man must have burnt the shrine, and borne the gods out; but the gods do not avenge everything on the spot. That man who has done this will no doubt be driven away out of Valhalla, and never come in thither."

Just then up ran four of the Earl's men, and told them ill tidings; for they said they had found three men slain in the field, and Thrand wounded to the death.

"Who can have done this?" says the Earl.

"Killing-Hrapp," they say.

"Then he must have burnt down the shrine," says the Earl.

They said they thought he was like enough to have done it.

"And where may he be now?" says the Earl.

They said that Thrand had told them that he had laid down in a thicket.

The Earl goes thither to look for him, but Hrapp was off and away. Then the Earl set his men to search for him, but still they could not find him. So the Earl was in the hue and cry himself, but first he bade them rest a while.

Then the Earl went aside by himself, away from other men, and bade that no man should follow him, and so he stays a while. He fell down on both his knees, and held his hands before his eyes; after that he went back to them, and then he said to them, "Come with me".

So they went along with him. He turns short away from the path on which they had walked before, and they came to a dell. There up sprang Hrapp before them, and there it was that he had hidden himself at first.

The Earl urges on his men to run after him, but Hrapp was so swift-footed that they never came near him. Hrapp made for Hlada. There both Thrain and Njal's sons lay "boun" for sea at the same time. Hrapp runs to where Njal's sons are.

"Help me, like good men and true," he said, "for the Earl will slay me."

Helgi looked at him and said —

"Thou lookest like an unlucky man, and the man who will not take thee in will have the best of it."

"Would that the worst might befall you from me," says Hrapp.

"I am the man," says Helgi, "to avenge me on thee for this as time rolls on."

Then Hrapp turned to Thrain Sigfus' son, and bade him shelter him.

"What hast thou on thy hand?" says Thrain.

"I have burnt a shrine under the Earl's eyes, and slain some men, and now he will be here speedily, for he has joined in the hue and cry himself."

"It hardly beseems me to do this," says Thrain, "when the Earl has done me so much good."

Then he showed Thrain the precious things which he had borne out of the shrine, and offered to give him the goods, but Thrain said he could not take them unless he gave him other goods of the same worth for them.

"Then," said Hrapp, "here will I take my stand, and here shall I be slain before thine eyes, and then thou wilt have to abide by every man's blame."

Then they see the Earl and his band of men coming, and then Thrain took Hrapp under his safeguard, and let them shove off the boat, and put out to his ship.

Then Thrain said, "Now this will be thy best hiding place, to knock out the bottoms of two casks, and then thou shalt get into them".

So it was done, and he got into the casks, and then they were lashed together, and lowered over-board.

Then comes the Earl with his band to Njal's sons, and asked if Hrapp had come there.

They said that he had come.

The Earl asked whither he had gone thence.

They said they had not kept eyes on him, and could not say.

"He," said the Earl, "should have great honour from me who would tell me where Hrapp was."

Then Grim said softly to Helgi —

"Why should we not say. What know I whether Thrain will repay us with any good?"

"We should not tell a whit more for that," says Helgi, "when his life lies at stake."

"Maybe," said Grim, "the Earl will turn his vengeance on us, for he is so wroth that some one will have to fall before him."

"That must not move us," says Helgi, "but still we will pull our ship out, and so away to sea as soon as ever we get a wind."

So they rowed out under an isle that lay there, and wait there for a fair breeze.

The Earl went about among the sailors, and tried them all, but they, one and all, denied that they knew aught of Hrapp.

Then the Earl said, "Now we will go to Thrain, my brother-in-arms, and he will give Hrapp up, if he knows anything of him".

After that they took a long-ship and went off to the merchant ship.

Thrain sees the Earl coming, and stands up and greets him kindly. The Earl took his greeting well and spoke thus —

"We are seeking for a man whose name is Hrapp, and he is an Icelander. He has done us all kind of ill; and now we will ask you to be good enough to give him up, or to tell us where he is."

"Ye know, Lord," said Thrain, "that I slew your outlaw, and then put my life in peril, and for that I had of you great honour."

"More honour shalt thou now have," says the Earl.

Now Thrain thought within himself, and could not make up his mind how the Earl would take it, so he denies that Hrapp is there, and bade the Earl to look for him. He spent little time on that, and went on land alone, away from other men, and was then very wroth, so that no man dared to speak to him.

"Show me to Njal's sons," said the Earl, "and I will force them to tell me the truth."

Then he was told that they had put out of the harbour.

"Then there is no help for it," says the Earl, "but still there were two water-casks alongside of Thrain's ship, and in them a man may well have been hid, and if Thrain has hidden him, there he must be; and now we will go a second time to see Thrain."

Thrain sees that the Earl means to put off again and said —

"However wroth the Earl was last time, now he will be half as wroth again, and now the life of every man on board the ship lies at stake."

They all gave their words to hide the matter, for they were all sore afraid. Then they took some sacks out of the lading, and put Hrapp down into the hold in their stead, and other sacks that were tight were laid over him.

Now comes the Earl, just as they were done stowing Hrapp away. Thrain greeted the Earl well. The Earl was rather slow to return it, and they saw that the Earl was very wroth.

Then said the Earl to Thrain —

"Give thou up Hrapp, for I am quite sure that thou hast hidden him."

"Where shall I have hidden him, Lord?" says Thrain.

"That thou knowest best," says the Earl; "but if I must guess, then I think that thou hiddest him in the water-casks a while ago."

"Well!" says Thrain, "I would rather not be taken for a liar, far sooner would I that ye should search the ship."

Then the Earl went on board the ship and hunted and hunted, but found him not.

"Dost thou speak me free now?" says Thrain. "Far from it," says the Earl, "and yet I cannot tell why we cannot find him, but methinks I see through it all when I come on shore, but when I come here, I can see nothing."

With that he made them row him ashore. He was so wroth that there was no speaking to him. His son Sweyn was there with him, and he said, "A strange turn of mind this to let guiltless men smart for one's wrath!"

Then the Earl went away alone aside from other men, and after that he went back to them at once, and said —

"Let us row out to them again," and they did so.

"Where can he have been hidden?" says Sweyn.

"There's not much good in knowing that," says the Earl, "for now he will be away thence; two sacks lay there by the rest of the lading, and Hrapp must have come into the lading in their place."

Then Thrain began to speak, and said —

"They are running off the ship again, and they must mean to pay us another visit. Now we will take him out of the lading, and stow other things in his stead, but let the sacks still lie loose." They did so, and then Thrain spoke —

"Now let us fold Hrapp in the sail."

It was then brailed up to the yard, and they did so.

Then the Earl comes to Thrain and his men, and he was very wroth, and said, "Wilt thou now give up the man, Thrain?" and he is worse now than before.

"I would have given him up long ago," answers Thrain, "if he had been in my keeping, or where can he have been?"

"In the lading," says the Earl.

"Then why did ye not seek him there?" says Thrain.

"That never came into our mind," says the Earl.

After that they sought him over all the ship, and found him not.

"Will you now hold me free?" says Thrain.

"Surely not," says the Earl, "for I know that thou hast hidden away the man, though I find him not; but I would rather that thou shouldest be a dastard to me than I to thee," says the Earl, and then they went on shore.

"Now," says the Earl, "I seem to see that Thrain has hidden away Hrapp in the sail."

Just then up sprung a fair breeze, and Thrain and his men sailed out to sea. He then spoke these words which have long been held in mind since —

> Let us make the Vulture fly,
> Nothing now gars Thrain flinch.

But when the Earl heard of Thrain's words, then he said —

"Tis not my want of foresight which caused this, but rather their ill-fellowship, which will drag them both to death."

Thrain was a short time out on the sea, and so came to Iceland, and fared home to his house. Hrapp went along with Thrain, and was with him that year; but the spring after, Thrain got him a homestead at Hrappstede, and he dwelt there; but yet he spent most of his time At Gritwater. He was thought to spoil everything there, and some men even said that he was too good friends with Hallgerda, and that he led her astray, but some spoke against that.

Thrain gave the Vulture to his kinsman, Mord the reckless; that Mord slew Oddi Haldor's son, east in Gautawick by Berufirth.

All Thrain's kinsmen looked on him as a chief.

Chapter 88
Earl Hacon fights with Njal's sons

Now we must take up the story, and say how, when Earl Hacon missed Thrain, he spoke to Sweyn his son, and said —

"Let us take four long-ships, and let us fare against Njal's sons and slay them, for they must have known all about it with Thrain."

"'Tis not good counsel," says Sweyn, "to throw the blame on guiltless men, but to let him escape who is guilty."

"I shall have my way in this," says the Earl.

Now they hold on after Njal's sons, and seek for them, and find them under an island.

Grim first saw the Earl's ships and said to Helgi —

"Here are war ships sailing up, and I see that here is the Earl, and he can mean to offer us no peace."

"It is said," said Helgi, "that he is the boldest man who holds his own against all comers, and so we will defend ourselves."

They all bade him take the course he thought best, and then they took to their arms.

Now the Earl comes up and called out to them, And bade them give themselves up.

Helgi said that they would defend themselves so long as they could.

Then the Earl offered peace and quarter to all who would neither defend themselves nor Helgi; but Helgi was so much beloved that all said they would rather die with him.

Then the Earl and his men fall on them, but they defended themselves well, and Njal's sons were ever where there was most need. The Earl often offered peace, but they all made the same answer, and said they would never yield.

Then Aslak of Longisle pressed them hard, and came on board their ship thrice. Then Grim said —

"Thou pressest on hard, and 'twere well that thou gettest what thou seekest;" and with that he snatched up a spear and hurled it at him, and hit him under the chin, and Aslak got his death wound there and then.

A little after, Helgi slew Egil the Earl's banner-bearer.

Then Sweyn, Earl Bacon's son, fell on them, and made men hem them in and bear them down with shields, and so they were taken captive.

The Earl was for letting them all be slain at once, but Sweyn said that should not be, and said too that it was night.

Then the Earl said, "Well, then, slay them to-morrow, but bind them fast to-night".

"So, I ween, it must be," says Sweyn; "but never yet have I met brisker men than these, and I call it the greatest manscathe to take their lives."

"They have slain two of our briskest men," said the Earl, "and for that they shall be slain."

"Because they were brisker men themselves," says Sweyn; "but still in this it must be done as thou willest."

So they were bond and fettered.

After that the Earl fell asleep; but when all men slept, Grim spoke to Helgi, and said, "Away would I get if I could".

"Let us try some trick then," says Helgi.

Grim sees that there lies an axe edge up, so Grim crawled thither, and gets the bowstring which bound him cut asunder against the axe, but still he got great wounds on his arms.

Then he set Helgi loose, and after that they crawled over the ship's side, and got on shore, so that neither Hacon nor his men were ware of them. Then they broke off their fetters and walked away to the other side of the island. By that time it began to dawn. There they found a ship, and knew that there was come Kari Solmund's son. They went at once to meet him, and told him of their wrongs and hardships, and showed him their wounds, and said the Earl would be then asleep.

"Ill is it," said Kari, "that ye should suffer such wrongs for wicked men; but what now would be most to your minds?"

"To fall on the Earl," they say, "and slay him."

"This will not be fated," says Kari; "but still ye do not lack heart, but we will first know whether he is there now."

After that they fared thither, and then the Earl was up and away.

Then Kari sailed in to Hlada to meet the Earl, and brought him the Orkney scatts; so the Earl said —

"Hast thou taken Njal's sons into thy keeping?"

"So it is, sure enough," says Kari.

"Wilt thou hand Njal's sons over to me?" asks the Earl.

"No, I will not," said Kari.

"Wilt thou swear this," says the Earl, "that thou wilt not fall on me with Njal's sons?"

Then Eric, the Earl's son, spoke and said —

"Such things ought not to be asked. Kari has always been our friend, and things should not have gone as they have, had I been by. Njal's sons should have been set free from all blame, but they should have had chastisement who had wrought for it. Methinks now it would be more seemly to give Njal's sons good gifts for the hardships and wrongs which have been put upon them, and the wounds they have got."

"So it ought to be, sure enough," says the Earl, "but I know not whether they will take an atonement."

Then the Earl said that Kari should try the feeling of Njal's sons as to an atonement.

After that Kari spoke to Helgi, and asked whether he would take any amends from the Earl or not.

"I will take them," said Helgi, "from his son Eric, but I will have nothing to do with the Earl."

Then Kari told Eric their answer.

"So it shall be," says Eric. "He shall take the amends from me if he thinks it better; and tell them this too, that I bid them to my house, and my father shall do them no harm."

This bidding they took, and went to Eric's house, and were with him till Kari was ready to sail west across the sea to meet Earl Sigurd.

Then Eric made a feast for Kari, and gave him gifts, and Njal's sons gifts too. After that Kari fared west across the sea, and met Earl Sigurd, and he greeted them very well, and they were with the Earl that winter.

But when the spring came, Kari asked Njal's sons to go on warfare with him, but Grim said they would only do so if he would fare with them afterwards out to Iceland. Kari gave his word to do that, and then they fared with him a-sea-roving. They harried south about Anglesea and all the Southern isles. Thence they held on to Cantyre, and landed there, and fought with the landsmen, and got thence much goods, and so fared to their ships. Thence they fared south to Wales, and harried there. Then they held on for Man, and there they met Godred, and fought with him, and got the victory, and slew Dungal the king's son. There they took great spoil. Thence they held on north to Coll, and found Earl Gilli there, and he greeted them well, and there they stayed with him a while. The Earl fared with them to the Orkneys to meet Earl Sigurd, but next spring Earl Sigurd gave away his sister Nereida to Earl Gilli, and then he fared back to the Southern isles.

Chapter 89
Njal's Sons and Kari come out to Iceland

That summer Kari and Njal's sons busked them for Iceland, and when they were "all-boun" they went to see the Earl. The Earl gave them good gifts, and they parted with great friendship.

Now they put to sea and have a short passage, and they got a fine fair breeze, and made the land at Eyrar. Then they got them horses and ride from the ship to Bergthorsknoll, but when they came home all men were glad to see them. They flitted home their goods and laid up the ship, and Kari was there that winter with Njal.

But the spring after, Kari asked for Njal's daughter, Helga, to wife, and Helgi and Grim backed his suit; and so the end of it was that she was betrothed to Kari, and the day for the wedding-feast was fixed, and the feast was held half a month before mid-summer, and they were that winter with Njal.

Then Kari bought him land at Dyrholms, east away by Mydale, and set up a farm there; they put in there a grieve and housekeeper to see after the farm, but they themselves were ever with Njal.

Chapter 90
The Quarrel of Njal's Sons with Thrain Sigfus' Son

Hrapp owned a farm at Hrappstede, but for all that he was always at Gritwater, and he was thought to spoil everything there. Thrain was good to him.

Once on a time it happened that Kettle of the Mark was at Bergthorsknoll; then Njal's sons told him of their wrongs and hardships, and said they had much to lay at Thrain Sigfus' son's door, whenever they chose to speak about it.

Njal said it would be best that Kettle should talk with his brother Thrain about it, and he gave his word to do so.

So they gave Kettle breathing-time to talk to Thrain.

A little after they spoke of the matter again to Kettle, but he said that he would repeat few of the words that had passed between them, "for it was pretty plain that Thrain thought I set too great store on being your brother-in-law".

Then they dropped talking about it, and thought they saw that things looked ugly, and so they asked their father for his counsel as to what was to be done, but they told him they would not let things rest as they then stood.

"Such things," said Njal, "are not so strange. It will be thought that they are slain without a cause, if they are slain now, and my counsel is, that as many men as may be should be brought to talk with them about these things, that thus as many as we can find may be ear-witnesses if they answer ill as to these things. Then Kari shall talk about them too, for he is just the man with the right turn of mind for this; then the dislike between you will grow and grow, for they will heap bad words on bad words when men bring the matter forward, for they are foolish men. It may also well be that it may be said that my sons are slow to take up a quarrel, but ye shall bear that for the sake of gaining time, for there are two sides to everything that is done, and ye can always pick a quarrel; but still ye shall let so much of your purpose out, as to say that if any wrong be put upon you that ye do mean something. But if ye had taken counsel from me at first, then these things should never have been spoken about at all, and then ye would have gotten no disgrace from them; but now ye have the greatest risk of it, and so it will go on ever growing and growing with your disgrace, that ye will never get rid of it until ye bring yourselves into a strait, and have to fight your way out with weapons; but in that there is a long and weary night in which ye will have to grope your way."

After that they ceased speaking about it; but the matter became the daily talk of many men.

One day it happened that those brothers spoke to Kari and bade him go to Gritwater. Kari said he thought he might go elsewhither on a better journey, but still he would go if that were Njal's counsel. So after that Kari fares to meet Thrain, and then they talk over the matter, and they did not each look at it in the same way.

Kari comes home, and Njal's sons ask how things had gone between Thrain and him. Kari said he would rather not repeat the words that had passed, "but," he went on, "it is to be looked for that the like words will be spoken when ye yourselves can hear them".

Thrain had fifteen house-earles trained to arms in his house, and eight of them rode with him whithersoever he went. Thrain was very fond of show and dress, and always rode in a blue cloak, and had on a guilded helm, and the spear — the Earl's gift — in his hand, and a fair shield, and a sword at his belt. Along with him always went Gunnar Lambi's son, and Lambi Sigurd's son, and Grani, Gunnar of Lithend's son. But nearest of all to him went Killing-Hrapp. Lodinn was the name of his serving-man, he too went with Thrain when he journeyed; Tjorvi was the name of Loddin's brother, and he too was one of Thrain's band. The worst of all, in their words against Njal's sons, were Hrapp and Grani; and it was mostly their doing that no atonement was offered to them.

Njal's sons often spoke to Kari that he should ride with them; and it came to that at last, for he said it would be well that they heard Thrain's answer.

Then they busked them, four of Njal's sons, and Kari the fifth, and so they fare to Gritwater.

There was a wide porch in the homestead there, so that many men might stand in it side by side. There was a woman out of doors, and she saw their coming, and told Thrain of it; he bade them to go out into the porch, and take their arms, and they did so.

Thrain stood in mid-door, Killing-Hrapp and Grani Gunnar's son stood on either hand of him; then next stood Gunnar Lambi's son, then Lodinn and Tjorvi, then Lambi Sigurd's son; then each of the others took his place right and left; for the house-earles were all at home.

Skarphedinn and his men walk up from below, and he went first, then Kari, then Hauskuld, then Grim, then Helgi. But when they had come up to the door, then not a word of welcome passed the lips of those who stood before them.

"May we all be welcome here?" said Skarphedinn.

Hallgerda stood in the porch, and had been talking low to Hrapp, then she spoke out loud —

"None of those who are here will say that ye are welcome."

Then Skarphedinn sang a song.

> Prop of sea-waves' fire, thy fretting
> Cannot cast a weight on us,
> Warriors wight; yes, wolf and eagle
> Willingly I feed to-day;
> Carline thrust into the ingle,
> Or a tramping whore, art thou;
> Lord of skates that skim the sea-belt,
> Odin's mocking cup I mix.

"Thy words," said Skarphedinn, "will not be worth much, for thou art either a hag, only fit to sit in the ingle, or a harlot."

"These words of thine thou shalt pay for," she says, "ere thou farest home."

"Thee am I come to see, Thrain," said Helgi, "and to know if thou will make me any amends for those wrongs and hardships which befell me for thy sake in Norway."

"I never knew," said Thrain, "that ye two brothers were wont to measure your manhood by money; or, how long shall such a claim for amends stand over?"

"Many will say," says Helgi, "that thou oughtest to offer us atonement, since thy life was at stake."

Then Hrapp said, "'Twas just luck that swayed the balance, when he got stripes who ought to bear them; and she dragged you under disgrace and hardship, but us away from them."

"Little good luck was there in that," says Helgi, "to break faith with the Earl, and to take to thee instead."

"Thinkest thou not that thou hast some amends to seek from me?" says Hrapp, "I will atone thee in a way that, methinks, were fitting."

"The only dealings we shall have," says Helgi, "will be those which will not stand thee in good stead."

"Don't bandy words with Hrapp," said Skarphedinn, "but give him a red skin for a grey."

"Hold thy tongue, Skarphedinn," said Hrapp, "or I will not spare to bring my axe on thy head."

"'Twill be proved soon enough, I dare say," says Skarphedinn, "which of us is to scatter gravel over the other's head."

"Away with you home, ye 'Dung-beardlings!'" says Hallgerda, "and so we will call you always from this day forth; but your father we will call 'the Beardless Carle.'"

They did not fare home before all who were there had made themselves guilty of uttering those words, save Thrain; he forbade men to utter them.

Then Njal's sons went away, and fared till they came home; then they told their father.

"Did ye call any men to witness of those words?" says Njal.

"We called none," says Skarphedinn; "we do not mean to follow that suit up except on the battlefield."

"No one will now think," says Bergthora, "that ye have the heart to lift your weapons."

"Spare thy tongue, mistress!" says Kari, "in egging on thy sons, for they will be quite eager enough."

After that they all talk long in secret, Njal and his sons, and Kari Solmund's son, their brother-in-law.

Chapter 91
Thrain Sigfus' Son's Slaying

Now there was great talk about this quarrel of theirs, and all seemed to know that it would not settle down peacefully.

Runolf, the son of Wolf Aurpriest, east in the Dale, was a great friend of Thrain's, and had asked Thrain to come and see him, and it was settled that he should come east when about three weeks or a month were wanting to winter.

Thrain bade Hrapp, and Grani, and Gunnar Lambi's son, and Lambi Sigurd's son, and Lodinn, and Tjorvi, eight of them in all, to go on this journey with him. Hallgerda and Thorgerda were to go too. At the same time Thrain gave it out that he meant to stay in the Mark with his brother Kettle, and said how many nights he meant to be away from home.

They all of them had full arms. So they rode east across Markfleet, and found there some gangrel women, and they begged them to put them across the Fleet west on their horses, and they did so.

Then they rode into the Dale, and had a hearty welcome; there Kettle of the Mark met them, and there they sate two nights.

Both Runolf and Kettle besought Thrain that he would make up his quarrel with Njal's sons; but he said he would never pay any money, and answered crossly, for he said he thought himself quite a match for Njal's sons wherever they met.

"So it may be," says Runolf; "but so far as I can see, no man has been their match since Gunnar of Lithend died, and it is likelier that ye will both drag one another down to death."

Thrain said that was not to be dreaded.

Then Thrain fared up into the Mark, and was there two nights more; after that he rode down into the Dale, and was sent away from both houses with fitting gifts.

Now the Markfleet was then flowing between sheets of ice on both sides, and there were tongues of ice bridging it across every here and there.

Thrain said that he meant to ride home that evening, but Runolf said that he ought not to ride home; he said, too, that it would be more wary not to fare back as he had said he would before he left home.

"That is fear, and I will none of it," answers Thrain.

Now those gangrel women whom they had put across the Fleet came to Bergthorsknoll, and Bergthora asked whence they came, but they answered, "Away east under Eyjafell".

"Then, who put you across Markfleet?" said Bergthora.

"Those," said they, "who were the most boastful and bravest clad of men."

"Who?" asked Bergthora.

"Thrain Sigfus' son," said they, "and his company, but we thought it best to tell thee that they were so full-tongued and foul-tongued towards this house, against thy husband and his sons."

"Listeners do not often hear good of themselves," says Bergthora. After that they went their way, and Bergthora gave them gifts on their going, and asked them when Thrain might be coming home.

They said that he would be from home four or five nights.

After that Bergthora told her sons and her son-in-law Kari, and they talked long and low about the matter.

But that same morning, when Thrain and his men rode from the east, Njal woke up early and heard how Skarphedinn's axe came against the panel.

Then Njal rises up, and goes out, and sees that his sons are all there with their weapons, and Karl, his son-in-law too. Skarphedinn was foremost. He was in a blue cape, and had a targe, and his axe aloft on his shoulder. Next to him went Helgi; he was in a red kirtle, had a helm on his head, and a red shield, on which a hart was marked. Next to him went Kari; he had on a silken jerkin, a gilded helm and shield, and on it was drawn a lion. They were all in bright holiday clothes.

Njal called out to Skarphedinn —

"Whither art thou going, kinsman?"

"On a sheep hunt," he said.

"So it was once before," said Njal, "but then ye hunted men."

Skarphedinn laughed at that, and said —

"Hear ye what the old man says? He is not without his doubts."

"When was it that thou spokest thus before?" asks Kari.

"When I slew Sigmund the white," says Skarphedinn, "Gunnar of Lithend's kinsman."

"For what?" asks Kari.

"He had slain Thord Freedmanson, my foster-father."

Njal went home, but they fared up into the Redslips, and bided there; thence they could see the others as soon as ever they rode from the east out of the dale.

There was sunshine that day and bright weather.

Now Thrain and his men ride down out of the Dale along the river bank.

Lambi Sigurd's son said —

"Shields gleam away yonder in the Redslips when the sun shines on them, and there must be some men lying in wait there."

"Then," says Thrain, "we will turn our way lower down the Fleet, and then they will come to meet us if they have any business with us."

So they turn down the Fleet. "Now they have caught sight of us," said Skarphedinn, "for lo! they turn their path elsewhither, and now we have no other choice than to run down and meet them."

"Many men," said Kari, "would rather not lie in wait if the balance of force were not more on their side than it is on ours; they are eight, but we are five."

Now they turn down along the Fleet, and see a tongue of ice bridging the stream lower down and mean to cross there.

Thrain and his men take their stand upon the ice away from the tongue, and Thrain said —

"What can these men want? They are five, and we are eight."

"I guess," said Lambi Sigurd's son, "that they would still run the risk though more men stood against them."

Thrain throws off his cloak, and takes off his helm.

Now it happened to Skarphedinn, as they ran down along the Fleet, that his shoe-string snapped asunder, and he stayed behind.

"Why so slow, Skarphedinn?" quoth Grim.

"I am tying my shoe," he says.

"Let us get on ahead," says Kari; "methinks he will not be slower than we."

So they turn off to the tongue, and run as fast as they can. Skarphedinn sprang up as soon as he was ready, and had lifted his axe, "the ogress of war," aloft, and runs right down to the Fleet. But the Fleet was so deep that there was no fording it for a long way up or down.

A great sheet of ice had been thrown up by the flood on the other side of the Fleet as smooth and slippery as glass, and there Thrain and his men stood in the midst of the sheet.

Skarphedinn takes a spring into the air, and leaps over the stream between the icebanks, and does not check his course, but rushes still onwards with a slide. The sheet of ice was very slippery, and so he went as fast as a bird flies. Thrain was just about to put his helm on his head; and now Skarphedinn bore down on them, and hews at Thrain with his axe, "the ogress of war," and smote him on the head, and clove him down to the teeth, so that his jaw-teeth fell out on the ice. This feat was done with such a quick sleight that no one could get a blow at him; he glided away from them at once at full speed. Tjorvi, indeed, threw his shield before him on the ice, but he leapt over it, and still kept his feet, and slid quite to the end of the sheet of ice.

There Kari and his brothers came to meet him.

"This was done like a man," says Kari.

"Your share is still left," says Skarphedinn, and sang a song.

> To the strife of swords not slower,
> After all, I came than you,
> For with ready stroke the sturdy
> Squanderer of wealth I felled;
> But since Grim's and Helgi's sea-stag
> Norway's Earl erst took and stripped,
> Now 'tis time for sea-fire bearers
> Such dishonour to avenge.

And this other song he sang —

> Swiftly down I dashed my weapon,
> Gashing giant, byrnie-breacher,
> She, the noisy ogre's namesake,
> Soon with flesh the ravens glutted;
> Now your words to Hrapp remember,
> On broad ice now rouse the storm,
> With dull crash war's eager ogress
> Battle's earliest note hath sung.

"That befits us well, and we wilt do it well," says Helgi. Then they turn up towards them. Both Grim and Helgi see where Hrapp is, and they turned on him at once. Hrapp hews at Grim there and then with his axe; Helgi sees this and cuts at Hrapp's arm, and cut it off, and down fell the axe.

"In this," says Hrapp, "thou hast done a most needful work, for this hand hath wrought harm and death to many a man."

"And so here an end shall be put to it," says Grim; and with that he ran him through with a spear, and then Hrapp fell down dead.

Tjorvi turns against Kari and hurls a spear at him. Kari leapt up in the air, and the spear flew below his feet. Then Kari rushes at him, and hews at him on the breast with his sword, and the blow passed at once into his chest, and he got his death there and then.

Then Skarphedinn seizes both Gunnar Lambi's son, and Grani Gunnar's son, and said —

"Here have I caught two whelps! but what shall we do with them?"

"It is in thy power," says Helgi, "to slay both or either of them, if you wish them dead."

"I cannot find it in my heart to do both — help Hogni and slay his brother," says Skarphedinn.

"Then the day will once come," says Helgi, "when thou wilt wish that thou hadst slain him, for never will he be true to thee, nor will any one of the others who are now here."

"I shall not fear them," answers Skarphedinn.

After that they gave peace to Grani Gunnar's son, and Gunnar Lambi's son, and Lambi Sigurd's son, and Lodinn.

After that they went down to the Fleet where Skarphedinn had leapt over it, and Kari and the others measured the length of the leap with their spear-shafts, and it was twelve ells (about eighteen feet, according to the old Norse measure).

Then they turned homewards, and Njal asked what tidings.

They told him all just as it had happened, and Njal said —

"These are great tidings, and it is more likely that hence will come the death of one of my sons, if not more evil."

Gunnar Lambi's son bore the body of Thrain with him to Gritwater, and he was laid in a cairn there.

Chapter 92
Kettle takes Hauskuld as his Foster-Son

Kettle of the Mark had to wife Thorgerda, Njal's daughter, but he was Thrain's brother, and he thought he was come into a strait, so he rode to Njal's house, and asked whether he were willing to atone in any way for Thrain's slaying?

"I will atone for it handsomely," answered Njal; "and my wish is that thou shouldst look after the matter with thy brothers who have to take the price of the atonement, that they may be ready to join in it."

Kettle said he would do so with all his heart, and Kettle rode home first; a little after, he summoned all his brothers to Lithend, and then he had a talk with them; and Hogni was on his side all through the talk; and so it came about that men were chosen to utter the award; and a meeting was agreed on, and the fair price of a man was awarded for Thrain's slaying, and they all had a share in the blood-money who had a lawful right to it. After that pledges of peace and good faith were agreed to, and they were settled in the most sure and binding way.

Njal paid down all the money out of hand well and bravely; and so things were quiet for a while.

One day Njal rode up into the Mark, and he and Kettle talked together the whole day, Njal rode home at even, and no man knew of what they had taken counsel.

A little after Kettle fares to Gritwater, and he said to Thorgerda —

"Long have I loved my brother Thrain much, and now I will show it, for I will ask Hauskuld Thrain's son to be my foster-child."

"Thou shalt have thy choice of this," she says; "and thou shalt give this lad all the help in thy power when he is grown up, and avenge him if he is slain with weapons, and bestow money on him for his wife's dower; and besides, thou shalt swear to do all this."

Now Hauskuld fares home with Kettle, and is with him some time.

Chapter 93
Njal takes Hauskuld to Foster

Once on a time Njal rides up into the Mark, and he had a hearty welcome. He was there that night, and in the evening Njal called out to the lad Hauskuld, and he went up to him at once.

Njal had a ring of gold on his hand, and showed it to the lad. He took hold of the gold, and looked at it, and put it on his finger.

"Wilt thou take the gold as a gift?" said Njal.

"That I will," said the lad.

"Knowest thou," says Njal, "what brought thy father to his death?"

"I know," answers the lad, "that Skarphedinn slew him; but we need not keep that in mind, when an atonement has been made for it, and a full price paid for him."

"Better answered than asked," said Njal; "and thou wilt live to be a good man and true," he adds.

"Methinks thy forecasting," says Hauskuld, "is worth having, for I know that thou art foresighted and unlying."

"Now I will offer to foster thee," said Njal, "if thou wilt take the offer."

He said he would be willing to take both that honour and any other good offer which he might make. So the end of the matter was, that Hauskuld fared home with Njal as his foster-son.

He suffered no harm to come nigh the lad, and loved him much. Njal's sons took him about with them, and did him honour in every way. And so things go on till Hauskuld is full grown. He was both tall and strong; the fairest of men to look on, and well-haired; blithe of speech, bountiful, well-behaved; as well trained to arms as the best; fairspoken to all men, and much beloved.

Njal's sons and Hauskuld were never apart, either in word or deed.

Chapter 94
Of Flosi Thord's Son

There was a man named Flosi, he was the son of Thord Freyspriest. Flosi had to wife Steinvora, daughter of Hall of the Side. She was base born, and her mother's name was Solvora, daughter of Herjolf the white. Flosi dwelt at Swinefell, and was a mighty chief. He was tall of stature, and strong withal, the most forward and boldest of men. His brother's name was Starkad; he was not by the same mother as Flosi.

The other brothers of Flosi were Thorgeir and Stein, Kolbein and Egil. Hildigunna was the name of the daughter of Starkad Flosi's brother. She was a proud, high-spirited maiden, and one of the fairest of women. She was so skilful with her hands, that few women were equally skilful. She was the grimmest and hardest-hearted of all women; but still a woman of open hand and heart when any fitting call was made upon her.

Chapter 95
Of Hall of the Side

Hall was the name of a man who was called Hall of the Side. He was the son of Thorstein Baudvar's son. Hall had to wife Joreida, daughter of Thidrandi the wise. Thorstein was the name of Hall's brother, and he was nick-named broadpaunch. His son was Kol, whom Kari slays in Wales. The sons of Hall of the Side were Thorstein and Egil, Thorwald and Ljot, and Thidrandi, whom, it is said, the goddesses slew.

There was a man named Thorir, whose surname was Holt-Thorir; his sons were these: Thorgeir Craggeir, and Thorleif crow, from whom the Wood-dwellers are come, and Thorgrim the big.

Chapter 96
Of the Change of Faith

There had been a change of rulers in Norway, Earl Hacon was dead and gone, but in his stead was come Olaf Tryggvi's son. That was the end of Earl Hacon, that Kark, the thrall, cut his throat at Rimul in Gaulardale.

Along with that was heard that there had been a change of faith in Norway; they had cast off the old faith, but King Olaf had christened the western lands, Shetland, and the Orkneys, and the Faroe Isles.

Then many men spoke so that Njal heard it, that it was a strange and wicked thing to throw off the old faith.

Then Njal spoke and said —

"It seems to me as though this new faith must be much better, and he will be happy who follows this rather than the other; and if those men come out hither who preach this faith, then I will back them well."

He went often alone away from other men and muttered to himself.

That same harvest a ship came out into the firths east to Berufirth, at a spot called Gautawick. The captain's name was Thangbrand. He was a son of Willibald, a count of Saxony, Thangbrand was sent out hither by King Olaf Tryggvi's son, to preach the faith. Along with him came that man of Iceland whose name was Gudleif. Gudleif was a great man-slayer, and one of the strongest of men, and hardy and forward in everything.

Two brothers dwelt at Beruness; the name of the one was Thorleif, but the other was Kettle. They were sons of Holmstein, the son of Auzur of Broaddale. These brothers held a meeting, and forbade men to have any dealings with them. This Hall of the Side heard. He dwelt at Thvattwater in Alftafirth; he rode to the ship with twenty-nine men, and he fares at once to find Thangbrand, and spoke to him and asked him —

"Trade is rather dull, is it not?"

He answered that so it was.

"Now will I say my errand," says Hall; "it is, that I wish to ask you all to my house, and run the risk of my being able to get rid of your wares for you."

Thangbrand thanked him, and fared to Thvattwater that harvest.

It so happened one morning that Thangbrand was out early and made them pitch a tent on land, and sang mass in it, and took much pains with it, for it was a great high day.

Hall spoke to Thangbrand and asked, "In memory of whom keepest thou this day?"

"In memory of Michael the archangel," says Thangbrand.

"What follows that angel?" asks Hall.

"Much good," says Thangbrand. "He will weigh all the good that thou doest, and he is so merciful, that whenever any one pleases him, he makes his good deeds weigh more."

"I would like to have him for my friend," says Hall.

"That thou mayest well have," says Thangbrand, "only give thyself over to him by God's help this very day."

"I only make this condition," says Hall, "that thou givest thy word for him that he will then become my guardian angel."

"That I will promise," says Thangbrand.

Then Hall was baptised, and all his household.

Chapter 97
Of Thangbrand's Journeys

The spring after Thangbrand set out to preach Christianity, and Hall went with him. But when they came west across Lonsheath to Staffell, there they found a man dwelling named Thorkell. He spoke most against the faith, and challenged Thangbrand to single combat. Then Thangbrand bore a rood-cross before his shield, and the end of their combat was that Thangbrand won the day and slew Thorkell.

Thence they fared to Hornfirth and turned in as guests at Borgarhaven, west of Heinabergs sand. There Hilldir the old dwelt, and then Hilldir and all his household took upon them the new faith.

Thence they fared to Fellcombe, and went in as guests to Calffell. There dwelt Kol Thorstein's son, Hall's kinsman, and he took upon him the faith and all his house.

Thence they fared to Swinefell, and Flosi only took the sign of the cross, but gave his word to back them at the Thing.

Thence they fared west to Woodcombe, and went in as guests at Kirkby. There dwelt Surt Asbjorn's son, the son of Thorstein, the son of Kettle the foolish. These had all of them been Christians from father to son.

After that they fared out of Woodcombe on to Headbrink. By that time the story of their journey was spread far and wide. There was a man named Sorcerer-Hedinn who dwelt in Carlinedale. There heathen men made a bargain with him that he should put Thangbrand to death with all his company. He fared upon Arnstacksheath, and there made a great sacrifice when Thangbrand was riding from the east. Then the earth burst asunder under his horse, but he sprang off his horse and saved himself on the brink of the gulf, but the earth swallowed up the horse and all his harness, and they never saw him more.

Then Thangbrand praised God.

Chapter 98
Of Thangbrand and Gudleif

Gudleif now searches for Sorcerer-Hedinn and finds him on the heath, and chases him down into Carlinedale, and got within spearshot of him, and shoots a spear at him and through him.

Thence they fared to Dyrholms and held a meeting there, and preached the faith there, and there Ingialld, the son of Thorsteinn Highbankawk, became a Christian.

Thence they fared to the Fleetlithe and preached the faith there. There Weatherlid the Skald, and Ari his son, spoke most against the faith, and for that they slew Weatherlid, and then this song was sung about it —

> He who proved his blade on bucklers,
> South went through the land to whet
> Brand that oft hath felled his foeman,
> 'Gainst the forge which foams with song;
> Mighty wielder of war's sickle
> Made his sword's avenging edge
> Hard on hero's helm-prop rattle,
> Skull of Weatherlid the Skald.

Thence Thangbrand fared to Bergthorsknoll, and Njal took the faith and all his house, but Mord and Valgard went much against it, and thence they fared out across the rivers; so they went on into Hawkdale and there they baptised Hall, and he was then three winters old.

Thence Thangbrand fared to Grimsness, there Thorwald the scurvy gathered a band against him, and sent word to Wolf Uggi's son, that he must fare against Thangbrand and slay him, and made this song on him—

> To the wolf in Woden's harness,

> Uggi's worthy warlike son,
> I, steel's swinger dearly loving,
> This my simple bidding send;
> That the wolf of Gods he chaseth, —
> Man who snaps at chink of gold —
> Wolf who base our Gods blasphemeth,
> I the other wolf will crush.

Wolf sang another song in return —

> Swarthy skarf from month that skimmeth
> Of the man who speaks in song
> Never will I catch, though surely
> Wealthy warrior it hath sent;
> Tender of the sea-horse snorting,
> E'en though ill deeds are on foot,
> Still to risk mine eyes are open;
> Harmful 'tis to snap at flies.

"And," says he, "I don't mean to be made a catspaw by him, but let him take heed lest his tongue twists a noose for his own neck."

And after that the messenger fared back to Thorwald the scurvy and told him Wolf's words. Thorwald had many men about him, and gave it out that he would lie in wait for them on Bluewoodheath.

Now those two, Thangbrand and Gudleif, ride out of Hawkdale, and there they came upon a man who rode to meet them. That man asked for Gudleif, and when he found him he said —

"Thou shalt gain by being the brother of Thorgil of Reykiahole, for I will let thee know that they have set many ambushes, and this too, that Thorwald the scurvy is now with his band At Hestbeck on Grimsness."

"We shall not the less for all that ride to meet him," says Gudleif, and then they turned down to Hestbeck. Thorwald was then come across the brook, and Gudleif said to Thangbrand —

"Here is now Thorwald; let us rush on him now." Thangbrand shot a spear through Thorwald, but Gudleif smote him on the shoulder and hewed his arm off, and that was his death.

After that they ride up to the Thing, and it was a near thing that the kinsmen of Thorwald had fallen on Thangbrand, but Njal and the eastfirthers stood by Thangbrand.

Then Hjallti Skeggi's son sang this rhyme at the Hill of Laws —

> Ever will I Gods blaspheme
> Freyja methinks a dog does seem,
> Freyja a dog? Aye! let them be
> Both dogs together Odin and she.

Hjallti fared abroad that summer and Gizur the White with him, but Thangbrand's ship was wrecked away east at Bulandsness, and the ship's name was "Bison".

Thangbrand and his messmate fared right through the west country, and Steinvora, the mother of Ref the Skald, came against him; she preached the heathen faith to Thangbrand and made him a long speech. Thangbrand held his peace while she spoke, but made a long speech after her, and turned all that she had said the wrong way against her.

"Hast thou heard," she said, "how Thor challenged Christ to single combat, and how he did not dare to fight with Thor?"

"I have heard tell," says Thangbrand, "that Thor was naught but dust and ashes, if God had not willed that he should live."

"Knowest thou," she says, "who it was that shattered thy ship?"

"What hast thou to say about that?" he asks.

"That I will tell thee," she says.

> He that giant's offspring slayeth
> Broke the new-field's bison stout,
> Thus the Gods, bell's warder grieving.
> Crushed the falcon of the strand;
> To the courser of the causeway
> Little good was Christ I ween,
> When Thor shattered ships to pieces
> Gylfi's hart no God could help.

And again she sang another song —

> Thangbrand's vessel from her moorings,
> Sea-king's steed, Thor wrathful tore,
> Shook and shattered all her timbers,
> Hurled her broadside on the beach;
> Ne'er again shall Viking's snow-shoe,
> On the briny billows glide,
> For a storm by Thor awakened,
> Dashed the bark to splinters small.

After that Thangbrand and Steinvora parted, and they fared west to Bardastrand.

Chapter 99
Of Gest Oddleif's Son

Gest Oddleif's son dwelt at Hagi on Bardastrand, He was one of the wisest of men, so that he foresaw the fates and fortunes of men. He made a feast for Thangbrand and his men. They fared to Hagi with sixty men. Then it was said that there were two hundred heathen men to meet them, and that a Baresark was looked for to come thither, whose name was Otrygg, and all were afraid of him. Of him such great things as these were said, that he feared neither fire nor sword, and the heathen men were sore afraid at his coming. Then Thangbrand asked if men were willing to take the faith, but all the heathen men spoke against it.

"Well," says Thangbrand, "I will give you the means whereby ye shall prove whether my faith is better. We will hallow two fires. The heathen men shall hallow one and I the other, but a third shall he unhallowed; and if the Baresark is afraid of the one that I hallow, but treads both the others, then ye shall take the faith."

"That is well-spoken," says Gest, "and I will agree to this for myself and my household."

And when Gest had so spoken, then many more agreed to it.

Then it was said that the Baresark was coming up to the homestead, and then the fires were made and burned strong. Then men took their arms and sprang up on the benches, and so waited.

The Baresark rushed in with his weapons. He comes into the room, and treads at once the fire which the heathen men had hallowed, and so comes to the fire that Thangbrand had hallowed, and dares not to tread it, but said that he was on fire all over. He hews with his sword at the bench, but strikes a cross-beam as he brandished the weapon aloft. Thangbrand smote the arm of the Baresark with his crucifix, and so mighty a token followed that the sword fell from the Baresark's hand.

Then Thangbrand thrusts a sword into his breast, and Gudleif smote him on the arm and hewed it off. Then many went up and slew the Baresark.

After that Thangbrand asked if they would take the faith now?

Gest said he had only spoken what he meant to keep to.

Then Thangbrand baptised Gest and all his house and many others. Then Thangbrand took counsel with Gest whether he should go any further west among the firths, but Gest set his face against that, and said they were a hard race of men there, and ill to deal with, "but if it be foredoomed that this faith shall make its way, then it will be taken as law at the Althing, and then all the chiefs out of the districts will be there".

"I did all that I could at the Thing," says Thangbrand, "and it was very uphill work."

"Still thou hast done most of the work," says Gest, "though it may be fated that others shall make Christianity law; but it is here as the saying runs, 'No tree falls at the first stroke'."

After that Gest gave Thangbrand good gifts, and he fared back south. Thangbrand fared to the Southlander's Quarter, and so to the Eastfirths. He turned in as a guest at Bergthorsknoll, and Njal gave him good gifts. Thence he rode east to Alftafirth to meet Hall of the Side. He caused his ship to be mended, and heathen man called it "Iron-basket". On board that ship Thangbrand fared abroad, and Gudleif with him.

Chapter 100
Of Gizur the White and Hjallti

That same summer Hjallti Skeggi's son was outlawed at the Thing for blasphemy against the Gods.

Thangbrand told King Olaf of all the mischief that the Icelanders had done to him, and said that they were such sorcerers there that the earth burst asunder under his horse and swallowed up the horse.

Then King Olaf was so wroth that he made them seize all the men from Iceland and set them in dungeons, and meant to slay them.

Then they, Gizur the White and Hjallti, came up and offered to lay themselves in pledge for those men, and fare out to Iceland and preach the faith. The king took this well, and they got them all set free again.

Then Gizur and Hjallti busked their ship for Iceland, and were soon "boun". They made the land at Eyrar when ten weeks of summer had passed; they got them horses at once, but left other men to strip their ship. Then they ride with thirty men to the Thing, and sent word to the Christian men that they must be ready to stand by them.

Hjallti stayed behind at Reydarmull, for he had heard that he had been made an outlaw for blasphemy, but when they came to the "Boiling Kettle" down below the brink of the Rift, there came Hjallti after them, and said he would not let the heathen men see that he was afraid of them.

Then many Christian men rode to meet them, and they ride in battle array to the Thing. The heathen men had drawn up their men in array to meet them, and it was a near thing that the whole body of the Thing had come to blows, but still it did not go so far.

Chapter 101
Of Thorgeir of Lightwater

There was a man named Thorgeir who dwelt at Lightwater; he was the son of Tjorfi, the son of Thorkel the long, the son of Kettle Longneck. His mother's name was Thoruna, and she was the daughter of Thorstein, the son of Sigmund, the son of Bard of the Nip. Gudrida was the name of his wife; she was a daughter of Thorkel the black of Hleidrargarth. His brother was Worm wallet-back, the father of Hlenni the old of Saurby.

The Christian men set up their booths, and Gizur the White and Hjallti were in the booths of the men from Mossfell. The day after both sides went to the Hill of Laws, and each, the Christian men as well as the heathen, took witness, and declared themselves out of the other's laws, and then there was such an uproar on the Hill of Laws that no man could hear the other's voice.

After that men went away, and all thought things looked like the greatest entanglement. The Christian men chose as their Speaker Hall of the Side, but

Hall went to Thorgeir, the priest of Lightwater, who was the old Speaker of the law, and gave him three marks of silver to utter what the law should be, but still that was most hazardous counsel, since he was an heathen.

Thorgeir lay all that day on the ground, and spread a cloak over his head, so that no man spoke with him; but the day after men went to the Hill of Laws, and then Thorgeir bade them be silent and listen, and spoke thus —

"It seems to me as though our matters were come to a dead lock, if we are not all to have one and the same law; for if there be a sundering of the laws, then there will be a sundering of the peace, and we shall never be able to live in the land. Now, I will ask both Christian men and heathen whether they will hold to those laws which I utter".

They all say they would.

He said he wished to take an oath of them, and pledges that they would hold to them, and they all said "yea" to that, and so he took pledges from them.

"This is the beginning of our laws," he said, "that all men shall be Christian here in the land, and believe in one God, the Father, the Son, and the Holy Ghost, but leave off all idol-worship, not expose children to perish, and not eat horseflesh. It shall be outlawry if such things are proved openly against any man; but if these things are done by stealth, then it shall be blameless."

But all this heathendom was all done away with within a few years' space, so that those things were not allowed to be done either by stealth or openly.

Thorgeir then uttered the law as to keeping the Lord's day and fast days, Yuletide and Easter, and all the greatest highdays and holidays.

The heathen men thought they had been greatly cheated; but still the true faith was brought into the law, and so all men became Christian here in the land.

After that men fare home from the Thing.

Chapter 102
The Wedding of Hauskuld, the Priest of Whiteness

Now we must take up the story, and say that Njal spoke thus to Hauskuld, his foster-son, and said —

"I would seek thee a match."

Hauskuld bade him settle the matter as he pleased, and asked whether he was most likely to turn his eyes.

"There is a woman called Hildigunna," answers Njal, "and she is the daughter of Starkad, the son of Thord Freyspriest. She is the best match I know of."

"See thou to it, foster-father," said Hauskuld; "that shall be my choice which thou choosest."

"Then we will look thitherward," says Njal.

A little while after, Njal called on men to go along with him. Then the sons of Sigfus, and Njal's sons, and Kari Solmund's son, all of them fared with him and they rode east to Swinefell.

There they got a hearty welcome.

The day after, Njal and Flosi went to talk alone, and the speech of Njal ended thus, that he said —

"This is my errand here, that we have set out on a wooing-journey, to ask for thy kinswoman Hildigunna."

"At whose hand?" says Flosi.

"At the hand of Hauskuld my foster-son," says Njal.

"Such things are well meant," says Flosi, "but still ye run each of you great risk, the one from the other; but what hast thou to say of Hauskuld?"

"Good I am able to say of him," says Njal; "and besides, I will lay down as much money as will seem fitting to thy niece and thyself, if thou wilt think of making this match."

"We will call her hither," says Flosi, "and know how she looks on the man."

Then Hildigunna was called, and she came thither.

Flosi told her of the wooing, but she said she was a proud-hearted woman.

"And I know not how things will turn out between me and men of like spirit; but this, too, is not the least of my dislike, that this man has no priesthood or leadership over men, but thou hast always said that thou wouldest not wed me to a man who had not the priesthood."

"This is quite enough," says Flosi, "if thou wilt not be wedded to Hauskuld, to make me take no more pains about the match."

"Nay!" she says, "I do not say that I will not be wedded to Hauskuld if they can get him a priesthood or a leadership over men; but otherwise I will have nothing to say to the match."

"Then," said Njal, "I will beg thee to let this match stand over for three winters, that I may see what I can do."

Flosi said that so it should be.

"I will only bargain for this one thing," says Hildigunna, "if this match comes to pass, that we shall stay here away east."

Njal said he would rather leave that to Hauskuld, but Hauskuld said that he put faith in many men, but in none so much as his foster-father.

Now they ride from the east.

Njal sought to get a priesthood and leadership for Hauskuld, but no one was willing to sell his priesthood, and now the summer passes away till the Althing.

There were great quarrels at the Thing that summer, and many a man then did as was their wont, in faring to see Njal; but he gave such counsel in men's lawsuits as was not thought at all likely, so that both the pleadings and the defence came to naught, and out of that great strife arose, when the lawsuits could not be brought to an end, and men rode home from the Thing unatoned.

Now things go on till another Thing comes. Njal rode to the Thing, and at first all is quiet until Njal says that it is high time for men to give notice of their suits.

Then many said that they thought that came to little, when no man could get his suit settled, even though the witnesses were summoned to the Althing, "and so," say they, "we would rather seek our rights with point and edge."

"So it must not be," says Njal, "for it will never do to have no law in the land. But yet ye have much to say on your side in this matter, and it behoves us who know the law, and who are bound to guide the law, to set men at one again, and to ensue peace. 'Twere good counsel, then, methinks, that we call together all the chiefs and talk the matter over."

Then they go to the Court of Laws, and Njal spoke and said —

"Thee, Skapti Thorod's son and you other chiefs, I call on, and say, that methinks our lawsuits have come into a deadlock, if we have to follow up our suits in the Quarter Courts, and they get so entangled that they can neither be pleaded nor ended. Methinks, it were wiser if we had a Fifth Court, and there pleaded those suits which cannot be brought to an end in the Quarter Courts."

"How," said Skapti, "wilt thou name a Fifth Court, when the Quarter Court is named for the old priesthoods, three twelves in each quarter?"

"I can see help for that," says Njal, "by setting up new priesthoods, and filling them with the men who are best fitted in each Quarter, and then let those men who are willing to agree to it, declare themselves ready to join the new priest's Thing."

"Well," says Skapti, "we will take this choice; but what weighty suits shall come before the court?"

"These matters shall come before it," says Njal — "all matters of contempt of the Thing, such as if men bear false witness, or utter a false finding; hither, too, shall come all those suits in which the Judges are divided in opinion in the Quarter Court; then they shall be summoned to the Fifth Court; so, too, if men offer bribes, or take them, for their help in suits. In this court all the oaths shall be of the strongest kind, and two men shall follow every oath, who shall support on their words of honour what the others swear. So it shall be also, if the pleadings on one side are right in form, and the other wrong, that the judgment shall be given for those that are right in form. Every suit in this court shall be pleaded just as is now done in the Quarter Court, save and except that when four twelves are named in the Fifth Court, then the plaintiff shall name and set aside six men out of the court, and the defendant other six; but if he will not set them aside, then the plaintiff shall name them and set them aside as he has done with his own six; but if the plaintiff does not set them aside, then the suit comes to naught, for three twelves shall utter judgment on all suits. We shall also have this arrangement in the Court of Laws, that those only shall have the right to make or change laws who sit on the middle bench, and to this bench those only shall be chosen who are wisest and best. There, too, shall the Fifth Court sit; but if those who sit in the Court of Laws are not agreed as to what they shall allow or bring in as law, then they shall clear the court for a division, and the majority shall bind the rest; but if any man who has a seat in the Court be outside the Court of Laws and cannot get inside it, or thinks himself overborne in the suit, then he shall forbid them by a protest, so that they can hear it in the Court, and then he has made all their grants and all their decisions void and of none effect, and stopped them by his protest."

After that, Skapti Thorod's son brought the Fifth Court into the law, and all that was spoken of before. Then men went to the Hill of Laws, and men set up new priesthoods: in the Northlanders' Quarter were these new priesthoods. The priesthood of the Melmen in Midfirth, and the Laufesingers' priesthood in the Eyjafirth.

Then Njal begged for a hearing, and spoke thus —

"It is known to many men what passed between my sons and the men of Gritwater when they slew Thrain Sigfus' son. But for all that we settled the matter; and now I have taken Hauskuld into my house, and planned a marriage for him if he can get a priesthood anywhere; but no man will sell his priesthood, and so I will beg you to give me leave to set up a new priesthood at Whiteness for Hauskuld."

He got this leave from all, and after that he set up the new priesthood for Hauskuld; and he was afterwards called Hauskuld, the Priest of Whiteness.

After that, men ride home from the Thing, and Njal stayed but a short time at home ere he rides east to Swinefell, and his sons with him, and again stirs in the matter of the marriage with Flosi; but Flosi said he was ready to keep faith with them in everything.

Then Hildigunna was betrothed to Hauskuld, and the day for the wedding feast was fixed, and so the matter ended. They then ride home, but they rode again shortly to the bridal, and Flosi paid down all her goods and money after the wedding, and all went off well.

They fared home to Bergthorsknoll, and were there the next year, and all went well between Hildigunna and Bergthora. But the next spring Njal bought land in Ossaby, and hands it over to Hauskuld, and thither he fares to his own abode. Njal got him all his household, and there was such love between them all, that none of them thought anything that he said or did any worth unless the others had a share in it.

Hauskuld dwelt long at Ossaby, and each backed the other's honour, and Njal's sons were always in Hauskuld's company. Their friendship was so warm, that each house bade the other to a feast every harvest, and gave each other great gifts; and so it goes on for a long while.

Chapter 103
The Slaying of Hauskuld Njal's Son

There was a man named Lyting; he dwelt at Samstede, and he had to wife a woman named Steinvora; she was a daughter of Sigfus, and Thrain's sister. Lyting was tall of growth and a strong man, wealthy in goods and ill to deal with.

It happened once that Lyting had a feast in his house at Samstede, and he had bidden thither Hauskuld and the sons of Sigfus, and they all came. There, too, was Grani Gunnar's son, and Gunnar Lambi's son, and Lambi Sigurd's son.

Hauskuld Njal's son and his mother had a farm at Holt, and he was always riding to his farm from Bergthorsknoll, and his path lay by the homestead at Samstede. Hauskuld had a son called Amund; he had been born blind, but for all that he was tall and strong. Lyting had two brothers — the one's name was Hallstein, and the other's Hallgrim. They were the most unruly of men, and they were ever with their brother, for other men could not bear their temper.

Lyting was out of doors most of that day, but every now and then he went inside his house. At last he had gone to his seat, when in came a woman who had been out of doors, and she said —

"You were too far off to see outside how that proud fellow rode by the farmyard!"

"What proud fellow was that," says Lyting, "of whom thou speakest?"

"Hauskuld Njal's son rode here by the yard," she says.

"He rides often here by the farmyard," said Lyting, "and I can't say that it does not try my temper; and now I will make thee an offer, Hauskuld [Sigfus' son], to go along with thee if thou wilt avenge thy father and slay Hauskuld Njal's son."

"That I will not do," says Hauskuld, "for then I should repay Njal, my foster father, evil for good, and mayst thou and thy feasts never thrive henceforth."

With that he sprang up away from the board, and made them catch his horses, and rode home.

Then Lyting said to Grani Gunnar's son —

"Thou wert by when Thrain was slain, and that will still be in thy mind; and thou, too, Gunnar Lambi's son, and thou, Lambi Sigurd's son. Now, my will is that we ride to meet him this evening, and slay him."

"No," says Grani, "I will not fall on Njal's son, and so break the atonement which good men and true have made."

With like words spoke each man of them, and so, too, spoke all the sons of Sigfus; and they took that counsel to ride away.

Then Lyting said, when they had gone away —

"All men know that I have taken no atonement for my brother-in-law Thrain, and I shall never be content that no vengeance — man for man — shall be taken for him."

After that he called on his two brothers to go with him, and three house-carles as well. They went on the way to meet Hauskuld [Njal's son] as he came back, and lay in wait for him north of the farmyard in a pit; and there they bided till it was about mid-even [six o'clock P.M.]. Then Hauskuld rode up to them. They jump up all of them with their arms, and fall on him. Hauskuld guarded himself well, so that for a long while they could not get the better of him; but the end of it was at last that he wounded Lyting on the arm, and slew two of his serving-men, and then fell himself. They gave Hauskuld sixteen wounds, but they hewed not off the head from his body. They fared away into the wood east of Rangriver, and hid themselves there.

That same evening, Rodny's shepherd found Hauskuld dead, and went home and told Rodny of her son's slaying.

"Was he surely dead?" she asks; "was his head off?"

"It was not," he says.

"I shall know if I see," she says; "so take thou my horse and driving gear."

He did so, and got all things ready, and then they went thither where Hauskuld lay.

She looked at the wounds, and said —

"'Tis even as I thought, that he could not be quite dead, and Njal no doubt can cure greater wounds."

After that they took the body and laid it on the sledge and drove to Bergthorsknoll, and drew it into the sheepcote, and made him sit upright against the wall.

Then they went both of them and knocked at the door, and a house-carle went to the door. She steals in by him at once, and goes till she comes to Njal's bed.

She asked whether Njal were awake? He said he had slept up to that time, but was then awake.

"But why art thou come hither so early?"

"Rise thou up," said Rodny, "from thy bed by my rival's side, and come out, and she too, and thy sons, to see thy son Hauskuld."

They rose and went out.

"Let us take our weapons," said Skarphedinn, "and have them with us."

Njal said naught at that, and they ran in and came out again armed.

She goes first till they come to the sheepcote; she goes in and bade them follow her. Then she lit a torch and held it up and said —

"Here, Njal, is thy son Hauskuld, and he hath gotten many wounds upon him, and now he will need leechcraft."

"I see death marks on him," said Njal, "but no signs of life; but why hast thou not closed his eyes and nostrils? see, his nostrils are still open!"

"That duty I meant for Skarphedinn," she says.

Then Skarphedinn went to close his eyes and nostrils, and said to his father—

"Who, sayest thou, hath slain him?"

"Lyting of Samstede and his brothers must have slain him," says Njal.

Then Rodny said, "Into thy hands, Skarphedinn, I leave it to take vengeance for thy brother, and I ween that thou wilt take it well, though he be not lawfully begotten, and that thou wilt not be slow to take it".

"Wonderfully do ye men behave," said Bergthora, "when ye slay men for small cause, but talk and tarry over such wrongs as this until no vengeance at all is taken; and now tidings of this will soon come to Hauskuld, the Priest of Whiteness, and he will be offering you atonement, and you will grant him that, but now is the time to act about it, if ye seek for vengeance."

"Our mother eggs us on now with a just goading," said Skarphedinn, and sang a song.

> Well we know the warrior's temper,
> One and all, well, father thine,
> But atonement to the mother,
> Snake-land's stem and thee were base;
> He that hoardeth ocean's fire
> Hearing this will leave his home;
> Wound of weapon us hath smitten,
> Worse the lot of those that wait!

After that they all ran out of the sheepcote, but Rodny went indoors with Njal, and was there the rest of the night.

Chapter 104
The Slaying of Lyting's Brothers

Now we must speak of Skarphedinn and his brothers, how they bend their course up to Rangriver. Then Skarphedinn said —

"Stand we here and listen, and let us go stilly, for I hear the voices of men up along the river's bank. But will ye, Helgi and Grim, deal with Lyting single-handed, or with both his brothers?"

They said they would sooner deal with Lyting alone.

"Still," says Skarphedinn, "there is more game in him, and methinks it were ill if he gets away, but I trust myself best for not letting him escape."

"We will take such steps," says Helgi, "if we get a chance at him, that he shall not slip through our fingers."

Then they went thitherward, Where they heard the voices of men, and see where Lyting and his brothers are by a stream.

Skarphedinn leaps over the stream at once, and alights on the sandy brink on the other side. There upon it stands Hallgrim and his brother. Skarphedinn smites at Hallgrim's thigh, so that he cut the leg clean off, but he grasps Hallstein with his left hand. Lyting thrust at Skarphedinn, but Helgi came up then and threw his shield before the spear, and caught the blow on it. Lyting took up a stone and hurled it at Skarphedinn, and he lost his hold on Hallstein. Hallstein sprang up the sandy bank, but could get up it in no other way than by crawling on his hands and knees. Skarphedinn made a side blow at him with his axe, "the ogress of war," and hews asunder his backbone. Now Lyting turns and flies, but Helgi and Grim both went after him, and each gave him a wound, but still Lyting got across the river away from them, and so to the horses, and gallops till he comes to Ossaby.

Hauskuld was at home, and meets him at once. Lyting told him of these deeds.

"Such things were to be looked for by thee," says Hauskuld. "Thou hast behaved like a madman, and here the truth of the old saw will be proved: 'but a short while is hand fain of blow'. Methinks what thou hast got to look to now is whether thou wilt be able to save thy life or not."

"Sure enough," says Lyting, "I had hard work to get away, but still I wish now that thou wouldest get me atoned with Njal and his sons, so that I might keep my farm."

"So it shall be," says Hauskuld.

After that Hauskuld made them saddle his horse, and rode to Bergthorsknoll with five men. Njal's sons were then come home and had laid them down to sleep.

Hauskuld went at once to see Njal, and they began to talk.

"Hither am I come," said Hauskuld to Njal, "to beg a boon on behalf of Lyting, my uncle. He has done great wickedness against you and yours, broken his atonement and slain thy son."

"Lyting will perhaps think," said Njal, "that he has already paid a heavy fine in the loss of his brothers, but if I grant him any terms, I shall let him reap the good of my love for thee, and I will tell thee before I utter the award of atonement, that Lyting's brothers shall fall as outlaws. Nor shall Lyting have any atonement for his wounds, but on the other hand, he shall pay the full blood-fine for Hauskuld."

"My wish," said Hauskuld, "is, that thou shouldest make thine own terms."

"Well," says Njal, "then I will utter the award at once if thou wilt."

"Wilt thou," says Hauskuld, "that thy sons should be by?"

"Then we should be no nearer an atonement than we were before," says Njal, "but they will keep to the atonement which I utter."

Then Hauskuld said, "Let us close the matter then, and handsel him peace on behalf of thy sons".

"So it shall be," says Njal. "My will then is that he pays two hundred in silver for the slaying of Hauskuld, but he may still dwell at Samstede; and yet I think it were wiser if he sold his land and changed his abode; but not for this quarrel; neither I nor my sons will break our pledges of peace to him: but methinks it may be that some one may rise up in this country against whom he may have to be on his guard. Yet, lest it should seem that I make a man an outcast from his native place, I allow him to be here in this neighbourhood, but in that case he alone is answerable for what may happen."

After that Hauskuld fared home, and Njal's sons woke up as he went, and asked their father who had come, but he told them that his foster-son Hauskuld had been there.

"He must have come to ask a boon for Lyting then," said Skarphedinn.

"So it was," says Njal

"Ill was it then," says Grim.

"Hauskuld could not have thrown his shield before him," says Njal, "if thou hadst slain him, as it was meant thou shouldst."

"Let us throw no blame on our father," says Skarphedinn.

Now it is to be said that this atonement was kept between them afterwards.

Chapter 105
Of Amund the Blind

That event happened three winters after at the Thingskala-Thing that Amund the blind was at the Thing; he was the son of Hauskuld Njal's son. He made men lead him about among the booths, and so he came to the booth inside which was Lyting of Samstede. He made them lead him into the booth till he came before Lyting.

"Is Lyting of Samstede here?" he asked.

"What dost thou want?" says Lyting.

"I want to know," says Amund, "what atonement thou wilt pay me for my father, I am base-born, and I have touched no fine."

"I have atoned for the slaying of thy father," says Lyting, "with a full price, and thy father's father and thy father's brothers took the money; but my brothers fell without a price as outlaws; and so it was that I had both done an ill-deed, and paid dear for it."

"I ask not," says Amund, "as to thy having paid an atonement to them. I know that ye two are now friends, but I ask this, what atonement thou wilt pay to me?"

"None at all," says Lyting.

"I cannot see," says Amund, "how thou canst have right before God, when thou hast stricken me so near the heart; but all I can say is, that if I were blessed with the sight of both my eyes, I would have either a money fine for my father, or revenge man for man; and so may God judge between us."

After that he went out; but when he came to the door of the booth, he turned short round towards the inside. Then his eyes were opened, and he said —

"Praised be the Lord! now I see what His will is."

With that he ran straight into the booth until he comes before Lyting, and smites him with an axe on the head, so that it sunk in up to the hammer, and gives the axe a pull towards him.

Lyting fell forwards and was dead at once.

Amund goes out to the door of the booth, and when he got to the very same spot on which he had stood when his eyes were opened, lo! they were shut again, and he was blind all his life after.

Then he made them lead him to Njal and his sons, and he told them of Lyting's slaying.

"Thou mayest not be blamed for this," says Njal, "for such things are settled by a higher power; but it is worth while to take warning from such events, lest we cut any short who have such near claims as Amund had."

After that Njal offered an atonement to Lyting's kinsmen. Hauskuld the Priest of Whiteness had a share in bringing Lyting's kinsmen to take the fine, and then the matter was put to an award, and half the fines fell away for the sake of the claim which he seemed to have on Lyting.

After that men came forward with pledges of peace and good faith, and Lyting's kinsmen granted pledges to Amund. Men rode home from the Thing; and now all is quiet for a long while.

Chapter 106
Of Valgard the Guileful

Valgard the guileful came back to Iceland that summer; he was then still heathen. He fared to Hof to his son Mord's house, and was there the winter over. He said to Mord —

"Here I have ridden far and wide all over the neighbourhood, and methinks I do not know it for the same. I came to Whiteness, and there I saw many tofts of booths and much ground levelled for building, I came to Thingskala-Thing, and there I saw all our booths broken down. What is the meaning of such strange things?"

"New priesthoods," answers Mord, "have been set up here, and a law for a Fifth Court, and men have declared themselves out of my Thing, and have gone over to Hauskuld's Thing."

"Ill hast thou repaid me," said Valgard, "for giving up to thee my priesthood, when thou hast handled it so little like a man, and now my wish is that thou shouldst pay them off by something that will drag them all down to death; and this thou canst do by setting them by the ears by tale-bearing, so that Njal's sons may slay Hauskuld; but there are many who will have the blood-feud after him, and so Njal's sons will be slain in that quarrel."

"I shall never be able to get that done," says Mord.

"I will give thee a plan," says Valgard; "thou shalt ask Njal's sons to thy house, and send them away with gifts, but thou shalt keep thy tale-bearing in the back ground until great friendship has sprung up between you, and they trust thee no worse than their own selves. So wilt thou be able to avenge thyself on Skarphedinn for that he took thy money from thee after Gunnar's death; and in this wise, further on, thou wilt be able to seize the leadership when they are all dead and gone."

This plan they settled between them should be brought to pass; and Mord said —

"I would, father, that thou wouldst take on thee the new faith. Thou art an old man."

"I will not do that," says Valgard. "I would rather that thou shouldst cast off the faith, and see what follows then."

Mord said he would not do that. Valgard broke crosses before Mord's face, and all holy tokens. A little after Valgard took a sickness and breathed his last, and he was laid in a cairn by Hof.

Chapter 107
Of Mord and Njal's Sons

Some while after Mord rode to Bergthorsknoll and saw Skarphedinn there; he fell into very fair words with them, and so he talked the whole day, and said he wished to be good friends with them, and to see much of them.

Skarphedinn took it all well, but said he had never sought for anything of the kind before. So it came about that he got himself into such great friendship with them, that neither side thought they had taken any good counsel unless the other had a share in it.

Njal always disliked his coming thither, and it often happened that he was angry with him.

It happened one day that Mord came to Bergthorsknoll, and Mord said to Njal's sons —

"I have made up my mind to give a feast yonder, and I mean to drink in my heirship after my father, but to that feast I wish to bid you, Njal's sons, and Kari; and at the same time I give you my word that ye shall not fare away giftless."

They promised to go, and now he fares home and makes ready the feast. He bade to it many householders, and that feast was very crowded.

Thither came Njal's sons and Kari. Mord gave Skarphedinn a brooch of gold, and a silver belt to Kari, and good gifts to Grim and Helgi.

They come home and boast of these gifts, and show them to Njal. He said they would be bought full dear, "and take heed that ye do not repay the giver in the coin which he no doubt wishes to get".

Chapter 108
Of the Slander of Mord Valgard's Son

A little after Njal's sons and Hauskuld were to have their yearly feasts, and they were the first to bid Hauskuld to come to them.

Skarphedinn had a brown horse four winters old, both tall and sightly. He was a stallion, and had never yet been matched in fight. That horse Skarphedinn gave to Hauskuld, and along with him two mares. They all gave Hauskuld gifts, and assured him of their friendship.

After that Hauskuld bade them to his house at Ossaby, and had many guests to meet them, and a great crowd.

It happened that he had just then taken down his hall, but he had built three out-houses, and there the beds were made.

So all that were bidden came, and the feast went off very well. But when men were to go home Hauskuld picked out good gifts for them, and went a part of the way with Njal's sons.

The sons of Sigfus followed him and all the crowd, and both sides said that nothing should ever come between them to spoil their friendship.

A little while after Mord came to Ossaby and called Hauskuld out to talk with him, and they went aside and spoke.

"What a difference in manliness there is," said Mord, "between thee and Njal's sons! Thou gavest them good gifts, but they gave thee gifts with great mockery."

"How makest thou that out?" says Hauskuld.

"They gave thee a horse which they called a 'dark horse,' and that they did out of mockery at thee, because they thought thee too untried, I can tell thee also that they envy thee the priesthood, Skarphedinn took it up as his own at the Thing when thou camest not to the Thing at the summoning of the Fifth Court, and Skarphedinn never means to let it go."

"That is not true," says Hauskuld, "for I got it back at the Folkmote last harvest."

"Then that was Njal's doing," says Mord. "They broke, too, the atonement about Lyting."

"I do not mean to lay that at their door," says Hauskuld.

"Well," says Mord, "thou canst not deny that when ye two, Skarphedinn and thou, were going east towards Markfleet, an axe fell out from under his belt, and he meant to have slain thee then and there."

"It was his woodman's axe," says Hauskuld, "and I saw how he put it under his belt; and now, Mord, I will just tell thee this right out, that thou canst never say so much ill of Njal's sons as to make me believe it; but though there were aught in it, and it were true as thou sayest, that either I must slay them or they me, then would I far rather suffer death at their hands than work them any harm. But as for thee, thou art all the worse a man for having spoken this."

After that Mord fares home. A little after Mord goes to see Njal's sons, and he talks much with those brothers and Kari.

"I have been told," says Mord, "that Hauskuld has said that thou, Skarphedinn, hast broken the atonement made with Lyting; but I was made aware also that he thought that thou hadst meant some treachery against him when ye two fared to Markfleet. But still, methinks that was no less treachery when he bade you to a feast at his house, and stowed you away in an outhouse that was farthest from the house, and wood was then heaped round the outhouse all night, and he meant to burn you all inside; but it so happened that Hogni Gunnar's son came that night, and naught came of their onslaught, for they were afraid of him. After that he followed you on your way and great band of men with him, then he meant to make another onslaught on you, and set Grani Gunnar's son, and Gunnar Lambi's son to kill thee; but their hearts failed them, and they dared not to fall on thee."

But when he had spoken thus, first of all they spoke against it, but the end of it was that they believed him, and from that day forth a coldness sprung up on their part towards Hauskuld, and they scarcely ever spoke to him when they met; but Hauskuld showed them little deference, and so things went on for a while.

Next harvest Hauskuld fared east to Swinefell to a feast, and Flosi gave him a hearty welcome. Hildigunna was there too. Then Flosi spoke to Hauskuld and said —

"Hildigunna tells me that there is great coldness with you and Njal's sons, and methinks that is ill, and I will beg thee not to ride west, but I will get thee a homestead in Skaptarfell, and I will send my brother, Thorgeir, to dwell at Ossaby."

"Then some will say," says Hauskuld, "that I am flying thence for fear's sake, and that I will not have said."

"Then it is more likely that great trouble will arise," says Flosi.

"Ill is that then," says Hauskuld, "for I would rather fall unatoned, than that many should reap ill for my sake."

Hauskuld busked him to ride home a few nights after, but Flosi gave him a scarlet cloak, and it was embroidered with needlework down to the waist.

Hauskuld rode home to Ossaby, and now all is quiet for a while.

Hauskuld was so much beloved that few men were his foes, but the same ill-will went on between him and Njal's sons the whole winter through.

Njal had taken as his foster-child, Thord, the son of Kari. He had also fostered Thorhall, the son of Asgrim Ellidagrim's son. Thorhall was a strong man, and hardy both in body and mind, he had learnt so much law that he was the third greatest lawyer in Iceland.

Next spring was an early spring, and men are busy sowing their corn.

Chapter 109
Of Mord and Njal's Sons

It happened one day that Mord came to Bergthorsknoll. He and Kari and Njal's sons fell a-talking at once, and Mord slanders Hauskuld after his wont, and has now many new tales to tell, and does naught but egg Skarphedinn and them on to slay Hauskuld, and said he would be beforehand with them if they did not fall on him at once.

"I will let thee have thy way in this," says Skarphedinn, "if thou wilt fare with us, and have some hand in it."

"That I am ready to do," says Mord, and so they bound that fast with promises, and he was to come there that evening.

Bergthora asked Njal —

"What are they talking about out of doors?"

"I am not in their counsels," says Njal, "but I was seldom left out of them when their plans were good."

Skarphedinn did not lie down to rest that evening, nor his brothers, nor Kari.

That same night, when it was well-nigh spent, came Mord Valgard's son, and Njal's sons and Kari took their weapons and rode away. They fared till

they came to Ossaby, and bided there by a fence. The weather was good, and
the sun just risen.

Chapter 110
The Slaying of Hauskuld, the Priest of Whiteness

About that time Hauskuld, the Priest of Whiteness, awoke; he put on his clothes,
and threw over him his cloak, Flosi's gift. He took his corn-sieve, and had his
sword in his other hand, and walks towards the fence, and sows the corn as he
goes.

Skarphedinn and his band had agreed that they would all give him a wound.
Skarphedinn sprang up from behind the fence, but when Hauskuld saw him
he wanted to turn away, then Skarphedinn ran up to him and said —

"Don't try to turn on thy heel, Whiteness priest," and hews at him, and the
blow came on his head, and he fell on his knees. Hauskuld said these words
when he fell —

"God help me, and forgive you!"

Then they all ran up to him and gave him wounds.

After that Mord said —

"A plan comes into my mind."

"What is that?" says Skarphedinn.

"That I shall fare home as soon as I can, but after that I will fare up to
Gritwater, and tell them the tidings, and say 'tis an ill deed; but I know surely
that Thorgerda will ask me to give notice of the slaying, and I will do that, for
that will be the surest way to spoil their suit. I will also send a man to Ossaby,
and know how soon they take any counsel in the matter, and that man will
learn all these tidings thence, and I will make believe that I have heard them
from him."

"Do so by all means," says Skarphedinn.

Those brothers fared home, and Kari with them, and when they came
home they told Njal the tidings.

"Sorrowful tidings are these," says Njal, "and such are ill to hear, for sooth
to say this grief touches me so nearly, that methinks it were better to have lost
two of my sons and that Hauskuld lived."

"It is some excuse for thee," says Skarphedinn, "that thou art an old man,
and it is to be looked for that this touches thee nearly."

"But this," says Njal, "no less than old age, is why I grieve, that I know better
than thou what will come after."

"What will come after?" says Skarphedinn.

"My death," says Njal, "and the death of my wife and of all my sons."

"What dost thou foretell for me?" says Kari.

"They will have hard work to go against thy good fortune, for thou wilt be
more than a match for all of them."

This one thing touched Njal so nearly that he could never speak of it without shedding tears.

Chapter 111
Of Hildigunna and Mord Valgard's son

Hildigunna woke up and found that Hauskuld was away out of his bed.

"Hard have been my dreams," she said, "and not good; but go and search for him, Hauskuld."

So they searched for him about the homestead and found him not.

By that time she had dressed herself; then she goes and two men with her, to the fence, and there they find Hauskuld slain.

Just then, too, came up Mord Valgard's son's shepherd, and told her that Njal's sons had gone down thence, "and," he said, "Skarphedinn called out to me and gave notice of the slaying as done by him".

"It were a manly deed," she says, "if one man had been at it."

She took the cloak and wiped off all the blood with it, and wrapped the gouts of gore up in it, and so folded it together and laid it up in her chest.

Now she sent a man up to Gritwater to tell the tidings thither, but Mord was there before him, and had already told the tidings. There, too, was come Kettle of the Mark.

Thorgerda said to Kettle —

"Now is Hauskuld dead as we know, and now bear in mind what thou promisedst to do when thou tookest him for thy foster-child."

"It may well be," says Kettle, "that I promised very many things then, for I thought not that these days would ever befall us that have now come to pass; but yet I am come into a strait, for 'nose is next of kin to eyes,' since I have Njal's daughter to wife."

"Art thou willing, then," says Thorgerda, "that Mord should give notice of the suit for the slaying?"

"I know not that," says Kettle, "for methinks ill comes from him more often than good."

But as soon as ever Mord began to speak to Kettle he fared the same as others, in that he thought as though Mord would be true to him, and so the end of their council was that Mord should give notice of the slaying, and get ready the suit in every way before the Thing.

Then Mord fared down to Ossaby, and thither came nine neighbours who dwelt nearest the spot.

Mord had ten men with him. He shows the neighbours Hauskuld's wounds, and takes witness to the hurts, and names a man as the dealer of every wound save one; that he made as though he knew not who had dealt it, but that wound he had dealt himself. But the slaying he gave notice of at Skarphedinn's hand, and the wounds at his brothers' and Kari's.

After that he called on nine neighbours who dwelt nearest the spot to ride away from home to the Althing on the inquest.

After that he rode home. He scarce ever met Njal's sons, and when he did meet them, he was cross, and that was part of their plan.

The slaying of Hauskuld was heard over all the land, and was ill-spoken of. Njal's sons went to see Asgrim Ellidagrim's son, and asked him for aid.

"Ye very well know that ye may look that I shall help you in all great suits, but still my heart is heavy about this suit, for there are many who have the blood feud, and this slaying is ill-spoken of over all the land."

Now Njal's sons fare home.

Chapter 112
The Pedigree of Gudmund the Powerful

There was a man named Gudmund the powerful, who dwelt at Modruvale in Eyjafirth. He was the son of Eyjolf the son of Einar. Gudmund was a mighty chief, wealthy in goods; he had in his house a hundred hired servants. He overbore in rank and weight all the chiefs in the north country, so that some left their homesteads, but some he put to death, and some gave up their priesthoods for his sake, and from him are come the greatest part of all the picked and famous families in the land, such as "the Point-dwellers" and the "Sturlungs" and the "Hvamdwellers," and the "Fleetmen," and Kettle the bishop, and many of the greatest men.

Gudmund was a friend of Asgrim Ellidagrim's son, and so he hoped to get his help.

Chapter 113
Of Snorri the Priest, and his stock

There was a man named Snorri, who was surnamed the Priest. He dwelt at Helgafell before Gudruna Oswif's daughter bought the land of him, and dwelt there till she died of old age; but Snorri then went and dwelt at Hvamsfirth on Sælingdale's tongue. Thorgrim was the name of Snorri's father, and he was a son of Thorstein codcatcher. Snorri was a great friend of Asgrim Ellidagrim's son, and he looked for help there also. Snorri was the wisest and shrewdest of all these men in Iceland who had not the gift of foresight. He was good to his friends, but grim to his foes.

At that time there was a great riding to the Thing out of all the Quarters, and men had many suits set on foot.

Chapter 114
Of Flosi Thord's son

Flosi hears of Hauskuld's slaying, and that brings him much grief and wrath, but still he kept his feelings well in hand. He was told how the suit had been set on foot, as has been said, for Hauskuld's slaying, and he said little about it. He sent word to Hall of the Side, his father-in-law, and to Ljot his son, that they must gather in a great company at the Thing. Ljot was thought the most hopeful man for a chief away there east. It had been foretold that if he could ride three summers running to the Thing, and come safe and sound home, that then he would be the greatest chief in all his family, and the oldest man. He had then ridden one summer to the Thing, and now he meant to ride the second time.

Flosi sent word to Kol Thorstein's son, and Glum the son of Hilldir the old, the son of Gerleif, the son of Aunund wallet-back, and to Modolf Kettle's son, and they all rode to meet Flosi.

Hall gave his word, too, to gather a great company, and Flosi rode till he came to Kirkby, to Surt Asbjorn's son. Then Flosi sent after Kolbein Egil's son, his brother's son, and he came to him there. Thence he rode to Headbrink. There dwelt Thorgrim the showy, the son of Thorkel the fair. Flosi begged him to ride to the Althing with him, and he said yea to the journey, and spoke thus to Flosi—

"Often hast thou been more glad, master, than thou art now, but thou hast some right to be so."

"Of a truth," said Flosi, "that hath now come on my hands, which I would give all my goods that it had never happened. Ill seed has been sown, and so an ill crop will spring from it."

Thence he rode over Arnstacksheath, and so to Solheim that evening. There dwelt Lodmund Wolf's son, but he was a great friend of Flosi, and there he stayed that night, and next morning Lodmund rode with him into the Dale.

There dwelt Runolf, the son of Wolf Aurpriest.

Flosi said to Runolf —

"Here we shall have true stories as to the slaying of Hauskuld, the Priest of Whiteness. Thou art a truthful man, and hast got at the truth by asking, and I will trust to all that thou tellest me as to what was the cause of quarrel between them."

"There is no good in mincing the matter," said Runolf, "but we must say outright that he has been slain for less than no cause; and his death is a great grief to all men. No one thinks it so much a loss as Njal, his foster-father."

"Then they will be ill off for help from men," says Flosi; "and they will find no one to speak up for them."

"So it will be," says Runolf, "unless it be otherwise foredoomed."

"What has been done in the suit?" says Flosi.

"Now the neighbours have been summoned on the inquest," says Runolf, "and due notice given of the suit for manslaughter."

"Who took that step?" asks Flosi.

"Mord Valgard's son," says Runolf.

"How far is that to be trusted?" says Flosi.

"He is of my kin," says Runolf; "but still, if I tell the truth of him, I must say that more men reap ill than good from him. But this one thing I will ask of thee, Flosi, that thou givest rest to thy wrath, and takest the matter up in such a way as may lead to the least trouble. For Njal will make a good offer, and so will others of the best men."

"Ride thou then to the Thing, Runolf," said Flosi, "and thy words shall have much weight with me, unless things turn out worse than they should."

After that they cease speaking about it, and Runolf promised to go to the Thing.

Runolf sent word to Hatr the wise, his kinsman, and he rode thither at once.

Thence Flosi rode to Ossaby.

Chapter 115
Of Flosi and Hildigunna

Hildigunna was out of doors, and said, "Now shall all the men of my household be out of doors when Flosi rides into the yard; but the women shall sweep the house and deck it with hangings, and make ready the high-seat for Flosi."

Then Flosi rode into the town, and Hildigunna turned to him and said —

"Come in safe and sound and happy kinsman, and my heart is fain at thy coming hither."

"Here," says Flosi, "we will break our fast, and then we will ride on."

Then their horses were tethered, and Flosi went into the sitting-room and sat him down, and spurned the high-seat away from him on the dais, and said —

"I am neither king nor earl, and there is no need to make a high-seat for me to sit on, nor is there any need to make a mock of me."

Hildigunna was standing close by, and said —

"It is ill if it mislikes thee, for this we did with a whole heart."

"If thy heart is whole towards me, then what I do will praise itself if it be well done, but it will blame itself if it be ill done."

Hildigunna laughed a cold laugh, and said —

"There is nothing new in that, we will go nearer yet ere we have done."

She sat her down by Flosi, and they talked long and low. After that the board was laid, and Flosi and his band washed their hands. Flosi looked hard at the towel and saw that it was all in rags, and had one end torn off. He threw it down on the bench and would not wipe himself with it, but tore off a piece of the table-cloth, and wiped himself with that, and then threw it to his men.

After that Flosi sat down to the board and bade men eat.

Then Hildigunna came into the room and went before Flosi, and threw her hair off her eyes and wept.

"Heavy-hearted art thou now, kinswoman," said Flosi, "when thou weepest, but still it is well that thou shouldst weep for a good husband."

"What vengeance or help shall I have of thee?" she says.

"I will follow up thy suit," said Flosi, "to the utmost limit of the law, or strive for that atonement which good men and true shall say that we ought to have as full amends."

"Hauskuld would avenge thee," she said, "if he had the blood-feud after thee."

"Thou lackest not grimness," answered Flosi, "and what thou wantest is plain."

"Arnor Ornolf's son, of Forswaterwood," said Hildigunna, "had done less wrong towards Thord Frey's priest thy father; and yet thy brothers Kolbein and Egil slew him at Skaptarfells-Thing."

Then Hildigunna went back into the hall and unlocked her chest, and then she took out the cloak, Flosi's gift, and in it Hauskuld had been slain, and there she had kept it, blood and all. Then she went back into the sitting room with the cloak; she went up silently to Flosi. Flosi had just then eaten his full, and the board was cleared. Hildigunna threw the cloak over Flosi, and the gore rattled down all over him.

Then she spoke and said —

"This cloak, Flosi, thou gavest to Hauskuld, and now I will give it back to thee; he was slain in it, and I call God and all good men to witness, that I adjure thee, by all the might of thy Christ, and by thy manhood and bravery, to take vengeance for all those wounds which he had on his dead body, or else to be called every man's dastard."

Flosi threw the cloak off him and hurled it into her lap, and said —

"Thou art the greatest hell-hag, and thou wishest that we should take that course which will be the worst for all of us. But 'women's counsel is ever cruel.'"

Flosi was so stirred at this, that sometimes he was bloodred in the face, and sometimes ashy pale as withered grass, and sometimes blue as death.

Flosi and his men rode away; he rode to Holtford, and there waits for the sons of Sigfus and other of his men.

Ingialld dwelt at the Springs; he was the brother of Rodny, Hauskuld Njal's son's mother. Ingialld had to wife Thraslauga, the daughter of Egil, the son of Thord Frey's priest. Flosi sent word to Ingialld to come to him, and Ingialld went at once, with fourteen men. They were all of his household. Ingialld was a tall man and a strong, and slow to meddle with other men's business, one of the bravest of men, and very bountiful to his friends.

Flosi greeted him well, and said to him, "Great trouble hath now come on me and my brothers-in-law, and it is hard to see our way out of it; I beseech thee not to part from my suit until this trouble is past and gone."

"I am come into a strait myself," said Ingialld, "for the sake of the ties that there are between me and Njal and his sons, and other great matters which stand in the way."

"I thought," said Flosi, "when I gave away my brother's daughter to thee, that thou gavest me thy word to stand by me in every suit."

"It is most likely," says Ingialld, "that I shall do so, but still I will now, first of all, ride home, and thence to the Thing."

Chapter 116
Of Flosi, Mord and the Sons of Sigfus

The sons of Sigfus heard how Flosi was at Holtford, and they rode thither to meet him, and there were Kettle of the Mark, and Lambi his brother, Thorkell and Mord, the sons of Sigfus, Sigmund their brother, and Lambi Sigurd's son, and Gunnar Lambi's son, and Grani Gunnar's son, and Vebrand Hamond's son.

Flosi stood up to meet them, and greeted them gladly. So they went down to the river. Flosi had the whole story from them about the slaying, and there was no difference between them and Kettle of the Mark's story.

Flosi spoke to Kettle of the Mark, and said —

"This now I ask of thee; how tightly are your hearts knit as to this suit, thou and the other sons of Sigfus?"

"My wish is," said Kettle, "that there should be peace between us, but yet I have sworn an oath not to part from this suit till it has been brought somehow to an end, and to lay my life on it."

"Thou art a good man and true," said Flosi, "and it is well to have such men with one."

Then Grani Gunnar's son and Lambi Sigurd's son both spoke together, and said —

"We wish for outlawry and death."

"It is not given us," said Flosi, "both to share and choose, we must take what we can get."

"I have had it in my heart," says Grani, "ever since they slew Thrain by Markfleet, and after that his son Hauskuld, never to be atoned with them by a lasting peace, for I would willingly stand by when they were all slain, every man of them."

"Thou hast stood so near to them," said Flosi, "that thou mightest have avenged these things hadst thou had the heart and manhood. Methinks thou and many others now ask for what ye would give much money hereafter never to have had a share in. I see this clearly, that though we slay Njal or his sons, still they are men of so great worth, and of such good family, that there will be such a blood feud and hue and cry after them, that we shall have to fall on our knees before many a man, and beg for help, ere we get an atonement and find our way out of this strait. Ye may make up your minds, then, that many will become poor who before had great goods, but some of you will lose both goods and life."

Mord Valgard's Son rode to meet Flosi, and said he would ride to the Thing with him with all his men. Flosi took that well, and raised a matter of a wedding with him, that he should give away Rannveiga his daughter to Starkad Flosi's brother's son, who dwelt at Staffell. Flosi did this because he thought he would so make sure both of his faithfulness and force.

Mord took the wedding kindly, but handed the matter over to Gizur the White, and bade him talk about it at the Thing.

Mord had to wife Thorkatla, Gizur the White's daughter.

They two, Mord and Flosi, rode both together to the Thing, and talked the whole day, and no man knew aught of their counsel.

Chapter 117
Njal and Skarphedinn Talk Together

Now, we must say how Njal said to Skarphedinn —

"What plan have ye laid down for yourselves, thou and thy brothers and Kari?"

"Little reck we of dreams in most matters," said Skarphedinn; "but if thou must know, we shall ride to Tongue to Asgrim Ellidagrim's son, and thence to the Thing; but what meanest thou to do about thine own journey, father?"

"I shall ride to the Thing," says Njal, "for it belongs to my honour not to be severed from your suit so long as I live. I ween that many men will have good words to say of me, and so I shall stand you in good stead, and do you no harm."

There, too, was Thorhall Asgrim's son, and Njal's foster-son. The sons of Njal laughed at him because he was clad in a coat of russet, and asked how long he meant to wear that?

"I shall have thrown it off," he said, "when I have to follow up the blood-feud for my foster father."

"There will ever be most good in thee," said Njal, "when there is most need of it."

So they all busked them to ride away from home, and were nigh thirty men in all, and rode till they came to Thursowater. Then came after them Njal's kinsmen, Thorleif crow, and Thorgrim the big; they were Holt-Thorir's sons, and offered their help and following to Njal's sons, and they took that gladly.

So they rode altogether across Thursowater, until they came on Laxwater bank, and took a rest and baited their horses there, and there Hjallti's Skeggi's son came to meet them, and Njal's sons fell to talking with him, and they talked long and low.

"Now, I will show," said Hjallti, "that I am not black-hearted; Njal has asked me for help, and I have agreed to it, and given my word to aid him; he has often given me and many others the worth of it in cunning counsel."

Hjallti tells Njal all about Flosi's doings. They sent Thorhall on to Tongue to tell Asgrim that they would be there that evening; and Asgrim made ready at once, and was out of doors to meet them when Njal rode into the town.

Njal was clad in a blue cape, and had a felt hat on his head, and a small axe in his hand. Asgrim helped Njal off his horse, and led him and sate him down in his own seat. After that they all went in, Njal's sons and Kari. Then Asgrim went out.

Hjallti wished to turn away, and thought there were too many there; but Asgrim caught hold of his reins, and said he should never have his way in riding off, and made men unsaddle their horses, and led Hjallti in and sate him down by Njal's aide; but Thorleif and his brother sat on the other bench and their men with them.

Asgrim sate him down on a stool before Njal, and asked —

"What says thy heart about our matter?"

"It speaks rather heavily," says Njal, "for I am afraid that we shall have no lucky men with us in the suit; but I would, friend, that thou shouldest send after all the men who belong to thy Thing, and ride to the Althing with me."

"I have always meant to do that," says Asgrim; "and this I will promise thee at the same time — that I will never leave thy cause while I can get any men to follow me."

But all those who were in the house thanked him, and said, that was bravely spoken. They were there that night, but the day after all Asgrim's band came thither.

And after that they all rode together till they come up on the Thingfield, and fit up their booths.

Chapter 118
Asgrim and Njal's Sons Pray for Help

By that time Flosi had come to the Thing, and filled all his booths. Runolf filled the Dale-dwellers' booths, and Mord the booths of the men from Rangriver. Hall of the Side had long since come from the east, but scarce any of the other men; but still Hall of the Side had come with a great band, and joined this at once to Flosi's company, and begged him to take an atonement and to make peace.

Hall was a wise man and good-hearted, Flosi answered him well in everything, but gave way in nothing.

Hall asked what men had promised him help? Flosi named Mord Valgard's son, and said he had asked for his daughter at the hand of his kinsman Starkad.

Hall said she was a good match, but it was ill dealing with Mord, "and that thou wilt put to the proof ere this Thing be over".

After that they ceased talking.

One day Njal and Asgrim had a long talk in secret.

Then all at once Asgrim sprang up and said to Njal's sons —

"We must set about seeking friends, that we may not be overborne by force; for this suit will be followed up boldly."

Then Asgrim went out, and Helgi Njal's son next; then Kari Solmund's son; then Grim Njal's son; then Skarphedinn; then Thorhall; then Thorgrim the big; then Thorleif crow.

They went to the booth of Gizur the White and inside it. Gizur stood up to meet them, and bade them sit down and drink.

"Not thitherward," says Asgrim, "tends our way, and we will speak our errand out loud, and not mutter and mouth about it. What help shall I have from thee, as thou art my kinsman?"

"Jorunn my sister," said Gizur, "would wish that I should not shrink from standing by thee; and so it shall be now and hereafter, that we will both of us have the same fate."

Asgrim thanked him, and went away afterwards.

Then Skarphedinn asked, "Whither shall we go now?"

"To the booths of the men of Olfus," says Asgrim.

So they went thither, and Asgrim asked whether Skapti Thorod's son were in the booth? He was told that he was. Then they went inside the booth.

Skapti sate on the cross bench, and greeted Asgrim, and he took the greeting well.

Skapti offered Asgrim a seat by his side, but Asgrim said he should only stay there a little while, "but still we have an errand to thee".

"Let me hear it," says Skapti.

"I wish to beg thee for thy help, that thou wilt stand by us in our suit."

"One thing I had hoped," says Skapti, "and that is, that neither you nor your troubles would ever come into my dwelling."

"Such things are ill-spoken," says Asgrim, "when a man is the last to help others, when most lies on his aid."

"Who is yon man," says Skapti, "before whom four men walk, a big burly man, and pale-faced, unlucky-looking, well-knit, and troll-like?"

"My name is Skarphedinn," he answers, "and thou hast often seen me at the Thing; but in this I am wiser than thou, that I have no need to ask what thy name is. Thy name is Skapti Thorod's son, but before thou calledst thyself 'Bristle-poll,' after thou hadst slain Kettle of Elda; then thou shavedst thy poll, and puttedst pitch on thy head, and then thou hiredst thralls to cut up a sod of turf, and thou creptest underneath it to spend the night. After that thou wentest to Thorolf Lopt's son of Eyrar, and he took thee on board, and bore thee out here in his meal sacks."

After that Asgrim and his band went out, and Skarphedinn asked —

"Whither shall we go now?"

"To Snorri the Priest's booth," says Asgrim.

Then they went to Snorri's booth. There was a man outside before the booth, and Asgrim asked whether Snorri were in the booth.

The man said he was.

Asgrim went into the booth, and all the others. Snorri was sitting on the cross bench, and Asgrim went and stood before him, and hailed him well.

Snorri took his greeting blithely, and bade him sit down.

Asgrim said he should be only a short time there, "but we have an errand with thee".

Snorri bade him tell it.

"I would," said Asgrim, "that thou wouldst come with me to the court, and stand by me with thy help, for thou art a wise man, and a great man of business."

"Suits fall heavy on us now," says Snorri the Priest, "and now many men push forward against us, and so we are slow to take up the troublesome suits of other men from other quarters."

"Thou mayest stand excused," says Asgrim, "for thou art not in our debt for any service."

"I know," says Snorri, "that thou art a good man and true, and I will promise thee this, that I will not be against thee, and not yield help to thy foes."

Asgrim thanked him, and Snorri the Priest asked —

"Who is that man before whom four go, pale-faced, and sharp-featured, and who shows his front teeth, and has his axe aloft on his shoulder?"

"My name is Hedinn," he says, "but some men call me Skarphedinn by my full name; but what more hast thou to say to me?"

"This," said Snorri the Priest, "that methinks thou art a well-knit, ready-handed man, but yet I guess that the best part of thy good fortune is past, and I ween thou hast not long to live."

"That is well," says Skarphedinn, "for that is a debt we all have to pay, but still it were more needful to avenge thy father than to foretell my fate in this way."

"Many have said that before," says Snorri, "and I will not be angry at such words."

After that they went out, and got no help there. Then they fared to the booths of the men of Skagafirth. There Hafr the wealthy had his booth. The mother of Hafr was named Thoruna, she was a daughter of Asbjorn baldpate of Myrka, the son of Hrosbjorn.

Asgrim and his band went into the booth, and Hafr sate in the midst of it, and was talking to a man.

Asgrim went up to him, and hailed him well; he took it kindly, and bade him sit down.

"This I would ask of thee," said Asgrim, "that thou wouldst grant me and my sons-in-law help."

Hafr answered sharp and quick, and said he would have nothing to do with their troubles.

"But still I must ask who that pale-faced man is before whom four men go, so ill-looking, as though he had come out of the sea-crags."

"Never mind, milksop that thou art!" said Skarphedinn, "who I am, for I will dare to go forward wherever thou standest before me, and little would I fear though such striplings were in my path. 'Twere rather thy duty, too, to get back thy sister Swanlauga, whom Eydis ironsword and his messmate Stediakoll took away out of thy house, but thou didst not dare to do aught against them."

"Let us go out," said Asgrim, "there is no hope of help here."

Then they went out to the booths of men of Modruvale, and asked whether Gudmund the powerful were in the booth, but they were told he was.

Then they went into the booth. There was a high seat in the midst of it, and there sate Gudmund the powerful.

Asgrim went and stood before him, and hailed him.

Gudmund took his greeting well, and asked him to sit down.

"I will not sit," said Asgrim, "but I wish to pray thee for help, for thou art a bold man and a mighty chief."

"I will not be against thee," said Gudmund, "but if I see fit to yield thee help, we may well talk of that afterwards," and so he treated them well and kindly in every way.

Asgrim thanked him for his words, and Gudmund said —

"There is one man in your band at whom I have gazed for awhile, and he seems to me more terrible than most men that I have seen."

"Which is he?" says Asgrim.

"Four go before him," says Gudmund; "dark brown is his hair, and pale is his face; tall of growth and sturdy. So quick and shifty in his manliness, that I would rather have his following than that of ten other men; but yet the man is unlucky-looking."

"I know," said Skarphedinn, "that thou speakest at me, but it does not go in the same way as to luck with me and thee. I have blame, indeed, from the slaying of Hauskuld, the Whiteness priest, as is fair and right; but both Thorkel foulmouth and Thorir Helgi's son spread abroad bad stories about thee, and that has tried thy temper very much."

Then they went out, and Skarphedinn said —

"Whither shall we go now?"

"To the booths of the men of Lightwater," said Asgrim.

There Thorkel foulmouth had set up his booth.

Thorkel foulmouth had been abroad and worked his way to fame in other lands. He had slain a robber east in Jemtland's wood, and then he fared on east into Sweden, and was a messmate of Saurkvir the churl, and they harried eastward ho; but to the east of Baltic side. Thorkel had to fetch water for them one evening; then he met a wild man of the woods, and struggled against him long; but the end of it was that he slew the wild man. Thence he fared east into Adalsyssla, and there he slew a flying fire-drake. After that he fared back to Sweden, and thence to Norway, and so out to Iceland, and let these deeds of derring do be carved over his shut bed, and on the stool before his high-seat. He fought, too, on Lightwater way with his brothers against Gudmund the powerful, and the men of Lightwater won the day. He and Thorir Helgi's son spread abroad bad stories about Gudmund. Thorkel said there was no man in Iceland with whom he would not fight in single combat, or yield an inch to, if need were. He was called Thorkel foulmouth, because he spared no one with whom he had to do either in word or deed.

Chapter 119
Of Skarphedinn and Thorkel Foulmouth

Asgrim and his fellows went to Thorkel foulmouth's booth, and Asgrim said then to his companions, "This booth Thorkel foulmouth owns, a great champion, and it were worth much to us to get his help. We must here take heed in everything, for he is self-willed and bad tempered; and now I will beg thee, Skarphedinn, not to let thyself be led into our talk."

Skarphedinn smiled at that. He was so clad, he had on a blue kirtle and gray breeks, and black shoes on his feet, coming high up his leg; he had a silver belt about him, and that same axe in his hand with which he slew Thrain, and which he called the "ogress of war," a round buckler, and a silken band round his brow, and his hair was brushed back behind his ears. He was the most soldier-like of men, and by that all men knew him. He went in his appointed place, and neither before nor behind.

Now they went into the booth and into its inner chamber. Thorkel sate in the middle of the cross-bench, and his men away from him on all sides. Asgrim hailed him, and Thorkel took the greeting well, and Asgrim said to him —

"For this have we come hither, to ask help of thee, and that thou wouldst come to the court with us."

"What need can ye have of my help," said Thorkel, "when ye have already gone to Gudmund; he must surely have promised thee his help?"

"We could not get his help," says Asgrim.

"Then Gudmund thought the suit likely to make him foes," said Thorkel; "and so no doubt it will be, for such deeds are the worst that have ever been done; nor do I know what can have driven you to come hither to me, and to think that I should be easier to undertake your suit than Gudmund, or that I would back a wrongful quarrel."

Then Asgrim held his peace, and thought it would be hard work to win him over.

Then Thorkel went on and said, "Who is that big and ugly fellow, before whom four men go, pale-faced and sharp-featured, and unlucky-looking, and cross-grained?"

"My name is Skarphedinn," said Skarphedinn, "and thou hast no right to pick me out, a guiltless man, for thy railing. It never has befallen me to make my father bow down before me, or to have fought against him, as thou didst with thy father. Thou hast ridden little to the Althing, or toiled in quarrels at it, and no doubt it is handier for thee to mind thy milking pails at home than to be here at Axewater in idleness. But stay, it were as well if thou pickedst out from thy teeth that steak of mare's rump which thou atest ere thou rodest to the Thing, while thy shepherd looked on all the while, and wondered that thou couldst work such filthiness!"

Then Thorkel sprang up in mickle wrath, and clutched his short sword and said —

"This sword I got in Sweden when I slew the greatest champion, but since then I have slain many a man with it, and as soon as ever I reach thee I will drive it through thee, and thou shall take that for thy bitter words."

Skarphedinn stood with his axe aloft, and smiled scornfully and said—

"This axe I had in my hand when I leapt twelve ells across Markfleet, and slew Thrain Sigfus' son, and eight of them stood before me, and none of them could touch me. Never have I aimed weapon at man that I have not smitten him."

And with that he tore himself from his brothers, and Kari his brother-in-law, and strode forward to Thorkel.

Then Skarphedinn said —

"Now, Thorkel foulmouth, do one of these two things: sheathe thy sword and sit thee down, or I drive the axe into thy head and cleave thee down to the chine."

Then Thorkel sate him down and sheathed the sword, and such a thing never happened to him either before or since.

Then Asgrim and his band go out, and Skarphedinn said —

"Whither shall we now go?"

"Home to out booths," answered Asgrim.

"Then we fare hack to our booths wearied of begging," says Skarphedinn.

"In many places," said Asgrim, "hast thou been rather sharp-tongued, but here now, in what Thorkel had a share methinks thou hast only treated him as is fitting."

Then they went home to their booths, and told Njal, word for word, all that had been done.

"Things," he said, "draw on to what must be."

Now Gudmund the powerful heard what had passed between Thorkel and Skarphedinn, and said —

"Ye all know how things fared between us and the men of Lightwater, but I have never suffered such scorn and mocking at their hands as has befallen Thorkel from Skarphedinn, and this is just as it should be."

Then he said to Einar of Thvera, his brother, "Thou shalt go with all my band, and stand by Njal's sons when the courts go out to try suits; but if they need help next summer, then I myself will yield them help".

Einar agreed to that, and sent and told Asgrim, and Asgrim said —

"There is no man like Gudmund for nobleness of mind," and then he told it to Njal.

Chapter 120
Of the Pleading of the Suit

The next day Asgrim, and Gizur the White, and Hjallti Skeggi's son, and Einar of Thvera, met together. There too was Mord Valgard's son; he had then let the suit fall from his hand, and given it over to the sons of Sigfus.

Then Asgrim spoke.

"Thee first I speak to about this matter, Gizur the White, and thee Hjallti, and thee Einar, that I may tell you how the suit stands. It will be known to all of you that Mord took up the suit, but the truth of the matter is, that Mord was at Hauskuld's slaying, and wounded him with that wound, for giving which no man was named. It seems to me, then, that this suit must come to nought by reason of a lawful flaw."

"Then we will plead it at once," says Hjallti.

"It is not good counsel," said Thorhall Asgrim's son, "that this should not be hidden until the courts are set."

"How so?" asks Hjallti.

"If," said Thorhall, "they knew now at once that the suit has been wrongly set on foot, then they may still save the suit by sending a man home from the Thing, and summoning the neighbours from home over again, and calling on them to ride to the Thing, and then the suit will be lawfully set on foot."

"Thou art a wise man, Thorhall," say they, "and we will take thy counsel."

After that each man went to his booth.

The sons of Sigfus gave notice of their suits at the Hill of Laws, and asked in what Quarter Courts they lay, and in what house in the district the defendants dwelt. But on the Friday night the courts were to go out to try suits, and so the Thing was quiet up to that day.

Many sought to bring about an atonement between them, but Flosi was steadfast; but others were still more wordy, and things looked ill.

Now the time comes when the courts were to go out, on the Friday evening. Then the whole body of men at the Thing went to the courts. Flosi stood south at the court of the men of Rangriver, and his band with him. There with him was Hall of the Side, and Runolf of the Dale, Wolf Aurpriest's son, and those other men who had promised Flosi help.

But north of the court of the men of Rangriver stood Asgrim Ellidagrim's son, and Gizur the White, Hjallti Skeggi's son, and Einar of Thvera. But Njal's sons were at home at their booth, and Kari and Thorleif crow, and Thorgeir Craggeir, and Thorgrim the big. They sate all with their weapons, and their band looked safe from onslaught.

Njal had already prayed the judges to go into the court, and now the sons of Sigfus plead their suit. They took witness and bade Njal's sons to listen to their oath; after that they took their oath, and then they declared their suit; then they brought forward witness of the notice, then they bade the neighbours on the inquest to take their seats, then they called on Njal's sons to challenge the inquest.

Then up stood Thorhall Asgrim's son, and took witness, and forbade the inquest by a protest to utter their finding; and his ground was, that he who had given notice of the suit was truly under the ban of the law, and was himself an outlaw.

"Of whom speakest thou this?" says Flosi.

"Mord Valgard's son," said Thorhall, "fared to Hauslkuld's slaying with Njal's sons, and wounded him with that wound for which no man was named when witness was taken to the death-wounds; and ye can say nothing against this, and so the suit comes to naught."

Chapter 121
Of the Award of Atonement between Flosi and Njal

Then Njal stood up and said —

"This I pray, Hall of the Side, and Flosi, and all the sons of Sigfus, and all our men too, that ye will not go away, but listen to my words."

They did so, and then he spoke thus —

"It seems to me as though this suit were come to naught, and it is likely it should, for it hath sprung from an ill root. I will let you all know that I loved Hauskuld more than my own sons, and when I heard that he was slain, methought the sweetest light of my eyes was quenched, and I would rather have lost all my sons, and that he were alive. Now I ask thee, Hall of the Side, and thee Runolf of the Dale, and thee Hjallti Skeggi's son, and thee Einar of Thvera, and thee Hafr the wise, that I may be allowed to make an atonement for the slaying of Hauskuld on my sons' behalf; and I wish that those men who are best fitted to do so shall utter the award."

Gizur, and Hafr, and Einar, spoke each on their own part, and prayed Flosi to take an atonement, and promised him their friendship in return.

Flosi answered them well in all things, but still did not give his word.

Then Hall of the Side said to Flosi —

"Wilt thou now keep thy word, and grant me my boon which thou hast already promised me, when I put beyond sea Thorgrim, the son of Kettle the fat, thy kinsman, when he had slain Halli the red."

"I will grant it thee, father-in-law," said Flosi, "for that alone wilt thou ask which will make my honour greater than it erewhile was."

"Then," said Hall, "my wish is that thou shouldst be quickly atoned, and lettest good men and true make an award, and so buy the friendship of good and worthy men."

"I will let you all know," said Flosi, "that I will do according to the word of Hall, my father-in-law, and other of the worthiest men, that he and others of the best men on each side, lawfully named, shall make this award. Methinks Njal is worthy that I should grant him this."

Njal thanked him and all of them, and others who were by thanked them too, and said that Flosi had behaved well.

Then Flosi said —

"Now will I name my daysmen [arbitrators] — First, I name Hall, my father-in-law; Auzur from Broadwater; Surt Asbjorn's son of Kirkby; Modolf Kettle's son" — he dwelt then at Asar — "Hafr the wise; and Runolf of the Dale; and it is scarce worth while to say that these are the fittest men out of all my company."

Now he bade Njal to name his daysmen, and then Njal stood up, and said —

"First of these I name, Asgrim Ellidagrim's son; and Hjallti Skeggi's son; Gizur the White; Einar of Thvera; Snorri the priest; and Gudmund the powerful."

After that Njal and Flosi, and the sons of Sigfus shook hands, and Njal pledged his hand on behalf of all his sons, and of Kari, his son-in-law, that they would hold to what those twelve men doomed; and one might say that the whole body of men at the Thing was glad at that.

Then men were sent after Snorri and Gudmund, for they were in their booths.

Then it was given out that the judges in this award would sit in the Court of Laws, but all the others were to go away.

Chapter 122
Of the Judges

Then Snorri the priest spoke thus — "Now are we here twelve judges to whom these suits are handed over, now I will beg you all that we may have no stumbling-blocks in these suits, so that they may not be atoned".

"Will ye," said Gudmund, "award either the lesser or the greater outlawry? Shall they be banished from the district, or from the whole land?"

"Neither of them," says Snorri, "for those banishments are often ill fulfilled, and men have been slain for that sake, and atonements broken, but I will award so great a money fine that no man shall have had a higher price here in the land than Hauskuld."

They all spoke well of his words.

Then they talked over the matter, and could not agree which should first utter how great he thought the fine ought to be, and so the end of it was that they cast lots, and the lot fell on Snorri to utter it.

Then Snorri said, "I will not sit long over this, I will now tell you what my utterance is, I will let Hauskuld be atoned for with triple manfines, but that is six hundred in silver. Now ye shall change it, if ye think it too much or too little."

They said that they would change it in nothing.

"This too shall be added," he said, "that all the money shall be paid down here at the Thing."

Then Gizur the White spoke and said —

"Methinks that can hardly be, for they will not have enough money to pay their fines."

"I know what Snorri wishes," said Gudmund the powerful, "he wants that all we daysmen should give such a sum as our bounty will bestow, and then many will do as we do."

Hall of the Side thanked him, and said he would willingly give as much as any one else gave, and then all the other daysmen agreed to that.

After that they went away, and settled between them that Hall should utter the award at the Court of Laws.

So the bell was rung, and all men went to the Court of Laws, and Hall of the Side stood up and spoke —

"In this suit, in which we have come to an award, we have been all well agreed, and we have awarded six hundred in silver, and half this sum we the daysmen will pay, but it must all be paid up here at the Thing. But it is my prayer to all the people that each man will give something for God's sake."

All answered well to that, and then Hall took witness to the award, that no one should be able to break it.

Njal thanked them for their award, but Skarphedinn stood by, and held his peace, and smiled scornfully.

Then men went from the Court of Laws and to their booths, but the daysmen gathered together in the freeman's church-yard the money which they had promised to give.

Njal's sons handed over that money which they had by them, and Kari did the same, and that came to a hundred in silver.

Njal took out that money which he had with him, and that was another hundred in silver.

So this money was all brought before the Court of Laws, and then men gave so much, that not a penny was wanting.

Then Njal took a silken scarf and a pair of boots and laid them on the top of the heap.

After that, Hall said to Njal, that he should go to fetch his sons, "but I will go for Flosi, and now each must give the other pledges of peace".

Then Njal went home to his booth, and spoke to his sons and said, "Now, are our suits come into a fair way of settlement, now are we men atoned, for all the money has been brought together in one place; and now either side is to go and grant the other peace and pledges of good faith. I will therefore ask you this, my sons, not to spoil these things in any way."

Skarphedinn stroked his brow, and smiled scornfully. So they all go to the Court of Laws.

Hall went to meet Flosi and said —

"Go thou now to the Court of Laws, for now all the money has been bravely paid down, and it has been brought together in one place."

Then Flosi bade the sons of Sigfus to go up with him, and they all went out of their booths. They came from the east, but Njal went from the west to the Court of Laws, and the sons with him.

Skarphedinn went to the middle bench and stood there.

Flosi went into the Court of Laws to look closely at his money, and said —

"This money is both great and good, and well paid down, as was to be looked for."

After that he took up the scarf, and waved it, and asked —

"Who may have given this?"

But no man answered him.

A second time he waved the scarf, and asked —

"Who may have given this?" and laughed, but no man answered him.

Then Flosi said —

"How is it that none of you knows who has owned this gear, or is it that none dares to tell me?"

"Who?" said Skarphedinn, "dost thou think, has given it?"

"If thou must know," said Flosi, "then I will tell thee; I think that thy father the 'Beardless Carle' must have given it, for many know not who look at him whether he is more a man than a woman."

"Such words are ill-spoken," said Skarphedinn, "to make game of him, an old man, and no man of any worth has ever done so before. Ye may know, too, that he is a man, for he has had sons by his wife, and few of our kinsfolk have fallen unatoned by our house, so that we have not had vengeance for them."

Then Skarphedinn took to himself the silken scarf, but threw a pair of blue breeks to Flosi, and said he would need them more.

"Why," said Flosi, "should I need these more?"

"Because," said Skarphedinn, "thou art the sweetheart of the Swinefell's goblin, if, as men say, he does indeed turn thee into a woman every ninth night."

Then Flosi spurned the money, and said he would not touch a penny of it, and then he said he would only have one of two things: either that Hauskuld should fall unatoned, or they would have vengeance for him.

Then Flosi would neither give nor take peace, and he said to the sons of Sigfus—

"Go we now home; one fate shall befall us all."

Then they went home to their booth, and Hall said —

"Here most unlucky men have a share in this suit."

Njal and his sons went home to their booth, and Njal said —

"Now comes to pass what my heart told me long ago, that this suit would fall heavy on us."

"Not so," says Skarphedinn; "they can never pursue us by the laws of the land."

"Then that will happen," says Njal, "which will be worse for all of us."

Those men who had given the money spoke about it, and said that they should take it back; but Gudmund the powerful said —

"That shame I will never choose for myself, to take back what I have given away, either here or elsewhere."

"That is well spoken," they said; and then no one would take it back.

Then Snorri the priest said, "My counsel is, that Gizur the White and Hjallti Skeggi's son keep the money till the next Althing; my heart tells me that no long time will pass ere there may be need to touch this money".

Hjallti took half the money and kept it safe, but Gizur took the rest.

Then men went home to their booths.

Chapter 123
An Attack Planned on Njal and his sons

Flosi summoned all his men up to the "Great Rift," and went thither himself.

So when all his men were come, there were one hundred and twenty of them.

Then Flosi spake thus to the sons of Sigfus —

"In what way shall I stand by you in this quarrel, which will be most to your minds?"

"Nothing will please us," said Gunnar Lambi's son, "until those brothers, Njal's sons, are all slain."

"This," said Flosi, "will I promise to you, ye sons of Sigfus, not to part from this quarrel before one of us bites the dust before the other, I will also know whether there be any man here who will not stand by us in this quarrel."

But they all said they would stand by him.

Then Flosi said —

"Come now all to me, and swear an oath that no man will shrink from this quarrel."

Then all went up to Flosi and swore oaths to him; and then Flosi said—

"We will all of us shake hands on this, that he shall have forfeited life and land who quits this quarrel ere it be over."

These were the chiefs who were with Flosi: — Kol the son of Thorstein broadpaunch, the brother's son of Hall of the Side, Hroald Auzur's son from Broadwater, Auzur son of Anund wallet-back, Thorstein the fair the son of Gerleif, Glum Hilldir's son, Modolf Kettle's son, Thorir the son of Thord Illugi's son of Mauratongue, Kolbein and Egil Flosi's kinsmen, Kettle Sigfus' son, and Mord his brother, Ingialld of the Springs, Thorkel and Lambi, Grani Gunnar's son, Gunnar Lambi's son, and Sigmund Sigfus' son, and Hroar from Hromundstede.

Then Flosi said to the sons of Sigfus —

"Choose ye now a leader, whomsoever ye think best fitted; for some one man must needs be chief over the quarrel."

Then Kettle of the Mark answered —

"If the choice is to be left with us brothers, then we will soon choose that this duty should fall on thee; there are many things which lead to this. Thou art a man of great birth, and a mighty chief, stout of heart, and strong of body, and wise withal, and so we think it best that thou shouldst see to all that is needful in the quarrel."

"It is most fitting," said Flosi, "that I should agree to undertake this as your prayer asks; and now I will lay down the course which we shall follow, and my counsel is, that each man ride home from the Thing and look after his household during the summer, so long as men's haymaking lasts. I, too, will ride home, and be at home this summer; but when that Lord's day comes on which winter is eight weeks off, then I will let them sing me a mass at home, and afterwards ride west across Loomnips Sand; each of our men shall have two horses. I will not swell our company beyond those which have now taken the oath, for we have enough and to spare if all keep true tryst. I will ride all the Lord's day and the night as well, but at even on the second day of the week, I shall ride up to Threecorner ridge about mid-even. There shall ye then be all come who have sworn an oath in this matter. But if there be any one who has not come, and who has joined us in this quarrel, then that man shall lose nothing save his life, if we may have our way."

"How does that hang together," said Kettle, "that thou canst ride from home on the Lord's day, and come the second day of the week to Threecorner ridge?"

"I will ride," said Flosi, "up from Skaptartongue, and north of the Eyjafell Jokul, and so down into Godaland, and it may be done if I ride fast. And now I will tell you my whole purpose, that when we meet there all together, we shall ride to Bergthorsknoll with all our band, and fall on Njal's sons with fire and sword, and not turn away before they are all dead. Ye shall hide this plan, for our lives lie on it. And now we will take to our horses and ride home."

Then they all went to their booths.

After that Flosi made them saddle his horses, and they waited for no man, and rode home.

Flosi would not stay to meet Hall his father-in-law, for he knew of a surety that Hall would set his face against all strong deeds.

Njal rode home from the Thing and his sons. They were at home that summer. Njal asked Kari his son-in-law whether he thought at all of riding east to Dyrholms to his own house.

"I will not ride east," answered Kari, "for one fate shall befall me and thy sons."

Njal thanked him, and said that was only what was likely from him. There were nearly thirty fighting men in Njal's house, reckoning the house-carles.

One day it happened that Rodny Hauskuld's daughter, the mother of Hauskuld Njal's son, came to the Springs. Her brother Ingialld greeted her well, but she would not take his greeting, but yet bade him go out with her. Ingialld did so, and went out with her; and so they walked away from the farmyard both together. Then she clutched hold of him and they both sat down, and Rodny said —

"Is it true that thou hast sworn an oath to fall on Njal, and slay him and his sons?"

"True it is," said he.

"A very great dastard art thou," she says, "thou, whom Njal hath thrice saved from outlawry."

"Still it hath come to this," says Ingialld, "that my life lies on it if I do not this."

"Not so," says she, "thou shalt live all the same, and be called a better man, if thou betrayest not him to whom thou oughtest to behave best."

Then she took a linen hood out of her bag, it was clotted with blood all over, and torn and tattered, and said, "This hood, Hauskuld Njal's son, and thy sister's son, had on his head when they slew him; methinks, then, it is ill owing to stand by those from whom this mischief sprang".

"Well!" answers Ingialld, "so it shall be that I will not be against Njal whatever follows after, but still I know that they will turn and throw trouble on me."

"Now mightest thou," said Rodny, "yield Njal and his sons great help, if thou tellest him all these plans."

"That I will not do," says Ingialld, "for then I am every man's dastard, if I tell what was trusted to me in good faith; but it is a manly deed to sunder myself from this quarrel when I know that there is a sure looking for of vengeance; but tell Njal and his sons to beware of themselves all this summer, for that will be good counsel, and to keep many men about them."

Then she fared to Bergthorsknoll, and told Njal all this talk; and Njal thanked her, and said she had done well, "for there would be more wickedness in his falling on me than of all men else".

She fared home, but he told this to his sons.

There was a carline at Bergthorsknoll, whose name was Saevuna. She was wise in many things, and foresighted; but she was then very old, and Njal's sons called her an old dotard, when she talked so much, but still some things which she said came to pass. It fell one day that she took a cudgel in her hand, and went up above the house to a stack of vetches. She beat the stack of vetches with her cudgel, and wished it might never thrive, "wretch that it was!"

Skarphedinn laughed at her, and asked why she was so angry with the vetch stack.

"This stack of vetches," said the carline, "will be taken and lighted with fire when Njal my master is burnt, house and all, and Bergthora my foster-child. Take it away to the water, or burn it up as quick as you can."

"We will not do that," says Skarphedinn, "for something else will be got to light a fire with, if that were foredoomed, though this stack were not here."

The carline babbled the whole summer about the vetch-stack that it should be got indoors, but something always hindered it.

Chapter 124
Of Portents

At Reykium on Skeid dwelt one Runolf Thorstein's son. His son's name was Hildiglum. He went out on the night of the Lord's day, when nine weeks were still to winter; he heard a great crash, so that he thought both heaven and earth shook. Then he looked into the west "airt," and he thought he saw thereabouts a ring of fiery hue, and within the ring a man on a gray horse. He passed quickly by him, and rode hard. He had a flaming firebrand in his hand, and he rode so close to him that he could see him plainly. He was as black as pitch, and he sung this song with a mighty voice —

> Here I ride swift steed,
> His flank flecked with rime,
> Rain from his mane drips,
> Horse mighty for harm;
> Flames flare at each end,
> Gall glows in the midst,
> So fares it with Flosi's redes
> As this flaming brand flies;
> And so fares it with Flosi's redes
> As this flaming brand flies.

Then he thought he hurled the firebrand east towards the fells before him, and such a blaze of fire leapt up to meet it that he could not see the fells for the blaze. It seemed as though that man rode east among the flames and vanished there.

After that he went to his bed, and was senseless a long time, but at last he came to himself. He bore in mind all that had happened, and told his father, but he bade him tell it to Hjallti Skeggi's son. So he went and told Hjallti, but he said he had seen "'the Wolfs ride,' and that comes ever before great tidings".

Chapter 125
Flosi's Journey from Home

Flosi busked him from the east when two months were still to winter, and summoned to him all his men who had promised him help and company. Each of them had two horses and good weapons, and they all came to Swinefell, and were there that night.

Flosi made them say prayers betimes on the Lord's day, and afterwards they sate down to meat. He spoke to his household, and told them what work each was to do while he was away. After that he went to his horses.

Flosi and his men rode first west on the Sand. Flosi bade them not to ride too hard at first; but said they would do well enough at that pace, and he bade all to wait for the others if any of them had need to stop. They rode west to Woodcombe, and came to Kirkby. Flosi there bade all men to come into the church, and pray to God, and men did so.

After that they mounted their horses, and rode on the fell, and so to Fish-waters, and rode a little to the west of the lakes, and so struck down west on to the Sand. Then they left Eyjafell Jokul on their left hand, and so came down into Godaland, and so on to Markfleet, and came about nones on the second day of the week to Threecorner ridge, and waited till mid-even. Then all had came thither save Ingialld of the Springs.

The sons of Sigfus spoke much ill of him, but Flosi bade them not blame

Ingialld when he was not by, "but we will pay him for this hereafter".

Chapter 126
Of Portents at Bergthorsknoll

Now we must take up the story, and turn to Bergthorsknoll, and say that Grim and Helgi go to Holar. They had children out at foster there, and they told their mother that they should not come home that evening. They were in Holar all the day, and there came some poor women and said they had come from far. Those brothers asked them for tidings, and they said they had no tidings to tell, "but still we might tell you one bit of news".

They asked what that might be, and bade them not hide it. They said so it should be.

"We came down out of Fleetlithe, and we saw all the sons of Sigfus riding fully armed — they made for Threecorner ridge, and were fifteen in company. We saw, too, Grani Gunnar's son and Gunnar Lambi's son, and they were five in all. They took the same road, and one may say now that the whole country-side is faring and flitting about."

"Then," said Helgi Njal's son, "Flosi must have come from the east, and they must have all gone to meet him, and we two, Grim, should be where Skarphedinn is."

Grim said so it ought to be, and they fared home.

That same evening Bergthora spoke to her household, and said, "Now shall ye choose your meat to-night, so that each may have what he likes best; for this evening is the last that I shall set meat before my household".

"That shall not be," they said.

"It will be though," she says, "and I could tell you much more if I would, but this shall be a token, that Grim and Helgi will be home ere men have eaten their full to-night; and if this turns out so, then the rest that I say will happen too."

After that she set meat on the board, and Njal said, "Wondrously now it seems to me. Methinks I see all round the room, and it seems as though the gable wall were thrown down, but the whole board and the meat on it is one gore of blood."

All thought this strange but Skarphedinn, he bade men not be downcast, nor to utter other unseemly sounds, so that men might make a story out of them.

"For it befits us surely more than other men to bear us well, and it is only what is looked for from us."

Grim and Helgi came home ere the board was cleared, and men were much struck at that. Njal asked why they had returned so quickly, but they told what they had heard.

Njal bade no man go to sleep, but to beware of themselves.

Chapter 127
The Onslaught on Bergthorsknoll

Now Flosi speaks to his men —

"Now we will ride to Bergthorsknoll, and come thither before supper-time."

They do so. There was a dell in the knoll, and they rode thither, and tethered their horses there, and stayed there till the evening was far spent.

Then Flosi said, "Now we will go straight up to the house, and keep close, and walk slow, and see what counsel they will take".

Njal stood out of doors, and his sons, and Kari and all the serving-men, and they stood in array to meet them in the yard, and they were near thirty of them.

Flosi halted and said — "Now we shall see what counsel they take, for it seems to me, if they stand out of doors to meet us, as though we should never get the mastery over them".

"Then is our journey bad," says Grani Gunnar's son, "if we are not to dare to fall on them."

"Nor shall that be," says Flosi; "for we will fall on them though they stand out of doors; but we shall pay that penalty, that many will not go away to tell which side won the day."

Njal said to his men, "See ye now what a great band of men they have".

"They have both a great and well-knit band," says Skarphedinn; "but this is why they make a halt now, because they think it will be a hard struggle to master us."

"That cannot be why they halt," says Njal; "and my will is that our men go indoors, for they had hard work to master Gunnar of Lithend, though he was alone to meet them; but here is a strong house as there was there, and they will be slow to come to close quarters."

"This is not to be settled in that wise," says Skarphedinn, "for those chiefs fell on Gunnar's house, who were so noble-minded, that they would rather turn back than burn him, house and all; but these will fall on us at once with fire, if they cannot get at us in any other way, for they will leave no stone unturned to get the better of us; and no doubt they think, as is not unlikely, that it will be their deaths if we escape out of their hands. Besides, I am unwilling to let myself be stifled indoors like a fox in his earth."

"Now," said Njal, "as often it happens, my sons, ye set my counsel at naught, and show me no honour, but when ye were younger ye did not so, and then your plans were better furthered."

"Let us do," said Helgi, "as our father wills; that will be best for us."

"I am not so sure of that," says Skarphedinn, "for now he is 'fey'; but still I may well humour my father in this, by being burnt indoors along with him, for I am not afraid of my death."

Then he said to Kari, "Let us stand by one another well, brother-in-law, so that neither parts from the other".

"That I have made up my mind to do," says Kari; "but if it should be otherwise doomed, — well! then it must be as it must be, and I shall not be able to fight against it."

"Avenge us, and we will avenge thee," says Skarphedinn, "if we live after thee."

Kari said so it should be.

Then they all went in, and stood in array at the door.

"Now are they all 'fey,'" said Flosi, "since they have gone indoors, and we will go right up to them as quickly as we can, and throng as close as we can before the door, and give heed that none of them, neither Kari nor Njal's sons, get away; for that were our bane."

So Flosi and his men came up to the house, and set men to watch round the house, if there were any secret doors in it. But Flosi went up to the front of the house with his men.

Then Hroald Auzur's son ran up to where Skarphedinn stood, and thrust at him. Skarphedinn hewed the spearhead off the shaft as he held it, and made another stroke at him, and the axe fell on the top of the shield, and dashed back the whole shield on Hroald's body, but the upper horn of the axe caught him on the brow, and he fell at full length on his back, and was dead at once.

"Little chance had that one with thee, Skarphedinn," said Kari, "and thou art our boldest."

"I'm not so sure of that," says Skarphedinn, and he drew up his lips and smiled.

Kari, and Grim, and Helgi, threw out many spears, and wounded many men; but Flosi and his men could do nothing.

At last Flosi said, "We have already gotten great manscathe in our men; many are wounded, and he slain whom we would choose last of all. It is now clear that we shall never master them with weapons; many now there be who are not so forward in fight as they boasted, and yet they were those who goaded us on most. I say this most to Grani Gunnar's son, and Gunnar Lambi's son, who were the least willing to spare their foes. But still we shall have to take to some other plan for ourselves, and now there are but two choices left, and neither of them good. One is to turn away, and that is our death; the other, to set fire to the house, and burn them inside it; and that is a deed which we shall have to answer for heavily before God, since we are Christian men ourselves; but still we must take to that counsel."

Chapter 128
Njal's Burning

Now they took fire, and made a great pile before the doors. Then Skarphedinn said.

"What, lads! are ye lighting a fire, or are ye taking to cooking?"

"So it shall be," answered Grani Gunnar's son; "and thou shalt not need to be better done."

"Thou repayest me," said Skarphedinn, "as one may look for from the man that thou art. I avenged thy father, and thou settest most store by that duty which is farthest from thee."

Then the women threw whey on the fire, and quenched it as fast as they lit it. Some, too, brought water, or slops.

Then Kol Thorstein's son said to Flosi —

"A plan comes into my mind; I have seen a loft over the hall among the crosstrees, and we will put the fire in there, and light it with the vetch-stack that stands just above the house."

Then they took the vetch-stack and set fire to it, and they who were inside were not aware of it till the whole hall was ablaze over their heads.

Then Flosi and his men made a great pile before each of the doors, and then the women folk who were inside began to weep and to wail.

Njal spoke to them and said, "Keep up your hearts, nor utter shrieks, for this is but a passing storm, and it will be long before ye have another such; and put your faith in God, and believe that He is so merciful that He will not let us burn both in this world and the next."

Such words of comfort had he for them all, and others still more strong.

Now the whole house began to blaze. Then Njal went to the door and said —

"Is Flosi so near that he can hear my voice?"

Flosi said that he could hear it.

"Wilt thou," said Njal, "take an atonement from my sons, or allow any men to go out?"

"I will not," answers Flosi, "take any atonement from thy sons, and now our dealings shall come to an end once for all, and I will not stir from this spot till they are all dead; but I will allow the women and children and house-carles to go out."

Then Njal went into the house, and said to the folk —

"Now all those must go out to whom leave is given, and so go thou out Thorhalla Asgrim's daughter, and all the people also with thee who may."

Then Thorhalla said —

"This is another parting between me and Helgi than I thought of a while ago; but still I will egg on my father and brothers to avenge this manscathe which is wrought here."

"Go, and good go with thee," said Njal, "for thou art a brave woman."

After that she went out and much folk with her.

Then Astrid of Deepback said to Helgi Njal's son —

"Come thou out with me, and I will throw a woman's cloak over thee, and tire thy head with a kerchief."

He spoke against it at first, but at last he did so at the prayer of others.

So Astrid wrapped the kerchief round Helgi's head, but Thorhilda, Skarphedinn's wife, threw the cloak over him, and he went out between them, and then Thorgerda Njal's daughter, and Helga her sister, and many other folk went out too.

But when Helgi came out Flosi said —

"That is a tall woman and broad across the shoulders that went yonder, take her and hold her."

But when Helgi heard that, he cast away the cloak. He had got his sword under his arm, and hewed at a man, and the blow fell on his shield and cut off the point of it, and the man's leg as well. Then Flosi came up and hewed at Helgi's neck, and took off his head at a stroke.

Then Flosi went to the door and called out to Njal, and said he would speak with him and Bergthora.

Now Njal does so, and Flosi said —

"I will offer thee, master Njal, leave to go out, for it is unworthy that thou shouldst burn indoors."

"I will not go out," said Njal, "for I am an old man, and little fitted to avenge my sons, but I will not live in shame."

Then Flosi said to Bergthora —

"Come thou out, housewife, for I will for no sake burn thee indoors."

"I was given away to Njal young," said Bergthora, "and I have promised him this, that we would both share the same fate."

After that they both went back into the house.

"What counsel shall we now take?" said Bergthora.

"We will go to our bed," says Njal, "and lay us down; I have long been eager for rest."

Then she said to the boy Thord, Kari's son —

"Thee will I take out, and thou shalt not burn in here."

"Thou hast promised me this, grandmother," says the boy, "that we should never part so long as I wished to be with thee; but methinks it is much better to die with thee and Njal than to live after you."

Then she bore the boy to her bed, and Njal spoke to his steward and said —

"Now shalt thou see where we lay us down, and how I lay us out, for I mean not to stir an inch hence, whether reek or burning smart me, and so thou wilt be able to guess where to look for our bones."

He said he would do so.

There had been an ox slaughtered and the hide lay there. Njal told the steward to spread the hide over them, and he did so.

So there they lay down both of them in their bed, and put the boy between them. Then they signed themselves and the boy with the cross, and gave over their souls into God's hand, and that was the last word that men heard them utter.

Then the steward took the hide and spread it over them, and went out afterwards. Kettle of the Mark caught hold of him, and dragged him out, he asked carefully after his father-in-law Njal, but the steward told him the whole truth. Then Kettle said —

"Great grief hath been sent on us, when we have had to share such ill-luck together."

Skarphedinn saw how his father laid him down, and how he laid himself out, and then he said —

"Our father goes early to bed, and that is what was to be looked for, for he is an old man."

Then Skarphedinn, and Kari, and Grim, caught the brands as fast as they dropped down, and hurled them out at them, and so it went on a while. Then they hurled spears in at them, but they caught them all as they flew, and sent them back again.

Then Flosi bade them cease shooting, "for all feats of arms will go hard with us when we deal with them; ye may well wait till the fire overcomes them".

So they do that, and shoot no more.

Then the great beams out of the roof began to fall, and Skarphedinn said —

"Now must my father be dead, and I have neither heard groan nor cough from him."

Then they went to the end of the hall, and there had fallen down a cross-beam inside which was much burnt in the middle.

Kari spoke to Skarphedinn, and said — "Leap thou out here, and I will help thee to do so, and I will leap out after thee, and then we shall both get away if we set about it so, for hitherward blows all the smoke."

"Thou shalt leap first," said Skarphedinn; "but I will leap straightway on thy heels."

"That is not wise," says Kari, "for I can get out well enough elsewhere, though it does not come about here."

"I will not do that," says Skarphedinn; "leap thou out first, but I will leap after thee at once."

"It is bidden to every man," says Kari, "to seek to save his life while he has a choice, and I will do so now; but still this parting of ours will be in such wise that we shall never see one another more; for if I leap out of the fire, I shall have no mind to leap back into the fire to thee, and then each of us will have to fare his own way."

"It joys me, brother-in-law," says Skarphedinn, "to think that if thou gettest away thou wilt avenge me."

Then Kari took up a blazing bench in his hand, and runs up along the cross-beam, then he hurls the bench out at the roof, and it fell among those who were outside.

Then they ran away, and by that time all Kari's upper-clothing and his hair were ablaze, then he threw himself down from the roof, and so crept along with the smoke.

Then one man said who was nearest —

"Was that a man that leapt out at the roof?"

"Far from it," says another; "more likely it was Skarphedinn who hurled a firebrand at us."

After that they had no more mistrust.

Kari ran till he came to a stream, and then, he threw himself down into it, and so quenched the fire on him.

After that he ran along under shelter of the smoke into a hollow, and rested him there, and that has since been called Kari's Hollow.

Chapter 129
Skarphedinn's Death

Now it is to be told of Skarphedinn that he runs out on the cross-beam straight after Kari, but when he came to where the beam was most burnt, then it broke down under him. Skarphedinn came down on his feet, and tried again the second time, and climbs up the wall with a run, then down on him came the wall-plate, and he toppled down again inside.

Then Skarphedinn said — "Now one can see what will come;" and then he went along the side wall. Gunnar Lambi's son leapt up on the wall and sees Skarphedinn; he spoke thus —

"Weepest thou now, Skarphedinn?"

"Not so," says Skarphedinn, "but true it is that the smoke makes one's eyes smart, but is it as it seems to me, dost thou laugh?"

"So it is surely," says Gunnar, "and I have never laughed since thou slewest Thrain on Markfleet."

Then Skarphedinn said — "He now is a keepsake for thee;" and with that he took out of his purse the jaw-tooth which he had hewn out of Thrain, and threw it at Gunnar, and struck him in the eye, so that it started out and lay on his cheek.

Then Gunnar fell down from the roof.

Skarphedinn then went to his brother Grim, and they held one another by the hand and trode the fire; but when they came to the middle of the hall Grim fell down dead.

Then Skarphedinn went to the end of the house, and then there was a great crash, and down fell the roof. Skarphedinn was then shut in between it and the gable, and so he could not stir a step thence.

Flosi and his band stayed by the fire until it was broad daylight; then came a man riding up to them. Flosi asked him for his name, but he said his name was Geirmund, and that he was a kinsman of the sons of Sigfus.

"Ye have done a mighty deed," he says.

"Men," says Flosi, "will call it both a mighty deed and an ill deed, but that can't be helped now."

"How many men have lost their lives here?" asks Geirmund.

"Here have died," says Flosi, "Njal and Bergthora and all their sons, Thord Kari's son, Kari Solmund's son, but besides these we cannot say for a surety, because we know not their names."

"Thou tellest him now dead," said Geirmund, "with whom we have gossiped this morning."

"Who is that?" says Flosi.

"We two," says Geirmund, "I and my neighbour Bard, met Kari Solmund's son, and Bard gave him his horse, and his hair and his upper clothes were burned off him."

"Had he any weapons?" asks Flosi.

"He had the sword 'Life-luller,'" says Geirmund, "and one edge of it was blue with fire, and Bard and I said that it must have become soft, but he answered thus, that he would harden it in the blood of the sons of Sigfus or the other Burners."

"What said he of Skarphedinn?" said Flosi.

"He said both he and Grim were alive," answers Geirmund, "when they parted; but he said that now they must be dead."

"Thou hast told us a tale," said Flosi, "which bodes us no idle peace, for that man hath now got away who comes next to Gunnar of Lithend in all things; and now, ye sons of Sigfus, and ye other Burners, know this, that such a great blood feud, and hue and cry will be made about this burning, that it will make many a man headless, but some will lose all their goods. Now I doubt much whether any man of you, ye sons of Sigfus, will dare to stay in his house; and that is not to be wondered at; and so I will bid you all to come and stay with me in the east, and let us all share one fate."

They thanked him for his offer, and said they would be glad to take it.

Then Modolf Kettle's son sang a song.

> But one prop of Njal's house liveth,
> All the rest inside are burnt,
> All but one, — those bounteous spenders,
> Sigfus' stalwart sons wrought this;
> Son of Gollnir now is glutted
> Vengeance for brave Hauskuld's death,
> Brisk flew fire through thy dwelling,
> Bright flames blazed above thy roof.

"We shall have to boast of something else than that Njal has been burnt in his house," says Flosi, "for there is no glory in that."

Then he went up on the gable, and Glum Hilldir's son, and some other men. Then Glum said, "Is Skarphedinn dead, indeed?" But the others said he must have been dead long ago.

The fire sometimes blazed up fitfully and sometimes burned low, and then they heard down in the fire beneath them that this song was sung —

> Deep, I ween, ye Ogre offspring!
> Devilish brood of giant birth,
> Would ye groan with gloomy visage

> Had the fight gone to my mind;
> But my very soul it gladdens
> That my friends who now boast high,
> Wrought not this foul deed, their glory,
> Save with footsteps filled with gore.

"Can Skarphedinn, think ye, have sung this song dead or alive?" said Grani Gunnar's son.

"I will go into no guesses about that," says Flosi.

"We will look for Skarphedinn," says Grani, "and the other men who have been here burnt inside the house."

"That shall not be," says Flosi, "it is just like such foolish men as thou art, now that men will be gathering force all over the country; and when they do come, I trow the very same man who now lingers will be so scared that he will not know which way to run; and now my counsel is that we all ride away as quickly as ever we can."

Then Flosi went hastily to his horse and all his men.

Then Flosi said to Geirmund —

"Is Ingialld, thinkest thou, at home, at the Springs?"

Geirmund said he thought he must be at home.

"There now is a man," says Flosi, "who has broken his oath with us and all good faith."

Then Flosi said to the sons of Sigfus — "What course will ye now take with Ingialld; will ye forgive him, or shall we now fall on him and slay him?"

They all answered that they would rather fall on him and slay him.

Then Flosi jumped on his horse, and all the others, and they rode away. Flosi rode first, and shaped his course for Rangriver, and up along the river bank.

Then he saw a man riding down on the other bank of the river, and he knew that there was Ingialld of the Springs. Flosi calls out to him. Ingialld halted and turned down to the river bank; and Flosi said to him —

"Thou hast broken faith with us, and hast forfeited life and goods. Here now are the sons of Sigfus, who are eager to slay thee; but methinks thou hast fallen into a strait, and I will give thee thy life if thou will hand over to me the right to make my own award."

"I will sooner ride to meet Kari," said Ingialld, "than grant thee the right to utter thine own award, and my answer to the sons of Sigfus is this, that I shall be no whit more afraid of them than they are of me."

"Bide thou there," says Flosi, "if thou art not a coward, for I will send thee a gift."

"I will bide of a surety," says Ingialld.

Thorstein Kolbein's son, Flosi's brother's son, rode up by his side and had a spear in his hand, he was one of the bravest of men, and the most worthy of those who were with Flosi.

Flosi snatched the spear from him, and launched it at Ingialld, and it fell on his left side, and passed through the shield just below the handle, and clove it all asunder, but the spear passed on into his thigh just above the knee-pan, and so on into the saddle-tree, and there stood fast.

Then Flosi said to Ingialld —

"Did it touch thee?"

"It touched me sure enough," says Ingialld, "but I call this a scratch and not a wound."

Then Ingialld plucked the spear out of the wound, and said to Flosi —

"Now bide thou, if thou art not a milksop."

Then he launched the spear back over the river. Flosi sees that the spear is coming straight for his middle, and then he backs his horse out of the way, but the spear flew in front of Flosi's horse, and missed him, but it struck Thorstein's middle, and down he fell at once dead off his horse.

Now Ingialld tuns for the wood, and they could not get at him.

Then Flosi said to his men —

"Now have we gotten manscathe, and now we may know, when such things befall us, into what a luckless state we have got. Now it is my counsel that we ride up to Threecorner ridge; thence we shall be able to see where men ride all over the country, for by this time they will have gathered together a great band, and they will think that we have ridden east to Fleetlithe from Threecorner ridge; and thence they will think that we are riding north up on the fell, and so east to our own country, and thither the greater part of the folk will ride after us; but some will ride the coast road east to Selialandsmull, and yet they will think there is less hope of finding us thitherward, but I will now take counsel for all of us, and my plan is to ride up into Threecorner-fell, and bide there till three suns have risen and set in heaven."

Chapter 130
Of Kari Solmund's Son

Now it is to be told of Kari Solmund's son that he fared away from that hollow in which he had rested himself until he met Bard, and those words passed between them which Geirmund had told.

Thence Kari rode to Mord, and told him the tidings, and he was greatly grieved.

Kari said there were other things more befitting a man than to weep for them dead, and bade him rather gather folk and come to Holtford.

After that he rode into Thursodale to Hjallti Skeggi's son, and as he went along Thurso water, he sees a man riding fast behind him. Kari waited for the man, and knows that he was Ingialld of the Springs. He sees that he is very bloody about the thigh; and Kari asked Ingialld who had wounded him, and he told him.

"Where met ye two?" says Kari.

"By Rangwater side," says Ingialld, "and he threw a spear over at me."

"Didst thou aught for it?" asks Kari.

"I threw the spear back," says Ingialld, "and they said that it met a man, and he was dead at once."

"Knowest thou not," said Kari, "who the man was?"

"Methought he was like Thorstein Flosi's brother's son," says Ingialld.

"Good luck go with thy hand," says Kari.

After that they rode both together to see Hjallti Skeggi's son, and told him the tidings. He took these deeds ill, and said there was the greatest need to ride after them and slay them all.

After that he gathered men and roused the whole country; now he and Kari and Ingialld ride with this band to meet Mord Valgard's son, and they found him at Holtford, and Mord was there waiting for them with a very great company. Then they parted the hue and cry; some fared the straight road by the east coast to Selialandsmull, but some went up to Fleetlithe, and other-some the higher road thence to Threecorner ridge, and so down into Godaland. Thence they rode north to Sand. Some too rode as far as Fishwaters, and there turned back. Some the coast road east to Holt, and told Thorgeir the tidings, and asked whether they had not ridden by there.

"This is how it is," said Thorgeir, "though I am not a mighty chief, yet Flosi would take other counsel than to ride under my eyes, when he has slain Njal, my father's brother, and my cousins; and there is nothing left for any of you but e'en to turn back again, for ye should have hunted longer nearer home; but tell this to Kari, that he must ride hither to me and be here with me if he will; but though he will not come hither east, still I will look after his farm at Dyrholms if he will, but tell him too that I will stand by him and ride with him to the Althing. And he shall also know this, that we brothers are the next of kin to follow up the feud, and we mean so to take up the suit, that outlawry shall follow and after that revenge, man for man, if we can bring it about; but I do not go with you now, because I know naught will come of it, and they will now be as wary as they can of themselves."

Now they ride back, and all met at Hof and talked there among themselves, and said that they had gotten disgrace since they had not found them. Mord said that was not so. Then many men were eager that they should fare to Fleetlithe, and pull down the homesteads of all those who had been at those deeds, but still they listened for Mord's utterance.

"That," he said, "would be the greatest folly." They asked why he said that.

"Because," he said, "if their houses stand, they will be sure to visit them to see their wives; and then, as time rolls on, we may hunt them down there; and now ye shall none of you doubt that I will be true to thee Kari, and to all of you, and in all counsel, for I have to answer for myself."

Hjallti bade him do as he said. Then Hjallti bade Kari to come and stay with him; he said he would ride thither first. They told him what Thorgeir had offered him, and he said he would make use of that offer afterwards, but said his heart told him it would be well if there were many such.

After that the whole band broke up.

Flosi and his men saw all these tidings from where they were on the fell; and Flosi said —

"Now we will take our horses and ride away, for now it will be some good."

The sons of Sigfus asked whether it would be worth while to get to their homes and tell the news.

"It must be Mord's meaning," says Flosi, "that ye will visit your wives; and my guess is, that his plan is to let your houses stand unsacked; but my plan is that not a man shall part from the other, but all ride east with me."

So every man took that counsel, and then they all rode east and north of the Jokul, and so on till they came to Swinefell.

Flosi sent at once men out to get in stores, so that nothing might fall short.

Flosi never spoke about the deed, but no fear was found in him, and he was at home the whole winter till Yule was over.

Chapter 131
Njal's and Bergthora's Bones Found

Kari bade Hjallti to go and search for Njal's bones, "for all will believe in what thou sayest and thinkest about them".

Hjallti said he would be most willing to bear Njal's bones to church; so they rode thence fifteen men. They rode east over Thurso-water, and called on men there to come with them till they had one hundred men, reckoning Njal's neighbours.

They came to Bergthorsknoll at mid-day.

Hjallti asked Kari under what part of the house Njal might be lying, but Kari showed them to the spot, and there was a great heap of ashes to dig away. There they found the hide underneath, and it was as though it were shrivelled with the fire. They raised up the hide, and lo! they were unburnt under it. All praised God for that, and thought it was a great token.

Then the boy was taken up who had lain between them, and of him a finger was burnt off which he had stretched out from under the hide.

Njal was borne out, and so was Bergthora, and then all men went to see their bodies.

Then Hjallti said — "What like look to you these bodies?"

They answered, "We will wait for thy utterance".

Then Hjallti said, "I shall speak what I say with all freedom of speech. The body of Bergthora looks as it was likely she would look, and still fair; but Njal's body and visage seem to me so bright that I have never seen any dead man's body so bright as this."

They all said they thought so too.

Then they sought for Skarphedinn, and the men of the household showed them to the spot where Flosi and his men heard the song sung, and there the roof had fallen down by the gable, and there Hjallti said that they should look. Then they did so, and found Skarphedinn's body there, and he had stood up hard by the gable-wall, and his legs were burnt off him right up to the knees, but all the rest of him was unburnt. He had bitten through his under lip, his eyes were wide open and not swollen nor starting out of his head; he had driven his axe into the gable-wall so hard that it had gone in up to the middle of the blade, and that was why it was not softened.

After that the axe was broken out of the wall, and Hjallti took up the axe, and said —

"This is a rare weapon, and few would be able to wield it."

"I see a man," said Kari, "who shall bear the axe."

"Who is that?" says Hjallti.

"Thorgeir Craggeir," says Kari, "he whom I now think to be the greatest man in all their family."

Then Skarphedinn was stripped of his clothes, for they were unburnt; he had laid his hands in a cross, and the right hand uppermost. They found marks on him; one between his shoulders and the other on his chest, and both were branded in the shape of a cross, and men thought that he must have burnt them in himself.

All men said that they thought that it was better to be near Skarphedinn dead than they weened, for no man was afraid of him.

They sought for the bones of Grim, and found them in the midst of the hall. They found, too, there, right over-against him under the side wall, Thord Freedmanson; but in the weaving-room they found Saevuna the carline, and three men more. In all they found there the bones of nine souls. Now they carried the bodies to the church, and then Hjallti rode home and Kari with him. A swelling came on Ingialld's leg, and then he fared to Hjallti, and was healed there, but still he limped ever afterwards.

Kari rode to Tongue to Asgrim Ellidagrim's son. By that time Thorhalla was come home, and she had already told the tidings. Asgrim took Kari by both hands, and bade him be there all that year. Kari said so it should be.

Asgrim asked besides all the folk who had been in the house at Bergth-orsknoll to stay with him. Kari said that was well offered, and said he would take it on their behalf.

Then all the folk were flitted thither.

Thorhall Asgrim's son was so startled when he was told that his foster-father Njal was dead, and that he had been burnt in his house, that he swelled all over, and a stream of blood burst out of both his ears, and could not be staunched, and he fell into a swoon, and then it was staunched.

After that he stood up, and said he had behaved like a coward, "but I would that I might be able to avenge this which has befallen me on some of those who burnt him".

But when others said that no one would think this a shame to him, he said he could not stop the mouths of the people from talking about it.

Asgrim asked Kari what trust and help he thought he might look for from those east of the rivers. Kari said that Mord Valgard's son, and Hjallti, Skeggi's

son, would yield him all the help they could, and so, too, would Thorgeir
Craggeir, and all those brothers.

Asgrim said that was great strength.

"What strength shall we have from thee?" says Kari.

"All that I can give," says Asgrim, "and I will lay down my life on it."

"So do," says Kari.

"I have also," says Asgrim, "brought Gizur the White into the suit, and have
asked his advice how we shall set about it."

"What advice did he give?" asks Kari.

"He counselled," answers Asgrim, "'that we should hold us quite still till
spring, but then ride east and set the suit on foot against Flosi for the manslaughter of Helgi, and summon the neighbours from their homes, and give due
notice at the Thing of the suits for the burning, and summon the same neighbours there too on the inquest before the court. I asked Gizur who should
plead the suit for manslaughter, but he said that Mord should plead it whether
he liked it or not, and now,' he went on, 'it shall fall most heavily on him that
up to this time all the suits he has undertaken have had the worst ending. Kari
shall also be wroth whenever he meets Mord, and so, if he be made to fear on
one side, and has to look to me on the other, then he will undertake the duty.'"

Then Kari said, "We will follow thy counsel as long as we can, and thou shalt
lead us".

It is to be told of Kari that he could not sleep of nights. Asgrim woke up
one night and heard that Kari was awake, and Asgrim said — "Is it that thou
canst not sleep at night?"

Then Kari sang this song —

> Bender of the bow of battle,
> Sleep will not my eyelids seal,
> Still my murdered messmates' bidding
> Haunts my mind the livelong night;
> Since the men their brands abusing
> Burned last autumn guileless Njal,
> Burned him house and home together,
> Mindful am I of my hurt.

Kari spoke of no men so often as of Njal and Skarphedinn, and Bergthora
and Helgi. He never abused his foes, and never threatened them.

Chapter 132
Flosi's Dream

One night it so happened that Flosi struggled much in his sleep. Glum Hilldir's
son woke him up, and then Flosi said —

"Call me Kettle of the Mark."

Kettle came thither, and Flosi said, "I will tell thee my dream".

"I am ready to hear it," says Kettle.

"I dreamt," says Flosi, "that methought I stood below Loom-nip, and went out and looked up to the Nip, and all at once it opened, and a man came out of the Nip, and he was clad in goatskins, and had an iron staff in his hand. He called, as he walked, on many of my men, some sooner and some later, and named them by name. First he called Grim the Red my kinsman, and Arni Kol's son. Then methought something strange followed, methought he called Eyjolf Bolverk's son, and Ljot son of Hall of the Side, and some six men more. Then he held his peace awhile. After that he called five men of our band, and among them were the sons of Sigfus, thy brothers; then he called other six men, and among them were Lambi, and Modolf, and Glum. Then he called three men. Last of all he called Gunnar Lambi's son, and Kol Thorstein's son. After that he came up to me; I asked him 'what news'. He said he had tidings enough to tell. Then I asked him for his name, but he called himself Irongrim. I asked him whither he was going; he said he had to fare to the Althing. 'What shalt thou do there?' I said. 'First I shall challenge the inquest,' he answers, 'and then the courts, then clear the field for fighters.' After that he sang this song —
"

> "'Soon a man death's snake-strokes dealing
> High shall lift his head on earth,
> Here amid the dust low rolling
> Battered brainpans men shall see:
> Now upon the hills in hurly
> Buds the blue steel's harvest bright;
> Soon the bloody dew of battle
> Thigh-deep through the ranks shall rise."

"Then he shouted with such a mighty shout that methought everything near shook, and dashed down his staff, and there was a mighty crash. Then he went back into the fell, but fear clung to me; and now I wish thee to tell me what thou thinkest this dream is."

"It is my foreboding," says Kettle, "that all those who were called must be 'fey'. It seems to me good counsel that we tell this dream to no man just now."

Flosi said so it should be. Now the winter passes away till Yule was over. Then Flosi said to his men —

"Now I mean that we should fare from home, for methinks we shall not be able to have an idle peace. Now we shall fare to pray for help, and now that will come true which I told you, that we should have to bow the knee to many ere this quarrel were ended."

Chapter 133
Of Flosi's Journey and Asking for Help

After that they busked them from home all together. Flosi was in long-hose because he meant to go on foot, and then he knew that it would seem less hard to the others to walk.

Then they fared from home to Knappvale, but the evening after to Broad-water, and then to Calffell, thence by Bjornness to Hornfirth, thence to Staffell in Lon, and then to Thvattwater to Hall of the Side.

Flosi had to wife Steinvora, his daughter.

Hall gave them a very hearty welcome, and Flosi said to Hall —

"I will ask thee, father-in-law, that thou wouldst ride to the Thing with me with all thy Thingmen."

"Now," answered Hall, "it has turned out as the saw says, 'but a short while is hand fain of blow'; and yet it is one and the same man in thy band who now hangs his head, and who then goaded thee on to the worst of deeds when it was still undone. But my help I am bound to lend thee in all such places as I may."

"What counsel dost thou give me," said Flosi, "in the strait in which I now am?"

"Thou shalt fare," said Hall, "north, right up to Weaponfirth, and ask all the chiefs for aid, and thou wilt yet need it all before the Thing is over."

Flosi stayed there three nights, and rested him, and fared thence east to Geitahellna, and so to Berufirth; there they were the night. Thence they fared east to Broaddale in Haydale. There Hallbjorn the strong dwelt. He had to wife Oddny the sister of Saurli Broddhelgi's son, and Flosi had a hearty welcome there.

Hallbjorn asked how far north among the firths Flosi meant to go. He said he meant to go as far as Weaponfirth. Then Flosi took a purse of money from his belt, and said he would give it to Hallbjorn. He took the money, but yet said he had no claim on Flosi for gifts, but still I would be glad to know in what thou wilt that I repay thee.

"I have no need of money," says Flosi, "but I wish thou wouldst ride to the Thing with me, and stand by me in my quarrel, but still I have no ties or kinship to tell towards thee."

"I will grant thee that," said Hallbjorn, "to ride to the Thing with thee, and to stand by thee in thy quarrel as I would by my brother."

Flosi thanked him, and Hallbjorn asked much about the Burning, but they told him all about it at length.

Thence Flosi fared to Broaddale's heath, and so to Hrafnkelstede, there dwelt Hrafnkell, the son of Thorir, the son of Hrafnkell Raum. Flosi had a hearty welcome there, and sought for help and a promise to ride to the Thing from Hrafnkell, but he stood out a long while, though the end of it was that he gave his word that his son Thorir should ride with all their Thingmen, and yield him such help as the other priests of the same district.

Flosi thanked him and fared away to Bersastede. There Holmstein son of Bersi the wise dwelt, and he gave Flosi a very hearty welcome. Flosi begged him for help. Holmstein said he had been long in his debt for help.

Thence they fared to Waltheofstede — there Saurli Broddhelgi's son, Bjarni's brother, dwelt. He had to wife Thordisa, a daughter of Gudmund the powerful, of Modruvale. They had a hearty welcome there. But next morning Flosi raised the question with Saurli that he should ride to the Althing with him, and bid him money for it.

"I cannot tell about that," says Saurli, "so long as I do not know on which side my father-in-law Gudmund the powerful stands, for I mean to stand by him on whichever side he stands."

"Oh!" said Flosi, "I see by thy answer that a woman rules in this house."

Then Flosi stood up and bade his men take their upper clothing and weapons, and then they fared away, and got no help there. So they fared below Lagarfleet and over the heath to Njardwick; there two brothers dwelt, Thorkel the allwise, and Thorwalld his brother; they were sons of Kettle, the son of Thidrandi the wise, the son of Kettle rumble, son of Thorir Thidrandi. The mother of Thorkel the allwise and Thorwalld was Yngvillda, daughter of Thorkel the wise. Flosi got a hearty welcome there; he told those brothers plainly of his errand, and asked for their help; but they put him off until he gave three marks of silver to each of them for their aid; then they agreed to stand by Flosi.

Their mother Yngvillda was by when they gave their words to ride to the Althing, and wept. Thorkel asked why she wept; and she answered —

"I dreamt that thy brother Thorwalld was clad in a red kirtle, and methought it was so tight as though it were sewn on him; methought too that he wore red hose on his legs and feet, and bad shoethongs were twisted round them; methought it ill to see when I knew he was so uncomfortable, but I could do naught for him."

They laughed and told her she had lost her wits, and said her babble should not stand in the way of their ride to the Thing.

Flosi thanked them kindly, and fared thence to Weaponfirth and came to Hof. There dwelt Bjarni Broddhelgi's son. Bjarni took Flosi by both hands, and Flosi bade Bjarni money for his help.

"Never," says Bjarni, "have I sold my manhood or help for bribes, but now that thou art in need of help, I will do thee a good turn for friendship's sake, and ride to the Thing with thee, and stand by thee as I would by my brother."

"Then thou hast thrown a great load of debt on my hands," said Flosi, "but still I looked for as much from thee."

Thence Flosi and his men fared to Crosswick. Thorkel Geiti's son was a great friend of his. Flosi told him his errand, and Thorkel said it was but his duty to stand by him in every way in his power, and not to part from his quarrel. Thorkel gave Flosi good gifts at parting.

Thence they fared north to Weaponfirth and up into the Fleetdale country, and turned in as guests at Holmstein's, the son of Bersi the wise. Flosi told him that all had backed him in his need and business well, save Saurli Broddhelgi's son. Holmstein said the reason of that was that he was not a man of strife. Holmstein gave Flosi good gifts.

Flosi fared up Fleetdale, and thence south on the fell across Oxenlava and

down Swinehorndale, and so out by Alftafirth to the west, and did not stop till
he came to Thvattwater to his father-in-law Hall's house. There he stayed half
a month, and his men with him and rested him.

Flosi asked Hall what counsel he would now give him, and what he should
do next, and whether he should change his plans.

"My counsel," said Hall, "is this, that thou goest home to thy house, and
the sons of Sigfus with thee, but that they send men to set their homesteads
in order. But first of all fare home, and when ye ride to the Thing, ride all
together, and do not scatter your band. Then let the sons of Sigfus go to see
their wives on the way. I too will ride to the Thing, and Ljot my son with all
our Thingmen, and stand by thee with such force as I can gather to me."

Flosi thanked him, and Hall gave him good gifts at parting.

Then Flosi went away from Thvattwater, and nothing is to be told of his
journey till he comes home to Swinefell. There he stayed at home the rest of
the winter, and all the summer right up to the Thing.

Chapter 134
Of Thorhall and Kari

Thorhall Asgrim's son, and Kari Solmund's son, rode one day to Mossfell to
see Gizur the White; he took them with both hands, and there they were at his
house a very long while. Once it happened as they and Gizur talked of Njal's
burning, that Gizur said it was very great luck that Kari had got away. Then a
song came into Kari's mouth.

> I who whetted helmet-hewer,
> I who oft have burnished brand,
> From the fray went all unwilling
> When Njal's rooftree crackling roared;
> Out I leapt when bands of spearmen
> Lighted there a blaze of flame!
> Listen men unto my moaning,
> Mark the telling of my grief.

Then Gizur said, "It must be forgiven thee that thou art mindful, and so we
will talk no more about it just now".

Kari says that he will ride home; and Gizur said "I will now make a clean
breast of my counsel to thee. Thou shalt not ride home, but still thou shalt
ride away, and east under Eyjafell, to see Thorgeir Craggeir, and Thorleif crow.
They shall ride from the east with thee. They are the next of kin in the suit,
and with them shall ride Thorgrim the big, their brother. Ye shall ride to Mord
Valgard's son's house, and tell him this message from me, that he shall take
up the suit for manslaughter for Helgi Njal's son against Flosi. But if he utters
any words against this, then shalt thou make thyself most wrathful, and make
believe as though thou wouldst let thy axe fall on his head; and in the second
place, thou shalt assure him of my wrath if he shows any ill will. Along with

that shalt thou say, that I will send and fetch away my daughter Thorkatla, and make her come home to me; but that he will not abide, for he loves her as the very eyes in his head."

Kari thanked him for his counsel. Kari spoke nothing of help to him, for he thought he would show himself his good friend in this as in other things.

Thence Kari rode east over the rivers, and so to Fleetlithe, and east across Markfleet, and so on to Selialandsmull. So they ride east to Holt.

Thorgeir welcomed them with the greatest kindliness. He told them of Flosi's journey, and how great help he had got in the east firths.

Kari said it was no wonder that he, who had to answer for so much, should ask for help for himself.

Then Thorgeir said, "The better things go for them, the worse it shall be for them; we will only follow them up so much the harder".

Kari told Thorgeir of Gizur's advice. After that they ride from the east to Rangrivervale to Mord Valgard's son's house. He gave them a hearty welcome. Kari told him the message of Gizur his father-in-law. He was slow to take the duty on him, and said it was harder to go to law with Flosi than with any other ten men.

"Thou behavest now as he [Gizur] thought," said Kari; "for thou art a bad bargain in every way; thou art both a coward and heartless, but the end of this shall be as is fitting, that Thorkatla shall fare home to her father."

She busked her at once, and said she had long been "boun" to part from Mord. Then he changed his mood and his words quickly, and begged off their wrath, and took the suit upon him at once.

"Now," said Kari, "thou hast taken the suit upon thee, see that thou pleadest it without fear, for thy life lies on it."

Mord said he would lay his whole heart on it to do this well and manfully.

After that Mord summoned to him nine neighbours — they were all near neighbours to the spot where the deed was done. Then Mord took Thorgeir by the hand and named two witnesses to bear witness, "that Thorgeir Thorir's son hands me over a suit for manslaughter against Flosi Thord's son, to plead it for the slaying of Helgi Njal's son, with all those proofs which have to follow the suit. Thou handest over to me this suit to plead and to settle, and to enjoy all rights in it, as though I were the rightful next of kin. Thou handest it over to me by law, and I take it from thee by law."

A second time Mord named his witnesses, "to bear witness," said he, "that I give notice of an assault laid down by law against Flosi Thord's son, for that he dealt Helgi Njal's son a brain, or a body, or a marrow wound, which proved a death wound; and from which Helgi got his death. I give notice of this before five witnesses" — here he named them all by name — "I give this lawful notice, I give notice of a suit which Thorgeir Thorir's son has handed over to me."

Again he named witnesses to "bear witness that I give notice of a brain, of a body, or a marrow wound against Flosi Thord's son, for that wound which proved a death wound, but Helgi got his death therefrom on such and such a spot, when Flosi Thord's son first rushed on Helgi Njal's son with an assault laid down by law. I give notice of this before five neighbours " — then he named them all by name — "I give this lawful notice. I give notice of a suit which Thorgeir Thorir's son has handed over to me."

Then Mord named his witnesses again "to bear witness," said he, "that I summon these nine neighbours who dwell nearest the spot" — here he named them all by name — "to ride to the Althing, and to sit on the inquest to find whether Flosi Thord's son rushed with an assault laid down by law on Helgi Njal's son, on that spot where Flosi Thord's son dealt Helgi Njal's son a brain, or a body, or a marrow wound, which proved a death wound, and from which Helgi got his death. I call on you to utter all those words which ye are bound to find by law, and which I shall call on you to utter before the court, and which belong to this suit; I call upon you by a lawful summons — I call on you so that ye may yourselves hear — I call on you in the suit which Thorgeir Thorir's son has handed over to me."

Again Mord named his witnesses, "to bear witness, that I summon these nine neighbours who dwell nearest to the spot to ride to the Althing, and to sit on an inquest to find whether Flosi Thord's son wounded Helgi Njal's son with a brain, or body, or marrow wound, which proved a death wound, and from which Helgi got his death, on that spot where Flosi Thord's son first rushed on Helgi Njal's son with an assault laid down by law. I call on you to utter all those words which ye are bound to find by law, and which I shall call on you to utter before the court, and which belong to this suit I call upon you by a lawful summons — I call on you so that ye may yourselves hear — I call on you in the suit which Thorgeir Thorir's son has handed over to me."

Then Mord said —

"Now is the suit set on foot as ye asked, and now I will pray thee, Thorgeir Craggeir, to come to me when thou ridest to the Thing, and then let us both ride together, each with our band, and keep as close as we can together, for my band shall be ready by the very beginning of the Thing, and I will be true to you in all things."

They showed themselves well pleased at that, and this was fast bound by oaths, that no man should sunder himself from another till Kari willed it, and that each of them should lay down his life for the other's life. Now they parted with friendship, and settled to meet again at the Thing.

Now Thorgeir rides back east, but Kari rides west over the rivers till he came to Tongue, to Asgrim's house. He welcomed them wonderfully well, and Kari told Asgrim all Gizur the White's plan, and of the setting on foot of the suit.

"I looked for as much from him," says Asgrim, "that he would behave well, and now he has shown it."

Then Asgrim went on —

"What heardest thou from the east of Flosi?"

"He went east all the way to Weaponfirth," answers Kari, "and nearly all the chiefs have promised to ride with him to the Althing, and to help him. They look, too, for help from the Reykdalesmen, and the men of Lightwater, and the Axefirthers."

Then they talked much about it, and so the time passes away up to the Althing.

Thorhall Asgrim's son took such a hurt in his leg that the foot above the ankle was as big and swollen as a woman's thigh, and he could not walk save with a staff. He was a man tall in growth, and strong and powerful, dark of hue in hair and skin, measured and guarded in his speech, and yet hot and hasty tempered. He was the third greatest lawyer in all Iceland.

Now the time comes that men should ride from home to the Thing, Asgrim said to Kari —

"Thou shalt ride at the very beginning of the Thing, and fit up our booths, and my son Thorhall with thee. Thou wilt treat him best and kindest, as he is footlame, but we shall stand in the greatest need of him at this Thing. With you two, twenty men more shall ride."

After that they made ready for their journey, and then they rode to the Thing, and set up their booths, and fitted them out well.

Chapter 135
Of Flosi and the burners

Flosi rode from the east and those hundred and twenty men who had been at the Burning with him. They rode till they came to Fleetlithe. Then the sons of Sigfus looked after their homesteads and tarried there that day, but at even they rode west over Thurso-water, and slept there that night. But next morning early they saddled their horses and rode off on their way.

Then Flosi said to his men —

"Now will we ride to Tongue to Asgrim to breakfast, and trample down his pride a little."

They said that were well done. They rode till they had a short way to Tongue. Asgrim stood out of doors, and some men with him. They see the band as soon as ever they could do so from the house. Then Asgrim's men said —

"There must be Thorgeir Craggeir."

"Not he," said Asgrim. "I think so all the more because these men fare with laughter and wantonness; but such kinsmen of Njal as Thorgeir is would not smile before some vengeance is taken for the Burning, and I will make another guess, and maybe ye will think that unlikely. My meaning is, that it must be Flosi and the Burners with him, and they must mean to humble us with insults, and we will now go indoors all of us."

Now they do so, and Asgrim made them sweep the house and put up the hangings, and set the boards and put meat on them. He made them place stools along each bench all down the room.

Flosi rode into the "town," and bade men alight from their horses and go in. They did so, and Flosi and his men went into the hall, Asgrim sate on the cross-bench on the dais. Flosi looked at the benches and saw that all was made ready that men needed to have. Asgrim gave them no greeting, but said to Flosi—

"The boards are set, so that meat may be free to those that need it."

Flosi sat down to the board, and all his men; but they laid their arms up against the wainscot. They sat on the stools who found no room on the benches; but four men stood with weapons just before where Flosi sat while they ate.

Asgrim kept his peace during the meat, but was as red to look on as blood.

But when they were full, some women cleared away the boards, while others brought in water to wash their hands. Flosi was in no greater hurry than if he had been at home. There lay a pole-axe in the corner of the dais. Asgrim caught it up with both hands, and ran up to the rail at the edge of the dais, and made a blow at Flosi's head. Glum Hilldir's son happened to see what he was about to do, and sprang up at once, and got hold of the axe above Asgrim's hands, and turned the edge at once on Asgrim; for Glum was very strong. Then many more men ran up and seized Asgrim, but Flosi said that no man was to do Asgrim any harm, "for we put him to too hard a trial, and he only did what he ought, and showed in that that he had a big heart".

Then Flosi said to Asgrim, "Here, now, we shall part safe and sound, and meet at the Thing, and there begin our quarrel over again".

"So it will be," says Asgrim; "and I would wish that, ere this Thing be over, ye should have to take in some of your sails."

Flosi answered him never a word, and then they went out, and mounted their horses, and rode away. They rode till they came to Laugarwater, and were there that night; but next morning they rode on to Baitvale, and baited their horses there, and there many bands rode to meet them. There was Hall of the Side, and all the Eastfirthers. Flosi greeted them well, and told them of his journeys and dealings with Asgrim. Many praised him for that, and said such things were bravely done.

Then Hall said, "I look on this in another way than ye do, for methinks it was a foolish prank; they were sure to bear in mind their griefs, even though they were not reminded of them anew; but those men who try others so heavily must look for all evil".

It was seen from Hall's way that he thought this deed far too strong. They rode thence all together, till they came to the Upper Field, and there they set their men in array, and rode down on the Thing.

Flosi had made them fit out Byrgir's booth ere he rode to the Thing; but the Eastfirthers rode to their own booths.

Chapter 136
Of Thorgeir Craggeir

Thorgeir Craggeir rode from the east with much people. His brothers were with him, Thorleif crow and Thorgrim the big. They came to Hof, to Mord Valgard's son's house, and bided there till he was ready. Mord had gathered every man who could bear arms, and they could see nothing about him but that he was most steadfast in everything, and now they rode until they came west across the rivers. Then they waited for Hjallti Skeggi's son. He came after they had waited a short while, and they greeted him well, and rode afterwards all together till they came to Reykia in Bishop's-tongue, and bided there for Asgrim Ellidagrim's son, and he came to meet them there. Then they rode west across Bridgewater. Then Asgrim told them all that had passed between him and Flosi; and Thorgeir said—

"I would that we might try their bravery ere the Thing closes."

They rode until they came to Baitvale. There Gizur the White came to meet them with a very great company, and they fell to talking together. Then they rode to the Upper Field, and drew up all their men in array there, and so rode to the Thing.

Flosi and his men all took to their arms, and it was within an ace that they would fall to blows. But Asgrim and his friends and their followers would have no hand in it, and rode to their booths; and now all was quiet that day, so that they had naught to do with one another. Thither were come chiefs from all the Quarters of the land; there had never been such a crowded Thing before, that men could call to mind.

Chapter 137
Of Eyjolf Bolverk's Son

There was a man named Eyjolf. He was the son of Bolverk, the son of Eyjolf the guileful, of Otterdale. Eyjolf was a man of great rank, and best skilled in law of all men, so that some said he was the third best lawyer in Iceland. He was the fairest in face of all men, tall and strong, and there was the making of a great chief in him. He was greedy of money, like the rest of his kinsfolk.

One day Flosi went to the booth of Bjarni Broddhelgi's son. Bjarni took him by both hands, and sat Flosi down by his side. They talked about many things, and at last Flosi said to Bjarni —

"What counsel shall we now take?"

"I think," answered Bjarni, "that it is now hard to say what to do, but the wisest thing seems to me to go round and ask for help, since they are drawing strength together against you. I will also ask thee, Flosi, whether there be any very good lawyer in your band; for now there are but two courses left; one to ask if they will take an atonement, and that is not a bad choice, but the other is to defend the suit at law, if there be any defence to it, though that will seem to be a bold course; and this is why I think this last ought to be chosen, because ye have hitherto fared high and mightily, and it is unseemly now to take a lower course."

"As to thy asking about lawyers," said Flosi, "I will answer thee at once that there is no such man in our band; nor do I know where to look for one except it be Thorkel Geiti's son, thy kinsman."

"We must not reckon on him," said Bjarni, "for though he knows something of law, he is far too wary, and no man need hope to have him as his shield; but he will back thee as well as any man who backs thee best, for he has a stout heart; besides, I must tell thee that it will be that man's bane who undertakes the defence in this suit for the Burning, but I have no mind that this should befall my kinsman Thorkel, so ye must turn your eyes elsewhither."

Flosi said he knew nothing about who were the best lawyers.

"There is a man named Eyjolf," said Bjarni; "he is Bolverk's son, and he is the best lawyer in the Westfirther's Quarter; but you will need to give him much money if you are to bring him into the suit, but still we must not stop at that. We must also go with our arms to all law business, and be most wary of ourselves, but not meddle with them before we are forced to fight for our lives. And now I will go with thee, and set out at once on our begging for help, for now methinks the peace will be kept but a little while longer."

After that they go out of the booth, and to the booths of the Axefirthers. Then Bjarni talks with Lyting and Bleing, and Hroi Arnstein's son, and he got speedily whatever he asked of them. Then they fared to see Kol, the son of Killing-Skuti, and Eyvind Thorkel's son, the son of Askel the priest, and asked them for their help; but they stood out a long while, but the end of it was that they took three marks of silver for it, and so went into the suit with them.

Then they went to the booths of the men of Lightwater, and stayed there some time. Flosi begged the men of Lightwater for help, but they were stubborn and hard to win over, and then Flosi said, with much wrath, "Ye are ill-behaved! ye are grasping and wrongful at home in your own country, and ye will not help men at the Thing, though they need it. No doubt you will be held up to reproach at the Thing, and very great blame will be laid on you if ye bare not in mind that scorn and those biting words which Skarphedinn hurled at you men of Lightwater."

But on the other hand, Flosi dealt secretly with them, and bade them money for their help, and so coaxed them over with fair words, until it came about that they promised him their aid, and then became so steadfast that they said they would fight for Flosi, if need were.

Then Bjarni said to Flosi —

"Well done! well done! Thou art a mighty chief, and a bold outspoken man, and reckest little what thou sayest to men."

After that they fared away west across the river, and so to the Hladbooth. They saw many men outside before the booth. There was one man who had a scarlet cloak over his shoulders, and a gold band round his head, and an axe studded with silver in his hand.

"This is just right," said Bjarni, "here now is the man I spoke of, Eyjolf Bolverk's son, if thou wilt see him, Flosi."

Then they went to meet Eyjolf, and hailed him. Eyjolf knew Bjarni at once, and greeted him well. Bjarni took Eyjolf by the hand, and led him up into the "Great Rift". Flosi's and Bjarni's men followed after, and Eyjolf's men went also with him. They bade them stay upon the lower brink of the Rift, and look about them, but Flosi, and Bjarni, and Eyjolf went on till they came to where the path leads down from the upper brink of the Rift.

Flosi said it was a good spot to sit down there, for they could see around them far and wide. Then they sat them down there. They were four of them together, and no more.

Then Bjarni spoke to Eyjolf, and said —

"Thee, friend, have we come to see, for we much need thy help in every way."

"Now," said Eyjolf, "there is good choice of men here at the Thing, and ye will not find it hard to fall on those who will be a much greater strength to you than I can be."

"Not so," said Bjarni, "Thou hast many things which show that there is no greater man than thou at the Thing; first of all, that thou art so well-born, as all those men are who are sprung from Ragnar hairybreeks; thy forefathers, too, have always stood first in great suits, both here at the Thing, and at home in their own country, and they have always had the best of it; we think, therefore, it is likely that thou wilt be lucky in winning suits, like thy kinsfolk."

"Thou speakest well, Bjarni," said Eyjolf; "but I think that I have small share in all this that thou sayest."

Then Flosi said —

"There is no need beating about the bush as to what we have in mind. We wish to ask for thy help, Eyjolf, and that thou wilt stand by us in our suits, and go to the court with us, and undertake the defence, if there be any, and plead it for us, and stand by us in all things that may happen at this Thing."

Eyjolf jumped up in wrath, and said that no man had any right to think that he could make a catspaw of him, or drag him on if he had no mind to go himself.

"I see, too, now," he says, "what has led you to utter all those fair words with which ye began to speak to me."

Then Hallbjorn the strong caught hold of him and sate him down by his side, between him and Bjarni, and said —

"No tree falls at the first stroke, friend, but sit here awhile by us."

Then Flosi drew a gold ring off his arm.

"This ring will I give thee, Eyjolf, for thy help and friendship, and so show thee that I will not befool thee. It will be best for thee to take the ring, for there is no man here at the Thing to whom I have ever given such a gift."

The ring was such a good one, and so well made, that it was worth twelve hundred yards of russet stuff.

Hallbjorn drew the ring on Eyjolf's arm; and Eyjolf said —

"It is now most fitting that I should take the ring, since thou behavest so handsomely; and now thou mayest make up thy mind that I will undertake the defence, and do all things needful."

"Now," said Bjarni, "ye behave handsomely on both sides, and here are men well fitted to be witnesses, since I and Hallbjorn are here, that thou hast undertaken the suit."

Then Eyjolf arose, and Flosi too, and they took one another by the hand; and so Eyjolf undertook the whole defence of the suit off Flosi's hands, and so, too, if any suit arose out of the defence, for it often happens that what is a defence in one suit, is a plaintiff's plea in another. So he took upon him all the proofs and proceedings which belonged to those suits, whether they were to be pleaded before the Quarter Court or the Fifth Court. Flosi handed them over in lawful form, and Eyjolf took them in lawful form, and then he said to Flosi and Bjarni.

"Now I have undertaken this defence just as ye asked, but my wish it is that ye should still keep it secret at first; but if the matter comes into the Fifth Court, then be most careful not to say that ye have given goods for my help."

Then Flosi went home to his booth, and Bjarni with him, but Eyjolf went to the booth of Snorri the priest, and sate down by him, and they talked much together.

Snorri the priest caught hold of Eyjolf's arm, and turned up the sleeve, and sees that he had a great ring of gold on his arm. Then Snorri the priest said —

"Pray, was this ring bought or given?"

Eyjolf was put out about it, and had never a word to say. Then Snorri said —

"I see plainly that thou must have taken it as a gift, and may this ring not be thy death!"

Eyjolf jumped up and went away, and would not speak about it; and Snorri said, as Eyjolf arose —

"It is very likely that thou wilt know what kind of gift thou hast taken by the time this Thing is ended."

Then Eyjolf went to his booth.

Chapter 138
Of Asgrim, and Gizur, and Kari

Now Asgrim Ellidagrim's son talks to Gizur the White, and Kari Solmund's son, and to Hjallti Skeggi's son, Mord Valgard's son, and Thorgeir Craggeir, and says—

"There is no need to have any secrets here, for only those men are by who know all our counsel. Now I will ask you if ye know anything of their plans, for if you do, it seems to me that we must take fresh counsel about our own plans."

"Snorri the priest," answers Gizur the White, "sent a man to me, and bade him tell me that Flosi had gotten great help from the Northlanders; but that Eyjolf Bolverk's son, his kinsman, had had a gold ring given him by some one, and made a secret of it, and Snorri said it was his meaning that Eyjolf Bolverk's son must be meant to defend the suit at law, and that the ring must have been given him for that."

They were all agreed that it must be so. Then Gizur spoke to them —

"Now has Mord Valgard's son, my son-in-law, undertaken a suit, which all must think most hard, to prosecute Flosi; and now my wish is that ye share the other suits amongst you, for now it will soon be time to give notice of the suits at the Hill of Laws. We shall need also to ask for more help."

Asgrim said so it should be, "but we will beg thee to go round with us when we ask for help". Gizur said he would be ready to do that.

After that Gizur picked out all the wisest men of their company to go with him as his backers. There was Hjallti Skeggi's son, and Asgrim, and Kari, and Thorgeir Craggeir.

Then Gizur the White said —

"Now will we first go to the booth of Skapti Thorod's son," and they do so. Gizur the White went first, then Hjallti, then Kari, then Asgrim, then Thorgeir Craggeir, and then his brothers.

They went into the booth. Skapti sat on the cross-bench on the dais, and when he saw Gizur the White he rose up to meet him, and greeted him and all of them well, and bade Gizur to sit down by him, and he does so. Then Gizur said to Asgrim —

"Now shalt thou first raise the question of help with Skapti, but I will throw in what I think good."

"We are come hither," said Asgrim, "for this sake, Skapti, to seek help and aid at thy hand."

"I was thought to be hard to win the last time," said Skapti, "when I would not take the burden of your trouble on me."

"It is quite another matter now," said Gizur. "Now the feud is for master Njal and mistress Bergthora, who were burnt in their own house without a cause, and for Njal's three sons, and many other worthy men, and thou wilt surely never be willing to yield no help to men, or to stand by thy kinsmen and connections."

"It was in my mind," answers Skapti, "when Skarphedinn told me that I had myself borne tar on my own head, and cut up a sod of turf and crept under it, and when he said that I had been so afraid that Thorolf Lopt's son of Eyrar bore me abroad in his ship among his meal-sacks, and so carried me to Iceland, that I would never share in the blood feud for his death."

"Now there is no need to bear such things in mind," said Gizur the White, "for he is dead who said that, and thou wilt surely grant me this, though thou wouldst not do it for other men's sake."

"This quarrel," says Skapti, "is no business of thine, except thou choosest to be entangled in it along with them."

Then Gizur was very wrath, and said —

"Thou art unlike thy father, though he was thought not to be quite clean-handed; yet was he ever helpful to men when they needed him most."

"We are unlike in temper," said Skapti. "Ye two, Asgrim and thou, think that ye have had the lead in mighty deeds; thou, Gizur the White, because thou overcamest Gunnar of Lithend; but Asgrim, for that he slew Gauk, his foster-brother."

"Few," said Asgrim, "bring forward the better if they know the worse, but many would say that I slew not Gauk ere I was driven to it. There is some excuse for thee for not helping us, but none for heaping reproaches on us; and I only wish before this Thing is out that thou mayest get from this suit the greatest disgrace, and that there may be none to make thy shame good."

Then Gizur and his men stood up all of them, and went out, and so on to the booth of Snorri the priest.

Snorri sat on the cross-bench in his booth; they went into the booth, and he knew the men at once, and stood up to meet them, and bade them all welcome, and made room for them to sit by him.

After that, they asked one another the news of the day.

Then Asgrim spoke to Snorri, and said —

"For that am I and my kinsman Gizur come hither, to ask thee for thy help."

"Thou speakest of what thou mayest always be forgiven for asking, for help in the blood-feud after such connections as thou hadst. We, too, got many wholesome counsels from Njal, though few now bear that in mind; but as yet I know not of what ye think ye stand most in need."

"We stand most in need," answers Asgrim, "of brisk lads and good weapons, if we fight them here at the Thing."

"True it is," said Snorri, "that much lies on that, and it is likeliest that ye will press them home with daring, and that they will defend themselves so in likewise, and neither of you will allow the other's right. Then ye will not bear with them and fall on them, and that will be the only way left; for then they will seek to pay you off with shame for manscathe, and with dishonour for loss of kin."

It was easy to see that he goaded them on in everything.

Then Gizur the White said —

"Thou speakest well, Snorri, and thou behavest ever most like a chief when most lies at stake."

"I wish to know," said Asgrim, "in what way thou wilt stand by us if things turn out as thou sayest."

"I will show thee those marks of friendship," said Snorri, "on which all your honour will hang, but I will not go with you to the court. But if ye fight here on the Thing, do not fall on them at all unless ye are all most steadfast and dauntless, for you have great champions against you. But if ye are over-matched, ye must let yourselves be driven hither towards us, for I shall then have drawn up my men in array hereabouts, and shall be ready to stand by you. But if it falls out otherwise, and they give way before you, my meaning is that they will try to run for a stronghold in the 'Great Rift'. But if they come thither, then ye will never get the better of them. Now I will take that on my hands, to draw up my men there, and guard the pass to the stronghold, but we will not follow them whether they turn north or south along the river. And when you have slain out of their band about as many as I think ye will be able to pay blood-fines for, and yet keep your priesthoods and abodes, then I will run up with all my men and part you. Then ye shall promise to do us I bid you, and stop the battle, if I on my part do what I have now promised."

Gizur thanked him kindly, and said that what he had said was just what they all needed, and then they all went out.

"Whither shall we go now?" said Gizur.

"To the Northlanders' booth," said Asgrim.

Then they fared thither.

Chapter 139
Of Asgrim and Gudmund

And when they came into the booth then they saw where Gudmund the powerful sate and talked with Einer Conal's son, his foster-child; he was a wise man.

Then they come before him, and Gudmund welcomed them very heartily, and made them clear the booth for them, that they might all be able to sit down.

Then they asked what tidings, and Asgrim said —

"There is no need to mutter what I have to say. We wish, Gudmund, to ask for thy steadfast help."

"Have ye seen any other chiefs before?" said Gudmund.

They said they had been to see Skapti Thorod's son and Snorri the priest, and told him quietly how they had fared with each of them.

Then Gudmund said —

"Last time I behaved badly and meanly to you. Then I was stubborn, but now ye shall drive your bargain with me all the more quickly because I was more stubborn then, and now I will go myself with you to the court with all my Thingmen, and stand by you in all such things as I can, and fight for you though this be needed, and lay down my life for your lives. I will also pay Skapti out in this way, that Thorstein gapemouth his son shall be in the battle on our side, for he will not dare to do aught else than I will, since he has Jodisa my daughter to wife, and then Skapti will try to part us."

They thanked him, and talked with him long and low afterwards, so that no other men could hear.

Then Gudmund bade them not to go before the knees of any other chiefs, for he said that would be little-hearted.

"We will now run the risk with the force that we have. Ye must go with your weapons to all law-business, but not fight as things stand."

Then they went all of them home to their booths, and all this was at first with few men's knowledge.

So now the Thing goes on.

Chapter 140
Of the Declarations of the Suits

It was one day that men went to the Hill of Laws, and the chiefs were so placed that Asgrim Ellidagrim's son, and Gizur the White, and Gudmund the powerful, and Snorri the priest, were on the upper hand by the Hill of Laws; but the Eastfirthers stood down below.

Mord Valgard's son stood next to Gizur his father-in-law; he was of all men the readiest-tongued.

Gizur told him that he ought to give notice of the suit for manslaughter, and bade him speak up, so that all might hear him well.

Then Mord took witness and said — "I take witness to this that I give notice of an assault laid down by law against Flosi Thord's son, for that he rushed at Helgi Njal's son and dealt him a brain, or a body, or a marrow wound, which proved a death-wound, and from which Helgi got his death. I say that in this suit he ought to be made a guilty man, an outlaw, not to be fed, not to be forwarded, not to be helped or harboured in any need. I say that all his goods are forfeited, half to me, and half to the men of the Quarter, who have a right by law to take his forfeited goods. I give notice of this suit for manslaughter in the Quarter Court into which this suit ought by law to come. I give notice of this lawful notice; I give notice in the hearing of all men on the Hill of Laws; I give notice of this suit to be pleaded this summer, and of full outlawry against Flosi Thord's son; I give notice of a suit which Thorgeir Thorir's son has handed over to me."

Then a great shout was uttered at the Hill of Laws, that Mord spoke well and boldly.

Then Mord begun to speak a second time.

"I take you to witness to this," says he, "that I give notice of a suit against Flosi Thord's son, I give notice for that he wounded Helgi Njal's son with a brain, or a body, or a marrow wound, which proved a death-wound, and from which Helgi got his death on that spot where Flosi Thord's son had first rushed on Helgi Njal's son with an assault laid down by law. I say that thou, Flosi, ought to be made in this suit a guilty man, an outlaw, not to be fed, not to be forwarded, not to he helped or harboured in any need. I say that all thy goods are forfeited, half to me and half to the men of the Quarter, who have a right by law to take the goods which have been forfeited by thee. I give notice of this suit in the Quarter Court into which it ought by law to come; I give notice of this lawful notice; I give notice of it in the hearing of all men on the Hill of Laws; I give notice of this suit to be pleaded this summer, and of full outlawry against Flosi Thord's son, I give notice of the suit which Thorgeir Thorir's son hath handed over to me."

After that Mord sat him down.

Flosi listened carefully, but said never a word the while.

Then Thorgeir Craggeir stood up and took witness, and said — "I take witness to this, that I give notice of a suit against Glum Hilldir's son, in that he took firing and lit it, and bore it to the house at Bergthorsknoll, when they were burned inside it, to wit, Njal Thorgeir's son, and Bergthora Skarphedinn's daughter, and all those other men who were burned inside it there and then. I say that in this suit he ought to be made a guilty man, an outlaw, not to be fed, not to be forwarded, not to be helped or harboured in any need. I say that all his goods are forfeited, half to me, and half to the men of the Quarter, who have a right by law to take his forfeited goods; I give notice of this suit in the Quarter Court into which it ought by law to come. I give notice in the hearing of all men on the Hill of Laws. I give notice of this suit to be pleaded this summer, and of full outlawry against Glum Hilldir's son."

Kari Solmund's son declared his suits against Kol Thorstein's son, and Gunnar Lambi's son, and Grani Gunnar's son, and it was the common talk of men that he spoke wondrous well.

Thorleif crow declared his suit against all the sons of Sigfus, but Thorgrim the big, his brother, against Modolf Kettle's son, and Lambi Sigurd's son, and Hroar Hamond's son, brother of Leidolf the strong.

Asgrim Ellidagrim's son declared his suit against Leidolf and Thorstein Geirleif's son. Arni Kol's son, and Grim the red.

And they all spoke well.

After that other men gave notice of their suits, and it was far on in the day that it went on so.

Then men fared home to their booths.

Eyjolf Bolverk's son went to his booth with Flosi; they passed east around the booth, and Flosi said to Eyjolf —

"See'st thou any defence in these suits?"

"None," says Eyjolf.

"What counsel is now to be taken?" says Flosi.

"I will give thee a piece of advice," said Eyjolf. "Now thou shalt hand over thy priesthood to thy brother Thorgeir, but declare that thou hast joined the Thing of Askel the priest the son of Thorkettle, north away in Reykiardale; but if they do not know this, then may be that this will harm them, for they will be sure to plead their suit in the Eastfirther's court, but they ought to plead it in the Northlanders' court, and they will overlook that, and it is a Fifth Court matter against them if they plead their suit in another court than that in which they ought, and then we will take that suit up, but not until we have no other choice left."

"May be," said Flosi, "that we shall get the worth of the ring."

"I don't know that," says Eyjolf; "but I will stand by thee at law, so that men shall say that there never was a better defence. Now, we must send for Askel, but Thorgeir shall come to thee at once, and a man with him."

A little while after Thorgeir came, and then he took on him Flosi's leadership and priesthood.

By that time Askel was come thither too, and then Flosi declared that he had joined his Thing, and this was with no man's knowledge save theirs.

Now all is quiet till the day when the courts were to go out to try suits.

Chapter 141
Now Men go to the Courts

Now the time passes away till the courts were to go out to try suits. Both sides then made them ready to go thither, and armed them. Each side put war-tokens on their helmets.

Then Thorhall Asgrim's son said —

"Walk hastily in nothing, father mine, and do everything as lawfully and rightly as ye can, but if ye fall into any strait let me know as quickly as ye can, and then I will give you counsel."

Asgrim and the others looked at him, and his face was as though it were all blood, but great teardrops gushed out of his eyes. He bade them bring him his spear, that had been a gift to him from Skarphedinn, and it was the greatest treasure.

Asgrim said as they went away —

"Our kinsman Thorhall was not easy in his mind as we left him behind in the booth, and I know not what he will be at."

Then Asgrim said again —

"Now we will go to Mord Valgard's son, and think of naught else but the suit, for there is more sport in Flosi than in very many other men."

Then Asgrim sent a man to Gizur the White, and Hjallti Skeggi's son, and Gudmund the powerful. Now they all came together, and went straight to the court of Eastfirthers. They went to the court from the south, but Flosi and all the Eastfirthers with him went to it from the north. There were also the men of Reykdale and the Axefirthers with Flosi. There, too, was Eyjolf Bolverk's son. Flosi looked at Eyjolf, and said —

"All now goes fairly, and may be that it will not be far off from thy guess."

"Keep thy peace about it," says Eyjolf, "and then we shall be sure to gain our point."

Now Mord took witness, and bade all those men who had suits of outlawry before the court to cast lots who should first plead or declare his suit, and who next, and who last; he bade them by a lawful bidding before the court, so that the judges heard it. Then lots were cast as to the declarations, and he, Mord, drew the lot to declare his suit first.

Now Mord Valgard's son took witness the second time, and said —

"I take witness to this, that I except all mistakes in words in my pleading, whether they be too many or wrongly spoken, and I claim the right to amend all my words until I have put them into proper lawful shape. I take witness to myself of this."

Again Mord said —

"I take witness to this, that I bid Flosi Thord's son, or any other man who has undertaken the defence made over to him by Flosi, to listen for him to my oath, and to my declaration of my suit, and to all the proofs and proceedings which I am about to bring forward against him; I bid him by a lawful bidding before the court, so that the judges may hear it across the court."

Again Mord Valgard's son said —

"I take witness to this, that I take an oath on the book, a lawful until, and I say it before God, that I will so plead this suit in the most truthful, and most just, and most lawful way, so far as I know; and that I will bring forward all my proofs in due form, and utter them faithfully so long as I am in this suit."

After that he spoke in these words —

"I have called Thorodd as my first witness, and Thorbjorn as my second; I have called them to bear witness that I gave notice of an assault laid down by law against Flosi Thord's son, on that spot where he, Flosi Thord's son, rushed with an assault laid down by law on Helgi Njal's son, when Flosi Thord's son, wounded Helgi Njal's son with a brain, or a body, or a marrow wound, which proved a death-wound, and from which Helgi got his death. I said that he ought to be made in this suit a guilty man, an outlaw, not to be fed, not to be forwarded, not to he helped or harboured in any need; I said that all his goods were forfeited, half to me and half to the men of the Quarter who have the right by law to take the goods which he has forfeited; I gave notice of the suit in the Quarter Court into which the suit ought by law to come; I gave notice of that lawful notice; I gave notice in the hearing of all men at the Hill of Laws; I gave notice of this suit to be pleaded now this summer, and of full outlawry against Flosi Thord's son. I gave notice of a suit which Thorgeir Thorir's son had handed heard it. Then lots were cast as to the declarations, and he, Mord, drew the lot to declare his suit first".

Now Mord Valgard's son took witness the second time, and said —

"I take witness to this, that I except all mistakes in words in my pleading, whether they be too many or wrongly spoken, and I claim the right to amend all my words until I have put them into proper lawful shape. I take witness to myself of this."

Again Mord said —

"I take witness to this, that I bid Flosi Thord's son, or any other man who has undertaken the defence made over to him by Flosi, to listen for him to my oath, and to my declaration of my suit, and to all the proofs and proceedings which I am about to bring forward against him; I bid him by a lawful bidding before the court, so that the judges may hear it across the court."

Again Mord Valgard's son said —

"I take witness to this, that I take an oath on the book, a lawful oath, and I say it before God, that I will so plead this suit in the most truthful, and most just, and most lawful way, so far as I know; and that I will bring forward all my proofs in due form, and utter them faithfully so long as I am in this suit."

After that he spoke in these words —

"I have called Thorodd as my first witness, and Thorbjorn as my second; I have called them to bear witness that I gave notice of an assault laid down by law against Flosi Thord's son, on that spot where he, Flosi Thord's son, rushed with an assault laid down by law on Helgi Njal's son, when Flosi Thord's son, wounded Helgi Njal's son with a brain, or a body, or a marrow wound, which proved a death-wound, and from which Helgi got his death. I said that he ought to be made in this suit a guilty man, an outlaw, not to be fed, not to be forwarded, not to be helped or harboured in any need; I said that all his goods were forfeited, half to me and half to the men of the Quarter who have the right by law to take the goods which he has forfeited; I gave notice of the suit in the Quarter Court into which the suit ought by law to come; I gave notice of that lawful notice; I gave notice in the hearing of all men at the Hill of Laws; I gave notice of this suit to be pleaded now this summer, and of full outlawry against Flosi Thord's son. I gave notice of a suit which Thorgeir Thorir's son had handed over to me; and I had all these words in my notice which I have now used in this declaration of my suit. I now declare this suit of outlawry in this shape before the court of the Eastfirthers over the head of John, as I uttered it when I gave notice of it."

Then Mord spoke again —

"I have called Thorodd as my first witness, and Thorbjorn as my second. I have called them to bear witness that I gave notice of a suit against Flosi Thord's son for that he wounded Helgi Njal's son with a brain, or a body, or a marrow wound, which proved a death-wound, and from which Helgi got his death. I said that he ought to be made in this suit a guilty man, an outlaw, not he fed, not to be forwarded, not to be helped or harboured in any need; I said that all his goods were forfeited, half to me and half to the men of the Quarter who have the right by law to take the goods which he has forfeited; I gave notice of the suit in the Quarter Court into which the suit ought by law to come; I gave notice of that lawful notice; I gave notice in the hearing of all men at the Hill of Laws; I gave notice of this suit to be pleaded now this summer, and of full outlawry against Flosi Thord's son. I gave notice of a suit which Thorgeir Thorir's son had handed over to me; and I had all these words in my notice which I have now used in this declaration of my suit. I now declare this suit of outlawry in this shape before the court of the Eastfirthers over the head of John, as I uttered it when I gave notice of it."

Then Mord's witnesses to the notice came before the court, and spake so that one uttered their witness, but both confirmed it by their common consent in this form, "I bear witness that Mord called Thorodd as his first witness, and me as his second, and my name is Thorbjorn" — then he named his father's name — "Mord called us two as his witnesses that he gave notice of an assault laid down by law against Flosi Thord's son when he rushed on Helgi Njal's son, in that spot where Flosi Thord's son dealt Helgi Njal's son a brain, or a body, or a marrow wound, that proved a death-wound, and from which Helgi got his death. He said that Flosi ought to be made in this suit a guilty man, an outlaw, not to be fed, not to be forwarded, not to be helped or harboured by any man; he said that all his goods were forfeited, half to himself and half to the men of the Quarter who have the right by law to take the goods which he had forfeited; he gave notice of the suit in the Quarter Court into which the suit ought by law to come; he gave notice of that lawful notice; he gave notice in the hearing of all men at the Hill of Laws; he gave notice of this suit to be pleaded now this summer, and of full outlawry against Flosi Thord's son. He gave notice of a suit which Thorgeir Thorir's son had handed over to him. He used all those words in his notice which he used in the declaration of his suit, and which we have used in bearing witness; we have now borne our witness rightly and lawfully, and we are agreed in bearing it; we bear this witness in this shape before the Eastfirthers' Court over the head of John, as Mord uttered it when he gave his notice."

A second time they bore their witness of the notice before the court, and put the wounds first and the assault last, and used all the same words as before, and bore their witness in this shape before the Eastfirthers' Court just as Mord uttered them when he gave his notice.

Then Mord's witnesses to the handing over of the suit went before the court, and one uttered their witness, and both confirmed it by common consent, and spoke in these words — "That those two, Mord Valgard's son and Thorgeir Thorir's son, took them to witness that Thorgeir Thorir's son handed over a suit for manslaughter to Mord Valgard's son against Flosi Thord's son for the laying of Helgi Njal's son; he handed over to him then the suit, with all the proofs and proceedings which belonged to the suit, he handed it over to him to plead and to settle, and to make use of all rights as though he were the rightful next of kin; Thorgeir handed it over lawfully, and Mord took it lawfully".

They bore this witness of the handing over of the suit in this shape before the Eastfirthers' Court over the head of John, just as Mord or Thorgeir had called them as witnesses to prove.

They made all these witnesses swear an oath ere they bore witness, and the judges too.

Again Mord Valgard's son took witness.

"I take witness to this," said he, "that I bid those nine neighbours whom I summoned when I laid this suit against Flosi Thord's son, to take their seats west on the river-bank, and I call on the defendant to challenge this inquest, I call on him by a lawful bidding before the court so that the judges may hear."

Again Mord took witness.

"I take witness to this, that I bid Flosi Thord's son, or that other man who has the defence handed over to him, to challenge the inquest which I have caused to take their seats west on the river-bank. I bid thee by a lawful bidding before the court so that the judges may hear."

Again Mord took witness.

"I take witness to this, that now are all the first steps and proofs brought forward which belong to the suit. Summons to hear my oath, oath taken, suit declared, witness borne to the notice, witness borne to the handing over of the suit, the neighbours on the inquest bidden to take their seats, and the defendant bidden to challenge the inquest. I take this witness to these steps and proofs which are now brought forward, and also to this that I shall not be thought to have left the suit though I go away from the court to look up proofs, or on other business."

Now Flosi and his men went thither where the neighbours on the inquest sate.

Then Flosi said to his men —

"The sons of Sigfus must know best whether these are the rightful neighbours to the spot who are here summoned."

Kettle of the Mark answered —

"Here is that neighbour who held Mord at the font when he was baptised, but another is his second cousin by kinship."

Then they reckoned up his kinship, and proved it with an oath.

Then Eyjolf took witness that the inquest should do nothing till it was challenged.

A second time Eyjolf took witness —

"I take witness to this," said he, "that I challenge both these men out of the inquest, and set them aside" — here he named them by name, and their fathers as well — "for this sake, that one of them is Mord's second cousin by kinship, but the other for gossipry, for which sake it is lawful to challenge a neighbour on the inquest; ye two are for a lawful reason incapable of uttering a finding, for now a lawful challenge has overtaken you, therefore I challenge and set you aside by the rightful custom of pleading at the Althing, and by the law of the land; I challenge you in the cause which Flosi Thord's son has handed over to me."

Now all the people spoke out, and said that Mord's suit had come to naught, and all were agreed in this that the defence was better than the prosecution.

Then Asgrim said to Mord —

"The day is not yet their own, though they think now that they have gained a great step; but now some one shall go to see Thorhall my son, and know what advice he gives us."

Then a trusty messenger was sent to Thorhall, and told him as plainly as he could how far the suit had gone, and how Flosi and his men thought they had brought the finding of the inquest to a dead lock.

"I will so make it out," says Thorhall, "that this shall not cause you to lose the suit; and tell them not to believe it, though quirks and quibbles be brought against them, for that wiseacre Eyjolf has now overlooked something. But now thou shalt go back as quickly as thou canst, and say that Mord Valgard's son must go before the court, and take witness that their challenge has come to naught," and then he told him step by step how they must proceed.

The messenger came and told them Thorhall's advice.

Then Mord Valgard's son went to the court and took witness. "I take witness to this," said he, "that I make Eyjolf's challenge void and of none effect; and my ground is, that he challenged them not for their kinship to the true plaintiff, the next of kin, but for their kinship to him who pleaded the suit; I take this witness to myself, and to all those to whom this witness will be of use."

After that he brought that witness before the court.

Now he went whither the neighbours sate on the inquest, and bade those to sit down again who had risen up, and said they were rightly called on to share in the finding of the inquest.

Then all said that Thorhall had done great things, and all thought the prosecution better than the defence.

Then Flosi said to Eyjolf — "Thinkest thou that this is good law?"

"I think so, surely," he says, "and beyond a doubt we overlooked this; but still we will have another trial of strength with them."

Then Eyjolf took witness. "I take witness to this," said he, "that I challenge these two men out of the inquest" — here he named them both — "for that sake that they are lodgers, but not householders; I do not allow you two to sit on the inquest, for now a lawful challenge has overtaken you; I challenge you both and set you aside out of the inquest, by the rightful custom of the Althing and by the law of the land."

Now Eyjolf said he was much mistaken if that could be shaken; and then all said that the defence was better than the prosecution.

Now all men praised Eyjolf, and said there was never a man who could cope with him in lawcraft.

Mord Valgard's son and Asgrim Ellidagrim's son now sent a man to Thorhall to tell him how things stood; but when Thorhall heard that, he asked what goods they owned, or if they were paupers?

The messenger said that one gained his livelihood by keeping milch-kine, and "he has both cows and ewes at his abode; but the other has a third of the land which he and the freeholder farm, and finds his own food; and they have one hearth between them, he and the man who lets the land, and one shepherd".

Then Thorhall said —

"They will fare now as before, for they must have made a mistake, and I will soon upset their challenge, and this though Eyjolf had used such big words that it was law."

Now Thorhall told the messenger plainly, step by step, how they must proceed; and the messenger came back and told Mord and Asgrim all the counsel that Thorhall had given.

Then Mord went to the court and took witness, "I take witness to this, that I bring to naught Eyjolf Bolverk's son's challenge, for that he has challenged those men out of the inquest who have a lawful right to lie there; every man has a right to sit on an inquest of neighbours, who owns three hundreds in land or more, though he may have no dairy-stock; and he too has the same right who lives by dairy-stock worth the same sum, though he leases no land."

Then he brought this witness before the court, and then he went whither the neighbours on the inquest were, and bade them sit down, and said they were rightfully among the inquest.

Then there was a great shout and cry, and then all men said that Flosi's and Eyjolf's cause was much shaken, and now men were of one mind as to this, that the prosecution was better than the defence.

Then Flosi said to Eyjolf —

"Can this be law?"

Eyjolf said he had not wisdom enough to know that for a surety, and then they sent a man to Skapti, the Speaker of the Law, to ask whether it were good law, and he sent them back word that it was surely good law, though few knew it.

Then this was told to Flosi, and Eyjolf Bolverk's son asked the sons of Sigfus as to the other neighbours who were summoned thither.

They said there were four of them who were wrongly summoned; "for those sit now at home who were nearer neighbours to the spot".

Then Eyjolf took witness that he challenged all those four men out of the inquest, and that he did it with lawful form of challenge. After that he said to the neighbours —

"Ye are bound to render lawful justice to both sides, and now ye shall go before the court when ye are called, and take witness that ye find that bar to uttering your finding; that ye are but five summoned to utter your finding, but that ye ought to be nine; and now Thorhall may prove and carry his point in every suit, if he can cure this flaw in this suit."

And now it was plain in everything that Flosi and Eyjolf were very boastful; and there was a great cry that now the suit for the Burning was quashed, and that again the defence was better than the prosecution.

Then Asgrim spoke to Mord —

"They know not yet of what to boast ere we have seen my son Thorhall. Njal told me that he had so taught Thorhall law, that he would turn out the best lawyer in Iceland when ever it were put to the proof."

Then a man was sent to Thorhall to tell him how things stood, and of Flosi's and Eyjolf's boasting, and the cry of the people that the suit for the Burning was quashed in Mord's bands.

"It will be well for them," says Thorhall, "if they get not disgrace from this. Thou shalt go and tell Mord to take witness, and swear an oath, that the greater part of the inquest is rightly summoned, and then he shall bring that witness before the court, and then he may set the prosecution on its feet again; but he will have to pay a fine of three marks for every man that he has wrongly summoned; but he may not be prosecuted for that at this Thing; and now thou shalt go back."

He does so, and told Mord and Asgrim all, word for word, that Thorhall had said.

Then Mord went to the court, and took witness, and swore an oath that the greater part of the inquest was rightly summoned, and said then that he had set the prosecution on its feet again, and then he went on, "and so our foes shall have honour from something else than from this, that we have here taken a great false step".

Then there was a great roar that Mord handled the suit well; but it was said that Flosi and his men betook them only to quibbling and wrong.

Flosi asked Eyjolf if this could be good law, but he said he could not surely tell, but said the Lawman must settle this knotty point.

Then Thorkel Geiti's son went on their behalf to tell the Lawman how things stood, and asked whether this were good law that Mord had said.

"More men are great lawyers now," says Skapti, "than I thought I must tell thee, then, that this is such good law in all points, that there is not a word to say against it; but still I thought that I alone would know this, now that Njal was dead, for he was the only man I ever knew who knew it."

Then Thorkel went back to Flosi and Eyjolf, and said that this was good law.

Then Mord Valgard's son went to the court and took witness. "I take witness to this," he said, "that I bid those neighbours on the inquest in the suit which I set on foot against Flosi Thord's son now to utter their finding, and to find it either against him or for him; I bid them by a lawful bidding before the court, so that the judges may bear it across the court."

Then the neighbours on Mord's inquest went to the court, and one uttered their finding, but all confirmed it by their consent; and they spoke thus, word for word —

"Mord Valgard's son summoned nine of us thanes on this inquest, but here we stand five of us, but four have been challenged and set aside, and now witness has been borne as to the absence of the four who ought to have uttered this finding along with us, and now we are bound by law to utter our finding. We were summoned to bear this witness, whether Flosi Thord's son rushed with an assault laid down by law on Helgi Njal's son, on that spot where Flosi Thord's son wounded Helgi Njal's son with a brain, or a body, or a marrow wound, which proved a death wound, and from which Helgi got his death. He summoned us to utter all those words which it was lawful for us to utter, and which he should call on us to answer before the court, and which belong to this suit; he summoned us, so that we heard what he said; he summoned us in a suit which Thorgeir Thorir's son had handed over to him, and now we have all sworn an oath, and found our lawful finding, and are all agreed, and we utter our finding against Flosi, and we say that he is truly guilty in this suit. We nine men on this inquest of neighbours so shapen, utter this our finding before the Eastfirthers' Court over the head of John, as Mord summoned us to do; but this is the finding of all of us."

Again a second time they uttered their finding against Flosi, and uttered it first about the wounds, and last about the assault, but all their other words they uttered just as they had before uttered their finding against Flosi, and brought him in truly guilty in the suit.

Then Mord Valgard's son went before the court, and took witness that those neighbours whom he had summoned in the suit which he had set on foot against Flosi Thord's son had now uttered their finding, and brought him in truly guilty in the suit; he took witness to this for his own part, or for those who might wish to make use of this witness.

Again a second time Mord took witness and said —

"I take witness to this that I call on Flosi, or that man who has to undertake the lawful defence which he has handed over to him, to begin his defence to this suit which I have set on foot against him, for now all the steps and proofs have been brought forward which belong by law to this suit; all witness borne, the finding of the inquest uttered and brought in, witness taken to the finding, and to all the steps which have gone before; but if any such thing arises in their lawful defence which I need to turn into a suit against them, then I claim the right to set that suit on foot against them. I bid this my lawful bidding before the court, so that the judges may hear."

"It gladdens me now, Eyjolf," said Flosi, "in my heart to think what a wry face they will make, and how their pates will tingle when thou bringest forward our defence."

Chapter 142
Of Eyjolf Bolverk's Son

Then Eyjolf Bolverk's son went before the court, and took witness to this—

"I take witness that this is a lawful defence in this cause, that ye have pleaded the suit in the Eastfirthers' Court, when ye ought to have pleaded it in the Northlanders' Court; for Flosi has declared himself one of the Thingmen of Askel the priest; and here now are those two witnesses who were by, and who will bear witness that Flosi handed over his priesthood to his brother Thorgeir, but afterwards declared himself one of Askel the priest's Thingmen. I take witness to this for my own part, and for those who may need to make use of it."

Again Eyjolf took witness — "I take witness," he said, "to this, that I bid Mord who pleads this suit, or the next of kin, to listen to my oath, and to my declaration of the defence which I am about to bring forward; I bid him by a lawful bidding before the court, so that the judges may hear me".

Again Eyjolf took witness —

"I take witness to this, that I swear an oath on the book, a lawful oath, and say it before God, that I will so defend this cause, in the most truthful, and most just, and most lawful way, so far as I know, and so fulfil all lawful duties which belong to me at this Thing."

Then Eyjolf said —

"These two men I take to witness that I bring forward this lawful defence that this suit was pleaded in another Quarter Court, than that in which it ought to have been pleaded; and I say that for this sake their suit has come to naught; I utter this defence in this shape before the Eastfirthers' Court."

After that he let all the witness be brought forward which belonged to the defence, and then he took witness to all the steps in the defence to prove that they had all been duly taken.

After that Eyjolf again took witness and said —

"I take witness to this, that I forbid the judges, by a lawful protest before the priest, to utter judgment in the suit of Mord and his friends, for now a lawful defence has been brought before the court. I forbid you by a protest made before a priest; by a full, fair, and binding protest; as I have a right to forbid you by the common custom of the Althing, and by the law of the land."

After that he called on the judges to pronounce for the defence.

Then Asgrim and his friends brought on the other suits for the Burning, and those suits took their course.

Chapter 143
The Counsel of Thorhall Asgrim's Son

Now Asgrim and his friends sent a man to Thorhall, and let him be told in what a strait they had come.

"Too far off was I now," answers Thorhall, "for this cause might still not have taken this turn if I had been by. I now see their course that they must mean to summon you to the Fifth Court for contempt of the Thing. They must also mean to divide the Eastfirthers' Court in the suit for the Burning, so that no judgment may be given, for now they behave so as to show that they will stay at no ill. Now shalt thou go back to them as quickly as thou canst, and say that Mord must summon them both, both Flosi and Eyjolf, for having brought money into the Fifth Court, and make it a case of lesser outlawry. Then he shall summon them with a second summons for that they have brought forward that witness which had nothing to do with their cause, and so were guilty of contempt of the Thing; and tell them that I say this, that if two suits for lesser outlawry hang over one and the same man, that he shall be adjudged a thorough outlaw at once. And for this ye must set your suits on foot first, that then ye will first go to trial and judgment."

Now the messenger went his way back and told Mord and Asgrim.

After that they went to the Hill of Laws, and Mord Valgard's son took witness.

"I take witness to this that I summon Flosi Thord's son, for that he gave money for his help here at the Thing to Eyjolf Bolverk's son. I say that he ought on this charge to be made a guilty outlaw, for this sake alone to be forwarded or to be allowed the right of frithstow [sanctuary], if his fine and bail are brought forward at the execution levied on his house and goods, but else to become a thorough outlaw. I say all his goods are forfeited, half to me and half to the men of the Quarter who have the right by law to take his goods after he has been outlawed. I summon this cause before the Fifth Court, whither the cause ought to come by law; I summon it to be pleaded now and to full outlawry. I summon with a lawful summons. I summon in the hearing of all men at the Hill of Laws."

With a like summons he summoned Eyjolf Bolverk's son, for that he had taken and received the money, and he summoned him for that sake to the Fifth Court.

Again a second time he summoned Flosi and Eyjolf, for that sake that they had brought forward that witness at the Thing which had nothing lawfully to do with the cause of the parties, and had so been guilty of contempt of the Thing; and he laid the penalty for that at lesser outlawry.

Then they went away to the Court of Laws, there the Fifth Court was then set.

Now when Mord and Asgrim had gone away, then the judges in the East-firthers' Court could not agree how they should give judgment, for some of them wished to give judgment for Flosi, but some for Mord and Asgrim. Then Flosi and Eyjolf tried to divide the court, and there they stayed, and lost time over that while the summoning at the Hill of Laws was going on. A little while after Flosi and Eyjolf were told that they had been summoned at the Hill of Laws into the Fifth Court, each of them with two summons. Then Eyjolf said —

"In an evil hour have we loitered here while they have been before us in quickness of summoning. Now hath come out Thorhall's cunning, and no man is his match in wit. Now they have the first right to plead their cause before the court, and that was everything for them; but still we will go to the Hill of Laws, and set our suit on foot against them, though that will now stand us in little stead."

Then they fared to the Hill of Laws, and Eyjolf summoned them for contempt of the Thing.

After that they went to the Fifth Court.

Now we must say that when Mord and Asgrim came to the Fifth Court, Mord took witness and bade them listen to his oath and the declaration of his suit, and to all those proofs and steps which he meant to bring forward against Flosi and Eyjolf. He bade them by a lawful bidding before the court, so that the judges could hear him across the court.

In the Fifth Court vouchers had to follow the oaths of the parties, and they had to take an oath after them.

Mord took witness.

"I take witness," he said, "to this, that I take a Fifth Court oath. I pray God so to help me in this light and in the next, as I shall plead this suit as I know to be most truthful, and just, and lawful. I believe with all my heart that Flosi is truly guilty in this suit, if I may bring forward my proofs; and I have not brought money into this court in this suit, and I will not bring it. I have not taken money, and I will not take it, neither for a lawful nor for an unlawful end."

The men who were Mord's vouchers then went two of them before the court, and took witness to this —

"We take witness that we take an oath on the book, a lawful oath; we pray

God so to help us two in this light and in the next, as we lay it on our honour that we believe with all our hearts that Mord will so plead this suit as he knows to be most truthful, and most just, and most lawful, and that he hath not brought money into this court in this suit to help himself, and that he will not offer it, and that he hath not taken money, nor will he take it, either for a lawful or unlawful end."

Mord had summoned nine neighbours who lived next to the Thingfield on the inquest in the suit, and then Mord took witness, and declared those four suits which he had set on foot against Flosi and Eyjolf; and Mord used all those words in his declaration that he had used in his summons. He declared his suits for outlawry in the same shape before the Fifth Court as he had uttered them when he summoned the defendants.

Mord took witness, and bade those nine neighbours on the inquest to take their seats west on the river-bank.

Mord took witness again, and bade Flosi and Eyjolf to challenge the inquest.

They went up to challenge the inquest, and looked narrowly at them, but could get none of them set aside; then they went away as things stood, and were very ill pleased with their case.

Then Mord took witness, and bade those nine neighbours whom he had before called on the inquest, to utter their finding, and to bring it in either for or against Flosi.

Then the neighbours on Mord's inquest came before the court, and one uttered the finding, but all the rest confirmed it by their consent. They had all taken the Fifth Court oath, and they brought in Flosi as truly guilty in the suit, and brought in their finding against him. They brought it in in such a shape before the Fifth Court over the head of the same man over whose head Mord had already declared his suit. After that they brought in all those findings which they were bound to bring in in all the other suits, and all was done in lawful form.

Eyjolf Bolverk's son and Flosi watched to find a flaw in the proceedings, but could get nothing done.

Then Mord Valgard's son took witness. "I take witness," said he, "to this, that these nine neighbours whom I called on these suits which I have had hanging over the heads of Flosi Thord's son, and Eyjolf Bolverk's son, have now uttered their finding, and have brought them in truly guilty in these suits."

He took this witness for his own part.

Again Mord took witness.

"I take witness," he said, "to this, that I bid Flosi Thord's son, or that other man who has taken his lawful defence in hand, now to begin their defence; for now all the steps and proofs have been brought forward in the suit, summons to listen to oaths, oaths taken, suit declared, witness taken to the summons, neighbours called on to take their seats on the inquest, defendant called on to challenge the inquest, finding uttered, witness taken to the finding."

He took this witness to all the steps that had been taken in the suit.

Then that man stood up over whose head the suit had been declared and pleaded, and summed up the case. He summed up first how Mord had bade them listen to his oath, and to his declaration of the suit, and to all the steps and proofs in it; then he summed up next how Mord took his oath and his vouchers theirs; then he summed up how Mord pleaded his suit, and used the very words in his summing up that Mord had before used in declaring and pleading his suit, and which he had used in his summons, and he said that the suit came before the Fifth Court in the same shape as it was when he uttered it at the summoning. Then he summed up that men had borne witness to the summoning, and repeated all those words that Mord had used in his summons, and which they had used in bearing their witness, "and which I now," he said, "have used in my summing up, and they bore their witness in the same shape before the Fifth Court as he uttered them at the summoning". After that he summed up that Mord bade the neighbours on the inquest to take their seats, then he told next of all how he bade Flosi to challenge the inquest, or that man who had undertaken this lawful defence for him; then he told how the neighbours went to the court, and uttered their finding, and brought in Flosi truly guilty in the suit, and how they brought in the finding of an inquest of nine men in that shape before the Fifth Court. Then he summed up how Mord took witness to all the steps in the suit, and how he had bidden the defendant to begin his defence.

After that Mord Valgard's son took witness. "I take witness," he said, "to this, that I forbid Flosi Thord's son, or that other man who has undertaken the lawful defence for him, to set up his defence; for now are all the steps taken which belong to the suit, when the case has been summed up and the proofs repeated."

After that the foreman added these words of Mord to his summing up.

Then Mord took witness, and prayed the judges to give judgment in this suit.

Then Gizur the White said, "Thou wilt have to do more yet, Mord, for four twelves can have no right to pass judgment."

Now Flosi said to Eyjolf, "What counsel is to be taken now?"

Then Eyjolf said, "Now we must make the best of a bad business; but still, we will bide our time, for now I guess that they will make a false step in their suit, for Mord prayed for judgment at once in the suit, but they ought to call and set aside six men out of the court, and after that they ought to offer us to call and set aside six other men, but we will not do that, for then they ought to call and set aside those six men, and they will perhaps overlook that; then all their case has come to naught if they do not do that, for three twelves have to judge in every cause".

"Thou art a wise man, Eyjolf," said Flosi, "so that few can come nigh thee."

Mord Valgard's son took witness.

"I take witness," he said, "to this, that I call and set aside these six men out of the court" — and named them all by name — "I do not allow you to sit in the court; I call you out and set you aside by the rightful custom of the Althing, and the law of the land."

After that he offered Eyjolf and Flosi, before witnesses, to call out by name and set aside other six men, but Flosi and Eyjolf would not call them out.

Then Mord made them pass judgment in the cause; but when the judgment was given, Eyjolf took witness, and said that all their judgment had come to naught, and also everything else that had been done, and his ground was that three twelves and one half had judged, when three only ought to have given judgment.

"And now we will follow up our suits before the Fifth Court," said Eyjolf, "and make them outlaws."

Then Gizur the White said to Mord Valgard's son —

"Thou hast made a very great mistake in taking such a false step, and this is great ill-luck; but what counsel shall we now take, kinsman Asgrim?" says Gizur.

Then Asgrim said — "Now we will send a man to my son Thorhall, and know what counsel he will give us."

Chapter 144
Battle at the Althing

Now Snorri the priest hears how the causes stood, and then he begins to draw up his men in array below the "Great Rift," between it and Hadbooth, and laid down beforehand to his men how they were to behave.

Now the messenger comes to Thorhall Asgrim's son, and tells him how things stood, and how Mord Valgard's son and his friends would all be made outlaws, and the suits for manslaughter be brought to naught.

But when he heard that, he was so shocked at it that he could not utter a word. He jumped up then from his bed, and clutched with both hands his spear, Skarphedinn's gift, and drove it through his foot; then flesh clung to the spear, and the eye of the boil too, for he had cut it clean out of the foot, but a torrent of blood and matter poured out, so that it fell in a stream along the floor. Now he went out of the booth unhalting, and walked so hard that the messenger could not keep up with him, and so he goes until he came to the Fifth Court. There he met Grim the red, Flosi's kinsman, and as soon as ever they met, Thorhall thrust at him with the spear, and smote him on the shield and clove it in twain, but the spear passed right through him, so that the point came out between his shoulders. Thorhall cast him off his spear.

Then Kari Solmund's son caught sight of that, and said to Asgrim —

"Here, now, is come Thorhall thy son, and has straightway slain a man, and this is a great shame, if he alone shall have the heart to avenge the Burning."

"That shall not be," says Asgrim, "but let us turn on them now."

Then there was a mighty cry all over the host, and then they shouted their war-cries.

Flosi and his friends then turned against their foes, and both sides egged on their men fast.

Kari Solmund's son turned now thither where Arni Kol's son and Hallbjorn the strong were in front, and as soon as ever Hallbjorn saw Kari, he made a blow at him, and aimed at his leg, but Kari leapt up into the air, and Hallbjorn missed him. Kari turned on Arni Kol's son and cut at him, and smote him on the shoulder, and cut asunder the shoulder blade and collar bone, and the blow went right down into his breast, and Arni fell down dead at once to earth.

After that he hewed at Hallbjorn and caught him on the shield, and the blow passed through the shield, and so down and cut off his great toe. Holmstein hurled a spear at Kari, but he caught it in the air, and sent it back, and it was a man's death in Flosi's band.

Thorgeir Craggeir came up to where Hallbjorn the strong was in front, and Thorgeir made such a spear-thrust at him with his left hand that Hallbjorn fell before it, and had hard work to get on his feet again, and turned away from the fight there and then. Then Thorgeir met Thorwalld Kettle rumble's son, and hewed at him at once with the axe, "the ogress of war," which Skarphedinn had owned. Thorwalld threw his shield before him, and Thorgeir hewed the shield and cleft it from top to bottom, but the upper horn of the axe made its way into his breast, and passed into his trunk, and Thorwalld fell and was dead at once.

Now it must be told how Asgrim Ellidagrim's son, and Thorhall his son, Hjallti Skeggi's son, and Gizur the White, made an onslaught where Flosi and the sons of Sigfus, and the other Burners were; then there was a very hard fight, and the end of it was that they pressed on so hard, that Flosi and his men gave way before them. Gudmund the powerful, and Mord Valgard's son, and Thorgeir Craggeir, made their onslaught where the Axefirthers and Eastfirthers, and the men of Reykdale stood, and there too there was a very hard fight.

Kari Solmund's son came up where Bjarni Broddhelgi's son had the lead. Kari caught up a spear and thrust at him, and the blow fell on his shield. Bjarni slipped the shield on one side of him, else it had gone straight through him. Then he cut at Kari and aimed at his leg, but Kari drew back his leg and turned short round on his heel, and Bjarni missed him. Kari cut at once at him, and then a man ran forward and threw his shield before Bjarni. Kari cleft the shield in twain, and the point of the sword caught his thigh, and ripped up the whole leg down to the ankle. That man fell there and then, and was ever after a cripple so long as he lived.

Then Kari clutched his spear with both hands, and turned on Bjarni and thrust at him; he saw he had no other chance but to throw himself down side-long away from the blow, but as soon as ever Bjarni found his feet, away he fell back out of the fight.

Thorgeir Craggeir and Gizur the White fell on there where Holmstein the son of Bersi the wise, and Thorkel Geiti's son were leaders, and the end of the struggle was, that Holmstein and Thorkel gave way, and then arose a mighty hooting after them from the men of Gudmund the powerful.

Thorwalld Tjorfi's son of Lightwater got a great wound; he was shot in the forearm, and men thought that Halldor Gudmund the powerful's son had hurled the spear, but he bore that wound about with him all his life long, and got no atonement for it.

Now there was a mighty throng. But though we hear tell of some of the deeds that were done, still there are far many more of which men have handed down no stories.

Flosi had told them that they should make for the stronghold in the Great Rift if they were worsted, "for there," said he, "they will only be able to attack us on one side". But the band which Hall of the Side and his son Ljot led, had fallen away out of the fight before the onslaught of that father and son, Asgrim and Thorhall. They turned down east of Axewater, and Hall said —

"This is a sad state of things when the whole host of men at the Thing fight, and I would, kinsman Ljot, that we begged us help even though that be brought against us by some men, and that we part them. Thou shalt wait for me at the foot of the bridge, and I will go to the booths and beg for help."

"If I see," said Ljot, "that Flosi and his men need help from our men, then I will at once run up and aid them."

"Thou wilt do in that as thou pleasest," says Hall, "but I pray thee to wait for me here."

Now flight breaks out in Flosi's band, and they all fly west across Axewater; but Asgrim and Gizur the White went after them and all their host. Flosi and his men turned down between the river and the Outwork booth. Snorri the priest had drawn up his men there in array, so thick that they could not pass that way, and Snorri the priest called out then to Flosi —

"Why are ye in such haste, or who chase you?"

"Thou askest not this," answered Flosi, "because thou dost not know it already; but whose fault is it that we cannot get to the stronghold in the Great Rift?"

"It is not my fault," says Snorri, "but it is quite true that I know whose fault it is, and I will tell thee if thou wilt; it is the fault of Thorwalld cropbeard and Kol."

They were both then dead, but they had been the worst men in all Flosi's band.

Again Snorri said to his men —

"Now do both, cut at them and thrust at them, and drive them away hence, they will then hold out but a short while here, if the others attack them from below; but then ye shall not go after them, but let both sides shift for themselves."

The son of Skapti Thorod's son was Thorstein gapemouth, as was written before, he was in the battle with Gudmund the powerful, his father-in-law, and as soon as Skapti knew that, he went to the booth of Snorri the priest, and meant to beg for help to part them; but just before he had got as far as the door of Snorri's booth, there the battle was hottest of all. Asgrim and his friends and his men were just coming up thither, and then Thorhall said to his father Asgrim —

"See there now is Skapti Thorod's son, father."

"I see him, kinsman," said Asgrim, and then he shot a spear at Skapti, and struck him just below where the calf was fattest, and so through both his legs. Skapti fell at the blow, and could not get up again, and the only counsel they could take who were by, was to drag Skapti flat on his face into the booth of a turf-cutter.

Then Asgrim and his men came up so fast that Flosi and his men gave way before them south along the river to the booths of the men of Modruvale. There there was a man outside one booth whose name was Solvi; he was boiling broth in a great kettle, and had just then taken the meat out, and the broth was boiling as hotly as it could.

Solvi cast his eyes on the Eastfirthers us they fled, and they were then just over against him, and then he said — "Can all these cowards who fly here be Eastfirthers, and yet Thorkel Geiti's son, he ran by as fast as any one of them, and very great lies have been told about him when men say that he is all heart, but now no one ran faster than he".

Hallbjorn the strong was near by them, and said —

"Thou shalt not have it to say that we are all cowards."

And with that he caught hold of him, and lifted him up aloft, and thrust him head down into the broth-kettle. Solvi died at once; but then a rush was made at Hallbjorn himself, and he had to turn and fly.

Flosi threw a spear at Bruni Haflidi's son, and caught him at the waist, and that was his bane; he was one of Gudmund the powerful's band.

Thorstein Hlenni's son took the spear out of the wound, and hurled it back at Flosi, and hit him on the leg, and he got a great wound and fell; he rose up again at once.

Then they passed on to the Waterfirther's booth, and then Hall and Ljot came from the east across the river, with all their band; but just when they came to the lava, a spear was hurled out of the band of Gudmund the powerful, and it struck Ljot in the middle, and he fell down dead at once; and it was never known surely who had done that manslaughter.

Flosi and his men turned up round the Waterfirther's booth, and then Thorgeir Craggeir said to Kari Solmund's son —

"Look, yonder now is Eyjolf Bolverk's son, if thou hast a mind to pay him off for the ring."

"That I ween is not far from my mind," says Kari, and snatched a spear from a man, and hurled it at Eyjolf, and it struck him in the waist, and went through him, and Eyjolf then fell dead to earth.

Then there was a little lull in the battle, and then Snorri the priest came up with his band, and Skapti was there in his company, and they ran in between them, and so they could not get at one another to fight.

Then Hall threw in his people with theirs, and was for parting them there and then, and so a truce was set, and was to be kept throughout the Thing, and then the bodies were laid out and borne to the church, and the wounds of those men were bound up who were hurt.

The day after men went to the Hill of Laws. Then Hall of the Side stood up and asked for a hearing, and got it at once; and he spoke thus —

"Here there have been hard happenings in lawsuits and loss of life at the Thing, and now I will show again that I am little-hearted, for I will now ask Asgrim and the others who take the lead in these suits, that they grant us an atonement on even terms;" and so he goes on with many fair words.

Kari Solmund's son said —

"Though all others take an atonement in their quarrels, yet will I take no atonement in my quarrel; for ye will wish to weigh these manslayings against the Burning, and we cannot bear that."

In the same way spoke Thorgeir Craggeir.

Then Skapti Thorod's son stood up and said —

"Better had it been for thee, Kari, not to have run away from thy father-in-law and thy brothers-in-law, than now to sneak out of this atonement."

Then Kari sang these verses —

> Warrior wight that weapon wieldest
> Spare thy speering why we fled,
> Oft for less falls hail of battle,
> Forth we fled to wreak revenge;
> Who was he, faint-hearted foeman,
> Who, when tongues of steel sung high,
> Stole beneath the booth for shelter,
> While his beard blushed red for shame?

> Many fetters Skapti fettered
> When the men, the Gods of fight,
> From the fray fared all unwilling
> Where the skald scarce held his shield;
> Then the suttlers dragged the lawyer
> Stout in scolding to their booth,
> Laid him low amongst the riffraff,
> How his heart then quaked for fear.

> Men who skim the main on sea stag
> Well in this ye showed your sense,
> Making game about the Burning,
> Mocking Helgi, Grim, and Njal;
> Now the moor round rocky Swinestye,
> As men run and shake their shields,
> With another grunt shall rattle

When this Thing is past and gone.

Then there was great laughter. Snorri the priest smiled, and sang this between his teeth, but so that many heard —

> Skill hath Skapti us to tell
> Whether Asgrim's shaft flew well;
> Holmstein hurried swift to flight,
> Thorstein turned him soon to fight.

Now men burst out in great fits of laughter.

Then Hall of the Side said —

"All men know what a grief I have suffered in the loss of my son Ljot; many will think that he would be valued dearest of all those men who have fallen here; but I will do this for the sake of an atonement — I will put no price on my son, and yet will come forward and grant both pledges and peace to those who are my adversaries. I beg thee, Snorri the priest, and other of the best men, to bring this about, that there may be an atonement between us."

Now he sits him down, and a great hum in his favour followed, and all praised his gentleness and good-will.

Then Snorri the priest stood up and made a long and clever speech, and begged Asgrim and the others who took the lead in the quarrel to look towards an atonement.

Then Asgrim said —

"I made up my mind when Flosi made an inroad on my house that I would never be atoned with him; but now Snorri the priest, I will take an atonement from him for thy word's sake and other of our friends."

In the same way spoke Thorleif crow and Thorgrim the big, that they were willing to be atoned, and they urged in every way their brother Thorgeir Craggeir to take an atonement also; but he hung back, and says he would never part from Kari.

Then Gizur the White said —

"Now Flosi must see that he must make his choice, whether he will be atoned on the understanding that some will be out of the atonement."

Flosi says he will take that atonement; "and methinks it is so much the better," he says, "that I have fewer good men and true against me".

Then Gudmund the powerful said —

"I will offer to hansel peace on my behalf for the slayings that have happened here at the Thing, on the understanding that the suit for the Burning is not to fall to the ground."

In the same way spoke Gizur the White and Hjallti Skeggi's son, Asgrim Ellidagrim's son and Mord Valgard's son.

In this way the atonement came about, and then hands were shaken on it, and twelve men were to utter the award; and Snorri the priest was the chief man in the award, and others with him. Then the manslaughters were set off the one against the other, and those men who were over and above were paid for in fines. They also made an award in the suit about the Burning.

Njal was to be atoned for with a triple fine, and Bergthora with two. The slaying of Skarphedinn was to be set off against that of Hauskuld the Whiteness priest. Both Grim and Helgi were to be paid for with double fines; and one full man-fine should be paid for each of those who had been burnt in the house.

No atonement was taken for the slaying of Thord Kari's son.

It was also in the award that Flosi and all the Burners should go abroad into banishment, and none of them was to sail the same summer unless he chose; but if he did not sail abroad by the time that three winters were spent, then he and all the Burners were to become thorough outlaws. And it was also said that their outlawry might be proclaimed either at the Harvest-Thing or Spring-Thing, whichever men chose; and Flosi was to stay abroad three winters.

As for Gunnar Lambi's son, and Grani Gunnar's son. Glum Hilldir's son, and Kol Thorstein's son, they were never to be allowed to come back.

Then Flosi was asked if he would wish to have a price put upon his wound, but he said he would not take bribes for his hurt.

Eyjolf Bolverk's son had no fine awarded for him, for his unfairness and wrongfulness.

And now the settlement and atonement was handselled, and was well kept afterwards.

Asgrim and his friends gave Snorri the priest good gifts, and he had great honour from these suits.

Skapti got a fine for his hurt.

Gizur the White, and Hjallti Skeggi's son, and Asgrim Ellidagrim's son, asked Gudmund the powerful to come and see them at home. He accepted the bidding, and each of them gave him a gold ring.

Now Gudmund rides home north, and had praise from every man for the part he had taken in these quarrels.

Thorgeir Craggeir asked Kari to go along with him, but yet first of all they rode with Gudmund right up to the fells north. Kari gave Gudmund a golden brooch, but Thorgeir gave him a silver belt, and each was the greatest treasure. So they parted with the utmost friendship, and Gudmund is out of this story.

Kari and Thorgeir rode south from the fell, and down to the Rapes, and so to Thurso-water.

Flosi, and the Burners along with him, rode east to Fleetlithe, and he allowed the sons of Sigfus to settle their affairs at home. Then Flosi heard that Thorgeir and Kari had ridden north with Gudmund the powerful, and so the Burners thought that Kari and his friend must mean to stay in the north country; and then the sons of Sigfus asked leave to go east under Eyjafell to get in their money, for they had money out on call at Headbrink. Flosi gave them leave to do that, but still bade them be ware of themselves, and be as short a time about it as they could.

Then Flosi rode up by Godaland, and so north of Eyjafell Jokul, and did not draw bridle before he came home east to Swinefell.

Now it must be said that Hall of the Side had suffered his son to fall without a fine, and did that for the sake of an atonement, but then the whole host of men at the Thing agreed to pay a fine for him, and the money so paid was not less than eight hundred in silver, but that was four times the price of a man; but all the others who had been with Flosi got no fines paid for their hurts, and were very ill pleased at it.

Chapter 145
Of Kari and Thorgeir

Those two, Kari Solmund's and Thorgeir Craggeir, rode that day east across Markfleet, and so on east to Selialandsmull. They found there some women. The wives knew them, and said to them —

"Ye two are less wanton than the sons of Sigfus yonder, but still ye fare unwarily."

"Why do ye talk thus of the sons of Sigfus, or what do ye know about them?"

"They were last night," they said, "at Raufarfell, and meant to get to Myrdale to-night, but still we thought they must have some fear of you, for they asked when he would be likely to come home."

Then Kari and Thorgeir went on their way and spurred their horses.

"What shall we lay down for ourselves to do now," said Thorgeir, "or what is most to thy mind? Wilt thou that we ride on their track?"

"I will not hinder this," answers Kari, "nor will I say what ought to be done, for it may often be that those live Long who are slain with words alone; but I well know what thou meanest to take on thyself, thou must mean to take on thy hands eight men, and after all that is less than it was when thou slewest those seven in the sea-crags, and let thyself down by a rope to get at them; but it is the way with all you kinsmen, that ye always wish to be doing some famous feat, and now I can do no less than stand by thee and have my share in the story. So now we two alone will ride after them, for I see that thou hast so made up thy mind."

After that they rode east by the upper way, and did not pass by Holt, for Thorgeir would not that any blame should be laid at his brother's door for what might be done.

Then they rode east to Myrdale, and there they met a man who had turf-panniers on his horse. He began to speak thus —

"Too few men, messmate Thorgeir, hast thou now in thy company."

"How is that?" says Thorgeir.

"Why," said the other, "because the prey is now before thy hand. The sons of Sigfus rode by a while ago, and mean to sleep the whole day east in Carlinedale, for they mean to go no farther to-night than to Headbrink."

After that they rode on their way east on Arnstacks heath, and there is nothing to be told of their journey before they came to Carlinedale-water.

The stream was high, and now they rode up along the river, for they saw their horses with saddles. They rode now thitherward, and saw that there were men asleep in a dell and their spears were standing upright in the ground a little below them. They took the spears from them, and threw them into the river.

Then Thorgeir said —

"Wilt thou that we wake them?"

"Thou hast not asked this," answers Kari, "because thou hast not already made up thy mind not to fall on sleeping men, and so to slay a shameful manslaughter."

After that they shouted to them, and then they all awoke and grasped at their arms.

They did not fall on them till they were armed.

Thorgeir Craggeir runs thither where Thorkel Sigfus' son stood, and just then a man ran behind his back, but before he could do Thorgeir any hurt, Thorgeir lifted the axe, "the ogress of war," with both hands, and dashed the hammer of the axe with a back-blow into the head of him that stood behind him, so that his skull was shattered to small bits.

"Slain is this one," said Thorgeir; and down the man fell at once, and was dead.

But when he dashed the axe forward, he smote Thorkel on the shoulder, and hewed it off, arm and all.

Against Kari came Mord Sigfus' son, and Sigmund Sigfus' son, and Lambi Sigurd's son; the last ran behind Kari's back, and thrust at him with a spear; Kari caught sight of him, and leapt up as the blow fell, and stretched his legs far apart, and so the blow spent itself on the ground, but Kari jumped down on the spear-shaft, and snapped it in sunder. He had a spear in one hand, and a sword in the other, but no shield. He thrust with the right hand at Sigmund Sigfus' son, and smote him on his breast, and the spear came out between his shoulders, and down he fell and was dead at once. With his left hand he made a cut at Mord, and smote him on the hip, and cut it asunder, and his backbone too; he fell flat on his lace, and was dead at once.

After that he turned sharp round on his heel like a whipping-top, and made at Lambi Sigurd's son, but he took the only way to save himself, and that was by running away as hard as he could.

Now Thorgeir turns against Leidolf the strong, and each hewed at the other at the same moment, and Leidolf's blow was so great that it shore off that part of the shield on which it fell.

Thorgeir had hewn with "the ogress of war," holding it with both hands, and the lower horn fell on the shield and clove it in twain, but the upper caught the collar bone and cut it in two, and tore on down into the breast and trunk. Kari came up just then, and cut off Leidolf's leg at mid-thigh, and then Leidolf fell and died at once.

Kettle of the Mark said — "We will now run for our horses, for we cannot hold our own here, for the overbearing strength of these men".

Then they ran for their horses, and leapt on their backs; and Thorgeir said —

"Wilt thou that we chase them? if so, we shall yet slay some of them."

"He rides last," says Kari, "whom I would not wish to slay, and that is Kettle of the Mark, for we have two sisters to wife; and besides, he has behaved best of all of them as yet in our quarrels."

Then they got on their horses, and rode till they came home to Holt. Then Thorgeir made his brothers fare away east to Skoga, for they had another farm there, and because Thorgeir would not that his brothers should be called truce-breakers.

Then Thorgeir kept many men there about him, so that there were never fewer than thirty fighting men there.

Then there was great joy there, and men thought Thorgeir had grown much greater, and pushed himself on; both he and Kari too. Men long kept in mind this hunting of theirs, how they two rode upon fifteen men and slew those five, but put those ten to flight who got away.

Now it is to be told of Kettle, that they rode as they best might till they came home to Swinefell, and told how bad their journey had been.

Flosi said it was only what was to be looked for; "and this is a warning that ye should never do the like again".

Flosi was the merriest of men, and the best of hosts, and it is so said that he had most of the chieftain in him of all the men of his time.

He was at home that summer, and the winter too.

But that winter, after Yule, Hall of the Side came from the east, and Kol his son. Flosi was glad at his coming, and they often talked about the matter of the Burning. Flosi said they had already paid a great fine, and Hall said it was pretty much what he had guessed would come of Flosi's and his friends' quarrel. Then he asked him what counsel he thought best to be taken, and Hall answers —

"The counsel I give is, that thou beest atoned with Thorgeir if there be a choice, and yet he will be hard to bring to take any atonement."

"Thinkest thou that the manslaughters will then be brought to an end?" asks Flosi.

"I do not think so," says Hall; "but you will have to do with fewer foes if Kari be left alone; but if thou art not atoned with Thorgeir, then that will be thy bane."

"What atonement shall we offer him?" asks Flosi.

"You will all think that atonement hard," says Hall, "which he will take, for he will not hear of an atonement unless he be not called on to pay any fine for what he has just done, but he will have fines for Njal and his sons, so far as his third share goes."

"That is a hard atonement," says Flosi.

"For thee at least," says Hall, "that atonement is not hard, for thou hast not the blood-feud after the sons of Sigfus; their brothers have the blood-feud, and Hamond the halt after his son; but thou shalt now get an atonement from Thorgeir, for I will now ride to his house with thee, and Thorgeir will in anywise receive me well; but no man of those who are in this quarrel will dare to sit in his house on Fleetlithe if they are out of the atonement, for that will be their bane; and, indeed, with Thorgeir's turn of mind, it is only what must be looked for."

Now the sons of Sigfus were sent for, and they brought this business before them; and the end of their speech was, on the persuasion of Hall, that they all thought what he said right, and were ready to be atoned.

Grani Gunnar's son and Gunnar Lambi's son said —

"It will be in our power, if Kari be left alone behind, to take care that he be not less afraid of us than we of him."

"Easier said than done," says Hall, "and ye will find it a dear bargain to deal with him. Ye will have to pay a heavy fine before you have done with him."

After that they ceased speaking about it.

Chapter 146
The Award of Atonement with Thorgeir Craggeir

Hall of the Side and his son Kol, seven of them in all, rode west over Loomnip's Sand, and so west over Arnstacksheath, and did not draw bridle till they came into Myrdale. There they asked whether Thorgeir would be at home at Holt, and they were told that they would find him at home.

The men asked whither Hall meant to go.

"Thither to Holt," he said.

They said they were sure he went on a good errand.

He stayed there some while and baited their horses, and after that they mounted their horses and rode to Solheim about even, and they were there that night, but the day-after they rode to Holt.

Thorgeir was out of doors, and Kari too, and their men, for they had seen Hall's coming. He rode in a blue cape, and had a little axe studded with silver in his hand; but when they came into the "town," Thorgeir went to meet him, and helped him off his horse, and both he and Kari kissed him and led him in between them into the sitting-room, and sate him down in the high seat on the dais, and they asked him tidings about many things.

He was there that night. Next morning Hall raised the question of the atonement with Thorgeir, and told him what terms they offered him; and he spoke about them with many fair and kindly words.

"It may be well known to thee," answers Thorgeir, "that I said I would take no atonement from the Burners."

"That was quite another matter then," says Hall; "ye were then wroth with fight, and, besides, ye have done great deeds in the way of manslaying since."

"I daresay ye think so," says Thorgeir, "but what atonement do ye offer to Kari?"

"A fitting atonement shall be offered him," says Hall, "if he will take it."

Then Kari said —

"I pray this of thee, Thorgeir, that thou wilt be atoned, for thy lot cannot be better than good."

"Methinks," says Thorgeir, "it is ill done to take an atonement, and sunder myself from thee, unless thou takest the same atonement as I."

"I will not take any atonement," says Kari, "but yet I say that we have avenged the Burning; but my son, I say, is still unavenged, and I mean to take that on myself alone, and see what I can get done."

But Thorgeir would take no atonement before Kari said that he would take it ill if he were not atoned. Then Thorgeir handselled a truce to Flosi and his men, as a step to a meeting for atonement; but Hall did the same on behalf of Flosi and the sons of Sigfus.

But ere they parted, Thorgeir gave Hall a gold ring and a scarlet cloak, but Kari gave him a silver brooch, and there were hung to it four crosses of gold. Hall thanked them kindly for their gifts, and rode away with the greatest honour. He did not draw bridle till he came to Swinefell, and Flosi gave him a hearty welcome. Hall told Flosi all about his errand and the talk he had with Thorgeir, and also that Thorgeir would not take the atonement till Kari told him he would quarrel with him if he did not take it; but that Kari would take no atonement.

"There are few men like Kari," said Flosi, "and I would that my mind were shapen altogether like his."

Hall and Kol stayed there some while, and afterwards they rode west at the time agreed on to the meeting for atonement, and met at Headbrink, as had been settled between them.

Then Thorgeir came to meet them from the west, and then they talked over their atonement, and all went off as Hall had said.

Before the atonement, Thorgeir said that Kari should still have the right to be at his house all the same if he chose.

"And neither side shall do the others any harm at my house; and I will not have the trouble of gathering in the fines from each of the Burners; but my will is that Flosi alone shall be answerable for them to me, but he must get them in from his followers. My will also is that all that award which was made at the Thing about the Burning shall be kept and held to; and my will also is, Flosi, that thou payest me up my third share in unclipped coin."

Flosi went quickly into all these terms.

Thorgeir neither gave up the banishment nor the outlawry.

Now Flosi and Hall rode home east, and then Hall said to Flosi —

"Keep this atonement well, son-in-law, both as to going abroad and the pilgrimage to Rome, and the fines, and then thou wilt be thought a brave man, though thou hast stumbled into this misdeed, if thou fulfillest handsomely all that belongs to it."

Flosi said it should be so.

Now Hall rode home east, but Flosi rode home to Swinefell, and was at home afterwards.

Chapter 147
Kari comes to Bjorn's House in the Mark

Thorgeir Craggeir rode home from the peace-meeting, and Kari asked whether the atonement had come about. Thorgeir said that they now fully atoned.

Then Kari took his horse and was for riding away.

"Thou hast no need to ride away," says Thorgeir, "for it was laid down in our atonement that thou shouldst be here as before if thou chosest."

"It shall not be so, cousin, for as soon as ever I slay a man they will be sure to say that thou wert in the plot with me, and I will not have that; but I wish this, that thou wouldst let me hand over in trust to thee my goods, and the estates of me and my wife Helga Njal's daughter, and my three daughters, and then they will not be seized by those adversaries of mine."

Thorgeir agreed to what Kari wished to ask of him, and then Thorgeir had Kari's goods handed over to him in trust.

After that Kari rode away. He had two horses and his weapons and outer clothing, and some ready money in gold and silver.

Now Kari rode west by Selialandsmull and up along Markfleet, and so on up into Thorsmark. There there are three farms all called "Mark". At the midmost farm dwelt that man whose name was Bjorn, and his surname was Bjorn the white; he was the son of Kadal, the son of Bjalfi. Bjalfi had been the freedman of Asgerda, the mother of Njal and Holt-Thorir; Bjorn had to wife Valgerda, she was the daughter of Thorbrand, the son of Asbrand. Her mother's name was Gudlauga, she was a sister of Hamond, the father of Gunnar of Lithend; she was given away to Bjorn for his money's sake, and she did not love him much, but yet they had children together, and they had enough and to spare in the house.

Bjorn was a man who was always boasting and praising himself, but his housewife thought that bad. He was sharpsighted and swift of foot.

Thither Kari turned in as a guest, and they took him by both hands, and he was there that night. But the next morning Kari said to Bjorn —

"I wish thou wouldst take me in, for I should think myself well housed here with thee. I would too that thou shouldst be with me in my journeyings, as thou art a sharpsighted, swift-footed man, and besides I think thou wouldst be dauntless in an onslaught."

"I can't blame myself," says Bjorn, "for wanting either sharp sight, or dash, or any other bravery; but no doubt thou camest hither because all thy other earths are stopped. Still, at thy prayer, Kari, I will not look on thee as an everyday man; I will surely help thee in all that thou askest."

"The trolls take thy boasting and bragging," said his housewife, "and thou shouldst not utter such stuff and silliness to any one than thyself. As for me, I will willingly give Kari meat and other good things, which I know will be useful to him; but on Bjorn's hardihood, Kari, thou shalt not trust, for I am afraid that thou wilt find it quite otherwise than he says."

"Often hast thou thrown blame upon me," said Bjorn, "but for all that I put so much faith in myself that though I am put to the trial I will never give way to any man; and the best proof of it is this, that few try a tussle with me because none dare to do so."

Kari was there some while in hiding, and few men knew of it.

Now men think that Kari must have ridden to the north country to see Gudmund the powerful, for Kari made Bjorn tell his neighbours that he had met Kari on the beaten track, and that he rode thence up into Godaland, and so north to Goose-sand, and then north to Gudmund the powerful at Modruvale.

So that story was spread over all the country.

Chapter 148
Of Flosi and the Burners

Now Flosi spoke to the Burners, his companions —

"It will no longer serve our turn to sit still, for now we shall have to think of our going abroad and of our fines, and of fulfilling our atonement as bravely as we can, and let us take a passage wherever it seems most likely to get one."

They bade him see to all that. Then Flosi said —

"We will ride east to Hornfirth; for there that ship is laid up, which is owned by Eyjolf nosy, a man from Drontheim, but he wants to take to him a wife here, and he will not get the match made unless he settles himself down here. We will buy the ship of him, for we shall have many men and little freight. The ship is big and will take us all."

Then they ceased talking of it.

But a little after they rode east, and did not stop before they came east to Bjornness in Hornfirth, and there they found Eyjolf, for he had been there as a guest that winter.

There Flosi and his men had a hearty welcome, and they were there the night. Next morning Flosi dealt with the captain for the ship, but he said he would not be hard to sell the ship if he could get what he wanted for her. Flosi asked him in what coin he wished to be paid for her; the Easterling says he wanted land for her near where he then was.

Then Eyjolf told Flosi all about his dealings with his host, and Flosi says he will pull an oar with him, so that his marriage bargain might be struck, and buy the ship of him afterwards. The Easterling was glad at that. Flosi offered him land at Borgarhaven, and now the Easterling holds on with his suit to his host when Flosi was by, and Flosi threw in a helping word, so that the bargain was brought about between them.

Flosi made over the land at Borgarhaven to the Easterling, but shook hands on the bargain for the ship. He got also from the Easterling twenty hundreds in wares, and that was also in their bargain for the land.

Now Flosi rode back home. He was so beloved by his men that their wares stood free to him to take either on loan or gift, just as he chose.

He rode home to Swinefell, and was at home a while.

Then Flosi sent Kol Thorstein's son and Gunnar Lambi's son east to Horn-firth. They were to be there by the ship, and to fit her out, and set up booths, and sack the wares, and get all things together that were needful.

Now we must tell of the sons of Sigfus how they say to Flosi that they will ride west to Fleetlithe to set their houses in order, and get wares thence, and such other things as they needed. "Kari is not there now to be guarded against," they say, "if he is in the north country as is said."

"I know not," answers Flosi, "as to such stories, whether there be any truth in what is said of Kari's journeyings; methinks, we have often been wrong in believing things which are nearer to learn than this. My counsel is that ye go many of you together, and part as little as ye can, and be as wary of yourselves as ye may. Thou, too, Kettle of the Mark, shalt bear in mind that dream which I told thee, and which thou prayedst me to hide; for many are those in thy company who were then called."

"All must come to pass as to man's life," said Kettle, "as it is foredoomed; but good go with thee for thy warning."

Now they spoke no more about it.

After that the sons of Sigfus busked them and those men with them who were meant to go with them. They were eight in all, and then they rode away, and ere they went they kissed Flosi, and he bade them farewell, and said he and some of those who rode away would not see each other more. But they would not let themselves be hindered. They rode now on their way, and Flosi said that they should take his wares in Middleland, and carry them east, and do the same in Landsbreach and Woodcombe.

After that they rode to Skaptartongue, and so on the fell, and north of Eyjafell Jokul, and down into Godaland, and so down into the woods in Thors-mark.

Bjorn of the Mark caught sight of them coming, and went at once to meet them.

Then they greeted each other well, and the sons of Sigfus asked after Kari Solmund's son.

"I met Kari," said Bjorn, "and that is now very long since; he rode hence north on Goose-sand, and meant to go to Gudmund the powerful, and methought if he were here now, he would stand in awe of you, for he seemed to be left all alone."

Grani Gunnar's son said —

"He shall stand more in awe of us yet before we have done with him, and he shall learn that as soon as ever he comes within spearthrow of us; but as for us, we do not fear him at all, now that he is all alone."

Kettle of the Mark bade them be still, and bring out no big words.

Bjorn asked when they would be coming back.

"We shall stay near a week in Fleetlithe," said they; and so they told him when they should be riding back on the fell.

With that they parted.

Now the sons of Sigfus rode to their homes, and their households were glad to see them. They were there near a week.

Now Bjorn comes home and sees Kari, and told him all about the doings of the sons of Sigfus, and their purpose.

Kari said he had shown in this great faithfulness to him, and Bjorn said —

"I should have thought there was more risk of any other man's failing in that than of me if I had pledged my help or care to any one."

"Ah," said his mistress, "but you may still be bad and yet not be so bad as to be a traitor to thy master."

Kari stayed there six nights after that.

Chapter 149
Of Kari and Bjorn

Now Kari talks to Bjorn and says —

"We shall ride east across the fell and down into Skaptartongue, and fare stealthily over Flosi's country, for I have it in my mind to get myself carried abroad east in Alftafirth."

"This is a very riskful journey," said Bjorn, "and few would have the heart to take it save thou and I."

"If thou backest Kari ill," said his housewife, "know this, that thou shalt never come afterwards into my bed, and my kinsmen shall share our goods between us."

"It is likelier, mistress," said he, "that thou wilt have to look out for something else than this if thou hast a mind to part from me; for I will bear my own witness to myself what a champion and daredevil I am when weapons clash."

Now they rode that day east on the fell to the north of the Jokul, but never on the highway, and so down into Skaptartongue, and above all the homesteads to Skaptarwater, and led their horses into a dell, but they themselves were on the look-out, and had so placed themselves that they could not be seen.

Then Kari said to Bjorn —

"What shall we do now if they ride down upon us here from the fell?"

"Are there not but two things to be done," said Bjorn; "one to ride away from them north under the crags, and so let them ride by us, or to wait and see if any of them lag behind, and then to fall on them."

They talked much about this, and one while Bjorn was for flying as fast as he could in every word he spoke, and at another for staying and fighting it out with them, and Kari thought this the greatest sport.

The sons of Sigfus rode from their homes the same day that they had named to Bjorn. They came to the Mark and knocked at the door there, and wanted to see Bjorn; but his mistress went to the door and greeted them. They asked at once for Bjorn, and she said he had ridden away down under Eyjafell, and so east under Selialandsmull, and on east to Holt, "for he has some money to call in thereabouts," she said.

They believed this, for they knew that Bjorn had money out at call there.

After that they rode east on the fell, and did not stop before they came to Skaptartongue, and so rode down along Skaptarwater, and baited their horses just where Kari had thought they would. Then they split their band. Kettle of the Mark rode east into Middleland, and eight men with him, but the others laid them down to sleep, and were not ware of aught until Kari and Bjorn came up to them. A little ness ran out there into the river; into it Kari went and took his stand, and bade Bjorn stand back to back with him, and not to put himself too forward, "but give me all the help thou canst".

"Well," says Bjorn, "I never had it in my head that any man should stand before me as a shield, but still as things are thou must have thy way; but for all that, with my gift of wit and my swiftness I may be of some use to thee, and not harmless to our foes."

Now they all rose up and ran at them, and Modolf Kettle's son was quickest of them, and thrust at Kari with his spear. Kari had his shield before him, and the blow fell on it, and the spear stuck fast in the shield. Then Kari twists the shield so smartly, that the spear snapped short off, and then he drew his sword and smote at Modolf; but Modolf made a cut at him too, and Kari's sword fell on Modolf's hilt, and glanced off it on to Modolph's wrist, and took the arm off, and down it fell, and the sword too. Then Kari's sword passed on into Modolf's side, and between his ribs, and so Modolf fell down and was dead on the spot.

Grani Gunnar's son snatched up a spear and hurled it at Kari, but Kari thrust down his shield so hard that the point stood fast in the ground, but with his left hand he caught the spear in the air, and hurled it back at Grani, and caught up his shield again at once with his left hand. Grani had his shield before him, and the spear came on the shield and passed right through it, and into Grani's thigh just below the small guts, and through the limb, and so on, pinning him to the ground, and he could not get rid of the spear before his fellows drew him off it, and carried him away on their shields, and laid him down in a dell.

There was a man who ran up to Kari's side, and meant to cut off his leg, but Bjorn cut off that man's arm, and sprang back again behind Kari, and they could not do him any hurt. Kari made a sweep at that same man with his sword, and cut him asunder at the waist.

Then Lambi Sigfus' son rushed at Kari, and hewed at him with his sword. Kari caught the blow sideways on his shield, and the sword would not bite; then Kari thrust at Lambi with his sword just below the breast, so that the point came out between his shoulders, and that was his death-blow.

Then Thorstein Geirleif's son rushed at Kari, and thought to take him in flank, but Kari caught sight of him, and swept at him with his sword across the shoulders, so that the man was cleft asunder at the chine.

A little while after he gave Gunnar of Skal, a good man and true, his death-blow. As for Bjorn, he had wounded three men who had tried to give Kari wounds, and yet he was never so far forward that he was in the least danger, nor was he wounded, nor was either of those companions hurt in that fight, but all those that got away were wounded.

Then they ran for their horses, and galloped them off across Skaptarwater as hard as they could; and they were so scared that they stopped at no house, nor did they dare to stay and tell the tidings anywhere.

Kari and Bjorn hooted and shouted after them as they galloped off. So they rode east to Woodcombe, and did not draw bridle till they came to Swinefell.

Flosi was not at home when they came thither, and that was why no hue and cry was made thence after Kari.

This journey of theirs was thought most shameful by all men.

Kari rode to Skal, and gave notice of these manslayings as done by his hand; there, too, he told them of the death of their master and five others, and of Grani's wound, and said it would be better to bear him to the house if he were to live.

Bjorn said he could not bear to slay him, though he said he was worthy of death; but those who answered him said they were sure few had bitten the dust before him. But Bjorn told them he had it now in his power to make as many of the Sidemen as he chose bite the dust; to which they said it was a bad look out.

Then Kari and Bjorn ride away from the house.

Chapter 150
More of Kari and Bjorn

Then Kari asked Bjorn —

"What counsel shall we take now? Now I will try what thy wit is worth."

"Dost thou think now," answered Bjorn, "that much lies on our being as wise as ever we can?"

"Ay," said Kari, "I think so surely."

"Then our counsel is soon taken," says Bjorn. "We will cheat them all as though they were giants; and now we will make as though we were riding north on the fell, but as soon as ever we are out of sight behind the brae, we will turn down along Skaptarwater, and hide us there where we think handiest, so long as the hue and cry is hottest, if they ride after us."

"So will we do," said Kari; "and this I had meant to do all along."

"And so you may put it to the proof," said Bjorn, "that I am no more of an everyday body in wit than I am in bravery."

Now Kari and his companion rode as they had purposed down along Skaptarwater, till they came where a branch of the stream ran away to the south-east; then they turned down along the middle branch, and did not draw bridle till they came into Middleland, and on that moor which is called Kringlemire; it has a stream of lava all around it.

Then Kari said to Bjorn that he must watch their horses, and keep a good look-out; "but as for me," he says, "I am heavy with sleep".

So Bjorn watched the horses, but Kari lay him down, and slept but a very short while ere Bjorn waked him up again, and he had already led their horses together, and they were by their side. Then Bjorn said to Kari —

"Thou standest in much need of me, though! A man might easily have run away from thee if he had not been as brave-hearted as I am; for now thy foes are riding upon thee, and so thou must up and be doing."

Then Kari went away under a jutting crag, and Bjorn said —

"Where shall I stand now?"

"Well!" answers Kari, "now there are two choices before thee; one is, that thou standest at my back and have my shield to cover thyself with, if it can be of any use to thee; and the other is, to get on thy horse and ride away as fast as thou canst."

"Nay," says Bjorn, "I will not do that, and there are many things against it; first of all, may be, if I ride away, some spiteful tongues might begin to say that I ran away from thee for faintheartedness; and another thing is, that I well know what game they will think there is in me, and so they will ride after me, two or three of them, and then I should be of no use or help to thee after all. No! I will rather stand by thee and keep them off so long as it is fated."

Then they had not long to wait ere horses with pack-saddles were driven by them over the moor, and with them went three men.

Then Kari said —

"These men see us not."

"Then let us suffer them to ride on," said Bjorn.

So those three rode on past them; but the six others then came riding right up to them, and they all leapt off their horses straightway in a body, and turned on Kari and his companion.

First, Glum Hilldir's son rushed at them, and thrust at Kari with a spear; Kari turned short round on his heel, and Glum missed him, and the blow fell against the rock. Bjorn sees that, and hewed at once the head off Glum's spear. Kari leant on one side and smote at Glum with his sword, and the blow fell on his thigh, and took off the limb high up in the thigh, and Glum died at once.

Then Vebrand and Asbrand the sons of Thorbrand ran up to Kari, but Kari flew at Vebrand and thrust his sword through him, but afterwards he hewed off both of Asbrand's feet from under him.

In this bout both Kari and Bjorn were wounded.

Then Kettle of the Mark rushed at Kari, and thrust at him with his spear. Kari threw up his leg, and the spear stuck in the ground, and Kari leapt on the spear-shaft, and snapped it in sunder.

Then Kari grasped Kettle in his arms, and Bjorn ran up just then, and wanted to slay him, but Kari said —

"Be still now. I will give Kettle peace; for though it may be that Kettle's life is in my power, still I will never slay him."

Kettle answers never a word, but rode away after his companions, and told those the tidings who did not know them already.

They told also these tidings to the men of the Hundred, and they gathered together at once a great force of armed men, and went straightway up all the water-courses, and so far up on the fell that they were three days in the chase; but after that they turned back to their own homes, but Kettle and his companions rode east to Swinefell, and told the tidings there.

Flosi was little stirred at what had befallen them, but said no one could tell whether things would stop there, "for there is no man like Kari of all that are now left in Iceland".

Chapter 151
Of Kari and Bjorn and Thorgeir

Now we must tell of Bjorn and Kari that they ride down on the Sand, and lead their horses under the banks where the wild oats grew, and cut the oats for them, that they might not die of hunger. Kari made such a near guess, that he rode away thence at the very time that they gave over seeking for him. He rode by night up through the Hundred, and after that he took to the fell; and so on all the same way as they had followed when they rode east, and did not stop till they came to Midmark.

Then Bjorn said to Kari —

"Now shalt thou be my great friend before my mistress, for she will never believe one word of what I say; but everything lies on what you do, so now repay me for the good following which I have yielded to thee."

"So it shall be; never fear," says Kari.

After that they ride up to the homestead, and then the mistress asked them what tidings, and greeted them well.

"Our troubles have rather grown greater, old lass!"

She answered little, and laughed; and then the mistress went on to ask —

"How did Bjorn behave to thee, Kari?"

"Bare is back," he answers, "without brother behind it, and Bjorn behaved well to me. He wounded three men, and, besides, he is wounded himself, and he stuck as close to me as he could in everything."

They were three nights there, and after that they rode to Holt to Thorgeir, and told him alone these tidings, for those tidings had not yet been heard there.

Thorgeir thanked him, and it was quite plain that he was glad at what he heard. He asked Kari what now was undone which he meant to do.

"I mean," answers Kari, "to kill Gunnar Lambi's son and Kol Thorstein's son, if I can get a chance. Then we have slain fifteen men, reckoning those five whom we two slew together. But one boon I will now ask of thee."

Thorgeir said he would grant him whatever he asked.

"I wish, then, that thou wilt take under thy safeguard this man whose name is Bjorn, and who has been in these slayings with me, and that thou wilt change farms with him, and give him a farm ready stocked here close by thee, and so hold thy hand over him that no vengeance may befall him; but all this will be an easy matter for thee who art such a chief."

"So it shall be," says Thorgeir.

Then he gave Bjorn a ready-stocked farm at Asolfskal, but he took the farm in the Mark into his own hands. Thorgeir flitted all Bjorn's household stuff and goods to Asolfskal, and all his live stock; and Thorgeir settled all Bjorn's quarrels for him, and he was reconciled to them with a full atonement. So Bjorn was thought to be much more of a man than he had been before.

Then Kari rode away, and did not draw rein till he came west to Tongue to Asgrim Ellidagrim's son. He gave Kari a most hearty welcome, and Kari told him of all the tidings that had happened in these slayings.

Asgrim was well pleased at them, and asked what Kari meant to do next.

"I mean," said Kari, "to fare abroad after them, and so dog their footsteps and slay them, if I can get at them."

Asgrim said there was no man like him for bravery and hardihood.

He was there some nights, and after that he rode to Gizur the White, and he took him by both hands. Kari stayed there some while, and then he told Gizur that he wished to ride down to Eyrar.

Gizur gave Kari a good sword at parting.

Now he rode down to Eyrar, and took him a passage with Kolbein the black; he was an Orkneyman and an old friend of Kari, and he was the most forward and brisk of men.

He took Kari by both hands, and said that one fate should befall both of them.

Chapter 152
Flosi goes Abroad

Now Flosi rides east to Hornfirth, and most of the men in his Thing followed him, and bore his wares east, as well as all his stores and baggage which he had to take with him.

After that they busked them for their voyage, and fitted out their ship.

Now Flosi stayed by the ship until they were "boun". But as soon as ever they got a fair wind they put out to sea. They had a long passage and hard weather.

Then they quite lost their reckoning, and sailed on and on, and all at once three great waves broke over their ship, one after the other. Then Flosi said they must be near some land, and that this was a ground-swell. A great mist was on them, but the wind rose so that a great gale overtook them, and they scarce knew where they were before they were dashed on shore at dead of night, and the men were saved, but the ship was dashed all to pieces, and they could not save their goods.

Then they had to look for shelter and warmth for themselves, and the day after they went up on a height. The weather was then good.

Flosi asked if any man knew this land, and there were two men of their crew who had fared thither before, and said they were quite sure they knew it, and, say they —

"We are come to Hrossey in the Orkneys."

"Then we might have made a better landing," said Flosi, "for Grim and Helgi, Njal's sons, whom I slew, were both of them of Earl Sigurd Hlodver's son's bodyguard."

Then they sought for a hiding-place, and spread moss over themselves, and so lay for a while, but not for long, ere Flosi spoke and said —

"We will not lie here any longer until the landsmen are ware of us."

Then they arose, and took counsel, and then Flosi said to his men —

"We will go all of us and give ourselves up to the Earl; for there is naught else to do, and the Earl has our lives at his pleasure if he chooses to seek for them."

Then they all went away thence, and Flosi said that they must tell no man any tidings of their voyage, or what manner of men they were, before he told them to the Earl.

Then they walked on until they met men who showed them to the town, and then they went in before the Earl, and Flosi and all the others hailed him.

The Earl asked what men they might be, and Flosi told his name, and said out of what part of Iceland he was.

The Earl had already heard of the Burning, and so he knew the men at once, and then the Earl asked Flosi — "What hast thou to tell me about Helgi Njal's son, my henchman?"

"This," said Flosi, "that I hewed off his head."

"Take them all," said the Earl.

Then that was done, and just then in came Thorstein, son of Hall of the Side. Flosi had to wife Steinvora, Thorstein's sister. Thorstein was one of Earl Sigurd's bodyguard, but when he saw Flosi seized and held, he went in before the Earl, and offered for Flosi all the goods he had.

The Earl was very wroth a long time, but at last the end of it was, by the prayer of good men and true, joined to those of Thorstein, for he was well backed by friends, and many threw in their word with his, that the Earl took an atonement from them, and gave Flosi and all the rest of them peace. The Earl held to that custom of mighty men that Flosi took that place in his service which Helgi Njal's son had filled.

So Flosi was made Earl Sigurd's henchman, and he soon won his way to great love with the Earl.

Chapter 153
Kari goes Abroad

Those messmates Kari and Kolbein the black put out to sea from Eyrar half a month later than Flosi and his companions from Hornfirth.

They got a fine fair wind, and were but a short time out. The first land they made was the Fair Isle; it lies between Shetland and the Orkneys. There that man whose name was David the white took Kari into his house, and he told him all that he had heard for certain about the doings of the Burners. He was one of Kari's greatest friends, and Kari stayed with him for the winter.

There they heard tidings from the west out of the Orkneys of all that was done there.

Earl Sigurd bade to his feast at Yule Earl Gilli, his brother-in-law, out of the Southern Isles; he had to wife Swanlauga, Earl Sigurd's sister; and then too came to see Earl Sigurd that king from Ireland whose name was Sigtrygg. He was a son of Olaf rattle, but his mother's name was Kormlada; she was the fairest of all women, and best gifted in everything that was not in her own power, but it was the talk of men that she did all things ill over which she had any power.

Brian was the name of the king who first had her to wife, but they were then parted. He was the best-natured of all kings. He had his seat in Connaught, in Ireland; his brother's name was Wolf the quarrelsome, the greatest champion and warrior; Brian's foster-child's name was Kerthialfad. He was the son of King Kylfi, who had many wars with King Brian, and fled away out of the land before him, and became a hermit; but when King Brian went south on a pilgrimage, then he met King Kylfi, and then they were atoned, and King Brian took his son Kerthialfad to him, and loved him more than his own sons. He was then full grown when these things happened, and was the boldest of all men.

Duncan was the name of the first of King Brian's sons; the second was Margad; the third, Takt, whom we call Tann, he was the youngest of them; but the elder sons of King Brian were full grown, and the briskest of men.

Kormlada was not the mother of King Brian's children, and so grim was she against King Brian after their parting, that she would gladly have him dead.

King Brian thrice forgave all his outlaws the same fault, but if they misbehaved themselves oftener, then he let them be judged by the law; and from this one may mark what a king he must have been.

Kormlada egged on her son Sigtrygg very much to kill King Brian, and she now sent him to Earl Sigurd to beg for help.

King Sigtrygg came before Yule to the Orkneys, and there, too, came Earl Gilli, as was written before.

The men were so placed that King Sigtrygg sat in a high seat in the middle, but on either side of the king sat one of the earls. The men of King Sigtrygg and Earl Gilli sate on the inner side away from him, but on the outer side away from Earl Sigurd, sate Flosi and Thorstein, son of Hall of the Side, and the whole hall was full.

Now King Sigtrygg and Earl Gilli wished to hear of these tidings which had happened at the Burning, and so, also, what had befallen since.

Then Gunnar Lambi's son was got to tell the tale, and a stool was set for him to sit upon.

Chapter 154
Gunnar Lambi's Son's Slaying

Just at that very time Kari and Kolbein and David the white came to Hrossey unawares to all men. They went straightway up on land, but a few men watched their ship.

Kari and his fellows went straight to the Earl's homestead, and came to the hall about drinking time.

It so happened that just then Gunnar was telling the story of the Burning, but they were listening to him meanwhile outside. This was on Yule-day itself.

Now King Sigtrygg asked —

"How did Skarphedinn bear the Burning?"

"Well at first for a long time," said Gunnar, "but still the end of it was that he wept." And so he went on giving an unfair leaning in his story, but every now and then he laughed out loud.

Kari could not stand this, and then he ran in with his sword drawn, and sang this song —

> Men of might, in battle eager,
> Boast of burning Njal's abode,
> Have the Princes heard how sturdy
> Seahorse racers sought revenge?
> Hath not since, on foemen holding
> High the shield's broad orb aloft,
> All that wrong been fully wroken?
> Raw flesh ravens got to tear.

So he ran in up the hall, and smote Gunnar Lambi's son on the neck with such a sharp blow, that his head spun off on to the board before the king and the earls, and the board was all one gore of blood, and the Earl's clothing too.

Earl Sigurd knew the man that had done the deed, and called out —

"Seize Kari and kill him."

Kari had been one of Earl Sigurd's bodyguard, and he was of all men most beloved by his friends; and no man stood up a whit more for the Earl's speech.

"Many would say, Lord," said Kari, "that I have done this deed on your behalf, to avenge your henchman."

Then Flosi said — "Kari hath not done this without a cause; he is in no atonement with us, and he only did what he had a right to do".

So Kari walked away, and there was no hue and cry after him. Kari fared to his ship, and his fellows with him. The weather was then good, and they sailed off at once south to Caithness, and went on shore at Thraswick to the house of a worthy man whose name was Skeggi, and with him they stayed a very long while.

Those behind in the Orkneys cleansed the board, and bore out the dead man.

The Earl was told that they had set sail south for Scotland, and King Sigtrygg said —

"This was a mighty bold fellow, who dealt his stroke so stoutly, and never thought twice about it!"

Then Earl Sigurd answered —

"There is no man like Kari for dash and daring."

Now Flosi undertook to tell the story of the Burning, and he was fair to all; and therefore what he said was believed.

Then King Sigtrygg stirred in his business with Earl Sigurd, and bade him go to the war with him against King Brian.

The Earl was long steadfast, but the end of it was that he let the king have his way, but said he must have his mother's hand for his help, and be king in Ireland, if they slew Brian. But all his men besought Earl Sigurd not to go into the war, but it was all no good.

So they parted on the understanding that Earl Sigurd gave his word to go; but King Sigtrygg promised him his mother and the kingdom.

It was so settled that Earl Sigurd was to come with all his host to Dublin by Palm Sunday.

Then King Sigtrygg fared south to Ireland, and told his mother Kormlada that the Earl had undertaken to come, and also what he had pledged himself to grant him.

She showed herself well pleased at that, but said they must gather greater force still.

Sigtrygg asked whence this was to be looked for?

She said there were two vikings lying off the west of Man; and that they had thirty ships, and, she went on, "they are men of such hardihood that nothing can withstand them. The one's name is Ospak, and the other's Brodir. Thou shalt fare to find them, and spare nothing to get them into thy quarrel, whatever price they ask."

Now King Sigtrygg fares and seeks the vikings, and found them lying outside off Man; King Sigtrygg brings forward his errand at once, but Brodir shrank from helping him until he, King Sigtrygg, promised him the kingdom and his mother, and they were to keep this such a secret that Earl Sigurd should know nothing about it; Brodir too was to come to Dublin on Palm Sunday.

So King Sigtrygg fared home to his mother, and told her how things stood.

After that those brothers, Ospak and Brodir, talked together, and then Brodir told Ospak all that he and Sigtrygg had spoken of, and bade him fare to battle with him against King Brian, and said he set much store on his going.

But Ospak said he would not fight against so good a king.

Then they were both wroth, and sundered their band at once. Ospak had ten ships and Brodir twenty.

Ospak was a heathen, and the wisest of all men. He laid his ships inside in a sound, but Brodir lay outside him.

Brodir had been a Christian man and a mass-deacon by consecration, but he had thrown off his faith and become God's dastard, and now worshipped heathen fiends, and he was of all men most skilled in sorcery. He had that coat of mail on which no steel would bite. He was both tall and strong, and had such long locks that he tucked them under his belt. His hair was black.

Chapter 155
Of Signs and Wonders

It so happened one night that a great din passed over Brodir and his men, so that they all woke, and sprang up and put on their clothes.

Along with that came a shower of boiling blood.

Then they covered themselves with their shields, but for all that many were scalded.

This wonder lasted all till day, and a man had died on board every ship.

Then they slept during the day, but the second night there was again a din, and again they all sprang up. Then swords leapt out of their sheaths, and axes and spears flew about in the air and fought.

The weapons pressed them so hard that they had to shield themselves, but still many were wounded, and again a man died out of every ship.

This wonder lasted all till day.

Then they slept again the day after.

But the third night there was a din of the same kind, and then ravens flew at them, and it seemed to them as though their beaks and claws were of iron.

The ravens pressed them so hard that they had to keep them off with their swords, and covered themselves with their shields, and so this went on again till day, and then another man had died in every ship.

Then they went to sleep first of all, but when Brodir woke up, he drew his breath painfully, and bade them put off the boat. "For," he said, "I will go to see Ospak."

Then he got into the boat and some men with him, but when he found Ospak he told him of the wonders which had befallen them, and bade him say what he thought they boded.

Ospak would not tell him before he pledged him peace, and Brodir promised him peace, but Ospak still shrank from telling him till night fell.

Then Ospak spoke and said — "When blood rained on you, therefore shall ye shed many men's blood, both of your own and others. But when ye heard a great din, then ye must have been shown the crack of doom, and ye shall all die speedily. But when weapons fought against you, that must forbode a battle; but when ravens pressed you, that marks the devils which ye put faith in, and who will drag you all down to the pains of hell."

Then Brodir was so wroth that he could answer never a word, but he went at once to his men, and made them lay his ships in a line across the sound, and moor them by bearing their cables on shore at either end of the line, and meant to slay them all next morning.

Ospak saw all their plan, and then he vowed to take the true faith, and to go to King Brian, and follow him till his death-day.

Then he took that counsel to lay his ships in a line, and punt them along the shore with poles, and cut the cables of Brodir's ships. Then the ships of Brodir's men began to fall aboard of one another when they were all fast asleep; and so Ospak and his men got out of the firth, and so west to Ireland, and came to Connaught.

Then Ospak told King Brian all that he had learnt, and took baptism, and gave himself over into the king's hand.

After that King Brian made them gather force over all his realm, and the whole host was to come to Dublin in the week before Palm Sunday.

Chapter 156
Brian's Battle

Earl Sigurd Hlodver's son busked him from the Orkneys, and Flosi offered to go with him.

The Earl would not have that, since he had his pilgrimage to fulfil.

Flosi offered fifteen men of his band to go on the voyage, and the Earl accepted them, but Flosi fared with Earl Gilli to the Southern Isles.

Thorstein, the Son of Hall of the Side, went along with Earl Sigurd, and Hrafn the red, and Erling of Straumey.

He would not that Hareck should go, but said he would be sure to be the first to tell him the tidings of his voyage.

The Earl came with all his host on Palm Sunday to Dublin, and there too was come Brodir with all his host.

Brodir tried by sorcery how the fight would go, but the answer ran thus, that if the fight were on Good Friday King Brian would fall but win the day; but if they fought before, they would all fall who were against him.

Then Brodir said that they must not fight before the Friday.

On the fifth day of the week a man rode up to Kormlada and her company on an apple-grey horse, and in his hand he held a halberd; he talked long with them.

King Brian came with all his host to the Burg, and on the Friday the host fared out of the Burg, and both armies were drawn up in array.

Brodir was on one wing of the battle, but King Sigtrygg on the other.

Earl Sigurd was in the mid battle.

Now it must be told of King Brian that he would not fight on the fast-day, and so a shieldburg was thrown round him, and his host was drawn up in array in front of it.

Wolf the quarrelsome was on that wing of the battle against which Brodir stood; but on the other wing, where Sigtrygg stood against them, were Ospak and his sons.

But in mid battle was Kerthialfad, and before him the banners were borne.

Now the wings fall on one another, and there was a very hard fight, Brodir went through the host of the foe, and felled all the foremost that stood there, but no steel would bite on his mail.

Wolf the quarrelsome turned then to meet him, and thrust at him thrice so hard that Brodir fell before him at each thrust, and was well-nigh not getting on his feet again; but as soon as ever he found his feet, he fled away into the wood at once.

Earl Sigurd had a hard battle against Kerthialfad, and Kerthialfad came on so fast that he laid low all who were in the front rank, and he broke the array of Earl Sigurd right up to his banner, and slew the banner-bearer.

Then he got another man to bear the banner, and there was again a hard fight.

Kerthialfad smote this man too his death blow at once, and so on one after the other all who stood near him.

Then Earl Sigurd called on Thorstein the son of Hall of the Side, to bear the banner, and Thorstein was just about to lift the banner, but then Asmund the white said —

"Don't bear the banner! for all they who bear it get their death."

"Hrafn the red!" called out Earl Sigurd, "bear thou the banner."

"Bear thine own devil thyself," answered Hrafn.

Then the Earl said —

"'Tis fittest that the beggar should bear the bag;" and with that he took the banner from the staff and put it under his cloak.

A little after Asmund the white was slain, and then the Earl was pierced through with a spear.

Ospak had gone through all the battle on his wing, he had been sore wounded, and lost both his sons ere King Sigtrygg fled before him.

Then flight broke out throughout all the host.

Thorstein Hall of the Side's son stood still while all the others fled, and tied his shoe-string. Then Kerthialfad asked why he ran not as the others.

"Because," said Thorstein, "I can't get home to-night, since I am at home out in Iceland."

Kerthialfad gave him peace.

Hrafn the red was chased out into a certain river; he thought he saw there the pains of hell down below him, and he thought the devils wanted to drag him to them.

Then Hrafn said —

"Thy dog, Apostle Peter! hath run twice to Rome, and he would run the third time if thou gavest him leave."

Then the devils let him loose, and Hrafn got across the river.

Now Brodir saw that King Brian's men were chasing the fleers, and that there were few men by the shieldburg.

Then he rushed out of the wood, and broke through the shieldburg, and hewed at the king.

The lad Takt threw his arm in the way, and the stroke took it off and the king's head too, but the king's blood came on the lad's stump, and the stump was healed by it on the spot.

Then Brodir called out with a loud voice —

"Now let man tell man that Brodir felled Brian."

Then men ran after those who were chasing the fleers, and they were told that King Brian had fallen, and then they turned back straightway, both Wolf the quarrelsome and Kerthialfad.

Then they threw a ring round Brodir and his men, and threw branches of trees upon them, and so Brodir was taken alive.

Wolf the quarrelsome cut open his belly, and led him round and round the trunk of a tree, and so wound all his entrails out of him, and he did not die before they were all drawn out of him.

Brodir's men were slain to a man.

After that they took King Brian's body and laid it out. The king's head had grown fast to the trunk.

Fifteen men of the Burners fell in Brian's battle, and there, too, fell Halldor the son of Gudmund the powerful, and Erling of Straumey.

On Good Friday that event happened in Caithness that a man whose name was Daurrud went out. He saw folk riding twelve together to a bower, and there they were all lost to his sight. He went to that bower and looked in through a window slit that was in it, and saw that there were women inside, and they had set up a loom. Men's heads were the weights, but men's entrails were the warp and wed, a sword was the shuttle, and the reels were arrows.

They sang these songs, and he learnt them by heart–

THE WOOF OF WAR.

See! warp is stretched
For warriors' fall,
Lo! weft in loom
'Tis wet with blood;
Now fight foreboding,
'Neath friends' swift fingers,
Our gray woof waxeth
With war's alarms,
Our warp bloodred,
Our weft corseblue.

This woof is y-woven
With entrails of men,
This warp is hardweighted
With heads of the slain,

Spears blood-besprinkled
For spindles we use,
Our loom ironbound,
And arrows our reels;
With swords for our shuttles
This war-woof we work;
So weave we, weird sisters,
Our warwinning woof.

Now War-winner walketh
To weave in her turn.
Now Swordswinger steppeth,
Now Swiftstroke, now Storm;
When they speed the shuttle
How spear-heads shall flash!
Shields crash, and helmgnawer
On harness bite hard!

Wind we, wind swiftly
Our warwinning woof.
Woof erst for king youthful
Foredoomed as his own,
Forth now we will ride,
Then through the ranks rushing
Be busy where friends
Blows blithe give and take.

Wind we, wind swiftly
Our warwinning woof,
After that let us steadfastly
Stand by the brave king;
Then men shall mark mournful
Their shields red with gore,
How Swordstroke and Spearthrust
Stood stout by the prince.

Wind we, wind swiftly
Our warwinning woof;
When sword-bearing rovers
To banners rush on,
Mind, maidens, we spare not
One life in the fray!
We corse-choosing sisters
Have charge of the slain.

Now new-coming nations
That island shall rule.
Who on outlying headlands
Abode ere the fight;
I say that King mighty
To death now is done,
Now low before spearpoint
That Earl bows his head.

Soon over all Ersemen
Sharp sorrow shall fall,
That woe to those warriors
Shall wane nevermore;
Our woof now is woven.
Now battle-field waste,
O'er land and o'er water
War tidings shall leap.

Now surely 'tis gruesome
To gaze all around,
When bloodred through heaven
Drives cloudrack o'er head;
Air soon shall be deep hued
With dying men's blood
When this our spaedom
Comes speedy to pass.

So cheerily chant we
Charms for the young king,
Come maidens lift loudly
His warwinning lay;
Let him who now listens
Learn well with his ears,
And gladden brave swordsmen
With bursts of war's song.

Now mount we our horses,
Now bare we our brands,
Now haste we hard, maidens,
Hence far, far away.

Then they plucked down the woof and tore it asunder, and each kept what she had hold of.

Now Daurrud goes away from the slit, and home; but they got on their steeds and rode six to the south, and the other six to the north.

A like event befell Brand Gneisti's son in the Faroe Isles.

At Swinefell, in Iceland, blood came on the priest's stole on Good Friday, so that he had to put it off.

At Thvattwater the priest thought he saw on Good Friday a long deep of the sea hard by the altar, and there he saw many awful sights, and it was long ere he could sing the prayers.

This event happened in the Orkneys, that Hareck thought he saw Earl Sigurd, and some men with him. Then Hareck took his horse and rode to meet the Earl. Men saw that they met and rode under a brae, but they were never seen again, and not a scrap was ever found of Hareck.

Earl Gilli in the Southern Isles dreamed that a man came to him and said his name was Hostfinn, and told him he was come from Ireland.

The Earl thought he asked him for tidings thence, and then he sang this song—

> I have been where warriors wrestled,
> High in Erin sang the sword,
> Boss to boss met many bucklers.
> Steel rung sharp on rattling helm;
> I can tell of all their struggle;
> Sigurd fell in flight of spears;
> Brian fell, but kept his kingdom
> Ere he lost one drop of blood.

Those two, Flosi and the Earl, talked much of this dream. A week after, Hrafn the red came thither, and told them all the tidings of Brian's battle, the fall of the king, and of Earl Sigurd, and Brodir, and all the Vikings.

"What," said Flosi, "hast thou to tell me of my men?"

"They all fell there," says Hrafn, "but thy brother-in-law Thorstein took peace from Kerthialfad, and is now with him."

Flosi told the Earl that he would now go away, "for we have our pilgrimage south to fulfil".

The Earl bade him go as he wished, and gave him a ship and all else that he needed, and much silver.

Then they sailed to Wales, and stayed there a while.

Chapter 157
The Slaying of Kol Thorstein's Son

Kari Solmund's son told master Skeggi that he wished he would get him a ship. So master Skeggi gave Kari a long-ship, fully trimmed and manned, and on board it went Kari, and David the white, and Kolbein the black.

Now Kari and his fellows sailed south through Scotland's Firths, and there they found men from the Southern Isles. They told Kari the tidings from Ireland, and also that Flosi was gone to Wales, and his men with him.

But when Kari heard that, he told his messmates that he would hold on south to Wales, to fall in with Flosi and his band. So he bade them then to part from his company, if they liked it better, and said that he would not wish to beguile any man into mischief, because he thought he had not yet had revenge enough on Flosi and his band.

All chose to go with him; and then he sails south to Wales, and there they lay in hiding in a creek out of the way.

That morning Kol Thorstein's son went into the town to buy silver. He of all the Burners had used the bitterest words. Kol had talked much with a mighty dame, and he had so knocked the nail on the head, that it was all but fixed that he was to have her, and settle down there.

That same morning Kari went also into the town. He came where Kol was telling the silver.

Kari knew him at once, and ran at him with his drawn sword and smote him on the neck; but he still went on telling the silver, and his head counted "ten" just as it spun off the body.

Then Kari said —

"Go and tell this to Flosi, that Kari Solmund's son hath slain Kol Thorstein's son. I give notice of this slaying as done by my hand."

Then Kari went to his ship, and told his shipmates of the manslaughter.

Then they sailed north to Beruwick, and laid up their ship, and fared up into Whitherne in Scotland, and were with Earl Malcolm that year.

But when Flosi heard of Kol's slaying, he laid out his body, and bestowed much money on his burial.

Flosi never uttered any wrathful words against Kari.

Thence Flosi fared south across the sea and began his pilgrimage, and went on south, and did not stop till he came to Rome. There he got so great honour that he took absolution from the Pope himself, and for that he gave a great sum of money.

Then he fared back again by the east road, and stayed long in towns, and went in before mighty men, and had from them great honour.

He was in Norway the winter after, and was with Earl Eric till he was ready to sail, and the Earl gave him much meal, and many other men behaved handsomely to him.

Now he sailed out to Iceland, and ran into Hornfirth, and thence fared home to Swinefell. He had then fulfilled all the terms of his atonement, both in fines and foreign travel.

Chapter 158
Of Flosi and Kari

Now it is to be told of Kari that the summer after he went down to his ship and sailed south across the sea, and began his pilgrimage in Normandy, and so went south and got absolution and fared back by the western way, and took his ship again in Normandy, and sailed in her north across the sea to Dover in England.

Thence he sailed west, round Wales, and so north, through Scotland's Firths, and did not stay his course till he came to Thraswick in Caithness, to master Skeggi's house.

There he gave over the ship of burden to Kolbein and David, and Kolbein sailed in that ship to Norway, but David stayed behind in the Fair Isle.

Kari was that winter in Caithness. In this winter his housewife died out in Iceland.

The next summer Kari busked him for Iceland. Skeggi gave him a ship of burden, and there were eighteen of them on board her.

They were rather late "boun," but still they put to sea, and had a long passage, but at last they made Ingolf's Head. There their shin was dashed all to pieces, but the men's lives were saved. Then, too, a gale of wind came on them.

Now they ask Kari what counsel was to be taken; but he said their best plan was to go to Swinefell and put Flosi's manhood to the proof.

So they went right up to Swinefell in the storm. Flosi was in the hall. He knew Kari as soon as ever he came into the hall, and sprang up to meet him, and kissed him, and sate him down in the high-seat by his side.

Flosi asked Kari to be there that winter, and Kari took his offer. Then they were atoned with a full atonement.

Then Flosi gave away his brother's daughter Hildigunna, whom Hauskuld the priest of Whiteness had had to wife, to Kari, and they dwelt first of all at Broadwater.

Men say that the end of Flosi's life was, that he fared abroad, when he had grown old, to seek for timber to build him a hall; and he was in Norway that winter, but the next summer he was late "boun"; and men told him that his ship was not seaworthy.

Flosi said she was quite good enough for an old and death-doomed man, and bore his goods on shipboard and put out to sea. But of that ship no tidings were ever heard.

These were the children of Kari Solmund's son and Helga Njal's daughter — Thorgerda and Ragneida, Valgerda, and Thord who was burnt in Njal's house. But the children of Hildigunna and Kari were these, Starkad, and Thord, and Flosi.

The son of Burning-Flosi was Kolbein, who has been the most famous man of any of that stock.

And here we end the saga of Burnt Njal.

THE STORY OF GISLI THE OUTLAW

Chapter 1
The Thrall's Curse

AT the end of the days of Harold Fairhair there was a mighty lord in Norway whose name was Thorkel Goldhelm, and he dwelt in Surnadale in North Mæren. He had a wedded wife, and three sons by her. The name of the eldest was Ari, the second was called Gisli, and the third Thorbjorn. They were all young men of promise. There was a man too, named Isi, who ruled over the Fjardarfolk. His daughter's name was Ingibjorga, and she was the fairest of women. Ari, Thorkel's son, asked her to wife, and she was wedded to him. He got a great dower with her, and amongst the rest that she brought with her from her home was a man named Kol: he was of high degree, but he had been taken captive in war, and was called a Thrall. So he came with Ingibjorga to Surnadale. Thorkel gave over to his son Ari a rich farm up in the dale, and there he set up his abode, and was looked on as a most rising man.

But now our story goes on to tell of a man named Bjorn, nicknamed Bjorn the Black. He was a Bearsark, and much given to duels. Twelve men went at his heel, and besides he was skilled in the black art, and no steel could touch his skin. No wonder he was unbeloved by the people, for he turned aside as he listed into the houses of men, and took a way their wives and daughters, and kept them with him as long as he liked. All raised an outcry when he came, and all were fain when he went away. Well, as soon as this Bjorn heard that Ari had brought home a fair wife with a rich dower, he thought he would have a finger in that pie. So he turned his steps thither with his crew, and reached the house at eventide. As soon as Ari and Bjorn met, Bjorn told him that he wanted to play the master in that house, and that Ingibjorga, the housewife, should be at his beck and call whenever he chose. As for Ari, he said he might please himself, go away or stay, so he let Bjorn have his will. But Ari said he would not go away, nor would he let him play the master there.

"Very well!" says Bjorn, "thou shalt have another choice. I will challenge thee to fight on the island, if thou darest, three days from this, and then we will try whose Ingibjorga shall be; and he, too, shall take all the other's goods who wins the day. Now, mind, I will neither ransom myself with money, nor will I suffer any one else to ransom himself. One shall conquer and the other die."

Ari said he was willing enough to fight; so the Bearsarks went their way and busked them to battle. To make a long story short, they met on the island, and the end of their struggle was, that Ari fell; but the Bearsark was not wounded, for no steel would touch him.

Now Bjorn thought he had won wife, and land, and goods, and he gave out that he meant to go at even to Ari's house to claim his own. Then Gisli, Ari's brother, answered and said: "It will soon be all over with me and mine if this disgrace comes to pass, that this ruffian tramples us under foot. But this shall never be, for I will challenge thee at once to battle to-morrow morning. I would far rather fall on the island than bear this shame."

"Well and good," says Bjorn; "thou and thy kith and kin shall all fall one after the other, if ye dare to fight with me."

After that they parted, and Gisli went home to the house that Ari had owned. Now the tidings were told of what had happened on the island, and of Ari's death, and all thought that a great blow to the house. But Gisli goes to Ingibjorga, and tells her of Ari's fall, and how he had challenged Bjorn to the island, and how they were to fight the very next morning.

"That is a bootless undertaking," said Ingibjorga, "and I fear it will not turn out well for thee, unless thou hast other help to lean on."

"Ah!" said Gisli, "then I beg that thou and all else who are likeliest to yield help will do their best that victory may seem more hopeful than it now looks."

"Know this," says Ingibjorga, "that I was not so very fond of Ari that I would not rather have had thee. There is a man," She said, "who, methinks, is likeliest to be able to help in this matter, so that it may be well with thee."

"Who is that?" asks Gisli.

"It is Kol, my foster-father," was the answer; "for I ween he has a sword that is said to be better than most others, though he seems to set little store by it, for he calls it his 'Chopper;' but whoever wields that sword wins the day."

So they sent for Kol, and he came to meet Gisli and Ingibjorga.

"Hast thou ever a good sword?" asked Gisli.

"My sword is no great treasure," answers Kol; "but yet there are many things in the churl's cot which are not in the king grange."

"Wilt thou not lend me the sword for my duel with Bjorn?" said Gisli.

"Ah!" said Kol, "then will happen what ever happens with those things that are treasures–you will never wish to give it up. But for all that, I tell thee now that this sword will bite whatever its blow falls on, be it iron or aught else; nor can its edge be deadened by spells, for it was forged by the Dwarves, and its name is 'Graysteel.' And now make up thy mind that I shall take it very ill if I do not get the sword back. when I claim it."

"It were most unfair," says Gisli, "that thou shouldst not get back the sword after I have had the use of it in my need."

Now Gisli takes the sword, and the night glides away, Next morn, ere they went from home to the duel, Thorbjorn called out to Gisli his brother, and said: "Which of us twain now shall fight with the Bearsark to-day, and which of us shall slaughter the calf?"

"My counsel," said Gisli, "is, that thou shalt slaughter the calf while I and Bjorn try our strength." He did not choose the easiest task.

So they set off to the island, and Gisli and Bjorn stood face to face on it. Then Gisli bade Bjorn strike the first blow. "No one has ever made me that offer before," said Bjorn; "indeed no one has ever challenged me before this day save thou." So Bjorn made a blow at Gisli, but Gisli threw his shield before him, and the sword hewed off from the shield all that it smote from below the handle. Then Gisli smote at Bjorn in his turn, and the stroke fell on the tail of the shield and shore it right off, and then passed on and struck off his leg below the knee. One other stroke he dealt him and took off his head. Then he and his men turned on Bjorn's followers, and some are slain and some chased away into the woods.

After that Gisli goes home and got good fame for this feat, and then he took the farm as his heritage after Ari his brother; and he got Ingibjorga also to wife, for he would not let a good woman go out of the family. And time rolls on, but he did not give up the good sword, nor had Kol ever asked for it.

One day they two met out of doors, and Gisli had "Graysteel" in his hand, and Kol had an axe. Kol asked whether he thought the sword had stood him in good stead, and Gisli was fall of its praises. "Well now" said Kol, "I should like to have it back if thou thinkest it has done thee good service in thy need."

"Wilt thou sell it?" says Gisli.

"No," says Kol.

"I will give thee thy freedom and goods, so that thou mayest fare whither thou wilt with other men."

"I will not sell it," says Kol.

"Then I will give thee thy freedom, and lease or give thee land, and besides I will give thee sheep and cattle and goods as much as thou needest."

"I will not sell it a whit more for that," says Kol.

"Indeed," says Gisli, "thou art too wilful to cling to it thus. Put thine own price on it—any sum thou choosest in money—and be sure I will not stand at trifles if thou wilt come to terms in some way. Besides, I will give thee thy freedom and a becoming match if thou hast any liking for any one."

"There is no use talking about it," says Kol; "I will not sell it whatsoever thou offerest. But now it just comes to what I feared at first, when I said it was not sure whether thou wouldest be ready to give the sword up if thou knewest what virtue was in it."

"And I too;" says Gisli, "will say what will happen. Good will befall neither of us, for I have not the heart to give up the sword, and it shall never come into any other man's hand than mine if I may have my will."

Then Kol lifts up his axe, while Gisli brandished "Graysteel;" and each smote at the other. Kol's blow fell on Gisli's head, so that it sank into the brain, but the sword fell on Kors head, and did not bite; but still the blow was so stoutly dealt that the skull was shattered and the sword broke asunder. Then Kol said:

"It had been better now that I had got back my sword when I asked for it; and yet this is but the beginning of the ill-luck which it will bring on thy kith and kin." Thus both of them lost their lives.

Chapter 2
Kolbein's Killing

Now after that Ingibjorga longed to get away from Surnadale, and went home to her father with her goods. As for Thorbjorn, he looked about for a wife, and went east across the Keel to Fressey, and wooed a woman named Isgerda, and got her. After that he went back home to Surnadale and set up housekeeping with his father. Thorkel Goldhelm lived but a little while afterwards ere he fell sick and died, and Thorbjorn took all the heritage after his father. He was afterwards called Thorbjorn Soursop, and he dwelt at Stock in Surnadale. He and Isgerda had children. Their eldest son was Thorkel, the second Gisli, and the third Ari, but he was sent at once to be fostered at Fressey, and he is little heard of in this story. Their daughter's name was Thordisa. She was their eldest child. Thorkel was a tall man and fair of face, of huge strength, and the greatest dandy. Gisli was swarthy of hue, and as tall as the tallest: 'twas hard to tell how strong he was. He was a man who could turn his hand to anything, and was ever at work-mild of temper too. Their sister Thordisa was a fair woman to look on, high-minded, and rather hard of heart. She was a dashing, forward woman.

At that time there were two young men in Surnadale, whose names were Bard and Kolbein. They were both well-to-do, and though they were not akin, they had each a little before lost their father on a cruise to England. Hella was the name of Bard's house, and Granskeid was where Kolbein dwelt. They were much about the same age as Thorbjorn's sons, and they were all full of mirth and frolic. This was just about the time when Hacon Athelstane's foster-child was king of Norway.

Well, we must go on to say that this Kolbein, of whom we have spoken, grew very fond of coming to Thorbjorn's house, and when there thought it best sport of all to talk with Thordisa. Before long other folk began to talk about this; and so much was said about it that it came to her father's ears, and he thought he saw it all as clear as day. Then Thorbjorn spoke to his sons, and bade them find a cure for this. Gisli said it was easy enough to cure things in which there was no harm.

"If we are to speak, don't say things which seem as though you wanted to pick a quarrel."

"I see," said Thorbjorn, "that this has got wind far too widely, and that it will be out of our power to smother it. Nevertheless, too, it seems much more likely that thou and thy brother are cravens, with little or no feeling of honour."

Gisli went on to say, "Don't fret thyself, father, about his coming. I will speak to him to stop his visits hither."

"Ah!" cried out Thorbjorn, "thou art likelier to go and beg and pray him not to come hither, and be so eager as even to thank him for so doing, and to show thyself a dastard in every way, and after all to do nothing if he does not listen to thy words!"

Now Gisli goes away, and he and his father stayed their talk; but the very next time that Kolbein came thither, Gisli went with him on his way home when he left, and spoke to him, and says he will not suffer him to come thither any longer; "for my father frets himself about thy visits: for folks say that thou beguilest my sister Thordisa, and that is not at all to my father's mind. As for me, I will do all I can, if thou dost as I wish, to bring mirth and sport into thy house."

"What's the good;" said Kolbein, "of talking of things which thou knowest can never be? I know not whether is more irksome to me, thy father's fretfulness, or the thought of giving way to his wish. 'Verily the words of the weak are little worth.'"

"That is not the way to take it," answers Gisli. "The end of this will be, that at last when it comes to the push I will set most store by my father's will. Methought now it was worth trying whether thou wouldest do this for my word's sake; then thou mightest have asked as much from me another time; but I am afraid that we shall not like it, if thou art bent on being cross-grained."

To that Kolbein said little, and so they parted. Then Gisli went home, and so things rested for a while, and Kolbein's visits were somewhat fewer and farther between than they had been. At last he thinks it dull at home, and goes oftener to Thorbjorn's house. So one day when he had come thither Gisli sat in the hall and smithied, and his father and his brother and sister were there too. Thorkel was the cheeriest towards Kolbein; and these three–Thorkel, and Thordisa, and Kolbein–all sat on the cross-bench. But when the day was far spent, and evening fell, they rose up and went out. Thorbjorn and Gisli were left behind in the hall, and Thorbjorn began to say:

"Thy begging and praying has not been worth much; for both thy undertaking was girlish, and indeed I can scarce say whether I am to reckon thee and thy brother as my sons or my daughters. Tis hard to learn, when one is old, that one has sons who have no more manly thoughts than women had in olden times, and ye two are utterly unlike my brothers Gisli and Ari."

"Thou hast no need," answered Gisli, "to take it so much to heart; for no one can say how a man will behave till he is tried."

With this Gisli could not bear to listen longer to his father's gibes, and went out. Just then Thorkel and Kolbein were going out at the gate, and Thordisa had turned back for the hall. Gisli went out after them, and so they all walked along together. Again Gisli besought Kolbein to cease his visits, but Kolbein said he weened that no good would come of that. Then Gisli said:

"So you set small store by my words, and now we shall lay down our companionship in a worse way than I thought."

"I don't see how I can help that," said Kolbein.

"Why," said Gisli, "one of two things must happen: either that thou settest some store by my words, or if thou dost not, then I will forsake all the friendship that has been between us."

"Thou must settle that as thou pleasest," says Kolbein; "but for all that I cannot find it in my heart to break off my visits."

At that Gisli drew his sword and smote at him, and that one stroke was more than enough for Kolbein.

Thorkel was very vexed at the deed, but Gisli bade his brother be soothed. "Let us change swords," he said; "and take thou that with the keenest edge."

This he said, mocking; but Thorkel was soothed, and sate down by Kolbein.

Then Gisli went home to his father's hall, and Thorbjorn asked:

"Well, how has thy begging and praying sped?"

"Well," says Gisli, "I think I may say that it has well sped; because we settled ere we parted just now that Kolbein should cease his visits, that they might not anger thee."

"That can only be," said Thorbjorn, "if he be dead."

"Then be all the better pleased," says Gisli, "that thy will hath been done in this matter."

"Good luck to thy hand," said Thorbjorn. "Maybe after all that I have not daughters alone to my children."

Chapter 3
The Burning of the Old House

As for Thorkel, who had been Kolbein's greatest friend, he could not bear to be at home, nor would he change swords with Gisli, but went his way to a man called Duelling Skeggi, in the isle of Saxa. He was near akin to Kolbein, and in his house Thorkel stayed. In a little while Thorkel egged Skeggi on to avenge his kinsman, and at the same time to woo his sister Thordisa. So they went to Stock—for that was the name of Thorbjorn's farm—twenty of them together; and when they came to the house, Skeggi began to talk of King Thorbjorn's son-in-law, and of having Thordisa to wife. But Thorbjorn would not hear of the match. The story went that Bard, Kolbein's friend, had settled it all with Thordisa; and, at anyrate, Skeggi made up his mind that Bard was to blame for the loss of the match. So he set off to find Bard, and challenged him to fight on the isle of Saxa. Bard said he would be sure to come; he was not worthy to have Thordisa if he did not dare to fight for her with Skeggi. So Thorkel and Skeggi set out for Saxa with twenty-one men in all, and waited for the day fixed for the duel. But when three nights had come and gone, Gisli went to find Bard, and asks whether he were ready for the combat. Bard says, Yes; and asked whether, if he fought, he should have the match.

"Twill be time to talk of that afterwards," says Gisli.

"Well," says Bard, "methinks I had better not fight with Skeggi."

"Out on thee for a dastard!" says Gisli; "but though thou broughtest us all to shame, still for all that I will go myself."

Now Gisli goes to the isle with eleven men. Meantime Skeggi had come to the isle and staked out the lists for Bard, and laid down the law of the combat, and after all saw neither him nor any one to fight on the isle in his stead. There was a man named Fox, who was Skeggi's Smith; and Skeggi bade Fox to carve likenesses of Gisli and Bard: "And see," he said, "that one stands just behind the back of the other, and this laughingstock shall stand for aye to put them to shame."

These words Gisli heard in the wood, and called out:

"Thy house-carles shall have other handier work to do. Here behold a man who dares to do battle with thee!"

Then they stepped on the isle and fought, and each bore his own shield before him. Skeggi had a sword called "Warflame," and with it he smote at Gisli till the blade sang again, and Skeggi chaunted:

> "Warflame fierce flickered,
> Flaring on Saxa."

But Gisli smote back at him with his battle-axe, and took off the tail of his shield, and Skeggi's leg along with it; and as he smote he chaunted:

> "Grimly grinned Ogremaw,
> Gaping at Skeggi."

As for Skeggi, he ransomed himself from the island, and went ever after on a wooden leg. But Thorkel went home with his brother Gisli, and now their friendship was pretty good, and Gisli was thought to have grown a great man by these dealings.

That same winter Einar and Sigurd, the sons of Skeggi, set off from their house at Flydroness, with nigh forty men, and marched till they came in the night to Surnadale. They went first to Bard's house at Hella, and seized all the doors. Two choices were given him: the first, that he should lose his life; the other, that he should go with them against Thorbjorn and his sons. Bard said there were no ties between him and Thorbjorn and his sons. "I set most store on my life," he says; "as for the other choice, I think nothing of doing it."

So he set out with them, and ten men followed him. They were then in all fifty men. They come unawares on Thorbjorn's house at Stock. His men were so arranged that some of them were in the hall and some in the store-room. This store-room Gisli had built some years before, and made it in such wise that every plank had been cut asunder, and a loose panel left in the middle, and on the outside they were all fitted together, while within they were held by iron bolts and bars, and yet on the outside the planks looked as if they were all one piece. The weather that night was in this wise: the air was thick, and the wind sharp; and the blast stood right on to the store-room. Einar and Sigurd heaped a pile of wood both before the hall and the store-room, and set fire to them. But when those in the store-room were ware of this, they threw open the outer door. By the entry stood two large pails or casks of whey, and they took the whey in goat-skins and threw it on the fire, and quenched it thrice. But the foe made the pile up again a little way from the door on either side, and then the fire soon began to catch the beams of the house. The heads of the household were all in that store-room–Thorbjorn, and Thorkel, and Gisli, and Isgerda, and Thordisa. Then Gisli stole away from the doorway to the gable-end, and pushed back the bolts, and thrust out a plank. After that he passed out there, and all the others after him. No men were on the watch there, for they were all guarding the door to see that none came out; but no man was ware of what was happening. Gisli and his kindred followed the smoke away from the house, and so got to the woods, and when they got so far they, turned and looked back, and saw that the hall and the whole homestead were ablaze. Then Gisli chaunted–

> "Flames flare fierce o'er roof and rafter,
> High the hubbub, loud the laughter;
> Hist with croak, and bark with howl,
> Ravens flit and gray wolves prowl:
> Father mine, for lesser matter
> Erst I fleshed my maiden steel
> Hear me swear amid this clatter,
> Soon our foes my sword shall feel."

Now these are there in the waste, but their house burns to cold ashes. Those brothers, Einar and Sigurd, never left the spot till they made up their minds that Thorbjorn and his sons, and all his household, had been burnt inside. They were thirty souls who were burnt inside the hall. So wherever those brothers went they told this story, that Thorbjorn was dead and all his household. But Gisli and his kindred never showed themselves till the others were well away. Then they got force together by stealth, and afterwards they fare by night to Bard's house, and set fire to the homestead, and burnt it up, and the men who were inside it. When they had done that deed, they went back and set about rebuilding their house. All at once Gisli took himself off, and no man knew what had become of him; but when spring came he came with it. Then they set to work and sold their lands secretly, but their goods and chattels they carried off. Now it was plain that Thorbjorn and his sons meant to change their abode and leave Norway; and that was why Gisli had gone away, that he might be busy building their ship. And all this was done so silently that few knew they had broken up their household before they had gone on shipboard, thirty men told, besides women. After that they hold on their course for the sea, and lay to in a haven under the lee of an island, and meant to wait there for a fair wind.

One day when the weather was good Gisli and his brother got into their boats. Ten men stayed behind with their ship, and ten got into each of the boats; but Thorbjorn stayed by the ship. Gisli and his brother row north along the land, and steer for Flydroness; for Gisli says he wishes to look those brothers up ere he leaves Norway for good and all. But when they got to Flydroness they hear that Einar and Sigurd had gone from home to gather King Hacon's dues. So Gisli and his men turned after them, and lay in wait for them in the path which they knew they must take. Those brothers were fifteen in all, and so they met, and there was a hard light. The end of it was that Einar and Sigurd fell, and all their followers. Gisli slew five men and Thorkel three. When the fight was over, Gisli says he has got an errand to do up at the farm. And Gisli went up to the farm, and into the hall, and sees where Skeggi lies, and comes on him, and hews off his head. They sacked the house, and behaved as much like enemies as they could, and took all they could carry with them. After that they row to their ships, and landed on the island, and made a great sacrifice, and vowed vows for a fair wind, and the wind comes. So they put to sea, and have Iceland in their mind's eye.

Chapter 4
The Soursops in Iceland

Well, they had a long and hard passage, and are out more than a hundred days: they made the north of the island, and coasted it westward along the Strand, and so on west off the firths. At last they ran their ship into Dyrafirth, at the mouth of the Hawkdale river. Then they unlade their ship and set up tents, and it was soon noised abroad that a ship had come. There was a man named Thorkel who dwelt at Alvidra, on the north side of Dyrafirth: he was a wealthy man of good birth. In Springdale, on the south side of the firth, dwelt another Thorkel, the son of Eric. At that time all the land round the west firths was settled. This Thorkel, Eric's son, sold land in Hawkdale to Thorbjorn Soursop, for he was so called after he quenched the fire with the sour whey; the inner bight of the stream was already settled, and Thorgrim Bottlenose was the name of the man who lived there. Far up the dale dwelt another Thorkel, and his nickname was "Faulty." He had a wife, and her name was Thorhalla; she was a sister of Thorgrim Bottlenose. Thorkel the Faulty was just what his nickname called him, but it could not be said that Thorhalla made any of his faults better, for she was worse than her husband. They had a son called Thorstein: he was tall and strong. In Tweendale, that turns aside from Hawkdale, dwelt a man whose name was Aunund: he was well to do, and a trustworthy man. So there, at Sæbol in Hawkdale, Thorbjorn, and Gisli, and Thorkel took up their abode, and Gisli built their house.

In the same neighbourhood dwelt Vestein, the son of Vestein. He was a seafaring man, but he had a house under Hest, a hill in Aunundarfirth. His sister's name was Auda. Just about this time Thorbjorn Soursop and Isgerda his wife died, and were buried in a howe in Hawkdale. Thorkel and Gisli took the homestead at Sæbol after him. A little after, Thorkel looked out for a wife. There was a man named Thorbjorn Sealnip. He dwelt at Talknafirth. His wife's name was Thordisa, and Asgerda was their daughter. Thorkel Soursop asked Asgerda to wife, and got her; but his brother Gisli wooed Auda, the sister of Vestein, and got her. So both of them went on living under the same roof at Sæbol in Hawkdale, and did not part their goods though they were married. The story goes on to say that one spring Thorkel of Alvidra had to make a journey south to Thorsness Thing, and Gisli and Thorkel, the Soursops, went with him. At that time Thorstein Codbiter dwelt on Thorsness. He was the son of Thorolf Mosttrarskegg. Thorgrim and Bork the Stout were the sons of Thorstein, and his daughter's name was Thordisa. When Thorkel had got through his business at the Thing, Thorstein Codbiter asked him and the Soursops to come to his house, and gave them good gifts, and ere they parted they asked Thorstein's sons to come and see them the spring after, west at the Dyrafirth Thing. So the winter passed over, and there were no tidings. Now the next spring comes, and the sons of Thorstein fared from home–Thorgrim and Bork and fourteen men more. When they came west to the Valsere Thing they met the Soursops there, and they asked the sons of Thorstein to come home with them after the Thing, for up to that time they had been guests of Thorkel of Alvidra. So they accepted the bidding, and fared home with the Soursops. But Thordisa, the sister of those brothers, seemed fair in the eyes of Thorgrim, and he lifted up his voice and asked for her, and she was then and there betrothed to Thorgrim, and the wedding-feast took place at once, and it was settled that she should have Sæbol for her dower, the farm where these brothers had dwelt before. Then Gisli and Thorkel went to Hol and set up their abode there; but Thorgrim took up his abode there in the west, and dwelt at Sæbol. Bork, his brother, had the management in Thorsness when his father Thorstein died, and there with him dwelt his nephews Quarrelsome Stein and Thorodd.

So those brothers-in-law dwell hard by as neighbours in Hawkdale, and are great friends. Thorkel. and Gisli built a fine house at Hol, so that it was soon no less a homestead than Sæbol: their lands touched and their friendship seemed likely to last. Thorgrim had the priesthood, and he was a great stay to those brothers. Now they fare in spring-time to the leet, forty men of them together and they were all in holiday clothes. There too, was Vestein, Gisli's brother-in-law, and every man of the Soursops following. Gest, the son of Oddleif, the wisest man in Iceland, had also come to that leet, and he turned into the booth of Thorkel the Wealthy of Alvidra. The Hawkdalemen sit at drink, while the rest of the freemen were at the court, for it was a Thing for trying suits. All at once there came into the Hawkdale booth a great oaf, Arnor by name, who spoke and said: "You Hawkdalemen are strange fellows, who take heed for naught but drink, and never go near the court where your followers have suits to settle. This is what all think, though I alone utter it."

Then Gisli said: "Let us go to the courts as soon as ever we can; maybe that others than Arnor utter this."

Now they go to the courts, and Thorgrim asks if there were any there who stood in need of their help, "for we will leave nothing undone to help our men, and they shall never be shorn of their rights so long as we stand straight."

Then Thorkel the Wealthy spoke and said: "This business that we have in hand is little worth. We will send and tell you as soon as we need your help."

Now men fell to talking about their band, how brave it was in attire, and about Thorgrim's haughty speech, and about his gallant bearing; and when men went home to their booths Thorkel the Wealthy said to Gest the Wise: "How long thinkest thou that the spirit of these Hawkdalemen will last? How long will they bear all before them?"

"They will not," said Gest, "be all of one and the same mind as they are now three springs hence."

But Arnor the oaf was by when Gest said this, and ran at once to the Hawk-dale booth, and told these words which had passed between Thorkel and Gest.

Then Gisli answered: "He must have said this because all feel it; but let us beware that it does not turn out true, for Gest says sooth about many things; and now methinks I see a plan by which we may well guard against it."

"What is that?"

"We shall bind ourselves by more lasting utterances than ever. Let us four take the oath of foster-brothers."

Well, they all thought that good counsel; and after that they went out of their booth to the point of the "ere," and there cut up a sod of turf in such wise that both its ends were still fast to the earth, and propped it up by a spear scored with runes, so tall that a man might lay his hand on the socket of the spear-head. Under this yoke they were all four to pass–Thorgrim, Gisli, Thorkel, and Vestein. Now they breathe each a vein, and let their blood fall together on the mould whence the turf had been cut up, and all touch it; and afterwards they all fall on their knees and were to take hands, and swear to avenge each the other as though he were his brother, and to call all the gods to witness.

But now, just as they were going to take hands, Thorgrim said: "I shall have quite enough on my hands if I do this towards Thorkel and Gisli, my brothers-in-law; but towards Vestein I have no tie to bind me to so great a charge." As he said this he drew back his hand.

"Then more will do the like," says Gisli, and drew back his hand. "I will be bound by no tie to the man who will not be bound by the same tie to my brother-in-law Vestein."

Now men began to think there was some weight in Gest's spaedom. But Gisli said to Thorkel: "All this happened as I foreboded, and this which we have done is of no good, for I guess that fate rules in this too."

Now men fare home from the leet, and all is still and tidingless.

Chapter 5
The Soursops Abroad

That summer, there came a ship from the sea into Dyrafirth, owned by two brothers, Norsemen. One's name was Thorir, and the other's Thorarinn. They were men from "the Bay," in South Norway. The story runs that Thorgrim the Priest rides to the ship, and buys of the captains wood worth four hundreds in woollen, and pays some of the price down, and promises to pay the rest. So the Easterlings made their ship snug at Sandwater-mouth and got winter-quarters for themselves and their men at the house of a man called Oddi who lived in Skutilsfirth. Now Thorgrim sends his son Thorodd to fetch home the wood, and bade him reckon it and know well every plank as he took it. So, he comes up to the ship, and thought the terms of the bargain were not so clear as Thorgrim had told him; for now the Easterlings were unwilling to keep to what they had agreed at first, and the end was that Thorodd spake ill words to the Easterlings. That they would not stand, and fell on him, and slew him there and then. After that the Easterlings left the ship, and took horse, and went to ride to their quarters in Skutilsfirth. They rode all that day and the night after, till they came to the dale which turns off from Skutilsfirth. Here they break their fast, and afterwards rode on again. Meanwhile Thorgrim had heard what had happened; how his son was slain, and the wood not handed over. Then he busked him for a journey, and had himself put across the firth. After the Easterlings he goes, all alone, and comes upon them as they lay and slept on a bit of mead. Thorgrim. wakes Thorarinn, and prods him with the butt of his spear. He springs up, and was about to draw his sword, for he knows Thorgrim, but Thorgrim thrusts his spear through him. Now Thorir wakes and would avenge his brother, but Thorgrim slew him too with his spear. So that is called Breakfastdale, where they broke their fast, and the, Easterlingsfall, where they lost their lives. Now Thorgrim goes home, and is famous for this deed. All that winter he stayed at home; but next spring the two brothers-in-law, Thorgrim and Thorkel, fitted out the ship which the Easterlings had owned for a foreign cruise, and they lade her with their goods, and were to sail for Norway. As for those Easterlings, they had been ill-doers in Norway, and were under a ban there. So they set sail the same summer, and Gisli also went aboard with his brother-in-law Vestein, and they sailed from Skeljawick in Steingrimsfirth. Aunund of Tweendale had care of Thorkel's and Gisli's farm while they were away, and Quarrelsome Stein took charge of Thorgrim's farm at Sæbol, along with his wife Thordisa.

At that time Harold Grayfell ruled over Norway. Thorgrim and Thorkel went north to Drontheim, and met the king there. They went in before him, and hailed him, and he was gracious to them. They became his thanes. They were well off both for goods and honour. As for Gisli and Vestein they were more than a hundred days out, and about the first day of winter came upon the coast of Hordaland in Norway, in a great fog and storm, at dead of night. Their ship was dashed to pieces, but they saved their goods and crew. There was a man off the coast called Beard-Bjalf. He owned a ship, and was on his way to Denmark. So Gisli and Vestein dealt with him for half the ship. He heard they were brave fellows, and gave them half the ship, and they repaid him at once by giving him more than half her worth in goods. So they held on their course for Denmark to that mart called Viborg. They stayed there that winter with a man called Sigrhadd. There they were all three in good fellowship–Gisli, Vestein, and Bjalf. They were great friends, and many gifts passed between them. At that time Christianity had come into Denmark, and Gisli and his companions were marked with the cross, for it was much the wont in those days of all who went on trading voyages; for so they entered into full fellowship with Christian men. Early the spring after, Bjalf fitted out his ship for Iceland. Now there was a man named Sigurd, a Norseman: he was a trading partner of Vestein's, and was then away west in England. He sent word to Vestein, and said he wished to cease partnership with him, for he thought he needed his goods no longer. So Vestein asked leave of Gisli to go to meet him; "for," he said, "I have money and goods to seek in that country."

"Thou shalt pledge me thy word first," said Gisli, "never to leave Iceland again, if thou comest safe back, unless I give thee leave."

To that Vestein agreed.

Next morning Gisli rises up early and goes to the smithy. He was the handiest of men, and had the quickest wit. So Gisli smithies a silver coin which weighed an ounce. He bent back the coin and broke it in two, and forged it with twenty teeth. When it was in two pieces there were ten teeth on one bit and ten on the other, but when they were put together it looked as though it were one whole; yet it might be taken asunder at once. Now Gisli takes the coin in two, and gives one half into Vestein's hand, and the other he keeps himself, He bids him keep that as a token if anything befell them which they thought of weight. "And," says Gisli, "we will only send these tokens between us if our life is at stake; and in truth my heart tells me we shall need to send them, though we do not see each other face to face."

With that they parted, and Vestein sails to England, but Gisli and Bjalf to Norway. That summer they set sail for Iceland, and had thriven well in goods and honour, and they ceased their partnership, and Bjalf bought back the half of the ship that Gisli owned. So Gisli goes home to his house in Dyrafirth with twelve men. That same spring Thorgrim and Thorkel fitted out their ship and came to Dyrafirth in the summer; and the very same day that Gisli had sailed into the mouth of the Hawkdale river Thorgrim and Thorkel sailed into it after him. So those brothers, Gisli and Thorkel, met; and that was a very joyful meeting.

So each of them went to his own home.

Chapter 6
Gisli and Thorkel Part

Thorkel the Soursop was very fond of dress and very lazy; he did not do a stroke of work in the housekeeping of those brothers; but Gisli worked night and day. It fell on a good drying day that Gisli set all the men at work hay-making, save his brother Thorkel. He alone of all the men was at home, and he had laid him down after breakfast in the hall, where the fire was, and gone to sleep. The hall was thirty fathoms long and ten broad. Away from it, and to the south, stood the bower of Auda and Asgerda, and there the two sat sewing. But when Thorkel wakes he goes toward the bower for he heard voices, and, lays him down outside close by the bower. Then Asgerda began to speak, and said:

"Help me, Auda dear; and cut me out a shirt for my husband Thorkel."

"I can't do that any better than thou," says Auda; "nor wouldst thou ask me to do it if thou wert making aught for my brother Vestein."

"All that touches Vestein is a thing by itself," says Asgerda; "and so it will be with me for many a day; for I love him more than my husband Thorkel, though we may never fulfil our love."

"I have long known," said Auda, "how Thorkel fared in this matter, and how things stood; but let us speak no more of it."

"I think it no harm," says Asgerda; "though I think Vestein a good fellow. Besides I have heard it said that ye two–thou and Thorgrim–often had meetings before thou wert given away in marriage."

"No wrong came of it to any man," said Auda, "nor has any man found favour in my eyes since I was given to Gisli. There has been no disgrace. Do pray stop this idle talk."

And so they did; but Thorkel had heard every word they spoke, and now he raised his voice and said:

> "Hear a great wonder,
> Hear words of doom;
> Hear matters mighty,
> Murders of men!"

After that he goes away indoors. Then Auda went on to say:

"Oft comes ill from women's gossip, and it may be so, and much worse, from this thing. Let us take counsel against it."

"Oh," says Asgerda, "I have bethought me of a plan which will stand me in good stead."

"What is it, pray?" says Auda.

"I will throw my arms round Thorkel's neck when we go to bed this evening, and be as kind to him as I can; and his heart will turn at that, and be will forgive me. I will tell him too that this was all stories, and that there is not a word of truth in what we chattered. But if he will be cross and hold me to it, then tell me some other plan; or hast thou any plan?"

"I will tell thee my plan in the twinkling of an eye," says Auda. "I will tell my husband Gisli all that gives me any trouble, whether it be good or ill. He will know how to help me out of it, for that will be best for me in the end."

At even Gisli came home from the hay-field. It was Thorkel's wont to thank his brother Gisli every day for the work he had done, but now he did not, and never a word said he to Gisli.

Then Gisli went up to Thorkel and said: "Does aught ail thee, brother, that thou art so silent?"

"I have no sickness," says Thorkel; "but this is worse than sickness."

"Have I done aught, brother," says Gisli, "that displeases thee?"

"Thou hast done nothing of the sort."

"That makes me glad at once; for the last thing that I wish is that anything should come between our love. But still I would so like to know what is at the root of thy sadness."

"Thou wilt know it soon enough," says Thorkel, "though thou dost not know it now."

Then Gisli goes away and says no more, and men go to bed when night came. Thorkel ate little that night, and was the first to go to bed. But when

Asgerda came to his bedside and lifted the bed-clothes, then Thorkel said to her:

"I do not mean to let thee sleep here to-night."

"Why, what is more fitting," she said, "than that I should sleep by my husband? Why hast thy heart so soon changed, and what is the matter?"

"Thou knowest very well, and I know it. It has been long hidden from me, but thy good name will not be greater if I speak it out."

"What's the good of talking like that?" she said. "Thou oughtest to know better than to believe the silly talk of us women, for we are ever chattering when we are alone about things without a word of truth in them; and so it was here."

Then Asgerda threw both her arms round his neck, and was soft and kind, and bade him never believe a word of it.

But Thorkel was cross, and bade her be off.

"Then," says Asgerda, "I will not strive with thee any longer for what thou wilt not grant. But I will give thee two choices: the first is, to treat all this as if it had been unspoken—I mean all that we have joked about, and to lay no faith on what is not true; the other is, that I take witness at once and be parted from thee. Then I shall do as I please, and maybe thou wilt then have something to tell of true hatred; and as for me, I will make my father claim at thy hand my dower and portion, and then surely thou wilt no longer be troubled with me as thy bed-fellow."

Thorkel was tongue-tied for a while. At last he said:

"My counsel to thee is to creep in on the side of the bed that belongs to thee. I can't waste all the night in keeping thee out."

So she goes to bed at once, and they make up their quarrel as though it had never happened. As for Auda, when she went to bed with her husband Gisli, she tells him all that she and Asgerda had said just as it happened, and begged him not to be wroth with her, but to give her good counsel if he saw any.

"For I know," she said, "that Thorkel will wish to see my brother Vestein dead, if he may have his way."

"I do not see," says Gisli, "any counsel that is good; but I will throw no blame on thee for this, because when things are once doomed, some one must utter the words that seem to bring them about."

Now that half-year passes away, and the flitting-days come. Thorkel tells his brother Gisli that he wishes to share all their goods between them, for he is going to join housekeeping with his brother-in-law Thorgrim.

"Brothers' goods are fairest to look on when they lie together, brother. Many things I see which whisper, 'Do not part.' It gladdens my heart to let things bide as they are. Do not let us part."

"Things cannot go on as they are," says Thorkel. "We cannot keep house together any longer, for there is great harm in this, that thou shouldest have all the toil and trouble about the farm, while I turn my hand to nothing which brings in any gain."

"Do not thou talk about that," says Gisli, "so long as I say never a word. I am well pleased with things as they are. Besides, we have gone through much together. We have been good friends and bad friends. We have borne bad luck and good luck as brothers. But we were always best off when we stood shoulder to shoulder, Do not let us change now."

"Well," says Thorkel, "there's no use in talking. I have made up my mind to share our goods, and they shall be shared. As I ask for them to be shared, thou shalt have the house and heritage, and I the goods and chattels."

"As for that," says Gisli, "if it must come to that, and we are to part, do as thou likest–share or choose. I care not what I do."

The end of it was that Gisli shared; and Thorkel chose the goods and chattels, and Gisli kept the land. In their household were two poor children whom they had taken in, the offspring of their kinsman Ingialld, and these two they parted: the boy's name was Geirmund, and the girls Gudrida. She stayed with Gisli, but Geirmund went with Thorkel. So Thorkel went away to his brother-in-law Thorgrim, and took up his abode with him; but Gisli had the farm at Hol to himself, and the household lacked nothing, but went on as well as before. And now the summer slips away, and the first winter night was nigh at hand.

Chapter 7
Vestein comes back to Iceland

Gisli made a feast, and bade his friends to it he wished to have a gathering, and so to welcome both the winter and his friends; but he had left off all heathen sacrifices since he had been in Viborg with Sigrhadd. He bade to the feast both the Thorkels and his cousins, the sons of Bjartmar. So that the day that the guests were looked for Gisli made ready his house. Then Auda, the housewife, spoke and said: "Now, methinks but one thing is wanting."

"What is that?" asked Gisli.

"This alone," said Auda, "that my brother Vestein is not here."

"Well," said Gisli, "we do not look at things in the same way. I would give much goods that he were not here, as I now ween he is."

There was a man of whom we have spoken before, Thorgrim Bottlenose; he dwelt at Nebstead, in the inner bight of the river. He was full of witchcraft and sorcery, and he was a wizard and worker of spells. This man Thorgrim. and Thorkel asked to their feast, for they had as large a gathering as Gisli Thorgrim, the priest of Frey, was a man well skilled in forging iron. So those three went aside together–the two Thorgrims and Thorkel. Then Thorkel brings out the broken bits of "Graysteel," which had fallen to his lot when they parted their heritage, and Thorgrim forged out of it a spear, and that spear was all ready by even and fitted to its haft. It was a great spear-head, and runes were on it, and it was fitted to a haft a span long.

And when this was being done there came Aunund of Tweendale to Gisli's house; and took him aside to talk, and tells him that Vestein his brother-in-law has come into the land, and is now at his house under Hest, and that he will be with him that evening. Then Gisli called his two house-carles, Hallvard and Havard, and bids them go on a message north to Aunundarfirth.

"Find now my brother-in-law Vestein; I am told he has come home. Bear him my greeting, and bid him sit quietly at home till I come to see him; for my will is, that he should not come-to this feast." Gisli gives them into their hands a purse, and in it half of the silver coin, for a token in case Vestein should not believe their story. Now the house-carles set off, and take ship out of Hawkdale, and row across to Brooksmouth. There they land, and go to a farmer named Bessi, who dwelt at Bessastead. To him Gisli had sent word that he should lend them two horses which he had, which were called "the Pair of Gloves." They were the fleetest horses in all the firths. He lent them the horses, and they got on their backs and rode till they came to Mossvale. After that they turned and rode along the firth.

But at the same time Vestein had started from home, and had got as far as beneath the sandhill at Mossvale, and then on to Holt. But the house-carles had ridden the upper road, and so they rode by and missed each other. There was a man named Thorvard who lived at Holt, and his house-carles were quarrelling over their work, and were striking at one another with their scythes, and gave one another bad wounds. Then Vestein came up and made them good friends again, so that both sides were well pleased. Then he rode on for Dyrafirth, and two Easterlings with him. By this time Gisli's house-carles had reached Hest. There they learn of Vestein's journey-how he had left home; and now they turn back after him as fast as they can. And when they come to Mossvale they see a train of men riding in the midst of the dale, and then a jutting crag hid them from their view. So they ride on up the dale, and when they come to Arnkelsbrink both their horses were foundered. But the house-carles run on;on foot, and call out. Vestein and his men heard them cry, and by that time they had got up on Gemladaleheath. So Vestein waited there till the others come up. But when they meet, the house-carles tell him their errand and show him the token. Then he takes the other half of the coin out of his purse, and put the two bits together, and grew red, as he said:

"Tis sooth every word of it, and I would have turned back had ye found me before; but now all the streams fall towards Dyrafirth, and I will ride thither, for I am eager to see my brother-in-law and my sister; 'tis long since we parted; but these Easterlings shall turn back. As for ye, ye shall go the shortest way, as ye are afoot; but tell Gisli and my sister that I am coming to them, for I hope to get there safe and sound."

Now they cross the firth, and come to Hol, and tell Gisli all that had happened on their journey, and that Vestein was on his way thither.

"So it must be, then," said Gisli.

Now Vestein rides the inner road round Dyrafirth, but the house-carles had a boat, as was said before, and so they were far quicker. Vestein comes to Luta, his kinswoman, in Lambdale–that is far up in the bight of the firth. She had him ferried across the top of the firth, and said to him:

"Beware of thyself, kinsman. Thou wilt need to take all care."

He said he would do all he could. Thence he was ferried over to Thingere, where a man dwelt whose name was Thorhall. Vestein went up to his house, and he lent him a horse. Vestein had with him his saddle and saddle-cloth, and rode with a streamer to his spear. Thorhall went with him on the way as far as Sandmouth, and offers to go with him as far as Gisli's house. Vestein said there was no need of that.

"Ah!" said Thorhall, "there have been many changes in Hawkdale since thou wert last here, and beware of thyself"

With these words they parted. Now Vestein rides till he comes to Hawkdale, and the evening was bright and starlit. But it so happened as he rode by Thorgrim's house at Sæbol in the dusk that they were tethering the cattle– Geirmund the lad, the kinsman of Thorkel and Gisli, and along with him a woman whose name was Rannveiga. She makes up the beds for the cattle, while he drives them into her; and so as they were at that work there rides Vestein round the 'town' and meets Geirmund. Then Geirmund said: "Come not thou in here at Sæbol, but go to Gisli, and beware of thyself."

Just then Rannveiga came out of the byre, and looked at the man and thought she knew him, for she had often seen Vestein. So when they had tethered the cattle in the byre they fell to wrangling about the stranger, who he could have been, and they were hard at it when they reached the house. Thorgrim and Thorkel were sitting before the fire when they came in-doors, and Thorgrim. asks if they had seen any one, and about what they were wrangling

"Oh!" said Rannveiga, "I thought I saw that Vestein rode here round our 'town,' and he had on a blue cape and held a big spear in his hand with a streamer fluttering on it."

"What sayest thou to that, Geirmund?" asked Thorgrim.

"I did not see clearly," he answered; "but I thought it was the house-carle of Aunund of Tweendale, and he had on Gisli's cape, and rode one of his master's horses, and in his hand he had a salmon-spear with a landing-net bound on it."

"Now one of you must be telling lies," said Thorgrim. "Go now over to Hol, Rannveiga, and find out what strangers have come thither."

So she went and stood at the door. Outside the doorway was Gisli, who greeted her and asked her to stay there, but she said she must go back home.

"What's thy errand?" he asked.

"I only wanted to have a word with Gudrida," she answered.

So Gisli called Gudrida, but when she came Rannveiga had nothing to say to her. Then Rannveiga said: "Where is the mistress Auda?"

"She is here," says Gisli, "inside the house. Auda, come and see Rannveiga," he calls out.

Then Auda went out to see Rannveiga, and asked what she wanted. But she said it was only about a little thing, and still she could not say what that little thing was.

So Gisli bade her do one thing or the other–stay there or go away; "for," he said, "'tis now getting so late that thou oughtest not to go back alone though the way be short."

Then she went home and was half as silly as she had been before, and she could tell nothing of any stranger that had come to Gisli's house.

Next morning Vestein made them bring in two bags which some of his lading was in, and which he had given over to Hallvard and Havard to bring. Out of these Vestein took seventy ells of hangings and a kerchief twenty ells long, all woven with a pattern of gold in three stripes. He also brought out two gilded basons. These treasures he took out, and to his sister he gave the kerchief, but to Gisli and Thorkel he gave the hangings and the basons between them, if Thorkel would take them. After that Gisli goes over to Sæbol, and both the Thorkels with him, to see his brother Thorkel; and now Gisli says that Vestein has come to stay with him, and he shows Thorkel the treasures, and tells him how they were given between them, and bade him take them; but Thorkel says:

"Thou art worthy to have them all alone, and I will not take them. It is not so very plain how I shall repay them."

So Gisli goes home, and Thorkel will not touch the gifts; and Gisli thought that things all went in one and the same way.

Chapter 8
Vestein's Slaying

It came out, too, at that feast that Gisli was restless at night, two nights together. He would not say what dreams he had, though men asked him.

Now comes the third night, and men go to their beds, and when they had slumbered a while a whirlwind fell on the house with such strength that it tore all the roof off on one side, and in a little while all the rest of the roof followed. Then rain fell from heaven in such a flood the like was never seen before, and the house began to drip and drip, as was likely when the roof was off Gisli sprang out of bed and called on his men to show their mettle, and save the hay-stacks from being washed away; and so he left the house, and every man with him, except a thrall, whose name was Thord the Hareheart, who was nearly as tall as Gisli. Vestein wanted to go with Gisli, but Gisli would not suffer it. So when they were all gone Auda and Vestein draw their beds from the wall, where the water dripped down on them, and turn them end on to the benches in the midst of the hall. The thrall too stayed in the house, for he had not heart enough to go out of doors in such a storm.

And a little before dawn some one stole softly into the hall, and stood over against Vestein's bed. He was then awake, and a spear was thrust then and there into his chest, right through his body. But when Vestein got the thrust, he sprang up and called out: "Stabbed! stabbed!" and with that he fell dead on the floor.

But the man passed out at the door.

Meanwhile Auda awakes, and sees what work was being done. Now Thord the Hareheart comes up, and she told him to pluck the weapon out of the wound, for in those days it was a settled thing that the man was bound to avenge the slain who took the weapon out of the wound, and it was called secret slaying, but not murder, if, when the deed was done, the weapon were left behind. But Thord was so afraid of the dead that he did not so much as dare to come nigh the spot. Then Gisli came in, and Spoke to the thrall, and bade him let it alone; and then Gisli went up and took the spear away, and cast it, all bloody as it was, into a chest, and let no man see it. After that he sat down on the bedside, and laid out the body as was the wont; and Gisli thought he had suffered a great loss, and many others with him.

Then Gisli said to Gudrida, his foster-child:

"Thou must go over to Sæbol, and find out what men are about there; and I send thee because I trust thee best of all in this and in all other things."

So she went to Sæbol, and found them already risen when she got there, and they were all sitting with their weapons.

There were both the Thorgrims and Thorkel. They were slow to greet her, for most of them had scarce a word to say. At last they ask her what news, and she tells them that Vestein was slain or murdered.

"We should have thought that great news once," said Thorkel.

Then Thorgrim went on: "We are bound to bury Vestein as worthily as we can. We will come and help to lay him in his howe. Tell Gisli we will come, too, this very day. Sooth to say, such a man's death is a great loss."

After that she went home, and tells Gisli that Thorgrim the priest sat with his helm on his head and his sword at his belt, and all his war-gear, when she went in; that Thorgrim Bottlenose had a pole-axe in his hand, and that Thorkel had a sword in his hand half-drawn. All men were up and about, and some of them armed, when she reached Sæbol.

"Just as I thought," said Gisli.

Now Gisli made ready to lay Vestein in his howe, and they meant to lay him in the sandhill which looks down on the tarn just below Sæbol, and as they were on their way with the body Thorgrim. came up with many men to meet them. And when they had heaped up the howe, and were going to lay the body in it, Thorgrim the priest goes up to Gisli, and says, "Tis the custom, brother-in-law, to bind the hellshoe on men, so that they may walk on them to Valhalla, and I will now do that by Vestein."

And when he had done it, he said

"I know nothing about binding on hellshoon if these loosen."

Then they sat down outside the howe and talked, and Gisli asks if any one thought he knew who had done that deed, but all thought it most unlikely that any there knew who had done this crime.

Thorkel asks Gisli: "How Auda bore her brother's death? Does she weep much?"

"I should think thou knowest well how she bears it. She shows it little and feels it much. I dreamed a dream," says Gisli, "the night before last, and last night too, but I will not tell it, nor say who did this slaying, but my dreams all point to it. Methought I dreamt the first night that an adder crept out of a house I know, and stung Vestein to death. And last night I dreamt that a wolf ran from the same house and tore Vestein to death; but I told neither dream up to this time, because I did not wish that any one should interpret them." Then he chaunted a song:

> "Twice I dreamt it! thrice I could not!
> Vestein, Woden's darling, would not
> Have been wakened thus I ween,
> When we sat in Vibjorg drinking,
> Never from the wine-cup shrinking,
> No man sitting us between."

Again Thorkel asks: "How bore Auda her brother's death? Does she weep sore?"

"Oft askest thou the same thing, kinsman," said Gisli, "and thou art very eager to know this."

Again Gisli chaunted a song:

> "Deep beneath her golden veil
> Rides her grief that lady pale
> Still down fields where roses blush
> Streams from slumber's fountain gush.
> From her heart dim mists arise,
> Filling all her beauteous eyes,
> Down her cheeks tears chase each other:
> Thus Auda mourneth for her brother."

And again he chaunted:

> "She the goddess, ring-bestowing,
> Sets the waves of sorrow flowing;
> From her golden eyebrows pressed,
> Down they dash upon her breast.
> Vestein's voice no longer singeth,
> Pearl on pearl his sister stringeth;
> Gems that round her dark eyes glisten:
> My song is o'er—no longer listen!"

Now these brothers go away both together, and as they went Thorkel said: "These have been great tidings, and to thee they must seem more mournful than to us; but after all, everyone must bear his own burden, for every one walks farthest with his own self. Now I would, brother, that thou dost not let this take such hold on thee that men should fall to wondering about it; and so my wish is, that we take to some sports, and that now everything should be with us as it hath been when we were the best friends."

"That is well spoken," said Gisli, "and I will willingly do that—only with this bargain, that if anything ever befalls thee which thou feelest as much as I do this, then thou shalt give me thy word to behave just as thou askest me to behave now."

To that Thorkel agreed, and after that they each go home, and Vestein's ale of heirship was brewed and drunk, and when that was done each man went to his own home, and all was quiet.

But men say that all that great storm was the work of Thorgrim Bottlenose, with his sorcery and witchcraft, and that he had so framed his spells as to get a good chance at Vestein while Gisli was not near him; for they did not dare to fall on him if Gisli were by. But after the storm Thorgrim, the priest of Frey, did the deed, and slew Vestein, as we have already said.

So now the sports were set afoot as though nothing had happened. Those brothers-in-law, Thorgrim and Gisli, were very often matched against each other, and men could not make up their minds which was the stronger, but most thought Gisli had most strength. They were playing at the ball on the tarn called Sedgetarn. On it there was ever a crowd. It fell one day when there was a great gathering that Gisli bade them share the sides as evenly as they could for a game.

"That we will with all our hearts," said Thorkel; "but we also wish thee not to spare thy strength against Thorgrim, for the story runs that thou sparest him; but as for me I love thee well enough to wish that thou shouldst get all the more honour if thou art the stronger."

"We have not put that yet to the proof," says Gisli "maybe the time may come for us to try our strength."

Now they began the game, and Thorgrim could not hold his own. Gisli threw him and bore away the ball. Again Gisli wished to catch the ball, but Thorgrim runs and holds him and will not let him get near it. Then Gisli turned and threw Thorgrim such a fall on the slippery ice that he could scarce rise. The skin came off his knuckles, and the flesh off his knees, and blood gushed from his nostrils. Thorgrim was very slow in rising. As he did so he looked towards Vestein's howe, and chaunted:

> "Right through his ribs,
> My spear-point went crashing;
> Why should I worry?
> Twas well worth this thrashing."

Gisli caught the ball on the bound, and hurled it between Thorgrim's shoulders so that he tumbled forwards, and threw his heels up in the air, and Gisli chaunted:

> "Bump on his back
> My big ball went dashing;

> Why should I worry?
> Twas I gave the thrashing."

Thorkel jumps up and says: "Now we can see who is the strongest or is the best player. Let us break off the game." And so they did.

Chapter 9
Thorgrim's Slaying

Now the games ceased, and the summer comes on, and there was rather a coldness between Thorgrim and Gisli. Thorgrim meant to have a harvest feast on the first night of winter, and to sacrifice to Frey. He bids to it his brother Bork, and Eyjolf the son of Thord, and many other great men. Gisli too made ready a feast, and bids to it his brothers-in-law from Arnafirth, and the two Thorkels; so that there were full sixty men at his house. There was to be a drinking-bout at each house, and the floor at Sæbol was covered with sedge won from Sedgetarn. Now when Thorgrim and his men were busy putting up the hangings in the hall, Thorgrim all at once said to Thorkel "Those hangings would come in well–those fine ones I mean–that Vestein wished to give thee; methinks there is great difference between your having them for a day or having them altogether. I wish thou wouldst send for them now."

"The man," said Thorkel, "who knows how to forbear is master of all knowledge. I will not send for them."

"Then I wilt" said Thorgrim; and with that he bade Geirmund go and fetch them.

"I have work to do," said Geirmund, "and I have no mind to go."

Then Thorgrim. goes up to him, and gave him a great buck-horse on the ear, and said:

"Be off with thee now, if thou likest it better."

"So I will," he said; "though I have less mind than ever but be sure I'll do my best to give thee the gray mare instead of thy horse. Then we shall be quits."

So he went away; but when he gets to Gisli's house, Gisli and Auda were hard at work putting up the hangings. Geirmund told his errand, and the whole story.

"Well, Auda," said Gisli, "wilt thou lend them the hangings?"

"Why ask me at all," says Auda, "when thou knowest that I would neither grant them this nor aught else that would do them any honour?"

"Did my brother Thorkel wish it?" asks Gisli.

"He was well pleased that I came for them."

"That alone is quite enough," said Gisli; and with that he gives him the rich hangings, and went back with him on the way. Gisli goes with him right up to the farm-yard, and then said:

"Things now stand in this wise: I think I have made thy errand turn out well, and now I wish thou wouldst be yielding to me in what I want. for gift answers to gift, you know, and one hand washes the other. My wish is, that thou wouldst push back the bolts of the three doors to-night. Think how thou wast bidden to set out."

"Will there be any risk to thy brother Thorkel?" said Geirmund.

"None at all," said Gisli.

"Then that shall come to pass," said Geirmund.

And now when he comes home he casts down the costly hangings, and Thorkel said:

"Unlike is Gisli to other men in long-suffering. He is far better than we."

"For all that," said Thorgrim. "we need these pretty things so let us e'en put them up."

After that the guests who were bidden came at even. Now the weather thickens, and a snow-drift falls that night and covers all paths.

Bork and Eyjolf came to the feast with a hundred and twenty men, and there were half as many at Gisli's house. Men took to drinking in the evening, and after that they go to bed and sleep.

Then Gisli said to Auda his wife:

"I have not given fodder to Thorkel the Wealthy's horse. Come now with me and undo the locks at the gate, and watch while I am away, and undo the locks again when I come back."

He takes the spear "Graysteel" out of the chest, and is clad in a blue cape, and in his kirtle and linen breeks and shoes. So he goes to the brook which runs between the farms, whence each drew water for its cattle. He goes down to the brook by the path, and then wades along it to the other path that led up to the other farm. Gisli knew all the ins and outs of the house at Sæbol, for he had built it himself. There was a way from the water into the byre. That was where he got in. There in the byre stood thirty cows, back to back; he knots together the tails of the kine, and locks up the byre, and makes it so fast that it cannot be opened if any one came from the inside. After that he goes to the dwelling-house, and Geirmund had done his work well, for there was not a bolt to any of the doors. Now he goes in and shuts the door again, just as it had been locked the evening before. Now he takes his time, and stands and spies about if any were awake, and he is soon aware that all men are asleep. There were three lamps in the hall. Then he takes some of the sedge from the floor, and makes a wisp of it, and throws it on one of the lights, and quenches it. Again he stands awhile, and spies if any man had awoke, and cannot find that any are awake. Then he takes another wisp and throws it at that light which stood next, and quenches that. Then he became aware that all men cannot be asleep; for he sees now a young man's arm comes toward the third light, and pulls down the lamp; and puts out the light.

Now he goes farther in along the house till he comes to the shut bed where Thorgrim and his sister Thordisa slept. The lattice was ajar, and there they are both in bed. Then he goes thither, and puts out his hand to feel, and touches her breast; for she slept on the outside.

Then Thordisa said: "Why is thy hand so cold, Thorgrim?" and wakes him up.

"Wilt thou that I turn to thee?" asked Thorgrim.

She thought he had laid his hand on her.

Then Gisli bides awhile, and warms his hand in his shirt but they two fell asleep again.

Now he takes hold of Thorgrim gently, so that he woke and turned towards Thordisa, for he thought she had roused him.

Then Gisli lifts the clothes off them with one hand, while with the other he thrusts Thorgrim through the body with "Graysteel," and pins him to the bed.

Now Thordisa, cries out: "Wake up men in the hall; my husband Thorgrim is slain!"

Gisli turns short away to the byre. He goes out where he had meant, and locks it up strongly behind him. Then he goes home by the same way, and his footsteps cannot be seen. Auda pushes back the bolts when he came home, and he gets into bed, and makes as though nothing had happened, or as though he had naught to do but sleep.

But down at Sæbol all the men were mad with drink, and knew not what to do. The deed came on them unawares, and so no course was taken that was of any good.

At last Eyjolf of Otterdale said: "Here have happened ill tidings, and great tidings, and all the folk have been bereft of their wits. It seems to me the best thing were to light the lamps, and run to the doors, that the manslayer may not get out."

And so it was done, and men thought when they could not lay hands on the manslayer, that it must have been some one in the house who had done the deed.

So time runs on till day came. Then they took Thorgrim's body and plucked out the spear, and he was laid out for burial, and sixty men followed him. So they fare to Gisli's house at Hol. Thord the Hareheart was out of doors early, and when he sees the band, he runs in and says that a host of men were marching on the house, and was quite out of breath.

"That is well," said Gisli, and chaunted a stave

> "Mighty man! my mind is easy;
> Too many have I done to death
> To be scared by tidings queasy,
> Uttered by idiots out of breath.
> No! I lie and take my slumber;
> Though this lord is stretched on earth
> Idle rumours without number
> Vex the folk and mar their mirth."

Now they come to the farm, Thorkel and Eyjolf, and go up to the shut-bed where Gisli and his wife slept; but Thorkel, Gisli's brother, stepped up first on to the floor, and stands at the side of the bed, and sees Gisli's shoes lying all frozen and snowy. He kicked them under the footboard, so that no other man should see them.

Now Gisli greets them and asks the news. Thorkel said there were both great and bad news, and asks what it might mean, and what counsel was best to take.

"Then there has been scant space between two great and ill deeds," said Gisli: "but we shall be ready enough to lay Thorgrim in his howe, and you have a right to ask that of us, for it is our bounden duty to do it with all honour."

They took that offer gladly, and all together went to Sæbol to throw up the howe, and lay Thorgrim in his ship.

Now they heap up the howe after the fashion of the olden time, and when they were just about to close the howe Gisli goes to the mouth of the stream, and takes up a stone so big that it looked like a rock, and dashes it down on the ship, so that every timber cracked again, and the whole ship creaked and groaned. As he did that he said:

"I know nothing of making a ship fast if any weather stirs this!"

Some now said that this looked very like what Thorgrim had done to Vestein when he spoke about the hellshoon.

Now they made them ready to go home from the howe, and Gisli said to his brother:

"Methinks I have a right to call on thee, brother, that our friendship should now be as good as when it was best. Now let us set some sports afoot."

Thorkel took that well enough, and they parted and went home. Gisli's house was now quite full, and the feast came to an end, and Gisli gives good gifts to his guests.

Chapter 10
Gisli Betrays Himself

Now Thorgrim's ale of heirship is brewed and drunk, and Bork gives good gifts to many of his friends. The next thing we have to say is, that Bork bargains with Thorgrim Bottlenose that he should work spells and charms, by which no man should be able to house or harbour him that had slain Thorgrim, however great their will might be, and that the slayer should have no rest on land. An ox nine winters old was given him for this; and now Thorgrim sets about his spells over his cauldron, and makes him a high-place, and fulfils his work with all witchcraft and wickedness. After that, the guests broke up, and each man went to his own abode.

And now, too, a thing happened which seemed strange and new. No snow lodged on the south side of Thorgrim's howe, nor did it freeze there. And men guessed it was because Thorgrim had been so dear to Frey for his worship's sake that the god would not suffer the frost to come between them.

Now Bork sets up his abode with Thordisa, and takes his brother's widow to wife, with his brother's goods; that was the rule in those days–wives were heritage like other things. But Thordisa was not single when this happened, and after a while she bears a son to Thorgrim, and he is sprinkled with water, and at first called Thorgrim, after his father; but as he grew up he was thought snappish and unyielding in temper, and so his name was changed to suit his mood, and he was called Snerrir the Snarler, and afterwards Snorro.

So Bork abode there that half-year, and the sports they had spoken of were set afoot. There was a woman named Audbjorga who dwelt at the top of the Dale at Anmarkstead. She was sister to Thorgrim Bottlenose. Her husband had been that Thorkel of whom we have spoken. Her son's name was Thorstein, and he was about the strongest man in all the west country, save Gisli. They are partners in the game at ball, Gisli and Thorstein and against them were matched Bork and Thorkel. One day a host of men came to see the game, for many were eager to behold the sport, and all wanted to know who was the strongest man and the best player. But here, as elsewhere, it happened that the players played with greater spirit when there were many lookers-on. It is said that Bork could not stand against Thorstein that day, and at last Bork got wroth, and broke asunder Thorstein's bat; but Thorstein gave him a fall, and sent him spinning along the slippery ice. But when Gisli sees that he says:

"Thorstein shall go on playing with Bork with all his might. I will change bats with thee."

So they changed bats, and Gisli sate him down and tries to put the broken bat to rights, and then he looks at Thorgrim's howe. There was snow on the ground, but on the south side of the howe there was no snow; and there, up on the steep brink sat Thordisa and many other women, who thought it fun to look on the game.

Then Gisli—woe worth the day!—chaunted this song:

> "O'er him who Thor's grim vizard wore
> Melt, wreath by wreath, snow-hangings hoar.
> Few have the wit to understand
> The riddle of this mound of land.
> I harmed him? No! I harmed him not;
> A mansion bright is here his lot;
> The priest unto his god I gave,
> And Frey now warms his servant's grave."

Thordisa heard these verses, and learned them by heart. She goes home, and understood their meaning at once.

Now they leave off playing, and Thorstein sets out to go home. There was a man named Thorgeir, called Thorgeir the Gorcock. He lived at Gorcockstead. There was another man named Berg; his nickname was Shortshanks. He lived at Shortshanks-mire, west of the river. Now as men fare home they talk about the games; and Thorstein and Berg from talking fell to quarrelling. Berg takes Bork's side, but Thorstein stands up for himself. At last Berg smote Thorstein with the back of his axe; but Thorgeir threw himself between them, so that Thorstein could not avenge himself. So he goes home to his mother Audbjorga, who binds up his wound, for the skin was broken, and she is ill-pleased at his plight.

All that night the carline could not sleep, so much did she take it to heart. The weather was cold, but still and bright.

But she goes once or twice round the house widdershins, and snuffs to all airts, and draws in the air. And as she did this the weather began to change, and there was a driving sleet, and after that a thaw; and a flood poured down the hillside; and a snowslip fell on the farm of Berg, and there twelve souls lost their lives, and the tokens of the landslip are still to be seen.

Now Thorstein goes to Gisli, and he sheltered him, and sent him south to Borgarfirth, and so abroad. But as soon as Bork heard of this black deed, he went straight to Anmarkstead, and made them seize Audbjorga, and takes her out to Saltness, and stones her with stones till she dies. And when this is noised abroad, Gisli goes from home to Nebstead, and seizes Thorgrim Bottlenose, and brings him to Saltness, and there a goatskin is drawn over his head, that his evil eye may be harmless, and he too is stoned to death, and buried by his sister's side, on the ridge between Hawkdale and Tweendale. And now all is quiet, and the spring draws on.

Now Bork makes up his mind to set off south to Thorsness, and thinks to change his abode thither, and thinks he has made rather a sorry figure there away west: lost such a man as Thorgrim was, and got no amends for it. Still he makes ready to go, and means first to set his house to rights, and then to make another journey to fetch his wife and goods. Thorkel too, the Soursop, makes up his mind to go with his brother-in-law Bork.

So men say that Thordisa, Gisli's sister, went with Bork a bit of the way, and as they went Bork said:

"I wish now thou wouldest tell me why thou wast all at once so sad last autumn when we broke up the games. Thou knowest thou saidst thou wouldst tell me ere I went away."

They had just then come to Thorgrim's howe as he uttered these words.

Then she stamps her foot on the ground, and says it was no use to fare farther. And now she tells him of the verses that Gisli had chaunted as he mended the bat and looked at Thorgrim's howe; and recites the verses.

"I ween," she said, "thou hast no need to look anywhere else for Thorgrim's manslayer, and thou mayst sue him for it with a safe heart, for he took the slaying on himself in those verses."

Then Bork grew awfully angry, and said:

"I will now turn back at once and slay Gisli. The best way is to waste no more time."

But Thorkel says he will not agree to that. "I am not quite sure whether this be true or not. Bear in mind the saw that says 'Women's counsel is always unlucky.' For even though this should be as bad as she has said, surely, Bork, it is better to follow the law of the land in this matter and make the man an outlaw; for thou hast the cause so made to thy hand that Gisli must be found guilty, even though he had some excuse. So that we shall be able to manage this suit as we choose if we take the right steps, and that is far better than spoiling everything by rushing on so madly against all reason."

The end was, that he had his way.

Chapter 11
Gisli an Outlaw

So Bork and his men rode on after that by the path over the sands till they get across the mouth of Sandwater; there they get off their horses and bait. Then Thorkel says he wishes to see his brother-in-law Aunund, and that he will ride on hard before them. But as soon as ever he was out of sight be rides straight for Hol, and says what had happened, and how Thordisa had given out that Gisli slew Thorgrim.

"Now," he says, "the story is in every man's mouth."

Gisli was silent a while, and then chaunted:

> "My sister loves to tire her head,
> But little thinks of Gudrun dead–
> Gudrun, that high-souled Gjuki's child,
> Who saw her husband slain, and smiled;
> Another husband she might have,
> But barren lies a brother's grave;
> And so, to 'venge her brother's fall,
> She slew her husband, sons, and all.

"And yet I never thought she would do this, for I think I have often shown that her dishonour was not a whit less felt by me than my own. Sometimes, too, I have had my life in peril for her sake, but now she deals me this death-blow. But what am I to look for at thy hands, kinsman, now that I have done such a deed?"

"This," said Thorkel, "I will warn thee if I am myself aware that men are about to lie in wait for thy life, but I will give thee no other help for which I may get into trouble. Methinks, too, thou hast much misdone against me–slain both my brother-in-law, and partner, and bosom friend."

"Well," says Gisli, "was it not to be looked for, for such a man as Vestein was, that some revenge must be had for his loss? I would not answer thee as thou answerest me; nor would I do as thou doest."

So those brothers parted, and now Thorkel rides back to meet Bork, and they ride west across the heath. Bork does not draw bridle till he comes south to Thorsness, and sets his house in order there. As for Thorkel Soursop he buys him land at Bardastrand at a place called "the Combe."

But when the summoning days are coming on Bork sets out with sixty men for the west firths, and means to summon Gisli to take his trial at Thorsness Thing, and Thorkel went with him, and Thorodd and Quarrelsome Stein,

Bork's nephews, the sons of Thordisa, the daughter of Thorstein Codbiter. There was an Easterling too, named Thorgrim, who went with them.

So they all fared till they came to Sandwatermouth. Then Thorkel says that he has some debts to call for at a farm called Hol, farther on in their way.

"I will ride on first," he says; and so he does. But as soon as ever he reached the farm he bade the housewife change horses with him.

"But let this horse of mine stand outside before the door,

saddled and bridled, and when they come by—my fellow-travellers—say I am indoors telling silver.'"

She did as he bade her—got him another horse; and he rides might and main to Hol, sees Gisli, and tells what was about to befall him. Gisli asks Thorkel again what counsel was best to take, and what countenance he will give him. But Thorkel answers as before that he will do naught else but warn him if any danger is about to befall him.

Now Thorkel rides away, and so shapes his course that he rode round behind Bork and his fellows, mounts his own horse, and overtakes them. He delays them as much as he can, and makes them lose much time. But as soon as those brothers parted—Thorkel and Gisli—Gisli takes two sledges, and drives off with them into the wood, with all his goods and chattels: he had already sold his land to Thorkel, Erie's son: and he takes Thord the Hareheart, his thrall, with him. Then Gisli said to Thord:

"Oft hast thou been faithful and obedient to me, and done my bidding, and I am bound to repay thee well." It was ever Gisli's wont to wear a blue cape, and he was often well clad; and now Gisli goes on to say:

"I will give thee this cape, friend; put it on at once, and get up on the last sledge. But I will lead the horses and wear thy cloak." So they did that, and Thord thanks him over and over again for the gift.

Again Gisli said:

"Bear in mind, though men may follow on our heels, never to answer a word if they call out to thee! But if the worst comes to the worst, and they try to do thee harm, jump down and run away into the wood, and let it shield us."

So they changed clothes. Thord was something like Gisli in bearing and gait, and a tall, proper man, but as to his courage and wit there was not a pin to choose between them; he had not a spark of either.

Now, Bork and his friends see Gisli going off into the wood, and run after them as hard as they can. But when Thord sees that, he jumps off the sledge in a trice, and runs nimbly among the trees. They all thought they knew Gisli, and press on after him, and call out to him, but he utters never a word. Then Thorgrim the Easterling hurls his spear after him, and hit the thrall between the shoulders, and he fell flat on his face, and needed no more.

Then Bork bawled out "Good luck. to thee for thy shot, thou happy man!"

As for the brothers Thorodd and Quarrelsome Stein, they spoke together and said: "We will e'en hold on after the thrall, and see if he shows any sport."

So they turned after him.

But when Bork and his friends came to the man in the blue cape they stripped him of it, and saw who it was. And now they think the deed not so lucky as they weened at first, for they saw it was only Thord the Hareheart.

As for those brothers, it is said they saw Gisli near enough to know him among the trees. Then one of them hurled a spear at

him, but he catches it in the air, and hurls it back, and it comes towards Thorodd's waist, and flies right through him. Then Stein turns back to meet his companions, and tells them what had happened.

After that they all went into the wood to beat it for Gisli. And lo! the Easterling sees that the twigs stirred in one place, and he casts a spear at a venture thither, and hits Gisli in the calf. But he sends the spear back again to its owner, and aims so that it struck the Easterling in the breast, and slew him there and then.

Now Bork and his men beat about the wood and cannot find him.; and then they turn back to Gisli's house and set the suit on foot against him, for now the proofs were as plain as day, and they had more than guesswork to go on. They did not plunder anything there. So Bork fares back home, little pleased with his journey.

Now Gisli goes up to the fell which stands by his farm, and there he binds his wounds. He stays there so long as Bork and his men are in his homestead, and thence be sees all that passes. As soon as they are gone he goes home and makes ready to leave Hol with all his household. He takes a boat and so flits his goods and cattle. Auda his wife went with him and Gudrida, his foster-child. He sails out of Dyrafirth as far as Husaness, and there lands. Gisli goes up to the farm, and meets a man, who asks him what man he was. Gisli told him what he pleased, but not the real truth. With that Gisli takes up a stone and throws it out on to the Holm, which lies off the land there, and bade the churl's son do the like when he got home, and said perhaps he would then know what man had been there. But there was never a man who could throw a stone so far; and here again it came out that Gisli was better than most others in feats of strength. After that he went on board his boat and rows round the ness, and across Arnarfirth, and across that firth that turns aside from Arnarfirth, and is called Geirthiofsfirth. There he set up his abode, and built a whole homestead, and dwelt there that winter.

The next thing that happens is that Gisli sends word to his brothers-in-law, Helgi, and Sigurd, and Vestgeir, to go to the Thing and offer an atonement for him, that he might not be outlawed. So they set off for the Thing the sons of Bjartmar, and could bring nothing to pass about the atonement; and men go so far as to say that they behaved very ill, so that they almost burst out into tears ere the suit was over. They were then very young, and Bork the Stout was so wroth they could do nothing with him.

When the Thing was over they went west and saw Thorkel the Wealthy of Alvidra, and tell him all that had happened, and begged him to see Gisli and tell him, for they said they did not dare to say to his face that he was an outlaw.

So Gisli was outlawed. That was the great news at that Thing. And Thorkel the Wealthy went and told Gisli. Then Gisli chaunted this stave:

"At Thorsness Thing
My suit at law
Had never failed
For quirk or flaw,
Had Vestein's heart,
That never blenched,
In Bjartmar's babies
Burned unquenched.

"They quailed, those kinsmen of my wife,
When all their souls should warm with strife.
To think that here was work to do,
And foes to foil and conquer too.
And so they fled the throng of men,
As when, with addle egg of hen,
The base-born thrall is pelted down
By all the riff-raff of the town.

"Evil tidings from the North,
An outlaw now I wander forth
A forfeit life by land and sea
None dares to speak a word for me
But still, O man in battle tried,
O bounteous man, whate'er betide,
Know this, that vengeance shall be mine
On those two caitiffs, Bork and Stein."

Both those namesakes, the Thorkels, say they will give him all the shelter they can, so that they run no risk of losing life or land. After that they went home.

Chapter 12
Gisli begins to dream

The next three years Gisli was sometimes in his house at Geirthiofsfirth, and sometimes with Thorkel the Wealthy, harboured by stealth. Other three years he spent in roaming over the land, and going from house to house asking help and countenance from great chiefs; but something always tripped him up everywhere, so that naught came of it. So mighty was that spell that Thorgrim's witchcraft had thrown on him that it was fated no chief should shelter him, and no one ever went heartily into his cause. After those six years were over he spent his time for the most part in Geirthiofsfirth, sometimes in his house, over which Auda ruled, and sometimes in the hiding-place which he had hollowed out for himself. That was on the north bank of the river. But he had another lair on the south bank among the crags, and there he lurked for the most part.

Now when Bork hears this, he set off from home, and seeks Eyjolf the Gray, who then dwelt in Arnarfirth in Otterdale, and begs him to hunt for Gisli, and slay him as an outlaw, and if he slew him, he said he would give him three hundreds in silver of the very best, and bade him leave no stone unturned to find him out. He takes the money, and gives his word to do his best. There was a man with Eyjolf named Helgi–Spy-Helgi by nickname; he was both swift of foot and sharp of eye, and he knew every inch of the firths. This man is sent to Geirthiofsfirth to find out if Gisli be there. He soon is aware of a man in hiding, but he knows not whether it be Gisli or another. So he goes back and tells Eyjolf how things stand. Eyjolf says at once it must be Gisli, and loses no time, but sets off with six men for Geirthiofsfirth; but he cannot find Gisli, and goes bootless back.

Gisli was a foresighted man and a great dreamer, and dreamt true. All wise men are of one mind that Gisli lived an outlaw longest of all men, save Grettir, the son of Osmund. Eighteen years was Grettir an outlaw. It is told that one autumn night Gisli was very restless as he slept, while he was in Auda's house, and when he wakes she asks him what he had dreamt?

"I have two women who are with me in my dreams," he answers; "one is good to me, but the other tells me naught but evil, and her tale is every day worse and worse, and she spaes me downright ruin. But what I just dreamed was this: Methought I came to a house or hall, and into that hall I went, and there I saw many of my friends and kinsfolk: they sat by fires and drank. There were. seven fires; some had burnt very low, but some still burned as bright as bright could be. Then in came my better dream-wife, and said these were tokens of my life, how much of it was still to come; and she counselled me so long as I lived to leave all old unbeliefs and witchcraft, and to be good to the deaf and the halt, and the poor and the weak." "Bear in mind," she said, "thou hast so many years yet to live as thou sawest fires alight." My dream was no longer than that. Then Gisli chaunted several staves:

> "Fires seven, the bard remembers,
> Lady, blazed within that hall;
> Men around those glowing embers
> Sate and drank like brothers all.
> One and all those inmates gladly
> Greeted Gisli as their guest;
> Gisli hailed them soft and sadly,
> Fitting words his thanks expressed.

> "Thus that weird wife, wise and witty,
> Spoke, and said to Norway's friend–
> Soft her voice and full of pity,–
> 'Man! behold thy journey's end;

Mark those seven fires burning,
Seven years to thee remain;
Then, to this abode returning,
Make thee merry, free from pain.'

"'Noble man!' the voice continues,
Shun the wizard's hateful lore;
Hero bold, of strongest sinews,
Seek the muse's golden store.
Bear in mind this precept hoary—
Naught so much defileth hearts
As wicked wit, as idle story;
Vile is witchcraft, black her arts.

"Stay thy hand, be slow to slaughter;
Rouse not men to seek thy life:
Come! thy word to wisdom's daughter
Be not first in stirring strife.
Man of noble nature, ever
Help the weak, the halt, the blind;
Hard the hand that opens never,
Bright and blest the generous mind."

Now Bork presses Eyjolf hard, and thinks he has not done so much as he said he would, and that there had been small return for the silver he had given him. He said he was quite sure Gisli was in Geirthiofsfirth, and if Eyjolf did not send some one to take Gisli's life, Bork said he must come and hunt him down himself: "For 'tis a shame that two such champions and chiefs as we think ourselves cannot get Gisli put out of the way."

Eyjolf was all alive again, and sends Spy-Helgi again round Geirthiofsfirth; and now he takes food with him, and is away a week, and lies in wait to catch sight of Gisli. At last one day he sees a man come out of a hiding-place, and knows Gisli at once. As soon as he sees him he goes back and tells Eyjolf what he had seen.

Now Eyjolf sets off with eight men, and makes for Auda's house in Geirthiofsfirth; but they do not find Gisli there, and now they beat all the thickets thereabouts, and still cannot find Gisli. Then they go back to Auda's house, and Eyjolf offers her a great sum of money if she will betray Gisli; but she would do nothing of the kind. Then they threatened to maim her, but it was all no good, and they had to go back as wise as they came. This was thought a most shameful journey for them; and Eyjolf stays at home all that autumn.

But though Gisli had not been hunted down, he sees plain enough that he must be taken, and that very soon, if he stays there. So he breaks up from home, and goes along the coast to Strand, and rides to see his brother Thorkel at "the Combe." He knocks at the door of the sleeping-house in which Thorkel is abed, and he gets up, goes out, and greets Gisli.

"I want to know, now," said Gisli, "if thou wilt yield me any help? I look to thee for comfort and countenance, for now I am hard pressed, and I have forborne to do this for a long time."

But Thorkel gave him the old answer, and said outright he would give him no help that might get himself into trouble. Silver and horses he would give him, if he needed them, or anything else, as he said before, but nothing besides.

"Now I see," said Gisli, "that thou wilt not help me. Give me now three hundred in wadmel, and make up your mind that henceforth I shall not often ask thy aid."

Thorkel does as he wishes, and gives him the woollen and some silver. Gisli said he would take what was given him, but added he would not behave so meanly were he in Thorkel's place. At their parting Gisli was very down-hearted.

Now he goes out to Vadil, to the mother of Gest, the son of Oddleif, and reaches her house before dawn, and knocks at the door. The housewife goes to the door. She was often wont to harbour outlaws, and she had an underground room. One end of it opened on the river-bank and the other below her hall. One way see the ruins of it still. Thorgerda—for that was heir name—made Gisli welcome. "I am willing enough thou shouldest stay here awhile, but I am sure I can't tell whether this is not mere old wife's talk."

Old wife's talk or not, Gisli was willing to take it as it was meant, and said he had not been so well treated by men that better things were not to be hoped for from women.

So Gisli stays there that winter, and he was never better cared for in all his outlawry than there.

As soon as ever the spring came Gisli fares back to Geirthiofsfirth, for he could not bear to be any longer away from Auda his wife, so much they loved each other. He is there that summer by stealth, and up to autumn. And now as the nights lengthen the dreams lengthen with them, and that worse dream-wife comes oftener and oftener to him, and he has hard nights. Once he says to Auda, when she asks him what he had dreamt, and his answer was in verse:

> "A weary wife now haunts my slumber;
> If dreams be true, as oft they be,
> Not many winters shall I number,
> No tongue shall 'Graybeard!' shout to me:
> This dream-wife bids me peak and pine,
> Vain 'tis to try to break her spell
> But little care I, darling mine!
> I dream, but slumber soft and well."

And now he tells her that that worse dream-wife was ever coming to him, and wishing to sprinkle blood over him, and to smear and bathe him in it; and that she looked spitefully on him. Then he chaunted:

> "Still my dreams are heavy-hearted,
> Still my evil genius lowers;
> All my mirth hath clean departed,
> Mine no more are blithesome hours:
> Sleep no sooner seals my eyelids
> Than a loathly wife appears,
> Bathed in blood and gore-bedabbled,
> Drenching me with dew of spears."

And again he chaunted:

> "Darling wife, I now have uttered
> All my mind about my dreams
> Nothing hidden, nothing muttered,
> Words of truth welled out in streams:
> Wrath now riseth hour by hour,
> Worse my foes shall feel my hand—
> High-born chiefs, whose haughty power,
> Marked me with an outlaw's brand."

Chapter 13
Gisli goes to Ingialld

Now all is quiet, and Gisli goes again to Thorgerda, and is with her another winter. But the summer after he goes back to Geirthiofsfirth, and is there till autumn draws near. Then he goes once more to his brother Thorkel and knocks at the door, but Thorkel will not go out of doors; so Gisli takes a staff and scores runes on it, and throws it in through a slit. Thorkel sees it and takes it up and looks at it. After that he arose and went out and greeted Gisli. "What news?" he asks, but Gisli says he has no news to tell.

"Now I am come to see thee, kinsman, for the last time; and now let me have some heartier help, and I will repay thee by never asking any more at thy hand."

But Thorkel answers now as before; offers him horse or boat, but withdraws from all other help. Gisli chooses the boat, and bids Thorkel shove her down with him. He does so, and gives him six measures of food, and a hundred ells of wadmel.

And so when Gisli had got into the boat Thorkel stands on the shore. Then Gisli said:

"Now thou thinkest thou standest with all four feet in the crib, and that thou art the friend of many great chiefs, and dreadest nothing at all. But I am an outlaw, and have the feud of many men, and know not where to lay my head; but for all that I can tell thee thou wilt be slain before I am slain. And now we must part worse friends than we ought, and never see each other again; but know this, I would not deal so by thee. Shoulder to shoulder, we would both share the same doom."

"I care not for thy ill-boding spaedom, nor how much thou braggest of thy bravery," said Thorkel; and so they parted.

Gisli rows for Hergilsisle in Broadfirth. There he takes out the tholes, and thwarts, and oars, and all that was loose in the boat, and then upsets and lets her drive with the tide in towards Ness. And now men guess who see the boat that Gisli must be drowned, since the boat is shattered and driven on shore; and they think he must have taken it from his brother Thorkel.

Now Gisli goes up to the farm in Hergilsisle. There dwells a man named Ingialld, and his wife's name was Thorgerda. Ingialld is Gisli's cousin by kinship, and had come out to Iceland with him. When they met he offered Gisli all the help and aid which he could show him, and Gisli took it gladly, and was quiet there for a time.

In Ingialld's household were a thrall and a woman slave. The man's name was Swart, and the woman's Bothilda. Ingialld had a son called Helgi, and he was an idiot, the biggest you ever saw, and utterly witless. He was so treated that a pierced stone was tied round his neck, and he grazed out of doors like a sheep, and he was called Ingialld's idiot. He was tall of growth, almost like a giant. So Gisli is there that winter, and builds a boat for Ingialld and many other things. But all that he did was easy to ken, for he was handier than almost any other man. Men wondered and wondered how it was that everything was so well made that Ingialld had, for he was not a skilful carpenter himself. Every summer Gisli went to Geirthiofsfirth; and so things go on for three winters since he had first began to dream, and the help Ingialld gave him stood him in the greatest stead. At last men began to lay their heads together about all this, and made up their minds after all that Gisli must be still alive, and have lived with Ingialld, and not be drowned as had been said. It strengthened what they said when they saw that Ingialld had three boats, all of them well built. So this gossip comes to the ears of Eyjolf the Gray, and it is again Spy-Helgi's lot to set off; and so he comes to Hergilsisle. Gisli is always in his earth-house whenever strangers come to the isle; but Ingialld is a good host, and offers Helgi shelter. So he stays there that night. Ingialld was a very busy man; he rowed out to sea every day that a boat would swim. So next morning, when he was ready to row away, he asks whether Helgi is not eager to be forwarded on his way, and why he lies a-bed. He says he is not quite himself, and puffs and blows, and rubs his forehead. Ingialld bade him lie there as still as he could, and goes off to sea, while Helgi groans and moans.

Now, it is said that Thorgerda goes to the earth-house and means to give Gisli his breakfast, but there was a panel between the larder and the room where Helgi lay. As soon as Thorgerda goes out of the larder Helgi climbs up to the top of the panel and sees that there is a meal of meat dished up for some one. Just then Thorgerda comes back, and Helgi turns him round as fast as he can, and topples down from the panel. Thorgerda asks why he behaves so, and why he clambers up to the roof like a thief, and cannot be still. He said he was so mad with pain that he couldn't be still: "Be so good as to lead me to my bed!" So she led him back to bed, and then she goes away with the dish of meat. But Helgi rises up straightway and follows her, and now he sees what is in the wind. Then he goes back, and lays him down again and sleeps in bed that day. Ingialld comes home at even, and goes to Helgi's bed and asks whether he were easier. He said he was on the way to be well, and begged to be put over from the isle next morning. So he is put across to Flat Isle, and thence he fares south to Thorsness, and says he has found out that Gisli is harboured by Ingialld. After that, Bork sets out from home, and there are fifteen of them in all, and they get on board a sailing boat, and sail from the south over Broadfirth. That day Ingialld had rowed out to the deep-sea fishing and Gisli with him; but his thrall and his maid were in another boat, and they lay near some islands called Skutilisles.

Now Ingialld sees a boat sailing from the south, and said: "I see something to my mind. Yonder sails a boat, and I think in that ship must be Bork the Stout, for her sails are striped with red."

"What's to be done now?" asks Gisli. "I want to know whether thou art so deep-thoughted as thou art brave and manly."

"My plan is soon made," said Ingialld, "though I am no long-headed fellow. Let us row as hard as we can to the isle, and then go up to the top of Vadsteinberg, and stand at bay so long as we can keep our feet."

"Just as I thought," said Gisli . "I knew thou wouldst choose what would show thy bravery; but I shall be paying thee a worse meed for all thy help than I mean if for my sake thou art to lose thy life. That shall never be; we must think of something else. Thou shalt row to the island and the thrall with thee, and ye two shall climb the hill and make ready to hold your own, and then they who are sailing round the Ness from the south will think I am the second man. But I will change clothes with the thrall, as I did once before, and I will get into the boat with Bothilda."

Then Ingialld did as Gisli advised, and he showed plainly enough that he was very wroth, and when they part Bothilda asked:

"What's to be done next?" and Gisli sang a stave

> "Maiden mine, what plan to take,
> Since we Ingialld must forsake;
> Now my tongue bursts forth in song,
> Maid in black, of muscle strong
> My heart is set to skim the seas,
> To ply the oar, to hug the breeze;
> But know, whatever be my doom,
> I care not whensoe'er it come."

Now they row south to meet Bork and his men, and show no token of being in any strait. Then Gisli laid it down how they were to behave.

"Thou shalt say that here on board the boat is the idiot, but I will sit in the stern and mock what thou sayest, and wrap me up in the nets, and every now and then almost throw myself overboard, and behave as madly as I can, and as soon as ever they have got a little way from us I will row with all my might, and try to put as much water between us as I can."

So now she rows to meet Bork and his men, and yet gave them a wide berth, and made as though she were seeking a fishing-bank. Now Bork calls out to her and asks if Gisli were on the isle.

"I don't know," she said, "but this I know, there is a man yonder who bears away the bell from all other men on the isle both in height and handicraft."

"Say you so?" said Bork. "Is he there now?"

"He was when I left home," she says.

"Pray, is Master Ingialld at home?" asked Bork.

"He rowed back to land long since," she said, "and his thrall with him, as I thought."

"That cannot have been," said Bork; "it must have been Gisli. Let us row after them as fast as we can."

"We think it fine fun," they answered, "to look at the idiot and all his mad pranks."

The men said she was in a sad plight when she had to lead such a fool about.

"I think so too," said she, "but I feel hurt that you laugh at him, and give me little pity."

"Have done with this stuff," said Bork. "Let us get on our course, for the prey is almost in our hands."

Chapter 14
Gisli slips through Bork's fingers

So they parted; and Bork and his men row to the isle, and land, and see the men on the Vadsteinberg, and make thither, and think they have done a good stroke of business. But all the while it was only Ingialld and his thrall who were up there.

Bork was the first to know the men, and said to Ingialld: "The best way is to give up Gisli, or tell where he is. Thou art a hound, and nothing else, when thou hast hidden away my brother's murderer, and all the while art my tenant. 'Twere well if thou gottest some harm, and it were best that thou wert slain."

"Well," says Ingialld, "I wear work-a-day clothes, and I don't care a button if they are torn to bits. I will sooner lose my life than not do Gisli all the good in my power, and keep him out of harm's way."

Men say that Ingialld gave most help to Gisli, and was the greatest gain to him; and it is also said that when Thorgrim Bottlenose worked his spells he used the words that "naught should help Gisli, though men tried to shelter him here on land;" but he forgot to add the out isles, and so his charm was only partly fulfilled, though it was fated to be fulfilled at last.

Bork thinks it not seemly to fall on his tenant Ingialld; so he turns away to the homestead and there seeks for Gisli, and cannot find him, as was likely.

Then they roam over the isle, and come at last to a spot where the idiot lay and grazed in a hollow, with the stone tied round his neck.

Then Bork says: "Well, I always heard strange stories about Ingialld's idiot, but I never thought he could be in two places at once. There's no use hunting here, and we have been so heedless, I never knew the like, nor do I know how we shall ever set it right. Why! that must have been Gisli in the boat alongside us, and be must have passed himself off as the idiot, for he is ready at everything, and is the biggest mockbird. 'Tis a shame to so many men if he slip through our fingers this time. Let us hasten after him, and let him not escape our clutches."

Then they jump into their boat and row after them, and ply the oars fast. They soon see that Gisli and the maid with a fair tide have got a good way across the sound, and each boat rowed smartly. But that boat goes faster through the water which has most men to pull, and they overhauled them so much that Bork and his men were just a spear's throw behind them when they got to land.

Then Gisli spoke to the maid, and said: "Now we must part, and here is a ring which thou shalt carry to Ingialld, and another to his wife, and tell them I say thou must have thy freedom, and send them these as tokens. My wish also is that Swart should be set free. Thou mayest well be called my deliverer, and I wish thee to profit by it,"

Now they part. Gisli leaps on shore and into some crags. It was at Hjardarness that he landed. The maid rowed off all dripping and reeking with her hard pull. Bork and his men had no time to waste on her alone in her boat, but rowed straight to shore, and Quarrelsome Stein was first out of the boat, and runs off to seek for Gisli. But as he clomb the crags Gisli stood in his path with his sword drawn, and smote him on the head, and cleft him to the chine, and down he toppled a dead man. Bork and his men land on the isle also for it was an island just off the mainland; but Gisli plunges into the strait and tries to swim to the main. Just then Bork hurled a spear at him, and smote him on the calf, and cut a piece out of it, and that was a great wound. Gisli gets rid of the spear, but loses his sword; for be was so weary he could not hold it. It was then dark and night. As soon as he came to land he runs into the wood, for then the land thereabouts was overgrown with trees. Now Bork and his men row to land and hunt for Gisli, and pen him up in the wood; for the wood was not deep, and he is so weary and stiff he can scarce walk a step, and is now ware of men on all sides of him. Now he takes a plan and goes down to the shore, and so comes along the water's edge in the dark to a farm called "the Howe" and there seeks a farmer named Ref (the Fox), who was the craftiest of men. Ref greets him, and asks the news. Gisli told him the whole truth, and all that had happened between him and Bork. Now Ref had a wife whose name was Elfdisa, fair of face, but the greatest shrew, and altogether a downright scold. That was her wont with others, but she and Ref hit it off very well together.

So when he had told Ref how things stood Gisli asks him for help.

"They will be here in the twinkling of an eye," said Gisli. "Now I am hard pressed, and there are few to stand by me."

"I will only help thee," says Ref, "if I may settle how thou art to be helped. Thou shalt have no share in it."

"With all my heart," says Gisli, "for I can't stir a step farther."

"Go indoors, then," says Ref; and so they did.

Then Ref said to Elfdisa:

"I must be so free as to send a man into thy bed."

And with that he takes all the clothes off the box-bed, and says that Gisli must crouch down in the straw at the bottom. Then he heaps the clothes and bedding on him, and last of all Elfdisa lies down atop of him.

"Stay where thou art, whatever happens," says Ref. At the same time he bids Elfdisa be as cross and snappish as ever she could be.

"Don't spare, but pour out all the bad words thou knowest—curses and oaths. But I will take the lead in talking with them, and turn my words as I think best."

Next time he goes out of doors he sees men coming. They were eight of Bork's band; but Bork himself stayed at Forcewater. But these were to come and seek for Gisli, and seize him if he had come thither.

So Ref stays out of doors and asks, "What tidings?"

"None but what thou must already know. Knowest thou aught of Gisli, or if he has passed this way."

"He hasn't passed by here," says Ref. "If he had tried it he would not have lived long. I don't know now why ye should think me less ready to slay Gisli than any other man; but I have just wit enough to see that the favour and friendship of such a man as Bork would be well worth winning."

"Well," they answered, "will it be against thy will if we search the house?"

"With all my heart! why not?" says Ref; "for I know ye will hunt all the more steadily in other places if ye know of a truth that he is not here. Pray, step in, and search for him as narrowly as ye can."

So they go indoors, but when Elfdisa heard their stamping, she bawled out what band of blackguards that might be, and what pack of fools it could be that knocked men up at night. Ref begged her to keep a smooth tongue in her mouth, but she did not spare them one of her foul words, and she yelled and hooted at them, so that they might be less able to hunt. Still they searched and searched, but still less than they would otherwise have done if the Goody had not pelted them with so much slang.

After that they go away and find nothing, and bid the farmer farewell, and he wished them a safe journey home. So they go back to Bork, and are sore grieved at their journey, and think they have got both harm and shame, and after all done nothing. Now all this was noised about the countryside, and men thought it was still the same story, and that Bork had still the same ill-luck at Gisli's hand.

Now Bork goes home and tells Eyjolf what ought to be done. Gisli stays with Ref half a month, and after that he goes away. They parted good friends, and Gisli gives him a knife and belt, and they were great treasures, though he had nothing else with him. After this Gisli goes to his wife in Geirthiofsfirth, and his fame waxed much after these deeds; and truth to say there never has been a man of readier hand or more daring heart than Gisli, but he was not a lucky man, as was proved from the very first.

Chapter 15
Thorkel's Slaying

Now the story goes on that next spring Bork fares to Thorskafirth Thing with a great company, and means to meet his friends there. Gest sails from the west from his house at Redsand on Bardastrand, and Thorkel Soursop comes too, each in his own ship. But just as Gest was ready to start two lads came to him ill-clad, with beggars staves in their hands. Men know this, that these two lads had a talk aside with Gest, that they beg a passage over the firth, and that he grants it. So they sail with him, and he takes them as far as Hallsteinsness. They landed just beyond the farm where Hallstein offered up his son, that a tree of sixty feet might be thrown up by the sea, and there are still to be seen the pillars of his high seat which he had made out of that tree. Thence the lads go up into Teigwood, and so go through the wood till they come to Thorskafirth Thing.

There was a man named Hallbjorn: he was a vagabond who roamed over the country, and not fewer men with him than ten or twelve. But when he came to the Thing he built himself a booth. Thither to the Beggar's Booth the lads go and ask for a lodging, and say they are beggars and runagates. He said he will find room for every one who asks him prettily.

"Here have I been," he said, "every year for many a spring, and I know all the chiefs and priests."

The lads said they would be very glad if he would take them under his wing and teach them wisdom.

"We are very curious to see mighty folk about whom great tales are told."

So Hallbjorn says if they will go down with him to the seastrand, that then he would know every ship as it ran in, and tell them all about it. They thanked him much for his gentleness.

Now they go down to the strand and look out at sea, and they soon see ships sailing up to the land. Then the elder lad began to ask:

"Who owns yon ship which now sails up nearest to us?"

"Gest the Wise," he answers, "of Hagi on Bardastrand."

"But who sail next, and run their ship up at the horn of the firth?"

"That is Thorkel Soursop."

They see now that Thorkel lands and sits him down while his men bore the lading from the ship as the tide rose. But Bork was busy setting up their booth; for the two brothers-in-law had one booth between them, and they were always good friends.

Thorkel had on a Greek hat and a gray cloak. He had a gold brooch on his shoulder, and a sword in his hand. In a little while Hallbjorn and the lads went up to where Thorkel was sitting. Now one of the lads, the elder, began to speak, and said:

"Pray who is this mighty man who sits here? Never have I seen a fairer or a nobler man."

He answered: "Thy words fall fair. My name is Thorkel."

The lad went on: "That sword which thou bearest in thy hand must be a treasure. Wilt thou let me look at it?"

"A strange fellow thou art," answers Thorkel; "but still I will let thee see it." And with that be banded him the sword.

The lad grasped the sword, drew off a step or two, snaps the peace-strings, and draws the sword.

But when Thorkel saw that he said:

"That I never gave thee leave to do. Why hast thou drawn the sword?"

"Neither did I ask thy leave," said the lad; and brandishes the sword, and smites Thorkel on the neck, and takes off his head at a stroke.

Now as soon as this happens up jumps Hallbjorn the Runagate; but the lad threw down the sword all bloody as it was, seizes his staff, and so they all ran with Hallbjorn, and all the beggars ran too, for they were almost mad with fright. So they ran by the booth which Bork was setting up.

Now men flocked round Thorkel, and no man could tell who had done the deed. Bork just then asked what was all that stir or fuss down where Thorkel sate. He said this just as the fifteen beggars tore along by his booth; and then the youngest lad, whose name was Helgi–Berg was he that did the deed–said.

"I don't know what they are mooting but methinks they are striving whether Vestein left only daughters behind him, or whether he had ever a son."

So Hallbjorn runs to his booth, but the lads take to the wood which was nigh to the spot, and no one can find them.

Now men run to Hallbjorn's booth, and ask what it all meant; but all the beggars could say was, that two young lads had joined their band, and that they were as much taken unawares as any one else, and hardly thought they should know them again. Yet they say something of their form and feature, and of their speech and discourse, what like it had been. And now Bork thinks he knows from the words which Helgi had uttered that it must have been Vestein's sons. After that he goes to Gest and takes counsel with him as what was best to do.

"I am most bound of all men," says Bork, "to take up the feud for my brother-in-law Thorkel. Methinks 'tis not unlikely that the sons of Vestein must have done this deed, for we know no other men than they who had any quarrel with Thorkel. Now it may well be they have got clear off for this time, but I will give much to have them outlawed at this very Thing; so give us counsel how the suit is to be followed up."

"I think," says Gest, "it is no easy matter to take this suit in hand, for methinks had I done the deed I could so hamper the suit, if it were about to be brought against me, by naming another man instead of myself, that the suit would come to naught. Maybe, methinks, he that did the deed had the same thought running in his head, and so he has thrown the blame on the boys."

And Gest was against bringing the suit against them, and threw cold water on it in every way.

Men thought it sooth that Gest had been in league with the lads all along, for he was their near kinsman. Then they cease talking, and the suit falls to the ground; but Thorkel is laid in his howe, after the fashion of the olden time, and men go away home from the Thing, and nothing else happened at it.

Now Bork is very ill-pleased with his doings, and though he ought to have been used to it, still he got great dishonour and disgrace from this matter of Thorkel.

As for the lads, they fare till they get to Geirthiofsfirth and lie out ten days. They reach Auda's house, and Gisli is at that time there. It was night when they came, and they knock at the door. Auda goes to the door and greets them, and asks what news. But Gisli lay all the while in his earth-house in his bed, and she raised her voice at once if he had need to be warned. They tell her of Thorkel's slaying, and how things stood. They also say how long they had been without food.

"I will send you on," says Auda, "over the ridge into Mossdale to the sons of Bjartmar, and I will give you food and tokens that they may take you under their wing, and I do this because I dare not ask Gisli to take you in."

So the lads go away into the wood, where they cannot be found, and eat their food, for it was long since they tasted any, and then they lay them down and sleep when they are full, for they were much worn with hunger and travel.

As for Auda she goes into Gisli and says

"Now I set great store upon knowing how thou wilt take something, and whether thou wilt honour me more than I am worth."

He caught her up at once and said: "I know thou art about to tell me the slaying of my brother Thorkel."

"So it is as thou guessest," said Auda; "the lads have come hither and wished thee to harbour them here for good and all, for they thought they could find shelter nowhere else."

"No!" he answers, "I cannot bear the sight of my brother's slayers and live under the same roof with them;" and up he jumps, and wants to draw his sword, and burst out into song:

> "Why should not Gisli draw the sword?
> Ha! soon shall vengeance be the word.
> What! Thorkel slain, and Gisli cool?
> Auda, thou tak'st me for a fool!
> All o'er the Thing, with 'bated breath,
> Men mourn for Thorkel done to death.
> One stalwart blow before I die,
> A brother's blood aloud doth cry."

But now Auda told him they had gone away; "for I had wit enough not to let them run this risk."

And Gisli said it was the best way that they never met, and then he soon softened down; and now all is quiet again.

Chapter 16
Spy-Helgi and Havard

It is said that now only two more years were left of those which the dream-wife had said he had to live. And as time goes on, and Gisli is in Geirthiofsfirth, all his dreams come back on him, and he has hard struggles in his sleep; and now the worse dream-wife comes oftener and oftener to him, though the better visits him sometimes. So it fell one night, as Gisli dreamed that the better dream-wife came to him, and she seemed to ride on a gray horse, and bids him go with her to her abode, and he went gladly. So they came to a house which was almost as large as a hall, and she leads him into that house, and he thought there were pillows of down on the benches, and that it was well furnished in everything. She bade him stay there and be happy: "Hither shalt thou fare when thou diest, and pass thy time in bliss and ease."

And now he wakes and chaunted these verses on what he had dreamt:

"Lo! the goddess shows her power,
Sets me on her palfrey gray,
Makes me ride unto her bower,
Bids me welcome every day:
All her words some comfort bringing,
Vowing ever to befriend;
In my ears soft sounds are ringing,
Still that music knows no end.

"There was many a slumb'rous pillow,
Strewn on benches in that hall,
Soft I sate as swan on billow,
Ah! my heart remembers all:
More–that lovely woman laid me
On a bed of softest down:
Grateful for the cheer she made me,
Straight my face forgot to frown.

"Then outspoke that bounteous woman–
'Mighty chief! thy foeman's bane,
Hither hasten, chased by no man;
Death shall set thee free from pain:
Then shalt thou–her speech pursuing–
'All these treasures call thine own;
Me, too, shalt thou win for wooing;

Happy we as birds new flown.' "

Now it is next to be said that Helgi the Spy was sent again round Geirthiofsfirth, and men deem it likely that Gisli is there. A man went with him whose name was Havard. He had come to Iceland from Norway the summer before, and was a kinsman of Gest the Wise. They gave out that they were sent into the wood to hew fuel for household use, but though this was the cloak of their journey, hidden under it was the design to hunt out Gisli, and see if they could find out his lurking-place. After they had been three nights in the wood spying about, on the last evening they see a fire burning in the cliffs and crags south of the river. That was just after sundown, and it was as dark as pitch. Then Havard asks Helgi what was to be done, "for thou must be more wont to these things than I can be."

"There is but one thing to be done," said Helgi, "and that is, to pile up a beacon on this hillock which we stand on, and then we shall find it when it is broad daylight, and then we shall see across from the beacon to the cliffs: 'tis but a short way to see."

So they take that plan, and when they had piled up the beacon Havard said he was worn out, and so tired he could scarce keep his eyes open. So he lay down to sleep. But Helgi keeps awake, and heaps up what yet failed to the beacon; and when he had ended his work Havard wakes, and bids Helgi go to sleep and he would watch. So Helgi sleeps awhile, and while he sleeps Havard sets to work and carries off the whole beacon, so that he did not leave one stone upon another in the dark. When he had done that, he takes up a huge stone and dashes it down on the rock close to Helgi's head, so that the earth shook again. Then Helgi jumps up, and is all of a quake and faint-hearted, and asks what ever is the matter.

"Well," said Havard, "there's a man in the wood, and very many such keepsakes have come hither during the night."

"That must have been Gisli. He must have found us out; and know, good fellow, we shall have every bone in our bodies broken if such grit falls on us. There is naught to be done but to be off as fast as possible."

Now Helgi runs off as fast as he can, but Havard follows him, and bids Helgi not to run away from him. But Helgi gave little heed, and ran as fast as he could lay legs to the ground.

At last they came to their boat, and jumped in, and dash the oars into the sea, and row like mad, and do not stay their course till they get to Otterdale, and then Helgi says he has found out where Gisli had hidden himself.

Eyjolf was up and stirring in a trice, and sets off at once with thirteen men, and both Helgi and Havard go with him. So they fare till they come to Geirthiofsfirth, and go through all the woods to search for the beacon and Gisli's lair, and found them nowhere.

Now Eyjolf asks Havard whereabouts they had piled up the beacon.

"I'm sure I can't tell," he answers; "I was so dead tired that I can't call to mind anything. Besides, Helgi piled up the beacon while I slept. Methinks 'tis not unlikely that Gisli was ware of us, and has carried away the beacon when it got light, and we had gone away."

Then Eyjolf said: "Everything seems doomed to go against us in this quest. We may as well turn back;" and so they did; but before they went Eyjolf says he wishes to go and see Auda.

Now they come to the house, and go indoors, and Eyjolf sate him down to talk with Auda. And this was how he began:

"I will make a bargain with thee, Auda. Thou shalt tell me where Gisli is, and I will give thee three hundreds in silver; those very pieces which I have taken as the price of his head. Thou shalt not be bound to stand by while we take his life. Besides all this, I will get thee a match which shall be far better in every way than this bath been. Thou must look also to this—how cheerless it is to be in this barren firth, and be cut off for ever from thy kinsmen and belongings, all because of Gisli's misdeeds."

"As for that," she says, "methinks it most unlikely we should ever agree upon a match which I should think as much worth as this; but still the old saw says: 'Fee is best for a 'fey' man.' Let me see then whether this fee is so much and fine as thou sayest."

So he pours out the silver into her lap, and she touches it with her hand, while he tells it over and presses her hard. Then her foster-daughter, Gudrida, fell a-weeping, and goes out and meets Gisli, and says:

"My foster-mother has now lost her wits, and will betray thee."

"Be of good heart," says Gisli; "that will never be. My brave Auda will never betray me."

With that he chaunted:

> "What! the folk, with wicked whisper,
> Say that she will me deceive?
> Auda faithless to her husband
> Never can my heart believe.
> No! her heart is staunch as ever;
> Auda plots no guile for me
> Auda wrongs her Gisli never;
> Vain the bribe of silver fee."

After that the lassie went home, and says never a word as to where she had been. By this time Eyjolf had told the silver, and then Auda said:

"This fee is no whit better or worse than thou hast said and now thou wilt no doubt let me do with it as I like."

Eyjolf jumped at that, and bade her do with it just as she chose.

So Auda takes the fee, and puts it into a big purse. After that she rises and runs to Eyjolf, and dashes the purse, silver and all, on Eyjolf's nose, so that the blood gushed out all over him; and as she smote him she said:

"Take that for thy silliness, and bad luck go with it! Didst thou ween I would sell my husband into the hands of such a wretch as thee. Take that, I say, and shame and blame go with it. Thou shalt bear in mind, vile fellow, so long as thou livest, that a woman hath beaten thee, and know thou shalt never work thy will whatever happens."

"Lay hands on," called out Eyjolf, "and slay her, though she be but a weak woman."

Then Havard spoke out and said: "Our journey is about as bad as it can be already without our doing this dastard's deed. Up men, and do not let him work his will."

"Sooth is the saw," said Eyjolf, "There are no foes like those of one's own house.'"

But Havard had many friends, and many a man was ready to stand by hint in this matter, and at the same time to save Eyjolf from disgrace; so he had to swallow his shame, and goes away home. But ere Havard leaves the house Auda said: "The debt that Gisli owes thee must not be long unpaid. Here is a ring which I wish thee to take."

"I would not have looked for this," says Havard.

"But for all that I will repay thee," says Auda. So she gave him the gold down on the nail for his help. So Havard takes horse and fares south to the Strand to Gest the Wise, for he will stay no longer with Eyjolf. As for Eyjolf, he fares home to Otterdale, and is ill-pleased with his journey; and this last seemed to men the most shameful of all.

Chapter 17
Gisli's Evil Dreams

So now that summer glides by, and Gisli abides in his earth-house, and is wary of himself, and does not mean to go away any more. For he thinks that the earths are stopped all round about him, and now the years of his dreaming are all spent. It chanced one night that summer that Gisli suffered much in his sleep. But when he wakes up Auda asks what he had dreamt. He says that worse dream-wife had come to him again and said thus—

"Now will I utterly crush all that the better dream-wife hath said to thee; and if I may have my way, none of those things that she hath spoken shall be of any good to thee."

Then Gisli chaunted:

> "Spoke the Valkyr, stern beholding—
> 'Ne'er shall ye twain woo and kiss,
> Day by day your love unfolding,
> All the gods forbid your bliss.
> Woden, lord of worlds and ages,
> Me hath sent to speak his will,
> Far from where the battle rages,
> Lo! his bidding I fulfil.'"

"Again I dreamed," says Gisli, "that yon wife came to me, and bound round my brow a bloody hood, and washed my head first in blood, and poured blood over me, so that I was all over gore." And he chaunted a song:

> "She, methought, her face all flushing,
> Bathed my locks in reddest blood,
> Flames of lightso rosy blushing,
> Woden's balm so bright and good
> Still I see her fingers glowing,
> Bright with gems and blazing rings,
> Steeped in blood so freely flowing,
> Welling from the wounds of kings."

Again Gisli chaunted:

> "Yes! that lady, dark as raven,
> Bound my brow with gory hood;
> All my hair was shorn and shaven–
> Sad the plight in which I stood:
> Still her hands were gore-bedabbled,
> Still her fingers dropped with blood;
> Something in my ear she babbled,
> Then I woke–to find thee good."

At last Gisli was so sore pressed with dreams that he grew quite afraid to be alone in the dark, and could not bear to be left by himself, for as soon as ever he shut his eyes the same wife appeared to him. One night it happened that Gisli struggled just a little in his sleep, and Auda asked what had happened.

"I dreamt," says Gisli, "that men came on us, and Eyjolf was along with them and many others beside, and we met, and I knew that there was merry work between us. One of their band came first, grinning and gaping, and methought I cut him asunder in the middle; and methought too he bore a wolf's head. Then many more fell on me, and methought I had my shield in my hand, and held my own a long while."

Then Gisli chaunted:

> "Methought that early on a morning
> My foes within my dwelling stood;
> Alone I met them, cravens scorning,
> Alone I carved the ravens' food.
> Fast and thick they fell around me–
> Woe is me! I was aware,
> Though chains of death not yet had bound me,
> My blood bedewed thy bosom fair."

And again he chaunted:

> "Well my trusty shield stood by me,
> Bold my heart with peril played
> Not a man of them came nigh me,
> Blithely sang my tuneful blade:
> Till at last my doom was spoken,
> Ten to one beat down my shield
> Well my death was then ywroken,
> Loud clashed swords on fated field."

And again he chaunted:

> "Thick I spread the ravens' table,
> One I swept like wind away,
> Ere those bitter foes were able
> Once to wound me in the fray
> Nay! my sword with temper eager
> Shore a leg from off a wight;
> Off he limped, so wan and meagre,
> Mine the pledge he lost in fight."

Now the autumn comes on and the dreams do not minish, but they rather go on waxing more and more. One night when Gisli struggled in his sleep Auda asked, as was her wont, what had happened. Gisli chaunted these verses:

> "Methought, O wife, the blood was flowing
> Down my sides in crimson rill;
> Tis but the debt of suffering owing,
> The toilsome task I must fulfil.
> Fairly won my wounds, no snarling,
> Others' wives for me must weep;–
> Such my visions, Auda darling,
> When my eyelids close in sleep.
>
> "Methought, O wife, with weapons bloody
> Both my close-set lips were scored;
> Those twin-sisters fair and ruddy
> Deeper blushed at kiss of sword.
> Still fond hope was ever smiling,
> Blooming like the fairest flower;
> 'Thou shalt scape'–such words beguiling
> Cheered me in that darksome hour.
>
> "Methought my foemen, axes wielding
> Both my arms at once lopped off;
> Wound on wound, no buckler shielding,
> Woe on woe, and bitter scoff.
> Worse I dreamt–my forehead splitting,

> Cleft in twain by force of hand,
> O'er my brow, like goblin flitting,
> Gaped and grinned the grisly brand.

> "Methought that lady wise and witty,
> Wearing crown of silver sheen;
> O'er me bowed her head in pity,
> Fast the pearls fell from her een.
> Mistress she of hoards unbroken,
> Bound my wounds with gentle skill;
> What, my love, doth this betoken?–
> Bodes it good or bodes it ill?"

Chapter 18
Gisli's Slaying

Now Gisli had stayed at home all that summer, and all had been quiet. At length the very last night of summer came. Then we are told Gisli could not sleep, nor could any of these three, Gisli, Auda, or Gudrida, sleep. The weather was in that wise that it was very still, and much rime-frost had fallen. Then Gisli says he will up and away from his house to his lurking-place south under the crags, and see if he can get rest there.

So they all three set out, and are clad in long loose kirtles, and the skirts of the kirtles swept the grass and left a track in the dew and rime. Gisli had a staff in his hand, and scored it with runes as he went, and the chips fell down. So they came to the lurking-place. He lays him down and tries to sleep, but the two women watched.

Then slumber steals over him, and he dreams that fowl came into the house called night-hawks: they are larger than ptarmigan, and they looked evil, and had been wallowing in gore and blood. Then Auda asked what he had dreamt.

"Still my dreams were not good," said Gisli, and chaunted a song:

> "Wife! what time I rose and hasted,
> Forth I wandered on the hills;
> O'er these regions wild and wasted
> Streams of song I poured in rills.
> Then I heard the night-hawk shrieking,
> Then I heard his mournful strain;
> Soon the dew of Woden reeking
> Shall this outlaw shed like rain."

And when this had happened they bear the voices of men, and there is Eyjolf come and fourteen men with him. They had already gone to the house, and see the trail in the dew, which pointed them out. But when they were ware of those men they clomb the crags hard by, where there was good vantage-ground, and each of the women had in her hand a great club. Now Eyjolf and his men try to come up to them from below, and he called out to Gisli:

"Thy best plan is not to fare farther away, and not to let thyself be hunted down like hare-hearted men, for thou art called a brave fellow. We have often met before, and we now wish this to be the last time."

"Come on like men," answered Gisli, "for I am not going to fare farther away. Besides it is thy bounden duty to be the first to fall on me, for thou hast greater ground for quarrel with me than these others who come along with thee?"

"I'm not going," says Eyjolf, "to leave it in your hands to place my men, but I will draw them up as I choose."

"Well!" says Gisli, "it was likeliest that such a hound as thou would not dare to cross swords with me."

Then Eyjolf said to Spy-Helgi:

"Twould be great fame for thee now wert thou to be first in leading the way up the crags to Gisli. Such a deed of derring-do would long be borne in mind."

"I have often proved," says Helgi, "that thou likest to have others before thee when there is any trial of courage; but now since thou eggest me on so hotly, well I will do my best, but mind thou backest me like a man, and keep as close to me as thou canst if thou art not altogether a milksop."

Now Helgi busks him to the work where he saw the likeliest place, and holds in his hand a big axe. Gisli was armed thus: he had in his hand his axe, and he was girt with a sword, and his shield was at his side. He had on a gray cloak, and had bound it round with a rope.

Now Helgi takes a run and rushes up the crags at Gisli. He hurried to meet him, and brandished his sword, and smote him on the loins, and exit him in two at the waist; and each half of the man fell down from the crags, each on its own side. Eyjolf got up in another place, and there Auda met him, and smites him on the arm with her club so that it lost all strength, and down he topples back again. Then Gisli spoke and said:

"Long ago I knew I was well wedded, though I never knew I was so well wedded as I am. But now thou hast yielded me less help than thou thoughtest, though thy meaning was good, for had I got at him they would both have gone the same path."

Then two men go to hold Auda and Gudrida, and think they have quite enough to do. And now twelve men rush at once on Gisli, and try to get up the crags. But he defends himself both with stones and weapons, so that great glory followed his deeds. And now one of Eyjolf's band runs up and calls out to Gisli:

"Lay down thy good arms that thou bearest, and give up at the same time Auda thy wife."

"Come and take them then like a man," answers Gisli, "for neither the arms I bear nor the wife I love are fit for any one else."

That man thrusts at Gisli with a spear, but Gisli smote off the spear-head

from the shaft with his axe, and the blow was so stout that the axe passed on to
the rock, and one horn of the edge broke off. Then he throws away the axe
and clutches his sword and fights with it, and shields himself with his shield.
They attack him bravely, but he kept them off like a man, and now they are
hard upon each other.

In that bout Gisli slew two men, and now four in all have fallen.

Still Eyjolf bade them fall on like men.

"We are getting the worst of it, but that would be worth little thought if we
could only make a good end of our business."

Just then, when they were least aware, Gisli whisked about and leaps up on
a crag that stands alone there, and is called Oneman's Crag. So he got away
from the cliffs, and then he turned at bay and fought. This took them quite
by surprise, and now they think that affairs are in a worse way than ever–four
men dead and all the rest weary and wounded.

And now there is a break in the onslaught. When they had taken breath
Eyjolf eggs on his men warmly, and gives his word to get them many fair
things, if they will only get at Gisli. It must be owned that Eyjolf had with him
picked men both in valour and hardihood.

It was a man named Sweyn who first was ready to attack Gisli, but Gisli
smites at him and cleaves him to the chine, and hurls him down from the crag.
And now they think they can never tell when this man's man-slayings will stop.
Then Gisli called out to Eyjolf:

"I wish to make those three hundreds in silver which thou hast taken as the
price of my head as dear-bought as I can. And I rather think thou wouldst give
other three hundreds in silver that we had never met, for thou wilt only take
disgrace in return for your loss of life."

Now they take counsel, and no one is willing to turn back for his life's sake.
So they fall on him from two sides, and two men are foremost in following
Eyjolf whose names are Thorir and Thord, kinsmen of Eyjolf. They were very
great swordsmen, and their onslaught was both hard and hot; and now they
gave him some wounds with spear-thrusts, but he still fought on with great
stoutness and bravery; and they got such knocks from him, both with stones
and strokes, that there was not one of them without a wound who came nigh
him, for Gisli was not a man to miss his mark. Now Eyjolf and his kinsmen
press on hard, for they felt that their fame and honour lay on it. Then they
thrust at him with spears, so that his entrails fall out; but he swept up the
entrails with his shirt and bound the rope round the wound.

Then Gisli called out and said they had better wait a while:

> "Wife so fair, so never failing,
> So truly loved, so sorely cross'd,
> Thou wilt often miss me wailing,
> Thou wilt weep thy hero lost.
> But my soul is stout as ever,
> Swords may bite, I feel no smart

> Father! better heirloom never
> Owned thy son than hardy heart."

That was Gisli's last song, and as soon as ever he had suing it he rushes down from the crag and smites Thord, Eyjolf's kinsman, on the head, and cleaves him down to the belt, but Gisli fell down on his body and breathed his last.

But they were all much wounded, Eyjolf's companions. Gisli there lost his life with so many great and sore wounds that it was a wonder to see. They say that he never turned his heel, and none of them saw that his strokes were lighter, the last than the first. There now ends Gisli's life, and it has always been said he was the greatest champion–though he was not lucky in all things.

Now they drag him down to the flat ground, and take away his sword, and bury him there in the gravel, and so go down to the sea. There on the sea-shore the sixth man breathed his last. Eyjolf offered Auda to take her with him, but she would not. After that Eyjolf fares home to Otterdale, and there, that same night, the seventh man breathes his last. An eighth lies bedridden from wounds twelve months, and then dies. As for the rest, they were healed, and got nothing but shame for their pains.

It has been said, in short, by one and all that there never was a more famous defence made by one man in times of which the truth is known.

Chapter 19
Thordisa's Welcome to Eyjolf

Now Eyjolf fares from home with eleven men to see Bork the Stout, and then he told him these tidings and the whole story.

Bork was merry at that, and bade Thordisa make Eyjolf welcome.

"Bear in mind now all thy old love for my brother Thorgrim, and be good to Eyjolf."

"I will weep for my brother Gisli," says Thordisa; "but will it not be welcome enough for Gisli's baneman if I make him some brose and serve it up?"

And that evening when she brought in the food she let fall the tray of spoons. Now Eyjolf had laid the sword that Gisli had borne between the table and his legs. Thordisa knows the sword, and as she stoops after the spoons she caught hold of the sword by the hilt and makes a stab at Eyjolf, and wished to run him through the middle, but she did not reckon that the hilt pointed up and caught the table; so she thrust lower than she would, and bit him on the thigh, and gave him a great wound.

Bork seizes Thordisa, and twists the sword out of her hand. All jump up and push away the board with the meat on it. Bork offered to let Eyjolf make his own award, and he laid it at the full price of a man, and said he would have laid it higher had not Bork behaved so well.

As for Thordisa, she took witness at once, and says she will be parted from Bork, for she will never come into his bed again; and she kept her word. After that she went and dwelt at Thordisastead, out on the Ere. But Bork stays behind at Helgafell till Snorro the Priest turned him out; and then Bork went to dwell at Glasswaterwood.

As for Eyjolf, he goes back home, and is ill-pleased with all he has done.

The sons of Vestein fare to Gest their kinsman, and call on him to send them, at his cost, abroad with their mother Gunnhillda, and Auda, Gisli's wife, and Gudrida, the daughter of Ingialld, and Geirmund, her brother. So they all sail for Norway from Whitewater in Borgarfirth. It was Gest who sent them away at his cost. They had a short passage, and came safe to Norway. There Berg walks along the street, and is looking out to hire them booth-room in the town. Two men were with him, and they meet two other men—one was clad in scarlet, and was a tall young man, and he asked Berg for his name. Berg told him at once the truth of himself and his kindred; for he thought it rather likely that he should gain good for his father than smart for him, for Vestein had made many friends on his voyages. But that man clad in scarlet drew his sword straightway and dealt Berg his death-blow. That man was Ari the Soursop, the brother of Gisli and Thorkel. Berg's companions go to the ship, a nd tell what had happened. The captain got them all out of the way, and Helgi took ship for Greenland. He got thither and throve, and was thought a brave fellow. Men were sent out to take his life, but it was not doomed that he should die so. Helgi was drowned out fishing, and that was thought great scathe. Auda. and Gunnhillda go to Denmark to Heathby. There they changed their faith, and went south to Rome, and did not come back. Geirmund stayed in Norway and married, and was well to do. His sister Gudrida was given away to a man, and she was thought a wise woman, and many men have come from her. Ari the Soursop sailed to Iceland, and landed in Whitewater, and sold his ship, and bought him land at Hammer; and there he dwelt some winters. Later on he lived on the Moors, and men have come from him too.

Here we end the Saga of Gisli the Soursop.

THE SAGA OF THE ERE-DWELLERS

Chapter 1
Herein Is Told How Ketil Flatneb Fares To West-Over-Sea

KETIL FLATNEB was hight a famous hersir in Norway; he was the son of Biorn Rough-foot, the son of Grim, a hersir of Sogn. Ketil Flatneb was a wedded man; he had to wife Yngvild, daughter of Ketil Wether, a hersir of Raumarik; Biorn and Helgi were hight their sons, but their daughters were these, Auth the Deep-minded, Thorun the Horned, and Jorun Manwitbrent. Biorn, the son of Ketil, was fostered east in Iamtaland with that earl who was called Kiallak, a wise man, and most renowned; he had a son whose name was Biorn, and a daughter hight Giaflaug. That was in the days when King Harald Hairfair came to the rule of Norway. Because of that unpeace many noble men fled from their lands out of Norway; some east over the Keel, some West-over-the-sea. Some there were withal who in winter kept themselves in the South-isles, or the Orkneys, but in summer harried in Norway and wrought much scathe in the kingdom of Harald the king.

Now the bonders bemoaned them of that to the king, and prayed him deliver them from that unpeace. Then Harald the king took such rede that he caused dight an army for West-over-the-sea, and said that Ketil Flatneb should be captain of that host. Ketil begged off therefrom, but the king said he must needs go; and when Ketil saw that the king would have his will, he betook himself to the faring, and had with him his wife and those of his children who were at home. But when Ketil came West-over-the-sea, some deal of fighting had he and his, and ever got the victory. He laid under him the South-isles, and made himself chief over them. Then he made peace with the mightiest chiefs West-over-the-sea, and made alliances with them, and therewithal sent the army back east. But when they met Harald the king, they said that Ketil Flatneb was lord of the South-isles, but that they wotted not if he would drag the rule west of the sea to King Harald. But when the king knew that, he took to himself those lands that Ketil owned in Norway.

Ketil Flatneb gave his daughter Auth to Olaf the White, who at that time was the greatest war-king West-over-the-sea; he was the son of Ingiald, the son of Helgi; but the mother of Ingiald was Thora, the daughter of Sigurd Worm-in-eye, the son of Ragnar Hairy-breeks. Thorun the Horned he gave in wedlock to Helgi the Lean, the son of Eyvind the Eastman and Rafarta, the daughter of Kiarfal, King of the Irish.

Chapter 2
Of Biorn Ketilson and Thorolf Most-Beard

Biorn the son of Ketil Flatneb was in Iamtaland till Kiallak the earl died; he gat to wife Giaflaug the earl's daughter, and thereafter fared west over the Keel, first to Thrandheim and then south through the land, and took to himself those lands which his father had owned, and drove away the bailiffs that King Harald had set over them. King Harald was in the Wick when he heard that, and thereon he fared by the inland road north to Thrandheim, and when he came there he summoned an eight-folks' mote; and at that mote he made Biorn Ketilson outlaw from Norway, a man to be slain or taken wheresoever he might be found. Thereafter he sent Hawk High-breeks and other of his warriors to slay him if they might find him. But when they came south beyond Stath, the friends of Biorn became ware of their journey and sent him tidings thereof. Then Biorn got him aboard a bark which he owned, with his household and chattels, and fled away south along the land, because that this was in the heart of winter, and he durst not make for the main. Biorn fared on till he came to the island called Most which lies off South-Hordaland, and there a man hight Rolf took him in, who was the son of Ornolf the Fish-driver. There lay Biorn privily the winter through. But the king's men turned back when they had settled Biorn's lands and set men over them.

Chapter 3
Thorolf Most-Beard Outlawed By King Harald Hairfair

Rolf was a mighty chief, and a man of the greatest largesse; he had the ward of Thor's temple there in the island, and was a great friend of Thor. And therefore he was called Thorolf. He was a big man and a strong, fair to look on, and had a great beard; therefore was he called Most-beard, and he was the noblest man in the island.

In the spring Thorolf gave Biorn a good long-ship manned with a doughty crew, and gave him Hallstein his son to bear him fellowship; and therewith they sailed West-over-the-sea to meet Biorn's kindred.

But when King Harald knew that Thorolf Mostbeard had harboured Biorn Ketilson the king's outlaw, then sent he men to see him and bade him begone from his lands, and fare as an outlaw even as Biorn his friend, but if he come and meet the king and lay the whole matter in his hand. This was ten winters after Ingolf Arnarson had fared out to take up his abode in Iceland, and that faring was grown to be very famous, because that those men who came out from Iceland told of good choice of land therein.

Chapter 4
Thorolf Most-Beard Comes Out To Iceland, And Sets Up House There

Thorolf Most-Beard made a great sacrifice, and asked of Thor his well-beloved friend whether he should make peace with the king, or get him gone from out the land and seek other fortunes. But the Word showed Thorolf to Iceland; and thereafter he got for himself a great ship meet for the main, and trimmed it for the Iceland-faring, and had with him his kindred and his household goods; and many friends of his betook themselves to faring with him. He pulled down the temple, and had with him most of the timbers which had been therein, and mould moreover from under the stall whereon Thor had sat.

Thereafter Thorolf sailed into the main sea, and had wind at will, and made land, and sailed south along and west about Reekness, and then fell the wind, and they saw that two big bights cut into the land.

Then Thorolf cast overboard the pillars of his high-seat, which had been in the temple, and on one of them was Thor carven; withal he spake over them, that there he would abide in Iceland, whereas Thor should let those pillars come a-land.

But when they drifted from off the ship they were borne towards the westernmost firth in sight, and folk deemed that they went in sooth no slower than might have been looked for.

After that came a sea breeze, and they sailed west about Snowfellsness and stood into the firth. There see they that the firth is mighty broad and long, with great fells rising on either side thereof. Then Thorolf gave name to the firth and called it Broadfirth. He took land on the south side of the firth, nigh the midmost, and laid his ship in the creek, which thereafter they called Templewick.

Thereafter they espied the land and found on the outermost point of a ness north of the bay that Thor was come a-land with the pillars. That was afterwards called Thorsness.

Thereafter Thorolf fared with fire through his land out from Staff-river in the west, and east to that river which is now called Thors-river, and settled his shipmates there. But he set up for himself a great house at Templewick which he called Templestead. There he let build a temple, and a mighty house it was. There was a door in the side-wall and nearer to one end thereof. Within the door stood the pillars of the high-seat, and nails were therein; they were called the Gods' nails. Therewithin was there a great frith-place. But off the inmost house was there another house, of that fashion whereof now is the choir of a church, and there stood a stall in the midst of the floor in the fashion of an altar, and thereon lay a ring without a join that weighed twenty ounces, and on that must men swear all oaths; and that ring must the chief have on his arm at all man-motes.

On the stall should also stand the blood-bowl, and therein the blood-rod was, like unto a sprinkler, and therewith should be sprinkled from the bowl that blood which is called "Hlaut", which was that kind of blood which flowed when those beasts were smitten who were sacrificed to the Gods. But round about the stall were the Gods arrayed in the Holy Place.

To that temple must all men pay toll, and be bound to follow the temple-priest in all farings even as now are the thingmen of chiefs. But the chief must uphold the temple at his own charges, so that it should not go to waste, and hold therein feasts of sacrifice.

Now Thorolf called that ness Thorsness which lieth between Swordfirth and Templewick; on the ness is a fell, and that fell Thorolf held in such worship that he laid down that no man unwashed should turn his eyes thither, and that nought should be done to death on the fell, either man or beast, until it went therefrom of its own will. That fell he called Holy Fell, and he trowed that thither he should fare when he died, and all his kindred from the ness. On the tongue of the ness whereas Thor had come a-land he made all dooms be held, and thereon he set up a county Thing.

And so holy a place that was, that he would nowise that men should defile the field with blood-shedding, and moreover none should go thither for their needs, but to that end was appointed a skerry called Dirtskerry.

Now Thorolf waxed of great largesse in his housekeeping, and had many men about him; for in those days meat was good to get both from the isles and from the take of the sea.

Chapter 5
Biorn Ketilson Comes West-Over-The-Sea, But Will Not Abide There

Now must we tell of Biorn, the son of Ketil Flatneb, that he sailed West-over-the-sea when he and Thorolf Most-beard sundered as is aforesaid.

He made for the South-isles; but when he came West-over-the-sea, then was Ketil Flatneb his father dead, but he found there Helgi his brother and his sisters, and they offered him good entertainment with them.

But Biorn saw that they had another troth, and nowise manly it seemed to him that they had cast off the faith that their kin had held; and he had no heart to dwell therein, and would not take up his abode there. Yet was he the winter through with Auth his sister and Thorstein her son.

But when they found that he would not be at one with his kindred, they called him Biorn the Easterner, and deemed it ill that he would not abide there.

Chapter 6
Biorn Comes Out To Iceland

Biorn was two winters in the South-isles before he dight him to fare to Iceland; with him in that faring was Hallstein Thorolfson; and they made haven at Broadfirth, and took land out from Staff-river, betwixt that and Lavafirth, by Thorolf's rede. Biorn dwelt at Burgholt in Bearhaven, and he was the most noble-hearted of men.

Hallstein, the son of Thorolf, deemed it less than manly to take land at the hands of his father; so he fared west over Broadfirth, and there took to himself land, and dwelt at Hallsteinsness.

Certain winters thereafter came out Auth the Deep-minded; and the first winter she was with Biorn her brother, but afterwards she made her own all the Dale-lands in Broadfirth between Skraumuhlaups-river and Daymeal-water, and dwelt at Hvamm.

In those days was all Broadfirth settled; but little need there is to speak of the land-taking of those men who come not into the story.

Chapter 7
Of The Kin Of Kiallak

There was a man hight Geirrod who took land from Thors-river eastward unto Longdale, and dwelt at Ere; with him came out Ulfar the Champion, to whom Geirrod gave lands round about Ulfar's-fell; with him too came Fingeir, son of Thorstein Snowshoe. He dwelt in Swanfirth, and his son was Thorfin, the father of Thorbrand of Swanfirth.

There was a man hight Vestar, son of Thorolf Bladderpate; he brought to Iceland his father, a man well on in years, and took land west away from Whalefirth, and dwelt at Onward-ere. His son was Asgeir, who dwelt there afterwards.

Biorn the Easterner died the first of these land-settlers, and was buried at Burgbrook. He left behind two sons: one was Kiallak the Old, who dwelt at Bearhaven after his father. Kiallak had to wife Astrid, daughter of Rolf the Hersir, and sister of Steinolf the Low. They had three children: Thorgrim the Priest was a son of theirs, and their daughter was Gerd, she whom Thorrood the Priest, son of Odd the Strong, had to wife; their third child was Helga, whom Asgeir of Ere had to wife.

From the children of Kiallak is sprung a great kindred, which is called the Kiallekings.

Ottar was the name of another son of Biorn; he married Gro, the daughter of Geirleif of Bardstrand. Their sons were these: Helgi, the father of Osvif the Wise, and Biorn, the father of Vigfus of Drapalith; but Vilgeir was the third son of Ottar Biornson.

Thorolf Most-beard married in his old age, and had to wife her who is called Unn; some say that she was daughter of Thorstein the Red, but Ari the Learned, son of Thorgils, numbers her not among his children. Thorolf and Unn had a son who was called Stein; that lad Thorolf gave to Thor his friend, and called him Thorstein, and the boy was very quick of growth.

Now Hallstein Thorolfson had to wife Osk, daughter of Thorstein the Red; Thorstein was their son; he was fostered at Thorolf's, and was called Thorstein the Swart; but his own son Thorolf called Thorstein Codbiter.

Chapter 8
Of Thorolf Halt-Foot

In those days came out Geirrid, the sister of Geirrod of Ere, and he gave her dwelling in Burgdale up from Swanfirth. She let build her hall athwart the highway, and all men should ride through it who passed by. Therein stood ever a table, and meat to be given to whomsoever had will thereto, and therefore was she deemed to be the greatest and noblest of women. Biorn, son of Bolverk

Blinding-snout, had had Geirrid to wife, and their son was called Thorolf, and was a mighty viking; he came out some time after his mother, and was with her the first winter. Thorolf deemed the lands of Burgdale but too narrow, and he challenged Ulfar the Champion for his lands, and bade him to the holm-gang because he was an old man and a childless. But Ulfar had liefer die than be cowed by Thorolf. They went to holm in Swanfirth, and Ulfar fell, but Thorolf was wounded in the leg, and went halt ever after, and therefore was he called Halt-foot. Now he set up house in Hvamm in Thorsriverdale. He took to himself the land after Ulfar, and was the most wrongful of men. He sold land to the freedmen of Thorbrand of Swanfirth; Ulfar's-fell to Ulfar, to wit, and Orligstead to Orlig; and they dwelt there long after. Thorolf Halt-foot had three children; his son was called Arnkel, but his daughter Gunnfrid, whom Thorbein of Thorbeinstead up on Waterneck east from Drapalith had to wife; their sons were Sigmund and Thorgils, but their daughter was hight Thorgerd, whom Vigfus of Drapalith had to wife. Another daughter of Thorolf was Geirrid, whom Thorolf the son of Heriolf Holkinrazi had to wife. They dwelt at Mewlithe; their children were Thorarin the Swart and Gudny.

Chapter 9
Of Thorstein Codbiter. Battle At Thorsness Thing

Thorolf Most-Beard died at Templestead, and then Thorstein Codbiter took his inheritance after him. He then took to wife Thora, daughter of Olaf Feilan and sister of Thord the Yeller, who dwelt at Hvamm in those days.

Thorolf was buried at Howness, west of Templestead.

At that time so great was the pride of the kin of Kiallak, that they thought themselves before all other men in that countryside; and so many were the kinsmen of Biorn that there was no kindred so mighty in all Broadfirth.

In those days Barne-Kiallak, their kinsman, dwelt in Midfell-strand, at the stead which is now called Kiallakstead, and a many sons he had who were of good conditions; they all brought help to their kin south of the firth at Things and folk-motes.

On a spring-tide at Thorsness Thing these brothers-in-law Thorgrim Kiallakson and Asgeir of Ere gave out that they would not give a lift to the pride of the Thorsness-folk, and that they would go their errands in the grass as otherwhere men do in man-motes, though those men were so proud that they made their lands holier than other lands of Broadfirth. They gave forth that they would not tread shoe for the going to the out-skerries for their easements.

But when Thorstein Codbiter was ware of this, he had no will that they should defile that field which Thorolf his father had honoured over all other places in his lands.

So he called his friends to him, and bade them keep those folk from the field by battle if they were minded to defile it.

In this rede were with him Thorgeir the son of Geirrod of Ere, and the Swanfirthers Thorfin and Thorbrand his son, Thorolf Halt- foot, and many other thingmen and friends of Thorstein.

But in the evening when the Kiallekings were full of meat they took their weapons and went out on to the ness; but when Thorstein and his folk saw that they turned off from the road that lay skerry-ward, they sprang to their weapons and ran after them with whooping and egging on. And when the Kiallekings saw that, they ran together and defended themselves.

But those of Thorsness made so hard an onset that Kiallak and his men shrunk off the field and clown to the foreshore, and then they turned against them therewith, and there was a hard battle between them; the Kiallekings were the fewer, but they had a chosen band. But now the men of Woodstrand were ware of this, Thorgest the Old and Aslak of Longdale; they ran thereto and went betwixt them; but both sides were of the fiercest, nor could they sunder them before they gave out that they would aid those who should hearken to their bidding to sunder.

Therewith were they parted, but yet in such wise that the Kiallekings might not go up on to the field; so they took ship, and fared away from the Thing.

There fell men of either side, the most of the Kiallekings; and a many were hurt. No truce could be struck, because neither side would handsel it, but swore to fall on each other as soon as it might be brought about. The field was all bloody whereas they fought, as well as there whereas the men of Thorsness had stood while the fight was toward.

Chapter 10
Peace Made

After the Thing the chiefs on either side sat at home with many men about them, and much ill blood there was between them. Their friends took this rede, to send word to Thord the Yeller, who was then the greatest chief in Broadfirth: he was akin to the Kiallekings, but closely allied to Thorstein; therefore he seemed to be the likeliest of men to settle peace between them. But when this message came to Thord, he fared thither with many men, and strove to make peace. He found that far apart were the minds of them; yet he brought about truce between them, and a meeting to be summoned. The close of the matter was that Thord should make it up, on such terms that whereas the Kiallekings laid down that they would never go their errands to Dirtskerry, Thorstein claimed that they should not defile the field now more than aforetime. The Kiallekings claimed that all they who had fallen on Thorstein's part should be fallen unhallowed, because they had first set on them with the mind to fight. But the Thorsnessings said that all the Kiallekings had fallen unhallowed because of their law-breaking at a Holy Thing.

But though the terms laid down were hard for the award, yet Thord yeasaid the taking it on him rather than that they should part unappeased. Now Thord thus set forth the beginning of the award: "Let hap abide as hap befell"; said that for no manslayings nor hurts which had happed at Thorsness should man-gild be paid. The field he gave out unhallowed because of the blood shed in wrath that had fallen thereon, and that land he declared now no holier than another, laying down that the cause thereof were those who first bestirred them to wounding others. And that he called the only peace-breaking that had betid, and said withal that no Thing should be held there thenceforward. But that they might be well appeased and friends thenceforth, he made this further award, that Thorgrim Kiallakson should uphold the temple half at his own costs, and answer for half the temple toll, and the Thingmen the other half. He should also help Thorstein thenceforth in all law-cases, and strengthen him in whatso hallowing he might bestow on the Thing, whereso it should next be set up.

Withal Thord the Yeller gave to Thorgrim Kiallakson Thorhild his kinswoman, the daughter of Thorkel Main-acre his neighbour; and thenceforth was he called Thorgrim the Priest. Then they moved the Thing up the ness, where it now is; and whenas Thord the Yeller settled the Quarter Things, he caused this to be the Quarter Thing of the Westfirthers, and men should seek to that Thing from all over the Westfirths. There is yet to be seen the Doom-ring, where men were doomed to the sacrifice. In that ring stands the stone of Thor over which those men were broken who were sacrificed, and the colour of the blood on that stone is yet to be seen.

And at that Thing was one of the holiest of steads, but there men were not forbidden to go their errands.

Chapter 11
Of Thorgrim The Priest The Death Of Thorstein Codbiter

Thorstein Codbiter became a man of the greatest largesse; he had ever with him sixty freedmen; he was a great gatherer of household stuff, and was ever going a-fishing.

He first let raise the homestead at Holyfell, and brought thither his household, and it was the greatest of temple-steads of those days.

Withal he let make a homestead on the ness near to where had been the Thing. That homestead he let make well arrayed, and he gave it afterwards to Thorstein the Swart, his kinsman, who dwelt there thenceforth, and was the wisest of men. Thorstein Codbiter had a son who was called Bork the Thick. But on a summer when Thorstein was five-and-twenty winters old, Thora bore him a man- child who was called Grim, and sprinkled with water. That lad Thorstein gave to Thor, and said that he should be a Temple- Priest, and called him Thorgrim.

That same harvest Thorstein fared out to Hoskuldsey to fish; but on an evening of harvest a shepherd-man of Thorstein's fared after his sheep north of Holyfell; there he saw how the fell was opened on the north side, and in the fell he saw mighty fires, and heard huge clamour therein, and the clank of drinking-horns; and when he hearkened if perchance he might hear any words clear of others, he heard that there was welcomed Thorstein Codbiter and his crew, and he was bidden to sit in the high-seat over against his father.

That foretoken the shepherd told in the evening to Thora, Thorstein's wife; she spake little thereon, and said that might be a foreboding of greater tidings.

The morning after came men west-away from Hoskuldsey and told these tidings: that Thorstein Codbiter had been drowned in the fishing; and men thought that great scathe. Thora went on keeping house there afterwards, and thereto joined himself with her he who is called Hallward; they had a son together, who was called Mar.

Chapter 12
Of Arnkel The Priest And Others

The sons of Thorstein Codbiter grew up at home with their mother, and they were the hopefullest of men; but Thorgrim was the foremost of them in all things, and was a chief as soon as he had age thereto. Thorgrim wedded west in Dyrafirth, and had to wife Thordis Sur's daughter, and betook himself west to his brothers- in-law Gisli and Thorkel.

Now Thorgrim slew Vestein Vesteinson at the harvest feast in Hawkdale; but the autumn next after, when Thorgrim was five-and- twenty years old, even as his father, Gisli his brother-in-law slew him at the harvest feast at Seastead. Some nights after Thordis his wife brought forth a son, and the lad was called Thorgrim after his father. A little thereafter Thordis was wedded to Bork the Thick, Thorgrim's brother, and betook her to housekeeping with him at Holyfell. Then fared Thorgrim her son to Swanfirth, and was there at fostering with Thorbrand; he was somewhat reckless in his youth, and was called Snerrir, but afterwards Snorri. Thorbrand of Swanfirth had to wife Thurid, daughter of Thorfin Selthorison from Redmell.

These were their children: Thorleif Kimbi was the eldest, the second was Snorri, the third Thorod, the fourth Thorfin, the fifth Thormod; their daughter was called Thorgerd; all these were foster-brethren of Snorri Thorgrimson.

At that time Arnkel, son of Thorolf Haltfoot, dwelt at Lairstead by Vadils-head; he was the biggest and strongest of men, a great lawman and mighty wise, and was a good and true man, and before all others, even in those parts, in luck of friends and hardihood; he was withal a Temple-Priest, and had many Thingmen.

Thorgrim Kiallakson dwelt at Bearhaven as is aforesaid, and he and Thorhild had three sons: Brand was the eldest; he dwelt at Crossness by Sealriver head. Another was Arngrim; he was a big man and a strong, large of nose, big-boned of face, bleak-red of hair, early bald in front; sallow of hue, his eyes great and fair; he was very masterful, and exceeding in wrongfulness, and therefore was he called Stir.

Vermund was the name of the youngest son of Thorgrim Kiallakson; he was a tall man and a slender, fair to look on; he was called Vermund the Slender. The son of Asgeir of Ere was called Thorlak; he had to wife Thurid, the daughter of Audum Stote of Lavafirth. These were their children: Steinthor, Bergthor, Thormod, Thord Wall-eye, and Helga. Steinthor was the foremost of the children of Thorlak; he was a big man and a strong, and most skilled in arms of all men, and he was the best knit of men, and meek of mood in every-day life. Steinthor is held for the third best man-at-arms of Iceland, along with these, Helgi, the son of Droplaug, and Vemund Kogr.

Thormod was a wise man and a peaceful. Thord Wall-eye was a very masterful man. Bergthor was the youngest, yet had he all the makings of a man in him.

Chapter 13
Of Snorri Thorgrimson

Snorri Thorgrimson was fourteen winters old when he fared abroad with his foster-brothers Thorleif Kimbi and Thorod. Bork the Thick gave him fifty hundreds in silver for his voyage. They had a good voyage, and came to Norway in harvest, and were the winter through in Rogaland.

Snorri abode with Erling Skialgson at Soli, and Erling was good to him because of the ancient friendship between their former kinsmen, Horda-Karl and Thorolf Most-beard to wit.

The summer after they fared out to Iceland and were late-ready. They had a hard outing of it, and came a little before winter to Hornfirth; but when the Broadfirthers dight them from shipboard, far asunder showed the array of the twain, Snorri and Thorleif Kimbi. Thorleif bought the best horse he could get, and had withal a fair-stained saddle, and glittering and fair-dight sword, and gold-inlaid spear, and his shield was dark blue and much gilded about; and all his clothes were well wrought withal. He had spent thereon pretty much all his faring-money; but Snorri was clad in a black cape, and rode a black mare, a good one. He had an ancient trough-saddle, and his weapons were little wrought for show. But the array of Thorod was between the two.

They rode from the east over the Side, and then as the road lay, west to Burgfirth, and so west across the Flats, and guested at Swanfirth. Thereafter Snorri rode to Holyfell, and was minded to abide there the winter through. Bork, however, took that matter slowly, and folk had much laughter over his array. Bork let out so much as that he had done unhappily with the faring-money, since it was all gone.

But one day in the beginning of winter, at Holyfell in came twelve men all armed. And there was come Eyolf the Gray, a kinsman of Bork and son of Thord the Yeller; he dwelt at Otterdale west in Ernfirth. But when folk asked for tidings, they said that they had slain Gisli Surson, and told of the men who were fallen before him or ever he fell. At these tidings was Bork exceeding glad, and bade Thordis and Snorri welcome Eyolf at their best, as a man who had thrust off so much shame from the hands of them and their kin.

Snorri let out little over those tidings, but Thordis said: "Cheer good enough for Gisli's bane if grout is given him."

Bork answered: "I meddle not with meals."

So Bork set Eyolf in the high-seat, and his fellows out from him, and they cast their weapons on the floor. Bork sat inside of Eyolf, and then Snorri Thordis bare in dishes of grout to the board, and had spoons withal; but when she set one before Eyolf, one of the spoons fell down for her. She stooped after it, and took Eyolf's sword therewith and drew it swiftly, and thrust it up under the board, and the thrust smote Eyolf's thigh, but the hilt caught against the board; yet was the hurt sore. Bork thrust the table away and smote at Thordis, but Snorri thrust Bork away, so that he fell over, and caught hold of his mother and set her down beside him, and said that enough were her heart-burnings though she were left unbeaten.

Then sprang up Eyolf and his men, and man caught hold of man; but such was the end of these matters that Bork handselled self-doom to Eyolf, and much fee he awarded himself for his hurt; and withal he fared away. But thereof waxed much ill-will betwixt the twain, Bork and Snorri.

Chapter 14
Snorri Gets Holyfell

At the Spring Thing the next summer Snorri claimed his father's heritage from Bork. Bork answered that he would yield him his heritage. "But I am loth," said he, "to share Holyfell asunder, though I see that it is meet for us not to dwell in one stead together. So I will redeem my share of the land." Snorri answered: "It is most fair that thou shouldst lay the land at as dear a price as thou wilt, but fair also that I choose which of us shall redeem it."

Bork thought over that matter, and so deemed that Snorri would not have loose money to give for the land if he should have to redeem it speedily, and he laid the worth of half the land at sixty hundreds of silver, having first set aside the islands, because he thought that he should get them at but little price when Snorri should have set up house and home otherwhere.

There followed therewith that the money should be straightway paid up, and nought of the money should be borrowed from other folk. "And choose thou now, Snorri, here on the spot which thou wilt take," said Bork.

Snorri answered: "This know I now, kinsman Bork, that thou deemest me sick of purse when thou layest down the land of Holyfell so good cheap; yet I choose to take to me my father's land at that price, so reach me out thine hand, and handsel me now the land."

"That shall not be," said Bork, "before every penny is first yolden."

Then said Snorri to Thorbrand his foster-father: "Did I hand over to thee any money last autumn?" "Yea," said Thorbrand, and therewith drew a purse from under his cape. Then was the silver told, and every penny paid for the land, and after that was left in the purse sixty hundreds of silver.

Bork took the money, and gave handsel to Snorri of the land.

Then said Bork: "More of silver hast thou got, kinsman, than we wotted; now I will that we give up the ill-will which was between us; and I will add this to thy well-doing, that we keep house both together at Holyfell these seasons, since thou hast little of live-stock."

Snorri answered: "Well then, thou shalt make the most of thy live-stock; but yet from Holyfell shalt thou get thee gone." And so must it be even as Snorri would.

But when Bork was ready to depart from Holyfell, Thordis went forth and named witnesses to this for herself, that she gave out that she was parted from Bork her husband, and gave that for the cause that he had smitten her, and she would not lie under his hand. Then were their goods divided, and Snorri stood forth for his mother because he was her heir. Then Bork took the lot which he had minded for another, that he got but a little price for the islands.

Thereafter Bork fared away from Holyfell, and west to Midfell-strand, and dwelt first at Borkstead between Orris-knoll and Tongue.

Chapter 15
Of Snorri The Priest, Of The Mewlithe-Folk

Snorri Thorgrimsom set up house at Holyfell, and his mother was over the housekeeping. Mar Hallwardson, his father's brother, betook himself thither with much live-stock, and was head over Snorri's household and husbandry. There Snorri held a thronged house of the greatest largesse.

Snorri was middling in height and somewhat slender, fair to look on, straight-faced and of light hue; of yellow hair and red beard; he was meek of mood in his daily ways; little men knew of his thought for good or ill; he was a wise man, and foreseeing in many things, enduring in wrath and deep in hatred; of good rede was he for his friends, but his unfriends deemed his counsels but cold.

He was now Warden of the Temple there; therefore was he called Snorri the Priest, and a great chief he became; but for his rule he was much envied, because there were many who for the sake of their kin thought they were of no less worth than he, but had more to fall back upon, because of their strength and proven hardihood.

Now Bork the Thick and Thordis Sur's daughter, had a daughter who was called Thurid, and was at this time wedded to Thorbiorn the Thick, who dwelt at Frodis-water. He was the son of Worm the Slender, who had dwelt there and had settled the land of Frodis- water; he had before had to wife Thurid of Broadwick, daughter of Asbrand of Combe; she was sister to Biorn, the Champion of the Broadwickers, who hereafter cometh again into this tale, and to Arnbiorn the Strong. These were the sons of Thorbiorn and Thurid: Ketil the Champion, Gunnlaug, and Hallstein.

But Thorbiorn of Frodis-water was overbearing and reckless with men lesser than he.

In those days dwelt at Mewlithe, Geirrid, daughter of Thorolf Halt-foot, with Thorarin the Swart, her son. He was a big man and a strong; ugly he was, and moody and quiet in his daily guise: he was called the Peace-maker. He had not much wealth to boast of, yet was his housekeeping gainful. So little of a meddler was he, that his foes said that he had no less the heart of a woman than a man. He was a married man, and his wife was called Aud; Gudny was his sister, whom Vermund the Slender had to wife.

At Holt, west of Mewlithe, dwelt a widow who was called Katla. She was fair to look upon, but yet not to all men's minds. Her son was called Odd; he was a big man and of good pith, a mighty brawler, and babbling, slippery, and slanderous.

Now Gunnlaug, the son of Thorbiorn the Thick, was eager to learn; he often stayed at Mewlithe, and learned cunning from Geirrid, Thorolt's daughter, because she knew much wizard lore. But on a day Gunnlaug came to Holt on his way to Mewlithe, and talked much with Katla; but she asked if he were minded once more for Mewlithe to pat the old carline's belly there. Gunnlaug said that was not his errand, "but thou art not so young, Katla, that it befits thee to cast Geirrid's eld in her teeth."

Katla answered: "I did not deem that we were so like herein; but it matters not," said she; "ye men deem that there is no woman beside Geirrid, but more women know somewhat than she alone."

Odd Katlason fared often to Mewlithe with Gunnlaug; but when they happened to go back late, Katla would often bid Gunnlaug to abide there at Holt, but he went home ever.

Chapter 16
Gunnlaug Is Witch-Ridden Geirrid Summoned, Of Thorarin

On a day at the beginning of that winter wherein Snorri first kept house at Holyfell, it befell that Gunnlaug Thorbiornson fared to Mewlithe, and Odd Katlason with him. Gunnlaug and Geirrid talked long together that day, and when the evening was far spent Geirrid said to Gunnlaug: "I would that thou go not home this evening, for there will be many ride-by-nights about, and oft is a fiend in a fair skin; but methinks that now thou seemest not over-lucky to look upon."

Gunnlaug answered: "No risk may there be to me," says he, "since we are two together."

She said: "No gain will Odd's help be to thee, and withal thou wilt thyself have to pay for thine own wilfulness."

Thereafter they went out, Gunnlaug and Odd, and fared till they came to Holt. Katla was by then in her bed; she bade Odd pray Gunnlaug to abide there. He said he had so done, "and he must needs fare home," said he. "Let him fare then as his fate he shapes," says she.

Gunnlaug came not home in the evening, and folk talked it over that he should be searched for; but the search came not off. But in the night, when Thorbiorn looked out, he found Gunnlaug his son before the door; and there he lay witless withal. Then was he borne in and his clothes pulled off; he was all black and blue about the shoulders, and the flesh was falling from the bones. He lay all the winter sick of his hurts, and great talk there was over that sickness of his. Odd Katlason spread that about that Geirrid must have ridden him; for he said that they had parted with short words that evening. And most men deemed that it was even thus.

This was about the summoning days. So Thorbiorn rode to Mewlithe and summoned Geirrid for this cause, that she was a ride-by-night and had brought about Gunnlaug's trouble. The case went to the Thorsness Thing, and Snorri the Priest took up the case for Thorbiorn his brother-in-law; but Arnkel the Priest defended the case for Geirrid his sister: a jury of twelve should give a verdict thereon. But neither of the two, Snorri or Arnkel, were deemed fit to bear witness, because of their kinship to the plaintiff and defendant.

Then was Helgi, the Priest of Templegarth, the father of Biorn, the father of Gest, the father of Shald-Ref, called to give out the twelve men's finding. Arnkel the Priest went to the doom and made oath on the stall-ring that Geirrid had not wrought the hurt of Gunnlaug; Thorarin made oath with him and ten other men, and then Helgi gave the verdict for Geirrid. And the case of Thorbiorn and Snorri came to nought, and thereof gat they shame.

Chapter 17
Strife At The Thorsness Thing; Snorri Goes Between

At this Thing Thorgrim Kiallakson and his sons strove with Illugi the Black about the jointure and dowry of Ingibiorg, Asbiorn's daughter, the wife of Illugi, which Tillforni had had in wardship.

At the Thing great storms befell, so that no man could come to the Thing from Midfell-strand, and a great drawback to Thorgrim's strength it was that his kin might not come.

Illugi had a hundred men and those a chosen band, and he pushed the case forward; but the Kiallekings went to the court, and would fain break it up.

Then there was a mighty throng, and men made it their business there to part them; but so the matter went, that Tinforni had to give up the money according to Illugi's claim. So says Odd the Skald in Illugi's lay:

"It was west at the Thorsness Thing fray was there foughten, And there was the man by hap ever upholden; The staff of the song from the helm that upriseth Was a-claiming the dowry amidst of the Mote. So the fair load of Fornir's scrip fell in the ending To the keen-witted wight one, the warrior that feedeth The swart swallow's brother that flits o'er the fight. But no easy matter was peace unto menfolk."

Chapter 18
Men Will Ransack At Mewlithe; Thorarin Falls To Fight

That summer died Thorgrim Kiallakson, whereon Vermund the Slender, his son, took the homestead at Bearhaven; he was a wise man, and marvellous wholesome of redes. Stir also had by then dwelt for some time at Lava, up from Bearhaven; he was a wise man and a hardy. He had to wife Thorbiorg, daughter of Thorstein Windy-Nose. Thorstein and Hall were their sons; Asdis was the name of their daughter, a manly-souled woman, and somewhat high-minded. Stir was a masterful man in the countryside, and had a many folk about him; he was held guilty at many men's hands, for that he wrought many slayings and booted none.

That summer came out a ship to the Salteremouth: half of it was owned by Northmen, and their skipper was called Biorn; he went to dwell at Ere with Steinthor. The other half was owned by South- islanders, and Alfgeir was their skipper; he went to dwell at Mewlithe with Thorarin the Swart, and with him a fellow of his who was called Nail, a big man, and swift of foot; he was Scotch of kin.

Now Thorarin had a good fighting horse up in the fells; and Thorbiorn the Thick withal had many stud horses together, which he kept on the fell-pastures, and he was wont to choose out of them in autumn horses for slaughter. But in the autumn it befell that Thorbiorn's horses were not to be found, though they were searched for far and wide: and that autumn the weather was somewhat hard.

In the beginning of winter Thorbiorn sent Odd Katlason south over the heath to a stead called Under-the-Lava, where there dwelt a man called Cunning-Gils, a foreseeing man, and a great man for spying after thefts and such like other matters as he was wistful to pry into. Odd asked whether it was outland men or out-parish men or neighbours who had stolen Thorbiorn's horses.

Cunning-Gils, answered: "Say thou to Thorbiorn even as I say, that I deem that those horses will not have gone far away from their pastures; but risky it is to tell of men's names, and it is better to lose one's own than that great troubles should arise therefrom."

Now when Odd came to Frodis-water, Thorbiorn deemed that Cunning-Gils had made a thrust at the Mewlithers in that matter. Odd said too that he had said as much as that they were the likeliest for the horse-stealing who were themselves penniless, and yet had lately got them increase of servants more than was their wont. In these words Thorbiorn thought that the Mewlithers were clearly meant.

After that rode Thorbiorn from home with eleven men. Hallstein, his son, was in that journey, but Ketil the Champion, another son of his, was then abroad; there was Thorir, the son of Ern of Ernknoll, a neighbour of Thorbiorn's and the briskest of men; Odd Katlason, too, was in this journey; but when they came to Holt to Katla, she did on Odd her son an earth-brown kirtle, which she had then newly made.

Thereafter they fared to Mewlithe, and there stood Thorarin and the home men out in the door when they saw the men coming.

Then they greeted Thorbiorn and asked for tidings. Thorbiorn said: "This is our errand here, Thorarin," says he, "that we are seeking after the horses which were stolen from me in the autumn; therefore we claim to ransack thine house."

Thorarin answered: "Is this ransacking taken up according to law; or have ye called any lawful law-seers to search into this case; or will ye handsel truce to us in this ransacking; or have ye sought further otherwhere for the doing of this ransacking?"

Thorbiorn answered: "We deem not that any ransacking need be pushed further."

Thorarin answered: "Then will we flatly refuse this ransacking, if ye begin and carry on the search lawlessly."

Said Thorbiorn: "Then shall we take that for sooth, that thou wilt be found proven guilty, if thou wilt not have the matter thrust off thee by the ransacking."

"Ye may do as ye please," said Thorarin.

Thereafter Thorbiorn made a door-doom, and named six men for that doom; and then Thorbiorn gave forth the case at Thorarin's hands for the horse-stealing.

Then came Geirrid out to the door, and saw what betid, and said: "Overtrue is that which men say, Thorarin, that thou hast more of the mind of a woman than a man, when thou bearest from Thorbiorn the Thick all shame soever; nor wot I why I have such a son."

Then said Alfgeir the Skipper, "We will give thee aid in whatsoever thou wilt bestir thyself."

Thorarin answered: "No longer will I stand here;" and therewith Thorarin and his folk ran out and would break up the court. They were seven in all, and therewithal both sides rushed into the fight. Thorarin slew a house-carle of Thorbiorn's, and Alfgeir another, and there fell also a housecarle of Thorarin's; but no weapons would bite on Odd Katlason.

Now the goodwife Aud calls out on her women to part them, and they cast clothes over the weapons.

Thereafter Thorarin and his men went in, but Thorbiorn rode off with his folk, and they put off the case to the Thorsness Thing. They rode up along the Creeks, and bound up their wounds under a stackyard that is called Combe-Garth.

But in the home-field at Mewlithe men found a hand whereas they had fought, and it was shown to Thorarin; he saw that it was a woman's hand, and asked where Aud was; it was told him that she lay in bed. Then he went to her, and asked whether she were wounded; she bade him pay no heed to that, but he was ware withal that her hand had been hewn off. Then he called to his mother, and bade her bind up the wound.

Then Thorarin rushed out with his fellows and ran after those of Thorbiorn, and when they were but a little from the garth they heard the babble of Thorbiorn and his folk; and Hallstein took up the word and said:

"Thorarin has thrust off from him the reproach of cowardice to-day."

"Boldly he fought," said Thorbiorn; "yet many become brave when brought to bay, but natheless are not over-brave between whiles."

Then said Odd: "Thorarin must needs be the bravest of men, but luckless will it be deemed that he so wrought as to cut off his wife's hand."

"Is that sure?" said Thorbiorn.

"Sure as day," says Odd. With that they jumped up, and made great shouting and laughter thereover.

In that very nick of time came up Thorarin and his folk, and Nail was the foremost; but when he saw them threaten with their weapons, he blenched and ran forth and up into the fell, and there became one witless with fear. But Thorarin rushed at Thorbiorn and smote his sword into his head, and clave it down to the jaw-teeth. Then Thorir Ernson with two others set on Thorarin, and Hallstein and another on Alfgeir. Odd Katlason with another man gat on to a fellow of Alfgeir's, and three of Thorbiorn's fellows on two of Thorarin's folk; and the fight was joined both fierce and fell. But so their dealings ended, that Thorarin cut the leg from Thorir at the thickest of the calf, and slew both his fellows. Hallstein fell before Alfgeir wounded to death; but when Thorarin was free, Odd Katlason fled with two men; he was not wounded, because no weapon might bite on his kirtle; all their other fellows lay on the field; and there too were slain two housecarles of Thorarin.

Then Thorarin and his men took the horses of Thorbiorn and his folk and rode home; and then they saw where Nail was running along the upper hill-side. And when they came to the home-field, they see that Nail had passed by the garth and made inward towards Buland's-head. There he found two thralls of Thorarin, who were driving their sheep from the Head; he told them of the meeting, and what odds in number of men there was; he said he knew for sure that Thorarin and his men were slain; and therewithal they see how men ride away from the homestead over the field.

Then Thorarin and his folk took to galopping in order to help Nail, that he might not run into the sea or over the cliffs; but he and those others, when they saw men riding eagerly, deemed that there must Thorbiorn be going. Then they all betook themselves to running afresh up on to the Head, till they came to that place which is now called Thrall-scree, and there Thorarin and his folk got Nail taken, because he had well-nigh broken his wind, but the thralls leapt over from the Head and were lost, as was like to be, because the Head is so high, that whatsoever leaps thereover must perish.

Thereafter Thorarin and his men rode home, and there was Geirrid in the door, and she asked how they had fared; but Thorarin sang this stave:

"The word of a woman wherewith I was wited Have I warded away now where war dared the warrior, He who slayeth the fire-flaught flaming in fight: (The share of the eagle was corpse-meat new slaughtered.) No yielding forsooth did I bear about yonder, Where, amidst of the corpse-worms I met him, The praiser manly the prayer of War-god beworshipped, Not often I boast me of deeds of my doing."

Chapter 19
The Lay Of The Mewlithers

For one night was Thorarin at home at Mewlithe, but in the morning Aud asked him what shift he was minded to seek for himself. "No will have I to turn thee out of my house," said she; "but I fear that there will be many a door-doom holden here this winter, for well I wot that Snorri the Priest must needs take up the case for Thorbiorn his brother-in4aw." Then sang Thorarin:

"The wakener of law-wrong shall nowise meseemeth This winter that waneth lay blood-wite on me, For yonder is Arnkel, and there, as my hope is, My life-warden liveth all praise-worth to win. Might I come but to Vermund and fare with the feeder Of the flame of the God of the field where the corpses Lie fallen in slaughter, then surely for me Might Hugin's son feed fat on field of the slain."

Chapter 20
The End Of Katla And Odd

Now Geirrid, the goodwife at Mewlithe, sent word to Lairstead that she was ware of this, that Odd Katlason had stricken off the hand from Aud; she said that she had Aud's own word therefor, and that Odd had made boast of it before his friends.

But when Arnkel and Thorarin heard this, they rode from home out to Mewlithe, twelve men all told, and were there through the night; but in the morning they rode out to Holt, from whence their going was seen.

Now at Holt was no man at home but Odd. Katla sat on the dais, and span yarn. She bade Odd sit beside her; "and be thou as near to me as thou may'st." She bade her women sit in their seats, "and be ye silent," quoth she, "and I will have words with them."

So when Arnkel and his folk came, they went in there, and when they came into the chamber, Katla greeted Arnkel and asked for tidings. Arnkel said he had nought to tell, and asked where was Odd. Katla said he had gone south to Broadwick. "Nor would he have foregone meeting thee if he had been at home, for that we trust thee well for thy manliness."

"That may be," said Arnkel, "but we will have a ransacking here."

"That shall be as ye will," said Katla, and bade her cookmaid bear light before them and unlock the meat bower, "that is the only locked chamber in the stead."

Now they saw, how Katla span yarn from her rock, and they searched through the house and found not Odd; and thereafter they fared away.

But when they were come a short space from the garth, Arnkel stood still and said:

"Whether now has Katla cast a hood over our heads, and was Odd her son there whereas we saw but a rock?"

"She is not unlike to have so done," said Thorarin, "so let us fare back." And that they did.

But when it was seen from Holt that they turned back, then said Katla to her women:

"Ye shall still sit in your seats, but I will go with Odd out into the fore-chamber." So when they were come out through the chamber door, she went into the porch over against the outer door, and combed Odd her son, and sheared his hair.

Then Arnkel and his folk fall in at the door, and saw where Katla was, and played with a he-goat of hers, and stroked his head and beard, and combed out his fell. Arnkel and his men went into the stove and saw Odd nowhere, but there lay Katla's rock on the bench, and thereby they deemed that Odd could never have been there.

Thereafter they went out and fared away. But when they came nigh to where they had turned before, Arnkel said: "Is it not in your mind that Odd was there in the likeness of that he-goat?"

"I wot not," said Thorarin, "but if we turn back now, then shall we lay hands on Katla."

"We will try once more then," said Arnkel, "and see what will happen;" and therewith they turned again.

But when their faring was seen, Katla asked Odd to come with her; and when they came out, she went to the ash-heap, and bade Odd lie down thereunder, "and abide thou there, whatsoever may come to pass."

Now when those of Arnkel came to the house, they ran in, and so into the chamber, and there sat Katla on the dais and span. She greeted them, and said that their visits came thick and fast. Arnkel said it was so; and therewith his fellows took the rock and hewed it asunder.

Then said Katla: "Ye will not have to say at home this eve that ye had no errand at Holt, since ye have slaughtered my rock."

Then went Arnkel and his folk and sought for Odd within and without, and saw nought quick save a house-boar that Katla owned, which lay under the ash-heap; and thereafter they fared away.

But when they were come halfway to Mewlithe, came Geirrid to meet them, with a workman of hers, and asked, how they had fared. Thorarin told her all about it. She said they had ill sought for Odd: "But I will that ye turn back again once more, and I will fare with you; nought will it avail to sail with leaf-sails whereas Katla is."

With that they turned back. Geirrid had a blue mantle over her; and when their coming was seen from Holt, Katla was told that now they were fourteen folk altogether, and one of them in coloured raiment.

Then said Katla: "Must not Geirrid the troll be coming there? Then may glamour only nowise be brought to bear."

With that she got up from the dais, and took the seat from under her, and there was a lid under that, and the dais was hollow within; therein she made Odd to go, and set everything right as it was before, and sat thereover; but she said withal that she felt somewhat uncouth.

But when those folk came into the chamber, it came to no greetings between them. Geirrid cast off her cloak and went up to Katla, and took a sealskin bag which she had had with her, and did it over Katla's head; and then her fellows bound it fast beneath. Then bade Geirrid break open the dais, and there was Odd found, and bound sithence; and after that those twain were brought up to Buland's-head.

There was Odd hanged, and as he spurned the gallows Arnkel said: "Ill is thy lot from thy mother; and so it is that thou hast verily had an ill mother."

Katla said: "True it may be that he has had no good mother, but the ill lot that he has had from me has not been by my will; but it is my will that all ye may have ill hap from me, and I hope withal that that may come to pass; nor shall it be hidden from you that I wrought that harm to Gunnlaug Thorbiornson wherefrom all these troubles have arisen."

"But thou, Arnkel," said she, "may'st have no ill hap from thy mother, because thou hast none alive; but herein were I fain that my spell may stand fast, that from thy father thou mightest have a lot as much the worse than Odd has had from me, as thou hast the more to risk than he; and I hope that this may be said before all is over, that thou hast an ill father."

Thereafter they stoned her with stones that she died under the Head there; and fared afterwards to Mewlithe, and were there through the night; but the next day they rode home. Now were all these tidings known at one time, and of that tale no folk thought harm: and so the winter wore.

Chapter 21
They Take Rede About The Blood-Feud

The next spring on a day Arnkel called to him for a talk Thorarin his kinsman, Vermund, and Alfgeir, and asked them what kind of help they deemed the friendliest for them: whether they would ride to the Thing; "and that we expend therein all our other friends," said he, "and then one of two things may hap: either that peace will be brought about, and then will your purses be shaken in atoning all who were slain there, or were hurt before you. That too may hap for one thing if the riding to the Thing is risked, that the troubles may wax, if so be the case is defended over-fiercely. But the other choice is to turn all our thoughts to this, that ye may fare abroad with all your loose goods, and let the lands be dealt with as fate may have it, such of them as may not be sold."

Of this kind of help was Alfgeir most fain. Thorarin also said that he saw not how he might have means to atone with money all those guilts which had been wrought in these matters. Vermund said that he would not part from Thorarin whether he would that he should fare abroad with him, or give him fighting-help here in the land. But Thorarin chose that Arnkel should help them to going abroad; so thereafter was a man sent out to Ere, to Biorn the Skipper, to turn all his mind to get the ship ready for them as soon as might be.

Chapter 22
Snorri Summons Thorarin

Now it must be told of Snorri the Priest that he took up the blood-feud for the slaying of Thorbiorn his brother-in-law; he also made Thurid his sister fare home to Holyfell, because the rumour ran that Biorn, the son of Asbrand from Combe, was wont to wend thither to meet her for her beguiling.

Now Snorri deemed that he saw through all the counsel of Arnkel and his friends, as soon as he learned of that ship getting ready for sea, namely, that they had no mind to deliver money atonements for those slayings; because that as yet no biddings of peace were coming forward from their hands; yet was all quiet up to the summoning days. But when that time came round Snorri gathered men, and rode up into Swanfirth with eighty men, because it was then the law to give out the summons for blood-guilt in the hearing of the slayers, or at their home, and not to summon the neighbours till the Thing.

But when Snorri's faring was seen from Lairstead; then men talked together whether they should set on him forthwith, because there were many men there together; but Arnkel said that that should not be; "Snorri's law shall we bear," said he, and he said that only that should be wrought as things stood which need drove them to.

So when Snorri came to Lairstead, no greetings there were betwixt them, and then Snorri summoned Thorarin and all those who had been at the slayings, to the Thorsness Thing.

Arnkel hearkened duly to the summoning, and thereafter Snorri and his band rode away and up into Ulfar's-fell, and when they were gone away, then Thorarin sang:

"O ground whereon groweth the fair flame of hands, Nought is it as if men were even now robbing The flinger abroad of the flame of the sword-storm, Of the law of the lands-folk, for me made all guilty. Though they, deft in dealing with roof-sun of Odin, Should lay me down guilty, and out of the law. Forsooth I can see it that more is their manflock; But yet may God give us the gain o'er the foemen."

Chapter 23
Of Vigfus And Biorn And Mar

Vigfus, the son of Biorn, the son of Ottar, dwelt at Drapalith, as is aforesaid; he had to wife Thorgerd, Thorbein's daughter; he was a mighty bonder, but exceeding violent. A sister's son of his dwelt with him who was called Biorn; he was a rash-spoken man and unyielding.

Now in the autumn, after the closing of the Mewlithe suits, were found the horses of Thorbiorn the Thick in the mountain, and the stallion had not been able to hold his pasture-ground before a stallion of Thorarin's, who had driven the other horses, which were all found dead.

That same autumn folk held a thronged sheep-folding at Tongue up from Holyfell, betwixt it and Lax-river; thither went to the folding the home-men of Snorri the Priest, and Mar Hallwardson, the father's brother of Snorri, was at the head of them. Helgi was the name of Snorri's shepherd. Biorn, the kinsman of Vigfus, lay on the fold-garth; he had a pike-staff in his hand. Now Helgi drew out sheep. Biorn on a time asked what sheep was that which he drew; and when that was looked to, there was the mark of Vigfus on the sheep.

Then said Biorn: "Thou art in a hurry to slip out the sheep to-day, Helgi."

"That is more like to befall thee," said Helgi, "who abide in the sheep-walks of men."

"Well, thief, what knowest thou of that?" said Biorn, and sprang up and drove at him with the staff so that he fell stunned. But when Mar saw that, he drew his sword and cut at Biorn, and the stroke fell on the arm up by the shoulder, and a great wound that was. Thereat men ran into two bands, but some went betwixt them, and they were parted, so that nought else happed to tell of. But the next morning rode Vigfus down to Holyfell and claimed boot for this shaming, but Snorri spoke, saying that he saw no odds between those haps that had befallen.

That Vigfus liked ill enough, and they parted with the greatest ill-will.

In the spring Vigfus brought a suit for the wounding to the Thorsness Thing, but Snorri set forth, that Biorn should be made guilty for the blow with the staff; and the end of the case was that Biorn was made guilty, because of the onslaught on Helgi, and got no boot for his wound, and his arm he bare ever after in a sling.

<h1 style="text-align:center">Chapter 24
Of Eric the Red</h1>

At this same Thing Thorgest the Old and the sons of Thord the Yeller brought a case against Eric the Red for the slaughter of the sons of Thorgest, who had been slain in the autumn when Eric fetched the settles to Broadlairstead; and very thronged was that Thing; but before it they had sat at home with crowded followings. While the Thing was toward, Eric fitted out a ship for the main in Eric's-creek in Oxisle, and in aid of Eric stood Thorbiorn Vifil's son, and Slaying-Stir, and the sons of Thorbrand of Swanfirth, and Eyolf, son of Aesa of Swineisle. But out of those that furthered Eric, Stir alone was at the Thing, and drew away from Thorgest all the men he might.

Stir prayed Snorri the Priest not to set on Eric after the Thing with those of Thorgest, and gave his word to Snorri in return, that he would help him another time, should he be holden by great troubles; and because of this promise Snorri let the case pass by. After the Thing those of Thorgest sailed with many ships into the islands; but Eyolf, son of Aesa, hid Eric's ships in Dimon's bay, and thither came Stir and Thorbiorn to meet Eric; and then did Eyolf and Stir after the fashion of Arnkel, for they went in company with Eric, each in his own skiff, as far as past Ellidis-isle.

In the voyage Eric the Red found Greenland, and was there three winters, and then he went to Iceland, and abode there one winter before he fared out to settle Greenland; but this befell fourteen winters before Christ's faith was made law in Iceland.

Chapter 25
Of Vermund And Thorarin In Norway; Of Those Bareserks

Now is it to be said of Vermund and Thorarin the Swart that they came up from the main as far north as Throndheim-mouth, and stretched in for Throndheim. In those days Earl Hakon, son of Sigurd, ruled over Norway; so Vermund went to the Earl, and became his man, but Thorarin went thence straightway that same autumn West-over-the-sea with Alfgeir, and Vermund gave them his share in the ship; and henceforward Thorarin has nought to do with this tale.

Earl Hakon abode at Hladir that winter, and Vermund was with him holden in great friendship, and the Earl did well to him, because he wotted that Vermund was of great kin out in Iceland.

With the Earl were two brothers, Swedes of kin, one called Halli, the other Leikner; they were big men of stature and strength, nor at that time were their peers herein to be found in Norway, nor far and wide otherwhere. They wrought Bareserkgang, and were not of the fashion of men when they were wroth, but went mad like dogs, and feared neither fire nor steel; but their daily wont was to be not ill to deal with, if nought was done to cross them; but they were straightway the most overreckless of men if anyone should beard them. Eric the Victorious, King of Sweden, had sent these Bareserks to the Earl, and gave him this warning therewith, that he should treat them well, and said, as was true, that of them might be the greatest avail if folk gave heed to their moods.

Now in the spring, when Vermund had been one winter with the Earl, he yearned for Iceland, and prayed the Earl for leave to fare thither. The Earl bade him go since he would, and bade him thus: "Think if there be anything in my power more than another which thou wilt take for thy furtherance, such as may be worthy and honourable for both of us."

But when Vermund had thought thereover, what thing he should ask of the Earl, it came into his mind that his ways would be greatly furthered in Iceland if he had such followers as those Bareserks were; and settled in his mind that he would pray the Earl to give him the Bareserks for his following; and this urged him to ask for them, that he deemed that his brother Stir lay heavy on his fortune, and dealt unjustly with him as with most others when he could bring his strength to bear on him. So he thought that Stir would deem it less easy to deal with him if he had such fellows as those two brothers were.

Now says Vermund to the Earl that he will take that honour from his hands, if he will give him for his safeguard and fellowship those Bareserks.

The Earl answered: "Now hast thou asked me for that which seems to me will in nowise be to thy gain, though I grant it thee. I deem that they will be to thee hard and high-minded as soon as thou hast aught to deal with them. I deem it beyond the power of most bonders: sons to curb them or hold them in fear, though they have been yielding enough in their service to me."

Vermund said that he would take them with that risk if the Earl would give him them into his power. The Earl bade him first ask the Bareserks if they would follow him. He did so, and asked if they would fare with him to Iceland, and give him fellowship and service; but he promised in return that he would do well to them in such matters as they deemed of need to them, and of which they knew how to tell him.

The Bareserks said that they had not set their minds on going to Iceland, and they wotted not if there were such chiefs there as would be meet for them to serve; "but if thou art so eager, Vermund, that we should fare to Iceland with thee, thou must look for it that we shall take it ill if thou givest not that which we ask for, if thou hast wherewithal." Vermund said that should never be, and thereafter he gat their yea to go to Iceland with him, if that were with the Earl's will and consent.

Now Vermund tells the Earl how things had gone, and the Earl settled that the Bareserks should fare with him to Iceland, "if thou deemest that most to thine honour;" but he bade him bethink him that he should deem that a cause for enmity if he ended ill with them, so utterly as they were now in his power; but Vermund said there was no need that things should come thereto.

Thereafter Vermund fared to Iceland with the Bareserks, and had a good voyage, and came home to his house in Bearhaven the same summer that Eric the Red went to Greenland, as is written afore.

Soon after Vermund came home, Halli the Bareserk fell to talk with Vermund about getting him a seemly match, but Vermund said he saw no hope that any woman of good kin would bind herself or her fortune to a Bareserk; so he hung back in that matter. But when Halli knew that, he burst out into wolfish mood and ill-will, and all went athwart betwixt them, and the Bareserks made themselves right big and rough with Vermund, so that he began to rue it that he had gotten him those Bareserks on hand.

Now in the autumn had Vermund a great feast, and bade Arnkel the Priest to him, and the men of Ere, and Stir his brother; and when the feast was over he offered to give the Bareserks to Arnkel, and calls that a thing of the fittest; but he will not take them.

Then Vermund asked Arnkel for counsel as to how he should rid himself of this trouble; but he put in a word that he had better give them to Stir, and said ir rather befitted him to have such men because of his overweening and iniquitous ways.

So when Stir was ready to go away, Vermund went to him and said: "Now will I, brother, that we lay aside the coldness which was between us before I fared abroad, and take to faithful kinship and loving-kindness; and therewith will I give thee those men that I have brought out, for thy strength and fellowship, nor do I know any men will dare to trust themselves to strife with thee if thou hast such followers as they are."

Stir answered: "I have good will, brother, to better our kinship; but that only have I heard about those men whom thou hast brought out hither, that by taking them, one shall rather get trouble than furtherance or good luck from them; nor will I that they ever come into my house, for full enough are my enmities though I get me no trouble from these."

"What counsel givest thou then, kinsman," said Vermund, "that I may put off this trouble from me."

"That is another case," said Stir, "to loose thee from thy troubles, than taking these men of thine hand as a friendly gift, and thus I will not take them; but it is the due of no man more than me to put off this thy trouble from thee, if we both have one way of thinking about it."

But though Stir spake so, Vermund chose that he should take to him the Bareserks, and the brothers parted in good love. Stir went home and the Bareserks with him, though they were not willing to this at first, and bade Vermund know that he had no right to sell or give them like unfree men; yet they said withal that it was more to their mood to follow Stir rather than Vermund; and things went very hopefully between them and Stir at first. The Bareserks were with Stir when he went west over Broadfirth to slay Thorbiorn Jaw who dwelt at Jawfirth. A lock-bed he had made exceeding strong with beams of timber, but the Bareserks brake that up, so that the naves outside sprang asunder; yet was Stir himself the bane of Thorbiorn Jaw.

Chapter 26
Of Vigfus And Swart The Strong. The Slaying Of Vigfus

The autumn when the Bareserks came to Stir, this happed withal, that Vigfus of Drapalith went to burn charcoal to the place called Selbrents, and three thralls with him, one of whom was Swart the Strong; but when they came into the wood Vigfus said: "Great pity it is, and so thou wilt deem it thyself, Swart, that thou shouldst be an unfree man, strong as thou art, and manly to look upon."

"Truly I deem it a great trouble," said Swart; "but it is not so with my will."

Vigfus said: "What wilt thou do that I give thee thy freedom?"

"I may not buy it with money, for I have it not," said he; "but such things as I may do I will not spare."

Said Vigfus: "Thou shalt go to Holyfell and kill Snorri the Priest, and thereafter shalt thou verily have thy freedom, and therewith will I give thee good fortune."

"Nay, I may not bring that about," said Swart.

"I shall give thee counsel," said Vigfus, "so that this may be brought about without any risk of thy life."

"Well, I will listen to it," said Swart.

"Thou shalt go to Holyfell and get into the loft that is over the outer door, and pull up the boards of the floor, so that thou may'st thrust a bill therethrough; then when Snorri goes out to his privy, thou shalt thrust the bill through the floor of the loft into his back so hard that it may come out at his belly; and then leap off out on to the roof and so over the wall, and let the mirk night cover thee."

So with this counsel went Swart to Holyfell, and broke open the roof over the outer door, and went into the loft thereby; and that was at such time as Snorri and his folk sat by the meal-fires. But in those days were the places of easement outside the houses. But when Snorri and his folk went from the fires they were minded for the place of easement, and Snorri went first, and got off out into the outer door before Swart could bring his onset about; but Mar Hallwardson came next, and Swart thrust the bill at him, and it smote the shoulder-blade, and glanced off out towards the armpit, and there cut itself through, and no great wound it was. Then Swart sprang out and over the wall, but the causeway stones were slippery under him, and he fell a great fall when he came down, and Snorri got hold of him before he got up.

Then they had a true tale of him, and he told them all that had been twixt him and Vigfus, and withal that he was burning charcoal under Selbrents.

Then was Mar's wound bound up, and thereafter Snorri set out with six men to Drapalith. And when they came up the hill-side they saw the fire whereat Vigfus and his folk burned charcoal. Withal they came unawares upon Vigfus and his men, and slew him, but gave life to the house-carles, and thereafter Snorri went back home; but the house-carles of Vigfus told these tidings at Drapalith.

Vigfus was laid in cairn the next day, and that same day went Thorgerd his wife into Lairstead to tell the tidings to Arnkel her kinsman, and bade him take up the blood-suit for the slaying of Vigfus. But he put that off from him, and said that that belonged to the Kiallekings, the kin of Vigfus; and above all would he have the case go to Stir, and said that it was fittest to him to take up the cause for Vigfus his kinsman; "for," said he, "he is a man who is fain to meddle in many things."

Now Thormod Trefilson sang this song about the slaying of Vigfus:

First the Folk-wielder Felled there the feller Of fight-boar gold-bristled, Vigfus men hight him. The wound-mews thereafter There were they tearing Full meat of fight-god, Biorn's heirship wearer.

Chapter 27
Arnkel Takes Up The Blood-Feud For Vigfus

Thereafter went Thorgerd out under Lava, and bade Stir take up the suit for

Vigfus his kinsman. He answered: "But I promised Snorri the Priest last spring, when he sat those suits of ours with the Thorgestlings, that I would not go against him with enmity in cases for the taking up of which there were many as nigh of kin as I. Now wert thou best to seek to Vermund my brother for this matter, or other kinsmen of ours."

So then Thorgerd fared out to Bearhaven, and prayed Vermund for aid, and said that the case came most home to him, "because Vigfus was wont to trust in thee the best of all his kin."

Vermund answered: "Now am I bound to lay down some good counsel for thee; yet am I loth to go into these matters instead of other kinsmen of ours, but I shall give thee help both with furtherance and counsel such as I may get done; but first I will that thou fare west to Ere and find Steinthor, Vigfus's kinsman; he is now at ease to fight, and it is now high time for him to try himself in some kind of case."

Thorgerd answered: "Much ye make me do for this suit, but I will not spare my labour if it be to its furtherance."

Thereafter she went west to Ere and found Steinthor, and bade him be leader of the case.

Steinthor answered: "Why dost thou bid me this? I am but a young man, and have had nought to do with the cases of men. But there are kinsmen of Vigfus nearer to him than I am, who are more forward than I withal; neither is it to be anywise hoped that I should take this case from their hands; but I shall not part myself from those of my kin who may have this blood-suit to look to."

No other answer got Thorgerd than this. So she made for home thereafter and then east again along the firths to find Vermund, and told him what things had come to, and said that the whole matter would be thrown over unless he became leader thereof.

Vermund answered: "It is not unlikely that some stir will be made concerning these matters for thy comforting. However, I shall now once more lay down a rede for thee if thou wilt but do thine utmost."

She answered: "Most things would I undergo therefor."

"Now shalt thou go home, and let dig up Vigfus thy husband, and take his head and bring it to Arnkel, and say to him thus, that that head would not have weighed with others the taking up of the blood-suit after him, if need there had been thereof."

Thorgerd said she wotted not where these things were coming to in the end, but she saw well enough that they spared her neither labour nor heartburn. "Yet even this will I undergo," said she, "if thereby the lot of my foes be made heavier than before."

Thereafter she fared home, and went in about this business as she was taught in all wise; and when she came to Lairstead she told Arnkel that the kin of Vigfus would that he should be the leader in taking up the blood-suit for the slaying of Vigfus, and that they all promised their help.

Arnkel said that he had said before whereto his mind was given about the suit.

Therewithal Thorgerd drew from under her cloak the head of Vigfus, and spake: "Here is now a head," said she, "that would not have begged off from taking up the suit for thee, if there had been need thereof."

Arnkel started back thereat, and thrust her from him, and said: "Go," says he, "and say so much to the kin of Vigfus, that henceforward they waver not more in their help against Snorri the Priest, than I shall in the leading of the suit; but so my mind tells me that, however the case goes, they shall lay land under foot or ever I do. But I see that these thy doings are by Vermund's counsel; but no need will he have to egg me on wheresoever we brothers-in-law are in one place."

Then went Thorgerd home. The winter wore, and in the spring Arnkel set afoot the case for the slaying of Vigfus against all those who had been at the slaying, except Snorri the Priest; but Snorri set forth a cross-suit for the unhallowing of Vigfus for plotting against his life and for the wounding of Mar; and men came thronging on both sides to the Thorsness Thing.

All the Kiallekings gave help to Arnkel, and theirs was the biggest company; and Arnkel pushed on the case with great eagerness.

But when the cases came into court, men went thereto, and the cases were laid to award by the urging and peace-making of men of good will; and so it befell that Snorri the Priest made a handsel as to the slaughter of Vigfus, and great fines were awarded; but Mar should be abroad for three winters. So Snorri paid up the money, and the Thing came to an end in such wise, that peace was made in all the suits.

Chapter 28
Of The Bareserks And The Wooing of Asdis, Stir's Daughter

Now that happed to tell of next which is aforewritten, that the Bareserks were with Stir, and when they had been there awhile, Halli fell to talking with Asdis, Stir's daughter. She was a young woman and a stately, proud of attire, and somewhat high-minded; but when Stir knew of their talk together, he bade Halli not to do him that shame and heartburn in beguiling his daughter.

Halli answered: "No shame it is to thee though I talk with thy daughter, nor will I do that to thy dishonour; but I will tell thee straightly that I have so much love in my heart for her, that I know not how to put it out of my mind. And now," said Halli, "will I seek for fast friendship with thee, and pray thee to give me thy daughter Asdis, and thereto in return will I put my friendship and true service, and so much strength through the power of my brother Leikner, that there shall not be in Iceland so much glory from two men's services as we two shall give thee; and our furtherance shall strengthen thy chieftainship more than if thou gavest thy daughter to the mightiest bonder of Broadfirth, and that shall be in return for our not being strong of purse. But if thou wilt not do for me my desire, that shall cut our friendship atwain; and then each must do as he will in his own matter; and little avail will it be to thee then to grumble about my talk with Asdis."

When he had thus spoken, Stir was silent, and thought it somewhat hard to answer, but he said in a while:

"Whether is this spoken with all thine heart, or is it a vain word, and seekest thou a quarrel?"

"So shalt thou answer," said Halli, "as if mine were no foolish word; and all our friendship lies on what thine answer will be in this matter."

Stir answered: "Then will I talk the thing over with my friends, and take counsel with them how I shall answer this."

Said Halli: "The matter shalt thou talk over with whomsoever pleases thee within three nights, but I will not that this answer to me drag on longer than that, because I will not be a dangler over this betrothal."

And therewithal they parted.

The next morning Stir rode east to Holyfell, and when he came there, Snorri bade him abide; but Stir said that he would talk with him, and then ride away.

Snorri asked if he had some troublous matter on hand to talk of. "So it seems to me," said Stir.

Snorri said: "Then we will go up on to the Holy Fell, for those redes have been the last to come to nought that have been taken there."

"Therein thou shalt have thy will," said Stir.

So they went upon to the mount, and there sat talking all day till evening, nor did any man know what they said together; and then Stir rode home.

But the next morning Stir and Halli went to talk together, and Halli asked Stir how his case stood.

Stir answered: "It is the talk of men that thou seemest somewhat bare of money, so what wilt thou do for this, since thou hast no fee to lay down therefor?"

Halli answered: "I will do what I may, since money fails me."

Says Stir: "I see that it will mislike thee if I give thee not my daughter; so now will I do as men of old, and will let thee do some great deed for this bridal."

"What is it, then?" said Halli.

"Thou shalt break up," says Stir, "a road through the lava out to Bearhaven, and raise a boundary-wall over the lava betwixt our lands, and make a burg here at the head of the lava; and when this work is done, I will give thee Asdis my daughter."

Halli answered: "I am not wont to work, yet will I say yea to this, if thereby I may the easier have the maiden for wife."

Stir said that this then should be their bargain.

Thereafter they began to make the road, and the greatest of man's-work it is; and they raised the wall whereof there are still tokens, and thereafter wrought the burg. But while they were at the work, Stir let build a hot bath at his house at Lava, and it was dug down in the ground, and there was a window over the furnace, so that it might be fed from without, and wondrous hot was that place.

Now when either work was nigh finished, on the last day whereon Halli and his brother were at work on the burg, it befell that thereby passed Asdis,

Stir's daughter, and close to the homestead it was. Now she had done on her best attire, and when Halli and his brother spake to her, she answered nought.

Then sang Halli this stave:

> "O fair-foot, O linen-girt goddess that beareth
> The flame that is hanging from fair limbs adown!
> Whither now hast thou dight thee thy ways to be wending,
> O fair wight, O tell me, and lie not in telling?
> For all through the winter, O wise-hearted warden
> Of the board of the chess-play, not once I beheld thee
> From out of the houses fare this-wise afoot,
> So goodly of garments, so grand of array."

Chapter 29
Of Thorod Scat-Catcher And Of Biorn Asbrandson, And Of The Slaying Of The Sons Of Thorir Wooden-Leg

There was a man called Thorod, who was of the Midfell-strand kindred. He was a trustworthy man and a great seafarer, and had a ship afloat. Thorod had sailed on a trading voyage west to Ireland and Dublin.

At that time Sigurd Lodverson, Earl of the Orkneys, had harried in the South-isles, and all the way west to Man. He had laid a tribute on the dwellers in Man; and when peace was made, the Earl left men to wait for the scat (and the more part thereof was paid up in burned silver), but he himself sailed away north to the Orkneys.

Now when they who had awaited the scat were ready to sail, the wind blew from the south-west, but when they had been at sea a while, it shifted to the south-east and east, and blew a great gale, and drove them north of Ireland. Their ship was broken to pieces on an unpeopled island there; and when they were in this plight there bore down on them Thorod the Icelander, late come from Dublin. The Earl's men hailed the chapmen for help, and Thorod put out a boat and went therein himself; and when they met, the Earl's men prayed him for aid, and promised him money to bring them home to the Orkneys to Earl Sigurd. But Thorod deemed he might not do that, since he was already bound for Iceland. But they prayed him hard, because they deemed that their wealth and their lives lay on their not being taken prisoners in Ireland or the South-isles, where they had harried erst. So the end of it was that he sold them his boat from his big ship, and took therefor a good share of the scat; and thereon they laid their boat for the Orkneys, but Thorod sailed boatless for Iceland.

He came upon the south coast of the land, and stretched west along the shore, and sailed into Broadfirth, and came safe and sound to Daymeal-ness, and in the autumn went to dwell with Snorri the Priest at Holyfell, and ever after was he called Thorod Scat-catcher.

Now this was a little after the slaying of Thorbiorn the Thick. And that winter was Thurid, the sister of Snorri the Priest, whom Thorbiorn the Thick had had to wife, abiding at Holyfell. A little while after his coming back to Iceland Thorod put forth the word and prayed Snorri to give him his sister Thurid; and seeing that he was wealthy of money, and that Snorri knew his conditions well, and that he saw that she needed much some good care, with all this it seemed good to Snorri to give him the woman; and he held their wedding in the winter there at Holyfell. But the spring after Thorod betook himself to keeping house at Frodis-water, and he became a good bonder and a trustworthy.

But so soon as Thurid came to Frodis-water Biorn Asbrandson got coming thither, and it was the talk of all men that there was fooling betwixt him and Thurid, and Thorod began to blame Biorn for his comings, yet that mended matters in no-wise.

At that time dwelt Thorir Wooden-leg at Ernknoll, and his sons Ern and Val were grown up by then, and were the hopefullest of men. Now they laid reproach on Thorod in that he bore with Biorn such shame as he dealt him, and they offered to follow Thorod if he would put an end to Biorn's comings and goings.

On a time Biorn came to Frodis-water and sat talking with Thurid. And Thorod was ever wont to be within doors when Biorn was there; but now they saw him nowhere. Then Thurid said: "Take thou heed to thy faring, Biorn; whereas I deem that Thorod is minded to put an end to thy coming hither; and I guess that they have gone to waylay thee; and he will be minded that ye two shall not meet with an equal band."

Then Biorn sang this song:

> "O ground of the golden strings, might we but gain it
> To make this day's wearing of all days the longest
> That ever yet hung twixt earth's woodland and heaven –
> Yea, whiles yet I tarried the hours in their waning –
> For, O fir of the worm that about the arm windeth,
> This night amongst all nights, 'tis I and no other
> Must turn me to grief now, and drink out the grave-ales
> Of the joys of our life-days, full often a-dying."

Chapter 30
Of The Evil Dealings Of Thorolf Halt-Foot

Now must it be told of Thorolf Halt-foot that he began to get exceeding old, and became very evil and hard to deal with by reason of his old age, and full of all injustice, and things went uneasily enough betwixt him and Arnkel his son.

Now on a day Thorolf rode in to Ulfar's-fell to find Ulfar the bonder. He was a great furtherer of field-work, and much spoken of for this, that he saved his hay quicker than other men, and was so lucky with sheep withal, that his sheep never died of clemming or from storms.

So when Thorolf met him, he asked him what counsel he gave him as to how he should set about his husbandry, and what his mind told him about the summer, if it would be dry or not.

Ulfar answered: "No better rede can I give thee than what I follow myself. I shall let bear out the scythe to-day, and mow down all I may this week, because I deem it will be rainy; but I guess that after that it will be very dry for the next half month."

So things went as he had said, for it was often seen that he could foretell the weather better than other men.

So Thorolf went home, and he had with him many workmen, and now he let straightway begin the out-meadow mowing; and the weather was even as Ulfar had said.

Now Thorolf and Ulfar had a meadow in common upon the neck, and either of them at first mowed much hay, and then they spread it, and raked it up into big cocks. But one morning early when Thorolf arose, he looked out and saw that the weather was thick, and deemed that the dry tide was failing, and called to his thralls to rise and carry the hay together, and work daylong all they might, "for it seems to me," quoth he, "that the weather is not to be trusted."

The thralls did on their clothes and went to the hay-work. But Thorolf piled up the hay and egged them on to work at their most might that it might speed at its fastest.

That same morning Ulfar looked out early, and when he came in, the workmen asked him of the weather, but he bade them sleep on in peace. "The weather is good," said he, "and it will clear off to-day. Therefore to-day shall ye mow in the home-field, but to-morrow will we save such hay as we have up on the neck."

Now the weather went even as he said; and when the evening was wearing on, Ulfar sent a man up to the neck, to look to the hay that stood there in cocks. But Thorolf Halt-foot carried hay with three draught-oxen the day through, and by the third hour after noontide they had saved all the hay that was his. Then he bade carry Ulfar's hay withal into his garth; and they did as he bade them.

But when Ulfar's messenger saw that, he ran and told his master. Then Ulfar went up on to the neck, and was exceeding wroth, and asked Thorolf why he robbed him. Thorolf said he heeded not what he said, and raved and was ugly to deal with, and they well-nigh came to blows. But Ulfar saw that he had no choice but to go away. So he went straightway to Arnkel, and told him of his scathe, and prayed for his warding, "else," he gave out, "all would be gone by the board."

Arnkel said he would bid his father pay boot for the hay, but said that none the less it sorely misgave him that nought would come of it.

So when father and son met, Arnkel bade his father pay Ulfar boot for the taking of the hay; but Thorolf said the thrall was far too rich already. Arnkel prayed him to do so much for his word as to atone for that hay. Then said Thorolf that he would do nought therefor but worsen Ulfar's lot; and therewith they parted.

Now when Arnkel met Ulfar, he told him of Thorolf's answer; but Ulfar deemed that Arnkel had followed up his case coldly, and said that he might have had his way with his father if he had chosen to do so.

So Arnkel paid Ulfar what he would for the hay; and when father and son next met, Arnkel claimed the price of the hay from his father, but Thorolf gave no better answers, and they parted in great wrath. But the next autumn Arnkel let drive from the fells seven oxen of his father's, and had them all slaughtered for his own household needs. That misliked Thorolf beyond measure, and he claimed their price of Arnkel; but he said that they should be in return for Ulfar's hay. Then Thorolf liked matters a great deal worse than before, and laid the whole thing on Ulfar, and said he should feel him therefor.

Chapter 31
Of Thorolf Halt-Foot And Snorri The Priest

That winter at Yule-tide had Thorolf a great drinking, and put the drink round briskly to his thralls, and when they were drunk, he egged them on to go up to Ulfar's-fell and burn Ulfar in his house, and promised to give them their freedom therefor. The thralls said they would do so much for their freedom if he would hold to his word. Then they went six of them together to Ulfar's-fell, and took a brushwood stack, and dragged it to the homestead, and set fire therein.

At that time Arnkel and his men sat drinking at Lairstead, and when they went to bed they saw fire at Ulfar's-fell. Then they went thereto forthwith, and took the thralls, and slaked the fire, and the houses were but little burned.

The next morning Arnkel let bring the thralls to Vadils-head, and there were they all hanged.

Thereafter Ulfar handselled all his goods to Arnkel, who became guardian over him. But this handselling misliked the sons of Thorbrand, because they deemed that to them belonged all the goods after Ulfar their freedman, and much ill-will arose here from between Arnkel and Thorbrand's sons. Nor might they henceforth have games together, which they had hitherto held, turn and turn about; in which games was Arnkel the strongest, but that man was the best to set against him, and the next strongest, who was called Freystein Rascal, and was the foster-son of Thorbrand, and his adopted son; for it was the talk of most men that his own son he was, but that his mother was a bondmaid. He was a manly man, and mighty of his hands.

Thorolf Halt-foot took it very ill of Arnkel that those thralls had been slain, and claimed atonement for them, but Arnkel flatly refused to pay a penny for them, and then was Thorolf worse pleased than afore.

But on a day he rode out to Holyfell to find Snorri the Priest, and Snorri bade him abide. But Thorolf said he had no need to eat his meat. "Therefor am I come, because I am fain thou shouldst set my matters straight, for I call thee chief of this countryside, and it is thy part to set right the lot of such men as have been wronged already."

"By whose means is thy lot brought low, goodman?" said Snorri.

"Through Arnkel, my son," answers Thorolf.

Said Snorri: "Thou shouldst not make plaint of that, because that thou shouldst be of one mind with him in all things: withal he is a better man than thou."

"That is not the way of it," says he, "because now of all men he tramples most on me, and now will I be thy close friend, Snorri, if thou wilt but take up the blood-suit for my thralls whom Arnkel let slay, nor will I bespeak all the blood-fines for myself."

Snorri answered: "I will not enter into the strife betwixt thee and thy son."

Says Thorolf: "Thou art no friend of Arnkel's; but mayhap thou deemest me niggard of my money. But it shall not be so now," says he. "I know thou wouldst fain have Crowness, and the wood thereon, which is the best possession in the countryside. Lo, I will handsel thee all that, if thou wilt but take up the suit for my thralls, and follow it up so mightily that thou shalt grow greater thereby, but they shall deem themselves put in the wrong who have wrought me shame; nor will I spare any man who has had part therein, be he more or less my kinsman."

Now Snorri deemed that he needed the wood greatly; and so it is said that he took handsel of the land, and took over the blood- suit for the thralls. But Thorolf rode home thereafter, and was well pleased therewith. But that was not talked of over-well by other folk.

In the spring Snorri set forth a case for the Thorsness Thing, at the hand of Arnkel, for the slaying of the thralls. Both sides came thronging to the Thing, and Snorri pushed forward the case. But when the suit came into court, Arnkel claimed for himself a verdict of not guilty, and set that forth as a defence that the thralls were taken with quickfire for the burning of a homestead.

Then Snorri set forth that the thralls were indeed out of the law on the field of deed, "but whereas thou didst bring them in to Vadils-head and slay them there, I deem that there they were not out of the law."

So Snorri pushed the case on, and set aside Arnkel's claim to a verdict of not guilty; and thereafter men busied themselves to make peace, and a bargain was come to, and those brethren, Stir and Vermund, should be umpires in the case; and they put the thralls at twelve ounces each, and the money should be paid there and then at the Thing. And when it was paid, Snorri gave the purse to Thorolf, who took it and said: "I had no mind when I gave thee my land, that thou wouldst follow up my suit with so little manhood, and I wot that Arnkel would not have withheld from me such boot for my thralls if I had left the matter to him."

"Now I say," said Snorri, "that thou hast no shame herein, but I will not stake my worth against thy evil lust and foul deeds."

Thorolf answers: "Most like it is that I shall not seek to thee in cases again; nor yet shall the woes of you folk of this country lie utterly asleep."

Thereafter men depart from the Thing, and Arnkel and Snorri misliked them of this end to the matter, but Thorolf thought worse yet of it, as was well meet.

Chapter 32
The Slaying Of Ulfar; Thorbrand's Sons Claim The Heritage

So it is said that this happened next to be told of, that Orlig of Orligstead fell sick, and when his sickness grew heavy on him, Ulfar his brother sat ever by him. Now of that sickness he died; but when he was dead, Ulfar sent forthwith for Arnkel, who went straightway to Orligstead, and he and Ulfar took to them all the goods that lay together there. But when Thorbrand's sons knew of the death of Orlig, they went to Orligstead, and laid claim to those same goods that there lay together, and claimed as their own what their freedman had had; but Ulfar said that it was his due to take the heritage after his brother. They asked what part Arnkel would take in this matter. Arnkel said that Ulfar should not be robbed of any man while their fellowship lasted and he might have his will.

Then Thorbrand's sons fare away, and first out to Holyfell, and told this to Snorri the Priest, and prayed him for his help in the case; but he said that he would not thrust into strife with Arnkel for this case, whereas they had done their part so slippery, that Arnkel and Ulfar had first laid hands on the goods. Then Thorbrand's sons said that he would rule there no longer if he did not heed such things as this.

The next autumn Arnkel had a great autumn feast in his house, and ever his wont was to ask Ulfar his friend to all biddings, and to see him off with gifts.

Now the day that men should depart from the feast at Lairstead, Thorolf Halt-foot rode from home, and went to see his friend Cunning-Gils, who dwelt at Thorswater-dale at Cunning-Gils- stead, and bade him ride with him east to Ulfar's-fell-neck, and a thrall of Thorolf's went with him, and when they came on to the neck Thorolf said:

"There will be Ulfar going from the feast, and belike he will journey with seemly gifts about him. Now would I, Cunning-Gils," said he, "that thou go meet him and waylay him under the garth at Ulfar's-fell, and slay him, and therefor will I give thee three marks of silver, and pay all weregild for the slaying; and then, when thou hast slain Ulfar, thou wilt have of him those good things which he has had of Arnkel. Then shalt thou run along Ulfar's-fell out to Crowness, and if any pursue thee let the wood cover thee, and then come and see me, and I shall see to thee that thou shalt take no harm."

Now whereas Cunning-Gils was a man of many children and very poor, he took the bait and went out under the towngarth at Ulfar's-fell, and there he saw how Ulfar came up from below with a good shield and a fair-dight sword that Arnkel had given him. So when they met, Cunning-Gils prayed to see the sword, and flattered Ulfar much, and said he was a great man, since he was deemed worthy to have such seemly gifts from chiefs. Ulfar wagged his beard, and handed to him the sword and shield. Cunning-Gils straightway drew the sword and thrust Ulfar through, and then took to his heels and ran out along Ulfar's-fell to Crowness.

Arnkel was out a-doors and saw how a man ran bearing a shield, and thought he should know the shield, and it came into his mind that Ulfar would not have given it up of his own good will. Then Arnkel called to his folk to run after the man; "and therewith," says he, "if this has befallen by my father's redes, and this man is Ulfar's banesman, then shall ye slay him, whoso he is, and not let him come before my eyes."

Then went Arnkel up to Ulfar's-fell, and there they found Ulfar dead. Thorolf Halt-foot saw Cunning-Gils run out along Ulfar's-fell with the shield, and thought he knew how it had fared between him and Ulfar. Then said he to his thrall that followed him: "Now shalt thou go to Karstead, and tell Thorbrand's sons to fare in to Ulfar's-fell, and not let themselves be robbed this time of their freedman's heritage as before; because Ulfar is now slain." So thereafter Thorolf rode home, and deemed he had done a good piece of business.

But those who ran after Cunning-Gils took him beneath a cliff which leads up from the sea. There they had a true tale out of him, and when he had told them all as it was, they slew him, and thrust him into earth beneath the cliff, but took his spoil and brought it to Arnkel.

Now the thrall of Thorolf came to Karstead, and told Thorbrand's sons the message of Thorolf, and so they went in to Ulfar's-fell; but when they came there, lo, there was Arnkel before them and many men with him. Then Thorbrand's sons gave out their claim to the goods that Ulfar had owned; but Arnkel brought forward against it the witness of those who were near at the handsel Ulfar had given him, and said that he would uphold it, because he said it had never been lawfully called in question, and bade them make no claim to the money; for he said he would hold to it, even as if it were his father's heritage.

Then Thorbrand's sons saw no choice but to come away, and they went once more out to Holyfell and found Snorri the Priest, and told him how things had befallen, and prayed for his help. Snorri said things had gone as before, that they had been one move too late in the game for Arnkel; "and ye shall not," said he, "grip out of Arnkel's hands aught of these goods, seeing that he has already got the chattels to him; and as to the lands, they lie about as near to one as to the other, and he will have them who has the strongest hand. And this is to be looked for herein that Arnkel will have the greater share of that, as in other dealings with you; and to tell truth, ye may well bear what many endure, because Arnkel rules now over every man's fortune in this countryside, and will do while he lives, whether that be longer or shorter."

Thorleif Kimbi answered: "True say'st thou, Snorri, and I deem it is to be excused in thee, though thou dost not set our matter with Arnkel right, since thou hast never held thine own against him in any due case that ye have had to do with together."

Thereafter Thorbrand's sons fared home, and took these things right heavily.

Chapter 33
Of The Death Of Thorolf Halt-Foot

Now Snorri the Priest let work Crowness wood, and let much wood cutting go on. Thorolf Halt-foot thought that the wood was spoilt thereby, and rode out to Holyfell, and bade Snorri give back the wood, and said that he had lent the wood and not given it. Snorri said that would be clearer when they bore witness who were by at the handselling, and said that he would not give up the wood unless they gave it against him. Then Thorolf took himself off, and was in the worst of minds. He rode in to Lairstead to see his son Arnkel.

Arnkel gave his father good welcome, and asked his errand there. Thorolf answered: "This is my errand, that I see it is amiss that there should be ill-liking betwixt us, and now I will that we lay that aside, and take to kindly ways. For unseemly it is for us to be at enmity together; and moreover it seems to me that we should be great men here in the district with thy hardihood and my good counsel."

"The better it would like me," said Arnkel, "the closer we should draw together."

"Now will I," says Thorolf, "that this shall be the beginning of our peace-making and friendship, that we two claim Crowness wood of Snorri the Priest. It seems to me very ill that he should rule our fortune, but now he will not give up to me my wood, and says I gave it him; and therein he lies," says he.

Arnkel answers: "Thou didst that for no friendship to me when thou gavest Snorri the wood, nor shall I do so much as for thy slandering to quarrel with Snorri about it; and though I wot that he has no due title to the wood, yet will I not that thou have so much for thy lust for evil as to gladden thee by strife twixt me and Snorri."

"Methinks," said Thorolf, "that this comes rather from thy poor heart than because thou begrudgest me sport over your strife."

"Think whatso true thou wilt," said Arnkel, "but as things stand, no strife will I have with Snorri for the wood."

Therewith father and son parted, and Thorolf fared home and liked his lot exceeding ill, and thought that now he might scarce get his oar in.

Thorolf Halt-foot came home in the evening and spake to no man, but sat down in his high-seat and would eat no meat that night, and he sat there after men went to bed, and in the morning, when men arose, there he sat on still, and was dead.

Then the housewife sent a man to Arnkel, and bade him tell him of the death of his father. Then Arnkel rode up to Hvamm, and some of his home-men with him. And when they came to Hvamm, then was Arnkel ware that his father was dead, and sat in his high-seat. But the folk were all full of dread, because to all folk his face seemed loathsome.

Now Arnkel went into the fire-hall, and so up along it behind the seat at Thorolf's back, and bade all beware of facing him before lyke-help was given to him. Then Arnkel took Thorolf by the shoulders, and must needs put forth all his strength before he brought him under. After that he swept a cloth about Thorolf's head, and then did to him according to custom. Then he let break down the wall behind him, and brought him out thereby, and then were oxen yoked to a sledge, and thereon was Thorolf laid out, and they drew him up into Thorswater-dale, and it was not without hard toil that he came to the stead whereas he should lie.

There they laid Thorolf in howe strongly; and then Arnkel rode to Hvamm and took to himself all the goods that were heaped up there, and which his father had owned. Arnkel was there three nights, and nought happed to tell of the while, and thereafter he rode home.

Chapter 34
Thorolf Halt-Foot Walks; The Second Burial Of Him

After the death of Thorolf Halt-foot many folk deemed it worse to be abroad as soon as the sun was getting low. But as the summer wore, men were ware of this, that Thorolf lay not quiet, and men might never be in peace abroad after sunset. And this happed withal that those oxen which had been yoked to Thorolf were troll-ridden, and all such cattle as came nigh to Thorolf's howe went mad, and bellowed till they died. Now the herdsman at Hvamm often came home in such wise that Thorolf had given chase to him. And so it befell in the autumn at Hvamm that one day neither herdsman nor beasts came home; and in the morning men went to seek them, and found the herdsman dead, a little way from Thorolf's howe, and he was all coal-blue, and every bone in him was broken. He was buried beside Thorolf. And of all the cattle that had been in the dale, some were found dead, and some fled into the mountains, and were never found again; and if fowls settled on Thorolf's howe, they fell down dead.

But so great trouble befell from this that no man durst feed his flocks up in the dale. Oft too was heard huge din abroad at Hvamm, and they were ware withal that the hall was ofttimes ridden. And when the winter came on

Thorolf was seen home at the house many a time, and troubled the goodwife the most. And great hurt gat many from this, but she herself was well-nigh witless thereat; and such was the end of it all, that the goodwife died from these troublings, and was brought up to Thorswater-dale and buried beside Thorolf.

Thereafter men fled away from the homestead, and now Thorolf took to walking so wide through the dale that he laid waste all steads therein, and so great was the trouble from his walking that he slew some men, and some fled away; but all those who died were seen in his company.

Now men bewailed them much of that trouble, and deemed that it was Arnkel's part to seek rede to better it. So Arnkel bade all those abide with him who had liefer be there than elsewhere; but whereso Arnkel was, no harm befell from Thorolf and his company.

So afeard were all men of this walking of Thorolf's that none durst go a journey that winter, what errands soever they had in the countryside. But when the winter had worn away the spring was fair; and when the ice was off the earth, Arnkel sent a man into Karstead for the sons of Thorbrand, and bade them go with him and bring Thorolf away from Thorswater-dale, and search for another abode for him.

Then, according to the laws of that time, it was due, as now, for all men, to bring dead folks to burial, if they were so summoned.

But when the sons of Thorbrand heard that, they said it lay nowise on them to put away the troubles of Arnkel or Arnkel's men; but thereat the old carle Thorbrand answered and said: "Nay, need there is," says he, "to fare on all such journeys as all men are bound in law to do, and that is now bidden of you which it beseemeth you not to gainsay."

Then said Thorod to the messenger: "Go thy ways and tell Arnkel that I will go on behalf of my brethren, and come to Ulfar's-fell and meet him there."

Now the messenger goes, and tells Arnkel, and he got ready to go, and he and his were twelve in all, and had with them yoke-oxen and digging tools; and they went first to Ulfar's-fell and met there Thorod, Thorbrand's son, and he and his were three.

They went up over the neck, and came into Thorswater-dale unto Thorolf's howe, and broke it open, and found Thorolf all undecayed, and most evil to look on.

They took him up from the grave, and laid him on a sledge, and yoked two strong oxen to it, and drew him up to Ulfar's-fell- neck, and by then were the oxen foundered, and others were taken that drew him up on to the neck, and Arnkel was minded to bring him to Vadils-head, and lay him in earth there. But when they came to the hill's brow the oxen went mad, and broke loose forthright, and ran thence away over the neck, and made out along the hillside above the garth of Ulfar's-fell, and so out to sea, and by then were both bursten.

But Thorolf was by then so heavy, that they could bring him no further; so they bore him to a little headland that was there beside, and laid him in earth there, and that is called sithence Halt-foot's Head.

Then let Arnkel raise a wall across the headland landward of the howe, so high that none might come thereover but fowl flying, and there are yet signs thereof. There lay Thorolf quiet as long as Arnkel lived.

Chapter 35

Arnkel Slays Hawk

Snorri the Priest let work Crowness wood for all that Thorolf Halt-foot had raised question about it; but that was seen of Arnkel that he deemed that the title of that wood had not gone according to law, and he deemed that Thorolf had beguiled him of his heritage in that he had given the wood to Snorri the Priest.

Now one summer Snorri the Priest sent his thralls to work in the wood, and they cut there much timber and piled it together, and then went home. Now while the timber was seasoning, the rumour ran that Arnkel would go fetch it. So it fell not out; but he bade a herdsman of his watch when Snorri the Priest let fetch the timber, and tell him thereof. But when the wood was dry, Snorri sent three thralls of his to fetch it; and he got Hawk, his follower, to go with the thralls for their aid. So they go, and bind the wood on twelve horses, and then take their way home. Arnkel's herdsman was ware of their ways, and told him thereof. He took his weapons and went after them, and came up with them west of Svelgriver twixt it and the Knolls, but as soon as he came up with them, Hawk leapt off his horse and thrust at Arnkel with a spear, and smote his shield, yet he gat no wound. Then Arnkel sprang from his horse and thrust with a spear at Hawk, and smote him in the midst, and he fell there on the place which is now called Hawks-river.

But when the thralls saw the fall of Hawk, they took to their heels and ran off on their way home, and Arnkel chased them all along beyond Oxbrents, and then turned back and drave home with him the wood-horses, and took the wood off them, and then let them loose, and bound the load-ropes on them, and they were then turned on their way out along the fell, and they went till they came home to Holyfell.

Now were these tidings told, but all was quiet through those seasons; but the next spring Snorri the Priest set on foot a suit for the slaying of Hawk to be heard at the Thorsness Thing, and Arnkel another for an onslaught for the unhallowing of Hawk. Both sides had great followings at the Thing, and men pushed forward the cases eagerly, but such was the end of it that Hawk was made guilty for the onslaught, and Snorri the Priest was nonsuited.

Therewith men ride home from the Thing, and there was much ill- blood betwixt men throughout the summer.

Chapter 36
Thorleif Would Slay Arnkel, And Is Slain

There was a man called Thorleif, an Eastfirther, who had been found guilty of an affair with a woman. He came to Holyfell in the autumn, and prayed Snorri the Priest to take him in, but he put him off, and they talked long together or ever he got him gone. Thereafter Thorleif went to Lairstead, and came there in the evening, and was there the next night.

Now Arnkel got up early in the morning and set to nailing together the boards of his outer door; and when Thorleif arose, he went to Arnkel, and prayed him to take him in.

He answered somewhat slowly, and asked if he had been to see Snorri the Priest.

"Yea, I have seen him," said Thorleif, "and he would nowise take me in; 'and indeed, it is little to my mind,' says he, 'to give following to such a man as will ever let himself be trodden underfoot by every man with whom he has to do.'"

"Meseems," says Arnkel, "that Snorri would nowise mend his bargains though he give thee meat and drink for thy following."

"Nay, here whereas thou art will I have leave to dwell, Arnkel," said Thorleif.

"It is not my wont," said Arnkel, "to take in out-country men."

So there they gave and took in talk awhile, and Thorleif ever held fast by his prayer, but Arnkel put him off.

Now Arnkel fell to boring holes in the door-ledge, and laid his adze down the while. Thorleif took it up, and heaved it up swiftly over his head with the mind to bring it down on Arnkel's skull, but Arnkel heard the whistle of it and ran in under the stroke, and heaved up Thorleif by the breast, and soon was proven the measure of either's strength, for Arnkel was wondrous strong. So he cast Thorleif down with so great a fall that he lay stunned, and the adze flew out of his hand, and Arnkel got hold thereof and smote it into Thorleif's head, and gave him his death-wound.

So the rumour ran that it was Snorri the Priest who sent that man for Arnkel's head, but Snorri made as if the story had nought to do with him, and let folk say what they would. And so those seasons slipped away that nought else is to be told of.

Chapter 37
The Slaying Of Arnkel

The autumn after, at winter-nights, Snorri the Priest had a great autumn-feast, and bade his friends thereto. Ale drinking they had thereat, and folk drank fast and were very merry with ale.

Now the talk fell on pairing men together by their worth, and as to who was the noblest man in the countryside or the greatest chief, and thereon were men not at one, as oft it haps when the talk falls on likening man to man. To most of them indeed it seemed that Snorri was the noblest man, but some named Arnkel, and Stir forsooth.

But as they talked hereover, then Thorleif Kimbi answered and said:

"Why do men bicker over such a matter," says he, "when all may see how it is?"

"What wilt thou say hereon, Thorleif," said they, "if thou splittest the case into so many fragments?"

"Much the greatest do I deem Arnkel," said he.

"What hast thou to back this with?" said they.

"That which is true," says he. "For I call Snorri the Priest and Stir but as one man, because of their affinity; but of Arnkel's home-men that Snorri has killed, none lie by his garth unatoned like as Hawk, Snorri's follower, whom Arnkel slew, lies here by Snorri's garth."

This men deemed a big word, true though it were, since the talk had gone so far; but hereat dropped that talk.

But whenas men went from the bidding, Snorri the Priest chose gifts for his friends. He led Thorbrand's sons down to their ship at Redwick-head; and as they parted Snorri went to Thorleif Kimbi and said:

"Here is an axe, Thorleif, which I will give thee; it is the longest handled of all I have, yet will it not reach Arnkel's head when he stacks his hay at Orligstead, if thou heavest it at him all the way from Swanfirth."

He took the axe and said: "Deem well," says he, "that I will not hang back in heaving this axe on Arnkel whenas thou hast wrought the revenge for Hawk thy follower."

Snorri answered: "That methinks is due from you to me, sons of Thorbrand, that ye have spies out to watch for a chance at Arnkel, but blame me then if I come not to meet you when aught may be done if ye make me ware thereof."

Therewith they parted, and both gave out that they were ready to plot against Arnkel's life, and Thorbrand's sons were to have a spy on his goings.

Early that winter was there much ice, and all firths were overlaid therewith. Freystein Rascal watched sheep in Swanfirth, and he was set to spy out an occasion against Arnkel.

Arnkel was a great man for work, and made his thralls work all day from sunrise to sunset. He had under him both the lands of Ulfar's-fell and Orligstead, for no one could be got to dwell on the lands for fear of the violence of Thorbrand's sons. Now in the winter it was Arnkel's wont to carry hay from Orligstead in the night in the new moons, because the thralls did other work at home by day. Nor did he heed if Thorbrand's sons were unware of the carrying of hay. Now on a night of winter before Yule, Arnkel arose and waked three of his thralls, one of whom was called Ofeig. Goodman Arnkel went with them up to Orligstead. Four oxen they had, and two sledges withal.

The sons of Thorbrand were ware of Arnkel's ways, and Freystein Rascal went that night over the ice to Holyfell, and came there by then men had been abed for a space. He took Snorri by the foot and waked him, and Snorri asked what he would. He answers: "Now has the old eagle taken flight to his quarry at Orligstead."

Snorri rose up and bade men clothe themselves. So when they were clad, they took their weapons and fared nine of them altogether over the ice to Swanfirth. And when they came to the bottom of the firth, Thorbrand's sons came to meet them, and were six in company.

Then they fared up to Orligstead, and by then they came there, one of the thralls had gone home with a load of hay, and Arnkel and the others were busy on a second.

Then saw Arnkel and his folk how armed men came up from the sea, and Ofeig said thereon that unpeace was at hand, and there was nought for it but to get them gone homeward.

Arnkel answered: "Good rede can I give thereto, and now shall we each of us do what each best liketh. Ye shall run home and wake up my following, and they will come quickly to meet me, but here in the rickyard is a good place to make a stand, and from hence will I defend myself if they come in warlike wise, for that meseems is better than running; nor shall I soon be overcome, and speedily will my men come to me, if ye do your errands in manly wise."

So when Arnkel had thus made an end of speaking, the thralls set off a-running; and Ofeig was the swiftest, but so afeard he was that he well-nigh went out of his wits, and ran off into the mountain and fell into a force there and was lost, and that is since called Ofeig's-force. The other thrall ran home to the stead, and when he came to the haybarn there was his fellow- thrall before him carrying in the hay. He called to the thrall as he ran to help bear in the hay to him, and belike the thrall was nowise loth of that work, so he went to help him.

Now it is to be said of Arnkel that he knew how Snorri the Priest and his folk went there, and he tore the runner from under the sledge, and had it up into the garth with him. The garth was very high outside, and within it was heaped up high as well; and a good fighting-stead it was. Hay was in the garth, but the garth-pieces of the stacks were cleared off.

Now when Snorri and his folk came to the garth, it is not told that any words befell there, but straightway they set on Arnkel, and chiefly with spear-thrust, which Arnkel put from him with the sledge-runner, and many of the spear-shafts were broken thereby, nor was Arnkel wounded; but when they had spent their shot-weapons, then Thorleif Kimbi ran at the garth and leapt up on to it with sword drawn, and Arnkel smote at him with the sledge-runner, and Thorleif dropped down away from the stroke out of the garth, and the runner smote against the garth wall, and up therefrom flew a piece of frozen turf; but the sledge-runner was broken at the mortice, and part thereof fell out over the garth. Arnkel had laid his sword and shield against a hayrick, and now he took up his weapons and defended himself therewith; but now he began to gather wounds, and withal they came up into the garth about him. Then Arnkel leapt

up on to the hayrick, and defended himself thence for a space, but such was
the end of the matter that he fell, and they covered him over there in the garth
with hay; and thereafter Snorri and his folk fared home to Holyfell.

Over the slaying of Arnkel, Thormod Trefilson made this stave:

> "Snorri the fight-strong
> Fetched for the wound-fowl
> Full feed with war-sword –
> Young he, and fame-fulfilled.
> O feeders of battle-fowl,
> Wild-fire of battle-storm
> Clave the life's coffer,
> Where Snorri felled Arnkel."

Chapter 38
The Blood-Suit For Arnkel

After the slaying of Arnkel, the heritage and blood-suit fell to women, and for
this reason the blood-suit was not pushed forward so strongly as men deemed
they might have looked for over so noble a man. But atonement was settled for
the slaying at the Thing, and the only outlawry was that Thorleif Kimbi should
abide abroad for three winters, because on him was laid the death-wound of
Arnkel.

But because the blood-suit was not so seemly as men deemed befitted such
a chief as was Arnkel, the rulers of the land made this law, that for the time to
come no woman and no man under sixteen winters old should be suitors in a
blood-suit. And that law has ever been holden to since.

Chapter 39
Of Thorleif Kimbi And His Dealings With Arnbiorn

Thorleif Kimbi took ship that same summer with chapmen who got ready in
Streamfirth, and was a messmate of the masters. In those days was it the wont
of chapmen to have no cooks, but the messmates chose by lot from amongst
themselves who should have the ward of the mess day by day. Then too was it
the wont of all the shipmen to have their drink in common, and a cask should
stand by the mast with the drink therein, and a locked lid was over it. But some
of the drink was in tuns, and was added to the cask thence as soon as it was
drunk out.

Now when they were nigh ready there came one forth upon the ledge of
rock by the booths. This man was great of growth, and had a bundle on his
back, and seemed to men somewhat uncouth. He asked for the ship-master,
and he was shown to his booth. So he laid down his bag at the booth-door and
went into the booth, and asked if the skipper would give him a passage over
the sea.

They asked him of his name, and he called himself Arnbiorn, the son of Asbrand of Combe, and said he fain would fare out and seek Biorn his brother, who had gone out some winters before, and had not been heard of since he went to Denmark.

The Eastmen said that the bulk was bound down, and they deemed it might not be undone. He said he had not more faring goods than might lie on the top of the bulk. But whereas they deemed him to have great need of faring, they took him to them, but he found himself in victual, and abode on the forecastle.

In his bag were three hundreds in wadmal, and twelve skins for sale, and his victual.

Now Arnbiorn was of good help and a brisk man, and the chapmen held him of good account.

They had a fair passage out and made Hordaland, and took land at an outskerry, and dight their victuals on land.

Thorleif Kimbi was the allotted mess-ward, and had to make porridge. Arnbiorn was aland and made porridge for himself, and had the mess-kettle which Thorleif was to have afterwards. Then went Thorleif aland and bade Arnbiorn give him his kettle, but he had not yet made his own porridge, but stirred the kettle while Thorleif stood over him. Now the Eastmen called aland from the ship and bade Thorleif get ready the meat, and said that he was just an Icelander because of his laziness. Then Thorleif lost his temper, and caught up the kettle and cast out Arnbiorn's porridge, and then turned away.

Arnbiorn had the stirring-stick in his hand, and therewith he smote at Thorleif and caught him on the neck, and the blow was not great, but whereas the porridge was hot, Thorleif was scalded on his neck. Then Thorleif said:

"These Northmen shall not mock us, since we be here two fellow- country-men together, that they must needs drag us apart like dogs; but I shall mind me of this when we are together in Iceland."

Arnbiorn answered nought. So they lay there three nights before they had a wind for land; then they brought their goods ashore.

Thorleif guested there, but Arnbiorn took ship with certain traders east to Wick, and thence to Denmark to seek for his brother Biorn.

Chapter 40
Of Biorn, The Champion Of The Broadwickers, And His Dealings With Thurid Of Frodis-Water

Thorleif Kimbi was two winters in Norway, and then went back to Iceland with the same chapmen as he had fared out with. They made Broadfirth and came to Daymeal-ness, and Thorleif went home to Swanfirth in the autumn, and made much of himself as his manner was.

That same summer came out to Lavahaven-mouth those brothers Biorn and Arnbiorn, and Biorn was afterwards called the Champion of the Broadwickers. Arnbiorn had by then brought home a pretty penny; and as soon as he came aland that summer he bought him land at Bank in Lavahaven, and set up house there the next spring. That winter he spent at Cnear with Thord Walleye, his brother-in-law. Arnbiorn was not a man for show, and was of few words in most matters, yet the stoutest and manliest of men in every wise. But Biorn his brother was a very stately man when he came out, and fair was his mien, for that he had shaped himself after the customs of outland chiefs. A far goodlier man was he than Arnbiorn, and in nothing of less skill than he, and in hardihood far more proven, for thereby he had gained renown in the outlands.

Now in the summer, when these were new come out, was appointed a great meeting of men north of the heath under Howebrent, in from Frodismouth. So those chapmen rode thither all of them, in coloured raiment, and when they came to the assembly, there were many there before them, and Thurid withal the goodwife of Frodis-water, and Biorn went to talk with her; and no man laid a word on them therefor, for they deemed that it was to be looked for that they should have much to say to each other, so long as it was since they met last.

Now that day men gave and took wounds, and one man from the Northcountry-men was brought to his death, and he was borne into a copse that was on the ere, and much blood ran from his wounds, and there stood a pool of blood in the copse. There was the youngling Kiartan, the son of Thurid of Frodis-water, with a little axe in his hand; he ran to the copse, and dipped the axe in the blood.

But when the folk from the south side of the heath rode south from the meeting, Thord Walleye asked Biorn how things had gone in the talk betwixt him and Thurid of Frodis-water. Biorn seemed well pleased thereabout. Then Thord asked Biorn if he had seen that day the youngling Kiartan, the son of Thurid and Thorod and them all together.

"Yea, I saw him," cried Biorn.

"In what wise didst thou deem of him?" said Thord.

Then sang Biorn this stave:

"The young tree I saw there, the eager-eyed sapling, The youngling, the very own image of her, That gem-bestrewn table; he ran to the tree-grove, Whence the brook of the Wolf, even Fenrir, was welling. They who waste wide the flame of Morn's river, meseemeth Have been hitherto heedful to hide from the stripling The name of the father who erewhile begat him, He who speedeth the steeds of the streams of the Ocean."

Chapter 41
Of Thorleif Kimbi And Thord Wall-Eye

That same spring at the Thorsness Thing, Thorleif Kimbi fell to wooing a wife, and prayed for Helga, daughter of Thorlak of Ere, and sister of Steinthor of that ilk; and Thormod her brother pressed this forward most, he who had to wife Thorgerd, daughter of Thorbrand, and sister of Thorleif Kimbi. But when the matter came before Steinthor, he took it up coldly, and must ask counsel of his brothers. So then they went to Thord Wall-eye, and when the matter was laid before him, he answered thus:

"I will not put this affair off on to other men, for herein may I be the shaper; so this I have to say to thee, Thorleif, that first must the porridge spots on thy neck be healed, wherewith thou wast burnt when thou wast beaten in Norway three winters agone, or ever I give thee my sister."

Thorleif answered: "I know not what my fortune may be therein; but whether that be avenged or not," says he, "my will it is that three winters pass not ere thou be beaten."

Thord answered: "I sit without fear in despite of thy threats."

But the next morning men had a turf-play beside the booth of the sons of Thorbrand, and as Thorlak's sons passed by, forth flew a great piece of turf, and smote Thord Wall-eye under the poll, and so great was the stroke, that he fell heels over head; but when he arose, he saw that Thorbrand's sons were laughing at him hugely. Then Thorlak's sons turned back and drew their swords, and they ran to meet one another, and forthwithal they fought together, and some were wounded, but none slain.

Steinthor had not been there, for he had been in talk with Snorri the Priest. So when they were parted, folk strove to bring about peace; and so it was settled that Snorri and Steinthor should be umpires in the matter. So the wounds of men and the onset were set one against the other, but the remnant over was atoned for; and all were called at one again whenas they rode home.

Chapter 42
Thorbrand's Sons Make An Onslaught On Arnbiorn

That summer a ship came out into Lavahaven-mouth, and another to Daymeal-ness. Snorri the Priest rode to the ship at Lavahaven, and fourteen men with him; but when they came south over the heath to Dufgusdale, six men all-armed rode after them, and there were the sons of Thorbrand. Snorri asked whither they were minded to fare, but they said they would go to the ship at Lavahaven-mouth. Snorri said that he would do their errands for them, and bade them go back home and not raise quarrels betwixt men; and he said that often little was needed for that matter among those who were unfriends together already, if they should chance to meet.

Thorleif Kimbi answered: "It shall not be told of us that we durst not ride through the countryside because of the Broadwickers; but thou mayest well ride home, if thou darest not to ride on thy ways when thou hast an errand."

Snorri answered nought, and so they rode forth over the necks, and so forth to Templegarth, and then west over the sands along the sea; but when they came anigh to the Mouth, Thorbrand's sons rode from the company up to Bank; and when they came to the homestead they leapt off their horses and were minded to enter, but might not break open the door. Then they leapt up on to the house, and fell to unroofing it.

Arnbiorn took his weapons, and warded himself from the inside of the house. He thrust out through the thatch, and that became woundsome to them. This was early in the morning, and the weather was bright and clear; and that morning had those of Broadwick arisen early, with the mind to ride to the ship; but when they came west of the shoulder of the fell, then saw they a man in coloured clothes up on the house-roof at Bank, and they wotted well that it was not the attire of Arnbiorn. Then Biorn and his folk spurred on their horses, and turned their way thitherward.

But when Snorri the Priest was ware that the sons of Thorbrand had ridden away from his company, he rode after them, and by then he and his came to Bank were those others working at their maddest for the unroofing of the house. Then Snorri bade them begone thence, nor work any unpeaceful deeds in his company, so whereas they had got no entrance there, they even gave up the onset as Snorri bade, and rode thereafter to the ship with Snorri.

Now those of Broadwick came to the ship that same day, and either side went with their own band, and great ill-will there was, and cross looks enow, but neither side set on another, yet the men of Broadwick were the most in number at the market. Snorri the Priest rode in the evening south to Templegarth, whereas Biorn dwelt as then with his son Guest, who was the father of Templegarth-Ref. The folk of Biorn the Champion of the Broadwickers offered Arnbiorn to ride after those of Snorri the Priest, but Arnbiorn would not have it so, but said that each should have what he had got. Those of Snorri rode home the next day, and the sons of Thorbrand were worse content with their lot than heretofore. And now the autumn began to wear.

Chapter 43
Of Egil The Strong

Now goodman Thorbrand had a thrall who was called Egil the Strong, the biggest and strongest of men, and he thought his life ill in that he was no free man, and would oft pray Thorbrand and his sons to give him his freedom, and offered to do therefor any such work as he might. So one evening Egil went with his sheep out to Burgdale in Swanfirth, and as the evening grew late, he saw an erne fly from the west over the firth. Now a great deerhound was with Egil, and lo, the erne swooped on the hound, and took him up in her claws, and flew back west over the firth straight for the howe of Thorolf Haltfoot, and vanished there, under the mountain; and a foreboding of tidings Thorbrand deemed this.

Now it was the wont of the Broadwickers in autumn, about the time of winter-nights, to have ball-play under the shoulder south of Cnear, and the place thereafter was called the Playhall-meads, and men betook themselves thither from all the countryside, and great play-halls were made there, wherein men abode and dwelt there a half month or more. Many chosen men there were as then in the countryside, and it was thickly peopled. Most of the young men were at the plays, except Thord Wall-eye; but he might not deal therein because of his too great eagerness, though he was not so strong that he might not play for that cause. So he sat on a chair and looked on the play. Those brethren withal, Biorn and Arnbiorn, were not deemed meet to play because of their strength, unless they played one against the other.

That same autumn Thorbrand's sons fell to talk with Egil that he should go to the ball-play and slay some one of the Broadwickers, either Biorn or Thord or Arnbiorn, in some wise, and that he should have his freedom after therefor; and some men say that that was done by Snorri's rede, and that he had so counselled that the thrall should try if he might get into the hall by stealth, and thence whereas he lurked do somewhat for the wounding of men; and he bade him go down the pass which is above Playhalls, and go down thence when the meal-fires were kindled; for he said it was mostly the way of the weather that a wind would blow off the lava in the evening and drive the smoke up into the pass. So he bade him abide his time to go down till the pass should be full of smoke.

Egil betook himself to this journey, and went first west over the firths, and asked after the sheep of the Swanfirthers, and made as if he were going a sheep-gleaning.

Now whilst he was on his way, Freystein Rascal was to watch the sheep in Swanfirth. So in the evening, when Egil had gone from home, Freystein went west over the river to the sheep, and when he came to that scree which is called Geirvor, and which goes down west of the river, he saw a man's head lying trunkless there and uncovered, and the head sang this stave:

> "With man's blood Geirvor
> Is reddened over,
> The skulls of men-folk
> Shall she cover."

Chapter 44
The Battle In Swanfirth

Snorri the Priest had sent word to his neighbours that they should bring their boats under Redwick-head; and he went thither with his home-men as soon as Steinthor's messenger was gone; and he went not before, because he thought he saw that the man had been sent to spy over his doings. So Snorri went up Swanfirth, and had nigh fifty men with three keels, and came to Karstead before Steinthor and his men. But when folk saw the coming of Steinthor and his men, the sons of Thorbrand cried out to go meet them, "and let them not get entry into the home-field, for that we have both a great company and a goodly."

Now they who were there were eighty men. But Snorri said: "Nay, we will not ward the homestead from them, and Steinthor shall have the law, for peaceably and wisely will he fare in his redes. So I will that all men abide within, and let no man cast any vain words at them in such wise as that the troubles of men be eked thereby."

With that all men went into the chamber, and men sat on the benches. But the sons of Thorbrand walked up and down the floor.

Now Steinthor and his folk rode up to the door; and for him it is said that he was in a red kirtle, and had pulled up the front skirts through his belt. A fair shield he had, and a helm, and was girt with a sword that was cunningly wrought; the hilts were white with silver, and the grip wrapped round with the same, but the strings thereof were gilded.

Steinthor and his folk leapt off their horses, and he went up to the door, and made fast to the doorpost a purse wherein were twelve ounces of silver. Then he named witnesses to the thrall's-gild being brought home according to law. The door was open, and a certain handmaid stood thereby, and heard the naming of the witnesses. Then she went into the chamber and said:

"Yea, both things are true, that Steinthor of Ere is a manly man, and moreover that he spoke well when he brought the thrall's-gild."

But when Thorleif Kimbi heard that, he ran out with the other sons of Thorbrand, and then all went forth who were in the chamber. Thorleif came first to the door, and saw where Thord Walleye stood before the doorway with his shield; but even therewith Steinthor went forth into the homefield. Thorleif took a spear which stood there in the doorway, and thrust it at Thord Wall-eye, and the thrust smote his shield and glanced off it unto the shoulder, and that was a great wound. After this men ran out and there was battle in the home-mead, and Steinthor was of the eagerest, and smote on either hand of him. But when Snorri the Priest came out he bade men stay the unpeace, and bade Steinthor ride away from the homestead, and said that he would not suffer men to ride after them. So Steinthor and his folks fared adown the mead, and men parted in such wise.

But when Snorri the Priest came back to the door, there stood Thorod his son with a great wound in his shoulder, and he was then twelve winters old. Snorri asked who had brought that about.

"Steinthor of Ere," said he.

And Thorleif Kimbi answered and said: "Now has he rewarded thee in meet wise, for that thou wouldst not have us chase him; but my rede it is that we part not thus."

"Yea, so shall it be now," said Snorri, "that we shall have more dealings with them." And he bade Thorleif withal tell the men to follow after them.

Now Steinthor and his folk were come down from the field when they saw the chase, and therewith they crossed the river and turned up on to the scree Geirvor, and made them ready for a stand; for a good fighting-stead was that because of the stones. But as Snorri's company came up the scree, Steinthor cast a spear over Snorri's folk for his good luck, according to ancient custom; but the spear sought a mark for itself, and in its way was Mar, the kinsman of

Snorri, who was straightway put out of the fight. So when that was told Snorri the Priest, he answered: "It is well that men should see," says he, "that he is not always in the best case that goeth the last."

So then befell a great battle, and Steinthor was at the head of his own folk, and smote on either hand of him; but the fair- wrought sword bit not whenas it smote armour, and oft he must straighten it under his foot. He made most for the place whereas was Snorri the Priest.

Stir Thorgrimson set on fiercely with Steinthor his kinsman, and his first hap was that he slew a man of the folk of Snorri the Priest, his son-in-law; but when Snorri saw that he cried to Stir:

"Thus, forsooth, thou avengest Thorod, the son of thy daughter, whom Steinthor of Ere has brought unto death; the greatest of dastards art thou."

Stir looked on him and said: "Speedily I may atone for that;" and he shifted his shield withal, and turned to the side of Snorri the Priest, and slew another man, but this time a man of Steinthor's band.

Now even herewith came up from Longdale the father and son, Aslak and Illugi the Red, and sought to go between them. Thirty men they had with them, and to that company joined himself Vermund the Slender.

So then they prayed Snorri the Priest to let stay the slaughter of men, and Snorri bade the Ere-dwellers come up and make a truce. Then Aslak, he and his, bade Steinthor take truce for his men. So Steinthor bade Snorri reach forth his hand, and he did so; but therewith Steinthor raised his sword aloft and cut at Snorri's arm, and great was the clatter of the stroke, for it smote the stall-ring, and well-nigh struck it asunder, but Snorri was nowise wounded.

Then cried out Thorod Thorbrandson: "No truce will they have! Well then, let us set on, and stay not till all the sons of Thorlak are slain."

But Snorri the Priest answered: "Turmoil enow it would bring to the countryside if all sons of Thorlak were slain, and the truce shall be holden to if Steinthor will, after the word aforesaid."

Then all bade Steinthor take the truce; and things went so far, that a truce was declared betwixt man and man until such time as they came back each one to his home.

Now it is to be told of the Broadwick folk that they knew how Snorri the Priest had fared with a flock to Swanfirth. So they take their horses and ride after Steinthor at their swiftest, and they were on Ulfar's-fell-neck whiles the fight was on the scree; and some men say that Snorri the Priest saw Biorn and his folk as they came up on the hill's brow, whenas he happened to turn and face them, and that for that cause he was so easy in the terms of the truce with Steinthor and his men.

So when Biorn and Steinthor met at Orligstead, Biorn said that matters had gone even after his guessing. "And my rede it is," said he, "that ye turn back now, and drive them hard."

But Steinthor said: "Nay, I will hold to the truce I have made with Snorri the Priest, in whatso ways matters may go betwixt us hereafter."

Thereafter they ride each to his own home, but Thord Wall-Eye lay wounded at Ere. In the fight at Swanfirth five men had fallen of Steinthor's company, and two of Snorri the Priest; but many were wounded on either side, for the fight had been of the hardest. So says Thorrood Trefilson in his Raven-lay:

"The feeder of swans Of wound-wave, in Swanfirth Made the erne full With feeding of wolfs' meat. There then, let Snorri Of five men the life-days Cut off in sword-storm: Such way shall foes pay."

Chapter 45
The Battle In Swordfirth

That summer, before the fight was in Swanfirth, a ship had come to Daymeal-ness, as is aforesaid. Now Steinthor of Ere had bought a ten-oarer at the ship; but when he was to bring it home there fell on him a great gale from the west, and they drave east past Thors-ness, and landed at Thinghall-ness, and laid the keel up in Gruflunaust, and went thence afoot over the necks to Bank, and thence fared home in a boat; but the ten-oarer he had not been able to go fetch through the autumn, so it lay still at Gruflunaust.

But one morning a little before Yule, Steinthor rose early, and said that he would go fetch his craft that lay east at Thinghall-ness; and there betook them to faring with him his brothers Bergthor and Thord Wall-eye, whose wound was by now pretty much healed, so that he was meet enow to carry weapons. Withal in Steinthor's company were two Eastmen, and they were eight in all.

So they were ferried over the firth into Dairyhead, and they went afoot in towards Bank, and thence came Thormod, their brother, who made the ninth of them. Now the ice stretched from Templesteadwick right up to Much Bank, and they went up along the ice, and so over the neck to Swordfirth, which lay all under ice. Such is the way of it, that when the sea ebbs, it leaves it all dry, and the ice lies on the mud at the ebb; but the skerries that were in the firth stood up above the ice, which was much broken about one of them, and the icefloes sloped down steeply from the skerry. Loose snow withal had fallen on the ice, and very slippery it was thereon.

Now Steinthor and his folk went to Thinghall-ness, and pushed out the boat from the boatstand, and took out of her both oars and deck, and laid them down on the ice, together with their clothes and the heaviest of their weapons. Then they dragged the craft in along the firth, and then west over the low neck to Templesteadwick, and right out to the edge of the ice; and then went after their clothes and the other matters. But as they went back into Swordfirth, they saw six men going from the south from Thinghall-ness, who went a great pace over the ice, and made for Holyfell. Then Steinthor and his men misdoubted them, that there would be going the sons of Thorbrand minded for the Yule-feast at Holyfell. Then Steinthor with his folk went swiftly out over the firth to the place where lay their clothes and weapons; and so it was as Steinthor had deemed, and these men were the sons of Thorbrand.

So when these beheld men running down the firth, they deemed they knew who they were, and thought the men of Ere were fain to meet them. So they fell to going at a great pace, and made for the skerry with the mind to make a stand there; and in this wise each came nigh to meeting the other, yet the sons of Thorbrand reached the skerry first. But as Steinthor and his folk came forth past the skerry, Thorleif Kimbi let drive a spear against their flock, and it smote Bergthor, son of Thorlak, in the midst, and straightway was he put out of the fight. Then he went away out on to the ice, and lay down, and Steinthor and his folk set on toward the skerry, but some went after their weapons. The sons of Thorbrand warded themselves well and in manly wise, and a good fighting-stead they had there, because the floes sloped steeply from the skerry and were wondrous slippery; thus wounding went slowly betwixt men, before those came back who had gone to fetch the weapons.

Steinthor and his men set on, six together, on the skerry, but the Eastmen went out on to the ice within bowshot, for they had bows, and there with they shot against those on the skerry, and gave many a wound.

Thorleif Kimbi cried out when he saw Steinthor draw his sword: "White hilts dost thou still wield aloft, Steinthor," says he; "but I wot not if thou raisest yet again a soft brand withal, as thou didst last autumn at Swanfirth."

Steinthor answers: "Ah! I will that thou prove ere we part whether I bear a soft brand or not."

Now slow work was the winning of the skerry, but when they had been thereat a long while, Thord Wall-eye made a dash at it, and would thrust at Thorleif Kimbi with a spear, for he was ever the foremost of his men. The thrust smote the shield of Thorleif, but even as Thord Wall-eye laboured over the blow his feet failed him on the slippery floe, and he fell on his back and slipped headforemost down from the skerry. Thorleif Kimbi leapt after him to smite him dead before he could get to his feet again, and Freystein Rascal followed Thorleif, and he had shoe-spikes on his feet. Then Steinthor ran thereto, and cast his shield over Thord even as Thorleif fetched a blow at him, and with the other hand he smote at Thorleif Kimbi, and smote the leg from him below the knee; and while that was a-doing Freystein Rascal thrust at Steinthor, aiming at his middle; and when Steinthor saw that, he leapt up aloft, and the thrust went between his legs, and these three things, whereof we have told even now, he did in one and the same nick of time. Then he ran to Freystein, and smote him on the neck with his sword, and loud was the clatter of that stroke. So he cried withal: "Art smitten, Rascal?"

"Smitten forsooth," said Freystein, "but yet no more than thou didst deem, for no wound have I therefrom." For in a hooded hat of felt was Freystein, with horn sewn into the neck thereof, and on that had the stroke fallen.

Then Freystein Rascal turned back skerryward, but Steinthor bade him run not, since he had no wound, and Freystein turned him round on the skerry, and now they made at each other hard and fast. Steinthor was in great risk of falling, for the floe was both steep and slippery, but Freystein stood firm on his spiked shoes, and smote both hard and oft; but such was the end of their dealings, that Steinthor brought his sword down on Freystein above his hips, and smote the man asunder in the midst.

Then they went on to the skerry, and stayed not till all Thorbrand's sons were fallen. Then cried out Thord Wall-eye that they should go betwixt head and trunk of all the sons of Thorbrand, but Steinthor said he had no will to bear weapons on men who lay alow.

So they came down from the skerry, and went to where Bergthor lay, who scarce had might to speak. So they brought him with them in over the ice, and so over the neck to the boat, and rowed in the boat out to Bank in the evening.

Now a shepherd of Snorri's had been at Oxbrents that day, and saw thence the fight at Swordfirth. So he went home straightway, and told Snorri the Priest how there had been a meeting that day at Swordfirth nowise friendly. So Snorri and his folk took their weapons, and went into the firth nine in company; but when they came there, Steinthor and his men had gone their ways and come aboard off the ice of the firth.

Then Snorri looked to the wounded men, and there was none slain save Freystein Rascal, but they were all nigh wounded to death.

Thorleif Kimbi cried out to Snorri, bidding go after Steinthor and his folk, and let no one of them escape. So Snorri the Priest went there whereas Bergthor had lain, and saw there great gouts of blood. Then he took up in his hand together blood and snow, and crushed it up, and put it in his mouth, and asked who had bled there. And Thorleif said it was Bergthor who had bled. Then Snorri said it was life-blood. "Like enow," said Thorleif; "from a spear it came."

"Methinks," says Snorri, "that is the blood of a doomed man; so we will not follow after them."

Then were Thorbrand's sons brought home to Holyfell and their wounds bound up. Thorod Thorbrandson had so great a wound in the back of his neck that he might not hold his head straight; he had on hose-breeches withal, and they were all wet with blood. A home-man of Snorri the Priest was about pulling them off; but when he fell to stripping them he could not get them off. Then he said: "No lie is that concerning you sons of Thorbrand, when folk say ye are showy men, whereas ye wear clothes so tight that they may not come off you."

Thorod said: "Belike thou pullest slovenly." And therewith the home-man set his feet against the bed-stock and pulled with all his might, but yet gat them off none the more.

Then Snorri the Priest went thereto, and felt along his leg, and found a spear stuck through his leg between the hough sinew and the leg bone, that had nailed together the leg and the breeches. Then said Snorri that the thrall was a measureless fool not to have thought of such a thing.

Snorri Thorbrandson was the briskest of those brothers, and he sat at table beside his namesake that evening. Curds and cheese they had to meat, but Snorri noted that his namesake made but little play with the cheese, and asked why he eat so slowly.

Snorri Thorbrandson answered that lambs found it the hardest to eat when they were first gagged.

Then Snorri the Priest drew his hand down his throat, and found an arrow sticking athwart his gullet and the roots of the tongue. Then Snorri the Priest took drawing-tongs and pulled out the arrow, and then Snorri Thorbrandson fell to his meat.

Then Snorri the Priest healed all the sons of Thorbrand. But when Thorod's neck grew together his head sat somewhat drawn backwards on his trunk, and he said that Snorri would heal him into a maimed man. Snorri said that he deemed the head would come straight when the sinews were knit together; but Thorod would have nought but that the wound should be torn open again, and the head set straighter. But all went as Snorri had guessed, and as soon as the sinews were knit together the head came right; yet little might Thord lout ever after. Thorleif Kimbi thenceforth went mostly with wooden leg.

Chapter 46
The Peace-Making After These Battles

Now when Steinthor of Ere and his men came to the boatstand at Bank, there they put up their craft, and the brothers went home to their steading, and the body of Bergthor was covered over with a tilt for the night. It is told that goodwife Thorgerd would not go to bed that night to Thormod her husband. But even therewith a man came up from the boatstand and told how Bergthor was dead; and when that was known she went to bed, nor is it said that any quarrel fell out betwixt them afterwards.

Steinthor went home to Ere in the morning, and no more fighting there was thenceforth through the winter. But in the spring, whenas time wore on to the days of summoning, men of good will bethought them that things had got to a sad plight, inasmuch as those men were unappeased and at strife together, who were the greatest in the countryside. So the best men who were friends of either side so brought it about that it came to seeking for peace betwixt them. And Vermund the Slender was chief of these, and with him were many men of good will, such as were allied to one side or the other, and thereof it came afterwards that truce was settled and they were brought to peace, and most men tell that these cases fell under Vermund's dooming; but he gave forth the award at the Thorsness Thing, and had with him the wisest men who were come there.

Now it is told of the peace-making that the slayings of men and onslaughts on either side were set off one against the other. The wound of Thord Wall-eye at Swanfirth was set against the wound of Thorod, son of Snorri the Priest. Against the wound of Mar Hallwardson and the stroke that Steinthor fetched at Snorri the Priest, were set the slayings of three men who fell in Swanfirth. The manslaughters which Stir made in either band were equalled; but in Swordfirth the slaughter of Bergthor and the wounds of Thorbrand's sons were set one against the other. But the slaying of Freystein Rascal met the death of one of those unnamed above who fell in Swanfirth out of Steinthor's company. Thorleif Kimbi had atonement for his lost leg; but the man who died out of Snorri's company in Swanfirth was set against the onset wherewith Thorleif Kimbi had set the fight agoing there.

Then were the wounds of other men set against each other, and what was deemed to be left over was booted for duly, and so men parted from the Thing appeased.

And that peace was well holden while Steinthor and Snorri were both alive.

Chapter 47
Of Thorod Scat-Catcher And Snorri And Biorn The Champion Of The Broad-Wickers

That same summer Thorod Scat-catcher bade Snorri his brother-in-law to a homefeast at Frodis-water, and Snorri went thither with eight men; but while Snorri was at the feast, Thorod complained to him that he deemed he had both shame and grief from the goings of Biorn Asbrandson, wherein he went to see his wife Thurid, the sister of Snorri the Priest, and said that it was Snorri's part to find rede for that trouble. So Snorri was at the feast certain nights, and Thorod led him away with seemly gifts. Snorri rode over the heath thence, and gave out that he would ride to the ship in Lavahavenmouth; and that was in summer at the time of mowing in the home-field. Now when he came south unto Combheath, then said Snorri: "Now shall we ride down from the heath unto Comb; and I will have you to know," says he, "that I will make an onset on Biorn, and take his life if occasion may serve; but not set on him in his house, because here are strong houses, and Biorn is brave and hardy, and we have but little strength. But hard have such great men as he is been to win in their houses, even when they were set on with more men; as the case of Geir the Priest and Gizur the White shows well enow; for with eighty men they fell on Gunnar of Lithend in his house when he was all alone, and some were hurt, and some slain, and they must needs draw off till Geir the Priest by his cunning found that Gunnar's shot was spent. Now, therefore," says he, "if Biorn is without, as is like, since the day is dry and good, I will that thou, kinsman Mar, fall to work on Biorn, but take heed of this first, that he is no mannikin, and therefore a greedy wolf will have a gripe, whereas he is, if he get not such a wound at the first onset as will speedily work his bane."

So when they rode down from the heath to the stead, they saw that Biorn was without in the home-mead working on a wain, and no man by him, and without weapons, save a little axe and a big whittle, with which he was widening the mortices of the wain; the whittle was a span long from the haft down.

Now Biorn saw how Snorri the Priest and his men rode down from the heath on to the mead, and straightway knew the men. Snorri the Priest was in a blue cape and rode first.

Such hasty rede took Biorn that he caught up the knife and turned swiftly to meet them, and when he came up to Snorri he caught hold of the sleeve of his cape with one hand, and held the knife in the other, in such wise as it was handiest to thrust it into Snorri's breast if need should be.

So Biorn hailed them when they met, and Snorri took his greeting; but Mar let his hands fall, because he deemed that Biorn looked like to do Snorri a mischief speedily if aught were done to break the peace against him.

Then Biorn turned on the road with Snorri and his folk, and asked for the common tidings; and still kept the hold he had got at the first. Then he fell to speech: "So it is, goodman Snorri, that I will not hide that I have played such a game with thee that ye may well hold me guilty, and it is told me that thy mind is heavy against me. Now best it is to my mind," says he, "if ye have any errand with me other than folk who go their ways hereby, that ye now show it forth; but if that be not so, then will I that ye say yea to my asking for truce, and then will I turn back, because I will not be led about like a fool."

"So lucky a hold thou hast of me in this our meeting," says Snorri, "that truce must thou have as at this time, whatever my mind was erst; but this I pray thee, that thou keep thyself henceforth from the beguiling of Thurid, for the wound betwixt us will not be healed if thou abidest as thou hast begun therein."

Biorn answered: "That only will I promise thee which lies in my might; nor do I wot if I have might enow for this, if Thurid and I are in one country together."

Snorri answered: "Nought holds thee here so much as that thou may'st not well take up thine abode away from this countryside."

Biorn answers: "True it is, even as thou say'st, and so shall it be, since thou thyself hast come to meet me thus; and whereas our meeting has gone in such wise, I will promise thee that thou and Thorod shall have no more grief of heart from the meetings of me and Thurid for the next winters."

"Then doest thou well," saith Snorri.

Therewithal they parted, and Snorri rode to the ship and then home to Holyfell. Next day Biorn rode south to the ship at Lavahaven, and took a berth for himself there that summer. Somewhat late ready were they, and they fell in with a northeaster, which prevailed long that summer, and nought was heard of that ship for long after.

Chapter 48
Of Thorbrand's Sons In Greenland

After the peace between the men of Ere and the Swanfirthers, Thorbrand's sons Snorri and Thorleif went out to Greenland. After Thorleif is called Kimbi's Bay in Greenland, betwixt the jokuls. So Thorleif lived to be old in Greenland, but Snorri went to Vineland the Good with Karlsefni, and in battle with the Skraelings in Vineland there fell Snorri Thorbrandson, the bravest of men.

Thorod Thorbrandson abode behind in Swanfirth, and had to wife Ragnhild, daughter of Thord, son of Thorgils the Eagle, who was the son of Hallstein, the Priest of Hallstein-ness, the thrall-owner.

Chapter 49
Of The Coming Of Christ's Faith To Iceland

Next it befell that Gizur the White and Hiallti his son-in-law came out to preach Christ's law; and all men in Iceland were christened, and the Christian faith was made law at the Althing. And Snorri the Priest brought it chiefly about with the Westfirthers that Christ's faith was taken of them; and as soon as the Thing was over, Snorri let build a church at Holyfell, and Stir, his father-in-law, another at Under-the-Lava. Now this whetted men much to the building of churches, that it was promised them by the teachers, that a man should have welcome place for so many men in the kingdom of Heaven as might stand in any church that he let build. Thorod Scat-catcher withal let make a church at his homestead of Frodis-water, but priests could not be got for the serving at the churches, though they were built, for in those days but few mass-priests there were in Iceland.

Chapter 50
Of Thorgunna And How She Came To Frodis-Water

The same summer that Christ's faith was made law in Iceland, a ship came from over the sea to Snowfell-ness, a keel of Dublin, whose folk were Erse and South-islanders, and a few Northmen. They lay off the Reef long through the summer, biding a wind to sail in over the firth to Daymeal-ness; so many men of the Ness went to chaffer with them. Now among her folk was a South-island woman named Thorgunna, and of her the shipmen told that she had such things among her faring-goods that the like of them would be hard to get in Iceland; but when Thurid the goodwife of Frodis- water heard thereof, she became exceeding wishful to see those fair things, for she was very fain of glitter and show. So she fared to the ship and found Thorgunna, and asked her if she had any woman's attire, something out of the common way. She said that she had no goods for sale, but let out that she had certain fair things, which she might show without shame at feasts or other meetings of men. Thurid prayed to see her fair things, and she granted it to her; and the wares seemed good to Thurid, and exceeding well shaped, but not beyond price.

Thurid offered to deal for the goods, but Thorgunna would not sell them, so Thurid bade her come dwell with her, for she knew that Thorgunna was rich of raiment, and thought to get the goods at her leisure.

Thorgunna answered: "I have good will to go dwell with thee, but I give you to know that I am loth to pay much for myself, because I am exceeding handy at work, and willing enough thereto; but no wet work will I do; and I myself too shall rule what I am to pay for myself from the wealth that I have."

So Thorgunna talked it all over unyieldingly enough, but Thurid would that she should go thither none the less, and her goods were borne from the ship: a great locked ark and a light chest, and they were brought to the house at Frodis-water.

So when Thorgunna came there she prayed to have a bed, and a berth was given to her in the inward part of the hall. There she unlocked her ark, and drew thereout bed-clothes all excellently wrought.

She covered over the bed with English sheets and a silken quilt, and took from the ark bed-curtains and all other bed-gear withal; and so good an array that was, that men deemed that of such goods they had never seen the like.

Then said goodwife Thurid: "Put a price for me on thy bed-gear."

But Thorgunna answered: "Nay, I will not lie in straw for thee, courteous though thou be, and grand of array."

That misliked the goodwife, and never after did she bid for the goods.

Thorgunna worked at the weaving day by day when no haymaking was, but when it was dry she worked at the saving of hay in the home- mead, and let make for herself a rake, which she alone must handle.

Thorgunna was a woman great of growth, thick and tall, and right full of flesh; dark-browed and narrow-eyed; her hair dark-red and plenteous; of exceeding good manners was she in her daily ways, and she went every day to church before she went about her work; yet not easy of temper was she, or of many words in her daily conversation. Most men deemed that Thorgunna must have come into her sixth ten of years, yet was she the halest of women.

In those days was Thorir Wooden-leg come to be harboured at Frodis-water, and Thorgrima Witchface his wife with him, and things went somewhat ill betwixt her and Thorgunna. Kiartan the goodman's son was the one with whom Thorgunna would have most dealings, and she loved him much, yet was he cold to her, wherefore she was often cross-grained of mood. Kiartan was by then of thirteen or fourteen winters, and was both great of growth, and noble to look on.

Chapter 51
It Rains Blood At Frodis-Water. Of Thorgunna, And How She Died And Was Buried At Skalaholt

The summer was something wet, but nigh autumn befell good drying weather, and the haymaking at Frodis-water was by then come so far that all the home-mead was mown, and nigh half thereof was fully dry. Then befell a good drying day, calm and clear, so that no cloud was seen in the heavens.

Goodman Thorod got up early in the morning and set folk awork, and some fell to carrying the hay, while others ricked it. But Thorod set the women to spreading it, and the work was shared betwixt them, and Thorgunna set to work at as much as a neat's winter-fodder.

So the work went on well the day long, but when it had well-nigh worn three hours from noon, a black cloud-fleck came across the heaven from the north above Skor, and swiftly drew over the heavens, and thitherward straight over the stead. Folk deemed they saw rain in that cloud, and Thorod bade men rake up the hay. But Thorgunna brought hers into ridges, nor would she fall to rake it up though she were so bidden.

The cloud-fleck came up swiftly, and when it stood over the homestead of Frodis-water, there followed therewith so great a darkness, that men might not see out of the home-field, or scarce their hands before them. Then fell so great a rain from the cloud that all the hay that was spread was wetted; but the cloud drew off swiftly and the weather cleared. Then men saw that it had rained blood in that shower. But that evening good drying weather set in again, and the blood dried off all the hay but that which Thorgunna had spread; that dried not, or the rake either which she had handled. Thurid asked Thorgunna what she thought that wonder might forbode. She said that she wotted not. "But that seems to me most like," says she, "that it will be the weird of some one of those that are here."

Thorgunna went home in the evening and into her berth, and put off her bloodied clothes, and then lay down in her bed and sighed heavily, and men deemed that she had fallen sick.

Now that shower had come nowhere else but to Frodis-water.

But Thorgunna might eat no meat that evening, but in the morning good-man Thorod came to her and asked her what end she looked to have of her ailing. She said that she was minded to think that she would not fall sick again.

Then she said: "I deem thee the wisest man of the homestead, therefore will I tell thee all my will as to what I would have made of the goods I leave behind me and of myself. For things will go," says she, "even as I say, though ye think there is little to be noted in me, and I deem it will avail but little to turn away from my behests; for things have begun in such wise, that to no narrow ends deem I they will come, if strong stays be not raised thereagainst."

Thorod answered and said: "Methinks there is no little likelihood that thou wilt have deemed aright about this; yet I will promise thee," says he, "to turn not from thy behests."

Then said Thorgunna: "This would I have done: I would be borne to Skalaholt if I die of this sickness, because my mind tells me that that stead will be for one while the most worshipped stead in the land; and I wot also," says she, "that there will be priests to do the singing over me; so I pray thee to bring me there, and of my goods shalt thou have so much as that thou wilt have no loss thereby; but from my undivided goods shall Thurid have the scarlet cloak that I own; and this I do to the end that she may be content that I see to my other goods in such wise as I will; but I will that thou take for the cost thou hast for me that which thou wilt, or that pleases her, from such things alone as I leave thereto. A gold ring I have which shall go to church with me, but I will that my bed and my bed-hangings be burned up with fire, for that they will be of no good to any man; and I say this not because I grudge anyone to enjoy those good things, if I knew that they would be of good avail to any; but now I say so much thereover," says she, "because I deem it ill that folk should have so much heavy trouble from me, as well I wot will be, if ye turn away from that which I now ordain."

Thorod promised to do after her bidding; and so the sickness grew on her after that, and Thorgunna lay there not many days before she died.

The corpse was first borne into the church there, and Thorod let make a chest for the corpse, and the next day he had the bed-gear borne out into the air, and brought faggots together, and let pile up a bonfire there beside. Then goodwife Thurid went to him and asked what he was minded to do with the bed-gear. He said that he would burn it up with fire, even as Thorgunna had charged.

She answered: "It mislikes me that such precious things should be burned."

Thorod said: "She spake much thereon, and how it would not do to turn aside from that she had laid down."

Thurid said: "Such words were of nought but her envious mind; she grudged that any should enjoy these, therefore did she lay such charge on thee; but nought ill-omened will come of it, in whatsoever way such things are departed from."

"I know not," said he, "that things will go well but if we do as she has bidden."

Then Thurid put her arms round his neck, and prayed him not to burn the bed-gear, and pressed him so eagerly that he changed his mind and she brought matters about in such wise that Thorod burned the bolster and the mattress, but she took to her the quilt and sheets, and all the hangings; and yet withal it misliked them both.

Thereafter was the burial journey got ready, and trusty men got to go with the corpse, and good horses that Thorod owned. The body was swathed in linen, but not sewn up, and then laid in the chest. So then they went south over the heath as the road lies, and nought is told of their journey till they came south past Valbiorns-vales. There they got amongst flows exceeding soft, and the corpse was often upset. Then they went south to Northwater, and crossed it by Isleford. Deep was the river, and a storm befell with much rain; but they came at last to a stead that was within Staffholts-tongue and is called Nether-ness, and there asked for guesting, but the bonder would give them no cheer; so whereas the night was at hand, they deemed they might go no further, for belike it was nought easy to deal with Whitewater by night; so they unloaded their horses, and bore the corpse into a house over against the outer door, and then went into the hall and did off their clothes, and deemed they would abide there unfed that night. But the home-men went to bed by daylight, and when they were abed, they heard a great clatter in the buttery, and so they went to see what was toward, if perchance thieves had not broken in there, and when they came to the buttery there was to behold a tall woman, naked, with nothing on her, busied at bringing out victuals. So when they saw her, they were so afeard they durst go nowhere anigh.

But when the corpse-bearers knew thereof they went there, and saw what was toward, that thither was Thorgunna come, and good it seemed to all not to meddle with her. So when she had wrought such things there as she would, she bore meat into the hall, and laid the table and set out meat thereon. Then spake the corpse-bearers to the bonder: "Maybe things will end so or ever we part that thou wilt deem that thou hast paid dear enough for not giving us any cheer."

Then said the goodman and goodwife: "We will surely give you meat, and do for you all other things that ye may need."

And forthwith, when the goodman had bidden them good cheer, Thorgunna went out of the hall and out adoors, and was not seen after. And after that, light was brought into the hall, and the wet clothes pulled off from the guests and dry clothes got them in their stead, and they went to table and crossed the meat, while the goodman had all the house besprinkled with holy water.

So the guests eat the meat, and none had harm therefrom, though Thorgunna had set it out.

There they slept through the night, and were in a most hospitable place belike; but in the morning they got them ready for their journey, and right well it sped with them; but wheresoever these haps were known, there it seemed best rede to most folk to give them all the cheer they stood in need of.

So after this nought befell to tell of in their journey. And when they came to Skalaholt, the good things were yielded up which Thorgunna had given thereto, and the priests took them, corpse and all, gladly enow, and there was Thorgunna laid in earth, but the corpse-bearers fared home, and all went well with their journey, and they all came home in good case.

Chapter 52
The Beginning Of Wonders At Frodis-Water

At Frodis-water was there a great fire-hall, and lock-beds in therefrom, as the wont then was. Out from the hall there were two butteries, one on either hand, with stock-fish stored in one, and meal in the other. There were meal-fires made every evening in the fire-hall, as the wont was, and men mostly sat thereby or ever they went to meat.

Now that same night that the corpse-bearers carne home, as men sat by the meal-fires at Frodiswater, they saw how by the panelling of the house-wall was come a half-moon, and all might see it who were in the house; and it went backward and withershins round about the house, nor did it vanish away while folk sat by the fires. So Thorod asked Thorir Wooden-leg what that might bode.

Thorir said it was the Moon of Weird, "and the deaths of men will follow thereafter," says he.

So a whole week this thing endured, that the Moon of Weird came in there evening after evening.

Chapter 53
Now Men Die At Frodis-Water, More Wonders

This happed next to tell of at Frodis-water, that the shepherd came in exceeding hushed. Little he said, and what he said was peevish; so men deemed it most like that he was bewitched, for he fared in distraught wise, and was ever talking to himself; and so things went on awhile.

But when two weeks of winter were worn, the shepherd came home on a night, and went straight to his bed and lay down, and in the morning when men carne to him he was dead. So he was buried at the church there.

A little after that great hauntings befell; and on a night as Thorir Wooden-leg went out for his needs, and turned off aside from the door, when he would go in again, he saw how the shepherd was come before the door. Then would he go in again, but the shepherd would nowise have it so; and Thorir was fain to get away, but the shepherd went at him, and got hold of him, and cast him homeward up against the door. At this he was affrighted exceedingly; yet he got him to his bed, and he was by then grown coal-blue all over.

Now from this he fell sick and died, and was buried there at the church; but ever after were the twain, the shepherd and Thorir Wooden-leg, seen in company, and therefrom were folk full of dread, as was like to be.

After Thorir's death a house-carle of Thorod fell sick, and lay there three nights or ever he died. Then one after another died, till six were dead; and by then it was hard on the Yule-fast, though at that time there was no fasting in Iceland.

Now the pile of stock-fish was so heaped up in the buttery that it filled it up, so that the door might not be opened, and it went right up to the tie-beam, and a ladder was needed to get the stock-fish from the top.

So one evening when men sat by the meal-fires, they heard how the stock-fish was being riven out of its skin, but when men looked thereto, they found there nought quick. But in the winter a little before Yule, goodman Thorod went out to Ness after his stock-fish. They were six together in a ten-oarer, and were out there night-long.

The same evening that Thorod went from home, it fell out at Frodis-water, when the meal-fires were lighted and men came gathering into the hall, that they saw how a seal's head came up through the floor of the fire-hall. A certain home-woman came forth first and saw that hap, and caught up a club that lay in the doorway, and drave it at the seal's head; but it rose up under the blow, and glared up at Thorgunna's bed-gear.

Then went a house-carle thereto, and beat on the seal, but at every blow it kept rising till it was up as far as below the flappers. Then fell the house-carle swooning, and all that were thereby were fulfilled of mighty dread.

Then the swain Kiartan ran thereto, and took up a great sledge- hammer and smote on the seal's head, and great was that blow, but the seal only shook its head and looked round about; but Kiartan smote one blow on another till the seal sank down therewith, as if he were at the knocking down of a peg; but he smote on till the seal went down so far that he might beat down the floor over the head of him. And so indeed it fell out the winter through, that all the portents dreaded Kiartan the most of all.

Chapter 54
The Death Of Thorod Scat-Catcher; The Dead Walk At Frodis-Water

The morning that Thorod and his men went out westaway from Ness, they were all lost off Enni; the ship and the fish drave ashore there under Enni, but the corpses were not found. But when this news was known at Frodiswater, Kiartan and Thurid bade their neighbours to the arvale, and their Yule ale was taken and used for the arvale. But the first evening whenas men were at the feast, and were come to their seats, in came goodman Thorod and his fellows into the hall, all of them dripping wet. Men gave good welcome to Thorod, for a good portent was it deemed, since folk held it for sooth that those men should have good cheer of Ran if they, who had been drowned at sea, came to their own burial-ale; for in those days little of the olden lore was cast aside, though men were baptized and were Christian by name.

Now Thorod and his company went down the endlong sitting-hall, which was double-doored, and went into the fire-hall, and took no man's greeting, and set them down by the fire. Then the homemen fled away from the fire-hall, but Thorod and his folk sat behind there till the fires slaked, and then gat them gone. And thus it befell every evening while the arvale lasted, that they came to the fire. Much talk was hereover at the arvale, and some guessed that it would leave off when the feast was over. The guests went home after the feast, and somewhat dreary was that household left.

Now the evening that the guests went away were the meal-fires made as wont was. But when they burned up, in came Thorod and his company all dripping wet, and they sat down by the fire and fell to wringing their raiment. And so when they were sat down, in came Thorir Wooden-leg and his six followers, and they were all be-moulded, and they shook their raiment and cast the mould at Thorod and his folk.

Then the home-men fled away from the fire-hall, as might be looked for, and had neither light nor warm stones nor any matter wherewith they had any avail of the fire.

But the evening next after were fires made in another chamber, and it was deemed that they would be less likely to come thither, but it fell not out so, and all went in the same way as the night before, and both companies came to the fires. The third evening Kiartan gave counsel to make a long fire in the fire-hall, and meal-fires in another chamber. So was it done, and this availed thus much, that Thorod and his folk sat by the long fire and the home-men by the little fire; and so things went till over Yuletide.

Now it befell that more and more were things going on in the stock-fish heap, and night and day men might hear how the stock- fish was torn. And after this the time came when need was of stock-fish, and men went to search the heap; and the man who went up thereon saw this to tell of, that up from the heap came a great tail as big as a singed neat's tail, and it was short- haired and seal-haired; he who went up on to the heap caught at the tail and tugged, and called on other men to come help, him. So folk fared up on to the heap, both men and women, and tugged at the tail, and got nought done, and they thought none otherwise than that the tail was dead; but lo, as they pulled, the tail drew down through their hands, so that the skin came off the palms of those who had the firmest hold thereon, and nought was known afterwards of that tail.

Then was the stock-fish heap taken down, and every fish therein was found torn from the skin, so that there was no fish found in his skin in the lower part of the heap; but nought quick was found therein.

After these haps Thorgrima Witch-face, the wife of Thorir Wooden- leg, fell sick and lay but a little while or she died, and the very same evening that she was buried, she was seen in the company of Thorir her husband. Then the sickness fell on folk anew after the tail was seen, and more women than men died; and yet six men died in that brunt. But some fled before those hauntings and ghosts. At harvest-tide there had been thirty serving-folk there, but eighteen were dead, and five fled away, and but seven were left behind at Goi.

Chapter 55
A Door-Doom At Frodis-Water

Now when those wonders had gone so far, one day Kiartan went east unto Holyfell to go see Snorri the Priest, his mother's brother, and asked rede of him what he should do in the matter of those wonders that had fallen on them. At that time was come to Holyfell the priest that Gizur the White had sent to Snorri the Priest. So Snorri sent the priest out to Frodis-water with Kiartan, as well as his son Thord Kausi, and six men more. Thereto he added the counsel to burn Thorgunna's bed-gear, and summon all those who walked, to a door-doom; and he bade the priest sing the hours there, and hallow water and shrive all folk. So these summoned men from the nighest steads on the road, and came to Frodis-water on the eve of Candlemas at such time as the meal-fires were lighted.

By then had goodwife Thurid fallen sick even in such wise as those who had died.

Now Kiartan went in straightway and saw how Thorod and his folk sat by the fire as their wont was. So he took down Thorgunna's bed-gear, and went into the fire-hall, and caught up brands from the fire, and went out therewith, and then was all the bed-array burned that Thorgunna had owned.

Thereafter Kiartan summoned Thorir Woodenleg, and Thord Kausi summoned goodman Thorod, in that they went about that household without leave, and despoiled men both of life and luck; all were summoned who sat by the fires.

Then was a door-doom named, and these cases put forward; and it was done in all matters even as at a doom of the Thing: verdicts were delivered, cases summed up, and doom given.

But as soon as the sentence on Thorir Woodenleg was given out, he arose and said: "Here have I sat while sit I might;" and thereafter he went out by the door before which the court was not set.

Then was the sentence on the shepherd passed. But when he heard it he stood up and said: "Go I now hencefrom; I ween erst it had more seemly been."

And when Thorgrima Witch-face heard the doom on her ended, she also arose and said: "Here while abiding was meet I abode."

Then they charged one after the other, and each arose as the sentence fell on him, and all said somewhat at their going forth; but ever it seemed by the words of each that they were all loth to depart. At last was judgment given on goodman Thorod, and when he heard it he stood up and said: "Meseems little peace is here; so get us all gone otherwhere;" and therewith he went out.

Then in walked Kiartan and his folk, and the priest bare hallowed water and the holy things throughout the house, and on the next day they sang all the hours and mass with great solemnity, and so there was an end thereafter to all walkings and hauntings at Frodis-water. But Thurid got better of her sickness so that she was healed.

In the spring after these wonders Kiartan took to him serving- folk, and dwelt long after at Frodis-water, and was the greatest of the doughty.

Chapter 56
Of Snorri The Priest And The Blood-Suit After Stir

Snorri the Priest dwelt at Holyfell eight winters after Christ's faith was made law in Iceland. The last winter he dwelt there was the one wherein his father-in-law Stir was slain at Iorvi in Flisa-wharf. Then Snorri the Priest went south thither after the corpse; and he went against Stir in the women's bower at Horseholt, whenas he was sitting upright and was holding the bonder's daughter by the middle.

That spring Snorri changed lands with Gudrun Osvif's daughter, and brought his household to Tongue in Saelings-dale; that was two winters after the slaying of Bolli Thorleikson, Gudrun's husband.

The same spring Snorri went south to Burgfirth with four hundred men to follow up the suit for the slaying of Stir. In his company was Vermund the Slender, the brother of Stir, who dwelt as then at Waterfirth; Steinthor of Ere withal, and Thorod Thorbrandson of Swanfirth; Thorleik Brandson of Crossness, the brother's son of Stir, also, and many other men of worth.

The furthest south they came was to Whitewater at Howeford over against By. There they found before them, south of the river, Illugi the Black, Kleppiarn the Old, Thorstein Gislison, Gunnlaug the Wormtongue, Thorstein Thorgilson of Hafsfirthisle, who had to wife Vigdis, the daughter of Illugi the Black; and many other men of account were there, with a band of more than five hundred men.

So Snorri the Priest and his folk might nowise ride south over the river, but set forth the suit when they had gone the furthest they might without risk, and Snorri summoned Guest for the slaying of Stir.

But this same suit Thorstein Gislison brought to nought for Snorri the Priest in the summer at the Althing.

The same summer Snorri the Priest rode south to Burgfirth, and took the life of Thorstein Gislison and Gunnar his son; and still was Steinthor of Ere with him, and Thorod Thorbrandson, and

Brand Hoskuldson, and Thorleik Brandson, and they were fifteen in all.

The next spring they met at the Thing of Thorsness, Snorri the Priest to wit, and Thorstein of Hafsfirthisle, the son-in-law of Illugi the Black. Thorstein was the son of Thorgils, the son of Thorfinn, the son of Seal-Thorir of Redmel, but his mother was Aud, the daughter of Alf-a-dales; but Thorstein was the cousin of Thorgils Arison of Reek-knolls, and Thorgeir Havarson, and Thorgils Hallason, and Bitter-Oddi, and those Swanfirthers, Thorleif Kimbi and the other sons of Thorbrand.

Thorstein had at that time set on foot many cases for the Thorsness Thing. So one day on the Thing-brent, Snorri the Priest asked if Thorstein had set on foot many suits for the Thing. Thorstein answered that he had set on foot certain ones.

Then said Snorri: "Now belike wilt thou that we further thy cases for thee, even as ye Burgrifthers furthered ours last spring."

Thorstein said: "I nowise long for this."

But when Snorri had so spoken, his sons and many other kinsmen of Stir laid heavy words thereto, and said that it would serve Thorstein right well, if every one of his suits there should come to an end as it now stood, and said it was right meet that he himself should now pay for that shame which he and Illugi his father-in4aw had done to them the past summer.

Thorstein answered few words thereto, and men went therewith from the Thing-brent. However, Thorstein and his kin, the men of Redmel, had brought together a great company, and when men should go to the courts, Thorstein got ready to push forward all these suits of his which he had set on foot for the courts to adjudge. But when the kin of Stir and folk allied to him knew that, they armed themselves, and went betwixt the courts, and the Redmel- folk as they would go to the courts, and a fight befell betwixt them.

Thorstein of Hafsfirthisle would pay no heed to aught but making for the place whereas Snorri the Priest was. Both big and stark was Thorstein, and a deft man-at-arms, but when he fell fiercely on Snorri, Kiartan of Frodis-water,

Snorri's sister's son, ran before him, and Thorstein and he fought long together, and their weapon-play was exceeding hard-fought.

But thereafter friends of both sides came thither, and went between them, and brought about truce.

After the battle spake Snorri to Kiartan his kinsman, and said: "Well wentest thou forth today, Broadwicking!"

Kiartan answered somewhat wrathfully: "No need to throw my kin in my teeth," said he. In this fight fell seven of Thorstein's men, but many were wounded on either side.

These matters were settled straightly at the Thing, and Snorri the Priest was the more generous in all peace-makings, because he would not that these matters should come to the Althing, whereas the slaughter of Thorstein Gislison was yet unatoned for; and it seemed to him that he would have full enough to answer to at the Althing, though this were not brought against him. About all these things, the slaying of Thorstein Gislison, and Gunnar his son, and also about the battle at the Thorsness Thing, thus sings Thorrood Trefilson in the Raven-song:

> "Again now the great-heart,
> The Rhine-fires waster,
> Slew two men in spear-storm
> South over the water.
> Thereafter lay seven
> Life-bereft on the Ness
> Of the bane of the troll-wives.
> Thereof are there tokens."

Chapter 57
Of Uspak Of Ere In Bitter And Of His Injustice

Whenas Snorri the Priest had dwelt a few winters at Saelings- dale-Tongue, there dwelt a man at Ere in Bitter called Uspak. He was a married man, and had a son called Glum, who was young in those days. Uspak was the son of Kiallak of Kiallak's-river of Skridinsenni. Uspak was the biggest and strongest of men; he was unloved and the most unjust of men, and had with him seven or eight carles who were much in the way of picking quarrels with men in those northern parts; they had ever a ship off the land, and took from every man his goods and his drifts as it seemed them good.

A man called Alf the Little dwelt at Thambardale in Bitter. He had wealth enow, and was the greatest of men in his housekeeping; he was a Thingman of Snorri the Priest, and had the ward of his drifts round Gudlaugs-head. Alf, too, deemed himself to feel cold from Uspak and his men, and made plaint thereof to Snorri the Priest whensoever they met.

Thorir, son of Gullhard, dwelt at Tongue in Bitter in those days. He was a friend of Sturla Thiodrekson, who was called Slaying-Sturla, who dwelt at

Stead-knoll in Saurby. Thorir was a rich bonder, and a foremost man among those of Bitter, and had withal the wardship of Sturla's drifts there in the north. Full oft was grey silver in the fire betwixt Thorir and Uspak, and now one now the other came off best.

Uspak was the foremost man there about Crosswater-dale and Enni.

One winter the hard weather came on early, and straightway was there earth-ban about Bitter, whereof men had great loss of live-stock; but some drave their beasts south over the heath.

The summer before had Uspak let build a work at his stead of Ere, a wondrous good fighting-stead, if men were therein for defence.

In the winter at Goi came on a great snowstorm and held on for a week; a great northern gale it was. But when the storm abated, men saw that the ice from the main was come thither all over the outer firth, but no ice was as then come into Bitter, so men went to scan their foreshores.

Now it is to be told, that out betwixt Stika and Gudlaugs-head was a great whale driven ashore; in that whale Snorri the Priest and Sturla Thiodrekson had the greatest share; but Alf the Little and more bonders yet had certain shares in it also. So men from all Bitter go thither and cut up the whale under the ordering of Thorir and Alf.

But as men were at the cutting they saw a craft come rowing from the other side of the firth from Ere, and knew it for a great twelve-oarer that Uspak owned.

Now these landed by the whale and went up there, fifteen men all-armed in company; and when Uspak came aland he went to the whale and asked who had the rule thereover. Thorir said that he was over the share that Sturla had, but Alf over his share and that of Snorri the Priest; and that of the other bonders each saw to his own share. Uspak asked what they would hand over to him of the whale. Thorir answers: "Nought will I give thee of the portion that I deal with; but I wot not but that the bonders will sell thee of that which they own. What wilt thou pay therefor?"

"Thou knowest, Thorir," said Uspak, "that I am not wont to buy whale of you men of Bitter."

"Well," said Thorir, "I am minded to think that thou gettest none without price."

Now such of the whale as was cut lay in a heap, and was not yet apportioned out; so Uspak bid his men go thereto and bear it down to his keel; and those who were at the whale had but few weapons except the axes wherewith they were cutting it up. But when Thorir saw that Uspak and his folk went at the whale, he called out to the men not to let themselves be robbed. Then they ran to the other side of the heap, and those about the uncut whale ran therefrom, and Thorir was the swiftest of them.

Uspak turned to meet him and fetched a blow at him with his axe-hammer, and smote him on the ear so that he fell swooning; but those who were nighest caught hold of him and dragged him to them, and stood over him while he lay in the swoon, but then was the whale not guarded.

Then came up Alf the Little and bade them not take the whale. Uspak answered: "Come not nigh, Alf; thin is thy skull and heavy my axe, and far worse than Thorir shalt thou fare, if thou makest one step further forward."

This wholesome counsel thus taught him Alf followed. Uspak and his folk bore the whale down to their keel, and had got it done or ever Thorir woke up. But when he knew what had betid, he blamed his men that they had done slothfully in standing by him while some were robbed and some beaten; and therewith he sprang up. But Uspak had by then got his keel afloat, and they thrust off from the land. Then they rowed west over the firth to Ere, and Uspak let none go from him who had been in this journey; but there they had their abode and got matters ready in the work.

Thorir and his folk shared the whale, and let the loss of that which was taken fall equally on all, even according to the share which each man owned in the whale, and thereafter all went home.

And now full great enmity there was betwixt Thorir and Uspak, but whereas Uspak had a many men, the booty was soon on the wane.

Chapter 58
Uspak Robs Alf The Little. Thorir Chases Uspak

Now on a night Uspak and his men went into Thambardale fifteen in company, and set on the house of Alf the Little, and drove him and all his men into the hall while they robbed there, and bore thence four horseloads of goods.

From Firth-horn men had gotten ware of their goings, and therefore was a man sent to Tongue to tell Thorir. Thorir gathered men, and he was eighteen strong, and they went down to the firth-bottom. Then Thorir saw where Uspak and his men had passed him, and went east on the other side of Firth-horn; and when Uspak saw the chase, he said:

"Men are coming after us, and there will Thorir be going," says he; "and now will he be minded to pay me back for my blow wherewith I smote him last winter. They are eighteen, but we fifteen, yet better arrayed. Now it will not be easy to see which of us will be fainest of blows; but those horses which we have taken from Thambardale will be fain of home, yet never will I let that be taken from me which we have laid hands on; so two of us who are the worst armed shall drive the laden horses before us out to Ere, and let those men who are at home come to meet us; but we thirteen will withstand these men even as we may."

So they did as Uspak bade. But when Thorir came up, Uspak greeted him, and asked for tidings, and was soft-spoken, that so he might delay Thorir and his folk. Thorir asked whence they had those goods. Uspak says: "From Thambardale."

"How camest thou thereby?" says Thorir.

Says Uspak: "They were neither given, nor paid, nor sold at a price."

"Will ye let them go, and give them into our hands?" said Thorir.

Uspak said he could not bring himself to that, and therewith they ran each at each, and a fight befell; and Thorir and his men were of the eagerest, but Uspak and his folk defended themselves well and manly, yet some were wounded, and some slain.

Thorir had a bear-bill in his hand, and therewith he ran at Uspak and smote at him, but Uspak put the thrust from him, and whereas Thorir had thrown all his might into the blow, and there was nought before the bill, he fell on his knees and louted forward. Then Uspak smote Thorir on the back with: his axe, and loud rang the stroke; and Uspak said: "That shall stay thy long journeys, Thorir," says he.

"Maybe," says Thorir; "yet methinks a full day's journey may I go for all thee and that stroke of thine."

For Thorir had a chain-knife round his neck, as the fashion then was, and had cast it aback behind him, and the blow had come thereon, and he had but been scratched in the muscles on either side of his spine, and little enough withal.

Then ran up a fellow of Thorir's and smote at Uspak, but he thrust forth his axe, and the blow took the shaft thereof and struck it asunder, and down fell the axe. Then cried out Uspak, and bade his men flee away, and himself fell to running; but as soon as Thorir arose, he cast his bill at Uspak and smote him on the thigh, and cut through it on the outer side of the bone. Uspak drew the bill from the wound and cast it back, and it smote the man in the midst who had erst cut at Uspak, and down he fell dead to the earth.

Thereafter away ran Uspak and his following, and Thorir and his company chased them out along the foreshores well-nigh to Ere. Then came folk from the homestead, both men and women, and Thorir and his folk turned back.

And no more onslaughts were made on either side thenceforth through the winter.

At that meeting fell three of Uspak's men and one of Thorir's, but many were wounded on either side.

Chapter 59
Uspak And His Men At The Strands. They Give Up Their Work

Snorri the Priest took up all the cases of Alf the Little at the hands of Uspak and his men, and made all those guilty at the Thorsness Thing; and after the Thing he went home to Tongue, and sat at home until the time came for the court of forfeiture to sit; and then he went north to Bitter with a great company. But when he came there, then was Uspak gone with all his; and they had gone north to the Strands fifteen in company, and had five keels. They were at the Strands through the summer, and did there many unpeaceful deeds.

They set them down north in Wrackfirth, and gathered men to them, and thither came he who is called Raven and was bynamed the Viking. He was nought but an ill-doer, and had lain out north about the Strands. There they wrought great warfare with robbing and slaying of men, and held all together till towards winter-nights.

Then gathered together the Strand-men, Olaf Eyvindson, of Drangar, and other bonders with him, and fell on them. They had there a work once more about their stead in Wrackfirth, and were well-nigh thirty in company. Olaf and his folk sat down before the work, and hard to deal with they deemed it to be. So both sides talked together, and the evil-doers offered to get them gone from the Strands, and do no more unpeaceful deeds there henceforth, while the others should depart from before the work; and whereas they deemed it nowise an easy play to have to do with them, they took that choice, and both sides bound themselves by oath to this settlement, and the bonders fared home withal.

Chapter 60
Uspak Goes Back To Ere In Bitter: He Robs And Slays

Now is it to be told of Snorri the Priest that he went to the court of forfeiture north in Bitter, as is written afore, but when he came to Ere, then was Uspak gone. So Snorri held the court of forfeiture there according to law, and laid hands on all the forfeit goods, and divided them betwixt those men as had had the most ill deeds done them, Alf the Little to wit, and the other men who had had harm from robberies. Thereafter Snorri the Priest rode home to Tongue, and so wore the summer.

Now Uspak and his men went from the Strands about the beginning of winter-nights, and had two big boats. They went in past the Strands, and then south across the bay to Waterness. There they went up and robbed, and loaded both the boats up to the gunwale, and then stretched north away over the bay into Bitter and landed at Ere, and bore their spoil up into the work. There had Uspak's wife and his son Glum abode the summer through, with but two cows. Now on the very same night that they came home, they rowed both the boats down to the firth-bottom, and went up to the farm at Tongue, and broke into the house there, and took goodman Thorir from his bed, and led him out and slew him. Then they robbed all the goods that were stored there within doors, and brought them to the boats, and then rowed to Thambardale, and ran up and brake open the doors there, as at Tongue.

Alf the Little had lain down in his clothes, and when he heard the door broken open, he ran out to the secret door that was at the back of the house, and went out there through and ran up the dale. But Uspak and his folk robbed all they might lay hands upon, and brought it to their boats, and then went home to Ere with both boats laden, and brought both the liftings into the work. They brought the boats into the work withal, and filled them both with water, and then closed the work, and the best of fighting-steads it was. So thereafter they sat there the winter long.

Chapter 61
Snorri Sends For Thrand The Strider

Alf the Little ran till he came to Tongue to Snorri the Priest, and told him of his troubles, and egged him on hard to go north against Uspak and his folk. But Snorri the Priest would first hear from the north what more they had done than driving Alf from the north, or whether they meant to have a settled abode there in Bitter. A little after came tidings from Bitter in the north of the slaying of Thorir and the array which Uspak had there, and it was heard tell of men that they would not be easily won.

Then Snorri the Priest let fetch Alf's household and such goods as were left behind, and all those matters came to Tongue and were there the winter long. Snorri's unfriends laid blame on him, in that he was held by folk slow to set Alf's matters right. Snorri let them say what they would about it, and still was nought done.

Now Sturla Thiodrekson sent word from the west that he would straightway get ready to set on Uspak and his company as soon as Snorri would, and said that it was no less due of him than of Snorri to go that journey. The winter wore on till past Yule, and ever were ill deeds of Uspak and his company heard of from the north. The winter was hard, and all the firths were under ice.

But a little before Lent, Snorri the Priest sent out to Ness to Ingiald's-knoll, where dwelt a man called Thrand the Strider, and was the son of that Ingiald by whom the homestead is named at Ingiald's-knoll. Thrand was the biggest and strongest of men, and the swiftest of foot. He had been before with Snorri the Priest, and was said to be not of one shape whiles he was heathen; but the devilhood fell off from most men when they were christened.

Now Snorri sent word to Thrand, bidding him come thither to Tongue to meet him, and to get ready his journey in such guise as though he was to have certain trials of manhood on his hands. So when Thrand got Snorri's word he said to the messenger: "Thou shalt rest thyself here such time as thou wilt, but I will go at Snorri's message, so we may not journey together."

The messenger said that would be known when it was tried. But in the morning when the man awoke, lo, Thrand was clean gone. He had taken his weapons and gone east under Enni, and so as the road lay to Bulands-head, and then east across the firths to the stead called Eidi. There he took to the ice and went over Coalpit-firth and Seliafirth, and thence into Swordfirth, and so in over the ice right to the firth-end, and to Tongue in the evening, whenas Snorri was set down and at table.

Snorri welcomed him lovingly, and Thrand took his greeting and asked what he would of him, and said he was ready to go whither he would, if Snorri had will to set him about somewhat. Snorri bade him abide in peace through the night, and Thrand's wet clothes were pulled off him.

Chapter 62
Snorri And Sturla Win The Work At Ere In Bitter

The same night Snorri the Priest sent a man west to Stead-knolls to Sturla Thiodrekson, and bade him come meet him at Tongue north in Bitter the next day. Withal Snorri sent to the farmsteads thereabout, and summoned men to him, and then they went north over Gablefell-heath with fifty men, and came to Tongue in Bitter in the evening, and there was Sturla abiding them with thirty men.

They fared thence out to Ere in the night-tide, and when they were come there, Uspak and his folk went on to the wall of the work, and asked who ruled that company. They told him, and bade him give up the work, but Uspak said he would nowise yield it up.

"But we will give you the same choice that we gave to the men of the Strands," said he, "that we will get us gone from the countryside, and ye shall depart from our castle."

Then Snorri bade him offer no more of such guileful choices.

But the next day, as soon as it was light, they apportioned out the work amongst them for onset, and Snorri the Priest got that part of the work that Raven the Viking guarded, and Sturla the guard of Uspak; the sons of Bork the Thick, Sam and Thormod, fell on at one side, but Thorod and Thorstein Codbiter, the sons of Snorri the Priest, on the other.

Of weapons that they could bring to bear, Uspak and his folk had for the most part stones for their defence, and they cast them forth against their foes unsparingly; for those in the work were of the briskest.

The men of Snorri and Sturla dealt chiefly with shot, both shafts and spears; and they had got together great plenty thereof, because that they had long been getting ready for the winning of the work.

So the onset was of the fiercest, and many were wounded on either side, but none slain. Snorri and his folk shot so thick and fast, that Raven with his men gave back from the wall. Then Thrand the Strider made a run at the wall, and leaped up so high that he got his axe hooked over the same, and therewith he drew himself up by the axe-shaft till he came up on to the work. But whenas Raven saw that a man had got on to the work, he ran at Thrand, and thrust at him with a spear, but Thrand put the thrust from him, and smote Raven on the arm close by the shoulder, and struck off the arm. After that many men came on him, and he let himself fall down outside the wall, and so came to his own folk.

Uspak egged on his men to stand stoutly, and fought himself in right manly wise; and when he cast stones he would go right out on the wall.

But at last whenas he was putting himself very forward and casting a stone at Sturla's company, at that very nick of time Sturla shot a twirl-spear at him, which smote him in the midst, and down he fell outside of the work. Sturla straightway ran to him, and took him to himself, and would not that more men should be at the slaying of him, because he was fain that there should be but one tale to tell of his having been the banesman of Uspak. Another man fell on that same wall where the sons of Bork fell on.

Thereon the Vikings offered to give up the work, life and limb saved, and therewithal that they would lay all their case under the doom of Snorri the Priest and Sturla.

So whereas Snorri and his men had pretty much spent their shot, they said yea to this. So the.work was given up, and those within rendered themselves to Snorri the Priest, and he gave them all peace of life and limb, even as they had claimed. Both Uspak and Raven died forthwith, and a third man withal of their company, but many were wounded on either side. So says Thormod in the Raven-song:

> "Fight fell there in Bitter;
> The maker of stir meseems
> For the choughs of the war-maidens
> Brought home the quarry.
> Three leaders of sea-wain
> Lay life-void before him,
> The fanner of fight-pith.
> There Raven gat resting."

Chapter 63
Of The Walking Of Thorolf Halt-Foot. He Is Dug Up And Burned. Of The Bull Glossy

In those days dwelt Thorod Thorbrandson in Swanfirth, and had the lands both of Ulfar's-fell and of Orligstead; but to such a pass had come the haunting of Thorolf Halt-foot, that men deemed they might not abide on those lands. Lairstead withal was voided, because Thorolf straightway took to walking as soon as Arnkel was dead, and slew both men and beasts there at Lairstead; nor has any man had a heart to dwell there, by reason of these things.

Then when all things were waste there, Haltfoot betook himself to Ulfar's-fell, and wrought great trouble there, and all folk were full of dread as soon as they were ware of Halt-foot's walking. At last the bonder fared in to Karstead, and bemoaned himself of that trouble to Thorod, because he was tenant of him, and he said that it was the fear of men that Halt-foot would not leave off before he had wasted all the firth both of man and beast, "and if no rede is tried I can no longer abide there, if nought be done herein."

But when Thorod heard that, he deemed the matter ill to deal with. But the next morning he let bring his horse, and called his house-carles to him, and gathered men to him from the nighest steads withal; and then they fare out to Haltfoot's-head, and come to Thorolf's howe; and he was even yet unrotten, and as like to a fiend as like could be, blue as hell, and big as a neat; and when they went about the raising of him, they could in nowise stir him. So Thorod let set lever-beams under him, and thereby they brought him up from the howe, and rolled him down to the seaside, and cut there a great bale, and set fire to it, and rolled Thorolf thereinto, and burned all up to cold coals; yet long it was or ever the fire would take on him. There was a stiff breeze, which scattered the ashes wide about as soon as the bale began to burn; but such of the ashes as they might, they cast out seaward; and so when they had made an end of the business they went home.

Now it was the time of the night-meal whenas Thorod came home, and the women were at the milking; but as Thorod rode by the milking-stead a certain cow started from before him, and brake her leg. Then was she felt, but was found so meagre that it was not deemed good to slaughter her; so Thorod let bind up her leg; but she became utterly dry.

So when the cow's leg was whole again, she was brought out to Ulfar's-fell to fatten, because there the pasture was good, as it might be in an island.

Now the cow went often down to the strand and the place: whereas the bale had been litten, and licked the stones on which the ashes thereof had been driven; and some men say, that whenas the island-men went along the firth with lading of stockfish, they saw there the cow up on the hillside, and another neat with her, dapple-grey of hide, of which neat no man knew how it might be there.

So in the autumn Thorod was minded to slaughter the cow, but when men went after her, she was nowhere to be found. Thorod sent after her often that autumn, but found her not, and men deemed no otherwise than that the cow was dead or stolen away.

But a little short of Yule, early on a morning at Karstead, as the herdsman went to the byre according to his wont, he saw a neat before the byre-door, and knew that thither was come the broken-legged cow which had been missing. So he led the cow into the boose and bound her, and then told Thorod. Thorod went to the byre and saw the cow, and laid his hand on her, and now finds that she is with calf, and thinks good not to kill her; and withal he had by then done all the slaughtering for his household whereof need was.

But in the spring, when summer was a little worn, the cow bore a calf, a cow-calf, and then a little after another which was a bull, and it went hardly with her, so big he was, and in a little while the cow died. So this same big calf was borne into the hall; dapple-grey of hue he was and right goodly.

Now whenas both the calves were in the hall, this one and that first born, there was therein withal an ancient carline, Thorod's foster-mother, who was as then blind. She was deemed to have been foreseeing in her earlier days, but as she grew old, all she said was taken for doting; nevertheless, things went pretty much according to her words.

So as the big calf was bound upon the floor, he cried out on high, and when the carline heard that, she started sorely, and spoke: "The voice of a troll," quoth she, "and of nought else alive; do the best ye can and slay this boder of woe straight-way."

Thorod said he would nowise slay the calf; for that it was well worthy to be nourished, and that it would turn out a noble beast if it were brought up; therewith the calf cried out yet again.

Then spake the carline, all a-flutter: "Fair foster-son," says she, "prithee kill the calf, for ill shall we have of him if he be brought up."

So he answers: "Well, I will kill him if thou wilt have it so, foster-mother."

Then were both the calves borne out, and Thorod let kill the cow- calf, and bear the other out to the barn, and withal he bade folk take heed that the carline was not told that the bull-calf was yet alive.

Now this calf grew greater day by day, so that in spring when the calves were let out, he was no less than those which had been born in the early winter. He ran about the home-mead bellowing loudly when he was let out, even as a bull might, so that he was heard clearly in the house. Then said the carline: "Ah, the troll was not slain then, and we shall have more harm of him than words can tell."

The calf waxed speedily, and went about the home-mead the summer long, and by autumn-tide was so big, that few yearling neats were equal to him; well horned he was, and the fairest of all neat to look on, and he was called Glossy. When he was two years old, he was as big as a five-year-old ox, and he was ever at home with the cows; and when Thorod went to the milking-stead, Glossy would go to him and sniff at him and lick his clothes all about, and Thorod would pat and stroke him. He was as tame both to man and beast as a sheep, but ever when he bellowed he gave forth a great and hideous voice, and when the carline heard, she started sorely thereat. When Glossy was four winters old, he would not be driven by women, children, or young men; and if the carles went up to him, he would rear up, and go on in perilous wise, and yet would give way before them if hard pressed.

Now on a day Glossy came home to the byre and bellowed wondrous loud, so that he was heard as clearly in the house as though he were hard thereby. Thorod was in the hall and the carline by him, who sighed heavily and said:

"Of no account dost thou hold my word concerning the slaughtering of the bull, foster-son."

Thorod answered: "Be content, foster-mother," says he; "Glossy shall live on till autumn, and then be slaughtered, when he has got the summer's flesh oil him."

"Over-late will it be then," says she.

"That is a hard matter to tell," says Thorod. But as they spake, again the bull gave forth a voice, bellowing yet worse than before. Then sang the carline this song:

> "O shaker of snow on the hair's hall that shineth,
> Forth out of his head is the herd-leader sending
> A voice and a crying that bodeth us blood;
> And the life-days of men now his might overlayeth.

He who shaketh the green-sward will teach thee the heeding
Of the place where thine earth-gash for thee is a-gaping.
O foster-son mine, now full clearly I see it,
That the horned beast in fetters is laying thy life."

Chapter 64
The Last Tidings Of Biorn The Champion Of The Broadwickers

There was a man named Gudleif, the son of Gunnlaug the Wealthy of Stream-firth, the brother of Thorfin, from whom are come the Sturlungs. Gudleif was much of a seafarer, and he owned a big ship of burden, and Thorolf, the son of Loft-o'-th'-Ere, owned another, whenas they fought with Gyrd, son of Earl Sigvaldi; at which fight Gyrd lost his eye.

But late in the days of King Olaf the Holy, Gudleif went a merchant voyage west to Dublin, and when he sailed from the west he was minded for Iceland, and he sailed round Ireland by the west, and fell in with gales from east and north-east, and so drove a long way west into the main and south-westward withal, so that they saw nought of land; by then was the summer pretty far spent, and therefore they made many vows, that they might escape from out the main.

But so it befell at last that they were ware of land; a great land it was, but they knew nought what land. Then such rede took Gudleif and his crew, that they should sail unto land, for they thought it ill to have to do any more with the main sea; and so then they got them good haven.

And when they had been there a little while, men came to meet them whereof none knew aught, though they deemed somewhat that they spake in the Erse tongue. At last they came in such throngs that they made many hundreds, and they laid hands on them all, and bound them, and drove them up into the country, and they were brought to a certain mote and were doomed thereat. And this they came to know, that some would that they should be slain, and othersome that they should be allotted to the countryfolk, and be their slaves.

And so, while these matters are in debate, they see a company of men come riding, and a banner borne over the company, and it seemed to them that there should be some great man amongst these; and so as that company drew nigh, they saw under the banner a man riding, big and like a great chief of aspect, but much stricken in years, and hoary withal; and all they who were there before, worshipped that man, and greeted him as their lord, and they soon found that all counsels and awards were brought whereas he was.

So this man sent for Gudleif and his folk, and whenas they came before him, he spake to them in the tongue of the Northmen, and asked them whence of lands they were. They said that they were Icelanders for the more part. So the man asked who the Icelanders might be.

Then Gudleif stood forth before the man, and greeted him in worthy wise, and he took his greeting well, and asked whence of Iceland he was. And he told him, of Burgfirth. Then asked he whence of Burgfirth he was, and Gudleif told him. After that he asked him closely concerning each and all of the mightiest men of Burgfirth and Broadfirth, and amidst this speech he asked concerning Snorri the Priest, and his sister Thurid of Frodiswater, and most of all of the youngling Kiartan, who in those days was gotten to be goodman of Frodiswater.

But now meanwhile the folk of that land were crying out in another place that some counsel should be taken concerning the ship's crew; so the big man went away from them, and called to him by name twelve of his own men, and they sat talking a long while, and thereafter went to the man-mote.

Then the big man said to Gudleif and his folk: "We people of the country have talked your matter over somewhat, and they have given the whole thing up to my ruling; and I for my part will give you leave to go your ways whithersoever ye will; and though ye may well deem that the summer wears late now, yet will I counsel you to get you gone hence, for here dwelleth a folk untrusty and ill to deal with, and they deem their laws to be already broken of you."

Gudleif says: "What shall we say concerning this, if it befall us to come back to the land of our kin, as to who has given us our freedom?"

He answered- "That will I not tell you; for I should be ill- content that any of my kin or my foster-brethren should make such a voyage hither as ye would have made, had I not been here for your avail; and now withal," says he, "my days have come so far, that on any day it may be looked for that eld shall stride over my head; yea, and though I live yet awhile, yet are there here men mightier than I, who will have little will to give peace to outland men; albeit they be not abiding nearby whereas ye have now come."

Then this man let make their ship ready for sea and abode with them till the wind was fair for sailing; and or ever he and Gudleif parted, he drew a gold ring from off his arm, and gave it into Gudleif's hand, and therewithal a good sword, and then spake to Gudleif: "If it befall thee to come back to thy fosterland, then shalt thou deliver this sword to that Kiartan, the goodman at Frodiswater; but the ring to Thurid his mother."

Then said Gudleif: "And what shall we say concerning the sender of these good things to them?"

He answered: "Say that he sends them who was a greater friend of the goodwife of Frodiswater than of the Priest of Holyfell, her brother; but and if any shall deem that they know thereby who owned these fair things, tell them this my word withal, that I forbid one and all to go seek me, for this land lacks all peace, unless to such as it may befall to come aland in such lucky wise as ye have done; the land also is wide, and harbours are ill to find therein, and in all places trouble and war await outland men, unless it befall them as it has now befallen you."

Thereafter they parted. Gudleif and his men put to sea, and made Ireland late in the autumn, and abode in Dublin through the winter. But the next summer Gudleif sailed to Iceland, and delivered the goodly gifts there, and all men held it for true that this must have been Biorn the Broadwick Champion; but no other true token have men thereof other, than these even now told.

Chapter 65
The Kindred Of Snorri The Priest; The Death Of Him

Snorri the Priest dwelt at Tongue for twenty winters, and at first had a power there somewhat begrudged, while those brawlers were alive, Thorstein Kuggison to wit, and Thorgils the son of Halla, besides other of the greater men who bore him ill-will. Withal he cometh into many stories, and of him the tale also telleth in the story of the Laxdale men, as is well known to many; whereas he was the greatest friend of Gudrun, the daughter of Osvif, and of her sons. He also hath to do with the story of the Heathslaughters, and most of all men, next indeed to Gudmund the Rich, lent aid to Bardi after the manslayings on the Heath.

But as he grew older, ill-will against him began to wane, chiefly by reason of those who bore him envy growing fewer. His friendships were greatly bettered by his knitting alliances with the greatest chiefs in Broadfirth and wide about elsewhere.

He married his daughter Sigrid to Brand the Bounteous, the son of Vermund the Slender; Kolli, the son of Thormod, the son of Thorlak, the brother of Steinthor of Ere, had her to wife thereafter; and they, Kolli and Sigrid, had house in Bearhaven.

His daughter Unn he married to Slaying-Bardi; Sigurd, the son of Thorir Hound of Birch-isle in Halogaland, had her to wife afterwards, and their daughter was Ranveig, whom Jon, the son of Arni, the son of Arni, the son of Arnmod, had to wife; their son was Vidkunn of Birch-isle, whilome one of the foremost among the barons of Norway.

His daughter Thordis, Snorri married to Bolli, son of Bolli, and from them is sprung the race of the Gilsbeckings.

His daughter Hallbera, Snorri married to Thord, the son of Sturla Thiodrekson, whose daughter was Thurid, the wife of Haflidi Marson, and from them a mighty kindred has sprung.

Thora his daughter, Snorri married to Keru-Bersi, the son of Haldor, the son of Olaf of Herdholt; Thorgrim the Burner afterwards had her to wife, and from them a great and a noble kin has sprung.

The other daughters of Snorri were married after his death. Thurid the Wise, the daughter of Snorri, Gunnlaug, the son of Steinthor of Ere, had for wife; but Gudrun, the daughter of Snorri the Priest, was wedded to Kalf of Sunhome. Thorgeir of Asgarths-knolls married Haldora, Snorri's daughter. Alof, Snorri's daughter, Jorund Thorfinnson had to wife; he was brother to Gudlaug of Streamfirth.

Haldor, the son of Snorri the Priest, was the noblest of his sons; he kept house in Herdholt in Laxdale. From him are come the Sturlungs and the Waterfirth folk. The second noblest son of Snorri the Priest was Thorod, who abode at Spaewife's-fell in Skagastrand.

Mani, the son of Snorri, dwelt at Sheepfell; his son was Liot, who was called Mana-Liot and was accounted of as the greatest among the grandsons of Snorri the Priest.

Thorstein, the son of Snorri, dwelt at Bathbrent, and from him are sprung the Asbirnings in Skagafiord, and a great stock withal.

Thord Kausi, Snorri's son, dwelt in Dufgusdale.

Eyolf, the son of Snorri, dwelt at Lambstead on the Mires.

Thorleif, the son of Snorri the Priest, dwelt on Midfell-strand; from him are sprung the men of Ballara.

Snorri, the son of Snorri the Priest, dwelt in Tongue after his father.

Klepp was hight a son of Snorri whose abiding-place men wot nought of, nor know men any tales to tell of him.

Snorri died in Saelings-dale-Tongue one winter after the fall of King Olaf the Holy. He was buried at the church he let rear at Tongue; but at the time the church was moved, his bones were taken up and brought down to the place whereas the church now is; and a witness thereat was Gudny, Bodvar's daughter, the mother of those sons of Sturla: Snorri, Thord, and Sighvat, to wit; and she said that they were bones of a man of middle height, and not right big. At that same time were also taken out of earth the bones of Bork the Thick, the father's brother of Snorri the Priest; and she said that they were mighty big. Then, too, were dug out the bones of the carline Thordis, the daughter of Thorbiorn Sur, the mother of Snorri the Priest; and Gudny said that they were small bones of a woman, and as black as if they had been singed.

All these bones were buried again in earth where the church is now.

And herewith endeth the Story of the Thornessings, the Ere-Dwellers and the Swanfirthers.

THE SAGA OF THE HEATH SLAYINGS

Chapter 1
Thorarin Bids Bardi Concerning The Choosing Of Men

NOW Bardi and his brethren had on hand much wright's work that summer, and the work went well the summer through, whereas it was better ordered than heretofore. Now summer had worn so far that but six weeks thereof were left. Then fares Bardi to Lechmote to meet Thorarin his fosterer; often they talked together privily a long while, and men knew not clearly what they said.

"Now will there be a man-mote," says Thorarin, "betwixt the Hope and Huna-water, at the place called Thing-ere. But I have so wrought it that heretofore none have been holden.

"Now shalt thou fare thither and prove thy friends; because now I look for it that many men will be together there, since man-motes have so long been put off. In crowds they will be there, and I ween that Haldor thy foster-brother will come thither. Crave thou fellowship of him and avail, if thine heart is anywise set on faring away from the country-side and the avenging of thy brother.

"A stead there is called Bank, lying west of Huna-water;" there dwelt a woman hight Thordis, by-named Gefn, a widow; there was a man with her over her housekeeping, hight Odd, a mighty man of his hands, not exceeding wealthy nor of great kin, but a man well renowned. "Of him shalt thou crave following; for he shall rule his answer himself."

"In that country is a place called Blizzard-mere, where are many steads, one of which is Middleham;" there dwelt a man hight Thorgisl; he was by kin mother's sister's son of Gefn's-Odd; a valiant man and a good skald, a man of good wealth, and a mighty man of his hands. "Call thou on him to fare with thee."

"A stead there is hight Bowerfell, twixt Swinewater and Blanda; it is on the Necks to the westward." There dwelt a man hight Eric, by-named Wide-sight; he was a skald and no little man of might. "Him shalt thou call to thy fellowship."

"In Longdale is a house called Audolfstead," where dwelt the man hight Audolf; "he is a good fellow and mighty of his hands; his brother is Thorwald." He is not told of as having aught to do with the journey; he dwelt at the place called Evendale, which lieth up from Swinewater. "There are two steads so called." He was the strongest man of might of all the North-country. "Him shalt thou not call on for this journey, and the mood of his mind is the reason for why."

"There is a stead called Swinewater;" and there dwelt the man hight Summerlid, who was by-named the Yeller, wealthy of fee and of good account. There dwelt in the house with him his daughter's son who hight Thorliot, Yeller's fosterling, a valiant man. "Pray him to be of thy fellowship."

A man hight Eyolf dwelt at Asmund's-nip, "which is betwixt the Water and Willowdale." "Him shalt thou meet and bid him fare with thee; he is our friend."

"Now meseemeth," saith he, "that little will come of it though thou puttest this forward at the man-mote; but sound them there about the matter, and say thou. that they shall not be bound to fare with thee, if thou comest not to each one of them on the Saturday whenas it lacketh yet five weeks of winter. And none such shalt thou have with thee who is not ready to go, for such an one is not right trusty. Therefore shalt thou the rather choose these men to fare with thee than others of the country- side, whereas they are near akin to each other; they are men of good wealth, and so also their kinsmen no less; so that they are all as one man. Withal they are the doughtiest men of all who are here in Willowdale, and in all our parishes; and they will be best willed towards thy furtherance who are most our friends. Now is it quite another thing to have with one good men and brave, rather than runagates untried, men of nought, to fall back upon, if any trouble happen. Now withal thy home-men are ready to fare with thee, and thy neighbours, who are both of thy kindred and thine alliance: such as Eyolf of Burg thy brother- in-law, a doughty man, and a good fellow."

"There is a stead called Ternmere in Westhope, where dwell two brothers." One was hight Thorod, the other Thorgisl; they were the sons of Hermund, and nephews of Bardi as to kinship; men of good wealth, great champions, and good of daring. "These men will be ready to fare with thee."

Two brothers yet are named who lived at Bardi's home, one hight Olaf, the other Day, sons of a sister of Bardi s mother, and they had grown up there in Gudmund's house; "they be ready to fare with thee."

Two men more are named, one hight Gris and by-named Kollgris, a man reared there at Asbiorn's-ness. He was a deft man and the foreman of them there, and had for long been of good-will toward them.

The other hight Thord, by-named Fox; he was the fosterling of Thurid and Gufimund. They had taken him a little bairn from off the road, and had reared him. He was a full ripe man, and well of his hands; and men say that there was nought either of word or deed that might not be looked for of him; Gudmund and his wife loved him much, and made more of him than he was of worth. "This man will be ready to fare from home with thee."

Now are the men named who were to fare with Bardi.

And when they had held such talk, they sundered.

Chapter 2
Of Bardi's Way-Fellows

The Lord's day cometh Bardi to Lechmote, and rideth on thence to the man-mote; and by then he came was much folk there come, and good game is toward. Now were men eager for game, whereas the man-motes had been dropped so long. Little was done in the case, though men were busy in talk at that meeting.

Now the foster-brethren Haldor and Bardi fell to talk together, and Bardi asks whether he would fare with him somewhat from out the country-side that autumn. Says Haldor: "Belike it will be found that on my part I utter not a very manly word, when I say that my mind is not made up for this journey. Now all things are ready for my faring abroad, on which faring I have been twice bent already. But I have settled this in my mind, if ever perchance I may have my will, to be to thee of avail that may be still greater, shouldst thou be in need of it, and ever hereafter if thou be hard bestead; and this also is a cause hereof, that there are many meeter than I for the journey that, as my mind tells me, thou art bent on."

Bardi understood that so it was as he said, and he said that he would be no worse friend to him than heretofore.

"But I will bid thee somewhat," says Haldor; "it befell here last summer, that I fell out with a man hight Thorarin, and he was wounded by my onslaught. He is of little account for his own sake, but those men claim boot for him of whose Thing he is, and of much account are they. Now it is not meet for me to put Eilif and Hoskuld from the boot, so I will thou make peace for me in the matter, as I cannot bring myself to it, whereas I have nay- said hitherto to offer them atonement."

Then goeth Bardi forthwith to meet Eilif and Hoskuld, and straightway takes up the word on behalf of Haldor, and they bespeak a meeting between themselves for the appeasing of the case, when it lacked four weeks of winter, at the Cliffs, Thorarin's dwelling.

Now cometh Bardi to speech with Gefn's-Odd that he should fare with him south to Burgfirth.

Odd answereth his word speedily: "Yea, though thou hadst called on me last winter, or two winters ago, I had been all ready for this journey."

Then met Bardi Thorgisl, the sister's son of Odd's mother, and put the same words before him. He answereth: "That will men say, that thou hast not spoken hereof before it was to be looked for, and fare shall I if thou willest."

Then meeteth he Arngrim, the fosterling of Audolf, and asked him if he would be in the journey with him; and he answereth: "Ready am I, when thou art ready."

The same talk held he with all them afore-named, and all they took his word well.

Now spake Bardi: "In manly wise have ye dealt with me herein; now therefore will I come unto you on the Saturday, when it lacketh five weeks of winter; and if I come not thus, then are ye nowise bound to fare with me."

Now ride men home from the man-mote, and they meet, the foster- father and son, Thorarin and Bardi, and Bardi tells him of the talk betwixt him and Haldor. Thorarin showed that it liked him well, and said that the journey would happen none the less though Haldor fared not. "Yea, he may yet stand thee in good stead. And know that I have made men ware of this journey for so short a while, because I would that as late as might be aforehand should it be heard of in the country of those Burgfirthers."

Chapter 3
Of Bardi And His Workman Thord The Fox

Now wears the time, till Friday of the sixth week, and at nones of that day home came the home-men of Bardi, and had by then pretty much finished with their hay-work.

Bardi and his brethren were without, when the workmen came, and they greeted them well. They had their work-tools with them, and Thord the Fox was dragging his scythe behind him.

Quoth Bardi: "Now draggeth the Fox his brush behind him."

"So is it," saith Thord, "that I drag my brush behind me, and cock it up but little or nought; but this my mind bodes me, that thou wilt trail thy brush very long or ever thou avenge Hall thy brother."

Bardi gave him back no word in revenge, and men go to table.

Those brethren were speedy with their meat, and stood up from table straightway, and Bardi goeth up to Thord the Fox and spake with him, laying before him the work he shall do that evening and the day after, Saturday to wit.

Forty haycocks lay yet ungathered together in Asbiorn's-ness; and he was to gather them together, and have done with it that evening. "Moreover, to-morrow shalt thou fare to fetch our bell- wether hight the Flinger, whereas our wethers be gone from the sheepwalks, and come into the home-pastures."

Now he bade Thord to this, because the wether was worse to catch than other sheep, and swifter withal. "Now further to-morrow shalt thou go to Ambardale, and fetch home the five-year-old ox which we have there, and slaughter him, and bring all the carcass south to Burg on Saturday. Great is the work, but if thou win it not, then shalt thou try which of us bears the brush most cocked thenceforward."

Thord answered and said that often he had heard his big threats; and thereof he is nowise blate.

Now rideth Bardi in the evening to Lechmote, and the brethren together, and Bardi and Thorarin talk together the evening through.

Chapter 4
Concerning Thord The Fox

Now it is to be told of Thord's business, how he got through with it. He gathered together the hay which had stood less safely; and when he came home, then was the shepherd about driving the sheep out to the Cliffs, and Thord rides the horse whereon he had been carting the evening long. Now he finds the flock of wethers to which he had been told off, but could not overhaul them till he got out to Hope-oyce; so he slaughters that wether and rideth home with the carcass. By this time he has foundered the horse; so he takes another, and gallops over the dale, as forthright the way lay, nor did he heed whether he was faring by night or by day. He cometh to Ambardale in early morn, and getteth the ox, and slaughtereth him and dighteth him, bindeth the carcass on his horse, and going his ways cometh home again, and layeth down the carcass. Then he taketh out the carcass of the wether, and when he cometh back one limb of the ox is gone. No good words spake Thord thereover; but a man owneth that he had taken it away, and bids him be nought so bold as to speak aught thereof unless he would have a clout. So Thord taketh the rest of the carcass, and fareth south to Burg as he had been bidden.

There Alof, the sister of Bardi, and her foster-mother taketh in the flesh-meat. The foster-mother also hight Alof, a wise woman, and foster-mother also of Bardi and the other sons of Gudmund. She was called Kiannok, and thus by that name were the two Alofs known apart. Alof, Bardi's fosterer, was wise exceedingly; she could see clearly a many things, and was well-wishing to the sons of Gudmund. She was full of lore, and ancient things were stored in her mind.

Chapter 5
Of The Horses Of Thord Of Broadford

Now must it be told what wise they talked together, Thorarin his fosterer and Bardi, before Bardi got to the road; they talked of a many things.

It was early of the Saturday morning, whereon he should go meet his fellows who were to fare with him. But when he was ready to ride, there were led forth two horses, white with black ears either of them. Those horses did Thord of Broadford own, and they had vanished away that summer from the Thing.

Now spake Thorarin: "Here are Thord's horses; thou shalt go and bring them to him, and take no reward therefor: neither is it worth rewarding; for I it was who caused them to vanish away, and they have been in my keeping, and hard enough matter for me has it been to see to their not being taken and used. But for this cause let I take these horses, that meseemed it would be more of an errand to ask after these horses than mere jades. So I have often sent men south to Burgfirth this summer to ask after them. Meseemed that was a noteworthy errand, and that they would not see through my device; and I have but newly sent a man south, and from the south will he come to-morrow, and tell us tidings of the South-country."

Now just then was there a market toward at Whitewater-meads, and ships were come from the main but a little while before these things befell.

Chapter 6
Bardi Gathers In His Following

Now rideth Bardi thence and cometh to Bank, whereas dwelt Thordis, and there stood a saddled horse and a shield there beside him, and they rode home to the house with much din in the home-mead over the hard field.

Without there was a man, and a woman with him, who was washing his head; and these were Thordis and Odd, and she had not quite done the washing of his head, and had not yet washed the lather therefrom.

So straightway when he saw Bardi he sprang up, and welcomed him laughing.

Bardi took his greeting well, and bade the woman finish her work and wash him better.

Even so he let her do, and arrayed himself and went with Bardi.

Now came they north over Blanda to Broadford, and brought Thord his horses.

It is to be told that, at that time in the week just worn, was Thorgisl Arason ridden north to Eyiafirth, whereas he was to be wedded at Thwartwater, and he was to be looked for from the north the next week after. Thord takes his horses well, and offers some good geldings as a reward. But Bardi said that he would take no reward therefor; and such, he said, was the bidding of him who had found the horses. "Thou, friend," saith he, "shalt be my friend at need."

Then Bardi rides into Longdale, and over the meadows close anigh to the stead of Audolf; and they saw how a man rode down from the home-mead, and they deemed it would be Arngrim their fellow; and he rideth with them.

Now ride they west over Blanda to Eric Widesight, and they came there by then the sheep were being tended at morning-meal time, betwixt noon and day-meal, and they come on the shepherd and ask him whether Eric were at home.

He said that Eric was a-horseback at sunrise, "and now we know not whither he has ridden."

"What thinkest thou mostlike as to where he has ridden?" says Bardi. For it cometh into his mind that he will have slunk away, and will not fare with them. But nought was it found to be so that he had slunk off away. Now they saw two men riding down along Swinewater; for thence from the stead one could see wide about, and they knew them for Eric Wide-sight and Thorliot, Yeller's fosterling. They met there whereas the water hight Laxwater falleth out of Swinewater, and either greeted the other well.

Now they ride till they come to Thorgisl of Middleham; they greeted each other well and ride away thence and come hard on Gorge-water. Then said Bardi that men should ride to the stead at Asmund's-nip and meet Eyolf Oddson. "There rideth a man," said he, "nor laggardly either, from the stead, and down along the river; and meseemeth," saith he, "that there will be Eyolf; I deem that he will be at the ford by then we come there; so ride we forth."

So did they, and saw a man by the ford, and knew him for Eyolf; and they met and greeted each other well. Then they go their ways and come to the place called Ash in Willowdale. Then there came riding up to meet Bardi and his fellowship three men in coloured raiment, and they met presently, whereas each were riding towards the other; and two sister's sons of Bardi were in that company, and one hight Lambkar and the other Hun; but the third man in their fellowship was a Waterdaler. They had all come out and landed west in Willowdale, but Gudbrand their father and Gudrun their mother dwelt west in Willowdale, at the stead called thereafter Gudbrandstead.

Now was there a joyful meeting betwixt those kinsmen, whereas Bardi met his sister's sons, and either told the other what tidings there were.

Bardi tells of his journey, whither he was bound.

These men were eighteen winters old, and had been abroad one winter. They were the noblest of men both for goodlihead and might, and goodly crafts and deftness, and moreover they would have been accounted of as doughty of deed even had they come already to their full age.

Now they took counsel together, and said that they were minded to betake them to the journey with them, but their fellow fared away into Willowdale.

Now Bardi rides till he comes to Lechmote, and tells his fosterer how matters stood. Thorarin says: "Now shalt thou ride home to Asbiorn's-ness; but to-morrow will I ride to meet thee, and Thorberg my son with me; and then will I ride on the way with you."

Chapter 7
Of The Egging-On of Thurid

Now fares Bardi home with his fellowship, and abides at home that night. On the morrow Kollgris arrays them breakfast; but the custom it was that the meat was laid on the board before men, and no dishes there were in those days. Then befell this unlooked- for thing, that three portions were gone from three men. Kollgris went and told Bardi thereof.

"Go on dighting the board," said he, "and speak not thereof before other men."

But Thurid said that to those sons of hers he should deal no portion of breakfast, but she would deal it.

Kollgris did even so, and set forth the board, a trencher for each man, and set meat thereon.

Then went in Thurid and laid a portion before each of those brethren, and there was now that ox-shoulder cut up in three.

Taketh up Steingrim the word and said: "Hugely is this carved, mother, nor hast thou been wont to give men meat in such measureless fashion. Unmeasured mood there is herein, and nigh witless of wits art thou become."

She answereth: "No marvel is this, and nought hast thou to wonder thereat; for bigger was Hall thy brother caryen, and I heard ye tell nought thereof that any wonder was that."

She let a stone go with the flesh-meat for each one of them; and they asked what that might betoken. She answereth: "Of that ye brethren have most which is no more likely for avail than are these stones (for food), insomuch as ye have not dared to avenge Hall your brother, such a man as he was; and far off have ye fallen away from your kinsmen, the men of great worth, who would not have sat down under such shame and disgrace as yea long while have done, and gotten the blame of many therefor."

Then she walked up along the floor shrieking, and sang a stave:

> "I say that the cravers of songs of the battle
> Now soon shall be casting their shame-word on Bardi.
> The tale shall be told of thee, God of the wound-worm,
> That thy yore-agone kindred with shame thou undoest;
> Unless thou, the ruler of light once a-lying
> All under the fish-road shall let it be done,
> That the lathe-fire's bidders at last be red-hooded.
> Let all folk be hearkening this song of my singing."

Chapter 8
How Foster-Father And Foster-Mother Array Bardi

Now Bardi and his flock ride their ways till they are but a little short of Burg. Then ride up certain men to meet them, who but Thorarin the Priest, Bardi's fosterer, and Thorberg his son.

They straightway fall to talk, and the fosterer and fosterling come to speech. "Nay, foster-father," saith Bardi, "great is the sword which thou layest there across thy knee."

"Hast thou not seen me have this weapon before, thou heedful and watchful?" saith Thorarin. "So it is, I have not had it before. And now shall we two shift weapons; I shall have that which thou now hast."

So did they; and Bardi asks whence it came to him. He told him, with all the haps of how it fared betwixt him who owned it and Lyng-Torfi, and how he had drawn him in to seek the weapons. "But Thorberg my son hath the other weapon, and Thorbiorn owns that, but Thorgaut owns that which thou hast. Most meet it seemed to me, that their own weapons should lay low their pride and masterful mood; therefore devised I this device, and therewithal this, that thou mightest avenge thee of the shame that they have done to thee and thy kindred. Now will I that thou be true to my counsel with me, such labour as I have put forth for thine honour."

Now ride they into the home-mead of Burg unto Eyolf, the brother- in-law of those brethren. There were two harnessed horses before the door when Bardi came into the garth; and on one of them was the victual of the brethren, and were meant for provision for their journey; and that was the meaning of the new-slain flesh- meat which Bardi let bring thither erst; but Alof their sister and Kiannok, Bardi's foster-mother, had dight the same.

Now Eyolf leaps a-horseback and is all ready to ride into the home-mead from the doors. Then came out a woman and called on Bardi, and said that he should ride back to the doors, and that she had will to speak with him; and she was Alof, his sister. He bade the others ride on before, and said that he would not tarry them.

So he cometh to the door and asketh her what she would. She biddeth him light down and come see his foster-mother. So did he, and went in. The carline was muttering up at the further end of the chamber, as she lay in her bed there. "Who goeth there now?" says she.

He answereth: "Now is Bardi here; what wilt thou with me, foster- mother?"

"Come thou hither," saith she; "welcome art thou now. Now have I slept," saith she, "but I waked through the night arraying thy victual along with thy sister. Come thou hither, and I will stroke thee over."

Bardi did according to her word, for he loved her much.

She fell to work, beginning with the crown of his head and stroked him all over right down to the toes.

Bardi said: "What feelest thou herein, and what art thou minded will be, that thou strokest me so carefully?"

She answereth: "I think well of it; nowhere meseemeth is aught in the way of a big bump, to come upon."

Bardi was a big man and stark of pith, and thick was the neck of him; she spans his neck with her hands, and taketh from her sark a big pair of beads which was hers, and winds it about his neck, and draggeth his shirt up over it.

He had a whittle at his neck in a chain, and that she let abide. Then she bade him farewell; and he rideth away now after his fellows; but she called after him, "Let it now abide so arrayed, as I have arrayed it; and meseemeth that then things will go well."

Chapter 9
Of Thorarin's Arraying

Now when he cometh up with his fellowship, they ride their ways. Thorarin fared long on the road with them, and layeth down, how they shall go about their journey, deeming that much lay on it that they should fare well.

"A place for guesting have I gotten you," saith he, "in Nipsdale, which ye shall take. The bonder whereas ye shall harbour to-night is one Nial. So it is told," said he, "that, as to other men, he is no great thane with his wealth, though he hath enough; but this I wot that he will take you in at the bidding of my word. But now is the man come hither who last night rode from Burgfirth and the south, he whom I sent south this week to wot tidings of the country-side. And this he knoweth clearly as a true tale, that Hermund Illugison will be at the market the beginning of this week with many other men of the country-side. This also ye will have heard, that those brethren, the sons of Thorgaut, have a business on their hands this summer, to wit, to mow the meadow which is called Goldmead; and now is the work well forward, so that it will be done on Wednesday of this week; so that they must needs be at home. Now I have heard that which they are wont to fall to speech of, those Gislungs, when there is any clatter or noise; then say they, 'What! Will Bardi be come?' and thereof make they much jeering and mocking for the shaming of you. Now it is also told north here, and avouched to be thoroughly true, that this have the men of the country-side agreed to, that if any tidings befall in the country such as be of men's fashioning, then shall all men be bound to ride after them, the reason thereof being that Snorri the Priest and his folk slept but a short way from the steads after that slaying and big deed of his. And everyone who is not ready hereto shall be fined in three marks of silver, if he belong to those who have 'thingfare-pay' to yield, from Havenfells to North-water, whereas there dwelleth the greatest number of the Thingmen of the Sidefolk and those of Flokis-dale. So ride ye on the Monday from Nial's, and fare leisurely and have night-harbour on the Heath" (thence gat it the name of Two-day's Heath), "and ye shall come to those two fighting-steads which be on the Heath, as ye go south, and look to it if they be as I tell you. There is a place called the Mires on the Heath, whence the fall of water is great; and in the northern Mire is a water whereinto reacheth a ness, no bigger at its upper part than nine men may stand abreast thereon; and from that mere waters run northward to our country-sides; and thither would I bid you to. But another fighting-stead is there in the southern Mire, which I would not so much have you hold as the other, and it will be worse for you if you shall have to make a shift there for safeguard. There also goeth a ness into the water. Thereon may eighteen men stand abreast, and the waters fall thence from that mere south into the country.

"But ye shall come south on Wednesday to the fell-bothies whenas all men are gone from the bothies all up and down Copsedale; for all the Sidemen have mountain business there, and there hitherto have tarried. Now meseemeth that ye will come thither nigh to nones of the day. Then shall two of your company ride down into the country-side there, and along the fell, and so to the Bridge, and not come into the peopled parts till ye are south of the river. Then shall ye come to the stead called Hallward-stead, and ask the goodman for tidings, and ask after those horses which have vanished away from the North-country. Ye shall ask also of tidings from the market. Then will ye see on Goldmead, whereas ye fare down along the river, whether men be a mowing thereon, even as the rumour goes.

"Then shall ye ride up along to the ford, and let the goodman show you the way to the ford; and so ride thence up towards the Heath and on to the Heath, whence ye may look down on Goldmead whereas ye fare along the river. Now on Wednesday morning shalt thou fare down on to the bridge, whence ye may see what may be toward in the country-side; and thou shalt sunder thy company for three places, to wit, the eighteen all told; but the nineteenth shall abide behind to heed your horses, and that shall be Kollgris, and let them be ready when ye need to take to them.

"Now six men shall be up on the bridge; and I shall make it clear who they shall be, and why it shall be arrayed that way. There shall be those kins-men Thorgisl of Middleham and Arngrim, and Eric Wide-sight, and Thorliot, Yeller's fosterling, and Eyolf of Asmund's-nip; and for this reason shall they sit there, because they would be the stiffest to thee and the hardest to sway whenas ye come into the country-side, and it behoveth you not that ye lack measure and quieting now and again.

"But midway shall sit other six: the brethren Thorod and Thorgisl of Tern-mere" (the sons of the brother of Bardi's father), "then the third man who came instead of Haldor; therewithal shall be the sons of thy mother's sister, Hun and Lambkar; and Eyolf, thy brother-in-law, for the sixth; they shall be somewhat more obedient to thy counsel, and not fare with suchlike fury. And for this reason shall they sit there, that they may look on the goings of men about the country-side.

"But ye six shall fare down (into the country), to wit, thou and Stein and Steingrim, thy brethren, and Olaf and Day and Thord. They will be the most obedient to thy word; yet shall ye have strength enough for those on the Mead.

"Now shall ye fare away forthright after ye have done them a scathe whereas the chase will not fail you, and less labour will they lay thereon, if there be but seen six men of you, and there will not be a great throng at your heels if so ye go on.

"Now shall ye ride away at your swiftest until ye are come to the northern fighting-stead upon the Heath; because that thence all verdicts go to the north, and therein is the greatest avail to you that so things should turn out.

"And yet I misdoubt me that thou wilt not bring this about, because of the frowardness of them that follow thee.

"Now must we sunder for this while, and meet we hail hereafter."

Chapter 10
Of Bardi's Two Spies

Now comes Bardi with his flock to Nial's in the evening. Nial is standing without, and bids them all guesting as one merry with ale; that they take, let loose their horses, and sit them down on either bench. Nial is without that evening, and his wife with him, dighting victual for their guests; but his young lad was within, and made game with them.

Bardi asked the lad if he had ever a whetstone. "I wot," saith he, "of a hard-stone which my father owns, but I durst not take it."

"I will buy it of thee," saith Bardi, "and give thee a whittle therefor."

"Yea," said the lad, "why then should I not strike a bargain with thee;" and goeth and findeth the hard-stone, and giveth it to Bardi. Bardi handles it, and taketh the whittle from his neck, and therewith was somewhat shifted the pair of beads which the carline had done about his neck, whereof is told sithence.

Now they whet their weapons, and the lad thinketh he hath done them a good turn, whereas they have what they needed. So there they abide the night through, and have good cheer.

They ride their ways on the Monday in good weather, and go not hard. Bardi asks of Eric Wide-sight what wise he deemed things would go. He answereth:

> "O Lime-tree, upbearer of board of the corpses,
> We nineteen together have gone from the Northland;

All over the Heath have we wended together,
And our will is to nourish the bloodfowl with victual.
But, O lad of the steed that is stalled on the rollers,
The steed of the sea-rover Heite, well wot we
That fewer shall wend we our ways from the Southland.
Now the mind of the singer is bent on the battle."

Chapter 11
Portents At Walls

Now must somewhat be told about the men of that country who now come into our matter. Thorbiorn Brunison rose up early at Walls, and bade his house-carle rise with him. "To-day shall we fare to Thorgaut to the stithy, and there shall we smithy."

Now that was early, just at the sun's uprising. Thorbiorn called for their breakfast, and nought is told of what of things was brought forward, but that the goodwife set a bowl on the board. Thorbiorn cried out that he was nought well served, and he drave the bowl betwixt the shoulders of her. She turned about thereat, and cried out aloud, and was shrewish of tongue, and either was hard on the other.

"Thou hast brought that before me," said he, "wherein there is nought save blood, and a wonder it is that thou seest nothing amiss therein."

Then she answereth calmly: "I brought nought before thee which thou mightest not well eat; and none the worse do I think of the wonder thou seest, whereas it betokens that thou shalt be speedily in hell. For assuredly this will be thy fetch."

He sang a stave:

> "The wealth-bearing stem that for wife we are owning,
> The black coif of widowhood never shall bear
> For my death; though I know that the field of the necklace
> All the days of my life neath the mould would be laying:
> She who filleth the ale round would give for my eating
> The apples of hell-orchard. Evil unheard of!
> But that wealth-bearing board now will scarcely meseemeth
> Have might for the bringing this evil about."

Chapter 12
The Slaying Of Gisli

Now has Bardi arrayed his folk in their lurking-places, as his fosterer had taught him, even as is aforesaid, and he tells them all what he had forecast in his mind.

Then they were somewhat better content therewith, and deemed that what was minded would be brought about; and they gave out that they liked this array, so to say, but they said nevertheless that to their minds the doings would be but little.

There was then a big wood on Whitewater-side, such as in those days were wide about the land here, and six of them sat down above the wood, and saw clearly what befell on Goldmead. Bardi was in the wood, and well-nigh he and the six of them within touch of them that were a-mowing. Now Bardi scans heedfully how many men were at the mowing; and he deemed that he did not clearly know whether the third man, who was white about the head, would be a woman, or whether it would be Gisli.

Now they went down from under the wood one after other; and it seemed first to those sons of Thorgaut as if but one man went there; and Thormod, who mowed the last in the meadow, took up the word. "There go men," said he.

"But it seemeth to me," said Gisli, "that but one man goeth there;" but they went hard, yet did not run.

"That is not so," said Ketil Brusi; "men are there, and not so few."

So they stood still, and looked thereon, and Ketil said: "Will not Bardi be there? That is not unlike him; and no man have I skill to know if yon be not he. And that wise was he arrayed last summer at the Thing."

Those brethren, Ketil and Thormod, looked on; but Gisli went on mowing and took up the word. "So speak .ye," said he, "as if Bardi would be coming from out of every bush all the summer. And he has not come yet."

Bardi and his folk had portioned out the men to them beforehand, that two should fall on each one of them. Bardi and Stein were to take Ketil Brusi, who was mighty of strength; Day and Olaf were to go against Gisli; Steingrim and Thord were to go against Thormod. So now they turn on them.

Now spake Ketil: "No lie it was that Bardi is come!"

They would fain catch up their weapons, but none of them gat hold of the weapons.

Now when they see into what plight they were come, Gisli and Ketil would run for the homemead garth, and Bardi and four of his fellows followed after them; but Thormod turns down to the river, and after him went Thord and Steingrim, and chased him into the river and stoned him from the shore; he got him over the river, and came off well.

Now came those brethren to the garth, and Ketil was the swifter, and leapt over it into the mead; but whenas Gisli leapt at the garth, a turf fell therefrom, and he slipped; therewith came up Bardi, who was the swiftest of those men, and hewed at him with the sword Thorgaut's-loom, and hewed off well-nigh all the face of him.

Straightway then he turns to meet his fellows, and tells them that something of a wound had been wrought. They said that the onset was but little and unwarrior-like. But he said that things would have to be as they were. "And now shall we turn back."

Needs must he rule, though it was much against their will.

But Ketil dragged Gisli in over the garth, and cast him on his back, and they saw that he was no heavy burden to him; and he ran home to the stead.

Thorbiorn and Thorgaut were in the stithy abiding till the house- carle should come back with the smithying stuff.

Now Thorgaut spake: "Yea, there is great noise and clatter; is not Bardi come?"

Even in that nick of time came Ketil into the stithy, and said: "That found Gisli thy son, that come he is;" and he cast him dead before his feet.

Now Bardi turns to meet his fellows, and said that he was minded that now man was come to be set against man. Quoth they, that the men were nowise equal, and that little had been done though one man had been slain, and so long a way as they had fared thereto.

So when all the fellowship met, then said they who had been higher up in the lurking-places, that full surely they would not have fared if they had known they should thus have to leave off in this way, that no more vengeance should follow after such a grief as had been done them, and they said that Gisli and Hall were men nowise equal. And they laid blame on Bardi, and said that they were minded to think that more would have been done if they had stood anear. Then they went to their horses, and said that they would have breakfast. Bardi bade them have no heed of breakfast, but they said that they had no will to fast. "And we know not how to think whatwise thou wouldst have come away if thou hadst done that wherein was some boldness."

Bardi said that he heeded not what they said. So they had their meat.

Chapter 13
The Call For The Chase

Now Thorgaut and Thorbiorn and Ketil, they talk together at home there. Thorgaut says that great is the hap befallen; "and the blow has lighted nigh to me; yet meseemeth that no less may be looked for yet, and I will that there be no tiding after them."

They say both that that shall never be. The women heard what had been said, and Ketil sends them out to Frodistead and Side-mull to tell the tidings; and then might each tell the other thence-forth, till the word should come into Thwartwater-lithe, and over Northwater-dale, for men to ride after them who have wrought this deed, and so put off from them forfeits and fines.

They fare then, and take their horses and ride to Highfell to see Arni Thorgautson; he there might welcome men allied to him, for thither was come Thorarin of Thwartwater-lithe, the father of Astrid his wife: thence ride they five together.

Now it is to be told of Thormod that he fared up along south of the river till he came to the Ridge. In that time south of the river was scantily housed. There were but few folk at home there, for the men were gone to Whitewater-meads, and the house- carles were at work. Eid was sitting at the chess, and his sons with him, the one hight Illugi, the other Eystein. Thormod tells him of the tidings that have befallen. There was, in those days and long after, a bridge over the river beside Biarnisforce. Eid nowise urged the journey, but his two sons grip their weapons and take to the way. The brethren go to Thorgisl of Hewerstead, and by then was come home Eyolf his son, who had come out to Iceland that same summer.

Thormod fares up to Hallkeldstead, and comes thither and tells the tidings. Tind was the one carle at home there; but men were come thither to the stithy.

A woman dwelt next thereto who hight Thorfinna, and was called the Skald-woman; she dwelt at Thorwardstead. She had a son hight Eyolf, and a brother who hight Tanni, and was called the Handstrong, for his might was unlike the sons of men; and of like kind was Eyolf, his sister's son; full-hearted in daring they were moreover. These had come to Tind for the smithying. But for that cause folk came not to Gilsbank, that Hermund was ridden to the ship and his house-carles with him.

Tind and the others were four, and Thormod the fifth, and it was now late in the day.

The sons of Eld came to Thorgisl the Hewer, and the folk there bestir them speedily, and fare thence six in company. Eyolf, the son of Thorgisl, fared with him and four others.

Chapter 14
The Chasing Of Bardi

Now must it be told what tidings Bardi and his folk see. He rideth the first of them, and somewhat the hardest, so that a gate's space was betwixt him and them; but they rode after him somewhat leisurely, and said that he was wondrous fearful.

Now see they the faring of men who chase them, and that flock was not much less than they themselves had. Then were Bardi's fellows glad, and thought it good that there would be a chance of some tale to tell of their journey.

Then spake Bardi: "Fare we away yet a while, for it is not to be looked for that they will spur on the chase any the less."

Then sang Eric Wide-sight a stave:

> "Now gather together the warriors renowned,
> Each one of them eager-fain after the fray.
> Now draweth together a folk that is fight-famed,
> Apace on the heathways from out of the Southland;
> But Bardi in nowise hard-counselled is bidding
> The warriors fare fast and be eager in fleeing
> The blast of the spear-storm that hitherward setteth,
> The storm of the feeders of fight from the South."

Chapter 15
The First Brunt Of Battle On The Heath

Now they come face to face, Bardi and the Southern men, who now got off their horses. Bardi's folk had arrayed them athwart the ness. "Go none of you forth beyond these steps," says Bardi, "because I misdoubt me that more men are to be looked for."

The breadth of the ness went with the rank of the eighteen of them, and there was but one way of falling on them. Says Bardi: "It is most like that ye will get the trying of weapons; but better had it been to hold the northernmost fight-stead, nor had any blame been laid upon us if we had so done; and better had it been for the blood-feuds. Yet shall we not be afraid, even though we are here."

There stood they with brandished weapons. On the one hand of Bardi stood Thorberg, and on the other side Gefn's-Odd, and on the other hand of them the brethren of Bardi.

Now those Southern men, they fall not on so speedily as the others looked for, for more folk had they to face than they had wotted of. The leaders of them were Thorgaut, Thorbiorn, and Ketil. Spake Thorgaut: "Wiser it were to bide more folk of ours; much deeper in counsel have they proved, inasmuch as they came but few of them within the country-side."

Now they fall not on; and when the Northern men see that, they take to their own devices. Saith Thorberg: "Is Brusi amidst the folk perchance?" He said that he was there.

Says Thorberg: "Knowest thou perchance this sword, which here I hold?" He said that he knew not how that should be looked for. "Or who art thou?"

"Thorberg I hight," says he; "and this sword Lyng-Torfi, thy kinsman, gave to me; thereof shalt thou abide many a stroke to-day, if it be as I will. But why fall ye not on, so boldly as ye have followed on to-day, as it seemeth to me, now running, and now riding."

He answereth: "Maybe that is a sword I own; but before we part to-day thou shalt have little need to taunt us."

Then said Thorberg: "If thou art a man full-fashioned for fight, why wilt thou tarry for more odds against us?"

Then Bardi took up the word: "What are the tidings of the country-side?"

Said Ketil: "Tidings are such as shall seem good to thee, to wit, the slaying of Gisli, my brother."

Saith Bardi: "We blame it nowise; and I deemed not that my work had been done anywise doubtfully. Come! Deemest thou, Ketil, that thou and thy father have nought at all wherefor to avenge you on us. I mind me that it was but a little since thou camest home, Ketil, bearing a back burden, a gift in hand for thy father. Now if thou bearest it not in mind, here is there a token thereof, this same sword, to wit, not yet dry of the brains of him."

And he shaketh the sword at him therewith.

This they might not abide, so now they run on them. Thorbiorn leaps at Bardi, and smites him on the neck, and wondrous great was the clatter of the stroke, and it fell on that stone of the beads which had been shifted whenas he took the knife and gave it to Nial's son; and the stone brake asunder, and blood was drawn on either side of the band, but the sword did not bite.

Then said Thorbiorn: "Troll! No iron will bite on thee."

Now were they joined in battle together, and after that great stroke he (Thorbiorn) turns him forthwith to meet Thorod, and they fall to fight together; Ketil goeth against Bardi, and Thorgaut against Thorberg. There lacked not great strokes and eggings-on.

The Southlanders had the lesser folk, and the less trusty.

Now first is to be told of the dealings betwixt Bardi and Ketil. Ketil was the strongest of men and of great heart. Long they had to do together, till it came to this, that Bardi slashed into the side of him, and Ketil fell. Then leapt Bardi unto Thorgaut and gave him his death-wound, and there they both lay low before the very weapon which they owned themselves.

Now is it to be told of Thorbiorn and Thorod. They fall to in another place; and there lacked not for great strokes, which neither spared to the other, most of them being huge in sooth. But one stroke Thorod fetched at Thorbiorn, and smote off his foot at the ankle-joint; but none the less he fought on, and thrust forth his sword into Thorod's belly, so that he fell, and his gut burst out.

But Thorbiorn, seeing how it had fared with his kinsmen (namely, Ketil and Thorgaut), he heeded nought of his life amidst these maimings.

Now turn the sons of Gudbrand on Thorbiorn. He said: "Seek ye another occasion; erst it was not for young men to strive with us." Therewith he leaps at Bardi and fights with him. Then said Bardi: "What! A very troll I deem thee, whereas thou tightest with one foot off. Truer of thee is that which thou spakest to me."

"Nay," quoth Thorbiorn, "nought of trollship is it for a man to bear his wounds, and not to be so soft as to forbear warding him whiles he may. That may be accounted for manliness rather; and so shouldst thou account it, and betroll men not, whereas thou art called a true man. But this shall ye have to say hereof before I bow me in the grass, that I had the heart to make the most of weapons."

There fell he before Bardi and won a good word.

Now lacks there never onset, but it came to this at last, that the Southern men gave way.

But it is told that there was a man hight Thorliot, a great champion, who had his abode at Walls; but some say that he was of Sleybrook: he fought with Eric Wide-sight; and before they fought, Eric sang this stave:

> "O warrior that reddenest the war-brand thin-whetted,
> 'Tis the mind of us twain to make shields meet together
> In the wrath of the war-fray. O bider of Wall-stead,

Now bear we no ruth into onset of battle.
O hider of hoards of the fire that abideth
In the fetter of earth, I have heard of thine heart,
High-holden, bepraised amongst men for its stoutness;
And now is the time that we try it together."

Chapter 16
The Second and Third Brunt Of Battle

Now is there somewhat of a lull; but therewith were seen six men a-riding: there were Thorgisl the Hewer, and Eyolf his son, and the sons of Eid. They see the evil plight of their folk, and that their lot was sinking much, and they were ill content therewith.

Now the sons of Gudbrand were ware that there was Eyolf, and they crave leave of Bardi to take his life and avenge them. For it had befallen, that whenas they were east-away he had thrust them from a certain gallery down into a muck-pit, and therein they had fared shamefully; so they would now avenge them; and they had made this journey with Bardi from the beginning that they might get the man.

Said Bardi: "Ye are doughty men, and of much worth, and much teen it were if ye were cast away. Still, I will see to it that your will have its way; but I will bid you go not from out the ranks." But they might not withhold themselves, and they run off to meet him eagerly, and they fall to fight. Eyolf was the greatest of champions, and a man of showy ways, like his father before him; full-fashioned of might, well proven in onslaught; and the battle betwixt them was long and hard; and suchwise it ended, that either was so wilful and eager, and so mighty of heart and hand, that they all lay dead at their parting.

Fast fought the sons of Eid withal, and go forward well and warrior-like; against them fought Stein and Steingrim, and now they all fight and do a good stroke of work; and there fall the sons of Eid, and Bardi was standing hard by, when they lost their lives.

Thorgisl the Hewer spared nought; he deemed great scathe wrought him by the death of his son. He was the mightiest man of his hands, and defter of weapons than other men. He heweth on either hand and deemeth life no better than death.

These are most named amongst the foremost herein, to wit, Thorgisl and Eric and Thorod.

Thorgisl spared him nought, and there was no man of the country who seemed to all a wayfellow of more avail than he. Thorgisl (son of Hermund, brother of Thorod) betook him to meet him; and they dealt long together, nor was either of them lacking in hardihood. Now Thorgisl (Hermundson) smites a stroke on him down his nose from the brow, and said:

"Now hast thou gotten a good mark befitting thee; and even such should more of you have."

Then spake Thorgisl (the Hewer): "Nought good is the mark; yet most like it is, that I shall have the heart to bear it manfully; little have ye yet to brag over." And he smote at him so that he fell and is now unfightworthy.

Now was there a lull for a while, and men bind their wounds.

Now is seen the riding of four men, and there was Tind and Tanni, Eyolf and Thormod; and when they came up they egg on much; and they themselves were of championship exceeding great; and battle was joined the third time.

Tanni fell on against Bardi, and there befell fight of wondrous daring.

Tanni hewed at him, and it fell out as before, that Bardi is hard to deal with, and the business betwixt them ended herewith, that Tanni fell before Bardi.

Eyolf went against Odd, and they fight, each of them the best of stout men. Now Eyolf smiteth at Odd, and it came on to his cheek and on to his mouth, and a great wound was that.

Then spake Eyolf: "Maybe the widow will think the kissing of thee worsened."

Odd answereth: "Long hath it been not over good, and now must it be much spoilt forsooth; yet it may be that thou wilt not tell thereof to thy sweetheart."

And he smote at him, so that he gat a great wound.

Here it befell as of the rest, that Bardi was standing hard by, and did him scathe.

Withal Thormod Thorgautson was a bold man, and went well forward. Eyolf of Burg fared against him, and got a sore hurt.

Now though these above said be the most named amongst the Northlanders, yet all of them fared forth well and in manly wise, whereas they had a chosen company.

So when these were fallen there was a lull in the battle. And now Thorberg spake that they should seek to get away; but eight men from the South were fallen, and three from the North. Now Bardi asks Thorod if he thought he would have the might to fare with them, and he gave out there was no hope thereof, and bids them ride off.

Now Bardi beheld his hurt, and therewithal they saw the band that now fared up from the South like a wood to look upon. So Bardi asks if they be minded to bide, but they said they would ride off; and so they did, and were now sixteen in company, and the more part of them wounded.

Chapter 17
Bardi Puts Away His Wife

Now it is to be told of Illugi that he cometh upon the field of deed, and seeth there things unlooked for, and great withal. Then sang Tind a song when Illugi asked how many they had been:

> "The stem of the battle-craft here was upbearing
> His spear-shaft with eight and with ten of the ash-trees
> That bear about ever the moon of the ocean;

With us five less than thirty men were they a-fighting.
But nine of the flingers of hail of the bow,
Yea, nine of our folk unto field there have fallen,
And surely meseemeth that dead they are lying,
Those staves of the flame by the lathe that is fashioned.

"Of the North the two cravers of heirship from Eid
In the field are they fallen as seen is full clearly,
And Gudbrand's two sons they fell there moreover,
Where the din of the spear-play was mighty mid men.
But never henceforward for boot are we biding;
Unless as time weareth the vengeance befall.
Now shall true folk be holding a mind of these matters,
As of sword-motes the greatest ere fought amongst men."

Chapter 18
The Speaking Out Of Truce

Now they hear a great din, in that many men ride to the river. Here was come Thorgisl Arason, having journeyed from the North- country from his bridal; in his company was Snorri the Priest, and eighty men together they rode.

Then said Bardi: "Let us drop our visors, and ride we into their band, but never more than one at a time, and then they will find out nothing, seeing that it is dark."

So Bardi rideth up to Snorri the Priest, having a mask over his face, and hath talk with him while they cross the ford, and tells him the tidings. And as they ride out of the river Snorri the Priest took up the word, and said:

"Here let us bait, Thorgisl, and tarry and talk together, before we betake ourselves to quarters for the night." Bardi and his were riding beside the company, and folk heeded it not. Thorgisl was minded in the evening for Broadlairstead.

Now when they had sat down, spake Snorri: "I am told, Thorgisl," says he, "that no man can set forth as well as thou the speech of truce and other in law matters."

"That is a tale that goeth not for much," says Thorgisl.

"Nay," says Snorri, "there must be much therein, since all men speak in one way thereof."

Thorgisl answers: "Truly there is nothing in it that I deliver the speech of truce better than other men, though it may be good in law notwithstanding."

Says Snorri: "I would that thou wouldst let me hear it."

He answers: "What need is there thereof? Are any men here at enmity together?"

He said he knew nought thereof, "but this can never be a misdoing; so do as I will."

So Thorgisl said it should be so, and therewithal he fell to speaking:

"This is the beginning of our speech of truce, that God may be at peace with us all; so also shall we be men at peace between ourselves and of good accord, at ale and at eating, at meets and at man-motes, at church-goings and in king's house; and wherever the meetings of men befall, we shall be so at one as if enmity had never been between us. Knife we shall share and shorn meat, yea, and all other things between us, even as friends and not foes. Should henceforth any trespass happen amongst us, let boot be done, but no blade be reddened. But he of us who tramples on truce settled, or fights after full troth given, he shall be so far wolf-driven and chased, as men furthest follow up wolves, Christian men churches seek, heathen men their temples tend, fires flare up, earth grows green, son names a mother's name, ships sail, shields glitter, sun shines, snow wanes, Fin skates, fir groweth, a falcon flieth the springlong day with wind abaft under both his wings standing, as heaven dwindles, the world is peopled, wind waxeth, water sheds to sea, and carles sow corn.

"He shall shun churches and Christian men, God's houses and men's, and every home but hell.

"Each one of us taketh troth from the other for himself and his heirs born and unborn, begotten and not begotten, named and not named, and each one giveth in turn troth, life troth, dear troth, yea, main troth, such as ever shall hold good while mold and men be alive.

"Now are we at one, and at peace wheresoever we meet on land or on water, on ship or on snowshoe, on high seas or horseback:

> "Oars to share,
> Or bailing-butt,
> Thoft or thole plank
> If that be needful."

Chapter 19
Snorri Tells The Whole Tale

And when Thorgisl had done giving out the words of truce, Snorri spoke: "Have thanks, friend; right well hast thou spoken, and it is clear enough that he who trespasseth there against is truly a truce-breaker, most especially if he be here present." And now Snorri tells the tidings which had befallen, and also this, that Bardi and his men had come into the band of Thorgisl and those with him.

In that band there were many friends and close kindred of the men of the South; moreover, Thorgisl had aforetime had for wife Grima, the daughter of Halkel, and sister of Illugi the Black.

Then said Thorgisl: "For this once we might well have done without thee, Snorri."

He answers: "Say not so, good friend; troubles between men have now grown full great, though here they be stayed."

So now Thorgisl would not go against the truce which he himself had bespoken, and so folk parted asunder.

Snorri rode away with a company of twenty men to Lechmote, and Bardi and his folk were with him, and Thorarin received them well, and cheery of mood they were and bespoke their counsels.

[Here a lacuna of one leaf in the old MS. interrupts the story, which begins again when, apparently at the Althing, the affairs of Bardi were settled at law.]

Chapter 20
Bardi's Affairs Settled

Then stands up an old man, Eid Skeggison to wit, and said: "We like it ill that men should bandy words about here, whether it be done by our men or others; to nought good will that come, while often evil proceedeth therefrom. It behoveth men here to speak what may tend to peace. I am minded to think that not another man among us has more to miss, nor that on any, much greater grief hath been brought than on me; yet a wise counsel do I deem it to come to peace, and therefore I shall have no ruth on anyone bandying words about here. Moreover, it is most likely now, as ever, that it will only come to evil if folk will be casting words of shame at each other."

He got good cheer for his speech. And now men search about for such as be likeliest for the peacemaking. Snorri is most chiefly spoken of as seeking to bring about the peace. He was then far sunk in age. Another such was Thorgisl, the friend of Snorri, for their wives were sisters. Now both sides did it to wit that matters should be put to award, and the pairing of man to man; though erst folk had been sore of their kinsmen.

Now we know no more to tell thereof than that the fallen were paired man to man, and for the award Snorri was chosen on behalf of Bardi, together with Gudmund, the son of Eyolf, while Thorgisl, the son of Ari, and Illugi, were appointed on behalf of the Southerners. So they fell to talking over the matter between them, as to what would most likely lead to peace. And it seemed good to them to pair men together in this wise:

The sons of Eid and the sons of Gudbrand were evened, as was also Thorod, the son of Hermund, and Thorbiorn. But now as to Hall Gudmundson, the Burgfirthers thought the mangild for him was pushed too far, so they drew off, and broke the peace; yet they knew that Bardi had set his heart on that matter. But of the close thereof this is to be told, that the sons of Thorgaut, Ketil and Gisli, were paired against Hall Gudmundson. In all there were nine lives lost of the Southerners, and now four from the North have been set off against five Gislungs; for nought else would like the kinsmen of Bardi because of the disparity of kin there was.

Then matters were talked over with both sides as to what next was most like to do. There were now four Southernmen unatoned, Thorgisl to wit, and

Eyolf his son, Tanni the Handstrong, and Eyolf, his sister's son.

Now Bardi declared that he was no man of wealth any more than his brothers or their kindred, "nor do we mean to claim money in atonement on our side."

Answered Snorri: "Yet it behoveth not, that neither fine nor outlawry come about." Bardi said he would not gainsay that people should go abroad, so that they were free to come back again, nor that then all the more of them should fare. "Yet one there is who cannot fare; for him let fee be yolden, though it may hap that ye deem ye have some guilt to square with him. My fellow Gris will not be found to be bitten by guilt." Hesthofdi, who now dwells at the place called Stead in Skagafirth, who was a kinsman of his, took him in.

So matters came about, that on this they made peace, as they were most willing to agree to men faring abroad. Now this was deemed to be about the only boot to be got, since Bardi might not bite at-fines; they hoped, too, that thereby unpeace would somewhat abate, and on the other hand they deemed no less honour done to themselves by their having to be abroad. By wise men it was deemed most like to allay their rage, so great as it was, if for a while they should not be living within one and the same land.

Fourteen of the men who had had share in the Heath-slaughters were to fare abroad, and be abroad for three winters, and be free to come back in the third summer, but no money should be found for their faring.

Thus were men appeased on these matters without taking them into court. And so it was accounted that Bardi and those who came forth for his avail had had the fuller share, for as hopeless as it had seemed for a while.

Chapter 21
Bardi Fares And Is Shipwrecked

Now Bardi sends men into the country-side. He and his had got rid of their land and stock in case this should be the end of the matter; the which they could not surely tell beforehand. The messenger was hight Thorod, and was by-named Kegward, not beloved of folk; he was to have three winters; he was akin to the sons of Gudround, wealthy in chattels withal. And now the purchase of their lands as aforesaid was all but settled.

Now there cometh withal a ship from the high seas into the mouth of Blanda, which was the keel of Haldor, Bardi's foster-brother.

Therewithal folk came back from the Thing, and when Haldor hears that Bardi must needs go abroad, he has the freight of the craft unshipped, and brings himself, ship and all, up into the Hope over against Bardi's house, and a joyful meeting was theirs.

"Kinsman," says Haldor, "ever hast thou handled matters well as concerning me; thou hast often been bounteous to me, nor didst thou wax wrath on me when I did not go with thee on that journey of thine, so therefore I will now promise thee some avail in return, as now thou shalt hear: this ship will I give thee with yard and gear."

Bardi thanked him, saying he deemed he had done the deed of a great man. So now he dights this craft, and has with him five- and-twenty men. Somewhat late they were bound for sea; then put off to the main, and are eleven days out at sea; but in such wise their faring befell that they wreck their ship against Sigluness in the north, and goods were lost, but the men saved.

Gudmund the Elder had ridden out to Galmastrand, and heareth the tidings and hasteneth homeward. And in the evening spake Eyolf, his son: "Maybe it is Bardi yonder on the other side, that we see from here." Many said it was not unlike.

"Now how wouldst thou go about it?" says Eyolf, even he, "if it should hap that he had been driven back here?"

He answers: "What seemeth good to thee?"

He answers: "To bid them all home here to guesting. Meet were that."

Gudmund answers: "Large of mind thou, nor wot I if that be altogether so ill counselled."

Answers Eyolf, even he: "Speak thou, hailest of men! Now I can tell thee that Bardi, he and his, have been driven back, and broken to splinters against Sigluness, and have lost the best part of their goods. From this thou wilt have honour."

So he closed his mouth; but Gudmund thought he liked the matter none the better for that, yet lets him have his will.

Chapter 22
Bardi's Abiding With Gudmund

So Eyolf dights him for the journey, and goes with five-and- twenty horses to meet them, and happens on them on Galmastrand. He greets them well, and bids them go home with him, by the will of his father.

They did so, and there they had to themselves the second bench throughout the winter; and Gudmund was cheery to them, and did to them after the fashion of a great man and well. And that was widely rumoured.

Einar, the son of Jarnskeggi, often bids them go to his house and stay with him. And thus now they are right happy.

Now we have to bring to mind, that it was Thorarin's rede that with Bardi there were men who were of great worth and had much to fall back upon. And they now sent to the west for their moneys, being still bent on faring abroad in the summer.

Chapter 23
Eric's Song On The Heathslayings

Some time that winter it befell that there was one who asked Eric the Skald as to what had befallen, and how many lives had been lost. He sang:

"Famed groves of the race-course whereon the sword runneth,
All up on the Heath 'twas eleven lay dead

In the place where the lime-board, the red board of battle,
Went shivering to pieces midst din of the shields.
And thereof was the cause of the battle, that erewhile
It was Gisli fell in with his fate and his ending
In the midst of the fray of the fire of the fight:
'Gainst the wielder of wound-shaft we thrust forth the onslaught."

Chapter 24
Bardi Goeth To Norway And Afterwards To Iceland Again

Now Bardi's fellows took their money and made them ready for faring abroad with a goodly deal of wealth.

Bardi and his brethren sent a word to say that they will have their lands to sell them, for they deem that they are in need of chattels. But he (Thorolf Kegward) would not give up the land, and claims that the bargain should stand even as it was erst purposed. So that now they must either forego their money or slay him.

Now Eyolf (Gudmundson) says he will hand over to them as much money as the land is worth, and that he will himself see to further dealings with Eyolf of Burg, and declareth that that summer he shall have him either killed or driven out of the lands, and made himself the owner thereof.

Now Bardi buys a ship which stood up in Housewick; and then he went abroad, and Eyolf saw them off with all honour, and now, this time, they fared well, and Bardi cometh up from the main north in Thrandheim-bay into the Cheaping, and has his ship drawn up and well done to withal.

At that time King Olaf the Holy ruled over Norway, and was now at the cheaping-stead. Bardi and his fellows went before the king, and they greeted the king well, even as beseemed, "and this is the way with us, lord," says Bardi, "that we would fain be of thy winter-guests."

The king answers in this way: "We have had news of thee, Bardi," says he, "that thou art a man of great kin, a mighty man of thine hands; moreover, that ye are doughty men, that ye have fallen in with certain great deeds, and have wreaked your wrongs, yet waited long before so doing. Howbeit ye have still some ancient ways about you, and such manner of faith as goeth utterly against my mind. Now for the reason that I have clean parted from such things, our will is not to take you in; yet shall I be thy friend, Bardi," says he, "for methinks that some great things may be in store for thee. But it may often befall to those who fall in with suchlike matters, should they grow to be over-weighty to deal with, then if there be certain ancient lore blended therewith, therein are men given to trow overmuch."

Then spake Bardi: "No man there is," says he, "whom I would rather have for a friend than thee, and thanks we owe thee for thy words."

Now that winter long Bardi had his abode in the town, and all men held him of good account. But the next spring he dights his ship for Denmark, and there he was for another winter, and was well beholden withal, though tidings be not told thereof.

Thereafter he dights his ship for Iceland, and .they came out upon the north of the land, and were in great straits for money.

By this time Gudmund was dead, and Eyolf came to see them and bid them come to his house, and anon each went to his own, all being now guiltless.

Eyolf gave up to Bardi and his brethren their lands inherited from their father, showing forth again his large-heartedness as before, nor was any other man such avail to them as he was.

Now Bardi betook himself to Gudbrand his brother-in-law, a wealthy man and of high kin withal, but said to be somewhat close-fisted.

But the brethren of Bardi went to Burg, the southernmost, to Eyolf their brother-in-law, and by that time their foster-mother was dead.

Now Eyolf redeemed all the land for the hand of those brothers, and buys Bardi out of his share, with chattels. And so the brothers now set up house on their father's lands, and they died there in old age – men of avail, though not abreast with the greatness of their family; they were married both, and men are come from them.

Chapter 25
The Second Wedding Of Bard

Bardi rideth to the Thing after he had been one winter here in the land. Then he wooed for himself a wife, hight Aud, daughter of Snorri the Priest, and betrothed to him she was, and the bridals were settled to be at Saelings-dale in the harvest tide, at the home of Snorri her father. It is not set forth what jointure there should go with her from home, though like enough it be that it would be a seemly portion. She was a right stirring woman and much beloved by Snorri. Her mother was Thurid, the daughter of Illugi the Red.

Bardi rides after the Thing to Waterdale to his alliances, being now well content with his journey and having good honour of men. And things turned out even as wise men had foreseen, that the peace amongst men was well holden, even as it had been framed erst, nor telleth the tale that aught of dealings they had further together.

Now Snorri dights the bridals in the harvest tide as had been settled, and a great multitude of folk gathered there; bravely the banquet turned out as might be looked for, and there Bardi and his wife tarry the winter long. But in the spring they get them away with all their belongings, and as good friends they parted, Snorri and Bardi.

Now Bardi goeth north to Waterdale, where he tarrieth with Gudbrand his brother-in-law. And in the following spring he dighteth a journey of his, and buyeth a ship and goeth abroad, and his wife with him. The tale telleth that the journey sped well with him, and he hove in from the main up against Halogaland, where the next winter long he dwelt in Thiotta with Svein, son of

Harek, being well accounted of, for men deemed they saw in him the tokens of a great man; so Svein held him dear, both him and his wife withal.

Chapter 26
The End Of Bardi

So it befell one morning, as they were both together in their sleeping loft, away from other folk, that Bardi would sleep on, but she would be rousing him, and so she took a small pillow and cast it into his face as if for sport. He threw it back again from him; and so this went on sundry times. And at last he cast it at her and let his hand go with it. She was wroth thereat, and having gotten a stone she throweth it at him in turn.

So that day, when drinking was at an end, Bardi riseth to his feet, and nameth witnesses for himself, and declareth that he is parted from Aud, saying that he will take masterful ways no more from her than from anyone else. And so fast was he set in this mind herein, that to bring words to bear was of no avail.

So their goods were divided between them, and Bardi went his ways next spring, and made no stay in his journey till he cometh into Garthrealm, where he taketh warrior's wages, and becometh one of the Vaerings, and all the Northmen held him of great account, and had him for a bosom-friend amongst themselves.

Always, when that king's realm was to be warded, he is on the ways of war, gaining good renown from his valiance, so that he has about him always a great company of men. There Bardi spent three winters, being much honoured by the king and all the Vaerings. But once it befell, as they were out on their war- galleys with an host and warded the king's realm, that there fell an host upon them; there make they a great battle, and many of the king's men fell, as they had to struggle against an overwhelming force, though ere they fell they wrought many a big deed; and therewithal fell Bardi amidst good renown, having used his weapons after the fashion of a valiant man unto death.

Aud was married again to a mighty man, the son of Thorir Hound, who was hight Sigurd. And thence are sprung the men of Birchisle, the most renowned among men.

And there endeth this story.

Book Catalog

Works by Our Authors

- *The Opium of Happiness* by Jeremy Hausotter. This book examines the Church's teachings on drugs and marijuana. It also contains about 70 pages of appendices of hard to find Church documents discussing drugs. ISBN: 978-1-964170-54-1
- *How to Win Tic Tac Toe Like a Champion* by Jeremy Hausotter. ISBN: 978-1-964170-58-9

Theology & Philosophy

- *Select Works* by **St. Ambrose**. ISBN: 978-1-964170-44-2
- **St. Thomas Aquinas**
  - *The Summa Theologiae: Prima Pars, Q. 1-119*. ISBN: 978-1-964170-23-7
  - *The Summa Theologiae: Prima Secundae, Q. 1-114.* ISBN: 978-1-964170-24-4
  - *The Summa Theologiae: Secunda Secundae, Q. 1-189.* ISBN: 978-1-964170-25-1
  - *The Summa Theologiae: Tertia Pars, Q. 1-90*. ISBN: 978-1-964170-27-5
  - *The Summa Theologiae: Supplementum, Q. 1-99.* ISBN: 978-1-964170-28-2
- *The Life of St. Anthony* by **St. Athanasius**. ISBN: 978-1-964170-20-6
- **St. Augustine**
  - *On Christian Doctrine, Doctrinal Treatises, and Moral Treatises* ISBN: 978-1-964170-63-3
  - *The Anti-Donatist Works*. ISBN: 978-1-964170-40-4
  - *The Anti-Manichean Works*. ISBN: 978-1-964170-67-1
  - *The Anti-Pelagian Works*. ISBN: 978-1-964170-65-7
- *The Art of Dying Well* by **St. Robert Bellarmine**. ISBN: 978-1-964170-62-6
- *Select Letters and Orations* by **St. Gregory Nazianzen**. ISBN: 978-1-964170-56-5
- **St. John Henry Newman**
  - *An Essay in Aid of a Grammar of Assent.* ISBN: 978-1-964170-52-7
  - *On the Development of Christian Doctrine*. ISBN: 978-1-964170-48-0
  - *Sermons Preached on Various Occasions*. ISBN: 978-1-964170-50-3
- *The Problem of Form in Painting and Sculpture* by **Adolf von Hildebrand**. ISBN: 978-1-964170-60-2

Papal Documents

- **The Papal Writings of John Paul II**
  - Vol. 1, *The Complete Encyclicals*. ISBN: 978-1-964170-21-3
  - Vol. 11, *Veritatis Splendor*. ISBN: 978-1-964170-09-1
  - Vol. 12, *Evangelium Vitae*. ISBN: 978-1-964170-10-7
  - Vol. 14, *Fides et Ratio*. ISBN: 978-1-964170-12-1
- **The Papal Writings of Benedict XVI**

– Vol. 1, *Select Papal Writings: The Encyclicals, Apostolic Exhortations, and Select Other Writings*. ISBN: 978-1-964170-14-5

Classics

- **The Complete Works of Fyodor Dostoevsky**

    – Vol. 8, *The Minor Novels and Novellas: The Insulted and the Injured, The House of the Dead*. ISBN: 978-1-964170-17-6

    – Vol. 9, *The Complete Short Stories*. ISBN: 978-1-964170-18-3

- *The Wind in the Willows* by **Kenneth Grahame**. ISBN: 978-1-964170-46-6

- **Greek and Roman Classics**

    – Vol. 1, *Homer's The Iliad and the Odyssey*, translated by Alexander Pope. ISBN: 978-1-964170-15-2

- **Norse Classics**

    – Vol. 1, *The Poetic and Prose Eddas*. ISBN: 978-1-964170-37-4

    – Vol. 2, *The Heimskringla*. ISBN: 978-1-964170-39-8

    – Vol. 3, *The Nibelungenlied* (prose translation). ISBN: 978-1-964170-33-6

    – Vol. 4, *The Norse Sagas, Part 1*. ISBN: 978-1-964170-35-0

    – Vol. 5, *The Norse Sagas, Part 2*. ISBN: 978-1-964170-29-9

    – Vol. 6, *The Norse Sagas, Part 3*. ISBN: 978-1-964170-31-2

- *20,000 Leagues Under the Sea* by **Jules Verne**. ISBN: 978-1-964170-42-8

Forthcoming Titles

- A volume on the dogma *no salvation outside of the Church* by Jeremy Hausotter.
- A volume on the hermeneutics of Vatican II by Jeremy Hausotter.
- The *Summa Contra Gentiles* by St. Thomas Aquinas.